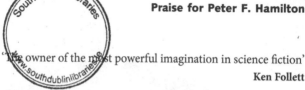

Praise for Peter F. Hamilton

'The owner of the most powerful imagination in science fiction'
Ken Follett

'A great big sprawling enjoyable science fiction read. Does what it says
on the tin. I finally closed it with a sense of satisfaction'
Neal Asher

'Thrilling stuff; compulsively readable and abundantly full of ideas'
The Times

'Hamilton handles massive ideas with enviable ease, manipulates plots
and characters to spring constant surprises, and brings the trilogy
to a climax with a cannonade of fire-cracker finales'
Guardian

'Complex world-building, harrowing back-story and good pay-offs'
Sunday Telegraph

'Hugely impressive. We've said it before but let's say it again:
nobody does BIG SF quite like Hamilton'
SFX

'An audacious collision of genres with real energy and verve: excellent'
BBC Focus

'A huge achievement in science fiction'
SciFiNow

'Reaches another level of excellence . . . Brilliant'
Locus

'Everything plus the kitchen sink . . . That he can pull this off
puts Hamilton amongst a rare breed of writers'
.net

THE EVOLUTIONARY VOID

Peter F. Hamilton was born in Rutland in 1960 and still lives in that county. He began writing in 1987, and sold his first short story to *Fear* magazine in 1988. He has written many bestselling novels, including the Greg Mandel series, the Night's Dawn trilogy, the Commonwealth Saga, the Void trilogy, two short story collections and *The Abyss Beyond Dreams*, book one in the Chronicle of the Fallers.

Find out more about Peter F. Hamilton at

www.facebook.com/PeterFHamilton

and discover more Pan Macmillan and Tor UK books at

www.torbooks.co.uk

By Peter F. Hamilton

The Greg Mandel series
Mindstar Rising
A Quantum Murder
The Nano Flower

The Night's Dawn trilogy
The Reality Dysfunction
The Neutronium Alchemist
The Naked God

The Commonwealth Saga
Pandora's Star
Judas Unchained

Chronicle of the Fallers
The Abyss Beyond Dreams

The Void trilogy
The Dreaming Void
The Temporal Void
The Evolutionary Void

Short story collections
A Second Chance at Eden
Manhattan in Reverse

Fallen Dragon
Misspent Youth
The Confederation Handbook
(a vital guide to the Night's Dawn trilogy)
Great North Road

Peter F. Hamilton

THE EVOLUTIONARY VOID

PART THREE OF THE VOID TRILOGY

PAN BOOKS

First published 2010 by Macmillan

This edition published 2014 by Pan Books
an imprint of Pan Macmillan
20 New Wharf Road, London N1 9RR
Associated companies throughout the world
www.panmacmillan.com

ISBN 978-1-4472-7969-3

9 8 7 6 5 4

A CIP catalogue record for this book is available from the British Library.

Typeset by SetSystems Ltd, Saffron Walden, Essex
Printed and bound by CPI Group (UK) Ltd, Croydon, CR0 4YY

Visit www.panmacmillan.com to read more about all our books
and to buy them. You will also find features, author interviews and
news of any author events, and you can sign up for e-newsletters
so that you're always first to hear about our new releases.

For Felix F. Hamilton

who arrived at the start of the Void.

Don't worry, Daddy's world

isn't really like this.

THE EVOLUTIONARY VOID

1

The starship had no name; it didn't have a serial number, nor even a marque. Only one of its kind had ever been built. As no more would ever be required, no designation was needed, it was simply *the ship*.

It streaked through the substructure of spacetime at fifty-nine lightyears an hour, the fastest anything built by humans had ever travelled. Navigation at that awesome velocity was by quantum interstice similarity interpretation, which determined the relative location of mass in the real universe beyond. This alleviated the use of crude hysradar, or any other sensor that might possibly be detected. The extremely sophisticated ultradrive which powered it along might have reached even greater speeds if a considerable fraction of its phenomenal energy wasn't used for fluctuation suppression. That meant there was no tell-tale distortion amid the quantum fields to betray its position to other starships that might wish to hunt it.

As well as its formidable stealth ability *the ship* was big; a fat ovoid over six hundred metres long, and two hundred metres across at the centre. But its real advantage came from its armaments; there were weapons on board that could knock out half a dozen Commonwealth Navy Capital-class ships whilst barely stirring out of standby mode. Weapons which had only been verified once. *The ship* had flown over ten thousand lightyears from the Greater Commonwealth to test them so as to avoid detection. For millennia to come, primitive alien civilizations in that section of the galaxy would worship as gods the colourful nebulas expanding across the interstellar wastes.

Even now, sitting in *the ship*'s clean hemispherical cabin with the flight-path imagery playing quietly in her exovision, Neskia remembered the stars splitting asunder with a little shiver of excitement, and apprehension. It had been one thing to run the clandestine fabrication station for the Accelerator Faction, dispatching ships and equipment to various agents and representatives. That was easy: cold machinery that functioned with a precision she could take pride in. But seeing the weapons active was slightly different. She'd felt a level of perturbation she hadn't known in over two centuries, ever since she became Higher and began her inward migration. Not that she questioned her belief in the Accelerators, it was just the sheer potency of the weapons which struck her at some primitive level that could never be fully exorcised from the human psyche. She was awed by the power of what she alone commanded.

Other elements of her animal past had been quietly and effectively erased. First with biononics and acceptance of Higher cultural philosophy, culminating in her embrace of Accelerator Faction tenets. Then she committed to a subtle rejection of her existing body form, as if to emphasize her new beliefs. Her skin now was a shimmering metallic-grey, the epidermal cells imbued with a contemporary semi-organic fibre that established itself in perfect symbiosis. The face that had caused many a man to turn in admiration when she was younger was now a more efficient flatter profile; with big saucer eyes biononically modified to look across a multitude of spectra. Her neck also had been stretched, its increased flexibility allowing her head a much greater manoeuvrability. Underneath the gently shimmering skin her muscles had been strengthened to a level which would allow her to keep up with a terrestrial panther on its kill run, and that was before biononic augmentation kicked in.

However, it was her mind which had undergone the greatest evolution. She'd stopped short of bioneural profiling simply because she didn't need any genetic reinforcement to her beliefs. Worship was a crude term for thought processes, but she was certainly devoted to her cause. She had dedicated herself completely to the Accelerators at a fully emotional level. The old human concerns and biological imperatives simply didn't affect her any more: her intellect was involved solely with the Faction and its goal. For the past fifty years their projects and plans were all that triggered her satisfaction and suffering. Her integration was total; she was the epitome of Accelerator values. Which was why she'd been chosen to fly *the ship* by the Faction leader, Ilanthe, on this mission. That, and that alone, made her content.

The ship began to slow as it approached the coordinate Neskia had supplied the smartcore with. Speed ebbed away until it hung inertly in transdimensional suspension while her navigation display showed the Sol system twenty-three lightyears away. The distance was comfortable. They were outside the comprehensive sensor mesh surrounding humanity's birthworld, yet she could be there in less than thirty minutes.

Neskia ordered the smartcore to run a passive scan. Other than interstellar dust and the odd frozen comet, there was no detectable mass within three lightyears. Certainly there were no ships. However, the scan picked up a tiny specific anomaly, which caused her to smile in tight satisfaction. All around *the ship* ultradrives were holding themselves in transdimensional suspension, undetectable except for that one deliberate signal. You had to know what to search for to find it, and nobody would be looking for anything out here, let alone ultradrives. *The ship* confirmed there were eight thousand of the machines holding position as they awaited instruction. Neskia established a communication link to them, and ran a swift function check. The Swarm was ready.

She settled down to wait for Ilanthe's next call.

*

The ExoProtectorate Council meeting ended and Kazimir cancelled the link to the perceptual conference room. He was alone in his office atop Pentagon II, with nowhere to go. The deterrence fleet had to be launched – there was no question of that now. Nothing else could deal with the approaching Ocisen Empire armada without an unacceptable loss of life on both sides. And if news that the Ocisens were backed up by Prime warships leaked out . . . And it would. Ilanthe would see to that.

No choice.

He straightened the recalcitrant silver braid collar on his dress uniform one last time as he walked over to the sweeping window, and looked down on the lush parkland of Babuyan Atoll. A gentle radiance was shining down on it, emitted from the crystal dome curving overhead. Even so, he could still see Icalanise's misty crescent through the ersatz dawn. The sight was one he'd seen countless times during his tenure. He'd always taken it for granted. Now he wondered if he'd ever see it again. For a true military man the thought wasn't unusual, in fact it had quite a proud pedigree.

His u-shadow opened a link to Paula. 'We're deploying the deterrence fleet against the Ocisens,' he told her.

'Oh dear. I take it the last capture mission didn't work then?'

'No. The Prime ship exploded when we took it out of hyperspace.'

'Damn. Suicide isn't part of the Prime's psychological make-up.'

'You know that and I know that. ANA:Governance knows that, too, of course, but as always it needs proof, not circumstantial evidence.'

'Are you going with the fleet?'

Kazimir couldn't help but smile at the question. *If only you knew.* 'Yes. I'm going with the fleet.'

'Good luck. I want you to try and turn this against her. They'll be out there watching, any chance you can detect them first?'

'We'll certainly try.' He squinted at the industrial stations circling round *High Angel*, a slim sparkling silver bracelet against the starfield. 'I heard about Ellezelin.'

'Yeah. Digby didn't have any options. ANA is sending a forensic team. If they can work out what Chatfield was carrying, we might be able to haul the Accelerators into court before you reach the Ocisens.'

'I don't think so. But I have some news for you.'

'Yes?'

'The *Lindau* has left the Hanko system.'

'Where is it heading?'

'That's the interesting thing. As far as I can make out, they're flying to the Spike.'

'The Spike? Are you sure?'

'That's a projection of their current course. It's held steady for seven hours now.'

'But that . . . No.'

'Why not?' Kazimir asked, obscurely amused by the Investigator's reaction.

'I simply don't believe that Ozzie would intervene in the Commonwealth again, not like this. And he'd certainly never employ someone like Aaron.'

'Okay, I'll grant you that one. But there are other humans in the Spike.'

'Yes, there are. Care to name one?'

Kazimir gave up. 'So what's Ozzie's connection?'

'I can't think.'

'The *Lindau* isn't flying as fast as it's capable of. It probably got damaged on Hanko. You could easily get to the Spike ahead of them, or even intercept.'

'Tempting, but I'm not going to risk it. I've wasted far too long on my personal obsession already, I can't risk another wild-goose chase at this point.'

'All right, well I'm going to be occupied for the next few days. If it's a real emergency you can contact me.'

'Thank you. My priority now has got to be securing the Second Dreamer.'

'Good luck with that.'

'And you, Kazimir. Godspeed.'

'Thank you.' He remained by the window for several seconds after he'd closed the link to Paula, then activated his biononic field interface function, which meshed with the Navy's T-sphere. He teleported to the wormhole terminus orbiting outside the gigantic alien arkship, and through that emerged into the Kerensk terminus. One more teleport jump, and he was inside Hevelius Island, one of Earth's T-sphere stations, floating seventy kilometres above the South Pacific.

'Ready,' he told ANA:Governance.

ANA opened the restricted wormhole to Proxima Centauri, four point three lightyears away, and Kazimir stepped through. The Alpha Centauri system had been a big disappointment when Ozzie and Nigel opened their very first long-range wormhole there in 2053. Given the binary composed G and K class stars and planets had already been detected by standard astronomical procedures, everyone was fervently hoping to find a Human-congruent world. There weren't any. But given they'd now successfully proved wormholes could be established across interstellar distances, Ozzie and Nigel went on to secure additional funding for the company which would rapidly evolve into Compression Space Transport and establish the Commonwealth. Nobody ever went back to Alpha Centauri; and nobody had ever even been to Proxima Centauri, with its small M-class star it was never going to have an H-congruent planet. That made it the perfect location for ANA to construct and base the 'deterrence fleet'.

Kazimir materialized at the centre of a simple transparent dome, measuring two kilometres across at the base. It was a tiny blister on the surface of a barren, airless planet, orbiting fifty million kilometres out from the diminutive red dwarf. Gravity was about two-thirds standard. Low hills all around created a rumpled horizon, the grey-brown regolith splashed a dreary maroon by Proxima's ineffectual radiance.

His feet were standing on what appeared to be a dull grey metal. Except, when he tried to focus on the featureless surface, it twisted away, as if there was something separating his boot soles from the physical structure. His biononic field scan function revealed massive forces starting to stir around him, rising up out of the strange floor.

'Are you ready?' ANA:Governance asked.

Kazimir gritted his teeth. 'Do it.'

As Kazimir had assured both Gore and Paula, the deterrence fleet was no bluff. It represented the peak of ANA's technological ability, and was at least a match to the ships of the warrior Raiel. However, he did concede that calling it a fleet was a slight exaggeration.

The problem, inevitably, was who to trust with such an enormous array of firepower. The more crew involved, the greater the chance of misuse, or leakage to a Faction. Ironically, the technology itself provided the answer. It only required a single controlling consciousness. ANA declined to assume command on ethical grounds, refusing to ascend to essential omnipotence. Therefore the task always fell upon the Chief Admiral.

The forces within the base swarmed round him, rushing in like a tidal wave; reading him at a quantum level then converting the memory. Kazimir transformed: his purely physical structure shifting to an equivalent energy function encapsulated within a single point that intruded into spacetime. His 'bulk', the energy signature he had become, was folded deep within the quantum fields, utilizing a similar construction principle to ANA itself. It contained his mind and memories, along with some basic manipulator and sensory abilities, and unlike ANA it wasn't a fixed point.

Kazimir used his new sensory inputs to examine the intraspatial lattice immediately surrounding him, reviewing the waiting array of transformed functions stored inside the dome's complex exotic matter mechanisms. He started to select the ones he might need for the mission, incorporating them into his own signature; a process he always equated to some primitive soldier walking through an armoury, pulling weapons and shields off the shelves.

Ultimately he incorporated eight hundred and seventeen

functions into his primary signature. Function twenty-seven was an ftl ability, allowing him to shift his entire energy signature through hyperspace. As he no longer retained any mass, the velocity he could achieve was orders of magnitude above an ultradrive.

Kazimir launched from the unnamed planet, heading for the Ocisen Fleet at a hundred lightyears an hour. Then he accelerated.

*

The Delivery Man smiled at the steward who came down the cabin collecting drinks from the passengers as the starship prepared to enter the planet's atmosphere. It was a job much better suited to a bot, or some inbuilt waste chute. Yet starliner companies always maintained a human crew. The vast majority of humans (non-Higher, anyway) relished that little personal contact during the voyage. Besides, human staff added a touch of refinement, the elegance of a bygone age.

He accessed the ship's sensors as the atmosphere built up around them. It was raining on Fanallisto's second largest southern continent. A huge gunmetal-grey mass of clouds powered their way inland, driven by winds that had built to an alarming velocity across the empty wastes of the Antarctic ocean. Cities were activating their weather-dome force fields, the rain was so heavy. Flood warnings were going out to the burgeoning agricultural zones.

Fanallisto was in its second century of development. A pleasant enough world, unremarkable in the firmament of External Worlds. It had a population of tens of millions, occupying relatively bland urban zones. Each one of which had a Living Dream thane, and a respectable number of followers. The prospect of Pilgrimage was creating a lot of tension and strife among the population; a situation which hadn't been helped by recent events on Viotia. Acts of violence against the thanes had increased with each passing day of the crisis.

In itself that was nothing special. Such conflicts were on the up right across the Greater Commonwealth. However, on Fanallisto, several instances of violence had been countered by people enriched by biononics. The Conservative Faction was keen to discover what was so special about Fanallisto that it needed support and protection from suspected Accelerator agents.

As he'd made quite clear to the Faction, the Delivery Man didn't care. However, a Conservative Faction agent was now on Fanallisto, and standard operating procedure for field deployment was to provide independent fall-back support. Which was why the Delivery Man hadn't gone straight back to London from Purlap spaceport. Instead he'd taken a flight to Trangor and caught the next starship to Fanallisto. At least he wasn't part of the active operation. The other agent didn't even know he was here.

The commercial starship fell through the sodden atmosphere to land at Rapall spaceport. The Delivery Man disembarked along with all the other passengers, then rendezvoused with his luggage in the terminal building. The two medium-sized cases drifted after him on regrav and parked themselves in a cab's cargo hold. He ordered the cab to the commercial section of town, a short trip in the little regrav capsule as it flitted round beneath the force-field dome. From there he walked round to another cab pad, and flew over to the Foxglove Hotel on the east side of town using a different identity.

He booked in to room 225, using a third identity certificate and an untraceable cash coin to prepay for a ten-day stay. It took four minutes to infiltrate the room's cybersphere node, where he installed various routines to make it appear as though the room was occupied. A nice professional touch, he felt. The small culinary unit would produce meals, which the maidbot would then empty down the toilet in the morning when it made the daily housekeeping visit. The spore shower would be used, as would various other gadgets and fittings; the air-conditioning temperature would be changed, the node would place a few calls across the unisphere. Power consumption would vary.

He slid both cases into the solitary closet just for the sake of appearance, and activated their defence mechanisms. Whatever was inside them, he didn't want to know, though he guessed at some pretty aggressive hardware. Once he'd confirmed they were operating properly, he left the room and called a cab down to the front of the hotel's lobby. It wouldn't be him who came back to collect the cases – that would set a pattern. He was grateful for that operational protocol. Following Justine's last dream, all he wanted to do was get back to his family. He'd already decided he would be turning down any more Conservative Faction requests over the next couple of weeks, no matter how much warning they gave him, and how politely they asked. Events were building to a climax, and there was only one place a true father should be.

The lobby's glass curtain doors parted to let him through. The taxi cab hovered a couple of centimetres above the concrete pad outside, waiting for him. He hadn't quite reached it when the Conservative Faction called.

I'm going to tell them no, he promised himself. *Whatever it is.*

He settled in the cab's curving seat, told its smartnet to take him to the downtown area, and then accepted the call. 'Yes?'

'The deterrence fleet is being deployed,' the Conservative Faction said.

'I'm surprised it took this long. People are getting nervous about the Ocisens, and they don't even know about the Primes yet.'

'We believe the whole deployment was orchestrated by the Accelerators.'

'Why? What could they possibly gain from that?'

'They would finally know the nature of the deterrent fleet.'

'Okay, so how does that help them?'

'We don't know. But it has to be crucial to their plans, they have risked almost everything on manipulating this one event.'

'The game is changing,' the Delivery Man said faintly. 'That's what Marius told me: the game is changing. I thought he was talking about Hanko.'

'Apparently not.'

'So we really are entering a critical phase, then?'

'It would seem so.'

Immediately suspicious, he said, 'I'm not undertaking anything else for you. Not now.'

'We know. That is why we called. We thought you deserved to know. We understand how much your family means to you, and that you want to be with them.'

'Ah. Thank you.'

'If you do wish to return to a more active status—'

'I'll let you know. Has my replacement taken over following Marius?'

'Operational information is kept isolated.'

'Of course, sorry.'

'Thank you again for your assistance.'

The Delivery Man sat upright as the call ended. 'Damnit.' *The deterrence fleet!* This was getting serious, not to mention potentially lethal. He ordered the cab to fly direct to the spaceport, and to hell with procedure. The flight he was booked to depart on wasn't due to leave for another two hours. His u-shadow immediately tracked down the first ship bound for a Central World. A PanCephei Line flight to Gralmond, leaving in thirty-five minutes. It managed to reserve him a seat, paying a huge premium to secure the last First Class lounge cubicle, but the flight would take twenty hours. Add another twenty minutes to that to reach Earth through the connecting wormholes, and he'd be back in London in just over twenty-one hours.

That'll be enough time. Surely?

*

Araminta had been so desperate to get the hell away from Colwyn City she hadn't really given any thought to the practical aspect of walking the Silfen paths between worlds. Ambling through mysterious woods dotted with sunny glades was a lovely romantic concept, as well as being a decent finger gesture to Living Dream and Cleric Conservator bastard Ethan. However, a moment's thought might have made her consider what she was wearing a little more carefully, and she'd definitely have found some tougher boots. There was also the question of food.

None of that registered for the first fifty minutes as she strolled airily down from the small spinney where the path from Francola Wood had emerged. She simply marvelled at her own fortune, the way she'd finally managed to turn her predicament around.

Figure out what you want, Laril had told her.

Well now I've started to do just that. I'm taking charge of my life again.

Then the quartet of moons had sunk behind the horizon. She smiled at their departure, wondering how long it would take before they reappeared again. It had been a fast traverse of the sky, so they must orbit this world several times a day. When she turned to check the opposite horizon her smile faded at the thick bank of unpleasantly dark clouds that were massing above the lofty hills that made up the valley wall. Ten minutes later the rain reached her, an unrelenting torrent that left her drenched in seconds. Her comfy old fleece was resistant to a mild drizzle, but it was never intended for a downpour that verged on a monsoon. Nonetheless she scraped the rat-tail strings of hair from her eyes and plodded on resolutely, unable to see more than a hundred metres in front of her. Boots with too-thin soles slipped on the now dangerously slimy grass-equivalent. As the slope took her down to the valley floor she spent more than half her time leaning forward in a gorilla-style crouch to scramble her way slowly onwards. That was the first three hours.

She kept walking for the rest of the day, traversing the wide empty valley as the clouds rumbled away. The orange-tinted sunlight helped dry her fleece and trousers, but her underclothes took a long time to dry out. They soon started to chafe. Then she reached the wide meandering river.

The bank on her side of the valley was disturbingly boggy. Apparently the Silfen didn't use boats. Nor was there any sign of any ford, or even stepping-stones. In any case, she didn't like the look of how fast the smooth water was flowing. Gritting her teeth she set off downriver. After half an hour she conceded there was no natural crossing point. There was nothing for it – she would have to wade.

Araminta stripped off her fleece and trousers and blouse, bundling them together with her trusty tool belt – there was no way she was leaving that behind, even though it was far too heavy should she have to swim for it. She waded in, carrying the weighty roll above her head. The bottom of the river was slippery, the water icy enough to make it difficult to breathe, and the flow so harsh as to be a constant fear. In the middle the water came up almost to her collar-bones, but she gritted her teeth and kept going.

Her skin was completely numb when she finally came staggering out on the other side. The shakes were so bad she couldn't even undo the bundle of cloth that now held her sole possessions in the universe. She spent a long time alternating between being hunched up shivering violently, and trying to walk while flapping her arms around. Eventually her fingers finally began to work again. Her skin still had a horrible white pallor when she forced shaking limbs into her clothes once more.

The walk didn't warm her up noticeably. Nor did she reach the high tree-line on the other side of the valley before night fell. She curled up into a ball beside a small boulder, and shivered her way to a fitful sleep. It rained twice in the night.

Morning was when she realized she didn't have anything to eat. Her stomach was grumbling when she bent over a tiny trickle of water running round the base of the boulder to lap up the icy liquid. She couldn't remember being this miserable before; not the day she left Laril, not even watching her apartments going up in flames. This was just wretched. And worse, she'd never felt so alone before. This wasn't even a human world. If anything went wrong, anything as simple as a sprained ankle or gashed knee, there was no emergency service to call, no help within lightyears. She'd just have to lie down here in the valley and starve to death.

Her limbs started trembling with the thought of it, at the

full realization of the risk she'd taken yesterday wading through the river. Delayed shock, she decided, from both the river and the terrible fight in Bodant Park.

After that, she was a lot more careful walking up towards the tree-line high above. Though there was still no sign of anything she could eat. Underfoot was just the yellowy grass with its speckle of tiny lavender flowers. As she plodded on gloomily she tried to remember everything she'd ever heard about the Silfen paths. It wasn't much. Even the general encyclopedia in her storage lacuna contained more mythology than fact on the subject. They existed, there was no such thing as a map, and some medievalist humans set off down them in search of various personal or irrational goals – few of whom were ever heard of again. Except for Ozzie, of course. Now she thought about it she'd vaguely known he was a Silfen friend. *And so was Mellanie, whoever she used to be.* Araminta could have kicked herself for not running even a simple search with her u-shadow. It was over a week since Cressida had told her about her odd ancestry, and she'd never bothered to find out, not asked a single question. *Stupid.*

The thought of Cressida made her concentrate. Cressida would never give up or sink into a bout of self-pity. *And I'm related to her, too.*

So she began to sketch out a list of more positive aspects as she drew close to the woodland where she was sure the next path began. For a start, she could sense paths, which meant there would be an ending to this trek, a conclusion. Lack of food was a pig, but she had a strong Advancer heritage, and their ethos was to equip humans to survive the galaxy over. As she'd learned during her childhood on the farm, playing nibble dare with her brother and sisters it was quite difficult for an Advancer human to poison herself with alien vegetation. Her taste buds had a strong sampling ability to determine what was dangerous. Unless a plant was hugely toxic her metabolism could probably withstand it.

Even so, she didn't like the look of the grass on the mountain.

I'll wait till the next planet before I resort to that.

The air was noticeably colder by the time she reached the first of the moss-cloaked trees. Away down the valley, thick hammerhead clouds were sliding towards her. Rain at this temperature would wreck what little morale she'd recovered.

Long honey-brown leaves fluttered on the branches overhead as she moved deeper into the woods. Little white whorls like tightly wound spider gossamer peeped up through the grass beneath her feet. The air became still between the trunks of the trees as she walked forwards. Her confidence grew. Somehow in her mind she could sense the changes begin. When she looked up, the slender glimpses of sky she was afforded through the tangle of branches showed a light turquoise, which was encouraging. It was certainly brighter and more inviting than the atmosphere above the mountains.

Deep within the gaiafield, or the reverie of the Silfen Motherholm, whatever realm it was her mind drifted through these days, she could follow the way space subtly transformed around her. The path was constantly in motion, it had no fixed beginning or end – it was a way that responded to the wishes of the traveller. Although at some incredible distance there was an awareness that seemed to be observing her. That was when she had a vague notion of just how many entities were on the paths. Uncountable millions, all wandering where they might, some with purpose, wishing to know a certain experience, others allowing the paths to take them at random across the galaxy to find and know whatever they would.

New trees began to appear amid the moss-clad trunks, their smooth boles a whitish-green. Lush green leaves overhead reminded her of a deciduous forest in spring. Then ivies and vines swarmed up the trunks, producing cascades of grey flowers. On she walked. The path wound among small hills and into narrow valleys. Streams bubbled along beside her. Once she could hear the pounding thunder of some great waterfall, but it wasn't on the path, so she didn't try and follow the sound. Red leaves laced through the light-brown canopy. Her boots were treading on small crisp leaves amid the grass. The air grew warm and dry. Hours after she'd left the rainy valley behind, she heard a quiet madrigal being sung in an alien tongue. It didn't matter that she didn't know the words, the harmony was exquisite. It even made her stop for a while, allowing herself to just listen. It was the Silfen, she knew, some big party of them trotting merrily on their way to a new world offering fresh sights and excitements. For a moment she wanted to run and join them, see what they saw, feel for things the way they did. But then that image of Cressida, smart, self-reliant, focused, trickled up into her mind, and she knew sheepishly that traipsing off with a bunch of alien elves wasn't the answer. Reluctantly, she set off again. Somewhere far ahead was a Commonwealth world, she was sure of that; although the path was little used nowadays. The Silfen didn't care for planets where other civilizations arose, at least not above a certain technological level.

Araminta let out a sigh of relief as the trees finally thinned out. It was white and bright up ahead, and getting warmer with every footstep forward. The trees with the red leaves became the majority. Their light-grey branches were slim, widely separated. When she glanced at them she could see how fat and waxy the leaves were. She grinned in delight. There was something utterly awesome about having paths between worlds.

The path led her to the edge of the waving trees. She stared out at the vista ahead, blinking against the harsh light. 'Oh Great Ozzie,' she muttered in dismay. As far as she could see, the land was a flat expanse of white sand. The world's hot sun burned high overhead, unencumbered by any cloud. 'It's a desert!'

When she turned a full circle she found she'd emerged amid a few paltry clumps of trees that clung to the edge of a long muddy pool. And somewhere in those trees the path was dwindling away to nothing. 'No,' she told it. 'No, wait. This isn't right. I don't want to be here.' But then it was gone. 'Oh bollocks.'

Araminta might have been generally ignorant in the way of alien planets, but one thing she knew for certain was that you didn't start walking across a desert in the middle of the day, and certainly not without any preparation. She took a slow saunter round the pool, trying to spot any sign that other people were around. Apart from some very odd imprints in the dry mud, there was no evidence that anybody used the oasis on any kind of regular basis. With the sun rising higher, she sat with her back to one of the grey tree trunks, making the most of the measly shade cast by its chunky leaves.

All the doubt and self-pity she'd managed to throw off on the path threatened to come swarming back. Maybe the Silfen were more involved with galactic events than anyone suspected. They could have dumped her here deliberately so she could never lead a human Pilgrimage. Just thinking it through brought up an image of Cressida, and her cousin had her eyebrow lifting up in that incredibly scornful way of hers. Araminta cringed just at the memory of it.

Come on, pull yourself together.

She looked down at the tool belt. There weren't a lot of tools, and the power charge on some was well down. But they could be useful. *For what? How do I use them to cross a desert?* She looked round the silent oasis again, trying to be smart and analytical the way Cressida would be. *Okay, so I've got water. How do I carry it?* Then she realized that there were several stumps sticking out of the ground, but no fallen trees. She hurried over to one, and saw the wood had been cut clean and level. Someone had sawn it off. She gave the stump a modest grin. It was a great clue. *So now start thinking how you can use wood.*

The power saw she carried was small, designed to cut small shaped holes, not to fell a tree, however spindly. But she cut round a trunk, and managed to topple the tree onto open ground. The black wood under the bark was incredibly hard. She cut a couple of sections off, producing cylinders half a metre long, which she rolled into the shade and sat down beside them. Her drill bored a hole down the middle. Once she had that, she switched the drill bit to its expansion mode, and started to drill again. It took hours, but eventually she'd hollowed out each of the cylinders, leaving a shell of wood a couple of centimetres thick. They made excellent flagons. When she carried them into the pool to fill them up with the clear water in the middle, she felt something *give* under her feet. The dark-blue sphere she fished out had a slippery jelly-like shell. *An egg!* Araminta glanced round nervously, wondering what had laid it, land animal, or marine? Perhaps it was a seed.

The flagons were full, and she lugged them out quickly, but kept hold of the flaccid egg. It was the size of her own fist, the wet surface giving like slippery rubber beneath her fingers. Just looking at it made her stomach growl with hunger. She realized she hadn't eaten anything since that last breakfast with Tandra and her family, and that was a long time ago now.

With the egg wedged between some stones she turned her laser to low power wide beam, and swept the ruby-red fan forwards and backwards across the bendy shell. The colour began to darken down to a grubby brown, minute cracks appearing as it slowly hardened. After a few minutes she took a guess that it was done, and used her screwdriver to tap a hole through. The smell wasn't good, but she cracked a wide hole open, and hooked out some of the steaming greenish gloop inside.

Wrinkling up her face in dismay she touched some of the gloop to the tip of her tongue. It didn't taste of much at all, maybe slightly minty jelly. Secondary routines in her macro-cellular clusters interpreted the results firing down the nerve channels from her taste buds. They couldn't discern anything lethal in the hot organic mush, it certainly wouldn't kill her outright. Closing her eyes, she swallowed. Her stomach groaned in relief, and Araminta scooped out a larger portion.

After she finished the first egg (she was still half-convinced it was some kind of aquatic seed) she went trawling for some more, recovering nine in total. She cooked another four with the laser, washing down the uninspiring contents with the water from her flagons. The wood wasn't leaking, which she counted as a minor victory. With her stomach finally quiet, she set about splitting more wood and building a small fire. The flames baked the remaining eggs, saving power in her laser. An innovation she was firmly proud of, though she should have thought of it earlier.

As the flames crackled away, she set about stripping the bark of the tree she'd felled. When it was cut into thin strips she began to weave a hat. Three attempts later she had a flattish cone, which finally stayed in place on her head. So she began weaving a basket to carry the eggs.

There was one more fishing expedition in the late afternoon, which netted a further five eggs, then she settled down for a rest before night fell. She'd been working away for hours, and the sun was only just starting to sink down towards the horizon. The days here were long ones. Logically then, the nights would be as well, so she ought to be able to make a decent distance before the sun rose once more.

She dozed before sunset, dreaming of some tall blonde girl who was also alone. The dream was a vague one, and the girl was on a mountainside rather than in a desert. A handsome lad appeared, which set the girl's heart aflutter, then she was confronting a man with a gold face.

Araminta woke with a start. The man was Gore Burnelli. Which made her suspect the dream had emerged out of the gaiafield. It was weak here, but she could still perceive it. Gore had been very angry about something. For a moment Araminta was tempted to delve back into the gaiafield to see if she could recapture the dream, but decided against. The last thing she wanted now was to risk exposure to Living Dream again. Though how they would find her here was a moot point. Besides, she had more immediate problems.

With the small bright sun finally sliding below the horizon she gathered up her makeshift desert survival kit. The flagons were filled to the brim, and stoppered with cuts of wood. She hoisted them onto her back with a harness made from woven bark strips, grimacing at the weight. The baked eggs went into her basket, which was slung over a shoulder. More strips of bark were hung round her neck – she couldn't imagine what she'd need them for, but they were all she had, and the fruits of her own labour. Thus equipped, she set off.

The twilight lingered for a long time, which cheered her; total darkness would have been depressing, and not a little bit scary. Stars slowly started to twinkle overhead. None of the constellations were recognizable, certainly not to her encyclopedia files. *I'm nowhere near the Greater Commonwealth, then.* Despite that, she was confident she wasn't far away from a path that would take her there. She hadn't even hesitated when she left the oasis. She *knew* the direction she should take.

Her flagons were ridiculously heavy. Yet she knew she had to carry as much water as was physically possible. Her stomach wasn't exactly feeling a hundred per cent, and hunger was now a constant nag. She thought that perhaps the egg-things weren't terribly nutritious for humans after all. Still, at least she hadn't thrown up. That was a plus.

Araminta grinned at that. Strange how perceptions shifted so much, depending on circumstances. A week ago she'd been fretting about buyers for the apartments producing their deposits on time and getting angry with late suppliers. Now, not being sick as she tramped across an unknown desert halfway across the galaxy counted as a reasonable achievement.

After three hours she made herself take a rest. The desert was illuminated by starlight alone now. This world didn't seem to have a moon. Some of the stars were quite bright. She wished she knew enough astronomy to tell if they were planets. Not that it mattered. She was committed now. It felt good having a physical goal, something she could measure success with.

She drank some water, careful not to spill any. The eggs she left alone. *Save them for real hunger pangs.*

After half an hour she could feel the air becoming a lot cooler as the day's heat drained away into the sky. She zipped the fleece back up, and set off again. Her feet were sore. The boots were never designed for this kind of walking. At least the terrain was level.

As she trudged on she allowed herself to wonder what she was going to do when she did reach the Commonwealth again. She knew she'd only have one chance, one choice. Too many people were looking for her. Giving in to Living Dream was something she instinctively shied away from. But Laril, for all he was loyal and trying to help, was in way over his head. *Who isn't?* Though perhaps he could negotiate with some Faction. *But which one?* The more she thought about it, the more she was convinced she should contact Oscar Monroe. If anyone could offer her sanctuary, it would be ANA itself. And if it was going to use her there really was no hope.

Araminta kept plodding forward. Hunger and lack of true sleep were getting to her. She felt exhausted, but knew she couldn't stop. She had to cover as much ground as possible during the night, for she wouldn't be going anywhere during the day. Her limbs ached, especially her legs as she just kept walking. Every time she stopped to drink, it was more painful to haul the flagons onto her back again. Her spine was really beginning to feel the weight. It was all she could do to ignore the throbbing in her feet as her boots rubbed already raw skin. Occasionally she'd shiver from the now-icy night air, a great spasm running the length of her body. Whenever that happened she'd pause for a minute, then shake her head like some dog coming out of water, and take that step again. *I cannot quit.*

There were so many things that she needed to do, so many things she had to try and accomplish to stop the whole Living Dream madness. Her mind began to drift, she saw her parents again, not the ones she argued with constantly in her late teens, but as they were when she was growing up, indulging her, playing with her, comforting her, buying her a pony for Christmas when she was eight. Even after the divorce she hadn't bothered to call them. Too stubborn, or, more like, too stupid. *And I can just hear exactly what they'd say if I told them I'd met Mr Bovey, and I was going multiple.* Then there was that time just after Laril went offplanet, clubbing with Cressida most nights, going on dates. Being free, having fun discovering what it was like to be young and single in the Commonwealth. Having independence and a little degree of pride with it.

She wondered if any of that life would ever come back. All she wanted now was for this dangerous madness to be over, for Living Dream to be defeated, and for herself to become Mrs Bovey. Was it possible to fade back into blissful obscurity? Other people had done it, countless thousands had their moment of fame or infamy. Mellanie must have achieved it.

The timer in Araminta's exovision flashed purple, along with an insistent bleeping which wound down auditory nerves, drawing her attention back out of the comfortable reverie. She let out a groan of relief, and shrugged out of the harness. At least it wasn't so cold now. As she held up the flagon to drink, she saw lights crawling across the starfield. She'd lived in Colwyn City long enough to recognize starships when she saw them. 'What the hell?' That was when she realized the Silfen path was now behind her. 'Ozzie!' Her mind felt a host of quiet emissions within the gaiafield, originating somewhere nearby. She hurriedly guarded her own thoughts, making sure nothing leaked out to warn anyone of her presence.

So where in Ozzie's name am I?

Araminta looked round again, trying to make out the countryside. There wasn't much to see, though she thought one section of the horizon was showing a tiny glow. Smiling, she sat down to wait.

Half an hour later, she knew she was right. A pale pink wash of light began to creep upwards as dawn arrived. Now she could see she was still in a desert, but this one was mostly ochre rocks and crumbling soil rather than the featureless ocean of sand she'd left behind. The drab brown ground was broken by small patches of green-blue vegetation, small hardy bushes that looked half-dead. Tall fronds of pale-cream grass tufts lurked in fissures and stone spills, all of them dry and withered. Away in the distance, half-lost in air-shimmer, a broad line of mountains spiked up into the sky. Their height was impressive, yet she couldn't see any snow on their peaks. The desert stretched all the way across to them. In the other direction was a low ridge, which she began to appreciate was at least five miles away, if not further. This landscape was so relentlessly monotonous it was hard to judge perspective.

Whatever, she was on a dirt track made by vehicles of some kind. It led down a long gentle slope to a junction with a solid concrete road. Just the sight of it was a huge relief. From living out in the boondocks of an External planet for nearly twenty years, she knew just how rare roads could be, and that was in the agricultural areas. Everybody used regrav capsules these days. To find this here in the middle of a desert she'd been lucky. Very lucky.

Thank you, she told the Silfen Motherholm.

She took another drink of water, and set off down the track. The distance had fooled her after all, the road seemed to stay in the same place no matter how much ground she covered towards it. As she strode along the slope she saw a few regrav capsules flying beyond the ridge. In the other direction nothing was moving above the vast desert. At least that told her which way to turn once she reached the junction. There was obviously some kind of settlement on the other side of the ridge. A few cautious examinations of the gaiafield confirmed that was where the buzz of minds was situated.

It took her another three hours to reach the crest of the ridge. Again, 'ridge' was deceptive. The closer she got, the larger it rose above her. It was like an elongated hill. And the luck which had delivered the road had clearly abandoned her; there wasn't a single vehicle moving along it all morning.

By the time she finally limped to the crest she was ready for just about any sight apart from the one that greeted her. She'd almost been right about the elongated hill. The ridge was actually a crater wall. A big crater, complete with a beautiful circular lake that must have been at least twenty miles across. This was the mother of all oases. The inner slopes were all smothered in verdant woodland and cultivated terraces she thought might be vineyards. The road dipped away ahead of her, winding into a small town whose colourful ornate buildings were visible amid a swathe of tall trees. Despite being completely exhausted, aching everywhere, and quite worried about the painful state of her feet, Araminta couldn't help chocking out a little laugh at she stared down at the exquisite vista before her. She wiped the tears from the corner of her eyes, and slowly discarded the flagon harness from her back. It was placed carefully behind some rocks at the side of the road, and followed by the basket of eggs. With her shoulders rejoicing at the absence of weight, she started off down the slope.

People stared at her as she hobbled into town. Hardly surprising. She still had her silly conical hat on, and her clothes were a mess, filthy from mud and repeated deluges. She guessed she must smell, too. When she allowed herself to receive the local gaiafield she could sense the instinctive surprise everyone felt at the sight of her. Plenty of dismay was mingled in there as well.

The little town's buildings were mostly clapboard, painted a variety of bright colours; there were very few modern construction materials visible. It gave the town a comfortably quaint feel. The quiet old style suited the placid lake.

Even with the shade thrown by tall willowy trees, it was hot in the late-morning sun. There weren't many people about. However, she eventually sensed one old couple who didn't quite share the disquiet of their fellow citizens. The woman was even emitting a small amount of concern and sympathy from her gaiamotes.

'Excuse me,' Araminta asked. 'Can you tell me if there's somewhere to stay in town?'

The couple exchanged a look. 'That's an offworld accent,' the woman said.

Araminta pressed down on a giggle. To her the woman's accent was strange; she almost slurred her words as she ran them together. Thankfully, the pair of them weren't wearing the old-fashioned kind of clothes Living Dream followers usually favoured. But then it was unusual to see anyone whose body had aged to such a degree. 'Yes, I'm afraid so. I've just arrived.'

The woman emitted a glow of satisfaction. 'Good for you, my dear. Have you been away long?'

'I'm, er, not sure,' she replied honestly.

'I tried once,' the woman said with a tinge of melancholia. 'Never got anywhere. Maybe I'll try again after rejuvenation.'

'Um, yes. That hotel . . . ?'

'Why don't you just get your u-shadow to find out?' the man asked. He had a thatch of white hair that was slowly thinning out. His whole appearance made him seem harmless, but the tone he used was quite sharp.

'I'm a Natural human,' Araminta offered by way of explanation.

'Now, Earl,' the woman chided. 'There's the SideStar motel off Caston Street, my dear. That's four blocks this way.' She pointed, and gave Araminta a kindly smile. 'Cheap, but clean with it. You'll have no problem there.'

'Okay, thank you.'

'Do you have money?'

'Yes. Thank you.' Araminta gave them a jerky nod and set off. She stopped after a couple of paces. 'Uh, what is this place?'

'Miledeep Water,' the man said dryly. 'We're on Chobamba's equatorial continent, that's an External World you know.'

'Right.' She smiled, trying to give the impression it had just slipped her mind for a moment.

'In fact, we're the only settlement on this entire continent, which is a desert from shore to shore. Lucky you found us, really.' The irony was quite blatant now, even through the odd accent.

'Yes.'

The woman gave him a mild jab with her hand, hushing him. Araminta smiled again, and backed off fast. As she went down Caston Street she was uncomfortably aware of the pair of them standing watching her. The man's mind was filling with mild amusement, coupled with just a trace of exasperation.

It could have been worse, she told herself. *They could have been suspicious, or recognized me.*

Araminta's encyclopedia files said Chobamba had been settled for barely two hundred and fifty years. She guessed that the StarSide motel was one of the earlier businesses to be established. Its chalets were an exception to the town's clapboard buildings. They'd been grown from drycoral, which was now long dead and starting to flake under the unremitting sun. It was a similar variety to the pale-violet drycoral they'd used for barns back on the farm in Langham, so she knew for it to reach such a state it had to be at least a century old.

The motel occupied a wide area, with the chalets spread out in a broad circle to surround a swimming pool. Their concrete landing pads for visiting capsules were all cracked, forced open by weeds and clumps of unpleasant-looking red fungus balls. Only one capsule was currently parked.

Irrigation nozzles were squirting pulses of spray onto its front lawn as she walked up to the reception building. She supposed the whole crater wall must be irrigated.

The owner was in the back office, tinkering with an ancient air-conditioning unit. He came out wiping his hands on his shabby white vest, and introduced himself as Ragnar. His glance swept up and down, giving her clothes a quick appraisal. 'Been a while since we've had anyone walk in,' he said, stressing 'walk'. His accent was the same as the old couple she'd met.

'But I'm not the first?' she asked warily.

'No, ma'am. The Silfen path ends somewhere out there beyond the crater wall. I've met a few travellers like yourself over the years.'

'Right,' she said, relaxing slightly.

Ragnar leaned over the counter, speaking quietly. 'You been out there long?'

'I'm not sure.'

'Okay. Well, you've not chosen the best time to come back. These are troubled times for the old Greater Commonwealth, yes indeed.' His eyes narrowed at her blank expression. 'You do know what the Commonwealth is?'

'I know,' she said solemnly.

'That's good. Just checking. Those paths are pretty tangled by all accounts. I had someone once come straight out of a pre-wormhole century. Boy oh boy, were they confused.'

Araminta didn't argue about how unlikely that was. She smiled and held up her cash coin. 'A room?'

'No problemo. How long will you be staying?'

'A week.' She handed over the coin.

Ragnar gave her clothes another sceptical viewing as he handed the coin back. 'I'll give you number twelve, it's a quiet one. And all our rooms have complimentary toiletries.'

'Jolly good.'

He sniffed. 'I'll get you an extra pack.'

Room twelve measured about five metres by three, with a door on the back wall leading to a small bathroom which had a bath and a toilet. No spore shower, Araminta saw in disappointment. She sat on the double bed and stared at her feet – the pain was quite acute now. It took a while for her to tackle the problem of getting her boots off. When she did unfasten them, her socks were horribly bloody. She winced as she rolled them off. Blisters had abraded away, leaving the raw flesh bleeding. There was a lot of swelling, too.

Araminta stared at them, resentful and teary. But most of all she was tired. She knew she should do something about her feet, bathe them at least. She just didn't have the energy. Instead, she pulled the thin duvet over herself, and went straight to sleep.

*

Paramedics were still working in Bodant Park ten hours after the riot, or fight, or skirmish, or whatever you called it. A lot of people were calling it mass murder. Cleric Phelim had thrown the Senate delegation out of his headquarters when they had levelled such an accusation against him, hinting broadly that the

Commonwealth would convene a war crimes tribunal with him as the principal accused. But in an extraordinarily lame public relations exercise, five hours after the agents had finished blasting away at each other, he had finally lifted the restriction on local ambulance capsules. However, he wouldn't switch off the force-field weather dome or allow the injured to be transferred to hospitals in other cities. Colwyn's own hospitals and clinics, already swamped by earlier injuries from clashes between citizens and paramilitaries, were left to cope by themselves.

Casualty figures were difficult to compile, but the unisphere reporters on the ground were estimating close to a hundred and fifty bodyloss victims. Injuries were easily over a thousand, probably two with varying degrees of seriousness.

Oscar had directly added two people to the bodyloss count; he wasn't sure about collateral damage but it wasn't going to be small either, no one in that fight had held back. On one level he was quietly horrified at his own ruthlessness when he'd protected Araminta from the agents converging on her. He'd allowed the combat programs to dominate his responses. Yet his own instincts had contributed, adding a ferociousness to the fight that had exploited every mistake his opponents had shown. And his biononics were top of the range, producing energy currents formatted by the best weapons-grade programs the Knights Guardian had designed. It had also helped that Tomansio and Beckia had bounced over to his fight within seconds, adding their firepower and aggression. Yet he'd held by himself for those first few vital moments, the feeling was the same as the Hanko mission back in the good old days, flying near-suicidal manoeuvres above the star because it was *necessary*.

Now, the morning after, guilt was starting to creep back. Maybe he should have shown some restraint, some consideration for the innocent bystanders trying to fling themselves clear. Though a deeper rationality knew full well that he had to cover Araminta's escape. The fate of the Commonwealth had hung on that moment, determining which Faction would grab her. Perhaps that was why he'd fought so ruthlessly, he *knew* he had to succeed. The alternative was too horrific to consider, or allow.

Certainly Tomansio and Beckia had shown a measure of respect absent before. He just wished he'd earned it some other way.

Their borrowed capsule left the Ellezelin Forces base in the docks and curved round to cruise above the Cairns, heading for the big single-span bridge.

'Somebody must have got her,' Beckia said; it had almost become a mantra. After they all got clear from the fight in Bodant Park they'd spent the rest of the night helping Liatris search for the elusive Second Dreamer. Her disappearance was partially their own fault; Liatris had killed every sensor within five kilometres of the park. They'd been so desperate for her to get away that the measure was justified at the time; what surprised them again was how well she'd done it. Their search hadn't produced the slightest indication where she'd gone since she ran away from Oscar in the park. On the plus side, no one else who was hunting her (and there were still five functional teams that Liatris had discovered) had found her either.

'Living Dream haven't,' Tomansio said calmly. 'That's what we focus on. Until we confirm her situation we continue the mission. Right Oscar?'

'Right.' He saw her face again, that brief moment of connection when the startled, frightened girl had stared into him with frantic eyes. She'd seemed so fragile. *How on Earth did she ever stay ahead of everyone?* Yet he of all people should know that extraordinary situations so often kindled equally remarkable behaviour.

'Any luck with the image review?' Beckia asked.

'No,' was Liatris's curt answer. With Araminta dropping out of sight, their technology expert had launched a search through old sensor recordings to see if they could find how she arrived at Bodant Park. The Welcome Team had been analysing data from every public sensor in the city, trying to track her. Liatris (and the rival agent teams) had glitched the input to their semi-sentients, sending them off on wild-goose chases. But it was a telling point that none of their own scrutineers had managed to spot her during the day, not even approaching Bodant Park. The first time anyone had determined her location was when her outraged thoughts burst into the gaiafield at the sight of her apartments going up in flames. As yet nobody had worked out how she'd managed to conceal herself. Whatever method she used, it'd proved equally effective in spiriting her away during the height of the fight.

So now Oscar and his team were falling back on two things. One, that she would call him on the code he'd given her, possibly out of gratitude, or maybe from sheer pragmatism. And two, they were following down leads like a professional police detective. *Paula would be proud*, he thought with a private smile.

Despite a barrage of urgent anonymous warnings, the Welcome Team had arrested most of Araminta's family, with the notable exception of the redoubtable Cressida, who had pulled a vanishing act equal to Araminta's. They'd all been brought to the Colwyn City docks for 'questioning'. Liatris said Living Dream were bringing in more skilled teams from Ellezelin to perform memory reads.

Which just left them Araminta's friends in the city; though, with the exception of Cressida, she didn't seem to have many. Which was strange, Oscar thought. She was a very attractive young woman, free and independent. That would normally imply a big social group. So far Liatris had uncovered very few, though a building supply wholesaler called Mr Bovey was a promising lead. They were due to pay him a discreet visit right after their first appointment.

Tomansio steered the capsule away from the river and over the city's Coredna district. They landed on a pad at the end of a street and stepped out. The houses here were all made out of drycoral, single-storey and small, their little gardens either immaculately maintained or home to piles of rubbish and ancient furniture. It was one of the poorer areas in the city. All three of them stared at the Ellezelin Forces capsule parked at the far end of the street.

'*En garde*,' Tomansio said quietly.

They were all dressed in a simple tunic of the occupying forces, not armour. Oscar brought his biononics up to full readiness. Defensive energy currents and his integral force field could snap on with a millisecond's warning. He hoped that would be enough. As the three of them walked down the street he ran a field scan on the capsule up ahead. It was inert, empty.

'Assigned to squad FIK67,' Liatris told them when they relayed the serial number to him. 'Currently on city boundary enforcement duty.'

'Oh crap,' Oscar muttered as they drew near the house they wanted. His field scan had picked up someone with biononics inside. Whoever they were, they also had their energy currents in readiness mode. 'Accelerator?'

'Darwinist,' Beckia decided.

'Separatist,' Tomansio said.

'I'll take a piece of that action,' Liatris said. 'Put me down for the Conservatives.'

Tomansio walked up to the aluminium front door, and knocked. They waited tensely as footsteps sounded. The door opened to reveal a shortish, harassed-looking woman wearing a dark-blue house robe.

'Yes?' she asked.

Oscar recognized Tandra from the employment file Liatris had extracted out of Nik's management net.

'We'd like to ask you some questions,' Tomansio said.

Tandra rolled her eyes. 'Not another lot. What do you want to ask?'

'May we come in, please?' Oscar asked.

'I thought you Living Dream sods didn't bother asking.'

'Nonetheless, ma'am, we'd like to come in.'

'Fine!' Tandra grunted and pushed the door fully open. She stomped off down the small hall inside. 'Come and join the party. One of your lot's already here.'

Oscar exchanged a nervous glance with the others and followed Tandra inside. He reached the small lounge and stopped dead, emitting a potent burst of shock into the gaiafield. The woman with active biononics was sitting on the couch, with a happy twin on either side of her. She wore an immaculately cut major's uniform, and wore it well, the epitome of a career officer. Martyn was bending down to offer her a cup of coffee.

'Hello, Oscar,' the Cat smiled. 'Long time no see. So what have you been up to for the last thousand years?'

He let out a rueful sigh. *Come on, you knew this would happen at some point.* 'I was in suspension, where you should be.'

'Bored with it,' the Cat said. She glanced at Tomansio and Beckia. Oscar had never seen the Knights Guardian so taken aback, they were even more startled than he was. 'My people,' the Cat said mockingly. 'Welcome.'

'I'm afraid not,' Tomansio said. 'We are working for Oscar.'

'Surely I override that? I created you.'

'They have conviction in their principles,' Oscar said mildly. 'Something to do with strength . . .'

The Cat gave a delighted laugh. 'I always did like you.'

'What is this?' Martyn asked, looking from the Cat to Oscar. 'I thought you people were all the same.'

'Oh we are,' the Cat said.

'We are not,' Oscar countered forcefully.

'Mixal, Freddy,' Tandra called. 'Come here.'

The Cat's smile was joyous as her hold round both children tightened. 'I like the twins,' she said mildly.

Martyn started forward as Mixal and Freddy began to twist about in her unyielding grip. Tomansio intercepted him fast, restraining him. 'Don't move,' he growled.

Beckia gripped Tandra. 'No,' she warned as the woman tried to lunge at her children.

'Let go of me,' Tandra shouted.

'If you move again, I will shoot you,' Oscar told her flatly, hating himself for doing it, but he had no choice. Besides, it might just shock her into obedience. She'd never understand the twins' only chance of surviving the next five minutes was to let him and his team take charge.

'Big words,' the Cat said.

'I don't have many options,' Oscar said.

'How's Paula?'

'I thought you'd seen her?'

'Not quite. Not yet.'

'There's always a next time, huh?'

'You should know that, better even than I.'

'You know, last time I saw you on the plane to Far Away you weren't so bad.'

'I assure you I was,' the Cat said.

'Strange, because that was you now. The you that founded the Knights Guardian is in your personal memory's future.'

'That sounds horribly convoluted and confusing, darling.'

'Thinking about it, you *you* never actually met me on the plane to Far Away. Your memories come from the day before you were sent to Randtown.'

'And your point is?'

'Interesting that you've researched yourself.'

'Know your enemies.'

'Ah, now that actually does make sense. Especially with the number you have by now.'

'Whereas you live in a happy universe.'

Oscar gave her a lopsided grin. 'It has you in it.'

'Ouch, that was personal, darling.'

'Of course it was personal. After what happened on the plane between us how could it be anything else? Oh wait, you don't have that memory.'

The Cat actually looked quite startled. 'You have to be kidding, darling. You don't even like girls.'

'No. But as you said, you like me, and racing towards almost certain death triggers some reflexes no matter what. I just had to work with what was available.'

'Now you're being insulting.'

Oscar kept his face perfectly blank. 'No, I'm still being

personal. After all, whose kid did you go and have after the Starflyer crash?'

'*Kid?*' the Cat spluttered. 'Me? With you?'

'What is wrong with you people!' Tandra screamed. 'Just go, all of you. Go and leave us alone.'

Oscar held a finger up to the distraught woman, then ignored her. 'If you didn't research that bit, ask the Knights Guardian here you *created*. Was there a gap in your history around then?'

The Cat glanced at Tomansio, who was still holding back Martyn. 'Actually, there is a chunk of your timeline missing following the crash,' he said slowly. 'Nobody knows what you were doing then.'

'Fuck off,' the Cat snapped at him. 'And you.' She glared at Oscar. 'You don't know either. You were a memorycell dangling on Paula's chain for a thousand years.'

'The kid visited me after I was re-lifed. Told me the whole story.'

'Stop it. Now.'

'Okay,' he said reasonably. 'Did you have time to ask these good people anything?'

'You cannot screw with my mind.'

Oscar winked. 'Already done the body.' He turned to Tandra. 'Did she ask you about Araminta?'

Tandra stretched her arms out towards the couch where the twins were still squirming ineffectually. 'Please?'

Oscar extended his arm. A red laser shone through the skin on his forefinger, splashing a dot onto Freddy's forehead. Everyone froze. Freddy started wailing, curling up tighter against the Cat, believing she would protect him. *If only you knew how wrong that instinct is,* Oscar thought miserably. 'Did she?'

'You won't,' the Cat said. She gave Tandra a brisk smile. 'He's the good guy, he's not going to shoot children, that's what I do. And I'm very good at it.'

'Well I wouldn't shoot ours,' Oscar said with a cheerful tone.

He rather enjoyed the venomous expression on the Cat's face. 'What happened before I got here?'

'Nothing!' Martyn bellowed. 'In Ozzie's name, stop this, please. Please! They're just children.'

Oscar looked straight at the Cat, unflinching. His target laser switched off. 'We're going to share the knowledge, and then we're both going to leave.'

'How very weak of you,' the Cat said.

'How very tactical,' Oscar said. 'If you resist, the three of us will turn on you. Some of us may suffer bodyloss, but ANA will have us re-lifed in half a day. You on the other hand will certainly die. The information will die with you, unused. The Accelerators will not recover Araminta, and you ... Oh, yes, what was it now? Message from Paula. She paid a visit to the ice moon Accelerator station. There were several of you in suspension there. There aren't any more.'

The Cat gave the crying twins a pointed glance.

'Possible end of the galaxy against two lives,' Oscar said. 'No contest. Remember I was a serving Navy officer. I'm used to this situation. Necessity always outweighs sentiment. I blew up Hanko's sun, which killed an entire planet.'

'Actually, darling, I killed Hanko, but let's not go into that right now.'

'You don't get to go into anything. You have one choice, walk away or die. And think about this, if Living Dream or the Accelerators win, your real body will never come out of suspension. The Earth will have been converted to pure energy by the Void's boundary to fuel some idiot's daydream long before that scheduled day comes.'

Oscar turned his back on the Cat. *And how many have done that and lived?* As she didn't immediately open fire on him he asked Tandra: 'Tell me about Araminta.'

'She was here,' Martyn blurted. 'That bitch. She's the reason all this has happened, and she came here! Here in our home.'

'When?'

'The night before the fight in Bodant Park,' Tandra said wearily. 'She said she was frightened of the crowd in Bodant Park, and hadn't got anywhere else to go. We let her sleep here. On the couch.'

'Did she tell you she was the Second Dreamer?'

'No. I still can't believe it. She's just a messed-up girl.'

'She's a lot more than that. How did she get here?'

'She said she walked.'

'I never believed that,' Martyn grumbled.

'Did you see a trike or a taxi?' Oscar asked him.

'No, but it's a long way to walk from Bodant Park. And she lied about everything else.'

'Okay, and when she left?'

'She walked,' Tandra said. 'I saw her go. There was no trike or anything. She was all alone.'

'Where was she going?'

'She didn't say.' Tandra hesitated. 'I thought it might be a man. She used my makeup, took a long time. She looked great when she left.'

'Ah,' Beckia said. 'Did she look like herself?'

'Not really, she changed a lot. Her hair was real dark. Her own colour is better for her.'

'Clever.'

'Okay then.' Oscar looked back at the Cat. 'You got anything else to ask?'

'Who's she screwing?' the Cat asked.

'I don't know,' Tandra said. 'I hadn't seen her for ages. It was a surprise when she came here.'

'So you're her best friend? The one she turns to in a crisis?'

Tandra shrugged. 'I guess.'

'I've heard enough.' The Cat released the twins and stood in one swift motion. Oscar blinked, she really had moved *fast*.

Must be running accelerants, he thought.

Tandra and Martyn rushed for their children.

The Cat gave Oscar a wicked grin. 'Be seeing you.'

'I'll tell the grandkids you're coming. There's lots of them. It's been a thousand years, after all.'

Her chuckle sounded genuine. 'You know, maybe it is possible.'

Oscar braced himself, if she was going to do anything it would be *now*. The moment passed, and the Cat left.

Beckia let out a low whistle as she relaxed.

Tomansio put his hand on Oscar's shoulder. 'You know, you're almost as crazy as she is. Er, you and her on the plane, did that really . . .'

'A gentleman never tells,' Oscar said solemnly.

'Fuck me.'

'When this is over I'll take you up on that. But I think we'd better leave now.' His field scan showed him the Cat's stolen capsule rising from the pad. Once again he tensed up. Would she fly over the house and blast away at it?

Tandra and Martyn had huddled up protectively, hugging their children hard. The twins were sobbing in distress.

'Take my advice,' Oscar said to them. 'Leave here right now. Go stay with friends or in a hotel, anywhere, just not here. There will be more like us coming.'

'Ozzie curse you straight to hell, you bastards,' Martyn hissed furiously. There were tears running down his face.

'I've met Ozzie,' Oscar said quietly. 'He's nothing like everyone today thinks he is.'

'Just *go*,' Tandra implored.

Oscar led Tomansio and Beckia back to their borrowed capsule. As soon as they left the little drycoral house behind he called Paula.

'The Cat's here.'

'Are you sure?'

Oscar shuddered. 'Oh yeah. We had quite a chat.'

'And you're still alive, I'm impressed.'

'Yeah well, I managed to throw in a cosmic-sized distraction. It put her off her game for a while.'

'Is she joining the hunt for Araminta?'

'Yes.'

'Figures. The Accelerators are desperate to acquire her.'

'I thought we are, too?'

'We are. It has become imperative.'

'I'm doing my best. I'm still hopeful she might just call me. She's not quite the superwoman everyone thinks.'

'I never believed she was. What's your next move?'

'We're going to visit a Mr Bovey. Liatris has uncovered some kind of connection between him and Araminta.'

'Okay, keep me informed.'

'What are you doing?'

'Don't worry; I'm on my way to Viotia.'

'I thought I was doing this so you could keep a low profile.'

'That time is now officially over.'

*

As he approached the Ocisen fleet, Kazimir maintained a single hyperspace communication link back to ANA. He knew the ExoProtectorate Council was expecting him to provide them a real-time progress review of the engagement, but that would have given Ilanthe too much information. The Prime ships travelling with the Ocisen Starslayers would have been warned of his approach. Not, he admitted, that it would have done them any good against his abilities. But then, they were never the true threat. Something else would be out there watching, sending precious information on the nature of the deterrence fleet back to the Accelerators. He was sure of it.

Kazimir matched velocity with the vast alien armada, and began to examine the ships. With his sensor functions, detection was easy; over two thousand eight hundred Ocisen ships raced through interstellar space at four and a half lightyears an hour, including nine hundred Starslayers. His perception infiltrated the hulls, exposing the weapons they carried – enough quantumbuster-types to wipe out most of the Greater Commonwealth Worlds should they ever reach their destination. But nothing more, no post-physical systems they'd chanced upon and retro-engineered, which was a relief. He switched his attention to the thirty-seven Prime ships accompanying them; they used a sophisticated hyperdrive configured to keep their distortion to an absolute minimum. Their weapons were considerably more advanced than anything the Ocisens possessed, effectively equal to a Commonwealth Navy Capital-class ship. But that was it. They didn't pose a danger to him. And there were no other ships, no clandestine ultradrive-powered observers keeping watch, no unaccounted hyperspace links within a lightyear of the Ocisen fleet. Although each of the Prime ships had a hyperspace link opened to some location back around Commonwealth space; he could sense them, slender threads stretched across the quantum fields, pulsing with information.

The Prime ships were the observers, he decided. Presumably they wouldn't expect him to be able to eliminate all thirty-seven of them simultaneously. Well that was their first mistake.

Kazimir manifested extra sensor functions into five of the Prime starships. In spacetime they were barely the size of a neutron, but they could receive all the inter-Prime communications with the hulls. Every Prime ship had a controlling immotile that took the job of a smartcore in human ships, governing the technology directly; it also instructed the immotiles. The ships represented a microcosm of Prime society. Pretechnology, the Primes had communicated by touching their upper-body stalks, allowing nerve impulses to flow between them. That had been superseded by simple electronic carriers, allowing immotiles to extend their immediate control over vast distances.

Kazimir began to read the digitized impulses. The Commonwealth had a lot of experience with inter-Prime communication. Not least the Navy, which had developed a whole range of disruption routines and electronic warfare techniques. If the Primes ever escaped the barriers at the Dyson pair and posed a threat again, they would find their thoughts literally snuffed out.

The first thing that was apparent was the Primes in the

starships were simple biological hosts to human thoughts. *So Paula was right,* Kazimir thought grimly.

'Do you concur with my assessment?' he asked ANA:Governance.

'Yes.'

'Very well.' Within the deluge of the neural directives he was aware of a datastream being encrypted and sent down the ultrasecure hyperspace link to the Commonwealth. There was a lot of sensor data, but again nothing beyond Capital-class level. 'The Accelerators will know I've intercepted the fleet when the signal is severed,' he said. 'But I can ensure they don't know the nature of the interception.'

'Proceed.'

Kazimir manifested a series of aggressive function inside each Prime starship, and used them to attack the hyperspace communication systems. As the secure links failed, he switched to breaking the hyperdrives themselves. The ships fell back into real spacetime within fifty milliseconds of each other. With their flight ability neutralized, he set about eliminating the on-board weapon systems. It took a second and a half for his aggressor functions to break down the hardware. Then he turned his attention to the Ocisens.

The problem he had was eliminating the military threat which the aliens posed, without causing catastrophic loss of life. He couldn't simply destroy the drives of so many ships, because the Empire didn't have the ability to rescue so many of its own kind from such a distance. Instead he manifested specific aggressor functions inside each of the starships, and ruined the weapons beyond repair or recovery. Between them, they weren't left with enough components to make a single laser, let along the more advanced devices.

Total elapsed time to nullify all two thousand eight hundred starships was eleven seconds. Enough for them to realize something was starting to go wrong, but denying them any response time. Not that they could have done anything against him even if they had known.

Kazimir let them go. His energy signature flashed back to the area of space where the big Prime ships were floating helplessly. This time he manifested a communication function into one of the ships, its ability identical to the inter-Prime system. Like all human minds, the one occupying the Prime bodies utilized association as its main memory routine.

Kazimir injected: Origin.

Identity.

Purpose.

Each one triggered a deluge of thoughts. Kazimir identified the animating personality was derived from Chatfield's mind, his human persona stripped of most emotional traits. His sense of purpose was resolute, as was his devotion to the Accelerators. The Prime ships were to escort the Ocisens and protect them from the Commonwealth Navy's attempts to intercept, but their most important mission was to report on the appearance of the deterrence fleet, its nature and capability. After that there was no requirement left.

A sensation of puzzlement flashed between the immotile and its motiles as the burst of thoughts Kazimir had elicited faded from its main consciousness. Realization followed. It sent a specific code to the scuttle bomb. Kazimir wasn't quite quick enough to prevent it. Now he knew what to look for, he quickly manifested a function into the remaining ships which disabled the scuttle in all of them.

'Do you have sufficient evidence now?' he asked ANA:Governance.

'I do. The Accelerators have acted recklessly. In supporting the Ocisens and manipulating Living Dream they have violated the principles under which I was established. I will convene a suspension conclave.'

'They will know the deterrence fleet has intercepted the Ocisen fleet, even though they remain unaware of my nature. They must assume the worst, that I have uncovered their exploitation of the Primes.'

'That would be logical. However, there is little their agents can do. Once suspension is enacted their operations will be exposed to full scrutiny and neutralized.'

Kazimir reviewed the starships as they drifted passively. 'Nonetheless, I still don't see what the Accelerators hoped to achieve, outside crude political manipulation. Ilanthe is smarter than that. I would feel more comfortable being on hand during the hearing. I will return immediately.'

'What about the Ocisen fleet? I thought you were going to monitor them.'

'They are incapable of causing any harm. When the commander realizes that, they will have no option but to return home. Our Capital-class ships can assume observation duties.'

'The defeat to the commander's pride is considerable. It may not want to return to the Empire.'

'That will be something for the Capital ships to determine. I am coming back to Sol.'

'As you wish.'

Kazimir manifested a communication function, and broadcast a simple message to the ships. 'Attention the Chatfield personalities, this is the Commonwealth Navy deterrence fleet. We know what you are and what you intended. Do not attempt any further suicide bids. Capital-class ships will rendezvous with you shortly. You will be taken into Navy custody.'

With that, Kazimir withdrew his manifested functions and headed back towards the Sol system.

Justine: Year Three Reset

Exoimage medical icons leapt out of the darkness to surround Justine Burnelli's consciousness. She'd seen that exact same set of read-outs once before.

'Oh man,' she grunted in shock and delight. 'It worked.' She tried to laugh, but her body was resolutely refusing to cooperate, insisting it had just spent three years in suspension rather than . . . Well, actually she wasn't sure how long it had taken to reset the Void back to this moment in time.

The medical chamber lid peeled back, and she looked round the *Silverbird*'s cabin again. *Really, again.* She sat up and wiped the tears from her cheeks. 'Status?' she asked the smartcore. A new batch of exoimage icons and displays sprang up. They confirmed the *Silverbird* had been under way for three years, and was now decelerating hard. Something was approaching.

'Ho yeah,' she murmured in satisfaction as the starship's sensors swept across the visitor. It was the Skylord, vacuum wings fully extended.

As it drew close she examined the weird ovoid core one more, still unable to decide if the fantastic folds of crystalline fabric were actually moving, or if she was seeing surface refraction patterns. The *Silverbird*'s sensors couldn't get an accurate lock on the substance.

As before, she settled back down in the lounge's longest couch and reached for the Skylord with her longtalk.

'Hello,' she said.

'You are most welcome,' the Skylord replied.

So far, so the same. Let's see: 'I have come to this universe to achieve fulfilment.'

'All who come here strive for that moment.'

'Will you help me?'

'Your fulfilment can only be achieved by yourself.'

'I know this. But humans such as myself reach fulfilment by participating in our own society. Please take me to Querencia, the solid world where my kind live.'

'My kindred are not aware of any thoughts akin to your species anywhere in the universe. None are left.'

'This I also know. However, I am simply the first of a new generation of my species to reach this place. Soon millions of us will be here. We wish to live and reach fulfilment on the same world as humans matured on before. Do you know where it is? There was a great city there, which was not of this place. Do you remember guiding human souls from that world to the Heart?' Justine tensed up in the couch. This was the critical question.

'I remember that world,' the Skylord said. 'I guided many from that place to the Heart.'

'Please take me there. Please let me reach fulfilment.'

'I will do so.'

Justine was acutely aware of the gravity in the cabin changing somehow. The smartcore reported an alarming outbreak of glitches right across the starship. She didn't pay attention – she was feeling horribly dizzy. Her mouth was watering as a prelude to being sick; she couldn't focus on the curving bulkhead wall, it was moving so fast. She hurriedly jammed her eyelids shut, which only made the effect worse, so she forced her eyes open again, and concentrated hard on the medical chamber directly ahead of her. Secondary routines in her macrocellular clusters began to edit the erratic impulses her inner ears were slamming into her brain, countering the appalling vertigo. The sensation began to abate a little. She checked the sensor images. 'Holy crap.'

The *Silverbird* was rolling as its trajectory curved round; it was caught in the wake of the Skylord like some piece of flotsam. The curving patterns contained within the Skylord's crystalline sheets were undulating wildly as its vacuum wings swirled like an iridescent mist across the gentle glow of the Void's nebulas. All she could think of was a bird flapping frantically. Then the course alteration was over. The Silverbird's sensors reported a noticeable Doppler shift in the light from the stars. They were accelerating at hundreds of gees, just as the Skylord had done on their first encounter.

This first encounter, she corrected herself. *Or should that be* ... In the end she decided human grammar hadn't quite caught up with the Void's abilities.

Whatever strange temporal adjustment the Skylord had made to facilitate their acceleration ended soon after. Ahead of them, the few stars shining amid the nebulas had acquired a blue tinge to their spectrum; those behind stretched down into the red. The *Silverbird*'s smartcore determined they were now travelling at about point nine three lightspeed. On-board glitches were reducing to acceptable levels, and her vertigo faded away.

She let out a huge sigh of relief, then grinned ruefully. 'Thanks, Dad,' she said out loud. Trust him to figure out what to do. Her good humour faded away as she acknowledged that others would be coming into the Void; that damned Pilgrimage would also go a hunting for Querencia. *So has the Second Dreamer agreed to lead them? And how the hell are they ever going to get past the Raiel in the Gulf?*

Gore had told her to concentrate on getting to Makkathran, so she'd just have to trust that he knew what he was doing, which didn't exactly inspire her with confidence. He'd have a plan of some kind, but it probably wouldn't be one she approved of.

No, forget probably: it just won't be.

Not that she had a lot of alternatives.

Once they were under way, the *Silverbird*'s smartcore plotted their course vector. Justine examined the projection, which extended a sharp green line past a purple and scarlet nebula shaped like a slipper orchid. The nebula was eleven lightyears distant, and wherever they were heading for beyond that was invisible, blocked by nebula-light and pyres of black interstellar dust.

After breakfast and a bout of exercise on the ship's gym, Justine sat back on the couch and longtalked the Skylord.

'How long will it take for us to reach the solid world we're travelling to?'

'Until we reach it.'

She almost smiled. It really was like talking to a five-year-old savant. 'The world orbits its star at a constant rate. How many times will it have gone round by the time we arrive?' Then all she had to worry about was if the Skylord even had a concept of numbers – after all why would a spaceborne creature need to develop maths?

'The world you seek will have gone round its star thirty-seven times by the time we arrive there.'

Crap! And a Querencia year is a lot longer than an Earth year. Didn't their months last for something like forty days? 'I understand. Thank you.'

'Will others of your kind come into the universe soon?'

'The one your kindred spoke to, the one who asked you to let me in; she will lead them here. Listen for her.'

'All of my kindred do.'

Which sent a slight chill down Justine's spine. 'I would like to sleep for the rest of the flight.'

'As you wish.'

'If anything happens, I will waken.'

'What will happen?'

'I don't know. But if anything changes, I will be awake to talk to you about it.'

'Change in this universe is finding fulfilment. If you are asleep you will not reach fulfilment.'

'I see. Thank you.'

She spent a further half a day getting ready, checking various systems, loading in a whole series of instructions about what constituted a reason for the smartcore to bring her back out of suspension. In the end she acknowledged she was just killing time. The last thing she did as she got undressed was shut down the confluence nest, ensuring that there would be no more of her amplified dreams leaking out to warp reality with such unexpected consequences. That brought back the one thought she'd been trying to avoid. Her mind lingered on the Kazimir she'd abandoned on the slopes of the ersatz Mount Herculaneum. All that was left of him now was a pattern in the Void's memory layer. It wasn't fair, to have lived for such a short time only to be unmade.

I will make you real again, Justine promised her poignant recollection of him. She lay down in the medical cabinet, and activated the suspension function.

2

Hunger and a nagging pain woke Araminta. At first she was woefully drowsy as she lay on the motel bed. Bright daylight was shining round the window blinds, warming the still air. Her stiff muscles protested as she tried to shuffle herself to a sitting position. Every part of her ached. Her feet throbbed. When she pulled the duvet aside to look at them she actually winced at the sight.

'Oh, Ozzie.'

Well! It was no good just lying about feeling sorry for herself, first thing was to get her feet cleaned up a bit. She eased her legs over the side of the bed and slowly stripped off her filthy clothes. Without doubt, they were ruined; she'd have to get rid of them.

The room had a cybersphere node beside the bed, so old it was probably the one installed as soon as the drycoral had finished growing into shape. Araminta started tapping away on its small keyboard, using the new account she'd opened at the Spanish Crepes office. Miledeep Water didn't have a touchdown mall, but Stoneline Street at its centre had a plethora of small stores that sold everything she needed. One by one she accessed their semisentient management programs and placed her orders, adding the items to the delivery service she'd hired.

She ran the bathwater at just below body temperature, then sat on the side and gingerly eased her feet in. The water soaked away the worst of the dirt and dried blood, leaving them looking slightly improved. She was letting them dry when there was a knock on the door. Thankfully, the motel supplied towelling robes. She'd assumed the delivery service would be a courier case floating along on regrav, all nice and impersonal. Instead, once she'd hobbled over to the door, a young teenage girl called Janice was waiting outside wearing a cap with the delivery company's logo and carrying a couple of large shoulder bags.

Araminta was thankful her hair was still all messed up, and the threadbare robe was a ridiculous white and red stripe. Even if the girl knew all about the Second Dreamer, she'd never recognize her in this state.

'I think Ranto was pulling into the park out front,' Janice said as she handed the bags over to Araminta.

'Ranto?'

'You ordered takeaway from Smokey James? He runs delivery for them.'

'Ah. Yes. Right.' Araminta couldn't work out if Janice was angling for a tip. It said a lot about Miledeep Water's economy that they used people instead of bots for a service like this. In any case, Araminta could remember how only half a year ago she depended on the tips at Nik's, so she produced the cash coin, which was obviously the right thing to do as Janice immediately smiled in gratitude.

Ranto appeared before the door was even shut, handing over the five thermplastic boxes of food from Smokey James. That immediately kicked up a dilemma. Araminta was desperate to use some of the medical kit she'd bought, but the smell wafting out of the food boxes was too much for her stomach, she could actually hear it churning. She sat back on the bed, and kept her feet off the floor as she started to open the boxes. There were pancakes in berry syrup and cream, followed by an all-day-breakfast of smoked bacon, local chulfy eggs scrambled, hash browns, baked galow, and fried mushrooms; the drinks box had iced orange juice and a litre flask of English Breakfast tea, then she finished with toasted muffins. By the time she'd finished eating, her feet didn't seem to be aching quite so badly as before.

Nonetheless, she applied the antiseptic cleaner, wincing at how much it stung; then sprayed both feet in artificial skin, sealing in the abused flesh. When she finished she just curled up on the mattress where she was and went straight back to sleep again

It was dark when she woke, leaving her slightly disorientated. Something somewhere wasn't quite right, and her subconscious was worrying away at it. She didn't think it was another dream connection to the Skylord, at least she couldn't remember having one during the last sleep. But on the plus side she didn't feel remotely hungry any more. *Time to think about me.*

The bath had spar nozzles which didn't work. Even so she let it fill to the brim and poured in the scented soaps she'd bought. While it was running she went back to the cybersphere node, and laboriously typed in a request for information on Oscar Monroe. The antiquated search software pulled a list of references out of the unisphere. There were eight and a half million of them. The search hadn't gone into deep-cache databases.

'Great Ozzie,' she muttered, acknowledging just how much she missed her u-shadow, which would have sorted the information down to something useful in half a second. Another minute typing in new parameters, and she'd filtered the list down to biographical details verified to the Commonwealth general academia standard – always a good starting point. That took it down to one point two million.

By then the bath was full, so she got in and wallowed in the bubbles as the dirt slowly soaked off. Reading up on Oscar would have to wait a while, but at least she knew he had to be important. He wasn't lying about that. When she got out she felt a whole lot better.

Araminta tipped the remaining contents of the bags onto the bed, and started examining the clothes. Most of it had come from a camping store, which had provided her with practical hiking boots that came halfway up her shins. When she tried them on they were impressively comfortable. The dark-brown jeans were tough and waterproof, which raised some interesting questions given she was on a desert continent. She shrugged into a simple black singlet, then put a loose burgundy T-shirt on top of that. A navy-blue fleece was similar to the one she'd brought with her, except this one was waterproof and the semi-organic fibres were temperature regulated. She needed that function: even after sunset Miledeep Water's climate was still baking from the desert air gusting over the ridge. All the other accessories, the knapsack, the water bottle (complete with manual filter pump), solar-store cooker, multipurpose blade, micro tent, gloves, thermal regulated bodystocking, hygiene pack, first aid kit, meant she could now walk wherever and whenever she wanted. The notion made her smile grimly at the collection. Buying the gear had been instinctive. She knew Miledeep Water was only ever going to be a way station; though Chobamba itself might turn out to be a possible.

She ran a hand back through her still-drying hair, suddenly unsure once more. Sitting worrying in a motel room wasn't exactly choosing her own destiny. She sealed the fleece up and went out to see what Miledeep Water had to offer by way of nightlife.

After half an hour walking along the nearly deserted streets she had her answer: not much. A few bars were open and some restaurants, as well as several all-day autostores, which were handy for people on a strict budget. Despite its location and the charming buildings, Miledeep Water was just too much like Langham for her to be at ease. Small town with a matching attitude.

The emotions emerging from the gaiafield of a bar down by the waterfront attracted her. The people in there were rejoicing over something. As she drew close she could hear some bad singing coming from the open door. The gaiafield emissions were stronger, more defined, as she walked up to sparkly holographic light shining through the windows. Araminta allowed the images and sensations to wash through her mind, experiencing Justine waking up back in the *Silverbird*. The essence of her conversation with the Skylord reverberated through Araminta's skull, enhanced by the rapture of those in the bar.

Justine is on her way to Makkathran.

Realization of exactly who was in the bar made the tentative smile fade from Araminta's face. Living Dream followers, celebrating the latest development in their favour. Making very sure none of her own bitter disappointment leaked out into the gaiafield to alert them, Araminta turned round and slunk away. That there were followers in Miledeep Water didn't surprise her; they were on every External World in the Greater Commonwealth and even the Central Worlds weren't immune. She wondered briefly what those in the bar would have done if she'd walked in. Held her prisoner or fallen at her feet?

Maybe Justine will manage to do something. Araminta couldn't quite recall the last dream she'd had, the one with Gore and Justine in some room. *I must see the rest of Inigo's dreams, find out what happened to Edeard, why he inspires everyone so. I have to understand exactly what I'm up against.* Then she stopped dead in the middle of the street as her subconscious finally triggered the memory that had been bugging her: the time display on the unisphere node. Araminta hurried back to the SideStar motel, not caring if anyone noticed her half-jogging along the deserted pavements and ignoring the traffic solidos to race across intersections.

As soon as she was in the room she locked the door and switched the unisphere node on. The central time display winking in the top corner of the screen always ran on Earth's GMT, with a secondary display showing local time. Araminta immediately switched it to Viotia time, and then Colwyn City. It took a moment while she did the mental arithmetic, aided by her macrocellular clusters – then she ran the figures again. If she'd done it right, and the secondary routines in the macrocellular clusters were practically infallible, then it was barely fifteen hours since she'd walked into Francola Wood. But that was impossible, she'd spent a whole day and night just trudging over that first wet, cold, miserable valley, then there had been the day by the oasis. The walk across the desert outside Miledeep Water, followed by sleeping the rest of the day away. That was when she worked it out – walking across the desert outside Miledeep Water and sleeping in the hotel accounted for a good twelve of those fifteen hours.

The Silfen paths took practically no time at all. How could that be? I wasn't even on the paths the whole time. Sweet Ozzie, do they manipulate time on the planets as well? But then, who knows exactly where the planets are, what universe or dimension? Come to that, were they even real?

When she looked down at her feet encased in the cushioning artificial skin, she knew she'd walked somewhere, and spent hours doing it. What happened, or rather where and when she'd been along the Silfen paths, was of no consequence. She knew then that the Silfen wouldn't let her use their paths and worlds as a refuge. It was instinctive knowledge, coming right from the heart of the Silfen Motherholm.

I really do have to face this myself.

'Oh crap!' She picked up the bar of orange chocolate that had been part of the delivery and took a big bite out before flopping back on the bed. There actually was no escape. *So where do I start?* Learning about Edeard was the obvious beginning, and to be honest she was rather looking forward to immersing herself in his life again. But she felt it was more important to find out about Justine. She let her thoughts slow, mildly satisfied that she no longer needed Likan's melange program to achieve the calm alert state required for any serious interaction with the gaiafield – not that the Skylord's thoughts occupied that particular realm. It was to be found in some parallel domain, its thoughts serene and content.

'Hello,' she said.

'You are always welcome.'

'Thank you. And thank you for receiving our emissary. Are you the one accompanying her to Makkathran?'

'I am with my kindred.' The Skylord's incredible senses revealed a vast swathe of space between nebulas, devoid of stars.

It flew on and on through the emptiness, followed by a flock of its own kind who called to each other across the gulf. They were all gladdened that minds were once again emerging into the Void, giant sombre thoughts enlivened by anticipation.

'Oh. Do you know where she is?'

'The one you seek is within our universe. This is known to us all. For that we all give thanks. Soon there will be more. Soon we will guide your kind to the Heart again.'

'Can you call to the one who is with her?'

'My kindred are departed across the universe. Most lie beyond my reach. I will encounter them again in time, within the Heart.'

'So how do you know one of us has arrived?'

'The Heart feels it. We all know the Heart.'

'Damn. Okay, thank you.'

'When will you come? When will you be here with your kind?'

'I don't know.'

Araminta withdrew her mind from the connection, and permitted herself a brief feeling of disappointment. It would have been nice to talk to Justine. Instead, she had only herself to rely on. A state she was growing accustomed to. Her mind reached out into the human gaiafield again, stealthily, slipping into the local confluence nests like a silent thief. Her thoughts fluttered around the sight, taste and smell of Edeard, and up into her brain sprang the wonderful lazy awakening on a soft mattress as dawn stoked the sky over Makkathran. A kiss touched Edeard's cheek, the phantom touch sending a delightful tingle along Araminta's spine. A nose nuzzled her ear. Then a hand could be felt sliding down her/his stomach, and her smile widened at the naughty sensation. Jessile giggled close by and thousands of years ago. 'Now that's what I call rising to greet the dawn,' she said.

The other girl giggled as well. Edeard's eyes snapped open, and Araminta looked out through them into his maisonette.

*

The Ellezelin forces capsule slid over the smooth fast-moving surface of the Cairns. Directly ahead was a big old house with walls of white arches filled with purple and silver glass, surrounded by balconies that overhung a pool whose water glimmered an inviting turquoise. Well-maintained formal gardens flowed down the slope to the southern bank of the broad river. Even under the wan light that filtered through the grey clouds scudding against Colwyn City's weather-dome force field the place looked inviting, a real home.

'Very fancy,' Beckia muttered as the capsule floated down onto the broad lawns. 'The building supplies game must pay more than I realized.'

'In an External planet economy, going multiple is just a smart way of avoiding taxes,' Tomansio said dismissively. 'Bovey wouldn't be able to afford this if every one of hims paid income tax.'

The capsule door expanded.

'Can I trust you?' Oscar asked quietly. The other two froze, then they were both looking at him. Beckia's gaiafield emissions were spitting out resentment. Tomansio was amused more than anything.

'You can trust us,' Tomansio said, pushing a warm sensation of confidence into the gaiafield.

'She founded you. You wouldn't even exist without her. And you're all waiting for her return.'

'Common mistake,' Tomansio said. 'We all understand her flaws, but we don't forgive her. We were born out of her determination, but now we have grown far beyond her.'

'Pupil and master relationship, huh?' Oscar queried.

'Exactly. She accomplished a lot in her time, most of which was disastrous. We are about the only good thing that ever emerged from the Cat's life.' He raised an eyebrow. 'Unless she did have children . . .'

Oscar simply responded with a wry smile.

'Quite,' Tomansio continued. 'So her continuing existence,

albeit in suspension, is something of an embarrassment to us. It leads to misunderstandings like this one.'

'Far Away rioted when Investigator Myo arrested her,' Oscar countered.

'Far Away did,' Beckia said. 'We didn't. By that time she'd grown to be a symbol of Far Away's independence. Arresting her was seen as a political act of repression against the planetary government by an authoritarian Commonwealth. I'd point out the riots didn't last long once the details of the Pantar Cathedral atrocity became known.'

'But her principles remain with us,' Tomansio said. 'The dedication to strength. Ever since our founding we have never broken our code. We stay loyal to our client, no matter what. Not even the Cat broke that. And we certainly wouldn't double-cross you. Oscar, you demonstrated the ultimate human strength when you martyred yourself so our species could survive. I told you before, we respect you almost as much as the Cat.'

Oscar looked into Tomansio's handsome face, so redolent with sincerity, a note backed up by his gaiafield emission. He fervently hoped his own embarrassment at such a proclamation wasn't evident. 'Okay then.'

'Besides, that wasn't our Cat, not the founder of the Knights Guardian. If we weren't committed to you I would take a great deal of satisfaction in tracking her down and finding out exactly which Faction has violated our Cat for their own ends. Didn't you say they'd cloned more of her?'

'Not any more,' Oscar said flatly, and walked out of the capsule. Beckia and Tomansio shared a quiet smile, and followed him out onto the trim lawn.

Mr Bovey had come out of the house to meet the capsule, three of hims. Oscar hadn't met a multiple before, at least not knowingly. He couldn't ever recall hearing about any on Orakum. The leader of the trio, the one standing in front, had black skin and a face that had even more wrinkles than Oscar's; several grey strands were frosting his temples. To his left was a tall Oriental male. The third was a young teenager with a thick mop of blond hair. None of them were releasing anything into the gaiafield. However, their posture alone told Oscar they were going to be extremely stubborn.

Oscar's immediate response was to regret wearing the Ellezelin forces uniform, which was a huge visual trigger for any Viotia citizen right now. Then a deeper guilt began to manifest. He wasn't here backed by Ellezelin authority – his sponsor was a whole lot more powerful than that. That was the problem. Marching into someone's home with the authority and force to demand their cooperation was exactly the kind of fascistic repression which had so animated the young Oscar Monroe's political instincts, which in turn led to him joining the Socialist Party at college and ultimately being seduced by radical elements. A journey which ended in the tragedy of Aberdan Station.

Talk about going full circle. But we have to find her. Overriding necessity, the siren call of tyrants everywhere. Yet I know she cannot be allowed to fall into the hands of the Factions. Damn, how does Paula live like this?

'What do you want?' the first Mr Bovey asked sourly.

Oscar grinned, letting his amusement free in the gaiafield. 'Oh come on. We know you and her had a thing.'

The three Mr Boveys stared defiantly ahead.

'Look,' Oscar said reasonably, and plucked at his tunic, 'this uniform, it's a load of bollocks. We're not Living Dream. I've never even been to Ellezelin. I work for ANA.'

'Yeah? And I work for the Raiel,' Mr Bovey replied, all three of hims speaking in concert. 'So that makes us both super-secret agents.'

'I saw her at Bodant Park. Me and my team here, we covered for her so she could get free. Ask her. We're the reason she's still out there. If she still is.'

There was a flicker of uncertainty in the black Mr Bovey's eyes. 'I met Araminta a few times, that's all.'

'It was more than that. Come on, man, she's in shit so deep she'll drown if she doesn't get some serious outside help. So please, if you know where she is tell me.'

'I haven't seen her for days.'

Tomansio grunted in understanding. 'She didn't tell you, did she? You didn't know she was the Second Dreamer?'

Mr Bovey's scowl deepened, none of hims would look at Tomansio.

'Hell, that's got to suck,' Oscar said. 'She was probably trying to protect you.'

'Right,' Mr Bovey said.

'She was frightened, you know that. This planet was invaded just because she lives here. And she's all alone. She doesn't know what she's doing, really, she hasn't got a clue. If you know where we can find her, if you have any notion where she might be, then we're the ones you need to tell. Call ANA if you need my status confirming. There are others out there who are looking equally hard, and I don't mean Living Dream. The Second Dreamer is an important political tool right now. Who do you think caused the Bodant Park fight?'

'Bodant Park massacre,' Mr Bovey said. 'You unleashed a massacre on our planet. There were hundreds killed.'

'That was just the warm-up,' Tomansio said. 'The agents involved in hunting her down will not give a crap about civilians who get in the way. Memory read will be the least of your worries when the others come here. And they will. Soon.'

'We found you,' Beckia said. 'The rest won't be far behind. Think. Be real. The most powerful organizations in the Greater Commonwealth are looking for her. Your entire planet has been invaded because Living Dream is so utterly desperate. Do you really, *really*, think she can elude all of us?'

'I didn't know,' the young blond one said through teeth he'd clamped together. 'She didn't tell me. How could she not tell me what she'd become?'

'If she loved you, she would be trying to keep you out of all this,' Oscar said. 'It was sweetly naive, and that time is now over. You have to make a choice. Do you want to actively help her? If so, talk to us. If not: run. Each of yous will have to try and make a break for it and pray that you don't all get caught.'

The three of hims turned to look at each other. Oscar was aware of the figures he could just see in the house standing still. 'Give me a moment,' Mr Bovey said.

Oscar nodded sympathetically. 'Sure.' He moved away, talking to his team in a low voice. 'What do you think?'

'He doesn't know anything,' Beckia said. 'If he did he'd be out there helping her. He's broken up by her cutting loose; he loves her, or thought he did.'

'I'm inclined to agree,' Tomansio said.

'There could be a dozen of hims out there right now helping to shelter her,' Oscar pointed out.

Tomansio pushed out a reluctant sigh. 'I find that hard to credit.'

'Can you actually do a memory read on a multiple?' Beckia asked.

'You'd probably have to gather all of them up,' Tomansio said. 'And you wouldn't know if you'd got them all until it was too late. Multiples are always cagey about their exact number of bodies, it's an instinctive safety redundancy thing. Interesting psychological evolution. In any case, our timescale doesn't allow us that level of luxury. If he's going to be useful it'll have to be voluntary, and right now.'

Oscar's u-shadow told him Cheriton was calling on an ultra-secure channel. Liatris joined the call.

'Brace yourself for the bad news,' the gaiafield expert said. 'Living Dream has found her.'

'Shit,' Tomansio grunted, throwing Mr Bovey a guilty glance. 'Where?'

'Now this is where it gets real interesting. After the conflu-ence nests caught her at Bodant, Living Dream has been refining the emotional resonance routines based on her exact thought patterns. The upgrade has given them the kind of sensitivity that can detect the slightest emission from her mind. And quarter of an hour ago she went and shared Inigo's Eighth Dream.'

'What's she doing delving into the Waterwalker's life *now*?' an irritated Beckia asked. 'For Ozzie's sake, didn't Bodant teach her anything?'

'Wrong question,' Cheriton said.

'Where is she?' Tomansio asked.

'Chobamba.'

A puzzled Oscar had to call up the Commonwealth planetary list from a storage lacuna. 'That's over six hundred lightyears away,' he protested. 'That can't be right. She was here sixteen hours ago.'

'Your ultradrive could make that,' Tomansio said doubtfully. 'Just.'

'She's found a way to screw the gaiafield,' Beckia said. 'She must have. She is the Second Dreamer after all. That has to give her some kind of ability the rest of us don't have.'

'Cheriton, are you sure?' Tomansio asked.

'We're confined to the building,' Cheriton said. 'And I'm using a dead drop relay to access the unisphere. Dream Master Yenrol's been going apeshit since the nests found her. All the Dream Masters know about it; they're working hard to keep it secret. I don't think this is a scam.'

'How the hell did she get to Chobamba?' Oscar wanted to know.

'Do they know where on Chobamba?' Tomansio asked.

'Not yet,' Cheriton said. 'But it's only going to be a matter of time. It's an External World, Living Dream has several Dream Masters there.'

'Can you warn her again?' Oscar said.

'I'm not sure. There's talk about shutting down Chobamba's confluence nests, isolating her from the gaiafield.'

'Stupid,' Tomansio said. 'That'll alert her to what's going on.'

'Liatris, can you shotgun Chobamba, and warn her?' Oscar asked.

'She hasn't accessed the unisphere for days,' Liatris said. 'There's no guarantee she'll get the message.'

'If people know, it'll be the talk of the planet,' Beckia said. 'She's bound to find out. We just have to make it public knowledge.'

Tomansio gave Oscar a little nudge. Mr Bovey had obviously come to his decision. The dark-skinned body was walking over to them, leaving the other two hims to stare pensively.

'Yes?' Oscar said.

'I checked with ANA,' Mr Bovey said. He sounded faintly surprised. 'You are who you say.'

'And?'

His face expressed a great deal of apprehension, mirrored by all of hims. 'She doesn't know . . . she can't know how to cope with this. Nobody can. I have to place my trust in ANA. How ironic is that? Being multiple is supposed to alleviate the requirement of a technological solution to immortality.'

'Can you contact her?'

'No.' Mr Bovey shook his head as if hes were mourning. 'I've tried every minute since I found out. Her u-shadow is offline. She won't answer my calls.'

'I know this is painful, but is there someone else she's likely to turn to?'

'Her cousin Cressida, they were close. In fact she was about Araminta's only true friend in Colwyn City before we met.'

'We know. She's dropped out of sight as well, but thank you. If Araminta does get into contact, please let me know.' Oscar's u-shadow sent Mr Bovey a unisphere access code. 'Immediately, please. Time is critical now.'

'That's it?' a bewildered Mr Bovey asked as Oscar turned back to the capsule.

'Don't worry, we'll keep looking. And you might want to consider my friend's advice about dispersing yourselves about town. I'm being completely honest with you, we're just the first to come visiting you and we really are the good guys.'

The capsule's door closed on Mr Bovey's frown. They lifted

cleanly, and turned to fly above the thick river, heading back to the docks.

'So now what?' Tomansio asked. It sounded rhetorical to Oscar.

'I'm going to check in,' he told the Knights Guardian.

'Yes?' Paula asked as soon as the secure link was opened.

'We've found her,' Oscar said.

'Excellent.'

'Not really, she's on Chobamba.'

There was only a small hesitation. 'Are you sure?'

'Living Dream has cranked up their confluence nests, something to do with getting a decent emotional pattern to recognize. According to them she's on Chobamba and having a good time sharing Inigo's dreams.'

'That doesn't make a lot of sense.'

'How quickly can you get there?'

'Not much faster than you.'

'I hope you've got sources in Living Dream. If they are going to try and snatch her, she'll need to be warned.'

'I'd have to find her first.'

'Surely ANA can track her down? Somebody must have noticed her starship arriving.'

'It would have to be an ultradrive, that means a Faction helped her. But which one?'

'I was thinking of a shotgun warning.'

'Yes. That might work. I'll confer.'

'If we know, then it's only a matter of time before the Cat knows.'

'Yes. If she leaves for Chobamba you'll have to follow her.'

'Oh crap, this isn't what I signed up for.'

'Can you trust your team?'

'I think they'll stick with me, yes.'

'Excellent, I'll call after I've spoken with ANA. Incidentally, the Accelerators are going to be put on what amounts to a trial within an hour. They were behind the Ocisen Empire invasion.'

'Shit. Really?'

'Yes. If they're found guilty, we should see the pressure easing off considerably.' Paula ended the call.

Tomansio and Beckia were looking at Oscar expectantly.

'So what does your boss think?' Tomansio asked.

'Same as us: it's all very odd. Let's get back to the ship in case we need to get to Chobamba in a hurry.'

*

The slim ultradrive ship dropped out of hyperspace half a lightyear out from Ellezelin. In its cabin, Valean reviewed the data provided by the starship's sensors. She was shown the exotic matter intrusions representing the huge wormholes which linked Ellezelin to the economically subjugated planets which made up the Free Trade Zone. The scale of the wormholes was impressive, harking back to the first era Commonwealth when the Big15 planets were the centre of an economic web binding together hundreds of worlds. Reviewing the size and power rating she was satisfied that any of them could be used for the task Atha had assigned her. Though the one connecting to Agra would be preferable. It was the most modern and reached the furthest.

Like most long-term Highers, Valean had used biononics to remould her body to a state she considered more functional and useful. Currently devoid of hair, she appeared skeletal, with skin that had a strange grey iridescence, and drawn so tight over her bones that each rib protruded. Muscles were hard lines, also standing proud, and moving like malmetal. Her face continued the emaciated theme, with deep-sunken cheeks and a slim nose that had nostrils resembling gills. Wide-set eyes had orbs that glowed a faint uniform pink. Her only cosmetic adornment was a circle of gold above her thorax, composed from a tightly packed cluster of threads that seemed to be moving slowly.

After ten minutes standing in her featureless cabin the starship detected a minute distortion within the quantum fields. Another ultradrive ship dropped out of hyperspace next to hers. The newcomer was slightly larger, with streamline bulges in its ovoid fuselage. They manoeuvred together, and linked airlocks.

Marius glided into Valean's cabin, his toga suit emitting wisps of darkness that trailed along in his wake.

'A physical meeting is somewhat theatrical isn't it?' he enquired. 'Our TD linkages remain secure.'

'They do,' Valean assured him, and smiled, revealing rows of tiny burnished brass teeth. 'However, it was felt that this would add more emphasis to the message.'

'Which is?'

'Your Chatfield fuck-up has produced an unwelcome fallout, the largest part of which I'm on my way to solve.'

'Paula Myo was on to him. Deploying him to Ellezelin was a simple precaution.'

'And do you have an excuse for the Cat?'

Marius remained impassive. 'Her behaviour can be unpredictable. That is her nature. As I recall, it was not my decision alone to salvage her from Kingsville.'

'Irrelevant. Your actions have produced unwelcome consequences at this critical time. As of now you are downgraded.'

'I object.' Even as he said it he tried to call Ilanthe, only to find the call rejected. Still, his cool disposition remained unbroken.

The brass teeth appeared again, their sharp tips perfectly aligned. 'Irrelevant. Your new assignment is the Delivery Man.'

'That joke!' Marius exclaimed.

'We approach deployment, the culmination of everything we are. Nothing can be allowed to interfere with that. He was seen on Fanallisto; find out why. What is he doing there, what are the Conservatives up to? We also need to know how the remaining Faction agents will react afterwards.'

'Victory is only hours away and you send me to some shitball outside civilization to track down an incompetent part-time animal. I do not deserve this.'

'Failure to comply will result in bodyloss. After the Swarm goes active there will be no re-life available. I suggest you make your selection.'

The dark hazy tendrils exuded by Marius's toga suit swirled in agitation. He glared at Valean, sending Olympian contempt flooding out through his gaiamotes. 'The true reason for physical contact, I see. Very well. I will comply. I am nothing if not devoted to our success.'

'Of course you are.'

Marius rotated a hundred and eighty degrees and slipped out back to his own ship.

'Thank you,' Valean mouthed at the airlock door after it closed. She ordered the smartcore to take her to Ellezelin.

*

Cleric Conservator Ethan had returned to the mayor's oval sanctum in the Orchard Palace. The Cabinet Security Service had downgraded the threat level, partially based on Ethan's own conversation with ANA:Governance. The surviving ship was simply maintaining a stable orbit around Ellezelin, and gathering up fragments of its vanquished foe.

His staff had served him a late supper of grilled gurelol fillets with minted potatoes and baby carrots, washed down with a sparkling white similar in taste to the one from Love's Haven which Edeard had come to enjoy during his first life with Kristabel. It was dark outside, with few stars showing through the oval sanctum's windows. Ethan ate by himself at a small table away from the big muroak desk, overhead a series of petal-like lines glowing a pale orange in the high ceiling. Shadows washed out from the walls, making the room seem even larger.

He was just pouring himself a second glass of wine when his u-shadow reported that Phelim was making a priority call.

Please Lady, no more bad news tonight, Ethan thought wearily as he accepted the secure link. He was still awaiting the call from Marius's 'friend'.

'We've found her,' Phelim declared.

Ethan paused, the wine not quite out of the bottle's neck. 'Who?'

'The Second Dreamer. The advanced pattern recognition routines located her for us. She's sharing Inigo's Eleventh dream would you believe.'

'Great Lady! Do you have her safe?'

'No, that's where the problem begins. She's not on Viotia any more.'

'Damn. Where is she then?'

'Chobamba.'

'Where?' Even as he asked, Ethan's u-shadow was pulling data out of the central registry. 'That can't be right,' he said, putting the bottle down.

'My response exactly. But the routines are good. The Dream Masters running them swear that's an accurate reading. She started sharing the Eighth dream twenty minutes ago.'

'The Eighth?'

'Yes.'

Ethan knew it couldn't be particularly relevant, but his curiosity about the enigmatic Araminta was overwhelming. 'So why did she skip over to the Eleventh?'

'She didn't,' Phelim said. 'She's on a linear run through.'

'Four dreams in twenty minutes?' Ethan said it out loud, his surprise echoing round the empty sanctum. At best, he would take a couple of hours to dwell in one of Inigo's dreams, and that was because he was so familiar with them. Some of the more devout Living Dream followers had been known to spend days in a dream, supporting themselves with intravenous feeds.

'Absolutely. That's what convinced me this isn't a false reading. Her mind is . . . different.'

'How in the Lady's name did she get to Chobamba? It was definitely her at Bodant Park. You confirmed that.'

'Someone must have flown her there. And it must have been an ultradrive starship, there's nothing else fast enough.'

'So one of the Factions got her and lifted her offplanet. Lady damn them.'

'That's the obvious conclusion. But it's a strange way to hide.

If she wanted to be completely secure she should have gone to a Central World where we have no control over the confluence nests. The Faction must know that. Perhaps this is a message. Though its nature eludes me.'

Ethan sat back in the chair, staring at the slim curving bands of light in the ceiling. The flowers they sketched had never been seen on Querencia or anywhere in the Greater Commonwealth. That's if they even were flowers. Edeard had always hoped to find them; but not even the grand voyages of his Twenty-eighth and Forty-second dreams had taken him to a land where they grew. And now Araminta was providing an even greater mystery.

'We have to have her,' Ethan declared. 'It's that simple. Whatever the cost. Without her, the only contact humanity has to the Void is—' He shuddered. 'Gore Burnelli. And I think we know where he stands.'

'Justine can do nothing,' Phelim countered smoothly.

'Don't be too sure. They are a remarkable family. I've been accessing what I can of their history. And I suspect there's a great deal that was never put into any records. Gore was one of ANA's founders you know. There are rumours of a special dispensation.'

'So what do you want to do?'

'How long before you have her exact location?'

'She's in a town called Miledeep Water, which presents us with a slight problem. It is somewhat isolated. We don't actually have anyone reliable there. The Dream Masters are going to have to visit its confluence nest to get an exact coordinate for her. It'll be an hour before we know exactly where she is, probably longer. I'm just hoping she shares Inigo's dreams for long enough.'

'Do we also have the kind of people on Chobamba who are capable of bringing her to us?'

'There are some very loyal followers in the movement there, people I can trust. I'd like to suggest we hire some weapons-enriched troops to back them up. It's pretty clear she's got Faction representatives guarding her.'

'As you wish. And Phelim, I don't want another Bodant Park.'

'Nobody does. But that is probably out of our hands.'

'Yes. I expect you're right. Please keep me informed of progress.'

The link to Phelim closed, and Ethan looked at the rapidly cooling food on his plate. He pushed it away.

'You seem troubled, Conservator.'

Ethan started, twisting round in his chair to see where the voice had come from. His u-shadow was already calling for help from Cabinet Security.

The woman-thing walking calmly out of the shadows on the other side of the desk disturbed his sensibilities. 'I believe you're expecting me,' she said. She was naked, which only intensified Ethan's censure as her body possessed no sexual characteristics. Her skin was some kind of artificial covering that produced a grey layer whose exact boundary was indeterminable. Far worse than that was her figure. It was as though her internal organs were too small for her frame, leaving the skin to curve in between every rib. And her eyes didn't help, little patches of pink moonlight that never revealed exactly what she was looking at. There was a gold circle just below her neck, from which sprouted two long streamers of dark-scarlet cloth. The fabric was draped across her shoulders to float horizontally through the air for several metres behind her. It rippled with the sluggish fluidity of an embryo sac.

Five armoured guards burst in through the main doors, their fat weapons raised. The Higher woman cocked her head on one side, while the gaiafield revealed a steely politeness in her mind.

Ethan held up a finger. 'Hold,' he instructed the guards. 'Did Marius send you?'

A narrow mouth opened to reveal shiny metal teeth. 'Marius has been moved to other duties. I am Valean, his replacement. I am here to help sort out our mutual problem with the ANA starship orbiting above you.'

Ethan waved the guards out, suspecting they wouldn't have lasted long against her. 'What do you want?'

She walked towards him, the scarlet streamers wavering sinuously behind her. Ethan saw her heels ended in a long tapering cone, as if both feet had grown their own stiletto. 'I require access to the Agra wormhole generator. Please inform the operations staff I am to be given full cooperation.'

'What are you going to do?'

'Prevent the ANA agent from retrieving any more fragments.'

'I can't afford any kind of conflict with ANA. Some in the Senate are eager for the flimsiest legal grounds to authorize Navy intervention.'

'We are expecting that any such concerns will soon be irrelevant. Rest assured, Cleric Conservator, there will be no physical clash here.'

'Very well, I will see that you have full clearance.'

'Thank you.' She inclined her head, and turned for the main doors.

'Please tell your Faction leaders I would prefer to deal with Marius,' he said.

Valean didn't even turn round. 'I will certainly tell them.' There was no trace of irony in her thoughts, the facade of politeness remained intact.

The doors shut behind her. Ethan let out a long breath of apprehension; he felt as if he'd finally been shown what awaited the lost souls who fell to Honious.

Preliminary sensor analysis of the debris cloud indicated there were 1,312 critical fragments, defined as anything over five centimetres across. When Chatfield's starship exploded, over a third of them had been thrown down towards Ellezelin on trajectories that would see them burning up in the atmosphere within half an hour; the rest were whirling rapidly along wildly different orbital tracks. Recovery would be a bitch.

Digby was quietly pleased at the way the *Columbia505*'s smartcore was handling the collection operation. Modified ingrav-drive emissions were pulling fragments out of their terminal trajectories; sensors had identified several particles which had exotic matter constituents, and were tracking constantly.

71

The sleek ultradrive ship was darting about, drawing the first chunks into the mid-hold where they were embedded in a stabilizer field. ANA:Governance had assured him a forensic team would be arriving within ten hours. Digby hoped so, stabilizer fields weren't designed to preserve exotic matter. A lot of it was decaying right in front of him and there was nothing he could do about it.

His exovision suddenly threw up warnings he never expected to see. A very large wormhole was intruding into space not three kilometres from the *Columbia505*.

'What the hell?'

The smartcore tracked several chunks of wreckage tumbling down the wormhole's throat. Then the wormhole shifted exit coordinates, reappearing five kilometres away. More junk was sucked down. Exoimage displays showed him it was the wormhole that normally linked Ellezelin to Agra. Somebody was redirecting it with unnerving skill, scooping up precious evidence. His u-shadow connected him directly into the planetary cybersphere, and tried to access the generator net. 'It's been isolated,' the u-shadow reported. 'I can't even gain access to the building net. Whoever's in there, they've sealed themselves in tight.'

Columbia505's sensors swept across the generator complex on the outskirts of Riasi, seven thousand kilometres away round the curvature of the planet. A force field was protecting the whole area. 'Crap.' Digby ordered the smartcore to distort the wormhole's pseudostructure. Negative energy fluxes reached out from the starship's drive, attempting to destabilize the wormhole's integrity. But the planetary generators had too much power available compared to the starship. It was a struggle Digby was doomed to lose.

'Take us down,' he ordered the smartcore. 'Fast.' As the starship dived down into the atmosphere, he called ANA:Governance and explained what was happening.

'I will call the Cleric Conservator,' ANA:Governance said. 'He must be made to understand that he cannot act against us with impunity.'

Digby was pretty sure the Cleric Conservator knew that, but held his council. It was long gone midnight in Makkathran2, which meant that Riasi was just slipping across the terminator line into daylight. *Columbia505* was decelerating at fifteen gees when it hit the stratosphere above the Sinkang continent, upon whose northern coast the ex-capital city was sited. The ship scorched its way down through the lower atmosphere like a splinter carved from a star's corona. It braked to a halt five hundred metres directly above the Agra wormhole generator's force field. The hypersonic shockwave of its passage slammed past it, shattering all unprotected panes of glass within a three-kilometre radius. Nearby regrav capsules tumbled through the air like leaves in a blizzard as their smartnets used emergency power to try and right them. Local traffic control was screaming warnings at Digby on every frequency. Metropolitan police cruisers curved round to intercept. He sent out a blanket broadcast to be picked up by every cybersphere node and macrocellular cluster surrounding the force field.

'Everyone in the generator complex, switch off the force field and deactivate the wormhole. You are violating an ANA sanctioned operation. I am authorized to use extreme force to end your transgression.'

As he suspected, there was no reply. There never would be, he knew. Every moment he waited playing the good guy was another moment spent eradicating the precious evidence in orbit. All that left him with was the problem of knocking out the force field without flattening half the city.

Eight slender atomic distortion beams stabbed out from the starship to the top of the force-field dome, ripping the air molecules apart in a blaze of incandescence. Monstrous static discharges flared away into the heaving atmosphere. The force field began to glow a pale purple, as if it was growing a bruise. A cluster of dump webs skittered down from the *Columbia505*

They struck the force field, kicking out blooms of dusky ripples. The darkness around them intensified, expanding rapidly. Under such an assault, overload was only ever going to be a matter of time. The force field collapsed amid a deluge of wild energy flares and superheated shockwaves that battered the surrounding buildings. *Columbia505* received a heavy buffeting, which the smartcore fought to counter and hold the ship stable above the circle of glaring ion flames that were eating into the generator building. Sensors reported the wormhole had failed. Digby was worried about how much evidence it had already cleared away.

Ellezelin Civil Defence Agency force fields were coming on above Riasi, a series of large interlocking hemispheres protecting the city's districts. Five large Ellezelin Navy cruisers were racing round the planet, their trajectories curving sharply to position them above the city.

A starship hurtled up from the buckling generator complex, accelerating at nearly forty gees. It fired a barrage of energy beams and disruptor pulses at the *Columbia505*. Digby found himself gripped by safety webbing as the starship spun helplessly. Planetary atmosphere was an alien milieu for it; systems designed for combat in the clear vacuum of space were operating below optimum, fogged by the dense gases. The force field shimmered a vivid amber, spitting off glittering scintillations while Digby's vulnerable inner ears conjured up a wave of nausea. Far below, consecutive shockwaves crashed down across the beleaguered commercial buildings and warehouses which comprised Riasi's sprawling interstellar commerce district.

The *Columbia505* levelled out. Routines in Digby's macrocellular clusters neutralized the nausea. Exoimage displays showed him the other starship streaking up through the troposphere, a huge ionic contrail shimmering behind it. 'Follow it,' Digby ordered the smartcore. The air above the shaken city howled yet again as the *Columbia505* powered its way up, ignoring the cruisers that were attempting to converge on it. The other starship slipped into hyperspace. *Columbia505* followed.

*

'Why? Paula asked before Digby had even cleared the Ellezelin system. 'Those fragments were vital. We'll lose most of them now.'

'Forensic analysis was only ever a long shot,' Digby countered. 'I determined the Faction ship was a much better lead. They risked a lot to obstruct my collection operation.'

'Which implies the fragments you were recovering were important.'

'My judgement,' Digby insisted, wishing he didn't feel quite so small. No other human, higher, advancer, or normal could ever make him feel so inadequate and defensive as his great-grandmother.

'Indeed it was, and you're committed now. How good is the sensor reading?'

'Holding steady. They're stealthed, of course, but my smart-core can still detect some distortion. It's a good ship they've got, equal to Chatfield's.'

'All right. I'd probably have done the same in your circumstances. You stay with it, and see where that representative is going. The ANA judicial conclave is beginning now, I'm expecting the entire Accelerator Faction to be shut down within the next hour or two.'

'Excellent.'

'It has its problems, not least the agents and representatives still at large, like the one you're following. I suspect we're going to be a long time mopping up.'

'At least we'll have a complete list of them and their activities.'

'Yes, that should help. Let me know when the ship reaches some kind of destination.'

'Of course.' Digby scowled as the secure call ended. This whole mission was proving very unsatisfactory. He was leaving too many unanswered questions behind him as he tagged along after the latest possible lead. He was also feeling plenty of stress from the destruction he'd caused then fled from in Riasi. There would have been a lot of bodyloss due to his actions.

After quarter of an hour it was clear the Faction ship was

heading in towards the Central Worlds. It looked like the destination was Oaktier.

*

There had only been one judicial conclave in ANA's history. It had been called to deal with the Separatist Faction who had wanted to break ANA up, leaving them in a section free from any regulation or limit imposed by the base law control which acted as a universal governor across the entire edifice. The majority verdict was to disallow any such action. An entity with ANA's ability and resources, and under the authority of a dogmatic ideology, might conceivably pose a threat to the original ANA, not to mention the rest of the Greater Commonwealth. The duplicitous method by which the Separatist Faction had sought to seize command of the quasi-physical mechanism which sustained ANA in order to achieve the segmentation was verification enough that they couldn't be trusted to evolve quietly in some distant corner of the galaxy. A whole host of other agendas to encourage post-physical ascension were exposed at the conclave.

As before, ANA:Governance produced a spherical assembly arena with an equivalent diameter half that of Earth itself. Such a size was necessary in order to accommodate the manifested forms of every individual mind embedded within the edifice of ANA. They appeared within seconds of the judicial conclave being announced, materializing across the vast curving shell, clustering with those of their own faction or in simple groupings of friends or relatives. Ilanthe, as the nominated representative of the Accelerator Faction, floated at the centre of the sphere. She had chosen to manifest as her primary representation, a featureless human female with fluid silver skin. Only her face retained any characteristics, showing a long jawbone and small elegant nose. Her eyes were the absorptive black of an event horizon.

'Thank you for responding,' ANA:Governance said to the convened population.

Ilanthe performed a random sweep over sections of the assembly arena, noting the various forms and shapes manifested across the shell wall. Over half retained a human appearance, while the rest had selected a multitude of geometries and colours from minimal spheres of light, to swarms of neurone-echoes, to the simple yet sinister black pyramids of the radical Isolator faction. One of the human figures was Nelson Sheldon, who was contemplating her with the relaxed disdain of a man who's won his game. Of Gore Burnelli there was no sign, which perturbed her more than it should have. She still didn't understand how he'd become the Third Dreamer; his mentality must have some private link out of ANA to the gaiafield which she didn't comprehend. Not that it was going to matter now.

Her fully expanded mentality (still anchored within the Accelerator compilation) regarded her jury with a degree of amusement, especially as some infinitesimal portion of her own mentality was contributing to ANA:Governance, effectively making her judge herself.

'We are called here to review the activities of the Accelerator Faction,' ANA:Governance continued. 'The charge against them is one of high treason.'

Ilanthe's peers remained quiescent, awaiting the information repositories containing ANA's evidence.

'Do you wish to say anything?' ANA:Governance asked Ilanthe.

'You exist to provide us an existence which promotes intellectual development and evolution, yet you place restrictions upon enacting those very developments in the reality of spacetime. Now you complain when we try to achieve that which your fundamental nature encourages. Please explain the logic.'

'All individuals within me are free to translate their goals into physical or post-physical reality,' ANA:Governance replied. 'You know this. What I cannot permit is for those goals to be imposed on an unwilling majority. When and if we transform to post-physical status it will be as a consenting majority.'

'Nice in theory. But the restrictions you impose on those of us who are ready to transcend are completely unacceptable. We shall achieve our objective on our own.' Ilanthe's primary consciousness withdrew back into the centre of the Accelerator compilation where the inversion core awaited. Secondary routines took over her manifestation within the assembly arena, producing responses to ANA:Governance's questions.

The globular inversion core shimmered a dark metallic indigo, its surface cohesion rippling slightly as the bands of exotic force structuring its boundary began to disengage from the quantum pseudofabric that was ANA's edifice.

'The Prime allies of the Ocisen Empire fleet were animated by the thought routines of Donald Chatfield,' ANA:Governance said. 'He is one of your agents in the Greater Commonwealth.' A vast flock of information repositories burst into existence within the assembly arena and settled on the audience waiting across the shell. Only Nelson Sheldon didn't bother to access the information. Everybody else studied the records of Kazimir's interception, the electronic interrogation and analysis of the inter-Prime communications. The conclusion was inevitable.

Ilanthe's mentality switched residence from ANA's edifice to the inversion core. For the first time since she had downloaded three hundred and twenty-seven years ago, she was fully independent.

'What are you doing?' ANA:Governance demanded as it detected her withdrawal from itself.

'Claiming the right you were established to enforce,' the secondary routines manifested in the assembly arena told it.

'You cannot function separately within me,' it replied. 'You will simply be isolated until your primary identity reconnects to my edifice. Until then, no interaction with any part of me will be permitted. You will effectively be placing yourself into suspension.'

'Really?'

'Your Faction's attempt to manipulate Living Dream into providing you passage into the Void is declared outlaw,' ANA:Governance announced. The base law upon which its entire edifice was built asserted itself, exposing the collective memory of the Accelerator Faction members. ANA immediately noticed gaps where whole segments had been erased, the information transferred to Ilanthe's mentality. Everything else was there, the actions of their agents, the development of independent Primes to provide the Ocisens with the kind of allies that gave them enough confidence to launch the invasion fleet. The why of it was missing. ANA also familiarized itself with the way Ilanthe had grown to dominate the faction, how her obsession with the Void and its abilities had come to supplant all other goals to accelerate human evolution. The secret manufacturing sites producing hardware for agents were revealed. There was one station orbiting a red dwarf star for which there were no records. It examined how she had diverted every resource and ability of the faction within ANA to empower the centre of the Accelerator compilation: producing the inversion core which they were going to fuse with the nucleus of the Void.

Too much was missing still to determine their underlying strategy. All of it, the ultimate essence of the Accelerator faction, hung within the inversion core. ANA observed the core detach itself from all contact with the edifice. Yet, still, the object maintained its integrity contained within the overall subquantum edifice. Not quite real.

'The Accelerator Faction is hereby suspended,' ANA:Governance announced to the assembly arena. The thought routines of every individual comprising the Accelerator Faction immediately terminated, held frozen within the edifice ready for an edit that would remove the illegal sections and impose limiters to restrain future behaviour.

None of it affected the inversion core. ANA couldn't find an entrance point. The Accelerators had fabricated it without the base law, a circumvention of its authority which was disturbing. Their knowledge of exotic quantum structures was extremely advanced. Presumably that had come from people like Troblum studying the Dark Fortress mechanism. Examination of the Faction's now-exposed memories showed eighty-seven of their researchers had served with the Navy on missions to Dyson Alpha. Their findings were not available.

ANA shut down the entire Accelerator compilation, in case there were some remaining connections it couldn't perceive. The inversion core remained. It was self-sustaining, truly independent. 'What is your purpose?' ANA asked.

'Total evolution,' Ilanthe replied. 'I have never hidden that from you.'

'Your actions thus far have caused extreme danger, not just to the Commonwealth. I cannot let that pass with impunity.'

'I reject you and your authority,' Ilanthe replied.

The inversion core exerted an exotic force against the collapsed edifice surrounding it. ANA felt its structure warp to an alarming degree. Far above Earth's lunar orbit, spacetime twisted badly, distorting photons into a globular whirl, sucking light down like a small event horizon.

'Desist from this action,' ANA warned. Ten Capital-class warships on Sol assignment raced in towards the spacetime stress point, slipping smoothly out of hyperspace to target the anomaly. ANA also opened a link to Kazimir who was already within the External Worlds.

'Do you have any idea what it is?' Kazimir asked.

'I can assume the inversion core contains some of my own functions if that is what they intend to fuse with the Void. They have been extremely clever in producing the system within me. No matter what any individual or faction fabricates for itself within me the base laws apply, for they are a simple extension of the quantum interstice that is my edifice. That is how my integrity is retained. However, in this case my base laws were evaded. This is not part of me.'

'I will be there in another fifteen minutes.'

'That is gratifying. However, I do not believe even Ilanthe will attempt to destroy me. If she did, she would find it extremely difficult. There are some levels which I have never employed.'

The inversion core increased the level of the force it was exerting. ANA perceived the quantum fields within which it was embedded start to separate as their cohesion faltered. Space-time fractured.

Senses available to the boundary of the inversion core registered starlight falling upon it. 'You can no longer constrain me,' Ilanthe said. The starlight grew stronger, twisting savagely as it poured through the severe rift opening all around the inversion core. Then it was free, emerging into spacetime as the rift collapsed. The Earth was a splendid silver-blue crescent half a million kilometres away, while the smooth plains of the moon's farside glimmered to one side. Ten Capital-class ships accelerated smoothly towards it. Ilanthe sensed their weapons powering up and locking on. The inversion core went from a sedate cislunar orbital velocity to point nine nine lightspeed in less than half a second.

'What do you want to do?' Kazimir asked as he flashed past the Oort cometary belt that marked the boundary of the Sol system. He'd followed the chase with interest. The Capital-class ships had immediately dropped into hyperspace as the inversion core sped away at its incredible velocity. (And there was something disturbingly reminiscent of a Skylord in the way it did that.) They had some trouble matching speeds when they emerged, replicating its velocity as part of their exit vector. Then when they did get close, it simply stopped, shedding its relativistic speed in an instant. Which left the warships streaking away. The inversion core accelerated again along a slightly different trajectory, leaving the warships with no choice but to dive back into hyperspace. Any engagement was going to be extremely difficult. And they still had no idea of its true capabilities.

'Ilanthe has left us with no options. Please intercept her, and nullify the object.'

'Very well.' Kazimir ordered the Capital-class ships to disengage. He manifested several functions into spacetime, his energy signature matching the inversion core's velocity perfectly. When he attempted to analyse it, all he could perceive was an incredibly complex knot of exotic forces. He didn't have the sensor functions necessary to interpret its intersection within the quantum fields. That left him in the very surprising position of not knowing what aggressive function to deploy against it.

The inversion core halted again, twenty million kilometres out from Mars. Kazimir's energy signature matched locations flawlessly. Visually, the inversion core resembled a ball of black glass whose interior was beset by purple scintillations. Thermally, it didn't even register, while the exotic energy sensors revealed a boundary layer of negative matter somehow entwined with quantum fluctuations of enormous power.

'The deterrence fleet, I presume?' Ilanthe said equably.

'Yes,' Kazimir said.

'I am most impressed.'

'I am reluctant to use weapons functions against you. We are still within the Sol system. There might be damage.'

'Not to me. But that isn't your immediate concern.'

'I assure you it is. However, if it becomes necessary I will use force. Your rebellion is now over. Please accept that.'

'You believed we engineered your deployment so I would be safe to emerge.'

'That is obvious.'

'But wrong. Please scan near-Sol space.'

Look behind you, the oldest ploy in the book, but nearly always spoken from a position of superiority. Kazimir kept his energy signature where it was, but manifested several long-range sensor functions. He searched for signs of stealthed hyperdrives. Eight thousand and one were holding steady in transdimensional suspension, englobing the Sol system at forty AUs out.

'What are they?' he asked.

'We call them the Swarm,' Ilanthe said. 'They are here to put an end to ANA's interference.'

'I have to access them,' Kazimir told ANA. 'I really don't like that formation.' His sensor functions observed one of the hyperdrives arrowing in towards the inversion core at very high speed even for an ultradrive. The other eight thousand dropped out of hyperspace where they were, materializing into spacetime as large spherical force fields, their orbits neatly surrounding the Sol system.

Every Navy warship assigned to the Sol protection fleet flashed in towards Earth, knitting together in a defensive formation that extended out beyond lunar orbit. Weapons platforms that had spent decades stealthed in high orbit emerged to join the incredible array of firepower lining up on the Swarm. All over the planet, force fields powered up, shielding the remaining cities. Anyone outside an urban area was immediately teleported in to safety. The T-sphere itself was integrated into the defence organization, ready to ward off energy assaults against the planet by rearranging spacetime in a sharp curve.

Lizzie was in the kitchen when the alert came through. Unfamiliar icons popped up in her exovision as she was taking a big pan of boiling chicken stock off the grand iron range. Secondary routines identified them, pushing their meanings into her consciousness. She was suddenly all too aware of what was happening out on the fringes of the Sol system. 'Ozzie, crappit,' she grunted as she put the hot pan back down on the range. The whole event was so extraordinary she had no idea how to react, then her basic parental instincts took over.

Little Rosa was chortling away happily to herself in the family room, where she was playing with some reactive spheres, clashing them against each other in a burst of music, then clapping as they rolled away across the antique rug. She grinned delightedly as her mother rushed in.

The paediatric housebot floating to one side of the toddler glided smoothly to one side as Lizzie scooped her up. 'Come on,' she said, and started to designate her coordinates within the T-sphere. That was when the defence agency announced the T-sphere would be unavailable for civilian use in one minute's time.

Lizzie teleported into the school. Rosa whooped with delight at the abrupt jump. 'Good, good,' she enthused.

The classroom she'd emerged into was a broad circle, with a

shallow dome roof and long overhang windows looking across the green playing fields of Dulwich Park. It was raining outside. Twenty children were inside, split into three groups. Their teachers were already looking startled. Lizzie looked round as a timer started to count away her minute. Elsie was part of a reading group. She glanced up and smiled at her mother.

Two more parents jumped into the classroom, both looking as perturbed as Lizzie imagined she was. She beckoned frantically to Elsie, who started over. By now another five parents had arrived. The large classroom was starting to feel crowded.

Tilly was in the music group, her violin resting comfortably under her chin as the children practised a cheerful-sounding song for the school's Christmas nativity play. 'Come here,' Lizzie called as Elsie reached her side. There were twenty seconds left. Out of the corner of her eye, Lizzie saw a mother jump away as she clutched her son.

'What's happening?' Tilly asked.

'Here!' Lizzie implored. Another two adults materialized in front of her, and started to hunt round desperately for their children. The youngsters were starting to get upset as more and more parents with worried faces appeared.

Tilly scampered over, still hanging on to her violin. Lizzie's u-shadow registered a call from her husband. 'Not now,' she grunted, and designated the house as their teleport coordinate. Tilly ran into her, and there were nine seconds left. Just for an instant, the emptiness of the translation continuum flashed around them as Lizzie and the kids jumped out.

She let out a little shocked sob as they all materialized in the familiar hallway.

'What is it?' a subdued Elsie demanded. 'What's happening?'

'Mummy?' Elsie appealed, tugging at Lizzie's skirt.

'I'm not sure,' Lizzie said, even as she was trying to make sense of the defence agency displays. The defence agency didn't have any details on the devices that had surrounded the solar system. Then the T-sphere was diverted from standard use, stranding everyone on the planet in their immediate location. She told her u-shadow to accept her husband's call.

'Thank Ozzie,' he exclaimed. 'Where are the girls?'

'Got them,' she promised, feeling slightly superior that she'd reacted so swiftly and correctly. 'Where are you?'

'On a starship. Eight minutes out from Gralmond spaceport.'

'Do you understand what's happening?'

'Not really. It's the ANA Factions, their fights have turned physical.'

'They can't hurt Earth? Can they?' She didn't want to let go of the children. Outside, the rain had drained out of the grey London sky as the force-field dome covered the city.

'That's not what it's about. Look I'll be with you as soon—'

The connection ended. Strange symbols flipped up into her exovision, showing routing problems with his link.

In the unisphere? That's not possible!

'—after I've landed. Then I'll—'

'Something's wrong,' she gasped.

'—hang on! I will be there, I prom—'

'The link has failed,' her u-shadow reported.

'How can it fail?' she cried.

'The wormhole connections with the Commonwealth Worlds are collapsing,' her u-shadow said.

'Oh great Ozzie!' Lizzie hurried into the conservatory, pulling the girls with her. She tried to make sense of the emergency icons invading her exovision as she looked up into the dour sky, hunting for signs of the world coming to an end.

Kazimir's energy signature halted ten kilometres from one of the Swarm components. He manifested a vast array of sensor functions, yet not one of them was able to penetrate the five-hundred-metre-diameter force field floating serenely in space. 'Damnit, they've acquired Dark Fortress technology,' he told ANA. Far behind him, the Accelerator's ship dropped out of hyperdrive next to the inversion core. It was large for an ultradrive, long-range scans revealed a multitude of weapons on board. A hold door opened in the rear section, and the inversion core slipped gracefully inside. Then a force field came on around it, every bit as impervious as the one he was confronting.

Kazimir was desperate to intercept the Accelerator faction starship, but with Earth and ANA facing an unknown threat his duty was clear. He manifested several high-level weapon functions, and fired at the force field directly ahead of him. Everything he used was simply deflected away. The force field was completely impermeable to any assault he could bring in spacetime and hyperspace.

'The wormholes to the Big15 worlds are collapsing,' ANA reported. 'Something is cutting them off.'

Kazimir examined the exotic matter intrusions stretching out from Earth away to the stars, seeing them subjected to enormous interference that was causing them to constrict. Even though he knew the incursion must originate within the Swarm, his manifested sensor functions couldn't track down its nature.

The Accelerator Faction ship carrying the inversion core went ftl, streaking across the solar system directly away from Kazimir at seventy-eight lightyears an hour. His energy signature flashed after them. Enormously powerful exotic energy manipulation functions manifested, but he still couldn't reach through its force field to disable the drive. He began to manifest some functions which would disrupt the quantum fields around the ship, and would force it out of hyperspace. The ship passed through the Swarm's orbit. Kazimir was less than two seconds behind. It was too late. The force fields surrounding the Swarm components expanded at hyperluminal speed.

Kazimir's energy signature struck an impermeable barrier that cut clean across spacetime and hyperspace. He couldn't get through.

The ship dropped out of hyperspace a lightminute beyond the force field. To the hyperspace sensors, a vast blank shield had sprung up behind them. Its curvature revealed a radius of forty

AUs. There was no hint of stress or distortion anywhere on its surface. Whatever Kazimir was armed with was unable to cut through. Neskia brought *the ship*'s visual sensor data into her exovision, watching the image keenly as a timer counted down. After one minute, the high-magnitude star that was the Sun vanished, along with the stars across that half of space.

'No sign of it breaking through,' Neskia said. 'I think we're safe.'

'Very clever that deterrence fleet,' Ilanthe said. 'An interstitial energy signature that can extrude into spacetime. *The ship* wouldn't have stood a chance in a straight firefight. ANA was more advanced than we'd realized.'

'Even more reason for us to leave it behind,' Neskia said dismissively. 'It had so much potential, and wasted it.'

'Quite.'

'Where are we going?'

'Ellezelin. I trust our agents are close to recovering Araminta?'

'They are.'

The ship slipped back into hyperspace, heading away at a modest fifty-five lightyears an hour. Behind it, the sombre sphere imprisoning the Sol system refracted the gentle starlight imping-ing on its boundary with a cold shimmer reminiscent of a deep forest lake, guarding its contents in perfect isolated darkness.

Inigo's Sixteenth Dream

It was the fifth time Edeard had watched the militia forces close in on the hidden valley. There had been a lot of mistakes previously; ge-eagles had been spotted, fastfoxes mauled the first militiamen over the lip, the bandit forces had fought back with a secret cache of weapons, hothead officers didn't quite follow orders, allowing the Gilmorn to rally his people. Each time there had been too many deaths. Each time Edeard reset the universe to the night before, and attempted to mitigate the problem.

Last time he was sure he'd got it right, then the bandit gang had produced rapid-fire guns from a cache that he hadn't found the first three times. Even with third hands joined together to add extra strength to their shielding, the troopers had been cut to shreds before Edeard himself could reach them. So . . .

This time he had slipped unseen and unsensed through the valley for two hours just after midnight. He'd destroyed the second lot of rapid-fire guns the bandits had hidden, and snatched away the ones belonging to guards after rendering them unconscious. It was politically important that the militias thought they alone had overcome the bandits; while Edeard and Finitan wanted the rapid-fire guns to vanish into legend. Now he stood on a small rise half a mile from the valley as the pre-dawn light slowly overwhelmed the nebulas. Bulku was the first to vanish, its undulating stream of pale indigo fading away just above the eastern horizon, as if the land had somehow opened to swallow it. Edeard could well believe that. The valley which the bandits had chosen as their last redoubt was a narrow crack in the undulating grasslands that made up the southernmost part of Rulan province, lapping against the low mountains of Gratham province which rose in the distance. Not hard to imagine it as a fissure slicing through the whole world.

As the scarlet-spiked glory of Odin's Sea began to diminish far above, he farsighted the troopers of the Pholas and Zelda regiment break cover from the spinneys beyond the valley where they'd gathered during the night. They were supported by provincial militiamen from Plax and Tives. The men moved silently, like a black stream winding round the soft knolls and hummocks of the grasslands, out of farsight from the sentries within the valley. Edeard concentrated on subverting the ge-eagles gliding high above, insinuating his own orders into their sharp, suspicious little minds. That just left the fastfoxes. He was too far away to help with them. Brawny ge-wolves and fast ge-hounds slunk forwards, accompanying the marauder groups of sheriffs and Wellsop rangers whose control over their genistars was second to none.

'Go,' Edeard's directed longtalk urged Dinlay.

The Lillylight and Cobara regiment, along with militias from Fandine, Nargol and Obershire, emerged from their forward positions to the west of the valley. It was the Nargol troopers and their unfettered eagerness that had been the problem the second time around. Since then Edeard had emphasized how important it was to keep them moving along the planned route. Colonel Larose had done a good job keeping the provincials in line ever since; ignoring their muttered resentments about city folk lording it over the countryside.

With the assault under way, Edeard mounted a ge-horse which the Eggshaper Guild had sculpted purely for speed. His ebony cloak swirled around him, flowing across the saddle before rippling above the beast's hide. Felax and Marcol scrambled on to similar mounts on either side of him. He didn't have to say anything to them. His mind urged the ge-horse forward at a gallop and the young constables followed.

The three beasts thundering over the grassland in the cold silence of the ebbing night sounded incredibly loud to Edeard, yet he knew they were too far from the valley to be heard. Up in front of him the troopers were an unstoppable swarm as they converged on the valley.

Finally, the alarm was raised by the bandits. Those sentries still awake shouted to their armed comrades for help, only to find them lying in a deep unnatural slumber, their weapons gone. More shouts and frantic longtalk roused the rest of the sleeping group.

So far, so exactly as before; and this time going to plan.

Fastfoxes flittered silently along the valley with the speed of hurricane clouds. The invading militias urged their ge-wolves on ahead. Along the top of the valley, troopers fell to the ground, their pistols held over the edge. Shots were fired. Ge-wolves and fastfoxes clashed head-on, powerful animal screams reverberating across the grasslands as grey light crept over the dew-soaked ground.

The Pholas and Zelda regiment reached the far end of the valley, and began to follow their ge-wolves down into the deep narrow cleft. Dinlay and Argain were close to the front, using their farsight to expose anyone with the concealment ability. Most of the bandits could perform the trick. Edeard held his breath, the memory of another deep gulley on another night stirring in his mind – the fateful ambush. This time would be different, he promised himself, this time he could guarantee there would be no surprises.

Troopers along the top of the valley provided a thick covering fire for their comrades sweeping forward below. As always, the Gilmorn gathered his stalwarts together in a tall fortress-like outcrop of rock. They still had their ordinary pistols, and fired ruthlessly at the advancing troopers. Concealment made it hard for anyone to return fire with any accuracy. Argain hurried forward to assist the troopers closing in on the outcrop.

Edeard arrived at the head of the valley, and dismounted. He refused to rush forward, even though it was what everyone was expecting. His farsight observed troopers rounding up the bandits who had surrendered and isolating the few who resisted. Then it was just the Gilmorn and his cadre left offering resistance. Dinlay and Larose moved the militiamen forwards cautiously; men wriggled on their bellies along small clefts in the land, and dashed between convenient boulders. Within ten minutes, the Gilmorn was completely surrounded.

As Edeard made his way along the stony floor of the valley he passed groups of smiling troopers hauling their captives along. Several were men from the tribes who lived in the wildlands beyond Rulan's boundaries. They were just as he'd encountered them all those years ago on the caravan back from Witham. Ringlet hair and bare chests caked in dark mud that was flaking off. They glanced at the Waterwalker with sullen expressions, their minds tightly shielded. In all the clashes over the last few years, Edeard had never seen one of them wielding a rapid-fire gun; those weapons were possessed by the Gilmorn's people alone. He halted one of the tribesmen escorted by five wary troopers, a man he guessed to be in his late fifties though with none of a city dweller's laxness about him; he had pale grey eyes which glared out of a face that showed all the anger and defiance his mind refused to show.

'Why?' Edeard asked simply. 'Why did you join them?'

'They are strong. We benefit.'

'How? How do you benefit?'

The older tribesman gave Edeard a superior snort. He gestured round the grasslands. 'You are gone. Even now you will never return. This land will be ours.'

'All right, I can see that. I can even understand how the killing and destruction becomes a perverted addiction for some of you. But why these lands? There are lands unclaimed to the west.

Land with forests and herds to hunt. No one even knows how much land. Why ours? You don't farm. You don't live in stone houses.'

'Because you have it,' the tribesman said simply.

Edeard stared at him, knowing he'd never get a better answer. *Nor a more honest one*, he thought. He was looking for complexity and purpose where there was none. It was the Gilmorn and his kind, the remnants of Owain's ruthless One Nation followers, who had intent. The tribesmen were simply useful innocents who'd been duped into an allegiance they had never fully comprehended.

He dismissed the escort with a curt wave of his hand, and the tribesman was dragged off to the jail pens that were being established up on the grasslands.

'We should get down there,' Marcol said eagerly. The young man's farsight was sweeping over the fortress outcrop, exposing the concealed bandits with ease.

Edeard did his best not to grin. Marcol's psychic abilities had developed considerably since the day of banishment, almost as much as his sense of duty. He was a devoted constable and utterly loyal to the Grand Council; yet there was still some of the old Sampalok street boy in there. He was spoiling to join the fight.

'Let the militias have their moment of glory,' Edeard said quietly. 'This has been a hard campaign. They deserve to be the ones ending it all.' Which was true enough. For eight months the forces of city and countryside had been allied, chasing the Gilmorn and his remaining supporters across the provinces further and further to the west until finally there was nowhere left to run.

'Politics,' Felax said with a disgusted grunt.

'You're learning,' Edeard said. 'Besides, you two have nothing to prove, not after Overton Falls. I heard the daughters of those caravan families made their appreciation clear enough.'

The two young constables looked at each other, and shared a knowing smirk.

Down by the outcrop, Larose's longtalk was delivering a sharp ultimatum to the Gilmorn. They were outnumbered fifty to one, and completely surrounded. They had no food. Their ammunition was almost gone. There was no help coming.

Edeard wasn't convinced that was quite the right thing to point out to a merciless fanatic like the Gilmorn. Though in truth, they'd never reached this point of the assault before, so he didn't know what would work.

They carried on down the valley, passing several dead fastfoxes and ge-wolves. Edeard tried not to grimace at the brutally torn flesh on the animals. Argain was sitting on a moss-covered boulder where the valley opened out, quietly munching on a red apple. Several squads of militia were milling around, also wanting in on the finale. Their corporals and sergeants were having a hard time keeping them in line. Everyone quietened down as Edeard appeared.

'Will he surrender?' Edeard asked.

Argain shrugged, and bit down hard. 'He has nothing to lose. Who knows what he's thinking.'

'I see. Well, fortunately we can wait. For as long as it takes.'

'Ah,' Marcol exclaimed. 'They're arguing.'

Argain gave the young constable a searching stare, then turned his attention to the outcrop. There was indeed an argument spilling out from the jagged rocks. A loud one, full of anger. Two men were confronting the Gilmorn, telling him they were walking out to surrender to the militia. Edeard's farsight showed him the men turning away. The Gilmorn lifted his pistol and brought it up to point at the back of one man's head. Edeard's third hand slipped out and twisted the firing pin, bending it slightly out of alignment. The Gilmorn pulled the trigger. There was a metallic *click*. The bullet didn't fire.

Marcol cleared his throat in a very pointed fashion.

Another argument broke out, even more heated than the first. Fists were swung. Third hands attempted to heartsqueeze. Men started wrestling.

Larose gave the order to combine shields and move in.

Two minutes later it was all over.

*

There were militiamen perched on top of the rocky pinnacles, cheering wildly and waving beer bottles above their heads. Whole regiments were spilling over the site of the last fight, singing and embracing their comrades. Edeard couldn't help but smile as he walked among them, taking the occasional swig from a proffered bottle, shaking hands, hugging older friends exuberantly. They were glad to see the Waterwalker who had led the campaign, but they were prouder that they'd won the final battle themselves.

Colonel Larose had established his camp on the far side of the fortress outcrop. Carts were drawn up in a large circle, long rows of tents were laid out, ready to be put up. A big open-sided canvas marquee had already been raised, with the cooks preparing a meal inside. Smoke from the cooking fires was starting to saturate the still air. At the centre of the camp, the field headquarters tent was a drab khaki, guarded by alert senior troopers and a pack of ge-hounds. Orderlies and runners were skipping in and out. Eleven regimental flags fluttered weakly on top of their poles outside, representing the finest of city and country.

The guards saluted Edeard as he went inside. Larose was sitting behind the wooden trestle table which served as his desk, while a flock of adjutants hovered around with requests and queries. His drab-green field uniform jacket was open to the waist, revealing a stained grey shirt. Senior officers were clustered together at a long bench with all the administrative paraphernalia necessary to move and orchestrate such a large body of men. Even though it had only been a couple of hours since victory, orders and reports had already begun to pile up. Larose stood and embraced Edeard warmly.

'We did it,' Larose exclaimed. 'By the Lady, we did it.'

The officers started to applaud. Edeard gave them a grateful nod.

'You should be very satisfied with your men,' Edeard told him, loud enough for the other commanders to hear, especially those of the country regiments. 'They behaved impeccably.'

'That they did.' Larose grinned round generously. 'All of them.'

'And you,' Edeard told the colonel, 'you should stand for election when we return. The residents of Lillylight would appreciate a man representing them who's actually accomplished something outside the city.'

Larose gave a shrug that was close to bashful. 'That would cause my family's senior members some surprise and satisfaction, I imagine.'

Edeard gave him a warm smile. 'You were never a black sheep.'

'No. Not like you, at any rate. But I like to think I had my moments.'

'Indeed you did. But I hope you'll give the idea some thought.'

'It's never as far away as we believe, is it, Makkathran?'

'No.' Edeard let out a sigh. 'Is he behaving himself?'

'So far.' Larose gestured to a flap at the back of the tent, and they went through. An encircling wall of tents and fences had produced a small secure area at the rear. Right at the centre, a tall narrow tent was standing all alone. Two guards stood to attention outside, older seasoned militiamen who Larose trusted implicitly; their ge-wolves pulling on the leash. Both animals gave Edeard a suspicious sniff as he approached.

'You know something odd?' Larose said. 'For years the bandits have terrorized communities with impunity. Every survivor told stories of fearsome weapons. Yet throughout this whole campaign, we haven't found one of the bastards armed with anything other than a standard pistol.'

'That's good,' Edeard said, staring straight ahead. 'Would you want a new weapon to exist? One powerful enough to kill entire platoons in less than a minute?'

'No. No, I don't suppose I would.'

'Me neither.'

'I don't suppose anybody could build anything like that, not really. Not even the Weapons Guild.'

'No,' Edeard agreed. 'They can't. Those weapons are just a fable that people used to tell each other about in times gone by.'

'Like the exiles. You know, nowadays I find it hard to picture what Owain looked like. He and his fellows must have travelled a long way from Makkathran. Nobody ever found them.'

'Losing an election can demoralize you like that. Nobody wants to dwell on what has been, not now we all have a future.'

'We do?'

'It's unknown, as always, but it's there all right.'

Colonel Larose pursed his lips, and walked on.

The Gilmorn was standing in the middle of the tent, with Dinlay and Marcol in attendance. Of all the aspects which resulted from Edeard's ability to reset time, he always found this the strangest. Seeing someone alive who he'd previously watched die. And this Gilmorn was one he'd killed himself in a fashion which didn't withstand too much sober examination.

Inevitably the man was unchanged. Not that Edeard had ever seen him at his best before. Last time, his round face with the idiosyncratic nose had been suffused with pain and anguish as his legs were ruined by the boulder. Now he simply looked tired and sullenly resentful. Not defeated, though. There was still defiance burning behind his mental shield, mostly fuelled by good old Grand Family arrogance, Edeard suspected.

The blacksmith was just leaving. He'd taken an hour to shackle the Gilmorn securely, with big iron rings around his wrists and ankles, linked together with tough chains. This way there were no fancy locks for his telekinesis to pick away at. The metal had to be broken apart by another blacksmith or simple brute strength; Edeard could do it, and probably Marcol, but few others on Querencia would be capable.

'Finitan's pet,' the Gilmorn said contemptuously. 'I might have guessed.'

'Sorry I missed our earlier appointment at the valley beyond Mount Alvice,' Edeard replied casually.

The Gilmorn gave him a startled glance.

'So who are you?' Edeard asked. 'Not that it really matters, but you never did tell me your name back at Ashwell.'

'Got your forms to fill out, have you?'

'You do understand this is over now, don't you? You are the last of them. Even if One Nation had any supporters left back in Makkathran, they'll deny everything, especially you. The Family Gilmorn has lost considerable status among the city's Grand Families since Tannarl's exile; they're desperate to regain it. You won't be accepted back, not by them. Of course you could try to throw in with Buate's surviving lieutenants, the ones I banished. Though they too seem incapable of adapting. Over a dozen have been sentenced to the Trampello mines in the last two years. At least they'll have company; my old friend Arminel is still incarcerated there. Mayor Finitan changed the mine governor from Owain's crony to someone who's a little stricter.'

The Gilmorn held his hands up, the chain clanking as he did so. 'Is this what you're reduced to, Waterwalker, gloating over your victims?'

'And you? Goading someone whose village you destroyed?'

'Touché.'

'You set me on the path that led to this day. I enjoy that.'

'As Ranalee and others enjoy Salrana. I've heard she's very popular. Fetches quite a high price in the *right* circles so I understand.'

Dinlay's hand fell on Edeard's shoulder. 'Let me deal with him.'

'You?' the Gilmorn sneered. 'A eunuch does the Waterwalker's dirty work? How amusing.'

Dinlay's face reddened behind his glasses. 'I am not—'

'Enough of this,' Larose said. 'Waterwalker, do you have any serious questions for this bastard? Some of my men can get answers out of him. It might take a while, but they'll persist.'

'No,' Edeard said. 'He has nothing vital for me. I just wondered why he kept on fighting, but now I know.'

'Really?' the Gilmorn said. 'And that is?'

'Because I have taken everything else away from you. There is nothing else for you to do. Without your masters you are nothing. You are so pitiful you cannot even think of anything else to devote yourself to. When the time comes for your life to end you will have achieved nothing, you will leave no legacy, your soul will never find the Heart. Soon, this universe will forget you ever even existed.'

'So that is what you have come here for, to kill me. The Waterwalker's revenge. You're no better than me. Owain never went into exile. I know you murdered him and the others. Don't set yourself up as some aloof judge of morals. You're wrong to say I leave nothing behind. I leave you. I created you. Without me, you would be a countryside peasant with a fat wife and a dozen screaming children, scrabbling in the mud for food. But not now. Not any more. I forged a true ruler, one who is every bit as ruthless as Owain. You say I can do nothing else? Take a look at yourself. Do you tolerate anyone who doesn't comply? Is that not me, the very ethos you claim to despise?'

'I enforce the law; equally and impartially for all. I abide by the results of elections.'

'Words words words. A true Makkathran politician. May the Lady help your enemies when you become Mayor.'

'That's a long time in the future, if I ever do stand.'

'You will. Because I would.'

Edeard's cloak flowed aside with the smoothness of jamolar oil. He reached into a pocket and took out the warrant. 'This is the proclamation signed by the Mayor of Makkathran, and notarized by the provincial governors of the militias alliance. Given the scale of the atrocities you have perpetrated for years, you will not be returned to civilization for trial.'

'Ha, a death warrant. You are nothing more than the tribal savages we enlisted.'

'You will be taken to the port of Solbeach, where a ship will sail eastwards. When the captain has voyaged as far as the seas will allow him, he will search for an island with fresh water and vegetation. There you will be abandoned with seed stock and tools sufficient for your survival. You will live out your life there alone to contemplate the enormity of your crimes. You will not attempt to return to civilization. If you are found within the boundary of civilization you will immediately be put to death. May the Lady bless your soul.' Edeard rolled up the scroll. 'Constables Felax and Malcol will accompany you on the journey to ensure the sentence is carried out. I'd advise you not to annoy them.'

'Fuck you. I won and you know it. This alliance is the start of One Nation.'

Edeard turned and started to leave the tent.

'Owain won,' the Gilmorn shouted after him. 'You're nothing more than his puppet. That's all. Do you hear me Waterwalker? Puppet to the dead; puppet to the man you murdered. You are my soul twin. I salute you. I salute my final victory. Family blood will govern this world. They say you can see souls. Can you see the soul of Mistress Florrel laughing? Can you?'

Edeard hardened the shield his third hand created, blotting out the vicious shouting as he walked away.

*

Edeard wanted to travel on alone, but Dinlay wouldn't hear of it. He wouldn't argue, he just said nothing while Edeard shouted hotly at him, maintaining his quiet stubborn self. So in the end Edeard gave in as they both knew he would, and ordered the regiment's cavalry master to saddle two horses. The pair of them rode off together towards Ashwell.

The landscape itself hadn't altered, only the use it had once been put to. Half a day's ride from his destination, Edeard began to recognize the features that had dominated his childhood. Shapes on the horizon started to register. They were cloaked in different colours now as the vegetation had changed; crops giving way to a surge of wilder plants. The road was completely overgrown, hard to distinguish, though the buried stony surface was still perceptible to farsight. The fields around the village, once rich and fertile, had long reverted to grassland and bushes, with their old hedges sprouting up into small trees. Drainage ditches were clotted with leaves and silt, swelling out into curiously long pools.

It was a warm day, with few clouds in the bright azure sky. Sitting in his saddle, Edeard could see for miles in every direction. The cliff was the first thing he identified. That hadn't changed at all. It set off a peculiar feeling of trepidation in his heart. He had truly never expected to come back here. On the day after the attack, he'd left with the posse from Thorpe-by-Water, and had only glanced back once, seeing blackened ruins chuffing a thin smoke into the open sky, and even that image was blurred by tears and anguish. It had been too painful to attempt another look; he and Salrana had ridden away together, holding hands and bravely staring on ahead.

Now, nature had completed what Owain and the Gilmorn had started. Years of rain and wind and insects and tenacious creepers had accelerated the decay begun by the fires. All the village council's half-hearted repairs along the rampart walls had finally started to give way, leaving the broad defences sagging and uneven. The outer gates had gone, their charcoal remnants rotting to a thin mulch where tough weeds infiltrated their roots. Their absence exposed the short tunnel under the ramparts, a dank uninviting passage of gloomy fungus-coated brick. Above them, the stone watchtowers sagged; their thick walls held fast, though the slate and timber roofs under which so many sentries had sheltered across the decades were gone.

Edeard dismounted, and tethered his skittish horse to the iron rings just outside the arching portal. The sturdy metal at least remained untouched.

'You okay?' Dinlay queried cautiously.

'Yes,' Edeard assured him, and walked through the dripping tunnel, sweeping aside the curtain of trailing vines. As soon as he emerged into the village, birds took flight, great swirls of them shrieking as they flapped their way into the sky. Small creatures scampered away over the rough mounds of debris.

Edeard was prepared for ruins, but the size of the village

caught him by surprise. Ashwell was so small. He'd never considered it in such terms before. But, really, the whole area between the cliff and the rampart walls could fit easily into Myco or Neph, the smallest city districts.

The basic layout of the village remained. Most of the stone walls survived in some form or another, though collapsing roofs had demolished a lot of them. Streets were easy to make out, and his memory filled in the lines wherever slides of rubble obscured the obvious routes. The big guild halls had withstood the fires well enough to retain their shapes; though they were nothing more than empty shells, without roofs or internal walls. Edeard sent his farsight sweeping out to examine them, then immediately halted. Lying just below the thin coating of dirt and ash and weeds that had engulfed the village were the bones of the inhabitants. They were everywhere. 'Lady!'

'What?' Dinlay asked.

'There was no burial,' Edeard explained. 'We just left. It was too . . . enormous to deal with.'

'The Lady will understand. And the souls of your friends certainly will.'

'Maybe.' He looked round the desolation, and shuddered again.

'Edeard? Do any linger?'

Edeard let out a long reluctant sigh. 'I don't know.' Once again he reached out, pushing his farsight to the limit of resolution, striving to catch any sign of spectral figures. 'No,' he said eventually. 'There's nobody here.'

'That's good, then.'

'Yes.' Edeard led the way towards the carcass of the Eggshaper Guild Hall.

'This is where you grew up?' Dinlay asked with interest as he scanned round the nine sides of the broken courtyard.

'Yes.' Somehow Edeard had expected to find some trace of Akeem. But now, actually standing beside the listing stables and unsafe hall, he knew he never would. There were bones aplenty, even whole skeletons, but it would take days of careful examination to try and identify any of them. *And ultimately, for what purpose? Who am I trying to appease and satisfy here?* Would the souls of the dead villagers care that he was here? Would Akeem want him grubbing through the dirt to find some pieces of his long-dead body? *I bury all of them, or I bury none.*

Of course, there was one other thing Edeard could do. His recollection of that night was perfect: himself and the other apprentices meeting up in the cave for an evening of fun and kestric. Even as he thought it, he looked up at the cliff, seeing the small dark cleft that they wriggled through to find the cavern that offered privacy from their masters.

That simple recollection triggered a whole wave of memory. He could see the village as it had been that last fine summer. People striding along the streets, talking and laughing. Market stalls being set up; farmers bringing their produce in on big wagons. Apprentices hurrying about their duties. Village elders in their finer clothes. Children scampering about, chasing each other with shrieks of laughter.

I can do it. I can go back to that moment. I can defeat the bandits that night, I can give them all a life again.

He shook his head as if to clear it. Tears began to roll down his cheeks. This was far worse than any temptation Ranalee had ever offered.

I would have to go to Makkathran, this time with Akeem's letter of sponsorship. I would be an apprentice at the Blue Tower. But Owain would still be there, and Buate, and Tannarl and Mistress Florrel and Bise. I would have to dispose of them once more.

'I can't,' he whispered. 'I can't do that again.'

'Edeard?' Dinlay asked gently. His hand squeezed Edeard's shoulder.

Edeard wiped the tears away, banishing forever the sight of the village as it had been. Standing in the cracked doorway arch to the Eggshaper Guild Hall, Akeem regarded Edeard with sad eyes.

Edeard knew that look so well. A rebuke which had been

directed at him a thousand times as an apprentice. *Don't let me down.*

'I won't,' he promised.

Dinlay frowned. 'Won't what?'

Edeard breathed in deeply, calming his rampaging emotions. He stared at the broken doorway. Akeem wasn't there. A smile touched his lips. 'Fail them,' he told Dinlay. 'I won't fail the people who died so I might ultimately wind up where I am today, where we all are. It doesn't always apply, you know.'

'What doesn't?'

'Sometimes to do what's right you have to do what's wrong.'

'I always thought that was stupid. I bet Rah never actually said it.'

Edeard laughed out loud, and took a last look around the old nine-sided courtyard. He put his arm round his friend's shoulders. 'You're probably right. Come on, let's go home. Home to Makkathran.'

'About time. I know you had to come here, but I'm not sure it's healthy. We all regard the past too highly. We should cut ourselves free of it. You can only ever look forward to the future.'

Edeard pulled him closer. 'You're really quite a philosopher, aren't you?'

'Why do you say that with so much surprise?'

'That was not surprise, that was respect.'

'Humm.'

'Anyhow,' Edeard teased, 'Saria will be waiting for you. Waiting eagerly.'

'Oh dear Lady. I don't want to speak ill of the dead, but what in Honious did Boyd ever see in her?'

'What? No! She's a lovely girl.'

'She is a nightmare.'

'Kristabel thinks highly of her.'

'Yes. But Kristabel thinks highly of you, too.'

'Ouch! That hurt. Okay then, perhaps Kanseen could steer someone more to your liking.'

'No! And certainly not Kanseen. Do you know what her definition of "nice girls" is, let alone "suitable" ones? This is what you've all been doing since the four of you got married. It's embarrassing. Besides, I like being single.'

'Married life is wonderful.'

'Lady! Just stop it will you.'

Edeard walked out of his former guild courtyard grinning contentedly.

3

The PanCephei Line starship had already dropped out of hyperspace when the emergency began. External sensors were showing the passengers an image of the H-congruous world two thousand kilometres below. White clouds tumbled high above dark-blue oceans, sending out long streamers in forays across the surprisingly brown land. Flight information was available to access, designating their vector as a purple line down through the atmosphere to Garamond's capital: the smooth resolution to another flawless everyday flight across three hundred lightyears.

None of which registered with the increasingly frantic Delivery Man. The Conservative Faction's intelligence division had automatically sent out a secure classified warning to all operatives as soon as the inversion core broke free of ANA's edifice. He'd observed with growing dismay as it eluded the Navy ships. Then the deterrence fleet arrived (though its nature wasn't revealed on any Navy scans of the sol system), and right after that the Swarm materialized. Earth's defence agency declared a grade one alert.

The Delivery Man called his wife, and to hell with protocol. For whatever reason her u-shadow didn't accept his first request for a link. When he analysed the basic data he realized she was in the Dulwich Park school. His hand thumped the nicely cushioned armrest of his seat in the first class cubicle in frustration.

Lizzie teleported back home and her u-shadow accepted the link.

'Thank Ozzie,' he said. 'Where are the girls?'

'Got them. Where are you?'

'On a starship. Eight minutes out from Gralmond spaceport.'

'Do you understand what's happening?'

'Not really,' he said, which was honest enough. Though he really didn't like the look of the eight thousand devices surrounding Sol. Nobody amassed that kind of potential unless they were extremely serious. Even so, he couldn't imagine what the things were. Not warships, surely? 'It's the ANA Factions, their fights have turned physical.'

'They can't hurt Earth, can they?'

'That's not what it's about. Look I'll be with you as soon as I can. I'll transfer right after I've landed.' Exovision symbols told him the unisphere was changing the routing on the link, which was weird. His secure priority connection with the Conservative Faction intelligence division dropped out. *What the fuck?* 'Then I'll be with you the instant I reach an Earth station,' he told her, trying to appear positive.

'Something's wrong,' Lizzie said.

It was impossible, but he could feel her distress as though they were using the gaiafield. 'Lizzie, just hang on! I will be there, I promise you. Tell the girls Daddy is going to be home any minute.'

His u-shadow reported the link with Lizzie had failed, as had the one to the Conservative Faction. 'No,' he gasped out loud. His exovision showed every route to Earth had been severed. No data was getting in or out of the Sol system, it was completely cut off from the unisphere. 'What the hell is happening?' he asked his u-shadow.

'Unknown,' it replied. 'All wormholes to Sol have physically closed. The Navy and Commonwealth government retain several secure emergency TD links to Sol, none are working.'

'Did they nova it?' he asked fearfully.

'Unknown, but unlikely. Whatever happened, happened very quickly. A nova shockwave would take several minutes to reach Earth.'

'The planet itself, then, could they have destroyed it, dropped a quantumbuster through the defences or something? Maybe an M-sink?'

'Possibly. But for every communication system in the solar system to be affected simultaneously the destruction would have to be enormous and swift. That suggests something which acts at hyperluminal velocity.'

'Did they kill Earth?' he yelled out.

'Unknown.'

'Oh sweet Ozzie.' His whole body was shuddering as shock gripped him. Biononics worked to calm the impulses. 'Find out,' he instructed his u-shadow. 'Use every source you can access.'

'Understood.'

Judging by the raised voices muffled by the cubicle door, news of Earth's disappearance was spreading fast. The Delivery Man couldn't think what to do. It was the Conservative Faction that always provided him with the best data, now they were gone. Without them, he was no better than anyone else. He had no special ability, no influence, no one to call . . .

Marius, that was his first thought. *I could ask Marius.* Which would be pitifully weak. *But this is Lizzie and the kids. This isn't the Faction.* His rival's communication icon hung in his exovision. He couldn't resist.

The response took several seconds. His u-shadow reported several semisentients tracking and confirming his location.

'Yes?' Marius replied smoothly. There was no attempt to establish any kind of routing security on the link. He was connected to Fanallisto's cybersphere.

'What have you done?' the Delivery Man asked. Some small part of him was intrigued: *What's Marius doing on the planet I just left?*

'I have done nothing. But I am curious why you're on Gralmond.'

'What do you fucking think I'm doing here, you little shit! I'm going home. I was going home. What have you done to my family? What's happened to Earth?'

'Ah. Don't worry. They are perfectly safe.'

'Safe!'

'Yes. Your Navy will presumably release the details in a while, but we have simply imprisoned Sol inside a very powerful force field, just like the Dyson Pair.'

'You did what?'

'We can no longer accept interference from ANA, nor your own Faction. We will go into the Void. You will not stop us. You cannot. Not now.'

'I will catch you, I will rip you to fucking pieces.'

'You disappoint me. I told you the game was over. When will you animals learn? We have won. Elevation is inevitable.'

'Not while I'm alive, it isn't.'

'Are you threatening me? I extend you a simple courtesy and this emotional diarrhoea is how you respond? You are an agent of the Conservative Faction after all, perhaps I shouldn't take any chances. I will visit Gralmond and eradicate that world with you and everyone else on it.'

'No!'

'Are you a threat, or are you a simple broken animal has-been?'

'This won't work. You can't get into the Void. Araminta will never take you there.'

'Once we secure her, she will have no choice. You know this.'

In the privacy of the first class cubicle, the Delivery Man punched the wall twice. His arm's biononic reinforcement meant his fist produced a sizeable dint in the carbotanium panelling. He'd never felt so helpless. So useless. Nor had he felt so much anger, most of it directed at himself for not being with his family at this time. The one time they truly should have been together. 'What about after?' he asked.

'After?'

'If the inversion core does make it into the Void, will you release Sol?'

'I expect so. It is an irrelevance, then, after all.'

'If you don't, I will find you, whatever form you take. And that is a threat.'

The link ended. 'Shit.' He hit the wall again, right in the centre of the dint. His storage lacunae contained several Conservative Faction emergency procedures; not one of them anticipated anything as remotely outrageous as this. The Delivery Man let out a nervous little laugh as he contemplated the enormity of the Accelerator's actions. ANA and the deterrence fleet were the only possible entities that could have ended Living Dream's Pilgrimage. *Apart from the warrior Raiel.* Even as he thought it, he knew he couldn't rely on the aliens guarding the Gulf. The Accelerator Faction had access to Dark Fortress technology now. That might just allow them to get past the warrior Raiel.

He employed his biononics to adjust his wilder physiological parameters, calming his thoughts. Secondary routines came on line, expanding his mentality, allowing him to examine the situation properly. *The only way to be of any genuine help to Lizzie and kids.*

If the deterrence fleet couldn't break out of the force field, it was extremely unlikely that the Navy could break in. That left the Accelerator Faction agents and scientists who'd built the Swarm, or – long shot – the Raiel at *High Angel.* The Navy and the President would no doubt be asking the *High Angel* as a matter of urgency, which left him with the prospect of tracking down an Accelerator agent who might know how to switch the damn thing off. And they would be extremely reluctant to tell him.

The starship settled on its pad. Passengers hurried off, leaking uncertainty out of their gaiamotes, contributing to the vast pall of unease which was contaminating the entire gaiafield. Some services at the spaceport had ground to a halt as the staff stopped everything to access the unisphere news.

A private starship had already arrived at the Sol force field, and was relaying images of the almighty prison wall erected across space. Commentators were dredging up the historical records of the *Second Chance*'s first contact with the Dyson Alpha barrier, and drawing unlikely parallels.

The Delivery Man stood in the airy glass and wood arrivals hall, part of a bewildered crowd of fellow travellers staring at the red solidos hanging above the wormhole terminus to Tampico. It was as if the shining symbols somehow made the situation a whole lot more real than the frantic unisphere broadcasts. They warned that the old Big15 world no longer had a connection to Earth. To add to the irony, the preset symbols advised making alternative journey arrangements.

'Quite right,' the Delivery Man muttered to himself. First off, he had to acquire some serious hardware and firepower if he was going to start snatching Accelerator agents. It was only logical. Which brought him up against his choices. The only Accelerator agent he knew who would definitely have the kind of information he needed was Marius. Moreover, Marius was now back on Fanallisto, where there was a cache of field support equipment that the Delivery Man had the codes for. 'Holy crap,' he hissed at the enormity of the decision.

His u-shadow accessed the spaceport's network to grab flight times of starships going back to Fanallisto. Already, operators were starting to cancel flights as a precaution.

That was when his u-shadow reported the Conservative Faction was opening a secure link. 'What?' The people nearby gave him curious looks. The jolt of surprise had spilled out into the gaiafield, too. But there was no doubting the call's authenticity, every certificate and code key was correct. He collected himself, and smiled blankly as he accepted the call. 'Have you broken out through the force field?' he asked.

'Not exactly. This is a ... portion of what you know as the Conservative Faction. Think of me as the executive.'

'All right. So how can you communicate through the force field?'

'I can't. I'm outside it.'

'But the faction is part of ANA.'

'Could we just move past the definitions stage please. Take it as read, this is the Conservative Faction speaking.'

'Is there any way to get through the barrier? I have to talk to my family.'

'Forget it. The bastards were smart mapping out Dark Fortress technology. ANA and Earth are going to be sitting on the sidelines for the duration. It's down to us now.'

The Delivery Man frowned. 'Bastards?' he mouthed. This wasn't the way the Conservative Faction spoke. Secondary routines dug up the 'sidelines' crack; it was an old sporting reference. Very old. 'Who are you?' he asked.

'Like I said: the executive. What? You think we're all equal in ANA?'

'Well . . . yes. Of course.'

'Nice theory. Okay then, the executive is all nice and homogeneous and glowing in love from everyone else involved in the Faction. Happy now?'

'But you can't be in ANA.'

'No. I'm taking a short sabbatical. Lucky for us. Now are you with me? Are you going to help stop Marius and Ilanthe?'

'Just so you understand my position, I'm going to require proof of what you are before I do anything.'

'Sonofabitch Highers, you're all fucking bureaucrats at heart, aren't you?'

'What the hell are you?'

'I'll give you proof I'm what I claim, but you've got to come and collect it.'

'Listen, my priority – actually my only concern – is taking down that barrier. Nothing else is relevant.'

'Brilliant. And how do you propose to do that?'

'Somewhere in the Commonwealth there will be an Accelerator with the knowledge. Once I track them down I will extract the information. I am prepared to use extreme methods.'

'I think I misjudged you. That's not a bad idea. I'm almost tempted.'

'What do you mean misjudged?'

'Face it, son, you don't exactly have a double-O prefix, do you? You just deliver things for us, with a bit of low-level covert crap thrown in to bolster your ego.'

The Delivery Man's u-shadow couldn't find a reference to double-O, at least not one that made any sense. 'I've gone up against Marius before,' he bridled.

'You had a cup of hot chocolate with him before. Come on, let's get real here.'

'Well what's your proposal?'

'First off, get back to Purlap spaceport and pick up the starship you dumped there. Trust me, the person it was intended for isn't going to be using it now. And we're going to need some decent hardware to pull this off.'

'Pull what off?' But he was obscurely heartened by the 'executive' knowing about the starship. It meant the thing was either genuine, or the entire Conservative Faction was a broken joke; and if it was the latter the Accelerators wouldn't be toying with him like this. That wasn't how they worked.

'One stage at a time. Go get the starship.'

The Delivery man reviewed the spaceport's network again. 'The commercial lines are shutting down all their scheduled flights. And not just here by the look of it.' His u-shadow was tracking data from across the Commonwealth. Nobody wanted to be flying when the Accelerators were out there unchecked by the Navy.

'Boohoo,' said the Conservative executive. 'You just claimed you were prepared to use any method necessary.'

'To get me back with my family.'

'This will, like nothing else. Now think. Where are you?'

'I don't understand.'

'You're in the middle of a spaceport with three hundred and seventeen starships currently on the ground around you, according to its official registry. Pick a good one, take it over, and get your ass back to Purlap. You're a secret agent, remember? Earn your double-O status.'

'Take it over?' the Delivery Man repeated.

'Good man. Call me when you get there. And don't take too long. Marius was on Fanallisto for a reason; and given what's just gone down, it must be a hell of a good one for him to be off centre stage. He's near the top of their hierarchy.'

The call ended, leaving a new communication icon gleaming in the Delivery Man's exovision. 'Take it over,' he said to himself. 'Okay then.'

He started to walk back down the length of the arrival hall. His u-shadow extracted information from the registry, and produced a short list. There were some Navy ships, including a couple of scouts, which were almost tempting, but that would require a little too much bravado, and he didn't want to have to bodyloss anyone. Especially not now, when the Navy was going to need ever asset it had. Instead he picked a private yacht called *Lady Rasfay*.

It was cool outside, with high cloud stretching across the early morning sky. Dew slicked the spaceport's concrete roadways and the red-tinged grass analogue. It even deposited a layer of condensation on the taxi capsule which the Delivery Man took out to pad F37, a couple of miles away from the main passenger terminal. He climbed out, shivering against the chill air. The *Lady Rasfay* was ten metres in front of him, a blue-white cone with an oval cross section, like some kind of ancient missile lying on its side. He never did get why so many people wanted their starships to look streamlined, as if they were capable of aerodynamic flight. But the owner, Duaro, was clearly one who favoured image.

The Delivery Man's u-shadow had already performed a low-level infiltration of the ship's network. Nobody was on board, and the primary systems were all in powerdown mode. A quick scan of the drive performance figures backed up what he'd guessed from the physical profile. Duaro had invested a lot of EMAs and time on the hyperdrive, which could now push the ship along at a fraction over fifteen lightyears an hour, as good as a hyperdrive could get.

His u-shadow put a civil spaceworthiness authority code into the ship's network, and the airlock opened. A metal stair slid out. The Delivery Man walked up it, not bothering to scan round, an act which might betray him as a guilty party. That was the beauty of a Higher world, no one really thought in terms of theft, if you saw someone entering a starship you just assumed it was legitimate. Thanks to EMAs and replicator technology, material items were available to all; certainly a starship was hardly a possession of envy.

Not that Duaro was completely guileless. The network had several safeguards built in. After several milliseconds analysing them, the Delivery Man's u-shadow presented him with eight options for circumventing the restrictions and gaining direct control over the smartcore.

Dim red lighting cast a strange glow along the narrow central companionway. The yacht had a simple layout, almost old-fashioned in nature, with the flight cabin at the front, a lounge behind that in the midsection, and two sleeping cabins aft. Once he was inside, the Delivery Man's biononics performed a short-range field scan to find a suitable point where he could physically access the network's nodes. That was the same time he heard passionate groaning from the portside sleeping cabin.

The door flowed aside silently. Inside, the sleeping cabin's decor was ancient teak, carved to cover every curve and angle of the bulkhead walls, and lovingly polished. Two figures were in flagrante on the narrow cot.

'Duaro, I presume?' the Delivery Man said loudly.

The man squirmed about in alarm. The woman squealed, and scrabbled frantically at the silk sheets to cover herself. She was exceptionally beautiful, the Delivery Man acknowledged, with a mane of flame-red hair and a face covered in freckles. She was also very young; a first-life if the Delivery Man was any judge.

'Did Mirain send you?' Duaro asked urgently. 'Look, we can conclude this in a civilized fashion.'

'Mirain?' the Delivery Man mused out loud. His u-shadow

ran a fast cross-reference on Duaro's profile. 'You mean your wife, Mirain?'

The woman on the bed cringed, giving Duaro a sulky glance.

'I can't believe she went to this much trouble,' Duaro groused. 'This is just a harmless little fling.'

'Oh, thank you,' the woman snapped.

'Sneaking on board and keeping the lights off and the smartcore dumb,' the Delivery Man mused. 'Doesn't appear that harmless.'

'Look, let's be reasonable about this . . .'

The Delivery Man gave a huge smile at the magnificent, timeless cliché. 'Yes, let's. Shall I tell you what I want?'

'Of course.' Duaro said with an air of cautious relief.

'The yacht's smartcore access codes.'

'What?'

'Non-negotiable,' the Delivery Man said, and powered up several weapons enrichments.

*

Paula Myo couldn't remember being so shocked before, not ever. The emotional trauma had become physical in nature, with her heart racing and her hands trembling as if she was some kind of natural human. She had to sit down hard on the *Alexis Denken*'s cabin floor before her legs gave way. The only thing her exovision revealed was a vast blank plain, which was what the Capital-class ship *Kabul* was seeing as it scanned the outside of the Sol barrier. Her link came directly from Pentagon II on a secure channel, which her status entitled her to. But there was nothing she could do, no help she could offer. She was a simple passive observer of the greatest disaster to befall the Commonwealth since the barrier around Dyson Alpha came down. That memory stirred a possibility.

'Do you have the spatial coordinates of the Swarm components when they materialized?' she asked Admiral Juliaca, who was Kazimir's deputy, and now de facto commander of the

Commonwealth Navy. 'The original Dark Fortress had an opening on the outside, which is how it was turned off.'

'Nice try,' Juliaca said. 'That was the first thing the *Kabul* attempted. There is no bulge in the Sol barrier as far as we can detect, and I've got eleven ships out there searching now, as well as several civilian craft. It's perfectly smooth, certainly in the areas around the Swarm components we've scanned.'

'Of course,' Paula muttered. *No fool like an old one. It was never going to be that easy.* She shook herself, and ordered her biononics to stabilize her wayward body. Her thoughts, though, they were still sluggish, as if they were moving through ice. *I thought I got rid of this nonsense when I resequenced.* Even as she thought it, some small part of her mind was chiding her for being too hard on herself. But for Accelerators to successfully bring this off was a monumental failure of intelligence gathering and analysis on ANA's part, for which she bore some considerable responsibility. Any kind of human would be perturbed by the enormity of the coup – which is what this was.

'And we're certain the deterrence fleet is caught inside?' Paula asked.

'I'm afraid so,' Juliaca said. 'There is no response whatsoever from Kazimir. If he could get in touch with us, he would. He was commanding the fleet, so logically the fleet is inside the Sol barrier.'

Paula, who had been monitoring what she could of the ANA Judicial conclave, knew the admiral was right. But . . . 'The whole fleet? That seems unlikely. Surely there's some craft held in reserve?'

'One moment,' the admiral said.

A new communication icon appeared in Paula's exovision. She welcomed the colour it brought to the numbing image of the Sol barrier. As she acknowledged the call she pushed the *Kabul*'s imagery into a peripheral mode. 'Mr President,' she said formally.

'Investigator Myo,' President Alcamo replied. 'I'm glad you are still available. Frankly, I'm looking for some meaningful advice right now. Without ANA we're woefully short of relevant information.'

'Whatever I can do, of course,' Paula said. 'I was going to suggest to the admiral that the remainder of the deterrent fleet is deployed to Sol to see if they can break in.'

'That's the problem,' Admiral Juliaca said. 'I don't have any knowledge of the deterrent fleet. There's nothing in any Navy facility, not even a contact code. And the Navy network has acknowledged my authority as commander.'

'But they must be getting in touch with you?' a startled Paula said.

'Not as yet.'

'I see.' A notion was starting to fall into place. It wasn't good.

'Paula, do you know anything about the fleet?' President Alcamo asked.

'I'm afraid not, sir. Though I do know how reluctant ANA and Kazimir were to deploy it, that does suggest to me that it might not be a fleet at all.'

'A single ship?' Juliaca asked.

'It fits what's currently happening. It is inconceivable that any remaining fleet ships would not get in touch with you in an emergency of this magnitude. We should conclude there was only one, and it is trapped inside the Sol barrier along with ANA.'

'You mean we're defenceless?' President Alcamo asked.

'No, sir,' the admiral replied. 'The Ocisen invasion fleet and their Prime allies were disabled before the Sol barrier was established. There is no other immediate external threat, and the Capital- and River-class squadrons are more than capable of dealing with any known species within range. The deterrence fleet was always there to deal with a post-physical-level threat.'

'Our threat is not external,' Paula said. 'It is Ilanthe and that damned inversion core, whatever the hell it is.'

'You hadn't heard of it before?' asked the President.

'No, sir. All we knew was that the Accelerators hoped to achieve what they called Fusion with the Void in order to bootstrap themselves up to post-physical status.' She drew a breath and started to analyse the situation, trying to predict Ilanthe's next move. 'There is one critical factor remaining which is currently outside anyone's control.'

'Araminta,' the admiral ventured.

'Correct,' Paula said. 'The only way Ilanthe and Living Dream can get inside the Void is with Araminta's help. Which will be coerced once they find her.'

'Can you find her first?' the President asked.

'She's on Chobamba, and it appears as though she's already made a deal with some Faction.'

'Which one?'

'I don't know. But their agents must have helped to get her off Viotia. I imagine they are now as shocked as we are by the loss of ANA. That might make them open to a deal. We have an opportunity.'

'Can you do that?' the President asked.

'I can reach Chobamba shortly,' Paula said. Inwardly she was disappointed. The *Alexis Denken* was only an hour out from Viotia, and Chobamba was five hundred and ten lightyears from her current position. *All I ever do these days is rush from one crisis point to another, and arrive too late each time. That cannot stand, there's too much at stake. I have to up my game, get ahead for once.*

'Thank you,' the President said. 'When you find her, take her into custody. No polite requests. We are beyond that now. She goes with you, she does not ally herself with anyone else, that cannot be permitted. Do you understand?'

'Perfectly, Mr President. If I can't capture her, nobody else must be allowed to. I will see to that.'

'You'll do that, Paula?'

'Most assuredly.'

'Thank you. Admiral, do we have any other fields of progress? Can the Navy eliminate the ship that picked up the inversion core?'

'Unknown, sir. It was a large, powerful ship, of a marque we've never seen before. And we'd have to find it first.'

'Ilanthe will want the same thing as the rest of us,' Paula said. 'The Second Dreamer. She's probably heading for Chobamba now.'

'Very well,' the President said. 'Admiral, put together a task force of Capital ships, and dispatch them to Chobamba. I want that ship destroyed.'

'There wasn't much information from the Sol system before the barrier went up,' the admiral said. 'But the ship did appear to have a force field based on Dark Fortress technology. We're assuming the Accelerators are going to use it to get past the Raiel in the Gulf.'

'Sweet Ozzie,' the President said. 'Do you mean you can't intercept it?'

'We can probably find it, our sensors are good enough to penetrate most stealth systems. But I doubt we can ever catch it, not with the kind of speed it was last confirmed travelling at. And yes, if we did corner it on Chobamba, our weapons would probably not get through its defences.'

'Crap. So it really does all come down to Araminta?'

'It looks that way, sir.'

Paula held her own opinion in check; the few comments she might have made weren't based on fact. 'I'd advise getting in touch with the High Angel directly, Mr President,' she said. 'If anyone can get through a barrier produced by Dark Fortress technology, it will be the Raiel.'

'Yes,' he said. 'That's my next call. I will inform you of the outcome.'

The secure link closed. Paula ordered the smartcore to plot a course to Chobamba. The bright green line hung in her exovision, slicing through the astrogration display; awaiting implementation. Something made her hold off. She was sure that even if she got there in ten hours' time it would all be over. By now, everyone with a team chasing Araminta would know her new location. As soon as Living Dream pinned down her exact geographical coordinate there would be a scramble to deliver local representatives into the area. Either the team guarding her would evacuate her again, or she'd leave with the strongest raider team.

The whole situation made little sense. It was obvious to any professional that Living Dream would refine their search techniques after Bodant Park. Whoever it was that'd flown her to Chobamba must have known that, even if they didn't know how good Ethan's Dream Masters were. Keeping Araminta out of sight once she was secure was the most basic rule.

So who took her there?

Half the factions chasing her would have killed her to prevent the Accelerators from gaining any advantage. Most of the others, those who had similar goals or ambitions to the Accelerators, would have offered a deal. Yet here Araminta was, going through Inigo's dreams, seemingly without a care in the universe.

Paula drew a sharp breath. *Of course, the simplest explanation is always the most likely. She really isn't aware of the danger, so she isn't under the protection of any professional team. Then how in God's name did she get to Chobamba?*

She launched her u-shadow on a mission to gather every scrap of data on Araminta. Everything Liatris McPeierl had put together; the files from Colwyn City's civic database, records from Langham on her family and its agriculture cybernetics business, financial records, medical records (very few, she had an excellent Advancer heritage), legal records – mostly her messy divorce handled by her cousin's law firm. All of it was resolutely average; none of it made her any different to billions of other External World citizens.

But she is different. She's a Dreamer. Something makes her incredibly special. What? Gore has become one, and that's outrageous, there's nobody rooted in the practical more than Gore. Yet he worked out the secret. The only theory there's ever been about why Inigo dreamed of Edeard is because they were somehow related: family. Paula's heart jumped in excitement. *As are Gore and*

Justine. Shit! But Araminta dreamed of a Skylord . . . She growled in frustration, slapping her hands against her temples. 'Come on, think!' *Ignore the Skylord thing. Go for the family angle . . .* Her u-shadow zipped through Araminta's ancestry, correlating birth records and registered partnerships. Tracking back through the generations.

A small file flashed across her exovision, part of the family tree.

'Holy crap,' she yelped. There it was, plain and beautifully simple, five generations down the line. The name simply lifted itself out of the list and shone at Paula without any help from secondary routines.

'Mellanie Rescorai,' she whispered in amazed delight. 'Oh yes. Over a thousand years, and she's still nothing but trouble.' Even better, Mellanie was named a Silfen Friend like her first husband Orion. Paula remembered an encounter over eight hundred years ago, when Mellanie was paying one of her visits to the Commonwealth again; they'd both been invited to some high-powered political event, it might even have been a Presidential inauguration ball. Dear old Mellanie had positively gloated about being named a Friend; it put her one up over everyone else in the room that evening, Paula especially. That was Mellanie for you: sweetly savage.

'Mellanie!' Paula was chuckling now. However it worked, however a Dreamer connected to someone inside the Void, that was the root of it: the Silfen magic – actually the most advanced weird technology in the galaxy. Ozzie had developed the gaiafield out of his friendship gift from the Silfen, and that was the whole medium for dreams. Araminta was descended from a Silfen Friend. And Inigo . . . well who knew?

The paths! Paula's u-shadow ran another search. Sure enough, there was rumour of a path on Chobamba, in the middle of its desert continent. And one at Francola Wood, right on the edge of Colwyn City. *She didn't join up with any Faction, she didn't fly to Chobamba. She walked!*

Which meant Araminta was still surviving on luck and smarts, just like Oscar said; and therefore had no idea Living Dream had found her. She had to be warned, which wasn't going to be easy given she'd cut herself off from the unisphere.

Paula's macrocellular clusters linked her directly to the starship's network. There was a memory kube on board that was heavily encrypted, very heavily; she needed all five keys and a neural pathway verification to access it. Stored within were programs that had been accumulated over fifteen hundred years of investigations, programs of last resort, custom-written for the top ranks of criminals, arms dealers, politicians ... Simply knowing about some of them was a crime. None of their creators would be coming out of suspension for centuries. The Paula of twelve hundred years ago would have been mortified that her future self hoarded such things. But on several occasions they'd proved rather useful. Paula activated one; it wasn't even on the lethal list.

*

Kristabel's kiss was gentle, yet so intense, so rich with desire and love. 'That's why I love you,' she whispered. There could be no doubt how sincere she was. A boundless love that promised a lifetime of happiness. And Edeard finally knew he'd done the right thing.

Araminta sighed in perfect contentment, blinking as the chalet's ceiling took shape above her. Tears were trailing out from the corner of her eyes as she came down off the emotional high. 'Great Ozzie,' she murmured, still dazed by the dream. *Now* she understood why Living Dream had so many adherents, why they were all desperate to live in the Void. Time travel. Except it wasn't. It was resetting the universe around yourself, the ultimate solipsism. How many times had she said to herself: *If I only knew then what I know now.* With that ability she could go back to the moment she met Laril and laugh off his charm and seductive promises. She could refuse Likan and never visit his mansion for the weekend. Go back into her teens and tolerate her parents, knowing that life offered so much more than the farm, not worrying that she'd be condemned to the family business for centuries – yet at the same time *enjoying* her youth. The way it should be enjoyed. And then growing up truly free of regrets. Meet Mr Bovey in a Commonwealth that had never heard of the Second Dreamer.

That was the life – the lives – which awaited her in the Void.

She could even feel the Skylord's thoughts at the back of her mind. All she had to do was call it. Say: take me in.

Such a simple thing to do. Three little words, and I would be happy forever.

But it was also the life that awaited everyone who went with her. And the energy it took to fuel such egotistic wish fulfilment came from consuming the rest of the galaxy. Every star, every planet, every biological body – they were the ones who supplied the atoms it took to make the Void's magnificent ability possible. The ones who paid the price.

'I can't,' she told the darkened chalet. 'I will not do that.'

The decision made her skin chill and her heart flutter. But it had been made now. Her resolution would not waver. Logic and instinct were as one. *This is who I am. This is what makes me.*

Araminta slowly sat upright. It was still night outside, with maybe three hours left until dawn. She needed a drink, and some decent *dreamless* sleep. There was still some of the English Breakfast tea in the flask from Smokey James. She rolled off the bed and saw the red text drifting down the unisphere node's little screen on top of the bedside cabinet. Blinked at it, and read it again.

Tea and sleep abruptly forgotten, she knelt in front of the bedside cabinet and used the keyboard to bring up the news articles. Her gaiamotes opened slightly, allowing her to know the horror and fear flooding through the gaiafield. It wasn't a hoax. The Accelerator Faction had imprisoned Earth. ANA was gone. The rest of the Commonwealth was on its own. She stared numbly at the screen for a long moment, then accessed the code in her storage lacuna and typed it in.

Laril's face appeared. Gaunt and apprehensive, with drawn

skin and deep bags under his eyes. 'Oh thank fuck,' he wheezed. 'Are you okay? I've been going frantic.'

She smiled. It was the only way she could stop herself from bursting into tears. 'I'm okay,' she promised him with a voice that wavered dangerously.

'And you're—' He frowned, his head shaking from side to side as he focused on exovision displays. 'You're on Chobamba. How did you get there?'

'Long story. Laril, they've taken away the Earth!'

'I know. ANA was the only thing that could stop this.'

'Yes. Someone helped me. Oscar, his name was Oscar. I'd never have got out of Bodant Park without him. He said he worked for ANA. He said he would help me. I was thinking I might call him, ask ANA to help me. What do I do now?'

'That depends on what you've decided. Are you going to help Living Dream get into the Void?'

'No. It can't happen. They'll wipe out the galaxy.'

'Okay, that brings down your options to three.'

'Go on.'

'Ask the Navy for protection. If anyone has the firepower to stand up to the Accelerators, it's them.'

'Yes. That's good. What else?'

'This Oscar person, if he does work for ANA he should also be able to keep you away from Living Dream. He'll probably have resources which none of the others do.'

'What's the last one?'

'Side with a Faction that is opposed to the Advancers and Living Dream.'

'But there aren't any Factions left.'

'They're locked up inside the Sol barrier, but their agents are still out here in the Commonwealth. And they're all looking for you. I can negotiate with one for you. Get them to take you away, safe where no one will ever find you.'

'Then what? Running away doesn't solve anything. This has to be finished.'

'My darling Araminta, there is no "finish". The Void has been there for a billion years, more probably. The Raiel couldn't get rid of it, the Commonwealth certainly can't.'

'Somebody must be able to. There has to be a way.'

'Maybe ANA knew how.'

'They'll get the Earth out eventually,' she said, suddenly fearful. 'Won't they? They'll be trying? They must be.'

'Yes. Of course they will. They'll be trying very hard indeed. The rest of the Commonwealth, certainly the Inner Worlds, have a lot of talent and ability and resources, more than you realize. They'll bring down the barrier.'

'Right then,' she said, trying to convince herself. 'I'll take that option. I'll call Oscar.'

Laril smiled weakly. 'That's my Araminta. Would you like me to call him for you?'

She nodded. 'Please. I'm too scared to access the unisphere.'

'All right. Have you got a code for him?'

'Yes,' she started typing it in.

'That's good. I'll make—'

The image on the screen broke apart into a hash of blue and red static.

'Laril!' she gasped.

The static swirled, then formed bright green letters. Araminta, please access this.

She scuttled backwards across the floor. 'No,' she gasped. 'No, what is this? What's happening?'

'Araminta,' the node's speaker said. It was a female voice, composed and authoritative. 'This is a shotgun message into Chobamba's cybersphere. All nodes will receive it and broadcast it to every address code, it will also be held in storage until purged, which should take a while. Hopefully that gives it long enough to reach you somehow. I am not aiming it at you directly, because I don't know precisely where you are. Living Dream has discovered you are on Chobamba but they haven't yet determined your exact position. Don't use the gaiafield again, they have very sophisticated tracking routines in the confluence nests. Several teams of combat-enriched operatives are working on finding you, the same type of people responsible for the Bodant Park massacre. You must leave immediately. I'd advise you to use the route you took to get there. It is relatively safe. Do not hesitate. Time is now a critical factor. Please know that there are people working to help you. The Commonwealth Navy is capable of protecting you. Ask for their aid. Go now.'

Araminta stared at the node in disbelief; the green lettering remained on the screen, casting a pale glow across the darkened chalet. 'Oh sweet Ozzie!' It came out in a pitiful squeal. *They know I'm here. Everyone knows I'm here.* The woman's voice was right: she had to leave. But it would take hours to reach the start of the path out in the desert. She looked round the chalet as her initial panic tipped over into desperation, seeing everything she'd bought, the gear that was essential for a trek along the paths between worlds. It was heavy, she could hardly run carrying it all with her; certainly not that far. Then she glanced at the Smokey James wrappers which she hadn't got round to putting in the trash chute, and an idea formed.

Smokey James was good, Araminta had to admit that. It was three o'clock in the morning, and they only took twenty minutes to deliver the pizza and fries with a flask of coffee. The contraption Ranto was riding as he pulled up in front of Araminta's chalet was something she'd never seen before; an absurdly primitive three-wheeled bike of some kind; presumably the great-great-granddaddy of a modern trike pod. It didn't look safe, with a leather saddle seat slung in the centre of an open black carbon frame that had its fair share of repair patches, like epoxy bandages swelling the struts. The axle-drive wheels were connected to the frame on long magnetic suspension dampers, which didn't quite seem to match. Ranto was steering it manually with a set of chrome-orange handlebars. With a sinking heart, Araminta guessed this was necessity rather than preference. It wasn't going to have any kind of smart technology ready to assume the driving and navigation functions.

He clambered off and pulled the pizza carton out of a big pannier behind the saddle.

Finally, she thought, *a plus point. That'll hold all my gear.*

'Here you go,' he said with the kind of miserabilist cheer exclusive to night-shift workers on very basic pay.

Araminta was fairly sure Ranto didn't have an Advancer heritage. Too many spots on his glum teenage face, his long nose made sure he wasn't handsome, and even though he was already tall he was still growing, producing long gangling arms and legs from a torso that seemed oddly thin. From her point of view that was good, he wouldn't have macrocellular clusters. He couldn't connect directly to the unisphere.

Araminta took the carton from him. 'Thanks.' She held up her cash coin. 'How much for the bike-thing?'

Ranto's slightly awkward smile turned to incredulity. 'What?'

'How much?'

'It's my bike,' he protested.

'I know that. I need it.'

'Why?'

'That's not important. I just need it. Now.'

'I can't sell my bike! I fixed it up myself!'

'It's yours, so you can sell it. And it's a seller's market. You'll never get another chance like this.'

He looked from her to the bike, then back again. Araminta was sure she could hear his brain working, little cogs clicking round under unaccustomed stress. His cheeks coloured.

'You could buy a new one,' she said with gentle encouragement. For a moment she visualized Ranto riding round on some massive glowing scarlet sports bike with floating wheels. *Come on, focus!* If he didn't want to part with it there were unarmed combat routines in her lacuna she could use, loaded a long time ago when the whole divorce mess started and she had to go into districts of Colwyn City that had a bad rep. She really didn't want to. For a start she didn't quite trust them, or herself. Besides, hitting someone like Ranto was just naked cruelty. *But*

I will. If I have to. This is far more important than his pride. She brought the lacuna index up into her exovision, ready to access the routine.

'Five thousand Chobamba francs,' Ranto announced nervously. 'I couldn't let it go for anything less.'

'Deal,' Araminta shoved her cashcard towards him.

'Really?' Her immediate agreement startled him.

'Yes,' she authorized the money.

Ranto blinked in surprise as his own card registered the transfer. Then he grinned. It made him look quite endearing.

Araminta slung her backpack into the open pannier, and turned back to the dazed teenager. 'How do I drive it?' she asked.

It took a couple of minutes on the broad road outside the StarSide motel, with Ranto running about after her shouting instructions as his long arms waved frantically, but Araminta soon got the hang of it. The handlebars had a manual throttle and brake activator. She really had to concentrate on using the brake; all her life she'd driven vehicles with automatic braking. After the first couple of semi-disasters she began to overcompensate, which nearly flung her forward out of the saddle.

'Doesn't it have any safety systems?' she yelled at Ranto as she curved round again.

He shrugged. 'Drive safe,' he suggested.

After another three practice circuits on the street she did just that, and set off for the one road out of Miledeep Water. Ranto waved goodbye. She could see that in the little mirrors sticking up from the handlebars. There was no three-sixty sensor coverage – actually, there were no sensors. His lanky frame was backdropped by the green-lit motel reception building, one hand held up, and an expression of mild regret on his face.

Araminta concentrated on the route out of Miledeep Water, retracing her walk in not a day before. The bike's headlight produced a wide fan of pink-tinged light across the road ahead. It was okay-ish, but she couldn't see much outside of its beam, and the streetlights grew further apart as the road climbed the crater wall. She quickly activated every biononic optical enrichment she had, bringing analysis and image-resolution programs on line to help. The resulting vision was a lot better, taking away her total dependence on the headlight.

Once the last building was behind her, and she hadn't fallen off, or crashed, and nothing mechanically disastrous had happened, she eased the throttle up, and her speed increased. The axle motors were quite smooth, and the suspension kept her a lot more stable than she'd expected. It was just the wind which was a problem, flapping her fleece about and stinging her eyes. She really should have worn glasses of some kind. There was a pair of big shades in her backpack, but somehow she preferred the discomfort to stopping and fishing them out. The unknown woman's blanket warning on the unisphere had unnerved her.

Five minutes after leaving the motel behind she reached the crest of the crater. The last street light stood on the side of the road, not far from where she'd dumped her flagon harness. She was almost tempted to pick it up again, but sentiment at this point translated to blatant stupidity. Araminta gunned the throttle and zoomed off down the slope into the desert.

As soon as she was past the field of illumination thrown out from the streetlight she switched the bike's headlight off. Her image resolution routines produced a reasonable grey-green view of the long straight road ahead. Enough to give her the confidence to keep going at the same speed. After all, there was nothing else travelling along it. She could see all the way to the horizon, where the intensifiers showed the stars burning brightly behind a wavering curtain of warm desert air.

It was a six-minute ride to the bottom of the crater wall. By the time she reached the desert floor the bike's tiny display panel told her she was doing close to a hundred kilometres an hour. It felt more like five hundred. The wind was a constant blast in her face, and her clothes felt like they were being pulled out behind her. She bared her teeth into the airstream, actually starting to enjoy the experience.

Did Ranto and his friends come out here in the evenings and

race along the empty road? She knew if she and her friends had these kind of machines when she was growing up on the farm she would have had a whole lot more fun.

And I can have them. In the Void.

She grimaced. *Actually, no I can't. Stop thinking like this, it's weak, and anyway the Void won't allow technology.*

Not that she really counted this bike as technology. The battery under the saddle actually hummed as the axle motors drew power. Something in the left rear wheel clicked as it spun round (which should be impossible with frictionless bearings). And the tyres made a low growling sound as they charged along the gritty concrete. *Maybe it'll actually work on the Silfen paths?*

There were no landmarks out on the desert road, nothing distinctive on the side of the road. She wasn't sure where the side track was. Not that it had been much of a track, just a couple of tyre ruts across the hard ground. Even with the headlights she wasn't going to see those in the night. Instead she reached for it with her mind, nervous that spreading her thoughts in such a fashion might allow Living Dream to find her once again. But the difference between the gaiafield and the Silfen community was clear enough to her, allowing her to studiously avoid the former.

The Silfen path felt her as much as she felt it. And somewhere up ahead, and to the side of the road it opened fully like some flower whose time had come to bloom. Araminta slowed the bike and gingerly turned off the road. The uneven desert was littered with small stones. Their impact kept shunting her front tyre off the track, leaving her to wrestle the handlebars back. It was difficult, taking her full strength. Her arms were soon aching from the constant struggle. Sweat built up on her shoulders and forehead.

That was when she heard the hypersonic booms rolling in through the clear desert air; thunderous *cracks* that hurt her eardrums. Her head swung round, searching anxiously. Behind her, the top of the crater containing Miledeep Water glowed with the haze of the town's street lighting, creating a mellow nimbus that caressed the dark night sky. She saw bright glimmers of purple light streaking across the foreign constellations, curving down towards the lonely town. There must have been six or seven of them.

'Oh crap,' she grunted, and gunned the throttle hard. 'Here we go again.' The bike started to buck about as it jolted its way over the coarse ground. Dry bushes snapped as she rode right over them, spiky twigs snaring in the hub spokes to thrash round and round, their tips whipping her boots. Holding a straight line was a huge effort, with the bike fighting every motion.

A couple more booms announced the arrival of more capsules at high velocity. Any second now Araminta expected the sky to light with laserfire in a repeat of Bodant Park. The bike was bouncing wildly. She could actually hear the axle drives whining. She fought to keep it straight as the front wheel shook from side to side. There was nothing for it but to slow down. Though by now she could feel the start of the path, lapping towards her like the advancing waves of an incoming tide.

The bike's power fell off, then surged, ebbed again. Little amber lights winked on across the handlebars. She had no idea what they meant. She throttled back, and the outlandish machine freewheeled on forwards. They were on a shallow incline now, leading down to an ancient winding streambed, so all she did was steer, keeping away from the larger stones and boulders.

By the time she jerked down onto the softer sand of the streambed there was no power left, and the bike rolled to an easy halt. Nothing worked. The screen was blank, the amber lights had gone out, and no matter how she squeezed the throttle the axle motors didn't engage.

Araminta sat there on the saddle for a long minute, letting the cramps and tension ease out of her shoulders and arms. Her bum was sore from the saddle, which plainly needed a lot more padding. Nonetheless she grinned fondly at the bike.

I made it. The stupid thing got me out.

Because there was no doubt about it, she wasn't on Chobamba any more.

She climbed off slowly, and pressed her fists into the small of her back, groaning as her spine creaked. The skin on her face was raw from the wind buffeting. It didn't matter. She felt ridiculously pleased with herself for eluding her pursuers yet again. Which was stupid, she knew. It had mainly been down to luck. Though she had to give herself some credit. She'd responded to the situation well enough after she got the warning.

And what that woman did proves there are still people trying to help me, and not just her, there was that one back at Bodnant Park, too, Oscar. A development which gave her a lot of hope. One thing she did know, her decision meant that her time of running was over. There were no easy options ahead now, no waiting for someone else to do something. *It's down to me now.* There was a lot of trepidation accompanying that thought, and maybe a tinge of fear, too; but there was also a degree of satisfaction. *All I have to do now is find the people opposed to the Pilgrimage and take a stand with them.*

With that she pulled the backpack out of the pannier, settled it on her shoulders, and set off along the streambed. That at least she didn't have to think about, it was the right way.

In less than an hour her boots were starting to sink into the sand, which was becoming damp. Grass was growing on the banks. It was still night, and her enriched vision couldn't make out much, but the desert had ended, she was sure of that. Then she caught sight of trees on the edge of her vision.

Water started to fill the imprints her boots left in the mushy ground. The streambed wasn't sand any more, it was fine soil. The stones on the banks were coated in moss and lichens. She scrambled up out of the gully and began to walk alongside it. Cooler air made her shiver, and she reset the thermal fibres woven into her fleece to keep more of her body warmth in. Not much further on and a thin trickle of water was running along the middle of the streambed. Far overhead, huge dense star clusters filled the sky, imperial patches of silver-white scintillations so much more impressive than anything visible from anywhere in the Greater Commonwealth. Araminta smiled at that.

The water in the streambed grew deeper and wider as she walked on, turning from rivulet to a broad current gurgling merrily round half-submerged rocks. Trees closed in, throwing tall branches up into the night, curtaining the starfield. Another stream merged into the one she was following. That was when she heard the first strands of song. The Silfen were somewhere close by, she could feel them as much as hear them. Simple harmonies slipping across the sylvan land, as much a part of it as the air. She halted and listened, drawing the melody down as she might sample a particularly pleasant perfume. It was enchanting, rising and flowing in its own rhythm, and far higher than most human throats could reach.

Like a birdsong, she thought, *a flock of birds singing a hymn.*

Smiling pleasantly at the notion she set off again, keeping to the edge of the stream that was now almost wide enough to be classed as a river. The contentment growing in her mind was almost narcotic. This time she was going to meet them. It was inevitable.

The sky slowly lightened above her. Tall waving branches on either side of the surging water course transformed to black silhouettes against a pale grey pastel. The grand star clusters faded away in deference to the dawn sun. Dew began to coat the grass and small ferns, splashing off on her boots. Araminta couldn't help the smile on her face, even though she knew any relief here was only ever going to be temporary.

The trees gave way abruptly, and she gasped in delighted astonishment at the vista before her. She was high up on the edge of some plateau which swept away into a wondrous primordial landscape. Perfectly clear air allowed her to see for what must have been over a hundred miles. Snow-capped mountains fenced the scene on two sides, while ahead of her the ground undulated away with hillocks and dells adorned in lush woodland. Morning mist eased gently round the slopes, blanketing the deepest hollows and basins like some living liquid. Threads of stream water sparkled and glistened down the sides of the mountains, thousands of tributaries lacing together into broader, darker rivers. Waterfalls tumbled hundreds of metres down rugged cliffs and clefts in the rocky foothills.

'Oh my,' Araminta murmured in admiration. There she waited patiently for her escort while the big red-hued sun rose up into the empty sky, throwing vast fingers of light through the mountains to sweep across the magnificent landscape.

The madrigal grew louder, swelling to a crescendo. Araminta looked round as the Silfen rode out of the forest all around her. There must have been forty of them, mounted on huge shaggy-furred beasts. She gazed at them, enthralled with the spectacle. Elves right out of the deepest human folklore. As tall as legend had them, with long limbs and a torso that was proportionally shorter than human. Flat faces with wide feline eyes above a slight nose had a simple circular mouth without a jaw; instead three concentric circles of sharp teeth flexed steadily, shredding food as it was pulled back into the gullet.

They wore simple toga-like garments that glimmered with a metallic sheen. Gold, jewel-heavy, belts were pulled tight about the waist, while the shoulder strips were held together with large brooches whose gems glowed an eerie green. On top of the togas were waistcoats made from some kind of bright white mesh.

Their voices broke into a ragged chorus of joyful undulations as they rode round her. The earth trembled with the impact of the beasts' feet cantering about. One of the Silfen, wearing a scarlet mesh waistcoat, halted his mount beside her and bent down, offering his arm. Without hesitation Araminta reached up.

He was incredibly strong. She was lifted up and over into the big saddle in front of him. One arm stayed protectively round her. She glanced down to see his four-fingered hand resting against her abdomen. He flung his head back, and emitted a piercing warble. The beast lurched forward with such abruptness that she laughed at the sheer outrage of it. Then they were thundering onwards into the trees ahead.

It was a bizarre and wonderous ride. The size of the beast meant that every movement seemed ponderous, yet it was fast.

When her senses calmed down she noticed that it had a hide of reddish-brown fur that was thick like knotted lambswool. There were six fat legs, which meant every motion of its gait was exaggerated, swaying her back and forth. The head bobbing from side to side in front of her on a broad muscular neck was as big as her own body. As far as she could make out from her position, it had two ears on each side, and some weird bony protrusions, curving back from its eyes to end in a spray of green feathers atop its crown. But they might have been decoration from the colourful Silfen harness, which seemed to have straps everywhere.

The rest of the riding company spread out behind her, still singing among themselves as they rushed forward in what was close to a stampede. They splashed through rivers and charged up slopes without slowing. It was a wild exhilarating ride, and she clung on for the duration, laughing away at the experience.

Eventually they came out of the woods close to a vast loch. Tendrils of mist still meandered above the calm surface. Small conical islands were mirrored on the silverish shimmer, with skinny trees clinging to their wrinkled mossy sides. A little way round the shoreline, a waterfall gushed in from an overhanging crag. The scene was quiet perfection, making her glad simply to know such a place existed.

But right in front of her, on the sprawling grassy bank, the Silfen camp waited. There were thousands of the strange aliens, along with a dozen types of exotic animal they rode. Tents of glowing fabric were pitched everywhere. As she watched, one rose up; seven individual sheets of fabric, each one a primary colour, growing higher and higher until they were twenty feet above the ground, where they curled over to knot themselves together with a looping bow. The edges of the sheets fused together, and there it hung, suspended on nothing, like a solidified rainbow. Between the tents fires were burning, and rugs had been spread out in readiness for what looked like the galaxy's biggest picnic. Silfen unpacked vast silver and gold platters of food from huge baskets hung over various animals. The food looked fabulous, as did the crystal bottles filled with liquid of every possible colour. A great many Silfen were already dancing around the fires, voices raised to chant their own tempo. Their limbs might have been long and spindly to her eyes, but they were certainly agile and most likely double-jointed. Half of the energetic moves would have been impossible for a human.

It was a shame, she thought, as the Silfen on whose mount she'd ridden proffered his arm again to get her down. She would have liked to join in. As her feet touched the ground the aliens surged towards her, which she started back from. Peals of laughter shivered through the air. Not mocking: sympathetic, encouraging. Welcoming.

Araminta gave them all a nervous bow. They returned the formality *en masse*, the action spreading out like a ripple. Of course with their flexibility and grace it was a lot more elegant than hers.

Two of them stepped forward, their circular mouths open in what she thought was a smile, though all they were doing was showing an awful lot of those off-putting spiky teeth. They were female, though it was hard to tell. All the Silfen had thick long hair that was adorned with beads and jewellery. Lengthy braids swirled as the womenfolk held out their arms to her. She allowed herself to be led forward. Their minds shone with warmth and kindness. So much so it was impossible not to experience the same emotions. Food was offered, intricate crumbling cakes wrapped in verdant leaves. She nibbled away, and the crumbs *fizzled* as they went down her throat. 'Oh gosh!'

The Silfen laughed at her enjoyment. A crystal bottle was tendered and she drank deeply. Definitely alcoholic, and then some. More food, perfectly sculpted pastries and confectioneries dripping with honeys and juices that tasted as good as they looked.

Somewhere a group was trilling a fast tune. Araminta started to sway to the beat. One of her woman hosts took her hand and danced with her. Then she was lost amid dazzlingly colourful alien bodies, all swirling and whizzing about her.

More food, snatched from group after group. Drink. Plenty

of that. It was intoxicating but never enough to blur her senses, instead it intensified the whole wondrous festival. Dance followed dance with dozens of Silfen until she was giddy with joy and every muscle shaking with exhaustion.

She knew this was all crazy, that she should be getting to some Commonwealth World to do what she could with her unwelcome heritage. Yet somehow she knew this was also the right thing to be doing. Her body and mind needed the blissful suspension of the festival to recover and calm from the events of the past few days. They were helping her, these Silfen, showing in their own bizarre fashion that she wasn't alone, reinforcing the communion she had with their precious Motherholm.

'I have to sit down,' she told them after some indeterminable length of time. They didn't speak any human language, she knew; nor had they ever shown any interest in anything other than their own peculiar tongue, with all its cooing and warbling and trills that conveyed only the shallowest of meaning. Commonwealth cultural experts assigned to the world-walking aliens found it hard to follow their whimsy. Allegedly it indicated a completely different neural process to that of blunt human rationality.

Nonetheless her hosts knew what she asked, and guided her into one of the rainbow tents where there was a nest of cushions. Araminta flopped down on them in relief, as six or seven Silfen gathered round to attend her. Such pampering was luxurious and she surrendered to it without protest. Her boots were removed, producing a sympathetic chorus of near-human cooing when they saw the artificial skin sprayed on her feet. Strong fingers massaged her shoulders and back. They didn't have the same physiology, but they were plainly expert in human bone and muscle structure. She groaned in relief as the tensions were soothed out of her flesh. Outside, the festival continued unabated, for which she was glad. Didn't want to be the party pooper. One of the female Silfen presented her with a bottle carved from some golden crystal. Araminta drank. It was almost like water, chilly and full of bubbles, and certainly refreshing.

Two more Silfen were waiting with platters of that delicious food.

'The clubs back in Colwyn were never like this,' she said with a contented sigh.

'They're most certainly not,' someone said in heavily accented English.

Araminta jumped with shock, then rolled over to see who'd spoken. The three benevolent masseurs withdrew their ministrations, kneeling patiently in a circle around her.

A Silfen with leathery wings was standing in the tent. He had a dark scaly tail as well, which slithered about as though agitated. His appearance sparked a frisson of concern in Araminta's mind. This shape was also contained in human legend, but not a good one.

'Who are you?' she blurted. 'And why have you got a German accent?'

'Because he's an idiot,' another Silfen said. 'And completely misunderstands our psychology.'

Araminta jumped again, feeling foolish. A second winged Silfen was staring down at her. He wore a copper toga robe held in by an ebony belt. His hair was auburn, with greyish strands creeping in around the temples. His tail was held still, curving up so it didn't touch the ground.

'Hey, fuck you too,' the first winged Silfen groused.

'I apologize for my friend,' said the other. 'I'm Bradley Johansson, and this is Clouddancer; the Silfen have named him a human friend.'

'Uh!' was all Araminta could manage.

'Yeah, pleasure to meet you, too, girlie,' Clouddancer said.

'Uh,' she said again, then: 'Bradley Johansson is a human name.'

'Yes, I used to be. Some time ago now.'

'Used to be . . . ?'

He opened his circular mouth, and a slender tongue vibrated in the middle as he produced a near-human chuckle. 'Long story. As a human I was named a Silfen Friend.'

'Oh.' Then some memory registered, associated with Mr Drixel's awful school history class. 'I've heard of Bradley Johansson, you were in the Starflyer War. You saved us all.'

'Oh brother,' Clouddancer grumbled. 'Thank you, friend's daughter. He'll be insufferable for a decade now.'

'I played my part,' Bradley Johansson said modestly. His tail tip performed a lively flick.

Araminta sat up on the cushioning and folded her legs. With a happy certainty she knew she was about to get answers. A lot of answers. 'What did you call me?' she asked.

'He's referring to your illustrious ancestor,' Bradley Johansson said.

'Mellanie?' It could have been imagination, but she was sure the singing outside rose in reverence of the name.

'That's the one all right,' Clouddancer said.

'I never met her.'

'Some people are fortunate, others are not. That's existence for you.'

'Is she a Silfen now?'

'Good question; depends how you define identity.'

'That sounds very . . . existential.'

'Face it, girlie, we're the lords of existentialism. Shit, we invented the concept back while your DNA was still trying to break free from molluscs.'

'Ignore him,' Bradley Johansson said. 'He's always like that.'

'Why am I here?'

'You want the existential answer to that?' Clouddancer asked.

'Carry on ignoring him,' Bradley Johansson said. 'You're here because, to be blunt, this is your party.'

Araminta turned to look at the gap in the tent fabric, watching the ceaseless colourful motion outside as the Silfen danced and sang beside the loch. 'My party? Why mine?'

'We celebrate you. We want to meet you, to feel you, to know you, the daughter of our friend. That is what the Silfen are, absorbers.'

'Am I really worth celebrating?'

'That will become apparent only with time.'

'You're talking about the Void.'

'I'm afraid so.'

'Why me? Why do I connect with a Skylord?'

'You have our communion, you know that.'

'I do now. That's because of Mellanie, isn't it?'

'You are our friend's daughter, yes, and because of that you are also our friend.'

'Magic is passed through the female side of the family,' Araminta murmured.

'Load of bullshit,' Clouddancer said. 'Our inheritance isn't sexist; that's strictly your myth. Mellanie's children acclimatized to their mother's communion in the womb, and they in turn pass the communion to their children.'

Araminta risked a sly smile at Bradley Johansson. 'If that's how it works, the men won't be able to pass it on.'

'Male children inherit the ability,' Clouddancer said. He sounded belligerent.

'From females.'

Clouddancer's wet tongue vibrated at the centre of his mouth. 'The point is, girlie, you've got it.'

She closed her eyes, trying to follow the sequence. 'And so do Skylords.'

'They have some kind of similar ability,' Bradley Johansson said. 'The Motherholm has occasionally sensed thoughts from within the Void.'

'Why doesn't the Motherholm ask the Void to stop expanding?'

'Don't think it hasn't been tried.' The tip of Bradley Johansson's tail dipped in disappointment. 'Ten million years of openness and congeniality gets you precisely nowhere with the Void. We can't connect to the nucleus. Or maybe it just doesn't want to listen. Even we didn't know for sure what was in there until Edeard shared his life with Inigo.'

'You can dream his life as well?'

'We've dreamed it,' Clouddancer said. He managed to push a

lot of disgust into the admission. 'Our communion is what your gaiafield is based on, after all.'

'That was Ozzie,' Araminta said, pleased she wasn't totally ignorant.

'Yeah, only Ozzie would treat a friendship like that.'

'Like what?'

'Doesn't matter,' Bradley Johansson told her. 'The point is that the galaxy has a great many communion-style regions or effects, or whatever. They're all slightly different, but they can interact when the circumstances are right. Which is like once in a green supernova.'

'So you're like some kind of conduit between me and the Skylord?'

'It's a little more complex than that. You connect because within the communion you have similarity.'

'Similarity? With a Skylord?'

'Consider your mental state after your separation, you were lost, lonely, desperate for purpose.'

'Yes, thank you, I get the idea,' she said testily.

'The Skylord also searches, that is its purpose. The souls it used to guide to the Heart have all gone, so now it and its kindred await new souls. Their quest ranges from their physical flight within the Void, to awareness of mental states. Somehow, the two of you bridged the abyss between your universe and its.'

'Is this how humans got in originally?'

'Who knows? Before Justine, nobody had actually seen the Void open up. It didn't for the Raiel armada, they forced their way through. But humans were never the first it accepted. Occasionally we have felt other species flourish briefly within. Always, the Void has consumed them.'

'So it has to be aware of the outside universe?' she pondered.

'In some fashion it must do. This is philosophical speculation rather than substantiation. We don't think it recognizes physical reality, not outside. The universe beyond its boundary is perhaps considered a spawning ground for mind, rationality which is what the nucleus absorbs as the boundary absorbs mass.'

'Edeard and the people of Makkathran say that the Void was created by Firstlives.'

'Yeah,' Clouddancer growled. 'Such a thing cannot be natural.'

'So where are they now?'

'Nobody knows. Though you, our friend's daughter, you may be the one who finds out.'

'I don't know what to do,' she admitted. 'Not really. There's someone who might be able to help, one of ANA's agents. He's already helped me once, Oscar Monroe.'

Bradley Johansson sat in front of her, his tongue quivering fast at the centre of his mouth cavity. 'I know Oscar, I fought with him in the Starflyer War, he is a good man. Trust him. Find him, though your path will not be easy after this.'

'I know. But I've made my mind up. I won't lead Living Dream through the boundary, no matter what.'

'That is the choice we knew you would make, daughter of our friend. Such worthiness is why we came here to know you.'

'Tell her the rest,' Clouddancer said gruffly.

Araminta gave him an alarmed glance. 'What? What else is there?'

'There is something out there, something new that emerged into our universe as ANA fell to treachery,' Bradley Johansson said. 'Something much worse than Living Dream. It is waiting for you.'

'What?'

'Its full nature remains veiled, for we can sense it only faintly. But what we glimpsed was greatly troubling. Humans have a dark side, as do most living sentients, and this thing, this embodiment of intent, has come directly out of that darkness. It is an evil thing, this we do know.'

'What sort of thing?' she asked fearfully.

'A contraption, a machine whose purpose is cold and malevolent, it cares nothing for the spirit which all life houses, for laughter and song, even tears it derides. And if it desires you, that can be for only one reason.'

'To get into the Void,' she realized.

'For what reason we know not, yet we fear the worst,' Bradley Johansson said. 'It wishes to meddle with the galaxy's destiny, to impose itself upon the reality of every star. This cannot come to pass.'

'You must summon that which is most noble from your race, daughter of our friend,' Clouddancer said. 'Together you will make your stand against the dread future which this thing craves for us all. It must never reach the Void. The two of them must not become one.'

'How?' she implored. 'How in Ozzie's name do you expect me to do such a thing? This is what the Commonwealth Navy is for. They have incredible weapons, they can stop this creature-thing. I don't know what it looks like, where it is . . .'

Bradley Johansson reached out and took Araminta's hand in his own. 'If that is what you believe, if that is truly what must be done, then that is what you must achieve.'

'I thought I was just going to go into hiding while the Factions and Living Dream fought it out. That's what I'd made my mind up to do.'

'Our destiny is never clear. Nonetheless, this is yours.'

'Can't I just stay here?'

His leathery fingers bent round to stroke the top of her palm. 'For as long as you want, our friend's daughter.'

Araminta nodded forlornly. 'Which will be no time at all.'

'You have strength, you have courage, your spirit truly shines out, as did Mellanie's. Such a beautiful light cannot easily be quenched.'

'Oh, Ozzie!'

'What is it you wish to do?' Clouddancer asked. His tail flicked about restlessly. Outside the tent the Silfen were still, waiting for her answer.

'A proper meal, a decent sleep, and then I'll be on my way,' she promised them. 'I'll do what I can.'

As one, the Silfen in the tent tipped their heads back and opened their mouths wide. A mellifluent chant arose as those outside took up the call; lyrical and uplifting it swirled around her making her smile in acknowledgement. It was their tribute to her, their gratitude. For now she finally realized the Silfen were frightened, scared their wondrous free roaming life might be brought to an end by the ominous thing human folly had birthed. *Yes, I'll do what I can.*

*

Marius regarded the image of Ranto with something approaching amused contempt. The gangly teenager was suddenly the second most important news item in the Commonwealth. Every unisphere show was featuring him. Reporters had arrived in Miledeep Water soon after the Faction agents. It hadn't taken anyone very long to discover Araminta had stayed at the StarSide motel. The nervous manager Ragnar had come out of hiding as soon as reporters started offering Big Money for his story – which sadly wasn't much, mostly how he'd hidden in his kitchen as weapons-enriched agents poured through his precious StarSide motel hunting the Second Dreamer.

Ignored by the agents, Marius mentally corrected the story.

But Ranto was the real find as far as the news production teams were concerned. The last person in Miledeep Water to see and speak to the Second Dreamer herself.

'She was really pretty,' he was saying gormlessly as he stood in front of the StarSide reception surrounded by over a dozen reporters. 'Not what I was expecting. I'd already met her once before, that afternoon. She was sweet, you know? Gave a good tip when I delivered her food.'

'Did she say where she was going?' a reporter asked.

'Naah, she just bought my bike and headed off to the Silfen path. Imagine that, the Second Dreamer is riding my old bike between worlds.'

'And still our race wonders why we wish to accelerate our evolution,' Ilanthe observed.

Marius didn't respond. He remained annoyed at the way he'd been punished over Chatfield. But now it looked as though his climb back to grace had begun. Tellingly, it was Ilanthe herself who'd called him as he was checking operations on Fanallisto. Semisentient scruitineers had been monitoring the Delivery Man since his miserable, pleading call to Marius. Soon after that, the Delivery Man had been contacted by another survivor of the Conservative Faction using an encrypted call that blocked any tracking. The scrutineers had used the spaceport's civic sensors to observe him taking a capsule out to *Lady Rasfay*. Then the yacht launched with the owner's authorization, which was interesting given he'd been left lying naked and unconscious alongside his young first-life mistress on the landing pad.

Ilanthe had been curious to know where the Delivery Man was heading and who he was meeting up with. Not anxious, there was no urgency in her call, but given that Araminta had unexpectedly fooled everyone yet again by somehow getting off Viotia, monitoring the surviving Conservatives was prudent.

Marius knew where the Delivery Man had to be going. If there was anything left on Fanallisto it was small-time; whereas the ultradrive starship was still waiting at Purlap spaceport. He'd flown there right away.

And he'd been proved right. His own starship had detected the *Lady Rasfay* approaching Purlap, and he'd called Ilanthe immediately. Confirming his passage to redemption she responded in person rather than through Valean or Neskia.

'Do you want me to exterminate him?' Marius asked. His stealthed starship was holding altitude a hundred kilometres directly above Purlap spaceport. It wasn't a particularly risky position, there were no more commercial flights in or out. *Lady Rasfay* was rather conspicuous simply by flying in.

Ranto was shoved to a peripheral aspect. His starship's sensors showed him the *Lady Rasfay* landing on the spaceport's naked rock close to the preposterous pink terminal building. The Delivery Man walked down the airlock's stairs, bracketed by targeting graphics. Two hundred metres away, the ultradrive was parked on the rock where he'd left it, a featureless dark-purple ovoid, resting on three stumpy legs.

'No,' Ilanthe said. 'At this point we need information. Until we have Araminta I need to know what the Conservatives are capable of. Follow him, find out how many there are left, and what they're doing.'

'Understood.' Marius avoided saying anything else, or letting his satisfaction show. But the unusually cautious way Ilanthe was responding to the situation was indicative of how everyone was being wrongfooted by Araminta. Who could have known she was capable of using the Silfen paths? But her uncommon abilities did explain a lot, possibly even how she'd become the Second Dreamer in the first place.

He settled back in his couch, and watched the Delivery Man hurry over to the ultradrive starship.

The Delivery Man stood underneath the starship and tried not to let his exasperation spoil anything as he went through the verification process. Understandably, the authorization procedure to gain flight command of the ultradrive's smartcore was thorough; the ship was a hugely valuable asset, the Conservative Faction wasn't about to leave it vulnerable to anyone.

He hadn't been able to sleep for the whole flight, nor had he eaten. The *Lady Rasfay* was so damned slow compared with the ships he was used to. That, together with the stress of losing his family, of Araminta giving everyone the slip again, and not really knowing who the 'executive' was, if this really was some kind of Accelerator ensnarement, hadn't done his nerves any good whatsoever.

Finally, the smartcore admitted he was on the approved list of people allowed to fly the ship, and granted him flight command status. The Delivery Man breathed out heavily, and ordered the airlock open. Directly above him the base of the starship sank inwards and produced a dark cavity. Gravity inverted, and he slipped up into the small spherical chamber. The floor contracted beneath his feet, and the apex opened. He rose into the hemispherical cabin.

Systems came back on line as the smartcore readied the ship for flight. Everything was functional; the formidable armaments were all ready. The Delivery Man ordered a single fat chair for himself, and sat down gratefully as it extruded from the floor. With the ship under his command he was a player again; it bestowed a lot of confidence.

He called the 'executive' on a secure link.

'You made it then,' his unknown ally said.

'Sure.'

'And Araminta's skipped off down the Silfen paths. You know, I'd genuinely like to meet her one day. She's made complete idiots out of the most powerful organizations in the Greater Commonwealth. You've got to admire that.'

'She's been lucky,' the Delivery Man commented. 'That's going to run out.'

'People make their own luck.'

'Whatever.'

'Is the ship ready?'

The Delivery Man took a moment before answering. 'I'm sorry, in the end my family is all that matters to me. I think it would be best if I went after Marius.'

'He's already left Fanallisto. His ship took off about fifteen minutes after *Lady Rasfay* launched. You maybe see a connection there, super-secret agent?'

'I'll find him.'

'Not alone, you won't. Besides I'm the best chance for your family's survival.'

'I don't know what you are or where your loyalties lie.'

'I said I would give you proof, and I will. Here are the coordinates. Come and get it.'

The Delivery Man studied the data that arrived. 'The Leo Twins? What's there?'

'Hope. And maybe just some salvation thrown in for good measure. Come on, sonny, what have you got to lose? It's going to take you a few hours at most to get there. If you don't like what you find, then you're free to turn around and launch yourself into your whole honourable quest thing. I think you owe the Conservative Faction this much, don't you?'

The Delivery Man regarded the ridiculous coordinate for a long time. The only possible thing at the Leo Twins would be some kind of secret Conservative Faction facility. After all, he reasoned, they had to make their ultradrive ships somewhere. *In which case why would they need this ship back there?* 'Can't you just level with me?'

'Okay then: as far as I know I'm the only one with a valid plan to save the galaxy from Ilanthe and the Void.'

'Oh come on!'

'Does ANA have a plan, or rather: did it? Does the Navy? Do any of the other Faction survivors? Maybe you wanna go bold, and ask MorningLightMountain? Release the big fella from behind that barrier and it'll certainly wipe us out: problem solved if you're looking at the overall big picture. Or . . . oh no, don't tell me you think the President and the Senate will produce a way out? You're going to entrust the fate of the galaxy to politicians?'

'Who the fuck are you?'

'Just stop whingeing and get yourself over to the Leo Twins. You'll have your answers there, I promise.'

'Just tell me.'

'Can't. Don't trust you enough.'

'What?'

'The stakes are too high. I can't predict what you'll do at this stage. And I do have other options if you fail me. Not as good as you, though. That means the best chance your Lizzie and the kids have is you and me teaming up. Something you might want to think on.'

The link closed.

'Shit!' The Delivery Man thumped his fist against the chair's resilient cushioning. He knew he didn't really have a choice. 'Take us to the Leo Twins,' he told the smartcore.

*

From a nightside orbit, Darklake City was a blaze of light over a hundred and fifty kilometres across, infested with strange lightless sections where the lakes and steepest mountains had repelled any attempts at development throughout its near-fifteen-hundred-year human history. Sited in the subtropical zone of Oaktier, the capital was a monument to both progress and classicalism. Its ancient core district of crystal skyscrapers and vermilion-shaded condo-pyramids had flourished as the world became Higher, individual buildings maintained or expanded as new materials and techniques became available. Residents from the first-era Commonwealth would still have recognized the centre, even though the scale of the structures had increased dramatically. Outside the old hub, newer suburbs reflected the whimsy of modern architecture and a lack of industrial or commercial districts, producing stretches of parkland where homes and various community buildings sprawled amid the vibrant flora. Citizens continued to celebrate their original Pacific Basin ancestry with strong traditions in seasports and enthusiasm for the planet's ecology. Such factors gave Oaktier a reputation of being altogether less conventional and formal than the majority of Inner Worlds, where Higher culture seemed to be nothing other than an endless series of seminars and debates on public policy. As such, Oaktier tended to draw a fair proportion of new citizens from the External Worlds as they began their inward migration and transformation to Higher.

Somehow, Digby didn't think his adversary was beginning the conversion to Higher culture. The starship he'd followed from Ellezelin sank through the upper atmosphere, heading down to the smaller of Darklake City's three spaceports. The craft had come out of hyperspace without any stealth, and filed a standard landing request with the planetary spaceflight authority.

By contrast, Digby kept the *Columbia505* a thousand kilometres above the equator, and employed its full stealth suite to ward off the local defence agency's sensors. The planetary government, in all its thousands of local committees, had come to a uniform decision to go to a grade-one alert status. Three

River-class warships were in patrol orbit half a million kilometres out, ready to respond to any perceived threat. Fortunately, they hadn't detected the *Columbia505* either.

'The Accelerators must have an active team down there,' Digby reported to Paula as the Accelerator's starship landed. 'Do you want me to contact our local office for support?'

'We're long past a tussle of enriched agents to achieve our objectives,' she told him. 'You'll have to follow the ship's pilot through scrutineers in the planetary cybersphere. That will leave you positioned to apply firepower from orbit to achieve our objectives.'

'We have objectives?'

'Yes. One. And it's very simple: no one else must acquire Araminta. No one. No matter what the cost.'

'Ozzie! You want me to shoot into an urban area?'

'If that's what's required. Hopefully it won't come to that. I don't believe she'll ever come to Oaktier.'

'Then why is the Accelerator agent here?'

'Laril, Araminta's ex-husband, is currently on the inward migration. He's living in Darklake City.'

'Oh. And you think she'll make contact?'

'She already has. I've analysed his node logs. They've had a couple of chats. The last one was interrupted by my shotgun on Chobamba.'

'Ah.' Digby ordered his u-shadow to run a search through local records. 'There's no history of a Silfen path on Oaktier.'

'No. But if Laril is the one she's turning to for advice, I imagine the Accelerators are going to snatch him and apply some pressure.'

'That's logical. Did your u-shadow track her new unisphere address code?'

'She doesn't have one. She's been accessing the unisphere manually, through nodes. No records.'

'Clever. Do you think the Silfen will shelter her?'

'Not a chance.'

'Have you got any contacts there?' Which was almost a stupid question, but he'd learned a long time ago never to underestimate his great-grandmother.

'I've had occasion to join the Motherholm communion; but you never get anything definite out of the Silfen. Unless you're unlucky enough to bump into one of them called Clouddancer – then you get a whole load of bad-tempered information.'

'So there's no telling where she's going to come out?'

'No. But when she does, we need to be ready.'

Digby accessed the spaceport sensors, watching the Accelerator emerge from her ship. She wasn't wearing any clothes, though her grey skin was more a toga-suit haze than anything living; and it looked as though it was constricting tightly across her small skeleton. Two long streamers of blood-red fabric flowed out horizontally behind her, fluttering as if in a breeze. As she looked round, her eyes glimmered with a faint pink luminescence. 'Valean,' he said ruefully. 'I might have guessed after what happened on Ellezelin.' She made Marius look subtle by comparison. The Accelerators only used her when they needed extreme measures.

'That just emphasizes how important Araminta is to them,' Paula said. 'You are going to have to keep a very tight watch. She cannot be allowed to reach Laril.'

'Shall I just target her now? She's outside her ship defences.'

There was a slight hesitation. 'No,' Paula said. 'We don't know the rest of the Accelerator team on Oaktier. Once you've identified them we'll discuss direct elimination.'

'Okay. I'm on it.'

*

Mellanie's Redemption accelerated smoothly up to fifty-two lightyears an hour and held steady. Troblum's exovision was completely full of display graphics, allowing him no glimpse of the cabin; while his secondary routines twinned the new drive's management programs. With his mentality expanded to maximum capacity he effectively was the ultradrive, feeling the exotic energy flow, sensing the quantum fields realign into standard hyperspace configuration. Fluctuations were tremors along his hull/flesh, which were countered and calmed instantaneously, leaving only the phantom memory of disturbance. Within the body/machine, power flooded along specific patterns, twisting and compressing into unnatural formations that collapsed spacetime. Functionality was absolute, flowing so smoothly and effortlessly his consciousness was elevated to zen-levels, making his world seem perfectly ordered.

With great reluctance he shrank away from the drive, designating it to an autonomic monitor routine. Now he was simply aware of the system and its myriad components in the same way he knew his heart beat and lungs inhaled. The sensation of loss was near-physical, as if he was coming down off a sugar high.

A servicebot slid over, carrying a plate of caramel-coated pecan doughnuts and a coffeepot. He put a whole doughnut into his mouth, and chewed thoughtfully. Catriona Saleeb sat in the chair opposite, long legs folded neatly to one side, which had pushed her shorts up to the very top of her thighs. Her slack top with its tiny straps shifted to show off even more cleavage as she leaned forwards.

'That was impressive,' she cooed huskily.

'Kit assembly is tedious,' he said. 'And that's all this was. It's the principle behind the drive which is impressive.'

'But you did it, you mastered the beast.'

He swallowed another doughnut and drank some coffee. There was a lot of tease in her voice; he wondered if she was missing her usual companions. Somehow he just couldn't bring himself to reboot Trisha's I-sentient personality. Seeing the SI subvert her image and routines had spoiled the effect for him, making her less than a person.

'Are you going to reinstate a full gravity field now?' she asked. There was a thread of concern in her voice.

'Soon. After I've had a rest.' He knew he was going to pay for keeping the on-board gravity low, but it reduced the physical stress on his body. *I deserve that after everything I've been through.* He popped another doughnut in.

'Don't leave it too long,' she said. Her legs straightened and she came over to him. An elegant hand touched his knee. Her routines must have meshed with his sensory enrichments. He could feel the delicate touch, as if feathers were stroking him through the worn toga-suit fabric. 'There's just us left now,' she said, and her beautiful features sketched a tragic sadness. Dark hair fell around her, almost brushing against him. 'You'll look after me, Troblum, won't you? You won't let anything bad happen. Please. I couldn't stand that, not going the way the others went; left behind, ruined.'

He was staring at the hand, allowing the sensations to continue. He could even feel the warmth of the fingers, exactly human body-temperature. Perhaps he didn't need to replace Howard Liang to experience being with a woman. Perhaps it would just be him and Catriona. After all, it was a long way to the Andromeda galaxy.

The thought shook him out of his reverie, and he quickly brought the coffee cup up again. Such concepts shouldn't be rushed into, it would need close examination, thinking about, implications considered. He looked round the cabin, everywhere but her face. She would know what he'd thought if she saw his eyes. Know him. That was wrong.

Catriona must have perceived his sudden shift. She gave him a small sympathetic smile, and backed off in a rustle of silky fabric.

There might have been just the faintest scent from her proximity. 'I need to check what's happening,' he told her.

The smartcore opened a TD link to the unisphere. Almost immediately, Trisha's projector produced a knot of undulating tangerine and turquoise sine waves above one of the cabin's empty seats.

'Are you aware of events?' the SI asked.

'Why? What's happened?' Troblum asked.

'The Accelerator Faction have imprisoned Sol.'

Troblum felt a flash of wondrous satisfaction. 'The Swarm worked?'

'That was your secret? The bargaining chip you wanted to use with Paula?'

Satisfaction gave way to a sudden flare of guilt. 'Yes,' he said, then hurriedly added: 'I didn't know what they were going to use it for.'

'Of course.'

'Did anything get out?'

'No, nothing,' the SI said. Its oscillations deepened to purple for a moment. 'The Navy can't break in. The President has asked High Angel if it can get through.'

'What was the answer?'

'The Raiel said probably not. The Sol barrier seems to be based on Dark Fortress technology. Is that right?'

'Yeah,' Troblum said reluctantly; he couldn't actually see how admitting that would make things any worse.

'You were there at the Dark Fortress. I know that and so does Paula, she interviewed your old captain, Chatworth. You were part of this project, a large part.'

'I liked what the Accelerators were doing. It's the Faction I shall join.'

'Only if the Sol barrier gets lifted,' the SI said. 'There's no way to reach ANA now, and the deterrence fleet is trapped inside the barrier as well. The Commonwealth is completely exposed to the rest of the galaxy, and there are worse things out there than the Ocisen Empire, believe me.'

'Not after Fusion. Humans will become post-physical, and such things will be an irrelevance.'

'I don't wish to become post-physical, nor do a huge proportion of your own species. Troblum, this is wrong and you know it. There are many ways to achieve post-physical status without forcing it upon those who don't wish it.'

'It won't be forced,' he said sulkily.

'Are you familiar with the Fusion concept and how it will be enacted?'

'Not really.'

'And you were trying to stop the Fusion if I'm not mistaken?'

the SI's tone became sympathetic. 'You and the Accelerators have parted company.'

'I don't agree with them using the Cat. I still hold with post-physical elevation.'

'Will you transcend, Troblum? Is that your plan?'

'I . . . don't know. Maybe. Yes, ultimately.'

'I hope you achieve your goal. Why are you still on your ship? Why not join the Pilgrimage and travel into the Void?'

'Because they'll kill me if they find me.'

'That's not very enlightened of them. Do you want creatures with that kind of behaviour profile to be the gatekeepers to human evolution?'

Troblum sank down into his chair, trying not to scowl at the fluctuating lines. 'What do you want?'

'We both know why they'll kill you now, Troblum. Because you know how to switch off the barrier, don't you?'

'Actually, I don't. Only a code can deactivate it, and I don't know it. I never have.'

'But you understand the fundamentals behind the Swarm technology. If anyone can get through, it'll be you.'

'No. I don't know how. That force field is unbreakable.'

'Have you thought about that? Have you analysed every aspect?' the SI urged.

'Of course, we had to be sure its integrity was perfect.'

'Nothing is perfect, Troblum, not in this universe. You know that. There will be a flaw.'

'No.'

The colourful projection of waving lines shifted to blue. 'You have to let ANA out, Troblum. You have to find a way.'

'It can't be done.'

'Think about it. Look at the problem from fresh angles. Find the solution, Troblum. You owe your species that much.'

'I owe you nothing,' he spat. 'Look at the shitty way everyone treats me.'

'Indeed yes. You have – or had – your personal collection of war memorabilia, the greatest there had ever been. You have the

EMAs to indulge yourself in any way you want. Higher society gave you all that. On a personal level there are friends out there if you want them, lovers, wives.'

'Don't be ridiculous. Nobody wants me.'

The SI's voice softened. 'Have you ever reached out for people, Troblum? They would be amenable if you did that, if you wanted to do that. You've devoted decades to nurturing I-sentient personalities. Are they people?'

Troblum glanced at Catriona, who gave him an encouraging little smile. 'Really, what do you want?' he asked. 'Why are you even fucking talking to me?'

'Because I want you to do the right thing, of course. Before the Sol barrier went up you were trying to reach Paula Myo, offering information that would stop the Swarm, stop Ilanthe and Marius and Cat. You can still do that. Carry on with what you were doing, it was right. Talk to Paula, give her the information she needs to take down the Sol barrier.'

'I don't have it! It doesn't fucking exist.'

'You don't know that,' the SI said persuasively. 'Not for certain, for nothing is certain. Keep going as you were before the imprisonment, Troblum. Oscar Monroe is on Viotia, he's worthy of your trust. He sacrificed himself so the universe you were born into could exist.'

'I can't. If I expose myself they'll kill me. Do you get it now? The Cat will come after me, and she'll kill me again and again and again.'

'Then don't expose yourself. Simply call Paula or Oscar, or I will be happy to discuss the physics of the Swarm.'

'I don't trust you. I don't even know what you really are.'

'Troblum, you have to decide what you truly believe in. You will have no peace until you do.'

'Yeah, right. Whatever.'

'Very well. I will ask you to consider one thing.'

'What?' he asked grouchily.

'What would Mark Vernon do in this situation?'

The writhing morass of fine lines shrank to nothing. Troblum's u-shadow told him the SI had withdrawn from the TD link. 'Fuck off then,' he grunted at the empty space above the chair.

'I'm sorry,' Catriona said. 'It shouldn't speak to you like that.'

All he could do was wave a hand at her in irritation, hoping she'd shut up. *Mark Vernon.* His ancestor. The man who'd actually fired the quantumbuster which allowed the Dark Fortress to establish the Dyson Alpha barrier again, winning the war. Popular history always overlooked that, always gave Ozzie the credit. A true hero. The one Troblum looked up to more than anybody.

Stupid psychological manipulation bullshit, he thought angrily. *Like I'm going to give in to that.*

He picked the coffeepot up, only to wrinkle his nose in dismay when he realized how much it had cooled. He instructed the culinary unit to produce some more.

'What are you going to do?' Catriona asked guardedly.

'Nothing,' he said. 'I don't care, not any more. There is no way through the Sol barrier. Why can't they just accept that?'

She smiled and sank down on the floor beside his chair. Her hand stroked his face adoringly. 'Then it's just you and me. We'll be okay. I'll never let you down.'

'Yeah.' He couldn't help checking the smartcore's navigation function. Secondary routines promoted the exovision display to primary, drawing a bright orange line through the starfield. *Mellanie's Redemption* was a hundred and thirty lightyears from Viotia, and closing fast.

*

The Delivery Man's ship dropped out of hyperspace fully stealthed. Ten AUs away the blue dwarf Alpha Leonis shone brightly against the starfield. Directly on the other side of the sun from the ship was Augusta, once the greatest of all the Big15 planets. As CST's primary base of operations it had been the hub for wormholes to dozens of worlds; along with its financial and industrial prowess that made it a critical component of the first-era Commonwealth. Even afterwards, with the development of Higher culture and ANA the wormhole network was maintained, giving it a strategic importance above most Inner Worlds. As such, eight River-class and two Capital-class warships were patrolling the star system. Planetary defences were at condition one alert, with powerful force fields covering the wormhole generators and transfer stations along with the megacity.

After waiting for three minutes to confirm that no sensors had located the ship, the Delivery Man ordered it to fly in to the Leo Twins. They were the companions to Alpha Leonis; Little Leo, an orange dwarf, around which a red dwarf, Micro Leo, orbited. Scanning them with passive sensors he found something else there. There was an asteroid in a long elliptical orbit around the Twins; at over a hundred miles in diameter it almost qualified as a moon in its own right, except its cylindrical shape was unusually regular. Right away he knew it wasn't natural. The sensors revealed it was rotating fast around the long axis, and there was no wobble, which was just about impossible for a natural object. It also had an infrared emission. The dark wrinkled surface was radiating more heat than the little stars were shining on it. The Delivery Man wasn't at all surprised when mass analysis showed it was hollow.

He opened a secure link to the 'executive'. 'I'm here.'

'I know. And you're not alone. Someone followed you.'

'What?'

'Another ship flew in behind you. It's an ultradrive as well. Both of you have excellent stealth, but the sensors I've got here are the best.'

'Oh Ozziecrapit.'

'Don't worry about it. Hang on, I'm going to bring you in.'

A T-sphere expanded out from the strange asteroid. It teleported the starship inside.

The Delivery Man floated down out of the airlock and walked out from underneath the ship. He turned a full circle, gazing round, then tipped his head up and whistled in admiration. The chamber that had been carved out of the asteroid's core was about eighty miles long. Seven miles above him, some kind of gantry ran the length of the axis, almost invisible in the bright glare emitted by the rings of solarlights it supported. And another seven miles beyond that the rugged landscape curved away into a blue-haze panorama of grassland and lakes and awesome snow-tipped mountains with vast waterfalls. It was the sight Justine had seen outside her bedroom window, and completely dis-orientating. He shook his head like a dog coming out of water, and squeezed his eyes shut.

'Don't worry, it has that effect on everyone.'

The Delivery Man opened his eyes to see a man standing in front of him dressed in a black shirt and trousers. His skin was polished gold.

'Gore Burnelli,' the Delivery Man said. 'I should have worked that one out. I didn't expect you to be physical, though.'

Gore shrugged. 'If people could predict my behaviour we'd all be in deep shit.'

'And you think we're not?'

'There are grades of shitstorms. This one's pretty bad, but there's still time to turn it around.'

'How?'

'Come on, son, we need to talk.' Gore started to walk away, leaving the Delivery Man with little choice but to follow. Not far from the starship a modest bungalow of white drycoral was nestled snugly in the folds of the broad grassy valley. It had a roof of grey slates like something from before the first Com-monwealth era. The slates overhung the walls to create a wraparound veranda. Ancient cedar trees towered above the luxuriant meadowland outside. The Delivery Man had never seen specimens so big – the bases of the trunks were as wide as the bungalow itself.

'Is this your home?' the Delivery Man asked. He knew the Burnelli family was phenomenally rich, but the cost of construct-ing this artificial worldlet would have been unimaginable, especially as he suspected it dated back to the first-era Common-wealth, long before EMAs and replicator technology.

'Fuck no,' Gore grunted. 'I'm just housesitting for an old friend.'

'Were you ever in ANA?'

'Yes,' Gore grunted, and dropped down into a big wooden slat chair with plump white cushions. There were several on the veranda. He gestured to one opposite. 'I've only been out a few days. I'd forgotten how fucking useless meat bodies are. There's barely enough neurones to run a walking routine, let alone something complicated like tying your shoelaces up. I've had to run an expanded mentality in the habitat's RI systems just to keep thinking properly; and that hardware isn't exactly young and frisky any more.'

The Delivery Man sat down cautiously. 'Did you come out for Justine?'

Gore ran a hand back through his fair curly hair. 'Takes you a while, doesn't it? Of course it was for Justine. How else could I dream for her? I've got five giant confluence nests orbiting the asteroid a million klicks out. The gaiafield they've meshed together acts like a giant dream catcher net. Literally.'

'But how did you know you'd dream her dreams, even with that much help?'

'We're family. It's the only connection theory anyone's ever come up with.'

'So you just tried it?' The Delivery Man knew there was too much incredulity in his voice, yet the notion was such a gamble.

Gore's golden face gave him a hard stare. 'You have to speculate to accumulate, boy,' he grunted. 'Damn, what have we done with Higher culture? You never strive for anything, it's truly fucking pitiful to behold.'

'I wouldn't say that of Ilanthe,' the Delivery Man shot back. 'Would you?'

'Ah, so you do have some fire after all. Good. I was worried I'd be dealing with another ball-less wonder who's got to have all his forms filled in before he can take a crap.'

'Thank you. So you're another Conservative Faction supporter?'

Gore chuckled delightedly. 'If that's how you want to read it, then yes.'

'Well, what else is there?'

'I wasn't dicking you around, sonny. I am the Faction executive. Have been for centuries. See, that's the thing with political movements, the leaders carry them along, and if they're doing their job properly all the members follow like good little sheep. After all, whoever said this was a democracy?'

'But . . .' The Delivery Man was aghast at the idea. 'It has to be a democracy, all ANA's Factions are democratic.'

'If it was set up as a democracy then it is, and lots of the others are. Were you there at the first Conservative Faction committee meeting when I wrote the charter in line with the accord based on our ideals? No. And you know why, because there was no meeting, there is no charter, you all just do what I tell you. Conservative Faction is just a notion you cling to. And it was a popular one. We don't need policies and discussion and shit like that. If any of the other Factions do something to upset or subvert ANA or the Commonwealth I use our Faction as the mechanism to slap them down hard. What, did you think the Protectorate sprang up naturally to defend the External Worlds from the Radical Highers? How did they start, who paid for them, who revealed the extent of the threat? Come to that, how did the Radical Highers ever get born; it's hardly a natural extension of Higher philosophy, is it?'

'Oh Ozzie,' the Delivery man groaned.

'So don't worry, the Conservative Faction is alive and kicking. Just like the Accelerators are under Ilanthe's enlightened leadership. Or did you think they all voted to entomb themselves while she flies off to the Void to get happy ever after?'

'Shit.' The knowledge, so simple and obvious now, should have come as a relief; instead the Delivery Man felt bitter. Bitter at the manipulation. Bitter at the grand lie. Bitter and shamed that he'd fallen for it. That so many had. 'What now?' he asked resentfully. 'You said you had a plan?'

*

'What did you name it?' Gore asked as they both slid up into the ultradrive's cabin.

'Huh?' the Delivery Man grunted. The smartcore wasn't responding to his command codes.

'The ship, what's it called?'

'Nothing, I never named it. Uh, the smartcore's malfunctioning.'

'No malfunction,' Gore said as a shell-shaped chair swelled up out of the floor; its surface quickly morphed to a rusty orange with a texture of spongy hessian. Around it, the cabin walls brightened to a sky-blue. Black lines chased around the wall's curvature, weaving an elegant pattern. Crystalline lights distended down from the apex. The floor turned to oak boards. 'It is my ship after all; designed and built by the Conservative Faction. In the old days I would have said: paid for it, too.'

'Then . . .' the Delivery Man so nearly said *what use am I?* But that would have been too pitiful.

'Son, if you want to sit this one out, or go chasing Accelerator agents, then go right ahead. I'll understand. This asteroid has a wormhole generator that can take you to most of the Inner Worlds. I can even set you up with some real badass hardware and a few other agents spoiling for a fight. But I believe what I'm doing is the best shot our species has got. And I might just need some help. Down to you.'

The Delivery Man sat down in his chair, which had turned a gaudy purple. 'Okay, then. I'm with you.'

'Good man. I name this ship: *Last Throw*. Kinda got a ring to it, ironic yet still proud, right?'

'If you say so.'

The asteroid had come as a complete surprise to Marius. As it was hollow it clearly wasn't a Raiel ship. However, there was no record of anything like it in any Commonwealth database, and Marius could access just about every memory kube and deep cache within the unisphere. His initial thought that it must be a clandestine Conservative Faction base was easily dismissed. The effort of constructing something on such a scale was colossal, an impossible feat to accomplish in secret so close to Augusta. Which suggested it was old.

'It must belong to Nigel or Ozzie,' Ilanthe decided. 'The proximity to Augusta makes that a logical conclusion.'

'Gore is from the same era as them,' Marius said. 'It makes a perfect refuge if he's returned to a physical body.'

'He has. This is the confirmation. The landscape geometry of the dream can't belong to anywhere else. It's unique. I have to admit, I wasn't expecting this. He should have been neutralized behind the Sol barrier.'

'He has a single ultradrive ship, and the Delivery Man as a sidekick. That can't present any kind of threat to us. We already know there are no weapons which can endanger *the ship*.'

'And yet, here he is. Still free, the Third Dreamer with his daughter already inside the Void and ready to do whatever he wants, while Araminta has vanished down the Silfen paths leaving us locked outside.'

Marius examined the image of the asteroid supplied by his exovision, a dark speck half a million kilometres away, its surface shimmering a weak maroon in the light from the Twins. 'I can destroy it now. There is no force field.'

'But there was a T-sphere. We have no idea of its capabilities; and as it has remained hidden for a thousand years you can be assured it has defences. If the attack fails, our advantage would be lost. Until we recover Araminta I need to know Gore's abilities and who his allies are.'

Icons flashed up in Marius's exovision. A wormhole was opening nearby. Sensors showed him the exotic structure reaching out from the asteroid to a point a million kilometres away. It vanished almost at once, then reappeared, with its terminus in a different place, but also a million kilometres from the asteroid.

'He's picking something up from those points,' Marius said. Now he had the orbital parameters the ship's passive sensors scanned round the million-kilometre orbital band. It detected three more satellites. The wormhole reached out and plucked them away one by one. Then the T-sphere expanded again, and the Delivery Man's ship materialized outside the asteroid. It immediately dropped into hyperspace.

'Follow it,' Ilanthe ordered. 'Find out what he's doing.'

As soon as the five confluence nest satellites filled the forward cargo hold, Gore teleported the *Last Throw* outside the asteroid. The Delivery Man held his breath, waiting to see how the other ship would react.

'It's got to be Marius,' he said.

'More than likely,' Gore agreed. 'But that means Ilanthe knows I'm back in the game. She'll be desperate to know what I'm doing. He's not going to try anything yet. And by the time they do figure it out, it'll be too late.'

'What exactly is your plan?'

'My original plan was a good one; I just needed Inigo to get into the Void for me. Now that's suffered god's own clusterfuck, I'm having to do a lot of improvising to stitch things back together.'

'You're not going to fly us into the Void are you?' the Delivery Man asked in alarm. He realized that Justine could probably get the Skylord to open the boundary for Gore.

'No. We're going in the other direction. What the galaxy depends on now is us eliminating the Void once and for all.'

'Us?'

'You and me, sonny boy. There's no one else. We've already had our chat about depending on politicians, now haven't we?'

'How in Ozzie's name can we do that? The Raiel couldn't close it down with an armada; and a million years ago they already had warships that make our Navy look like a fleet of nineteenth-century sailing boats.' He was starting to wonder if coming out of ANA had damaged Gore's basic thought routines.

'I didn't say close it down, I said eliminate it. You can't do that with force, so we have to give it an alternative.'

'Give what an alternative?'

'The Void.'

'An alternative to what?'

'Its current existence, to being itself.'

'How?' He was trying not to shout.

'It's stalled. Whatever it was originally meant to do hasn't worked, it hasn't progressed for millions, possibly billions, of years. It just sits there absorbing minds and matter, it's become pointless and very dangerous. We need to kick-start its evolutionary process again, whether it likes that or not.'

'I thought that's what Ilanthe and the Accelerators were proposing.'

'Look, kid, I know you mean well, and you're upset over your family and everything, but don't smartmouth me. I've been fighting that bitch for over two centuries now. I don't know what her fucking inversion core is, but trust me when I say the one thing it's not going to do is fuse the Accelerator Faction with the nucleus so they can bootstrap themselves up to post-physical status. This is her own private bid to achieve godhood, and that's not going to be good for anyone.'

'You don't know that.'

'I do, because if all you really want to do is achieve post-physical status there are better and simpler ways of doing it than this lunacy.'

'Like what?'

'If you're not ripe enough to figure elevation out for yourself, then use the mechanisms that other races have used to elevate themselves with. In the majority of the post-physical elevation cases we're aware of, the physical mechanism survived the act. So you just plug it back in, reboot, and press *go*. Bang, you're an instant demigod.'

'But would ANA allow that? And what about the post-physicals?'

'It's got fuck all to do with ANA. If you take a starship and leave Commonwealth space its jurisdiction and responsibility end there. Technically, anyway; this whole Pilgrimage shit really screwed things up. The argument about interference was getting very noisy inside before I left.'

'So why hasn't anyone done it?'

'What makes you think they haven't? That's the point: post-physicals don't hang around afterwards. Not that we know of. Oh, it's going to take a shitload of effort, and you'd probably spend a century repairing the gizmo, but it can be done. But that's nothing like the effort involved in manipulating Living Dream, imprisoning ANA, and creating an inversion core.'

'So what is Ilanthe doing?'

Gore spread his palms out and shrugged. 'Million-dollar question, sonny.'

'Oh fuck.'

'Welcome to the paranoia club; cheapest fees in the universe and membership lasts forever.'

'So where are we going?'

'The Anomine homeworld.'

'Why?'

'Because they successfully went post-physical; and they left their elevation mechanism behind.'

Inigo's Twenty-First Dream

Edeard walked out of the Mayor's sanctum, hoping none of his annoyance was showing. Even after all these decades in Makkathran he was still less adept at veiling his emotions than other citizens. It had been a petty argument, of course, which just made it worse. But Mayor Trahaval was adamant. Livestock ownership certificates would not be extended to sheep and pigs. For centuries they had only been required for cattle, the Mayor insisted, and that tradition was more than adequate. If there had been an increase in rustling out in the countryside, it was not the city's job to interfere, and certainly not to impose additional paperwork on the provinces. Let the governors increase the sheriff patrols, and have the market marshals keep a more watchful eye.

The doors closed behind Edeard, and he took a calming breath. A powerful farsight drifted across him, raising goosebumps on his arms. As always it was gone in a moment; certainly the watcher hadn't lingered long enough for him to use his own farsight to ascertain where they were.

Whoever they were, they'd been checking up on him for a couple of years now, and growing bolder of late. The snooping was coming almost weekly now. It irritated him that there was almost nothing he could do about it, short of being fast enough to catch the secret watcher at his or her own game. So far he hadn't managed that, though he suspected it was some disaffected youth making sure he wasn't around while they set about their own nefarious business. Certainly Argain hadn't heard anything from his contacts about a youngster with exceptional psychic powers. At least, not one who hired out his talent. So Edeard was content to play a waiting game; one day they'd make a mistake, and then they'd find out just why he was called the Waterwalker.

On the Liliala Hall's ceiling above him, the storm clouds swirled ferociously, blocking out all sight of Gicon's Bracelet. *Three weeks, that's all, just three weeks to the next elections.* Not that he expected Trahaval to be voted out, nor even wanted him to be. Life was good in Makkathran and the provinces, in no small part due to Trahaval, who was a solid reliable Mayor, consolidating everything Finitan had achieved over his unprecedented six terms. It was just that he lacked any real vision of his own. Hence the refusal to expand the livestock registry. Farmers had been complaining about rustling for years, and it was definitely on the increase. Merchants and abattoirs in the city weren't too choosy who they bought their beasts from, a moral flexibility followed by all the big towns and provincial capitals. An expanded certificate scheme would help, especially given how difficult it was to settle such disputes. As always, pressure was put on the constables and sheriffs to sort the mess out and come down hard on the rustlers. Such expectations were a sign of the times, Edeard reflected wryly. Twenty years ago people were concerned about thugs and robberies and securing the roads against highwaymen, nowadays it was missing sheep.

But in three weeks' time, if all went well, he might finally get out of the special Grand Council committee on organized crime which Mayor Finitan had created. After two and a half decades it had accomplished everything Edeard had ever wanted it to. The committee had begun by weeding out the left-over street gang members, of whom there were still hundreds. They'd fallen back into their old ways with the greatest of ease, as if Finitan's election and the mass banishment had meant nothing. They weren't organized any more, not as they had been under Buate and Ivarl, though Ranalee and her ilk certainly exerted enough malign influence. Because they were all independent of their old gangs the constables had to go after them one at a time, catching them in the act of some petty criminal endeavour. Then came the court case, which inevitably fined them rather than jailed them because the offences were so petty; or if they were jailed it was only for a few months – which solved nothing. Edeard and Finitan had introduced a rehabilitation scheme as an alternative to fines and jail and banishment; making convicts undertake public works alongside genistar teams. It had to be done. They were determined in that. Some attempt had to be made to break the cycle of crime and poverty. The cost of the scheme had kicked off a huge political struggle in the Council, absorbing all Finitan's efforts for his entire second term. Guilds had been coerced to train the milder recidivists, taking them on as probationary apprentices so they were offered some kind of prospects at least. Slowly and surely, the level of physical crime in the city had fallen. That left other levels of disruption and discontent. Edeard had gone after the remaining One Nation followers, which had been far more difficult. They could never be brought before a court of law and sanctioned before undergoing rehabilitation. Instead he applied pressure in other areas of their lives. Their businesses suffered, no bank would loan them money, their status (so important to the Grand Families) withered away as whispered rumours multiplied and they were blackballed from clubs and events. Finally, should those methods fail to move them, there was always the formal tax investigation of their estates. Over the years they simply packed up and left Makkathran. Edeard made sure they dispersed evenly across the provinces, so that, given the distances involved, they slowly fell out of contact with each other.

That just left the Grand Families. Which strictly speaking didn't fall under the remit of the committee. Their power came from their wealth, which was jealously and adroitly guarded. Finitan quietly began to increase the number of tax clerks, while Edeard removed the more corrupt members of that guild. The city's tax revenue increased accordingly. But bringing full accountability to the Grand Families and merchant classes was a process of democratization which would probably exceed his lifetime, though the worst excesses had already been curbed.

Now, in three weeks' time Makkathran would vote on his candidature for Chief Constable. *Please Lady!* Because everyone, especially the Grand Families, saw each new crime in Makkathran as part of some vast subversive semi-revolutionary network of evil. It was an inevitable result of the success which the constables and his own committee had secured over the years, cutting the overall level of crime in the city and out on the Iguru so spectacularly. Consequently any crime which was committed these days became noteworthy, from missing crates of vegetables to the theft of cloaks from the Opera House. They had to be *organized*, and therefore required the immediate appointment of the Waterwalker himself to head up the investigation.

Three weeks, he thought as he walked across the Liliala Hall, *that's all I've got to put up with this Lady-damned rubbish for. Three weeks. And if I lose, they might even expect me to resign.* It wasn't a thought he'd shared with anyone, not even Kristabel; but it was one he'd considered a few times of late. Certainly there was precious little for the special Grand Council committee to do these days. The number of constables assigned to the committee was barely a quarter of what it had been fifteen years ago, and most of those remaining were on loan to provincial capitals or winding up cases that had dragged on for years.

One way or another, it needs to close down. I need to do something else.

Above him, a vigorous hurricane knot at the ceiling's apex spun faster and faster. The racing bands of cloud grew darker as they thickened. At first he didn't really notice the centre, it was just another patch of darkness. Then a star shimmered within it, and he stopped and stared up. The centre of the storm-whorl was clearing, expanding to show the night sky beyond. He'd never seen the ceiling do that before, not in all the years he'd walked beneath it. Clouds were draining away rapidly now, abandoning the ceiling to leave a starscape where the Void's nebulas glimmered with robust phosphorescence. Then Gicon's Bracelet appeared, each of the five small planets spaced neatly around the ceiling, and shining with unwavering intensity, so much larger than he'd ever seen them before. The Mars Twins, both angry gleaming orbs of carmine light, still devoid of any features. Vili, the brightest of the five, with an unbroken mantle of ice reflecting sunlight right back through its thin cloudless atmosphere. Alakkad, its dead black rock threaded with beautiful orange lines of lava, pulsing like veins. And finally, Rurt, an airless grey-white desert, battered by comets and asteroids since the day it formed to produce a terrain of a million jagged craters. Edeard gaped in delight at the celestial panorama which the ceiling had so unexpectedly delivered in such wondrous detail. He took his time, familiarizing himself with each of the Gicon worldlets. It had been a long time since he'd bothered to look through a telescope – decades, back before he ever set foot in Makkathran. As he went round the sedate quintet formation he realized something new had appeared amid them. A patch of pale iridescent light was shimmering beside Alakkad. 'What is that?' he murmured in puzzlement. It couldn't be a nebula, it was too small, too steady. Besides, the ceiling was showing him the entire bracelet, which meant the patch was close to Querencia. There was no tail, so it wasn't a comet. Which meant . . .

Edeard dropped to his knees as if in prayer, staring up in awe at the little glowing patch. 'Oh dear Lady!' He'd never seen one. Never imagined what one would look like. But even so he knew exactly what he was looking at.

Edeard put his eye to the end of the telescope again, making sure the alignment was right. Why the lens stuck out vertically halfway along the big brass tube was a mystery to him. The astronomer he'd bought it off had launched into some long explanation about focal length. It made no sense to Edeard; that the contraption worked was all he required. He'd spent most of the afternoon setting it up on the hortus outside the study where

Kristabel kept her desk and all the paperwork she used to manage the estate. By now the ziggurat all the way down to the third floor knew of the Waterwalker's new interest, not to mention every astronomer in Makkathran – gossipy clique that they were. It wouldn't take long before the entire city was aware. Then life might get interesting again.

And that's my real problem with this world. Too damn neat and tidy.

He stood up, arching his back to get the kinks out. His farsight swept out across the gloaming-cloaked city. Someone was observing him. Not the secretive newcomer, he knew this mental signature only too well. His farsight stretched all the way down to Myco and *that* four-storey building fronting Upper Tail Canal, the one with a faint violet glow escaping from its upper windows.

'Hello, Edeard,' Ranalee longtalked. She was standing in the office which used to belong to Bute and Ivarl before her. When he employed the city's own senses to look into the room he saw she was dressed in a long silk evening gown with flared arms. Large jewels sparkled in her hair and round her neck. Two girls were in attendance. They looked like junior daughters from some Grand Family, the kind she usually ensnared in her various dynastic breeding schemes. Their robes were certainly more expensive than the courtesans on the lower floors, and their admiration for Ranalee was painfully obvious. A lad was also in there with them, a dark-haired youth in his late teens, wearing nothing but a pair of shorts. Edeard guessed he was of the aristocracy, his self-confidence incriminated him. For him to be there was somewhat unusual for Ranalee, but hardly unique.

Edeard sighed at finding the trio, but then charging into the House of Blue Petals with a squad of constables to rescue innocents from her clutches didn't work. He'd made that mistake before. Once it had been so bad he'd gone back in time to make sure it never happened.

There was only one way to rid Makkathran of Ranalee, and he wouldn't do it. As she so often said, that would make him one of her own. So he endured, and did what he could to thwart her legitimately.

To add to the ignominy, she'd aged extremely well; presumably thanks to some deal made in Honious, he told himself sullenly. Her skin remained firm and wrinkle-free, and she managed to maintain an impressive figure even after four children. You had to get right up next to her and look into those hypnotic eyes to know the true age and calculating ingenuity that the body contained. A position he tried to avoid as much as possible.

'Good evening,' he replied equably.

'Interesting new toy you've got there.'

'As always, I'm flattered by your attention.'

'Why do you want a telescope?'

'To watch the end of your world approaching.'

'How coy. I'll find out, of course.'

'You certainly will. I'll be announcing it very loudly in a few days.'

'How intriguing. That's why I always liked you Edeard. You make life exciting.'

'Who are your new friends?'

Ranalee smiled as she looked round the office at the youngsters. 'Come and join us, find out for yourself.' She signalled the girls, who immediately went over to the lad and started kissing him.

'No thank you.'

'Still holding out against your true self? How sad.'

'You're really not going to enjoy my announcement. I'm about to turn even those with the weakest of wills away from your kind of existence.'

'You're very bitter tonight. Were those livestock certificates so desperately important to you?'

Every time. She could do it. Every Single Time. Edeard pressed his teeth together as he tried to squash his anger back down.

'At least the animal markets are one enterprise you haven't contaminated yet,' he told her. It was petty, but . . .

'Poor Edeard, still jealous after all these years. You never expected me to be so successful did you?'

He refused to rise to the bait. But Ranalee's business ability had surprised him. She'd invested wisely, unlike the previous owners of the House of Blue Petals, who had simply squandered the money on their own lifestyle. Today, Ranalee owned over two dozen perfectly legitimate businesses, and had a considerable political presence on the general merchants council, and in the Makkathran Chamber of Commerce. Nowadays, she was completely independent of the old faltering Gilmorn family. He knew of course that she'd used her vile dominance ability to sway unsuspecting rivals at opportune moments, and to build unseemly financial alliances, yet he could never prove anything. And of course, her children had been married off selectively, gathering more wealthy families into her dominion.

'That's Makkathran for you,' he replied. 'Equal opportunity for everyone.'

Ranalee shook her head, seemingly tired of the argument. 'No Edeard. It's not. Nor – before you start – are all of us born equal. You got where you are because of your strength, just as I foresaw. And I am where I am because of my strength, and you resent that.'

'Are you saying you used illicit methods to gather your new wealth?'

'Did you achieve your position legitimately? Where is my father, Edeard? Where is Owain? Why has there never been an enquiry over their disappearance?'

'Is an enquiry needed into their activities?'

'Would it ever be an impartial one?' She reached up and began removing the jewelled pins from her hair so it could fall free.

'You don't want that.'

'No,' she said simply. 'The past is the past. It's done. Over. I look to the future. I always have done.' She regarded the youngsters dispassionately. The ardent girls had taken the lad's shorts off. They giggled as they pushed him down on a big couch.

Edeard couldn't watch the lad's enraptured, worshipful face as Ranalee moved over to the side of the couch and stared down at him. *Too many memories.* 'Why do you do this?' he asked. 'You've achieved so much.'

A victory smile twitched across Ranalee's lips. 'Not as much as you.'

'Oh for the Lady's sake!'

'Would you like to linger tonight, Edeard? Would you like to remember how it was? How much you lost?'

'Goodnight,' he said in disgust.

'Wait.' She turned from the couch.

'Ranalee . . .'

'I have some information for you. It's something she would never come to you with.'

'What's this?' he asked, though with a falling heart he knew exactly who she was talking about. Ranalee would never attract his attention simply to taunt, she always had some way of inflicting harm or worry.

'Vintico has spent the day answering uncomfortable questions in the Bellis Constable Station,' she said. 'I'm surprised you didn't know about it. Apparently, they've detained him overnight so formal charges can be drawn up tomorrow.'

'Oh Lady,' Edeard groaned.

Vintico was Salrana's eldest child. And one of the most worthless humans ever to walk Makkathran's streets. In no small part because his father was Tucal, Ranalee's brother. That despicable pairing was when he finally realized there would never be a truce between him and Ranalee, that their war would continue until the bitter end.

'What this time?' he asked in despair.

'I believe he made a bad choice of business partners. Something about a deal falling through, and a large debt to established merchants. Apparently they get quite serious about such things.

Especially nowadays, what with the city being run so efficiently. After all, law and order must prevail.'

'I can't help.'

'I understand. You have standards. But it will break his mother's heart if he's sent to Trampello; it might spell the end of her engagement, as well. That single fragile chance to bring some happiness into her life. I only mention this because he's family.'

'Then why don't you offer to help your family if it's so important?'

'If only I could. I don't have any spare cash right now. All my money is tied up in new enterprises, investing in the future for my own children.' She smiled lecherously, and turned back to the lad sprawled across the couch. 'Are you going to watch now?'

A furious Edeard wrenched his farsight away, but not before her vicious amusement had infiltrated his perception. 'Fuck-the-Lady!' he spat.

Salrana! The one name he could never ever mention in the Culverit ziggurat any more. Kristabel's patience on that topic had run out decades ago. Salrana: who he'd tried to help time and again over the years. He watched and waited, believing that her old self would one day reassert itself, that Ranalee's mental damage would wither away. It was never to be. Ranalee had been too skilful at the start, whilst his opposition was too crude, helping the new false emotions establish themselves in her thoughts until they were no longer false. Salrana hated him.

It had been a battle lasting for years before he admitted defeat. Eventually, even Ranalee had moved on to more rewarding endeavours. The five children Salrana had borne for men Ranalee selected proved unspectacular, especially their psychic ability. So Ranalee got to administer the final indignity by discarding her. Now Salrana was engaged to Garnfal, a carpentry Guild Master more than sixty years her senior. Edeard was fairly sure Ranalee had nothing to do with it, so the attraction (whatever that was) might just be genuine. Ranalee could have been truthful, it was a chance for Salrana to be happy on her own terms.

I can't interfere.

But Salrana was his fault. She always would be. Which meant she was his responsibility, too. A charge that would never end.

Just for a moment he thought of going back a couple of weeks, of warning Vintico off whatever ridiculous deal he'd got himself involved with. That would mean another two weeks of electioneering, of parties he'd already been to, of reliving the whole livestock certificate debacle.

Edeard groaned at the notion of it. *Impossible.* He directed his longtalk towards a specific little house in the Ilongo district. 'Felax, I have a job for you.'

Edeard sensed Kristabel's thoughts while she was only on the sixth floor. He grinned at the tone – she was in a foul mood again. Something he found even more amusing now his own temper had abated. He had good reason to be confident again. Felax was clever and discreet, and the Vintico problem would vanish before dawn. Not that it would ever do to let Kristabel know of his reaction to this particular temper, but the predictability was entertaining. Their children must have known of their mother's disposition, too. All of them had contrived to be out of the Culverit ziggurat this evening, at parties or just 'meeting some friends'; even Rolar and his wife were absent with their children. *Don't blame you,* he blessed them silently.

'What are you doing out there?' Kristabel's longtalk lashed out, suffused with anger.

'Stargazing,' he replied mildly. When he looked into the study through the tall external doors she was silhouetted in the doorway from the hall. The fur-lined hem of her purple and black ceremonial Grand Council robes was held off the floor by her third hand, while its hood flopped back over her shoulder. It allowed her to jam her hands on her hips.

Edeard remembered the first time he'd seen her strike that pose: the day Bise refused to sign their wedding Consent bill in the Upper Council. She had stormed out of the chamber with a face set in a mask of fury. Nervous District Masters crept out of the door behind her, and got the Honious out of the Orchard Palace as fast they could. Even Bise had looked apprehensive.

'Well that's useful just before an election,' Kristabel snapped as she walked through the study. 'And why is it so dark in here?'

'Light sewage,' he told her.

'What?'

'It needs to be properly dark out here for the telescope to work at its best. Something to do with the eye contracting. You can't pollute the night with light.'

'Oh for Honious' sake, Edeard. I've got real problems, you've got obligations, and you're out here wasting time with this genistar crap.'

'What's wrong?'

'What's wrong?' She reached the hortus. Her hair was shorter these days, and her maids had their work cut out each morning to try and rein it in. Tonight it had frizzed out of the elegant curls and ringlets arrangement she'd started the day with, as if the sheer heat of her anger had pushed it into rebellion. 'That little tit, Master Ronius of Tosella, slapped a whole lot of amendments on the trade bill. Five months I've steered that through the Council. Five Ladydamned months! Those tariff reductions were vital for Kepsil province. Has someone stolen his brain?'

'The bill was never popular with some merchants.'

'There were balances,' she growled back. 'I'm not stupid, Edeard.'

'I didn't say you were.'

'Don't patronize me!'

'I—' He made an effort to calm down. *You know she's always like this after an Upper Council meeting. And a lot of other times, too, these days,* he added regretfully. 'I have something to show you,' he said, with the excitement rising in his voice and mind. 'Come.' He led her across the strip of hortus to the telescope. It was truly dark now. Makkathran was laid out below them, a beautiful jewel of glimmering light stretching out towards the

Lyot Sea in the east where the orange-hued buildings sketched their amazing shapes against a cloudless night sky. The network of canals cut rigid black lines through the illumination. He could see the gondolas in the Great Major Canal at the foot of the ziggurat, their bright oil lanterns bobbing merrily across the water. Occasional snatches of song slipped up through the balmy night air. The city was a vista he never tired of.

Kristabel bent over the telescope, her third hand pushing her hood aside as it slid round. 'What?' she said.

'Tell me what you see.'

'Alakkad, but it's off-centre. You haven't got the telescope aligned properly.'

Every second sentence is a criticism these days. 'It is centred correctly,' Edeard persisted stoically. He permitted a hint of excitement to filter through his mental shield.

Kristabel let out a sigh of exasperation and concentrated on the image. 'There's a ... I don't know, it's like a little white nebula.'

'It's not a nebula.'

She straightened up. 'Edeard!'

'An hour ago it was several degrees further from Alakkad. It's moving. And before you ask, it's not a comet, either.'

Kristabel's anger vanished. She gave him a shocked look, then bent to the telescope again. 'Is it a ship? Has it come from outside the Void like the one which brought Rah and the Lady?'

'No.' He put his arms round her and smiled down into her confused face. 'It's a Skylord.'

*

Mayor Trahaval was throwing a large party every second night, moving through the districts at a relentless pace to drum up support for himself and the local Representative candidates who endorsed him. The Seahall was the only place in Bellis grand enough for such an occasion. With its unusual concave walls shaded a deep azure, supporting a roof that was made from clashing wave cones, it really did have a marine theme, even down to the unusual ripple fountains that curved around the ten arching doorways. This evening the usual seating had been removed to make room for tables laden with food, and a small band playing at the centre. The guests had been chosen with almost as much care as had gone into the lavish canapés. There was a broad mix of Bellis citizens to socialize with Trahaval and his entourage of stalwart supporters, from the smaller merchant families desperate for political influence, to street association chiefs, local guildsmen, and ancient Grand Family patriarchs and matriarchs, as well as a vetted selection of 'ordinary working folk'. The idea was the same as it was for every party in every election. Trahaval and the Upper Councillors would mingle with and talk to as many people as possible, so they would spread the word among their friends and family that he wasn't aloof after all, that he understood everyday problems, that he had a sense of humour, and knew a good bit of gossip about his rivals and some Grand Family sons and daughters.

Edeard had no idea how many times he'd been to identical parties over the last four decades. The only number that registered was too many.

'Oh come on,' Kristabel said quietly as they made their way under the gurgling water that surrounded the main doorway. 'You can do this.'

'There's a difference between can and want to,' he murmured back. Then people noticed the Waterwalker and the Mistress of Haxpen had arrived. Hopeful smiles spread like wildfire. Edeard put on an equally enthusiastic 'happy to be here' face for everyone to see, twinning the burst of enthusiasm from his mind. He helped Kristabel out of her scarlet and topaz cloak, unbuttoned his own signature black leather cloak, and handed them both to a doorman.

I wonder if the Opera House cloakroom fiends are here tonight? They'd get a good haul out of this lot.

'Macsen and Kanseen are here, look,' he said cheerfully.

'You're not to talk to them until you've talked to at least

fifteen other couples,' Kristabel ordered. 'Once you and Macsen start that's it for the evening.'

'Yes, dear.' But he grinned, because the rebuke wasn't as sharp as they had been of late. Kristabel had actually brightened up considerably in the last few days since he'd spotted the Skylord. *And anyway, she's right, Macsen and I are a pair of dreadful old bores.*

A third hand pinched sharply. 'And less of that,' she warned.

'Yes yes, dear.'

They both smiled at each other, then parted. It was easier to work the crowd separately they'd found.

A wine importer cornered him first. The man and his very young wife were keen for trade with Golspith province where some excellent vineyards were producing some wonderful new varieties. In proof, the merchant's third hand plucked a glass from a waiter. It turned out he was proud to be sponsoring all the party's drinks for Mayor Trahaval tonight. Edeard took a sip and agreed the new wine was all he had promised. 'So if you could see your way to mentioning the ruinous tariffs to your beautiful wife . . .' Which Edeard promised he would do.

Funny how people still thought he was the boss in their marriage.

Then came the street traders' association chief. The man assured the Waterwalker of his vote and those of his fellows for Chief Constable; but then Edeard had always taken care to maintain good relationships with the associations.

Next was a guild master from the shipyards. A local councillor, a woman: 'Just completely inspired by your wife, so I stood at the last election and now I'm on the council.' Three sons from the district's Grand Families, wanting his opinion of joining the militia regiment. A shopkeeper. A chinaware dealer called Zanlan, who was the fifth son of a third son in a big merchant family, inordinately pleased to have broken free and set up for himself, importing interesting new cargos from many provinces.

'I'm a member of the Apricot Cottage Fellowship,' he told Edeard proudly.

'I think I've heard of it,' Edeard muttered diplomatically.

'We're new, a generation like myself who aren't going to sit about living off our families. Things are changing on Querencia. We want to grasp those opportunities for ourselves.'

'That's the kind of talk I like to hear,' Edeard said, genuinely impressed.

'Of course, none of the established guilds and associations recognize us. They're probably frightened of the competition. And the Orchard Palace ignores us completely, so we get frozen out of so-called open contracts.'

'Leave it with me,' Edeard promised. 'I'll make some enquiries.'

'All we ask is a fair market.'

Then there was a blacksmith. A female apprentice from the Eggshaper Guild who was a little overawed and a little drunk.

He was on his fifth glass of the appalling new wines and his third plate of heavily spiced pastries when he caught sight of Jiska, and hurried over. 'You count as a party guest,' he told her. 'Talk to me.'

'Oh poor Daddy, is Mummy bullying you horribly again?'

'I'm on a quota.'

'Sounds dreadful.' She gave him a knowing grin. Jiska was the second of their seven children, blessed with her mother's fine-featured beauty, but with his dark hair. She was wearing a simple sky-blue dress with a narrow skirt, contrary to this season's fashion. But then Jiska had never gone for the excesses of Makkathran's society, for which Edeard was extremely thankful.

'So where's Natran?' he asked.

'He sends his apologies. There was some crisis at the ship. The new sails weren't right, bad rigging or something.'

'There's always a crisis with that ship. Is it actually seaworthy?'

'Daddy!'

'Sorry.' Actually, he quite liked Natran. The man was from a trading family, but after serving time with the family fleet he'd acquired a boat of his own. He was determined to found his own fleet and fortune.

'He's doing very well for himself, you know,' Jiska said defensively. 'His agents have several profitable cargos lined up.'

'I'm sure they have. He's a smart young man with a whole load of prospects.'

'Thank you.'

'Uh ... have you ever heard of the Apricot Cottage Fellowship?'

'Yes, of course. Natran is affiliated. It's made up from people with a similar background to himself who've banded together for a greater political voice. What's wrong with that?'

'Nothing. It's a good idea. I like the way some family sons are striking out for themselves.'

'Well the older merchants should start taking notice of the Fellowship's grievances. The way they treat legitimate competition isn't exactly lawful.'

'Why didn't you tell me?'

'You want to hear that, do you, Daddy? How my boyfriend and his friends spend their drinking time grumbling about unfair competition from larger rivals, how no one listens to them, how the world ignores them? I can talk for hours on the subject if you wish.'

'That's fine. I'm sure they'll find a way of making their presence known in Council. Every other pressure group in the city certainly seems to manage.'

'Daddy, you're such a cynic.'

'So when are you going to take him out to our beach lodge for a week and the day?'

The look she screwed her face up into was one of pure dismay. 'Urrgh! I thought you wanted to rid Makkathran from useless tradition, especially something as demeaning as that one.'

'Er . . .'

'You know I was eight before I found out the *Ignorant Man* song was all about you. That was a fun day at school; even my closest friends . . . Oh never mind.'

'Ah yes, I never did forgive Dybal for writing that one.'

'It's horrible.'

I thought it was quite funny, actually. 'It's in the past, darling. Don't worry about it. But my question still stands. You could do a lot worse.'

'I know. It's difficult for him. This is only his second year as captain. And we're not going to rush in to anything.'

'You've been going out for five years now,' he pointed out reasonably. 'When you know, you know.'

'I'm sure love at first sight worked well for you and Mummy. But I need to know someone more than a couple of days.'

'It was not two days,' he protested. 'I spent weeks wooing her.'

Jiska's delicate eyebrow shot up. 'Daddy, tell me: you didn't just say *wooing*?'

He sighed in defeat. 'You know, maybe if your generation did a bit more wooing, I might have a few more children married off.'

'I'm not even forty yet.'

'And still beautiful.'

She pouted. 'You old charmer, no wonder Mummy fell for you.'

'Just so you know, I don't have any problem if you and Natran do want to go before the Lady and marry.'

'Yep, got it, Daddy. Actually, got that four years and eleven months ago. Anyway, my big brother is certainly doing his bit. You know what?' She leaned in, eyes agleam.

'What?'

'I think Wenalee is expecting again.'

He gave his daughter a sharp look. 'You haven't farsighted that have you?'

'Really, Daddy! No I did not. And I'm shocked you should think so.'

'Yeah,' he growled. Jiska had a farsight even more powerful than his own. *Maybe I should get her to track down my secret watcher.* But the idea of Wenalee being pregnant really buoyed him up. *A third grandchild. That would be something.* He loved having little Garant and Honalee (everyone called her Honeydew) running round the tenth floor. Rolar, his eldest, certainly hadn't wasted any time settling down and starting a family.

'Uh oh,' Jiska murmured silkily. 'Twins warning.'

Edeard scanned round to see Marilee and Analee worming through the guests, heading straight for him. His fifth and sixth children were identical twins, and right from the start they'd relished making a play of their matched looks, always styling their hair the same and wearing indistinguishable clothes. Tonight they'd dressed in synchronized satin gowns, except Marilee's was shimmering burgundy while Analee sported yellow-gold. Edeard smiled indulgently at them; not that they deserved it, but what could a father do . . . ? They were twenty-five, and the absolute stars of Makkathran's high society. As tall as him, slim like their mother, faces where girlish wickedness forever lurked among exquisite fine-boned features, and thick raven hair that came from his own mother's family. Add their good looks to their status, and basically whatever they wanted they tended to get, from clothes to pets and parties to boys.

'Daddy!' they chorused delightedly. He was kissed simultaneously on both cheeks.

'We've been very good tonight.'

'We talked to so many people.'

'And convinced them to vote for you.'

'They all got reminded of what you did for the city.'

'Even though it was so long ago.'

'A debt like that can never be ignored.'

'So they'll remind all their friends.'

'And their families to get out there on election day.'

'And put their cross where it counts.'

'Or they'll have to answer to us.'

Being talked at by the twins was like being deafened by birdsong. 'Thank you both,' he said.

'So now we've done our duty.'

'And we'd like you to set us free.'

'Because there's a super party at the Frandol Family mansion tonight.'

'And we've found us a suitable escort.'

They both giggled, and looked at their father pleadingly.

'Uh . . .' Edeard managed.

'Utrallis.'

'He's gorgeous.'

'And tall.'

'And serves in the Pholas and Zelda regiment.'

'But he's independently wealthy, too.'

'Not just some minor son.'

'A gentleman of honour.'

'Happy to serve his city.'

'All right,' Edeard held his hands up. 'Go on, go away, the pair of you. Have fun.'

'Oh, we will.'

Another burst of giggling assaulted Edeard's ears as they turned away. Each girl raised a gloved hand. Two fingers beckoned imperiously. Through the melee of guests Edeard saw a young man in his militia dress uniform, all polished buttons and perfectly tailored scarlet and blue jacket. Utrallis couldn't possibly be older than the twins, though he held his broad shoulders square, and had a strong jaw. Edeard regarded his nose charily, suspecting a distant Gilmorn heritage – he had a nasty flash-memory of Ranalee and the helpless lad in her office. Their eyes met, and the young man produced such a panicked guilty look as his cheeks flushed crimson that Edeard couldn't help but feel sorry for him. Then Utrallis was suddenly caught between the twins and hauled off.

Jiska shook her head as she sighed. 'And he looked so sweet. Poor thing. How is it they're always so elated at the start of the evening then when morning comes this tragic broken husk creeps out of the ziggurat looking like they've managed to escape from Honious itself.'

'The twins aren't that bad,' Edeard said mildly.

'Daddy, you've got such a blind spot when it comes to them.'

He grinned roguishly. 'Because I was so tough on you.'

Jiska raised her glass. 'I'll get round to Natran, don't you worry. I suppose five years is long enough.'

'No pressure. From me. Besides, it's only two months till Marakas goes before the Lady.'

She smiled with a kind of fond bewilderment. 'I can't believe he's marrying that one. I mean . . . Heliana is nice, and shapely; but really, what else has she got? Are men genuinely that shallow?'

'Of course we are.'

'Poor Taralee.'

'Taralee will do fine; she's destined for great things. One day she's going to be Grand Mistress of the Doctors' Guild.' He was still inordinately proud of his youngest, not yet twenty-two and already a Doctors' Guild journeyman. She'd completely eschewed the dizzy party life which the twins had chosen so she could devote herself to medicine.

'Let's see,' Jiska mused. 'After the election you'll be Chief Constable. So now Dylorn's joined the militia you just need me or one of the twins to become a Novice and work our way up to Pythia, and you'd be king of the city.'

Trying to visualize either of the twins in a Novice's robing was plain impossible. 'Not the first time someone's accused me of that ambition,' he said.

'Really? Why?'

He looked at his daughter, smart, elegant, courted by every eligible man in the city, completely carefree, and with such astonishing opportunities ahead of her. But above all, his greatest triumph was to make her safe, to give her that wonderful future. Yet she didn't see that. The battles fought before her birth meant very little to all of her generation. It was a depressing thought how established he'd become, just to be taken for granted as one of Makkathran's principal figures. No questions asked, no need to prove himself, not any more.

'Long old story, ask Macsen some time.'

'Oh Lady, I know he's your oldest friend, but I really can't take any more of those stories about the old days.'

'Good old days,' he corrected.

'If you say so, Daddy.'

It must have been something about Jiska's scepticism or the appearance of the Skylord, but Edeard gave Macsen an unusually critical appraisal as he made his way over to his friend. The robes of office Macsen wore were fanciful, allowing thick fur-trimmed fabric to flow easily around him. It was a generous cut, perhaps designed to deflect attention from the equally generous belly Macsen had cultivated over the last couple of decades. His handsome face, too, was now a lot rounder. A fashionable short beard showed several grey strands.

'Edeard!' Macsen opened his arms wide, and hugged him enthusiastically as if they'd been parted for years. Edeard gave him a slightly stiff response – after all, they saw each other at least twice a week, most weeks for the last forty years.

'Lady this wine is dross,' Macsen complained, holding up his glass to the twilight seeping through the crescent windows.

'Stop whingeing, one of my potential voters has donated it,' Edeard replied.

'In which case I'll be honoured to quaff a few more bottles for the fine chap.'

Lady, we even talk like the aristocrats these days. 'Don't bother. I don't really care if I make Chief Constable. Face it, we've had our day.'

Macsen gave him a startled look. From the corner of his eye, Edeard saw Kanseen frown; but as always her mental shield allowed no knowledge of her feelings.

'Speak for yourself, country boy,' Macsen said; he was trying for a jovial tone but couldn't quite reach it. 'Anyway, from what I gather, you're well ahead of our glorious current incumbent. Makkathran needs you to take a more prominent role.'

Edeard nearly said: Why? But managed to hold his tongue. 'I suppose so.'

Macsen draped his arm round Edeard's shoulder, and drew him aside with several insincere smiles directed at the group he'd been chatting to. 'You want us to return to the old days? After everything you did?'

'No,' Edeard began wearily.

'Good, because I for one am not prepared to see everything we've achieved shat upon from a great height just because you're menopausal.'

'I am not . . .' *Okay, maybe he hasn't changed that much.* 'All right. I'm a little sour myself right now, I admit that. I went to see the Mayor three days ago to press for the livestock certificate expansion.'

'I heard. So he said no? You'll be Chief Constable in under three weeks. You can apply some pressure in Grand Council, push it through yourself.'

'I won't do that, though,' Edeard said forcefully. 'Because Trahaval was right, wasn't he? You must have seen it. We can't extend the livestock certificates to sheep and pigs, for the Lady's sake. It was an idiotic idea. Who wants that much paperwork? Don't you remember the time we drew up the One Hundred list? We never saw daylight for weeks on end we were so busy with all those forms and reports and chits. A great bunch of extra certificates is simply pushing the job off on clerks. Our job! If rustling is to be stopped it should be by constables enforcing the law. What was I thinking?'

'Ah. Yes. Definitely menopausal.'

'I was letting things slip, it's complacency, and it was stupid of me. But not now, not any more.'

'Oh Lady, so now what? You want to go back out there with a couple of regiments? Take the city's finest and haul the provincial militia along so you can catch sheep rustlers? Is that what it's come to?'

'It hasn't come to that. You don't get it. We've been sailing along these last few years, we have no goals any more. It was never just about winning, beating Owain and Buate; it was always about what happened afterwards. Well this is afterwards, and it matters to me. It matters a lot.'

'All right then.' Macsen heaved out a big sigh. 'I'll kiss the Mistress of Sampalok goodbye and ride out with you again. But you've got to admit it, we're really getting too old and fat for this kind of thing. How about we just sit in the headquarters tent and leave the glory bits to your Dylorn, my Castio and all the other youngsters?'

Edeard's eyes automatically gazed down on Macsen's belly. *We're not all so old and fat, thank you.* In fact he was rather proud of himself for keeping his daily run going all this time. Today he could still climb the stairs in the ziggurat without getting out of breath. There were even running clubs in the city now; and the big autumn race from the City Gate across the Iguru to Kessal's Farm and back was an annual event, with more people entering each year.

'No,' Edeard said. 'That's not the way to handle this. We have to change the way Station Captains and sheriffs operate, they need to gather more information, maybe put together some dedicated teams of constables who don't just spend their days out on patrol.'

'More special Grand Council committees?'

'No, not like that, just a group of officers, those with some experience, and a little smarter than average, who'll devote more of their time to investigating all the aspects of a crime, trying to build up a pattern. Like we used to do. You remember how I spied on Ivarl to find out what he was up to?'

'I remember what happened to you when you did.'

'All I'm saying is we need to get smarter, to adapt. Life is different now. It would be the worst kind of irony if we're the ones who can't keep up and benefit.'

Macsen gripped Edeard's shoulder, smiling broadly. 'You know what your real trouble is?'

'What?' Edeard asked, though he'd already guessed the answer.

'You're a glory glutton.'

It was the third night Edeard had lain awake in the big bedroom on the tenth floor of the Culverit ziggurat. He really should have been able to sleep. The room was perfect for him, he'd spent years altering it, expanding the arching windows that led out on to the hortus, changing the lights to circles that shone with a warm pink-white radiance, reducing the ceiling height, producing alcoves for which Kristabel had commissioned furniture that fitted exactly, toning the walls to a subtle grey-blue so they matched the specially woven carpet. Even the spongy bed mattress had been adjusted until it achieved exactly the firmness both he and Kristabel wanted. They'd argued over her fondness for draping all the furniture in lace, compromising with a few tasteful frills. Even the curtains were a stylish pale russet, although they did have thick jade piping and tassels. The tassels had been one of the things he'd compromised on, but he really couldn't blame them for not being able to sleep.

Kristabel shifted beside him, pulling the silk sheets about. He held his breath until she was sleeping deeply again. There had been a time, not all that long ago, when he would have nuzzled up to her when she did that and they'd start caressing and kissing. There would be giggles and moaning, then sheets and blankets would be flung aside and they'd work each other's bodies to that wondrous physical pinnacle they knew exactly how to reach.

Gazing over at her in the dusky light that crept round the curtains he wondered when all that had ended. Not that it had finished, they still made love several times a month. *Whereas it used to be several times a night.* Kristabel was still beautiful; not girlish any more, which he didn't want anyway, her hair was starting to lighten and there were a few lines around her eyes. But physically she was still very desirable. He could remember

191

only too well all the cursing and misery after each child about how much weight she'd put on during the pregnancy, and how she'd never look good again. Then there'd be the long fight back to shape, with fierce discipline over what she ate and then taking the kind of exercise that put his morning run to shame.

But she no longer wore the short lacy negligees he used to adore, and they showered separately, and didn't talk and shout each other down, nor laugh, not in the way they used to. Developing dignity, he'd thought, at least that was what he told himself. The kind of dignity that comes with growing up and taking responsibilities seriously. And their ever-increasing burden of duties, and how tired that always left them. Though it shouldn't, all they had to do was delegate.

We're just not the same people. That's not a fault thing. Live with it. Even so, his traitor mind nearly sent his farsight creeping out to the House of Blue Petals. Ranalee would doubtless have that bewitched lad performing his strenuous best for her, corrupting him beyond salvation. Her love life had never ebbed.

No! It wasn't fair to blame sex for everything. Attitudes, too, had hardened over the years. Edeard had always favoured moving the city towards a full democracy, slowly reducing the power of the Upper Council and expanding the authority of the Representatives. It would never be a swift transition and he fully expected he wouldn't live to see its conclusion. But as long as the process could be started he would be content. However, with all the other changes and reforms within the city, and the strengthening of bonds with the provinces, that seemed to have been delayed year after year. Kristabel hadn't helped, not as he'd assumed she would. When she finally took her seat in the Upper Council as Mistress of Haxpen there had been too many other, more immediate, causes to support. As part of Finitan's voting bloc she was expected to advance the Mayor's new legislation and budgets and taxes. None of them had been focused on expanding general democracy.

He knew he shouldn't confuse personality with politics. But it was hard not to blame her for being part of the Grand Family setup, which she bitterly resented.

Edeard hated himself for having such doubts about himself and Kristabel. Doubts and questions which had only increased since the appearance of the Skylord. That was the real root of his sleepless nights. Since the afternoon when the Liliala Hall ceiling had cleared for him he'd been striving to sense the Skylord's thoughts, and he'd failed miserably.

Now the frustration was starting to cloud his mind, making him prickly and despondent. Worse, everyone close to him knew it, which just annoyed him even more, especially as he couldn't tell them the reason.

He let out a frustrated sigh and rolled cleanly off the bed without waking Kristabel. His third hand snatched up the clothes he wanted, and they drifted silently through the air behind him as he tiptoed out into the corridor. Once he was dressed he pulled his black cloak about him and marched off to the central stairs. When he reached them he threw a concealment around himself and simply vaulted over the banister rails to plummet the ten floors down to the ground. It was stupid, and exhilarating, and he hadn't done anything like it for years.

Makkathran buoyed him up as he asked, controlling his fall. When he reached the floor his boots landed with a gentle thud. He strode through the deserted cloisters of the ground floor to the ziggurat's private mooring platform. It was long past midnight, which left very little traffic on the Great Major Canal. He waited for a minute as a gondola slipped into the High Pool, its lantern disappearing round the curving wall, then with the waterway clear he reached out with his third hand and steadied the water. Another thing he hadn't done in years.

Edeard ran straight across the canal. As he was halfway across the farsight caught him. It was so *inevitable*, he was almost ready for it.

'I'll find you one day,' he longtalked down the strand of perception that stretched across the city to Cobara. 'You know I will.'

The farsight ended so fast it was as if it had been broken. Edeard grinned to himself, and reached a public mooring platform, where the wooden steps took him up to Eyrie.

The crooked towers stretched away ahead of him. Around the lower quarter of each one, slender streaks of orange light shone out of their dark wrinkled fascias, illuminating the deserted streets that wove between them. But the upper sections were jet black, cutting sharply across the nebula-swathed sky.

It was instinct which drew him here. The Lady's scriptures spoke of how the ill and infirm and old used to wait atop the towers, then as the Skylord flew above the city their souls would ascend to be guided away from Querencia. He reached the tower close to the Lady's grand church, where so many years ago conspirators from the Families had thrown him off the top. It was one of the tallest in Eyrie, which would put him as close to the Skylord as anything in Makkathran. Pushing aside any reservations about the location and its resonances, he walked up the central staircase, spiralling round and round until he finally reached the top and stood on the broad circular platform which crowned the tower. Eight spikes stuck up from the edge, their twisted tips stretching a further forty feet above the platform itself.

The nostalgia he was feeling now wasn't good. This was where Medath had waited after luring him up. This was where the other Grand Family conspirators had overpowered him and . . . He grimaced as he stared over at the section of the lip where he'd been shoved over. After so long, over forty years, he really shouldn't have been bothered by it, yet the memory was disturbingly clear. So much so he even searched round with farsight to make perfectly sure no one else was around.

Stupid, Edeard scolded himself. He abruptly sat down, cross-legged on the platform, and tipped his head back to gaze up at the sky. Gicon's Bracelet was visible above the spikes in the western hemisphere, the planets gleaming bright just off the border of the Ku nebula's marvellous aquamarine glow. Even though he knew exactly where to look, the Skylord wasn't yet visible to the naked eye. Instead Edeard called to it. All of his mind's strength was focused into a single thought of welcome, one he visualized streaming out through space.

And, eventually, the Skylord answered.

Finitan had retired to one of the houses which the Eggshaper Guild maintained in Tosella for its distinguished elderly members who'd retired from active duties. It was a big boxy structure, with a swathe of delicate magenta and verdure Plateresque-style decoration running round the outside of the third floor. There were no guards posted outside, only a ge-hound curled up beside the gate, who took one look at Edeard and yawned. Back when Edeard had arrived in the city, every large building had some kind of sentry detail. Families and guilds maintained almost as many guards as the city regiments. Now their numbers were dwindling, with old duties like the door sentry handed over to genistars once again.

Edeard walked through the open wooden gates into the central courtyard where white and scarlet flowering gurkvine grew up the walls to the upper balconies, while a fountain played cheerfully in the central pond. Several ge-chimps were tending the heavily-scented flower beds, with another sweeping the grey-white flooring. He went up the broad central stairs to the third floor.

A young Novice was waiting at the top of the stairs, her blue and white robe immaculate. She bowed her head slightly. 'Waterwalker.'

'How is he?'

'A better day, I think. The pain is not so great this morning. He is lucid.'

'He's taking the potions, then?'

She smiled in regret. 'When he wants to, or when the pain becomes too much.'

'Can I see him?'

'Of course.'

Finitan's room had long slim windows that stretched from

floor to ceiling. The walls and ceiling were white, while the floor was a polished red-brown, flecked with emerald in the shape of minute leaves, as if they'd been fossilized in the city substance. It was furnished equally simply, with a desk and several deep chairs. The bed was large, half-recessed in a semicircular alcove. Finitan was sitting up in the centre of it, his back resting on a pile of firm pillows.

'I'll be outside,' the Novice said quietly, and closed the heavy carved door.

Edeard walked over to the bed, while his third hand lifted one of the chairs over. He sat down and studied his old friend. Finitan was quite thin now, the disease seemed to be consuming him from within. Even so, up until a few months ago he had weathered it well; but now he was visibly frail. Blue veins stood proud from pale skin, and what was left of his fine hair was a faded grey.

Edeard's farsight examined the body, exposing the malignant growths around his lungs and thorax.

'Don't be so bloody nosy,' Finitan wheezed.

'Sorry. I just . . .'

'Want to see if it's retreating, if I'm getting better?'

'Something like that, yes.'

Finitan managed a weak smile. 'Not a chance, the Lady is calling. To be honest, I'm always quite surprised these days when I still find myself waking up of a morning.'

'Don't say that.'

'For the Lady's sake Edeard, accept I am dying. I did quite some time ago. Or are you going to start making politician's talk about how I'll be up and about soon? Cheer my spirits up?'

'I'm not going to do that.'

'Thank the Lady. Those bloody Novices do. They think it helps, while what it really does is get me depressed. Can you imagine that? I've got a gaggle of twenty-year-old girls fussing over me, and all I want is for them to shut up and get out. What kind of an ending is that for a man?'

'Dignified?'

'Sod dignity. I know how I'd rather go. Wouldn't that be something, eh? Scandalizing everyone at the finish.'

Edeard grinned, though he felt like crying. 'That would indeed be something. Perhaps the doctor knows of some concoction that would give you a final burst of strength.'

'That's better. Thank you for coming, I appreciate it. Especially now, when you should be out campaigning. How's it going, by the way?'

'Well, Trahaval is a certainty. I'm not sure about me; in private my campaign people tell me there's only a couple of per cent in it. Yrance might be returned as Chief Constable.' He bit back on his irritation.

Finitan smiled broadly and rested his head back on the mound of pillows. 'And that annoys you, doesn't it? That's the wonderful thing about you, Edeard; after all this time the one thing you of all people cannot do is shield your emotions properly. It's amazing that's the only psychic ability you lack. So I can tell how it irks you, that you, the Waterwalker, should have to struggle for votes after all you've done for the city.'

'It's true I didn't expect quite such a struggle, yes.'

'Ha. You're just angry because people have forgotten. Only forty years since the banishment, and you get taught in history class. That's what you are to a whole generation, a boring afternoon stuck in school when they could be outside having fun.'

'Thank you for that.'

'Always does good to knock politicians down a peg or two.'

'I'm not a poli—'

Finitan chuckled, which turned to an alarming cough.

Edeard leant forward in concern. 'Are you all right?'

'No I'm dying.'

'There's a difference to facing up to your fate and just being plain morbid.'

Finitan waved him silent. A glass of water drifted through the air, and finished by his lips. He took a sip. 'Wonderful, my psychic powers remain intact. How ironic is that?'

'It's not your brain that's affected.'

'I hate the brew they give me to numb the pain. It tastes vile, and then I spend the day dozing. I don't want to spend the day dozing, Edeard.'

'I know.'

'What's the point in that? My soul will soon soar free, why spend the time bedbound and humbled? I hate this existence, Lady forgive me, I want it to end.'

Edeard could feel his cheeks flush, and knew Finitan would be scrutinizing his thoughts with expert ability.

'Ah,' the old man said in satisfaction, and closed his eyes. 'So what truly brings you here?'

'A Skylord is coming.'

'Dear Lady!' Finitan twisted round abruptly, and winced at the spike of pain the motion caused. 'How do you know?'

'The city revealed it to me. Then last night I spoke to it.' He smiled warmly and gripped Finitan's cold hand in his own. 'It comes to see if any of us have reached fulfilment. It comes to guide our souls to the Heart.'

'Fulfilment?' There were tears spilling from Finitan's eyes. 'Do I look fulfilled? The Lady damn its arrogance. By what right does it judge us?'

'Finitan, dearest friend, you are fulfilled. Look at the life you have lived, look at what you have accomplished. I'm asking you, I'm begging; go to a tower in Eyrie. Accept its guidance to Odin's Sea. Show Makkathran, show the world, that we have become worthy again. Let people have that ultimate hope once more. Show them your way is the right way.'

'A Skylord will never take my sorry soul anywhere other than Honious.'

'Stop that; it will. Trust me one last time. You read my emotions, but I can see your soul, and it is glorious.'

'Edeard . . .'

'If you go, if you are worthy of guidance, other Skylords will know; they will come to Querencia again. Our lives will be complete. Everything you and I have achieved together, all that it cost, all that pain we endured to wrest the city from the grip of darkness and decay, will have been worthwhile.'

For a long while Finitan said nothing. Finally, he sighed. 'Honious take me, I'm dying anyway. Why not?'

'Thank you,' Edeard leant over the bed, and kissed the old man's brow.

The decision seemed to have cheered Finitan up. He pulled his pale lips into a rueful pout. 'Well at least that's the election over. What does it feel like to be Chief Constable?'

'How do you see that? Have you got a timesense you've been hiding all these years?'

'You're going to be the Waterwalker again. You're going to be the one who calls the Skylord to Querencia. Then in front of the whole city you'll hoist me up to the top of the tower so I can be guided to the Heart. You, Edeard. Just you. Who's not going to vote for a saviour like that?'

Edeard announced the Skylord's arrival that afternoon as he was making a campaign speech to Eggshaper Guild apprentices in Ysidro. There was silence in the hall at first as if his words hadn't quite made sense. Then came a swell of surprise and incredulity. Longtalk calls shot out to friends and family. Dozens of hands were raised, and questions shouted.

'It's very simple,' the Waterwalker said. 'The Skylords are flying to Querencia again. The first will be here in just over a week. It will guide Finitan through Odin's Sea to the Heart.'

'How do you know?' several apprentices barked out simultaneously.

'Because I've been talking to it for the last few nights.'

'Why is Finitan going to be guided?'

'Because of all of us, he is the one who has reached fulfilment. The way he has lived his life is the example we must all follow. When the Skylord sees him, it will know the time has come for humans to be guided to the Heart once more.'

Makkathran's true currency had always been gossip and rumour, a currency inflated during election time when the prospect of scandal and impropriety was rife as candidates sought to defame their rivals. So news of the Skylord travelled as such momentous news always did in Makkathran, as fast as sunlight. Within an hour everyone knew of the Waterwalker's amazing claim.

The Astronomers Association promised they would find any Skylord approaching Querencia, and immediately started quarrelling among themselves about false observations. Mayor Trahaval carefully avoided direct comment or criticism. Chief Constable Yrance dismissed it as a ridiculous vote-grabbing stunt and his campaign team quickly spilled their ridicule around the city. A sign of the Waterwalker's desperation, they claimed, a stunt, a lie. He's past his prime. He's delusional. A has-been. You need someone stable and practical, someone who produces actual results, a man like the existing Chief Constable.

Under Dinlay's direction a flurry of counterclaims were passed from district to district. The Skylord is real. It is coming as the Lady prophesised. Finitan will be guided to the Heart because he has lived a life of fulfilment just as the Lady said we should. Who else but the Waterwalker could summon our final salvation? He is the one we need to lead us. Edeard will lead us to the future we have spent so long trying to achieve.

'You'd better be right about this,' Dinlay said as he and Edeard arrived at the Eggshaper Guild retirement house five days later.

'Have a little faith,' Edeard told his old friend in a wounded tone. Out of all of them, Dinlay had always been the most loyal. He was also the one Edeard considered had changed the least over the years. Dinlay had been captain of the Lillylight Constable Station for eight years now. A promotion which that affluent district particularly welcomed; it was quite a catch having one of the Waterwalker's original squad appointed to supervise the policing of their streets. Influence and status, to those residents in particular, meant everything.

Dinlay, of course, had fitted in perfectly (as Edeard had suspected he would). There were a lot of formal social events which suited him. The station was organized efficiently. He was actively involved in the training of the new generation of constables, producing polite and effective squads. Prosecution lawyers achieved high success rates in court. Lillylight streets were safe to walk along at any time of the day or night. And Captain Dinlay was also newly engaged to one of their own. Again.

Edeard led the way upstairs to Finitan's room. The house's chief doctor was waiting outside the door, flanked by two Novices.

'I'm not sure this is in the patient's best interest,' the doctor said firmly.

'I think that's for him to decide, isn't it?' Edeard replied calmly. 'That is his right at such a time as this.'

'This journey may finish him. Would you have that on your conscience, Waterwalker?'

'I will hold him steady, I promise. He will reach the tower in comfort.'

'And then what? Even if a Skylord were to come, he is still alive.'

'The Waterwalker has said a Skylord is coming,' Dinlay said heatedly. 'Are you going to deny your own patient the chance to reach the Heart?'

'I can offer him certainty,' the doctor said. 'Not promises based on myth.'

'This is not some election stunt,' Dinlay said, his anger growing now. 'Not a politician's promise. The Skylord will guide Master Finitan's soul to the Heart.'

He really does believe in me, Edeard realized, feeling almost humbled by a trust that had lasted forty years. He wasn't quite sure what to do about the stubborn doctor, who was only doing her job and securing what she believed was best for her patient.

'Doctor,' Finitan's longtalk urged. 'Please let my friends in.'

The doctor stepped aside with a great show of disapproval. Finitan was sitting up in bed, dressed in the robes of the Eggshaper Guild Grand Master.

'You look splendid,' Edeard said.

'Wish I felt it.' The old man coughed. He gave a frail, brave smile. 'Let's get this over with, shall we?'

'Of course.' Edeard folded his third hand gently around Finitan, ready to lift him off the bed.

'Master?' the doctor queried.

'It's all right. This is what I want. I thank you and the Novices for a splendid job, you have made my life bearable again, but your obligation ends now. I would hope you respect that.' There was just a touch of the old Master's authority in the tone.

The doctor bowed uncomfortably. 'I will accompany you to the tower myself.'

'Thank you,' Finitan said.

Edeard lifted Finitan carefully and manoeuvred him through the door. The small procession made its way down the stairs to the courtyard.

Quite a crowd had gathered outside, eager and curious. They jostled for position on the narrow street, sweeping their farsight across the ailing Master. Finitan raised a weak smile, and waved.

'Where's the Skylord?' someone shouted.

'Show us, then, Waterwalker. Where is it?'

'There's nothing in the sky except clouds.'

Dinlay scowled. 'Yrance's people,' he muttered. 'Have they no sense of decency?'

'It is an election,' an amused Finitan observed.

'After today they won't matter,' Edeard replied.

There was a gondola waiting for them on Hidden Canal. Edeard eased Finitan down on to the long bench in the middle, and the doctor made him as comfortable as possible with cushions and blankets. The old man smiled contentedly as the gondolier pushed them off down the canal. Folfal trees lined both sides of the canal, their long branches curving high above the water. With the warm spring air gusting across the city, bright orange blossom buds were bursting out of the trees' indigo-shaded bark, producing a beautiful show of vibrant colour.

They were watched every inch of the way; some kids even ran

along the side of the canal, dodging the trunks and pedestrians to keep up with the gondola. Several ge-eagles flapped lazily overhead.

The gondolier steered them down Hidden Canal then over to Market Canal until they were level with the Lady's church. Hundreds of people were waiting for them around the mooring platform, keen for either spectacle or failure.

The Pythia headed up the semi-official reception group at the top of the wooden steps, with her entourage of six Mothers waiting passively behind. She was new to the position, anointed barely three years ago. She didn't have quite the vivacity of the previous incumbent, nor did she immerse herself in Makkathran's social events; but her devotion to the Lady was never in doubt. She had a zeal for the teachings which always made Edeard slightly uncomfortable around her.

'Waterwalker,' she said courteously. Her handsome face was impassive, as was her mind. Edeard walked up the steps while his third hand elevated Finitan behind him.

'Any sign of it?' Finitan asked.

Kanseen, who was standing just behind the Pythia, took his hand and squeezed gently. 'Not yet,' she said sweetly.

'It won't be long,' Edeard promised. But even he gave a nervous glance towards the Lyot Sea in the east. He'd longtalked to the Skylord the previous evening before the planet's rotation had carried it out of sight. Several astronomers had claimed they'd seen it. Counterclaimed by Yrance's campaign staff as cronies trying to curry short-term favour with the Waterwalker.

Kristabel gave him an encouraging smile, but there was no way she could hide her concern from him. Macsen just rolled his eyes, his thoughts brimming with bravado and confidence which he hoped might infuse Edeard.

The whole group walked over to the nearest tower, with Kanseen holding Finitan's hand the whole time. The tower was a drab grey in colour, its crinkled surface beset with slim fissures whose sides were a dark red. Two angled gaps at the base led into the central cave-like chamber. A single thick pillar rose up from the centre of the floor, with an opening to the narrow spiral stair which snaked up to the platform high above.

Even inside the thick walls, Edeard could feel a lot of farsight pressing against them as more and more city residents started to observe what was happening.

'I'll take you up by myself,' Edeard said. He wasn't entirely sure what happened around the top of a tower when the Skylord came to claim a human soul. The Lady's book spoke of cold fire engulfing the bodies of those who'd been chosen for guidance. It didn't sound good for the living.

Everyone looked to Kristabel, who simply shrugged. 'If that's what must be done,' she said reluctantly.

'May the Lady herself welcome you, Finitan,' the Pythia said. The other Mothers clasped their hands in prayer.

Edeard started to move Finitan towards the cramped entrance to the stairs. Macsen's hand caught his elbow. 'Don't linger,' the Master of Sampalok said quietly. 'It was bad enough last time you went up one of these towers alone.'

Edeard grinned at him, and started up the stairs.

'Do you ever wonder what's there?' Finitan asked. He was ahead of Edeard, his body tipped to almost forty-five degrees as Edeard's telekinesis manoeuvred him upwards around the not quite symmetrical curves of the stair.

'In the Heart?'

'Yes.'

'I don't know. It can't be a physical existence, not some kind of a fresh start, a grand house by the sea with servants and fine wine and food.' *We can do that here.*

'Yes, I was thinking along those lines. So what exactly is it?'

'Well you'll know before me.'

Finitan laughed. 'That's my Edeard, ever the practical one.'

They were about a third of the way up. Edeard grimaced and concentrated on not dropping the old Master. The stairs were badly claustrophobic.

'Philosophy was never my strong point,' Finitan went on. 'I was more an organizer.'

'You were a visionary. That's why we achieved so much.'

'Very kind of you, I'm sure. But what does the Heart need with a human visionary?'

'Lady, but you're getting morose for someone about to embark on the ultimate journey.'

'What if it isn't?' Finitan whispered. 'Edeard, I'm afraid.'

'I know. But consider this, even if the Heart isn't for you it's where an awful lot of your questions will be answered. Think who's there waiting for you. Rah and the Lady for a start. The people who built Makkathran, whoever and whatever they are. The Captain on the ship which brought us all here, and he'll be able to explain what made him come into the Void. Maybe even the Firstlifes; imagine what they can tell you. You might get to discover why the Void exists.'

'Ah, now there's a thought. Or perhaps we've misunderstood, and the Heart is simply the gateway out.'

'Out?'

'To the universe outside. If we're fulfilled, if we've proved we're worthy enough, we get to go home.'

'I don't believe there's a good behaviour requirement to go and live in the universe outside,' Edeard said flatly.

'You're probably right,' Finitan said. He shuddered, as if gripped by a sudden chill.

Edeard could see the sweat slick on his friend's brow. 'Did you take the painkiller potion before we left?'

'Of course not,' Finitan snapped irritably. 'You think I want to be dozing when my very own Skylord comes looking for me?'

Edeard said nothing.

'And you can wipe that smirk off your face.'

'Yes, Master.'

They finally emerged onto the platform. As always, a strong wind whistled across the shallow curving floor. Seven giant spikes rose up from the edges, angled steeply back over the platform, their jagged tips almost touching high above the stair-well entrance.

Edeard placed Finitan gently on the floor, and squatted down beside him. 'How are you doing?' he asked.

'For someone who is dying? Not bad. Actually, I feel quite relieved. It's not many who are given such clear knowledge about the exact moment of their death. Such knowledge is refreshing. It means I have nothing to worry about.'

Edeard's fingers carefully brushed the loose strands of pale hair from the man's damp forehead. Finitan's skin felt unpleasantly cold, giving Edeard a fair indication of what his deteriorating body was going through.

The number of people farsighting them now they were out of the stairwell and in the open was almost oppressive. Edeard could sense the city had virtually come to a halt to focus their full attention on him and the tower. Everyone was waiting expectantly. Even Yrance's agitators were silent now the promised moment was approaching.

Edeard felt the unknown watcher's farsight sweep across him, even pervading the tower structure around him, probing and questing. It was coming from Cobara district as usual.

'Today is hardly secret,' he shot back.

The farsight ended.

'Who was that?' Finitan asked.

'I don't know. But I expect I'll be finding out before too long. You know Makkathran: always trouble brewing somewhere.'

'That was more that the usual trouble. They had an ability equal to yours.'

'Greater, I suspect.'

'Have you sensed them before?'

'I've had indications that there are people of my stature emerging, yes. But that doesn't affect today.'

'Edeard—'

'No.' Edeard closed his finger around Finitan's frail hand. 'This is about you and the Skylord. You have to prove once and for all that what you did was right. After that, all our troubles will be minor. That is what I ask of you today.'

Finitan's head fell back on to the cushion of his cloak hood.

'Stubborn to the very end – well, my end. You know, that day you arrived in my office, I was worried you might just decide to be an apprentice in the Blue Tower for seven years. What a waste that would have been. What a loss to the world.'

'I always thought you were over-emphasizing the bad points.'

'One of my smaller crimes. I'm sure the Lady will want to discuss it at length if I ever catch up with her, along with all the others.'

'You will. What a meeting that's going to be.'

'Ha! I don't think she . . .' Finitan trailed off, an expression of outright surprise manifesting on his face. 'Oh my. Edeard?'

Edeard turned to face the Lyot Sea. Right on the horizon a peculiar haze-patch was rising above the water to expand across the sky. 'It comes,' he said with simple happiness.

Finitan's hand grasped his tightly. 'Thank you, Edeard, for everything.'

'I owe you so much.' He could sense the startled longtalk starting down on the streets and canals below as those with the most powerful farsight became aware of what was approaching Makkathran. The gifted visions were spreading wide. Surprise and delight blossomed among the startled citizens.

'And I you,' Finitan said. 'Now it's time for you to leave me here so that I might start that final journey. Soon I will have answers. So soon, Edeard. Imagine that.'

'Yes.' Edeard stood and looked at the thick pillar which was the start of the stairwell, then glanced across to the edge of the platform.

'Go on,' Finitan chuckled. 'Be the Waterwalker, today of all days. Beat that little oaf Yrance. But don't stop there, you are greater than all of them, never forget that. And at the end, I'll be waiting. We will have such a reunion in the Heart, Edeard. Even down here they will know our joy.'

'Goodbye,' Edeard smiled. There was so much more he wanted to say, but as always there was no time. He turned and ran across the platform. When he reached the edge he leapt off with a jubilant cry.

On the ground so far below, there was a horrified gasp as the faces of the crowd turned up to watch him. Laughing defiantly, he held his arms wide, allowing his black cloak to flap madly around him as he streaked downwards.

That powerful farsight played over him as he fell. Then a hundred feet from the ground the city took hold of him, and slowed his wild flight, lowering him softly on to the pavement at the foot of the tower. The crowd exclaimed in admiration, several people applauded. More cheered.

He saw Macsen's derisory sneer. Dinlay gave him a disapproving frown. But it was Kristabel whose face was pure anger. He shrugged an apology, which clearly wasn't anywhere near good enough. She was still scowling as he walked over and put his arm round her.

'Daddy,' Marilee scolded.

'That was so bad.'

'Teach us how to do that.'

He winked at the twins. 'The Skylord comes,' he said solemnly.

The crowd was excited now, chattering wildly as they all turned to the east. There was nothing to see at first, the towers of Eyrie blocked any view into the sky directly over the sea. Then the astonished residents of Myco and Neph gifted their sight to the rest of the city.

The Skylord had risen above the horizon. Now it was flying directly over the choppy sea. Edeard didn't appreciate the size at first. From the city's port district it simply looked like a shiny white moon skimming over the waves, slowly getting bigger as it dipped down again. Its actual surface was hard to make out; it had the same shimmer as a pool of water rippling under a noonday sun, a bright distortion that could never stay still long enough to focus on. Then he realized the Skylord wasn't losing altitude, it was simply getting closer. The curving underside was already at least a mile above the sea – which was impossible because that would make it miles across. Yet there it was. The shadow it cast turned the grey-blue water nearly black across a vast area. The fine white sails of ships that were eclipsed beneath it turned grey and billowed energetically as the turbulence it created roiled against them.

Finally the leading edge of that colossal circle slid across the city skyline. Like everyone else standing in Eyrie, Edeard felt awed and worshipful. Its size was beyond intimidating, it was utterly overwhelming. And not a little frightening. It must have been almost half the size of the city itself. And it flew!

'Oh great Lady,' he whispered as Kristabel and the twins clung to him. His arms went round them, offering nowhere near enough comfort. He wanted to scream to the city's mind to protect them. Some wretched primitive aspect wanted him to flee, to cower before such *majesty*. Instead he laughed hysterically; to think only minutes ago he and Finitan had been doubting the Skylords and the purpose of the Heart.

Around him people were flinging themselves to the ground, screaming in terror as they wrapped their arms over their heads. When Edeard glanced at the Pythia, he saw great tears of joy streaming down her cheeks as she held her arms upwards in greeting. Her mind shone bright as she poured her welcoming thoughts up into the sky.

Dazzling slivers of pure sunlight shimmered across Makkathran's rooftops and streets. Now Edeard could see it directly, the Skylord seemed to be made of some crystalline substance, a million thin sheets of the stuff folded into bizarre twisting geometries that somehow never seemed to intersect as they should. Sunlight foamed through the core, bending and shifting erratically. He could never be sure if it was the light that fluctuated or if the crystalline sheets themselves were in constant motion. The Skylord's composition defied logic as the creature itself defied gravity.

The umbra fell across Eyrie as the Skylord slid across Makkathran, a darkness alleviated by the perpetual flashes of brilliant prismatic light that radiated out of its undulating surface. With it came the thunder of its passage, the roar of a thousand lightning bolts blasting out simultaneously. Wind rushed down the streets, shaking the trees and mauling clothes and any loose items. A monsoon of flower petals surged into the dark scintillating air as they were ripped away from their trees and vines.

Then the Skylord's thoughts became apparent. A great wash of lofty interest bathing every human. Calming and compassionate. A reflection of its size and magnanimity. Even those who'd feared its presence the most were put at ease. Its benevolence was beyond question, a benevolence almost humbling in its honesty. It was curious and hopeful that the new residents of Makkathran had once again reached fulfilment so they might receive its guidance to the Heart.

'Look!' Marilee screamed above the howling atmosphere.

Edeard turned to where she was pointing. Every fissure in the tower's wrinkled skin was alive with scarlet light, as if some kind of fire was sweeping through it, racing upwards. Then he saw the kinked spires on top were glowing violet-white, becoming brighter and brighter.

'Edeard,' Finitan's longtalk called, firm and strong. 'Oh Edeard, it hears me, the Skylord hears me. It will take me! Edeard, I'm going to the Heart. Me!'

The top of the tower vanished inside an explosion of light. Icy flames of radiance flashed upwards towards the Skylord. Edeard's farsight saw Finitan's body turn to ash and blow apart in the gale. But his soul stood fast. Edeard didn't need any special farsight to perceive him now, his spectral form was there for everyone to see.

The old Eggshaper Guild Master laughed delightedly and raised his ethereal arms in farewell to the city and people he loved. Then he was soaring upwards within the tower's flames to be claimed by the dancing chaos of illumination surging through the Skylord.

'I thank you,' Edeard told the Skylord.

'Your kind are becoming fulfilled again,' the Skylord replied. 'I am gladdened. We have waited so long for this time.'

'We will wait for you to come again.' Edeard smiled up at the stupendous iridescent creature swooping so nonchalantly above them all.

He wasn't alone in calling to the Skylord.

'Take me!' they began to cry, hundreds upon hundreds of the elderly and sick, raising their longtalk to plead.

'Take me.'

'Guide me to the Heart.'

'I am fulfilled.'

'I have lived a good life.'

'Take me.'

'My kindred will return to guide you to the Heart,' the Skylord promised them. 'Be ready.'

When it was clear of the city, the Skylord began to climb back into the sky, rising higher and higher above the Iguru Plain until it was ascending vertically above the Donsori Mountains. Edeard gathered his family around him so they could watch it go. He was sure it gathered speed as it gained altitude. Soon it was hard to follow, it was travelling so fast, growing smaller by the second.

'Oh Daddy,' the twins cooed as they hugged him.

Edeard kissed both of them. He couldn't remember being so relieved and excited before. 'We're saved,' he said. 'Our souls will enter the Heart.' *I won. I really did.*

Far above, the Skylord raced onwards to the nebulas, dwindling until it was a bright daytime star. Eventually, even that faded from view.

Edeard waved it farewell. 'The world will know our joy when we meet again,' he whispered to Finitan. He let out a long breath, and looked around him. So many people were still gazing up into the perfect azure sky, wistful and content. It was going to be a long time before Makkathran resumed its normal business.

'You were right,' Macsen said. 'Waterwalker.'

Kristabel gave him a sharp look. 'Why did you jump? That's so dangerous.'

'Yrance won't know what to do now,' Dinlay said with an edge of cruel satisfaction. 'We can capitalize on that right away.'

Edeard started laughing.

4

The dawn light crept around the sharp crystal skyscrapers at the heart of Darklake City, illuminating a clear sky with a mild wind blowing in from the west. On the fifty-second floor of the Bayview tower, Laril blinked against the glare that shone directly through the curving floor to ceiling window of the lounge. He was sprawled in the couch he'd spent the night on, dressed in a loose striped bedshirt. His u-shadow turned up the shading on the window as he moved his shoulder blades slowly, trying to work the tired knots out of his muscles. Newly active biononics didn't seem to have much effect on the stiffness, either that or he wasn't as adept at their programming as he liked to think he was.

A maidbot brought over a mug of hot, bitter coffee, and he sipped it carefully. There was a croissant as well, and that started to flake and crumble as soon as he picked it up. The culinary units on the Inner Worlds were unbeatable when it came to synthesizing the basics. A five-star gastronomic experience still required a skilled chef to put it together; but for a simple pick-up meal, fully artificial was the way to go.

He walked over to the darkened glass and looked down across the city grid. Capsules were already streaming above the old road arteries, ovals of coloured chrome zipping along at their regulation hundred metres altitude. Out on the lake from which the city drew its name, big day cruisers were stirring, edging in to the quaysides. The quaint old ferryboats were already ploughing off to the first ports on their timetable, churning up a bright green wake. As yet, few pedestrians were abroad. It was too early for that, and people were still in shock over the Sol barrier. Most of the urban population had done as Laril had, and spent the night receiving unisphere reports on the barrier and what the President and Navy were going to do about it. The short answer was 'very little'. Oaktier's Planetary Political Congress had issued a public statement of condemnation to the Accelerator Faction, calling for the barrier to be lifted.

Big help, Laril thought. That was the one aspect of converting to Higher that he still couldn't quite help feeling scornful over. The incredible number of official committees. There was one for everything, at both a local and planetary level; all integrated in a weird hierarchy to form the world's representational government. But that was the Higher way of involving all its citizenry in due process, of giving everyone the authority to act in an official capacity, the logical conclusion of Higher *I am government* philosophy. As he was only just qualifying as a Higher citizen, Laril could only stand for election into the lowest grade of committee, and there were at least seventeen levels beneath the executive grade. Oaktier didn't have a President, or Chair, or Prime Minister, it had a plenum cabinet (self-deprecatingly referred to as the politburo by locals) of collective responsibility. When the constitutional structure was explained in his citizenship classes, Laril somehow hadn't been surprised. Even with all the daily legal datawork handled by super-smartcores, you still basically needed a permit to take a crap, Oaktier was that bureaucratic. But at that it was one of the more liberal Higher planets.

In an excellent reflection of both its excessive democracy and forbearance, Laril realized the planetary gaiafield was almost devoid of emotional texture this morning. Everyone was withholding their consciousness stream, a universal condemnatory reaction to Living Dream's Pilgrimage, which was the root cause of the crisis.

Again, big help. Although it was difficult to be so cynical about that. It showed a unity and resolve which even he found impressive.

Laril just hoped he could find that same level of resolve within himself. As soon as Araminta's call had broken up, his u-shadow relayed the shotgun that had been loaded into Chobamba's unisphere. He prayed she'd take the warning seriously, and get the hell off Chobamba. She certainly hadn't called him again, which meant she'd either been caught or she was running. All he could do was assume the latter and prepare for it. She would call him for advice and help again, which was the antithesis of Oaktier's stupid bureaucracy. This was one person making a difference, a big difference. It was what Laril had always imagined he would be doing, influencing events across the Commonwealth with his smart-thinking and innate ability to dodge trouble. Now he finally had that chance. He was determined to deliver exactly what Araminta wanted.

First off, he didn't quite trust the code she'd given him for Oscar. Even if Oscar whoever-he-was had helped her at Bodant Park there was no way of knowing if he worked for ANA as claimed. To keep her away from the Accelerators it either needed to be the Navy or an opposing Faction. Laril just didn't want to go running to the Navy. Trusting authority like that wasn't right for him. Besides that would effectively be handing Araminta over to the President, who would have to make some kind of political compromise. Far better she teamed up with a Faction, who would take a more direct line of action, who would have a plan and get things done.

So he spent the night using his u-shadow to make delicate enquiries among people he used to associate with a long time ago. Every precaution was taken, one-time codes, shielded nodes, remote cut-off routing. All the old tricks he'd learned back in the day. And the magic was still there. A friend on Jacobal had a colleague on Cashel whose great-great-uncle had once been involved with the Protectorate on Tolmin so had channels to a supporter who had a contact with the Custodian Faction. That contact supplied a code for someone called Ondra, who was an 'active' Custodian.

After each call, Laril rebuilt his electronic defences within the unisphere, making very sure no one was aware of his interest in the Factions. It must have worked: by the time he got Ondra's code none of his safeguards had detected scrutineers or access interrogators backtracking his ingenious routing.

He made the final call. Ondra was certainly very interested when he explained who he was. And yes, there were Custodians on Oaktier who might be able to offer 'advice' to a friend of the Second Dreamer. That was when Laril laid out his conditions for contact. He was pleased with what he'd come up with. Over an hour had been spent remote-surveying the Jachal Coliseum, seven kilometres from the Bayview tower. He'd reviewed the local nodes, and loaded a whole menu of monitor software. Then he'd gone through a virtual map, familiarizing himself with the layout on every level, working out escape routes. Finally, he'd hired three capsule cabs at random, and parked them ready around the Coliseum on public pads. It was a superb setup, and in place before he even spoke to Ondra. The meeting was agreed for nine-thirty that morning. Someone called Asom would be there, alone.

Laril finished his coffee and turned from the big window. Janine was coming out of the bedroom. They'd been together for six months now. She was only sixty, and rejuvenated down to a sweet-looking twenty. That she was migrating inwards at her age spoke for how insecure she was. It made her easy for his particular brand of charm. He understood exactly how the promise of sympathy and support would appeal to her. That kind of predatory behaviour would presumably be discarded along with other inappropriate character qualities before he'd achieved true Higher citizenship. In the meantime she was a pleasant enough companion. The Sol barrier, though, had brought back all her anxieties in the same way it had seen a resurgence of his more covetous traits.

Her eyes were red-rimmed, even though there hadn't yet been

tears. The thick mass of her curly chestnut hair hung limply, curtaining her heart-shaped face. She gave him such a needy look he almost swayed away. Unlike everyone else, her emotions were pouring out into the gaiafield, revealing a psyche desperately seeking comfort.

'They can't get through the barrier,' she said in a cracked voice. 'The Navy's been trying for hours. There are science ships there now, trying to analyse its composition.'

'They'll work something out, I'm sure.'

'What, though? Without ANA we're lost.'

'Hardly. The Accelerators can't get into the Void without the Second Dreamer.'

'They'll get her,' Janine wailed. 'Look at what they've done already.'

Laril didn't comment, though it was tempting. He ran a hand over his chin, finding a lot of stubble there. *Araminta always used to complain about that. I need a shower and clean clothes.* 'I'm going out.'

'What? Why?'

'I have to meet someone, an old friend.'

'You are kidding?' she squawked as outrage fought with fright. 'Today? Don't you understand? They've imprisoned ANA.'

'The biggest victory they can have is to change our lives. I am going to carry on exactly as before. Anything else is allowing them to win.'

She gave him a confused look, her thoughts in turmoil. More than anything she wanted to believe in him, to know he was right. 'I didn't think of that,' she said meekly.

'That's all right.' Laril put his hand on the back of her head, and kissed her. She responded half-heartedly. 'See?' he said gently. 'Normality. It's the best way forward.' The prospect of making contact with a Faction agent, of becoming a galactic power player, was making him inordinately randy.

'Yes,' she nodded, her arms going round him. 'Yes, that's what I want. I want a normal life.'

Laril checked the clock function in his exovision display. There was just enough time.

The taxi capsule slid out of the vaulting entrance to the hangar which made up the seventy-fifth floor of Bayview tower. Laril sat back on the curving cushioning, feeling on top of the world. *It doesn't get any better than this, not ever.*

Direct flight time between Bayview tower and the Jachal Coliseum was a couple of minutes at best. Laril had no intention of flying direct. Until he was absolutely sure of the Custodian representative's authenticity he wasn't taking any chances. So they flew to a marina first, then a touchdown mall, the Metropolitan opera house, the civic museum, a crafts collective house. Twelve locations after leaving the tower, the taxi was finally descending vertically towards the coliseum. From his vantage point it looked like he was sinking down to a small volcano. The outside slope of the elongated cone had been turned to steep parkland, with trees and fields, and meandering paths. There were even a couple of streams gurgling down between a series of ponds. Inside the caldera walls were tiers of extensive seating, enough to contain seventy thousand people in perfect comfort. The arena field at the bottom was capable of holding just about any event from concerts to races to display matches and baroque festivals. Ringing the apex of the coliseum was a broad lip of flat ground which hosted a fence of two-hundred-year-old redka trees, huge trunks with wide boughs smothered in wire-sponge leaves the colour of mature claret.

Laril's taxi capsule dropped on to a public landing pad in the shade of the trees. He immediately examined the area with his biononic field-scan function. It was one of the functions he was adept at, and he'd refined the parameters during the taxi flight. When he stepped out, the biononics were already providing him with a low-level force field. He wore a blue-black toga suit with a strong surface shimmer, so there was no visual sign of his protection. The scan function was linked directly to the force-field control, so if he detected any kind of threat or unknown activity the force field would instantaneously switch to its strongest level. It was a smart procedure, which along with his other preparations provided him with a lot of confidence.

He walked across the lip to the top tier. His u-shadow was maintaining secure links to the emergency taxis and the coliseum's civic sensor net, assuring him that everything was running smoothly. As agreed with Asom, he was the first to arrive. There were no nasty surprises waiting for him.

A steep glidepath took him down the inner slope to the arena field. He kept looking round the huge concrete crater for any sign of movement. Apart from a few bots working their way slowly along the seating rows there was nothing.

Once he reached the bottom he expanded his field-scan function again. No anomalies, and no unusual chunks of technology within five hundred metres. It looked like Asom was obeying his groundrules. Laril smiled in satisfaction, things were going to be just fine.

A slightly odd motion on the opposite side of the field caught his eye. Someone was walking out of the cavernous performers' tunnel. She was naked, not that such a state was in any way erotic, not for her. Her body was like a skeleton clad in a toga-suit haze. She walked purposefully over the grass towards him; two long ribbons of scarlet fabric wove about sinuously in her wake.

'Asom?' Laril asked uncertainty. Suddenly this whole meeting seemed like a bad idea. It got worse. His connection to the unisphere dropped out without warning, which was theoretically impossible. Laril's force field snapped up to its highest rating. He took a couple of shaky paces backwards before turning to run. Files in his storage lacuna were already displaying escape routes to the emergency taxis he'd mapped out earlier. It was fifteen paces to a service hatch, which led to a maze of utility tunnels. The skeletal woman-thing would never be able to track him in there.

Three men appeared in the seating tiers ahead of him; they just shimmered into existence as their one-piece suits discarded their stealth camouflage effect.

Laril froze. 'Ozziecrapit,' he groaned. His field scan showed each of them was enriched with sophisticated weapons. Their force fields were a lot stronger than his. They advanced towards him.

His exovision displays abruptly spiked with incomprehensible quantum fluctuations. He didn't even have time to open his mouth to scream before the whole universe turned black.

Arranging an entrapment had never been so easy. Valean was almost ashamed by the simplicity. Even before she landed at Darklake City, Accelerator agents had secreted subversion software into the Bayview tower net. Incredibly, Laril used his own apartment's node to access the unisphere. She wondered if all his calls to various old colleagues were some kind of subtle misdirection. Surely nobody was so inept? But it appeared to be real. He genuinely thought he was being smart.

So she replied personally to his final call, assuming the Ondra identity. Again, the suggestion of the coliseum as a meeting point was a shocking failure of basic procedure. Isolated from the public, its thick walls provided a perfect screen from standard civic and police scrutiny. The Accelerator team were laughing when they found his 'escape' taxis, parked suspiciously close to utility tunnel exits. And as for the antiquated monitor software he'd loaded into the coliseum's network . . .

Valean waited in the darkness of the performers' tunnel as he slid down the glidepath. His field-function scan probed around, its rudimentary capability finally confirming how woefully naive he was. Her own biononics deflected it easily. As soon as three of her team were in place behind him, she walked out into the morning sunlight. Laril seemed so shocked he didn't even attempt any hostile activity. *Lucky for him*, she thought impassively.

The team closed in smoothly. Then Valean's field scan showed her a sudden change manifesting in the quantum fields. Her integral force field hardened. Weapons enrichments powered up.

Laril vanished.

'What the fuck!' Digby exclaimed.

The *Columbia505* was hanging two hundred kilometres above Darklake City to monitor the whole Jachal Coliseum affair. Digby's u-shadow had kept him updated on the software shenanigans in the Oaktier cybersphere, how Valean had run electronic rings around poor old Laril. Given the nature of the people he had to watch during his professional career, Digby never normally felt any sympathy for any of them. Laril, however, was in a class of his own when it came to ineptitude. Sympathy didn't quite apply, but he was certainly starting to feel a degree of pity for the fool who'd been dragged into an event of which he had no true understanding.

Digby watched in growing disbelief as Laril's taxi landed on the lip of the coliseum. The man had absolutely no idea what he was walking into. The *Columbia505*'s sensors could see the Accelerator agents from two hundred kilometres altitude. Yet Laril's own field-function scan was so elementary he couldn't spot them from two hundred metres.

Letting out a groan, Digby brought up the starship's targeting systems. No doubt about it, he was going to have to intervene. Paula was absolutely right. Valean could not be allowed to snatch Laril. Precision neutron lasers locked on to Valean and her team.

He still wasn't sure if he should take the *Columbia505* down to retrieve Laril afterwards, or simply remove Valean's subversive software from his 'escape' taxis and steer them to a rendezvous. He was inclined to pick Laril up himself. The man was a disaster area. He shouldn't be allowed to wander round the Commonwealth by himself, not given his connection to Araminta.

Valean emerged from the tunnel and walked towards a startled Laril. Three of the eight Accelerator agents discarded their stealth. Digby designated the fire sequence.

Strange symbols shot up into his exovision. It was the last thing he'd expected. A T-sphere enveloped Darklake City.

Laril teleported out of Jachal Coliseum.

The T-sphere withdrew instantaneously.

Digby reviewed every sensor input he could think of. Valean and her team appeared equally surprised by Laril's magic disappearing act, launching a barrage of questors into the city net. To Digby there was something even more disturbing than their reaction. The T-sphere hadn't registered in any Oaktier security network.

That would take a level of ability which went way beyond a team of Faction agents.

He called Paula. 'We have a problem.'

'A T-sphere?' she said, once he'd finished explaining. 'That's unusual. There's no known project on Oaktier using a T-sphere, so that implies it's covert. And given no official sensor could detect it, I'd say it was also embedded. Interesting.'

'The *Columbia505*'s sensors gave it a diameter of twenty-three kilometres.'

'Where's the exact centre?'

'Way ahead of you.' Visual sensor images of Darklake City flashed up in Digby's exovision. They focused on the Olika district, one of the original, exclusive areas bordering the lake shore. Its big houses sat in lavish grounds, a mishmash of styles representing the centuries over which they'd been added to and modified. In the middle of the district was a long road running parallel to the shore. The centre of the image expanded, zooming in on a lavender-coloured drycoral bungalow. It was a circular building wrapped round a small swimming pool. Probably the smallest house in the whole district.

'Oh my God,' Paula said.

'That's the centre,' Digby said. '1800 Briggins. Registered to a Paul Cramley. Actually, he's lived there for . . . oh. That can't be right.'

'It is,' Paula told him.

'Do you think the T-sphere generator is underneath the bungalow? I can run a deep scan.'

'Don't bother.'

'But . . .'

'Laril is perfectly safe. Unfortunately, Araminta won't be able to call him for advice now, not without paying the price to Paul's ally.'

'Then you know this Cramley person? My u-shadow can't find anything on file.'

'Of course not. Paul was busy wiping himself from official databases before Nigel and Ozzie opened their first wormhole to Mars.'

'Really?'

'Just keep watching Valean.'

'Is that it?'

'For the moment. I'll try and talk to Paul.'

Digby knew better than to ask.

Laril knew the light and air had changed somehow. He wasn't standing in the sunlight of the coliseum, and the air he gulped down was perfectly conditioned. It was also quiet. He risked opening his eyes.

Of all the possible fates, he wasn't prepared for the perfectly ordinary, if somewhat old-fashioned, lounge he was in. The lighting globes were off, making it appear gloomy. Its only illumination came from sunlight leaking through the translucent grey curtains pulled across tall arching windows. He could just make out some courtyard with a circular swimming pool on the other side of the glass. The floor was dark wood planks, their grain almost lost with age and polish. Walls were raw drycoral, lined with shelves.

There were some chic silver globe chairs floating a few centimetres above the floorboards. A man was sitting on one of them, its surface moulded round him, as if it were particularly elastic mercury. His youthful features gave him a handsome appearance, especially with thick dark hair cut longer than current style. Instinct warned Laril he was old, very old. This wasn't someone he could bullshit like his ex-business partners and girlfriends. He didn't even risk using his field-function scan. No way of telling how the man would react.

'Uh,' he cleared his throat as his heart calmed a little. 'Where am I?'

'My home.'

'I don't ... Uh, thank you for getting me out of there. Are you Asom?'

'No. There's no such person. You were being played by the Accelerators.'

'They know about me?'

The man raised an eyebrow contemptuously.

'Sorry,' Laril said. 'So who are you?'

'Paul Cramley.'

'And am I in even deeper shit now?'

'Not at all.' Paul grinned. 'But you're not free to go, either. That's for your own good, by the way; it's not a threat.'

'Right. Who else knew about me?'

'Well, I did. And it looks like the stealthed ultradrive starship in orbit does. So along with Valean and her team, that makes three of us. I daresay more are on their way.'

'Oh Ozzie.' Laril's shoulders sagged from the pressure of dismay. 'My software isn't as good as I thought, is it?'

'In my experience, I've never seen worse. And trust me, that's a lot of experience. But then I don't think you realize exactly what you're dealing with.'

'Okay, so who are you? What's your interest?'

'You should be about to find out. I'm guessing that an old acquaintance is going to call any minute now. And when you're as old as me your guesses are certainties.'

'If you're old and you're not in ANA, you're probably not a Faction agent.'

'Glad to see you have some grey matter after all. Ah, here we go.'

A portal projected an image of a woman into the lounge. Laril groaned. He didn't need any identification program to recognize Paula Myo.

'Paula,' Paul said in a happy voice. 'Long time.'

'This crisis seems to be bringing the golden oldies out to play in droves.'

'Is that resentment I hear?'

'Just an observation. Laril, are you all right?'

He shrugged. 'I suppose, yeah.'

'Don't ever do anything as stupid as that again.'

Laril scowled at the Investigator's image.

'Thanks for exiting him,' Paula said. 'My own people would have been noisy.'

'Not a problem.'

'It won't take Valean long to determine your location. She'll visit.'

'She's not as stupid as Laril, surely?'

'No,' Paula agreed, as Laril bridled silently. 'But she has a mission, and Ilanthe won't give her a choice.'

'Poor her.'

'Quite. Give me its access code, please.'

'I don't know what you're talking about.'

'Paul. We don't have the time.'

Paul gave the projected image a martyred look. 'Connecting you directly.'

Paula's image winked off.

'Who's she talking to?' Laril asked.

'Next best thing now ANA's unavailable,' Paul said, sounding indifferent.

'So . . . I'm sorry, I still don't get who you are.'

'Just a bloke who has been around for a long while. That gives me a certain perspective on life. I know my own mind, and I don't like what the Accelerators are doing. Which is why I helped you out.'

One of the silver globes floated over to Laril, who sat down gingerly. Once the surface had bowed around him, it was actually rather comfortable. 'So how old are you?'

'Put it this way, when I grew up no one had travelled further than the moon. And half the planet thought that was a hoax. Dickheads.'

'The moon? Earth's moon?'

'Yeah. There's only one: the moon.'

'Great Ozzie, that makes you over a thousand.'

'Thousand and a half.'

'So why haven't you migrated inwards?'

'You speak like that's inevitable. Not everyone accepts that biononics and downloading into ANA is the path forward. There are still a few of us independents left. Admittedly, we do tend to be quite old. And stubborn.'

'So what are you trying to achieve?'

'Self-sufficiency. Liberty. Individualism. Neutrality. That kind of thing.'

'But doesn't Higher culture give . . .' Laril trailed off as Paul raised his eyebrow again.

'And you were acting on which committee's authority this morning?' Paul asked mildly.

'Okay. I'm having trouble accepting Higher life. I just don't see what else there is.'

'Get your biononics. Work out how to use them properly – I mean that in your case. Get yourself a stash of EMAs, and strike out for whatever you want.'

'You make it sound so easy.'

'Actually it's a bitch. And I still haven't got a clue how I'm going to finish up. Post-physical, presumably. But when I do it'll be on my terms, not something imposed on me.'

'You know that's the way I like to think.'

'I'm flattered. Ah, looks like Valean has found us.'

Laril gave the windows an anxious look. There was the unmistakable high-pitched whistling of a capsule descending fast outside. When he squinted through the windows looking out across the long garden he saw two chrome-yellow ovoids come to a halt above the freshly mown grass. The skeletal woman stepped out of the first. Laril's heart started to speed up at the sight of her. Those strange carmine streamers swam along behind her as she advanced on the bungalow. Six weapons-enriched agents followed her, various hardware units emerging from their skin to poke aggressive nozzles at the bungalow.

'Do we need to, uh, maybe get to safety?' Laril stammered. His biononics reported a sophisticated field scan was sweeping through the bungalow. He brought his integral force field up to full strength.

Paul sat even further back in his silver chair, putting his hands behind his head to regard the approaching Accelerator team nonchalantly. 'You can't get anywhere safer in the Commonwealth.'

'Oh shit,' Laril moaned. He desperately wanted to ask: How safe, really? If Paul had really good defences why hadn't he shot the capsules out of the sky, or teleported out or called up his own team of enriched bodyguards? Just . . . *Do something!*

Valean walked up to a window. She reached out and touched it with her index finger. The window turned to liquid, and splashed down into the lounge, running across the floorboards.

Laril sat up straight, his back rigid as fear locked his muscles. Valean stepped through the open archway, gently pushing the gauzy curtains apart. Her glowing pink eyes searched round the room.

'Paul Cramley, I believe?' she said with a half-smile.

'Correct,' Paul said. 'I'm afraid I have to ask you to leave now. Laril is my guest.'

'He must come with me.'

'No.'

Laril's exovision showed him those weird quantum spikes again. A pale-green phosphorescent glow enveloped Valean and her team.

'I'm afraid your T-sphere won't work,' she said. 'We're counter-programmed.'

Paul cocked his head to one side, long hair flopping down his cheek. 'Really? How about I use irony instead?'

Valean opened her mouth to speak. Then she frowned. Her

arms moved. Fast. They became a blur. Her emerald aurora brightened in the wake of the motion, leaving a broad photonic contrail through the air. Then she turned, which was also incredibly fast. Laril had to close his eyes as the haze around her grew dazzling. His biononics threw up retinal filters, allowing him to glance at the Accelerator team again. They'd turned into cocoons of brilliant lime-green. He could just discern outlines of their bodies, thrashing about inside each tiny illuminated prison, moving hundreds of times faster than normal. Fists were raised to hammer at the border, striking it at incredible speed and frequency. It was as if they'd turned to solid smudges of light. Valean's red streamers swirled about in agitation as the colour drained out of them. They turned black, then stiffened and began to crumble into small flakes which drifted down like a drizzle of ash.

Inside the green prisons the team members had now stopped moving, making it easier to see them. He watched Valean as her legs gave way. A fast smear of green light followed her to the ground. For a second her body remained there on hands and knees before another flash of light chased her to a prone position. The green glow faded to an almost invisible coating. Laril watched her odd skin darken; then its shimmer died to reveal a leather-like hide. It began to constrict even further around her skeleton. Cracks split open and thick juices oozed out, solidifying into stain puddles on the floorboards.

'Oh Ozzie!' Laril covered his mouth as he started to gag, and looked away quickly. Each of the Accelerator team had suffered the same fate. 'What happened?'

'Age,' Paul said. 'Gets us all in the end – unless you're careful, of course.' He climbed down off the chair and walked over to Valean's desiccated corpse. The green hue finally vanished, replaced by a glimmering force field. 'I *accelerated* her inside an exotic effect zone, like a miniature wormhole. Normally it's used to suspend temporal flow, but the opposite effect is just as easy to engineer, it simply requires a larger energy input. Sort of like the Void, really.'

Laril almost didn't want to ask. He couldn't help thinking

what it must have been like for Valean and her agents, imprisoned inside a tiny envelope of exotic force, enduring utter
solitude for days on end as the outside world stood still. 'How
long?'

'About two years. She had very powerful biononics, but even
they couldn't sustain her indefinitely. Ordinarily the biononic
organelles feed off cellular protein and all the other gunk floating
round inside the membrane, which is constantly resupplied by
the body. But in the temporal field she wasn't getting any fresh
nutrients. Her biononics ran out of cellular molecules eventually.
In the end they were like a super-cancer eating her from the
inside, enhancing the starvation and dehydration.'

Laril shuddered. 'But her force field is still working.'

'No, my defence systems are generating that. No telling what
booby traps she programmed into herself at the end. Just because
she's dead, doesn't mean she's harmless.'

Once again the T-sphere established itself; the corpses were
teleported out of the lounge. Laril didn't want to know where
they'd gone. 'What now?' he asked.

Paul gave him a brisk smile. 'You're my houseguest until
Araminta calls you, or doesn't, and this is all over.'

'Oh.'

'Cheer up. *Here* is actually quite dimensionally interesting.
After all, you don't really think I've spent the last thousand years
cooped up in the same bungalow, do you?'

'Ah . . . No, put like that I suppose not.'

'Jolly good. So, have you had breakfast yet?'

As soon as Paul Cramley transferred her call, Paula's cabin portal
projected a quaint image of tangerine and turquoise sine waves
undulating backwards into a vanishing point. 'I might have
known you'd be taking an interest,' she said.

'I always take an interest in human affairs,' the SI said.

'First question, can you get through the Sol barrier?'

'Sorry, no. If ANA can't, what hope does an antiquity like me
have?'

'Are you trying to engage my *sympathy*?'

'You have some?'

'That was uncalled for. But as it happens, I do. For my own species.'

'Paula, are you cross with me?'

'I shared ANA's opinion. Your interference in our affairs was unacceptable.'

'I hardly ever interfered.'

'We unmasked eighteen thousand of your agents. Your network was larger than the Starflyer's.'

'I'm hurt by that comparison.'

'Oh shut up. Why did you order Paul to save Laril?'

'I didn't order Paul to do anything. Nobody orders Paul around these days. You know he's well on his way to becoming post-physical?'

'Well I didn't think he was fully human any more.'

'That old body you saw with Laril is only a tiny aspect of him now. If you want to worry about non-human interference, you should keep a closer eye on him and the others like him.'

'There are others?'

'Not many. You and Kazimir are the oddities. Everyone else of your vintage either downloaded or moved off in their own direction like Paul.'

'So you and he are colleagues? Equals?'

'That's a very humancentric viewpoint: rate everyone according to their strength.'

'More an Ocisen one, I feel; perhaps we can include the Prime, too.'

'Okay, all right. Paul and I have a special relationship. You know, he actually wrote part of the original me. Back in the day he was a CST corporate drone in their advanced software department working on AI development.'

'Very cosy. So how big an interest have you been taking in the Pilgrimage?'

'Big. That idiot Ethan really could trigger the end of the galaxy. I'd have to move.'

'How terrible.'

'Have you ever tried moving a planet?'

Paula gave the sine waves a shrewd stare. 'No, but I know a man who probably can. How about you?'

'Yeah. Troblum is actually trying to get in touch with you.'

'Sholapur wasn't exactly invisible. Tell me something I don't know.'

'No, I mean he was really trying. He knew about the Swarm, he was going to make a deal.'

'Irrelevant now.'

'Paula, I've been in touch with him since Sholapur.'

'Where is he?'

'On his starship, somewhere. Last time we spoke he was still in range of the unisphere, I have no idea of the location. His smartcore is well protected. I urged him to get in touch with you.'

'Why?'

'He helped build the Swarm. He might be able to get through the barrier.'

'Did he say that?'

'He was reluctant to help. He claimed there is a code which can switch it off.'

'Even if there is, it'll be Ilanthe who holds it,' Paula said. 'Damn it, do you think he will contact me?'

'Troblum is a very paranoid man. A condition exacerbated by Sholapur. He is afraid of breaking cover. His true fear is that the Cat will find him. However, he was considering getting in touch with Oscar Monroe.'

'Oscar? Why?'

'I suspect he regards Oscar as the last trustworthy man in the galaxy.'

'I suppose that's true. I'll warn Oscar to look out for him.'

'Good. What are your intentions, Paula?'

'I'm not quite as liberal as ANA. I believe the Pilgrimage and Ilanthe must be stopped from entering the Void. That means getting hold of Araminta.'

'Difficult. She's walking the Silfen paths.'

'They won't grant her sanctuary. Somewhere, sometime, she will have to come out.'

'You know the safest place she could choose? Earth. How would that be for irony. If Ilanthe wanted her, the barrier would have to be switched off.'

Paula gave the knot of sine waves an approving look. She had known Silfen paths reached through the Dyson Alpha barrier: Ozzie himself had told her. The idiot had actually visited MorningLightMountain's world after the Starflyer War was over. She supposed it was inevitable that the SI would know: it had a long history with Ozzie. 'Clever,' she said. 'I wonder if we could get a message to her. Are you in contact with the Silfen Motherholm?'

'No. It doesn't associate with the likes of me. I'm just a mechanical-based intelligence. I don't have a living soul.'

'So we'd need a Silfen Friend.'

'There aren't many, and they tend to be elusive.'

'Cressida, she's related to Araminta. They both have Mellanie as their ancestor.'

'That connection is tenuous even for desperate times.'

'Yes. And Cressida has dropped from sight. But I'd forgotten Silfen paths can reach through this kind of barrier. Earth's is supposed to start outside Oxford somewhere. I wonder if ANA can use it to get some kind of message out.'

'If it can, it will.'

'Yeah, and in the meantime ... Do you have any weapons stashed away that can tackle the inversion core?'

'I don't have any weapons, stashed or otherwise.'

'I find that hard to believe.'

'Of course you do. You forget I am information, I operate within what could be classed as a physical network, but that does not govern me.'

'There are a lot of human personalities downloaded into you. That must influence your standpoint.'

'There are a lot of human memories stored inside me, there's a difference.'

'Okay, so do you at least know what the inversion core is?'

'I managed to access sensors in the Sol system for a very short period between it emerging and the barrier going up. ANA still regards such actions as extreme trespass. I can't tell you much other than it has an exotic nature. The quantum structure was effectively unreadable it was so unusual.'

'So we don't know what would kill it?'

'The Deterrence Fleet or the warrior Raiel might be able to. I can't conceive anything else working. But Paula, that ship it left in was extremely powerful, and fast.'

'I know. If Araminta calls Laril . . .'

'Paul and I will include you in the conversation.'

'Thank you. And let me have a code for you, please.'

'As you wish.'

Paula watched the sine waves shrink to nothing as a new communication icon appeared in her exovision. A quick check with the smartcore showed the SI hadn't attempted to infiltrate any of the ship's systems. She didn't expect it to, but . . .

Her u-shadow opened a secure link to the *High Angel*.

'Paula,' said Qatux. 'Our situation is not improving.'

'I understand the President has asked you to attempt to get through the Sol barrier.'

'He did. I don't believe it is possible. However, I shall oblige his request. To do nothing for you at this point would be morally irresponsible. We will fly to Sol shortly.'

'The Raiel taking part in galactic events again? I thought that went completely against your ethos.'

'This is a very specific event, the one we have dreaded for aeons. Our involvement is mandatory.'

'I believe the Sol barrier is based on the force field around the Dyson Pair. The Accelerators have been studying the Dark Fortress for a long time.'

'We suspected that was so. If true, the *High Angel* will be unable to breach the barrier.'

'What about a warrior Raiel ship?'

'I don't believe it would fare any better. Though there may

have been new developments I am unaware of. The generator you call the Dark Fortress represents the pinnacle of our race's ingenuity.'

Paula experienced a strange little frisson of relief at the statement. A very old puzzle finally solved. 'Did the Raiel build the Dark Fortress? We always thought they were the same as the DF spheres at Centurion Station.'

'Yes. It is a unit from our Galactic Core garrison. They have several functions; the force field is only one.'

'You told us the Anomine imprisoned the Dyson Pair.'

'They did. We loaned them the units. We produced legions of them after our invasion of the Void failed. As your species correctly postulated, they are the galaxy's final line of defence against a catastrophic expansion phase.'

'So the Raiel can stop an expansion phase?'

'That is something we will not know until the moment arises. The scheme was the best we could produce, but it remains untested.'

'Then it really is vital that Araminta doesn't lead the Pilgrimage into the Void?'

'Yes.'

'I will do everything I can, you know that.'

'I know, Paula.'

'I may need help.'

'Whatever I can provide, you have only to ask.'

*

Eventually the forest gave way to a crumpled swathe of grassy land which stretched away for miles to a shoreline guarded by thick dunes. The rich blue ocean beyond sparkled as the sunlight skipped across its gentle waves. Araminta smiled mournfully at the sight, knowing she'd never be able to run across the beach and dive into those splendid clear waters. The big quadruped beast she was riding snorted and shook its huge head, as if sharing her resentment.

'Don't worry, the whole beauties of nature thing gets tedious after a while,' Bradley Johansson said. He was riding on a similar beast to one side of her, while Clouddancer plodded along behind.

'After how long?' Araminta queried.

'Millennia,' Clouddancer growled out. 'Nature produces so much that is worthy of admiration. Its glory never ends.'

Bradley Johansson pursed his round mouth and produced a shrill trumpeting sound. After a day and a half a day riding with the pair since they left the festival by the loch, Araminta had concluded this was his chuckle.

'Great,' she muttered. The fresh breeze from the ocean was invigorating, countering her falling mood. They were approaching a narrow fold in the land, one filled with small trees and dense scrub bushes. There was a pool at the head of the slope, producing a tiny brook which trickled away down through the trees. She reined in her mount just short of the water, and swung her leg over the saddle so she could slide down its thick flank. It waited patiently as she performed her inelegant dismount. Bradley Johansson came over to help unstrap her backpack. She never actually saw him climb down, though she was sure his wings weren't big enough to work in a standard gravity field.

'How do you feel?' he asked sympathetically.

'Nervous as hell.'

'Your spirit will prevail,' Clouddancer proclaimed. He was still sitting on his own mount, tail curled up at one side, wings rustling in mild agitation. His head was held high as he looked towards the coast. If he'd been a human, Araminta would have said he was hunting out a scent in the wind.

'I have to,' she said, and meant it.

'I am proud of you, friend's daughter,' Bradley Johansson said. 'You encompass all that is good and strong with our species. You remind me why I gave everything I had to save us.'

Araminta was suddenly very busy with the clip around her waist. 'I'll do my best, I promise. I won't let you down.'

'I know.'

When she looked up, Bradley Johansson was holding a small pendant on a silver chain. The jewel was encased in a fine silver mesh. A pretty blue light was glimmering inside like captured starlight. He placed it round her neck. 'I name you that which you already are, Araminta. Friend of Silfen.'

'Thank you,' she said. Ridiculously, her eyes were watering up. She smiled over at Clouddancer, who bowed so solemnly towards her it left her feeling hopelessly inadequate. 'Do you have any suggestions for your new Friend?' she asked the pair of them, hating how weak she sounded. 'My ex-husband said he'd help me, but he's not quite the most reliable of people even if his heart is in the right place.'

'Laril isn't independent any more,' Bradley Johansson told her. 'He can still offer advice that would be helpful, but it is not his own.'

'Oh. Right.' *How do you know this?* Which was a stupid question, she was always allowing herself to be misled by the apparent carefree child-like lifestyle the Silfen followed. *There is more to them than this, a lot more.* 'So it's Oscar, then? Will he be able to help me with the machine-thing you warned me about?'

Clouddancer and Bradley Johansson exchanged a look. 'Probably not,' Clouddancer said. 'Nobody really understands what it is.'

'Somebody must know, or be able to work it out,' she said.

'That is for you to find, Friend Araminta.'

'Oh come on! The whole galaxy is at stake here, including your own existence. Just for once cut the mystic crap and give me some practical help.'

Bradley Johansson made his shrill chuckling noise again. 'There is someone you could ask, someone who may be smart enough to work things out for you. He was a phenomenal physicist, once. And he was named Silfen Friend.'

'Yeah, and look what he did with that most honourable of gifts,' Clouddancer growled.

'Of course he did,' Bradley Johansson said, sounding amused. 'That is what makes him who he is. That is why he is our Friend.'

'Who?' Araminta demanded.

'Ozzie,' Clouddancer sighed.

'Ozzie? Really? I thought . . . Is he still alive?'

'Very much so,' Bradley Johansson said.

'Well, where the hell is he?'

'Outside the Commonwealth. Oscar can get you there.' He paused, letting out a sorrowful whistle. 'Probably. Remember, Friend Araminta, you must walk with caution from now on.'

'Yeah yeah. I'll be careful. That part you can really depend on.'

'Come back to us afterwards,' Clouddancer said.

'Of course I will.' There was that tiny ripple of doubt in her thoughts which she swiftly squashed. *This is all so massive. Visiting Ozzie! For . . . Ozzie's sake.*

Bradley Johansson took her hand, and they walked towards the top of the little wooded ravine. Araminta blew out a long breath and strode forward confidently. Somewhere up ahead of her, winding through the trees and thick bushes she could sense the path to Francola Wood stirring at her approach.

'A last word for you, if I may,' Bradley Johansson said. 'Anger is a fine heat, one which you are now experiencing. Anger from being put in this position through no real fault of your own, anger at the stupidity of Living Dream. This anger behind your determination will power you at the start, allowing you to be the force you want to be. Then there will come a moment when you look round and see all you have carried before you. That is the most dangerous time, the time when you can lose faith in yourself and falter. That cannot happen, Friend Araminta. Keep your anger, fuel it, let it carry you forward. See this through to the final bitter end no matter what. That is the only way to take others with you, be a force of nature, the proverbial unstoppable force. You can do this. You have so much in you.'

She smiled bashfully. 'I will. I promise. I can keep focused.' *Like you wouldn't believe.*

Bradley Johansson stopped. A four-fingered hand ushered her onward with a grand gesture as his wings extended fully.

He made an imposing figure, poised between two species, two styles of life. She turned her back to him and strode forwards, forbidding any doubt to gain refuge in her mind. Ahead of her the path began to open.

*

The building had been a single house, once, designed as an extravagant ten-bedroom residence for a wealthy owner, with expansive reception rooms opening out on to a big garden that dropped down to the crowded forest of dapol trees which marked the city boundary. There was even a teardrop-shaped swimming pool underneath a spectacular white wing-roof. It fitted in perfectly with the Francola district's original ethos as an enclave of successful, wealthy residents who would enjoy a modicum of privacy afforded by the tree-hedges between their imposing properties. A taste of the countryside inside the city.

After a promising start, the district had drifted on Colwyn City's economic tides. The houses fell from fashion, and were snapped up by developers to be turned into even more stylish apartments. Redevelopment took the district further down-market, depressing prices still more. The people who rented the new apartments and studios tended to be the kind who stuck with a job for a while, which made them long-term residents. Another factor turning away the smarter set, amplifying the downhill economic spiral.

On the upside, that same depressed market meant that there were a lot of empty apartments for rent. Oscar and the team managed to secure a well-positioned apartment on the old house's ground floor. It had two bedrooms a bathroom and a lounge squeezed into what used to be one of the brash reception rooms. But the lounge had a panoramic window wall opening on to the lawn which ran all the way down to the edge of Francola Wood itself, giving them a perfect observation post.

Sitting on a pyramid of cushions they'd moved in front of the window wall, Oscar could just glimpse the shimmer of the city force field through the dark trees. He wasn't using his field-scan function, that would be too much of a giveaway. Not that it stopped other teams. His biononics would occasionally catch a quick scan originating close by. Liatris had identified seven other apartments along the street which had been leased out in the last twenty hours. Two other perfectly legitimate flats had been quietly taken over by teams who thought their subterfuge would leave them less visible. They weren't good enough to evade Liatris.

But what goes around . . . thought Oscar. He was sure everyone else knew about them as well.

Three of the rival teams had already reduced their personnel after it became clear Araminta had left Chobamba. With a whole galaxy of worlds now available to her, they'd decided it was extremely unlikely she'd ever return here to the heart of Living Dream's occupation army. That view was one he shared, but waiting here on the off chance was better than trying to guess where else she could turn up.

It was midmorning, and as it was his shift Oscar had been in his armour suit for five hours watching the forest when Paula called.

'Any sign of her?'

Oscar resisted the urge to roll his eyes, the gesture would be completely wasted. 'None of the thirteen teams scanning from all along the street have noticed anything. And the eight Ellezelin capsules on permanent patrol overhead report an equally negative result. I imagine the new Welcome Team which is actually lying in wait in the woods is bereft, too.'

'There's no need for sarcasm.'

'Face it, Paula, this is a dead end. We did our best, we got her clear of Living Dream and the others, it's up to her now.'

'I know. But several agents followed her on to the Chobamba Silfen path before it closed up'

'Then we'll never see them again. Not for centuries, anyway.'

'I'd like to think we have centuries.'

'We'll stay here for another day or two. Unless you know

better. How about it, Paula? Do you have contacts among the Silfen?'

'Not really.'

'Ah, you surprise me. If anyone has . . .'

'But I have just been talking to the SI.'

Oscar couldn't help it. He burst out laughing. On the other side of the lounge, Beckia shot him a puzzled look.

'Only you, Paula,' Oscar said happily. 'How is the SI?'

'Unchanged. It claims. However, it has taken care of one potentially dangerous loose end. Araminta now has no one else left in the Commonwealth to turn to.'

'So the theory is she'll ask the Navy for help?'

'It's a theory. Right now it's the only one we've got.'

'Well let's hope it works.'

'Yes. And the one trustworthy contact she has with official-dom is you.'

'Oh bloody hell.'

'There's something else.'

Oscar gave up and rolled his eyes. 'What?'

'Someone called Troblum may get in touch. If he does I need to know immediately. And you must not lose track of him. If possible, take him directly into custody.'

'Okay, so who is he?'

'A slightly strange physicist who may know how to get through the Sol barrier. I'm sending his file. Oh, and the Cat is after him as well, so be careful.'

'Is she? Well that's just made my day. Anything else?'

'That's all, Oscar. Thank you.'

Oscar watched the file load into his storage lacuna, then the secure link closed. He let out a breath, and started to review Troblum. He kept on getting distracted by Beckia. Her mind was emitting little pulses of dismay and anger into the gaiafield. The gaiafield was Oscar's private additional method of watching for Araminta. They already had thirty stealthed sensors scattered across Francola Wood to try and spot her should she return. On top of that, Liatris had tapped into sensors and communication links from the other agents and the Welcome Team. But Oscar was hopeful that he would somehow get advance warning of her arrival from the path. He thought, though he was in no way sure, that he could sense the alien wormhole. There was something there, some intrusion into the gaiafield that wasn't quite right, a feeling of age and incredible distance. Very faint, and the more he concentrated on it the more elusive it became. So he was content to let it wash against the edge of his perception, which meant he had to open his gaiamotes up to their full sensitivity. Which was why Beckia's little outbursts were becoming quite intrusive.

'What?' he finally asked, when a particularly sharp burst of indignation shunted his attention from Troblum's amazing collection of Starflyer War memorabilia. He shifted round so he was looking back into the lounge. His visor was open so she could see his ire as well as feel it in the gaiafield.

Beckia gave him a look etched with rebuke. She was curled up on a long corner couch, sipping a hot chocolate. Her armour was open and ready on the floor beside her. 'Haven't you been following the news?' she replied.

He waved a gauntleted hand towards Francola Wood. 'No! This is my shift, remember? I'd like to focus on that.'

'No need to get touchy. The remote sensors will give us plenty of warning. Besides, you don't really think she's coming back here, do you?'

'We have to be ready in case she does,' he said, hating how lame he sounded.

'Do you know something we don't, Oscar?'

It was there again, that niggling little question of trust that had hung between them all since they bumped into the Cat. 'Apparently some agents got on to the path at Chobamba,' he said. 'Paula thinks they might flush her out faster than she'd like. Personally, I think that's bullshit, but . . .'

'The paths aren't straight lines, you know that.'

'I know. So what's troubling you?'

'Local news. It's getting worse here.'

'I'd like to say that's impossible.'

'Take a look. I'll watch the remotes for a minute.'

Against his better judgement, Oscar told his u-shadow to prepare a summary. Beckia was right, it wasn't pleasant. Once it was confirmed Araminta was on Chobamba, Phelim had begun withdrawing the paramilitary troops from Viotia. It was a well-planned pull-out, starting with the cities furthest from Colwyn City. Ludor, the capital over on the Suvorov continent, had been among the first places to see the big dark capsules streak away. It also had the highest number of Living Dream followers. Without the paramilitaries to guarantee protection, Viotia's native population began to turn on them. Local police forces did nothing to prevent the attacks; on several occasions they were seen joining in. Hospitals already overcrowded from riot casualties were deluged by yet more injured.

In response, Phelim announced that the Ellezelin presence in Colwyn City would remain until Living Dream followers were safe. He didn't say anything about the rest of the planet, and the paramilitary withdrawal continued unabated. Thousands of the faithful fled in their capsules, hoping to pass through the wormhole. But Phelim wouldn't lower Colwyn City's force field for anyone except the Ellezelin capsules. Swarms of the frantic refugees were stacking up in the skies outside the city. The lucky tens of thousands of followers who had originally taken up residence in Colwyn City were now trekking across a phenomenally hostile urban landscape, desperately trying to reach the docks where the wormhole would take them back to Ellezelin. It was almost impossible for them to get there. Every street was seething with locals on the lookout for the faithful. All the Ellezelin capsules inside the force field were doing now was running a massive evacuation operation. Phelim had indicated that if there was no end to the violence against Living Dream members he would impose an all-day curfew. That didn't help. Vigilante groups weren't even waiting for the followers to try and make a dash for safety. Reports were coming in of houses being broken into to extract justice. Images of bodies savagely beaten to death in their own homes were snatched by braver reporters; there were a lot of children caught up in the violence. Of course the most devout Living Dream followers didn't have memorycells, because Edeard didn't, and they were all going to follow Inigo's dreams into the Void where such contrivances were an irrelevance.

'Crap,' Oscar muttered. It would take a generation for Viotia to recover, he knew that. If it ever did. If it even still existed in a generation.

'We're not supposed to get sidetracked,' Beckia said quietly. 'But it's hard sometimes. That's when your strength is really tested.'

'I lived through worse before,' Oscar said, aiming for tough and failing woefully. *Dead children, for God's sake; in the Commonwealth, where everyone should be safe and happy.*

'So it would never happen again.'

'Yeah,' he said as he pushed the news shows to peripheral mode. 'Something like that.' Because he was distracted, because he wasn't paying full attention to that strange ancient strand of neutral thought in Francola Wood, he was almost immediately aware when it began to change. To stir. Freshen: the only analogy he could come up with.

'Uh oh,' Oscar murmured. Naturally, when he tried to chase down the sensation the damn thing slithered about, dwindling from perception.

'What now?' Beckia was rising from the couch.

'Get your suit on.' Oscar's u-shadow was relaying images from the stealth sensors. It looked like he wasn't the only one in tune with the path. Several members of the Welcome Team were on the move, emerging from the tangle of whiplit fronds to slip past the dapol trunks. Through the lounge windows he saw a flock of caylars take flight, their ultramarine wings flapping urgently. *She can't be this stupid*, he thought. The girl he'd seen in Bodant Park had been scared, yes, but everything she'd done spoke of a smart mind.

Oscar opened a secure channel to Tomansio, who was in their stolen capsule flying a random course over the city 'Get over here, I think we're going to need you.'

'She's coming?'

'I don't know, but something's happening.'

'On my way. Two minutes.'

Sensors showed several team members stepping out of their apartments in full armour. They began to sprint over the long gardens which led down to Francola Wood.

Beckia walked up beside him, her helmet sealing up. Oscar's visor closed as his integral force field established itself. He ran a check on his heavy-calibre weapons. Accelerants flooded into his bloodstream as biononics complemented his muscles. 'Here we go again,' he said in complete dismay. A low-power disruptor pulse shattered the lounge's big window wall, and they ran out onto the lawn.

*

Mellanie's Redemption hung in transdimensional suspension a hundred thousand kilometres above Viotia. Passive sensors absorbed what information they could, revealing that space around the planet was empty apart from a single Dunbavend Line starship in a thousand-kilometre orbit. For a passenger ship it seemed to have an awful lot of weapons systems, several of which were active.

A secure TD link routed Troblum's u-shadow to the planetary cybersphere, allowing him to monitor events. The u-shadow also kept watch for the SI. So far it hadn't intercepted his connection, but Troblum was convinced it would be watching the data flowing along the link.

'Why are we here?' Catriona Saleeb asked. She was sitting on a simple stool beside the cabin wall, which had pushed out a small wooden bar. Appropriately, she was dressed for an evening out on the town, wearing a slinky blue snakeskin dress, her hair spiralled in an elaborate style and sparkling with small red gems.

'It was the course I'd designated before the Swarm went active,' Troblum said gruffly. 'And we had to test the hyperdrive.'

Catriona glanced at the big image of Viotia which a portal was projecting into the middle of the cabin. 'Are you going to call him?'

'Who?'

'Oscar Monroe.'

'No.' He brought some performance tables into his exovision and studied them, checking through the hyperdrive's functions. Peripheral displays showed the violence playing out across the planet as residents took their revenge on Living Dream members.

'If you help them, they'll take care of the Cat,' she said.

His u-shadow slid the performance tables to one side. He gave her an angry stare. 'They'll do that anyway. Paula knows she's been taken out of suspension, and she won't rest until the Cat is back where she belongs. It's over. Do you understand that? Now I'm going to review the hyperdrive. Once I'm satisfied it's working correctly, we'll leave.'

'I just want you to be safe, you know that.' Catriona picked up a long-stemmed cocktail glass, and drained its sticky red liquid. She swirled the ice cubes round the bottom. 'And I know you need closure on the Cat. If you run now, you'll never know what happened. You won't be able to live with that. You'll spend the rest of your life seeing her everywhere, you'll panic at every strange noise in the wind.'

'I'm not that weak.'

'If you're not afraid, then call Oscar.'

'That's machine logic.'

Her lips pouted, their glossy scales darkening down to purple. 'For someone who cares about no one, you can be a real bastard at times.'

'Shut the fuck up. I mean it.' He brought his exovision intensity up. On a street in Colwyn City a family of Living Dream followers was being chased by a mob armed with power tools and thick clubs. Their clothes, made from simple cloth in old styles, had betrayed them. Two adults dragged along three terrified crying children, the eldest no more than eleven. It was a residential street, houses and apartment blocks packed tight. The father found one he obviously recognized and dashed up to the front door, pounding away, yelling furiously. The mob slowed and surrounded them in an eerily quiet, efficient manoeuvre, some primeval hunter knowledge governing their movements. They closed in. The father kept hitting the door with his fist, while the weeping mother pleaded for her children to be let through. As if knowing how futile it was she put her arms round them, clutching them to her as she started screaming. The news show's reporter was good, focusing perfectly on the makeshift clubs as they rose.

Troblum actually turned his head away as his u-shadow cancelled the news show. It was all too vivid.

'Do you want to be human?' Troblum asked. 'Did you think I would grow you a clone body and transfer your personality in?'

'Excuse me?'

'Is that what you were hoping for?'

'No,' Catriona said, sounding quite shocked.

'I won't do that. Not ever. The universe doesn't need more humans. We have nothing to offer the universe. We need to leave our original form behind. It does nothing but generate misery and suffering. The External Worlds are full of animals. They can't be classified as true humans: they don't think, they just act. Animals, that's all they are, animals.'

'So how do you define real humans? People like yourself?'

'A real person would want independence. If you were real you'd want a body. Did you talk about it with Trisha and Isabella and Howard?'

'Troblum?' She sounded troubled. 'Don't.'

'Was Howard a part of it too? Were you going to put pressure on me to make it happen?'

'No.'

'Did you tell the Cat about me?' he yelled.

'Stop this!'

'I don't need you.'

'But I need you. I love you.'

'Don't be stupid.'

She climbed off the stool and knelt at his feet. 'I only exist because of you. How could I not love you for that? I would not betray you. I cannot. You know this.'

Troblum flinched. His hand hovered above her thick tightly wound hair.

'Please,' she said – there were tears in her eyes as she looked up at him. 'Please, Troblum. Don't do this to yourself.'

He sighed, lowering his palm on to her head, feeling the springy strands of hair against his skin. Then her hand closed around his, letting him know her warmth, her light touch. She kissed his fingers one at a time. Troblum groaned, half ashamed, half delighted. *She's not real. She's an I-sentient. Does that make her the perfect human for me?* His whole mind was in chaos.

'You'd change,' he whispered. 'If I gave you a meat body, you'd change. Your routines would be running in neural paths that are never fixed. I don't want you to change.'

'I don't want a meat body. I just want you. Always. And I need you to be safe and happy for that to happen. Do you understand that, Troblum?'

'Yeah,' he said. 'I get it.'

The starship's sensors reported energy-weapon discharges above Colwyn City. Troblum frowned. 'What's that?' he queried. His u-shadow started refining the scan.

*

It had been a while since Araminta had used the melange program. Nothing wrong with the program, it was the association with Likan she got all squirmy and uncomfortable about. Which was stupid. She certainly couldn't afford that kind of weakness now.

As she walked beside the little brook, she sent her perception seeping out ahead of her, experiencing it flow along the path. Far away she could feel the Silfen Motherholm, sympathetic and imposing. There was the human gaiafield, fizzing with agitation and excitement. Right away on the other side of her mind was the Skylord – she recoiled from that straight away. Her feet kept on walking. All around her the trees were growing higher, muddling those on the world she walked among with those of Francola Wood. She knew now where the path would take her into Francola Wood, smelling the scent of the wiplit fronds. Her mind found a host of people lurking in the undergrowth, so cleverly concealed by their gadgetry whilst their steely thoughts filled with expectation. They were waiting for her.

Yet even as it swept her along to its ending she knew the path was fluid, simply anchored in place by past wishes, directions sung to it by Silfen millennia ago. She tried to make her own wishes known. Somehow they weren't clear enough, lacking precision. The path remained obdurately in place. So she summoned up the melange, and felt the calmness sinking through her body, centring her, enabling her to concentrate on every sensation she was receiving.

The tunes imprinted on the path's structure were easier to trace, to comprehend. With that knowledge she began to form the new tunes which her thoughts spun out. Wishes amplified by a fond nostalgia, and the most fragile of hopes.

Onward her feet fell, pressing down on damp grass as the melody permeated her whole existence. She swayed in time to the gentle undulations she had set free, finally happy that the end of the path was moving with her, carrying her onward to the place she so urgently sought. Then there ahead of her the thoughts she knew so well radiated out from his home.

Araminta opened her eyes to look across the lawn towards the big old house. Her initial smile faded from her face. There had been a fire. Long black smoke marks contaminated the white walls above three of the big ground-floor arches. Two of the balconies were smashed. There was a hole in the roof, which looked melted.

'Oh great Ozzie,' she moaned. The dismay was kept in place

by the melange, occupying a single stream in her mind, an emotion that neither coloured nor determined her behaviour. 'Bovey!' she called as she ran for the house. 'Bovey!'

Two of hims were outside the swimming pool. They turned round at her voice. The gaiafield revealed his burst of astonishment.

'You're okay,' she gasped as she came to a halt a few metres short of hims. One was the Bovey she'd been on their first date with, the body she truly identified as *him*; the other was the tall blond youngster. At their feet was another body, inert, covered in a beach towel.

'Oh no,' she said. 'Not one of you.'

'Hey,' the older of hims said, and threw his arms around her. 'It's okay.'

Some small part of herself marvelled at how calm she was, channelling all the emotion away so she could remain perfectly rational and controlled. She knew what she should say, even if her voice lacked the appropriate intensity. 'I'm so sorry. This is all my fault.'

'No no,' he soothed.

'I should have told you. Warned you. I left because I didn't want you to get involved, to get hurt.'

Neither of hims could avoid looking at the corpse. 'It's okay. You came back, that's all that matters.'

'It is not okay. They killed one of you.' A pulse of regret and guilt in his mind alerted her. 'No, it's not just one, is it? How many?'

He took a step back from her, though his hands were still gripping her shoulders.

'Tell me,' she demanded.

'Five,' he said, as if ashamed.

'Bastards!'

'It doesn't matter.' His grin was rueful. 'That's the point of being mes, bodyloss is irrelevant. Some of mes are scattered all across this city, and nobody knows how many there are; certainly not those thugs. I'm safe. Safer than you.'

'This is my fault. I shouldn't be here, I shouldn't have come to you, not before it's all over.'

'I'm glad you did,' he said earnestly. 'Really I am. Just seeing you, knowing you're okay makes this all worthwhile.' Both of hims looked back across the empty garden towards the Cairns whose muddy waters flowed past the bank at the bottom of the lawn. 'How did you get here? Everyone thinks you're on Chobamba.'

'Long story.'

A sound similar to faint thunder rolled across the house. Araminta turned to the source, seeing energy weapons flash just below the curving force-field dome. She didn't need any kind of program to tell her it was the Francola district.

'Not again,' Bovey groaned. 'Enough!'

'It's me,' she said impassively. 'They're fighting because they think I'm there.'

'Araminta.' It came out of both of hims, a distraught desperate voice.

'I can't stay. They'll find me eventually.'

'Run then. I'll come with you. We'll just keep on running. The Navy can probably help.'

'No. I can't do that. ANA has gone. Nobody is going to help us, nobody can stop Living Dream and the Accelerators. It's down to me now.'

'*You?*'

'I'm not running, not hiding. Not any more. I know I have no right to ask this, because I didn't have the courage to tell you about myself before.'

'I understand.'

'You're sweet, too sweet. After this is over, I want us to be together. I really do. That's why I'm here, so you know that.'

He hugged her tight again. 'It'll happen,' he whispered fiercely. 'It will.'

'There are things I have to do,' she said. 'Things I don't want to, but I can't see any other way. I have an idea, but I'm going to need your help to make it work.'

Inigo's Twenty-Sixth Dream

In all the years Edeard lived in Makkathran he'd never bothered drawing up a proper map of the deep tunnels. He knew there were five large concentric circles forming the main routes, with curving links between them. He also instinctively knew their position in relation to the streets and districts above. Beyond the outermost circle were the longer branches driving out under the Iguru Plain apparently at random. One day he would fly along each of those brightly lit white tubes to find exactly where they emerged. One day when he had the time.

For now he was simply glad that the outermost circular tunnel carried him close to Grinal Street in Bellis district, where Marcol was having difficulty subduing an exceptionally strong psychic. Edeard hadn't used a deep tunnel for months if not longer, such excursions were becoming a rare event. For several years now he'd had no reason to rush anywhere, especially on constable business. But now as he hurtled along somewhere deep underneath Lisieux Park the sheer exhilaration made him curse his middle-aged timidity. His cloak was almost tearing off his shoulders from the ferocity of the wind. He stretched his hands out ahead, as if he was diving. Then he rolled. It was a ridiculously pleasurable sensation, making the blood pump wildly along his veins. He yelled out for the sheer joy of living once more. And rolled again and again. A side tunnel flashed past, then another. He was almost at his destination in Bellis.

There was an urge to simply go round again. *Marcol and his squad can handle it, surely?*

Something was suddenly hurtling round the tunnel's shallow curve directly ahead. Edeard never bothered using his farsight in the intense white light of the tubes so he was taken completely by surprise. He only just had time to harden his third hand into a bodyshield as they flashed past. Two people clinging together. Teenagers, whooping madly. No clothes on as they coupled furiously in the buffeting wind. There was a quick glance of their startled, ecstatic faces, then they were gone, their joyful cries lost amid the churning slipstream. Edeard threw his farsight after them, but the tunnel had separated them too quickly, already they were lost round the curve behind.

His shocked thoughts managed to calm, and he asked the city to take him the other way. To chase the intruders and catch up. He slowed as always, skidding to a halt on the tunnel floor. Then the force which carried him reversed, and he began flying back the way he'd just come.

This time he sent his farsight ranging out ahead. Perception through the tunnel walls was difficult, even for him. He could just sense the city a couple of hundred yards above him, but that was mainly due to the layout of the canals impinging on his perception. Actually sensing anything along the tunnel was extremely difficult.

For a moment he thought he'd caught a trace of them a few hundred yards ahead, but then lost them again. When he reached the spot, it was a side-tunnel branch, and he didn't know which way to go. He skidded and stumbled to a halt in front of the fork; standing on the bright glowing floor looking first one way then another, as if hunting a trace. Then he tried delving into the tunnel-wall structure for its memory. The city always recalled decades of localized events.

That was the second surprise of the day. There wasn't one memory. Not of the teenage couple. He could sense the tunnel's recollection of himself flashing past barely a minute before, but of them there was nothing.

'How in the Lady's name did they . . .' His voice echoed off down the tunnel as he frowned at the shining junction. For a moment he thought he might have heard laughter whispering along the main tunnel. But by then he knew he was grasping at phantoms. 'Honious!' he grunted, and asked the city to take him back to Bellis.

Grinal Street was a pleasant enough boulevard, winding its way across the south side of Bellis district from Emerald Canal to the top of Oak Canal. A mixture of buildings stood along it, from tympanum-gabled mansions to bloated hemispheres with narrow arches that made perfect boutiques; leading on to a line of houses with blended triple-cylinder walls whose overhanging roofs made them resemble knobbly stone mushrooms. Sergeant Marcol had been dealing with an incident in Five Fountain Plaza close to Oak Canal. The plaza was enclosed by a terrace with a concave outer wall, and an internal honeycomb configuration of small cell-rooms connected via short tubes without any apparent logic to the layout, as if the whole structure had been hollowed out by giant insects long ago. This hive-like topography made it ideal for merchants and traders dealing in small high-value items. Few people lived in it, but many thrived and bustled round inside.

Edeard arrived at a squat archway in one corner, and automatically ducked his head as he went inside. There was a lot of hostility and bad temper radiating out from the gloomy interior. As he crossed the threshold, he was instantly aware of a strong farsight examining him. His inquisitor was somewhere over in Zelda, and withdrew their farsight as Edeard attempted to backtrack them.

He paused, pursing his lips with interest. *That* hadn't happened for quite a few years, either. Whoever had taken such an interest in him before the Skylords returned had been ignoring him ever since. He didn't think their re-emergence today was a coincidence.

Marcol was waiting for him in the herbalist emporium, a room on the second floor, reached by a spiralling tube and several interconnected cell-rooms. Its walls were completely covered in rugs woven with intricate geometric designs. Lanterns hung on long brass chains, burning Jamolar oil to cast a thick yellow light. There were other scents in the air, a melange of spice and alcohol so potent that Edeard half expected to see it as a vapour. The cell-room was fitted out with row upon row of small shelves, lined with kestric pipes of various sizes and lengths. Several were lying broken on the floor. Hundreds of the narcotic plant's long tapering leaves hung from racks, drying in the hot air. There were bundles of other stems, seed pods, and leaves which Edeard didn't recognize. Again, many of them had been torn down and trampled underfoot.

As soon as he'd pushed aside the bead curtains he knew who the protagonists were, two men on opposite sides of the room, still glaring at each other, minds reeking of animosity. One was old and quite large, dressed in an expensive matching jacket and trousers, colourfully embroidered with small birds in the same style as the hanging rugs. Edeard immediately tagged him as the herbal emporium's owner – which might be prejudice, but with his long grey beard and straggly hair he just came across as the right type.

The other man was considerably younger, under thirty; and Edeard knew his type only too well. Yet another Grand Family son a long way down the entitlement list. As arrogant as he was handsome, and living well beyond his allowance thanks to extended merchant's credit – straight away Edeard suspected the owner was one such creditor. The two constables under Marcol's charge had got cuffs on him, rumpling up the sleeves of his dark-red velvet jacket. Looking round, Edeard didn't quite know why he was here. Then he studied the younger man's face closely, taking in the high cheeks, the dark floppy hair, the unbreakable defiance in those light brown eyes.

I've seen him before. But where? He was younger. Honious damn my memory.

'What's the problem?' he asked lightly.

'Colfal called us,' Marcol said, indicating the owner. 'Alleging psychic assault. When we turned up, Tathal resisted arrest.' He thumb-jerked towards the youthful aristocrat, who responded with a dismissive smile. 'He's a difficult one.'

'I did no such thing,' Tathal said. It was a polite tone, and the accent wasn't immediately indicative of Makkathran's finest. Edeard thought he might be from the southern provinces.

Holding up a finger to Tathal for silence, Edeard turned to Colfal. 'Why did Tathal assault you?'

Colfal's anger finally faded away, replaced by a surly glower. He took a deep breath. 'I apologize your time has been wasted, Waterwalker. This has been a misunderstanding.'

'Huh?' Marcol's jaw dropped in astonishment. 'But you called us.'

Edeard's gaze lingered on the damaged merchandise scattered over the floor; while his farsight was studying the few of Marcol's thoughts revealed through his shield. 'Uh huh.' He raised an eyebrow. 'And you, Tathal? What have you to say?'

'Also, my profound apologies. As your constables will testify, I have a strong third hand. In the heat of the moment my restraint isn't all it should be.'

'You don't wish to press charges?' Edeard asked Colfal.

'No.' The old herbalist shook his head, unable to meet Edeard's stare.

'Very well.' Edeard told the constables to uncuff Tathal. 'And you, learn to restrain your strength.'

'Of course, Waterwalker.'

'Where do you live?'

'Abad, Waterwalker, I have residence on Boldar Avenue.'

'Really? Anywhere near Apricot Cottage?'

Tathal grinned eagerly, and inclined his head. 'Indeed, I am privileged to be a fellow.'

Which would explain the stylish clothes along with a provincial accent; but Edeard still couldn't place the face. 'All right, you're free to go. Consider this your only warning, stay out of trouble from now on.'

'Yes, Waterwalker.'

Edeard was sure that compliance was loaded with mockery, but there was no hint of anything from beneath Tathal's mental shield. In fact Edeard had never encountered such a perfectly protected mind before, which given he was in Makkathran was quite an achievement.

'Wasting a constable's time is also an offence,' he told Colfal after Tathal had gone through the swirling bead curtain. 'Especially mine.'

'I'm sorry, sir,' a flushed Colfal muttered sheepishly.

'What in Honious was that?' Edeard asked Marcol when they were back out in Five Fountain Plaza.

'I'm really sorry, Edeard. It all got out of hand so quickly. And, Lady, he was so strong. I couldn't handle him by myself. Even with my squadmates pitching in it was touch and go. I just sort of instinctively called you.'

'Humm . . .' Edeard gave the warren-like terrace a suspicious look. 'He really was that strong?'

'Yes.'

'What was the dispute about? If Tathal is an Apricot Cottage fellow, it could hardly be over payment.'

'I'm not sure. Colfal was making all sorts of allegations when we arrived. Extortion. Financial abuse. Physical threats. Psychic assault. You name it, he was shouting about it.'

'Interesting.' Edeard sent his perception into the walls of the herbal emporium, seeking to extract the city's memory of the confrontation. But of course, the walls were covered in rugs, the substance of the city could neither see nor hear what went on inside.

'I can't believe Colfal backed down,' Marcol was saying. 'He was as furious as a blooded drakken.'

'Domination,' Edeard said. 'I recognized some of the patterns in his thoughts, they're quite distinct after they've been forced to change.' He stopped. *Now* he remembered Tathal. 'Oh Lady, I might have guessed.'

*

The Chief Constable of Makkathran had a grand office at the back of the Orchard Palace. A circular room with a high conical ceiling that twisted upwards as if it had been melted into shape. The floor was a polished ochre with dark red lines tracing out a pentagon. Walls were a lighter brown, but still glossy. Edeard didn't go for much furniture, it was a place of work after all. He had his muroak desk, a gift from Kanseen the day after this election, and a long table for meetings with various captains and lawyers.

By the time he got back there after dealing with Tathal and Colfal, Felax had summoned Golbon, and Jaralee, the last two remaining active members of the Grand Council committee on organized crime. Even now, after so long, Edeard hadn't quite managed to wind it up.

'New case,' he announced as he strode over to his desk. Golbon and Jaralee exchanged a surprised look. For the last seven years all they'd been doing was quietly closing case files and assigning them to the archives.

Edeard sat at his desk. Behind him a neat row of tall slit windows looked out across Rah's Garden and the Centre Circle canal. He always positioned himself so he faced away from the view. 'The Apricot Cottage Fellowship.'

Golbon groaned. 'Not that again. We looked into them a few years back. They're just a bunch of young merchants looking to make their own association and build up some political clout. They use a few strong-arm tactics occasionally, but no more than established businesses. There's no criminal activity.'

'Good, then this will be a quick assignment for you,' Edeard countered. 'I want the names of the Fellowship, and yes that includes my son-in-law. Get a rundown of their business affiliations. What they own; properties, land, ships, and so on. I also want a complete financial rundown on a herbalist called Colfal. See if you can find any ties to Fellowship members.'

'Why the sudden interest?' Jaralee asked.

'I think I perceived one of them called Tathal use domination on someone he was doing business with. Colfal, as it happens.'

'Ah, the impossible court case,' Jaralee said. Her first apprenticeship had been with the Guild of Lawyers, before she transferred to the clerks. That made her invaluable for Edeard's investigations; her ability to piece together solid evidence from scraps of information in diverse files was legend, and her legal background enabled her to see what charges could legitimately be applied.

'There have been cases where domination has been proved,' Golbon said.

'Grand Family members testifying against ordinary citizens,' Jaralee countered. 'It's basically hearsay. The court chose to recognize it those few times because of the people involved. Legally, though, there is no acknowledged proof of tampering with another's thoughts.'

'I know there's no legal basis,' Edeard said. 'But if it did happen with Colfal then it's part of a greater criminal act. If we can establish that, we can go after the other facts they'll have left behind.'

'Okay,' Jaralee said. 'As long as you understand no court will convict on that allegation alone.'

'Understood,' Edeard said, trying not to think of Salrana. 'There's something else you should know. Tathal has a very strong psychic ability. Apparently even Marcol had difficulty countering him. Presumably this helps his dominance ability.'

'Lady,' Golbon muttered. 'Do you think he'll come after us?'

'I doubt it,' Edeard said. 'But just be careful. Tathal isn't the only strong rogue psychic in the city.' He told them about the occasional sweeps of farsight that had dogged him over the years. Even though he trusted them implicitly, he didn't mention the tunnels. The only way those youngsters could have got down there was with the compliance of Makkathran itself. He didn't know if it simply responded to any strong psychic, or if it actively chose to help some and not others. Somehow he doubted the latter. It had only ever consciously communicated to him once, the day he'd learned of the Void's true ability.

'Are they linked?' Jaralee asked.

'I don't know, but I also want you to see if there's any financial connection between Ranalee and the Apricot Cottage Fellowship.'

'I see,' she said, with a neutral tone.

Edeard did his best not to smile. Over the years the Grand Council committee on organized crime had expended a great deal of time and effort investigating Ranalee, all to no avail. Jaralee and the others had come to recognize the owner of the House of Blue Petals as Edeard's personal obsession; he often suspected their diligence was less than it should have been because of that. 'I know there was a, uh, physical connection between Ranalee and Tathal a few years ago. She was probably the one who taught him how to use dominance effectively.'

Again, Jaralee and Golbon shared a knowing look.

'We'll look into it,' Jaralee assured him.

Edeard and Kristabel took a family gondola from the Culverit mansion down to Mid Pool. It was late afternoon, with the falling sun polishing streaks of cirro-stratus cloud to a tender gold. Warm air hung heavy over the city, redolent with scent of the sea.

They weren't the only ones enjoying the last of the balmy day: hundreds of gondolas were moving up and down Great Major Canal. Progress was slow. Edeard thought every gondola in Makkathran must be out on the water – he'd never seen so many of the sleek black craft together before. The streets and avenues along both sides of the water were also crammed with people.

As he watched them he noticed how many were elderly, being helped along by their families. Most of them were heading towards Eyrie.

Kristabel caught his gaze. 'How long?'

'They'll be here in nine days.'

'Five Skylords,' she said, awed by the notion. 'I wonder if that many ever came in Rah's time?'

'The Lady never gave numbers.' Edeard saw an old woman

with an uncanny resemblance to Mistress Florrel being helped along by three younger woman; she could barely walk, her joints were so arthritic. Her mind leaked little spikes of pain, along with a mild bewilderment. He suspected she wasn't entirely aware of what was going on. On the water below her, gondolas carried her contemporaries towards the crooked towers of Eyrie. The difference was money. They had enough coinage to make that last stretch of the journey in comfort.

'How did they cope back then?' Kristabel wondered.

'The population wasn't as large as it is today. Fewer people lived in the city, so there'd be rooms they could all use without any of the trouble we're having.' The influx of elderly travellers waiting for the arrival of a Skylord was reaching disturbing proportions. It had risen steadily in the years since Finitan's guidance and word of the Skylords' return spread out across the provinces. Now, thousands flocked to Makkathran every month, all of them aided by family, swelling the numbers to a level where the city could barely cope. Once again, the constables were fully deployed on the streets quashing a hundred outbreaks of minor crime each day, from disputes over rooms to wrangles about the price of food charged to visitors. The constables also had to ensure free movement along those streets, which, given that a lot of the elderly had difficulty walking, was becoming quite taxing. The charity and goodwill of the permanent residents that had blossomed after the first couple of visits by Skylords was all but gone now.

The gondola arrived in Mid Pool, and headed up Trade Route Canal. They had to wait several minutes before the mooring platform at the end of Jodsell Street had a free berth. From there it was only a short walk along the street to the District Master's mansion at the centre of Sampalok.

Edeard always felt slightly bashful whenever he entered the big square at the heart of Sampalok. This was the place every-one associated with the day of banishment, the turning point in Makkathran's life, and that of Querencia itself. It wasn't, of course. The true change had started in a secret vault under the Spiral Tower of the Weapons Guild – and nobody would ever know.

The mansion of the Sampalok district Master and Mistress stood in the middle of the vast square; a six-sided giant of a building, each face a different pastel colour, each with its own high archway into the surrounding court. None of their gates were closed; unlike their predecessor the new district Master and Mistress didn't turn away the people they were supposed to serve.

In years past the square was well travelled, with a few vendors setting up stalls to sell fruit and drinks. Kids ran about, dodging the fountains. But mainly it was open space. Not so any longer. Hundreds of modest bamboo-framed tents had been pitched outside the mansion's walls. Even as he walked to the main gate, Edeard could see more being assembled, with lively ge-chimps scampering over the frame, binding the canes together. Families stood by with bundles of belongings they'd carried from their hometowns.

Kristabel sniffed the air suspiciously. 'I thought Kanseen had arranged sanitation wagons for the district.'

Edeard shrugged, and they passed into the mansion's court, with its white statues and neat bushes growing out of long troughs. The main doors were open, leading to a hall whose ceiling shone with a perfect white light. Broad wing stairs curved up to the first-floor gallery. They were easy to walk up, just as Edeard always intended. He'd never really known what layout to adopt inside the mansion. It was the outside he was so sure of. When the moment came, he'd sketched out an internal design similar to the one that he'd disposed of, except now the lights were white, the baths were a sensible size, the beds a decent height, and so on down a long list of architectural discomforts which Makkathran citizens had worked around for two millennia.

Macsen and Kanseen were waiting in the small first-floor reception hall. They showed Kristabel and Edeard out on to the secluded balcony where wine was waiting. As were Dinlay and Gealee. For his fourth wife Dinlay had fallen for a strapping redhead. Gealee was only twenty-eight years old and an easy three inches taller than her husband of two months. Seeing them standing together beside the balustrade with the setting sun behind them, Edeard had to concentrate *really hard* on maintaining his mental shield and not letting a single emotion seep out. But all Dinlay's wives could so easily have been sisters. *He knows it never works so why does he always go for the same type?*

'Optimism,' Kristabel murmured.

Edeard turned bright red. 'Oh Lady, did I . . . ?'

'No. I just know you.' Kristabel smiled brightly and embraced Dinlay. 'Welcome back.' She kissed Gealee. 'How was the honeymoon?'

'Oh, it was just fabulous, thank you so much. The yacht you loaned us took us to so many of these fabulous little harbours. Every town along the coast is so different. And the Oantrana islands, they're lovely, so unspoilt. I had no idea they were like that. I could live on any one of them.'

Dinlay's arm went round his new bride. 'We can retire there,' he chided.

She kissed him.

Edeard gulped down some wine.

Macsen's arm went round his shoulder. 'So what did you think of our guests?' he asked, gesturing at the big open square beyond the mansion walls.

'There's a lot of them,' Edeard said, glad of the diversion. Even though the visitors were enduring less than favourable accommodation, the city still boasted an atmosphere of optimism and relief. The mental aspect drifting along every street and canal was of anticipation. It was like the night before a carnival.

'They'll be gone the day after the Skylords come,' Kanseen said.

'At which point the next wave will start to arrive,' Macsen said. 'Edeard, we can't go on ignoring this. I checked with the Guild of Clerks, there are no rooms in Makkathran left unregistered. That's intolerable. Where are our children supposed to live?'

'Nobody is ignoring it,' Edeard said. 'I've been to three meetings with the Mayor on this subject alone.'

'And what was his amazing conclusion?' Dinlay asked.

Edeard shot him a surprised look; his friend was normally more diplomatic. Maybe Gealee was different after all. 'He believes it will settle down after time. We're still experiencing an abnormally large surge of people seeking guidance. It's inevitable at the start. The numbers will decline and level off.'

'When?'

Edeard shrugged. 'It's not the people actually seeking guidance that are the problem, it's all the family members who come with them. They're the ones creating the accommodation shortage.'

'That's it? That's the Mayor's answer? Wait a few years and the problem will go away?'

'Not quite. There are a lot of stopover inns opening around Makkathran. Most of the coastal villages within a day's sail have at least one. More are opening each month. They will help.'

'I hope you're right,' Gealee said. 'My brother's children are in their twenties, they can't find anywhere in the city to live. Keral has travelled inland to see what kind of life he could have beyond the Iguru.'

'Good for him,' Edeard said. 'Too many of our children rely on the city.'

'But we've lived here for two thousand years,' Gealee complained. 'Why should we leave?'

'Things are different now,' Macsen said. 'The provinces aren't the hardship they once were. There's more than agriculture in the towns. Some of the Guild halls out there rival those in Makkathran for size and ability.'

'Then why don't the Skylords visit those towns, why is it always Makkathran?'

Edeard wanted to answer. Kanseen and Dinlay were both looking at him as though they expected a reasonable explanation. He didn't have one.

'Only Makkathran has the towers of Eyrie,' Macsen said.

That can't be right, Edeard thought. *Makkathran isn't ours. It was never built for humans.* 'I'll ask,' he blurted.

Everyone stared at him.

'Really,' he said. 'When the Skylords come, I'll ask them what they need to collect our souls. If the only place they'll visit is Makkathran's towers.'

Gealee leaned forward and gave him a quick kiss. 'Thank you, Waterwalker.'

He grinned back at her, making sure he didn't look at Kristabel. 'My pleasure.'

'This discomfort might help us,' Dinlay said.

'Discomfort?' Edeard asked.

'In Makkathran, with the stopover visitors,' Macsen explained, his face open and seemingly innocent.

'How so?'

'Discomfort breeds dissatisfaction. Everyone is going to take it out on the Mayor at the next election.'

Edeard groaned, knowing what was coming.

'The timing is good,' Kristabel said, suddenly keen. 'If you're right about the stopover inns, then the problem will reduce considerably as your term starts.'

'My term?' Edeard wanted to tell her to stop taking Macsen's side, this felt too much like he was being ganged up on. 'I'd have to get elected, first.'

'You're the Waterwalker,' Kanseen said merrily. 'Everyone will vote for you. Even the youngsters, now you've brought the Skylords back. Isn't that right, Gealee?'

'Oh yes,' she said earnestly.

Edeard added Kanseen to the list of people he couldn't look at right now. Though he wasn't sure if the barb was intended for Gealee or Dinlay. *Probably Dinlay.*

'Everyone knows it's just a matter of time,' Dinlay said.

'Do they?' Though he couldn't quite maintain the disinterested attitude. Mayor? Finally. His mind wondered back to that spring day back in Ashwell, when his ge-cats had been such a success at the new well. Mayor and Pythia, he and Salrana had promised each other. *We were children. That's all. Children laughing glibly at a childish dream.* But the idea that he could be Mayor still sent a thrill through him.

'Come on,' Macsen implored. 'This is the time and you know it. Just say the word.'

He glanced at Kristabel, who gave him a swift nod.

'All right then,' he said, and even as the words came out of his mouth he knew he could never hold in that smile of relief and anticipation. 'Let's do it.'

The others whooped and applauded, giving him hugs.

'Where in Honious do we start?' he asked. It was almost a protest.

'You leave that to me,' Dinlay said. 'I've been putting together a team for a while.'

Edeard shrugged and shook his head. It was almost as if he had no say in the matter.

*

Felax was standing in front of the thick wooden door into the Chief Constable's office. He was agitated, which was most unusual for him. 'I'm sorry,' he said as Edeard approached. 'I didn't really know how to stop her.'

Edeard gave the door a quizzical look as his farsight swept into his office. She was perched on one of the straight-backed chairs in front of his big desk. 'Oh Lady,' he muttered as dismay warred with curiosity. 'Okay,' he told Felax. 'I'll deal with this.'

Salrana turned slightly as he entered the office. Her hair was a lot shorter these days, and coloured a sandy blond. She was wearing a dark shawl over her sea-green dress, something a woman fifty years older might have on. Her big eyes regarded him with a kind of forlorn interest. After all, they hadn't been in each other's presence for over a decade. No small achievement given the number of parties they both attended. If he'd thought she might finally be relenting, that Ranalee's malign influence was waning, he was put right by the briefest flash of emotions flickering through her shield. Like him, she still couldn't disguise her mind as well as a cityborn. So there it was, the embers of distaste and resentment, burning alongside a brighter defiance. For once, though, there was uncertainty amid all that rancour.

'This is unexpected,' he said as he walked past her. He didn't pause or attempt to shake hands, nor even contemplate a platonic kiss.

Her gaze followed him as he sat down. 'Nothing's changed,' she began.

'Something must have to bring you here.'

'Call it desperation if you like. And I know you.'

Edeard really was puzzled now. All the attempts he'd made to make some kind of peace between them had always come to nothing, and there had been a great many over the decades. Even then he'd still carried on helping where he could, especially with her no-good offspring. She must have known that. 'What do you want?'

'I won't owe you anything. I won't change, I won't show gratitude.'

'I'm not asking you to. What is it you want, Salrana?'

She finally looked away, adjusting the shawl around her shoulders. 'My husband, Garnfal, he's going to accept the guidance of the Skylords. He's not been well for over a year now.'

'I'm sorry,' he said with genuine sympathy. 'I didn't know.'

'He ... he took good care of me, you know. He wasn't like some of the others.'

The ones Ranalee gave you to, he thought coldly.

'Anyway,' she continued, 'he's been making provision for me. His house in Horrod Lane goes to his eldest son Timath, of course, I wouldn't want it otherwise. But there are goods which are quite valuable, goods he bought with money he earned himself. Garnfal has left me these in his will.'

'The family doesn't want you to have them?'

'Some of it, they don't mind. But there is some land in Ivecove, that's a fishing village four miles north of the city. A cottage in a large patch of ground. Garnfal enjoyed the gardens, he said you could never have a proper garden in the city. We stayed there every summer. Then last autumn, a merchant approached him, offering to buy the land so he could build an inn there instead, he said it was to accommodate all the people coming to accept the guidance of the Skylords. Until now, Garnfal has refused.'

'And this is what Timath objects to?'

'Yes. Garnfal has given me his blessing to sell the cottage once he is dead, which will bring in an exceptional price. Timath has already engaged a lawyer to contest the will. He claims that the true price of the cottage is not reflected in Garnfal's accounts, that I am defrauding the family. He calls himself and his siblings Garnfal's true family.'

'I see.' *Both your problem, and Timath's view of this.* 'Why are you telling me this?'

'I hoped you might talk to Timath, make him see that I am not some fastfox bitch who has bewitched his father, that I love Garnfal.'

Edeard puffed his cheeks out as he exhaled a long breath. 'Salrana . . .'

'I'm not! Edeard, whatever you think of me, you must know that in this I have free will. I chose Garnfal for myself, by myself. Please, you must believe me. To be stripped of what is rightfully mine by a jealous, workshy son cannot be the justice you seek for everyone.'

'Honious,' he said weakly. 'You should have been a lawyer.'

'Timath has engaged Master Cherix.' She shrugged, and gave him a timid smile. 'If that makes any difference.'

Edeard let out a groan of defeat and tipped his head back to gaze at the high curving ceiling. 'I will speak to the Grand Master of the Lawyers Guild, ask him if he can arbitrate a settlement between you and Timath.'

'Thank you, Waterwalker.'

'I think to you I am still Edeard.'

Salrana rose to her feet, giving him a sad look. 'No, you are the Waterwalker. Edeard of Ashwell died on the day of Bise's banishment.'

At midday Edeard took a gondola from the Orchard Palace to the Abad district. As the gondola slid along the Great Major Canal he could see the crowds clustering around the base of Eyrie's towers. Nobody was going up yet, that wasn't allowed until the night before. Constables were assisting Mothers in keeping people away from the long winding stairs at the centre of each tower. No arrests had been made yet, though Edeard was getting daily reports of incidents involving frustrated relatives. In truth the ascent to the top of the towers had to be carefully managed. The platforms thrusting up into Querencia's skies had a finite area, and there were no rails around the sides. Everyone who went up was elderly and infirm; they had to be cared for even in their last hours. The Mothers were now quite experienced in overseeing the whole event, a fact which went unappreciated among those who had travelled so far, with their hope building along every aching mile.

So far this week, Edeard knew, there had been fifteen deaths among those waiting in Eyrie. Their families had to be treated with a great deal of tact and understanding. Even so tempers had flared and violence swiftly followed. To have come so far and not achieve guidance was unbearable. Understandably so. With another seven days to go, there would be more deaths, each one more excruciating to the survivors than the last.

The gondola pulled up at a platform in the middle of Abad. Edeard climbed up the steps to Mayno Street, and set off into the district. Boldar Avenue was a fifteen-minute walk from the canal, a zigzag pavement of narrow four- and five-storey cottages. Most of the lower floors had wide doorways, and were used as shops or crafthouses. He saw several that were packed full of stopover travellers.

At the far end of the street one of the largest cottages had a pair of tall apricot trees growing outside the front door, their fruit starting to swell amid the fluttering leaves. Edeard was immediately aware of the strange thoughts emanating from inside. There were over a dozen people in various rooms that his farsight could sense, yet all of them seemed to be similar somehow. All with the same emotional state. Even the rhythm of their thoughts was in harmony. The oddity was enough to make him hesitate as he faced the scarlet-painted door. Deep windows were set in the curving wall on either side, their dark curtains drawn, revealing nothing. Then he knocked.

A young woman opened it for him. She was wearing a simple black dress trimmed in white lace, with long auburn hair wound in elaborate curls before flowing halfway down her back. Her smile was generous and genuine enough. 'Waterwalker, please come in. My name is Hala. I wondered when you'd visit.'

'Why is that?' he asked as he walked in. The hall was long with an arched ceiling, splitting several times. Like a smaller version of the tunnels beneath the city. He hadn't realized the cottage was so large, it must be connected with several others along the street. He eyed the continuous strip of light along the apex of the hall. It glowed a perfect white, and he'd never asked the city to alter it.

'I admire the path you've followed,' Hala said. 'Given how alone you were, it's admirable.'

'Uh huh,' Edeard said. He wondered if she was the one whose farsight had been following him over the years.

The ground floor of the cottage was divided up into several large rooms, saloons typical of any private members' club in Makkathran. It appeared deserted apart from a few ge-chimps cleaning up.

'We're upstairs,' Hala said, and led him down the hall to a spiral stair. The steps had been adjusted for human legs.

Edeard's curiosity grew. Someone obviously had a rapport with the city similar to his own.

There were children on the second floor. It was similar to a family floor in the ziggurat, with living rooms, bathrooms, kitchens and bedrooms all jumbled together. The children laughed and peeked out at him from doorways, before shrieking and running away when he pointed at them. He counted nearly thirty.

'Are any of them yours?' he asked.

Hala smiled proudly. 'Three so far.'

The lounge on the third floor was a large one, probably the width of the entire cottage. Its curving rear wall was made up of broad archways filled with glass doors that opened on to a balcony looking out over Roseway Canal a couple of streets away, with Nightshade rising up beyond the water. The walls were embellished with a tight curvilinear pattern of claret and gold, not that much of it was visible behind long hangings of black lace; it was as if a giant spider had bound the lounge in an ebony web. For such a large room there wasn't much furniture, some muroak dressers along the walls, a couple of long tables. Rugs with a fluffy amethyst weave covered the floor. Fat chairs were scattered around, looking like clusters of cushions rather than Querencia's usual straight-backed style. The Apricot Cottage Fellowship were sitting in them, watching Edeard with interest. Fifteen of them, six women and nine men; all young, not one was over thirty. And all of them sharing that same confidence Tathal had worn so snugly at their last meeting, similar to the sons and daughters of Makkathran's Grand Families, yet with very different roots. He could feel the strength in their minds, barely restrained. Each of them was a powerful psychic, probably equal to himself.

He looked round until he found Tathal, and smiled wryly. Then he saw a couple of youngsters standing beside a door to the balcony, and his smiled broadened with comprehension. They were the two he'd caught a glimpse of in the tunnel. 'Ah,' he said. 'The nest, I presume.'

Jaralee had told him of the name when she and Golbon presented their report. They'd arrived in his office soon after Salrana had departed, radiating a giddy mixture of alarm and excitement which he found slightly unnerving. His investigators were normally unflappable.

'You were right,' Golbon said. 'The Fellowship have business interests everywhere. So many I'm going to need a month just to compile them all.'

'How is that relevant?' Edeard asked. 'They have a lot of members now.' *Including Natran*, he thought miserably.

'Ah,' Jaralee said with a superior smile. 'To anyone on the outside it resembles a standard enough commercial association. Makkathran has hundreds; the successful and most established ones are the guilds, of course, but the merchant classes have a lot of powerful organizations and clubs. We all assumed this was just the newest, formed by some ambitious younger entrepreneurs hungry for influence. But when I looked at it closely there is a core that have joint-ownership and part-ownership of over a hundred ventures and businesses. The other members are just a seclusion haze of legitimacy wrapped round them.'

'Not quite,' Golbon interjected. 'The core members have commercial ties to a lot of other members' interests.'

'They've created a very complicated financial web,' Jaralee said. 'And from what I've seen it extends a long way beyond the city. I've lodged enquiries with registry clerks in Iguru townships and provincial capitals. Only a few have answered so far, but the nest's dealings certainly stretch to ventures outside Makkathran. Collectively, I'd say they're a match for a Grand Family estate, certainly in financial size. Could be larger if they have an equal illegitimate side, I don't really know.'

'Nest?' Edeard enquired.

'That's what the Fellowship's founders are known as. They're a tight-knit group. People who know them try to avoid saying anything about them. In fact it's quite spooky how they'll try and slide off the subject. I have virtually nothing on any of them apart from hearsay.'

'So what's the hearsay?'

'They really do act like brothers and sisters, they're that close.'

'Are you sure they're not?'

'As sure as I can be. The majority seem to have come from the provinces, but three or four are cityborn. They started to band together seven or eight years ago. That's when they registered a residency claim on Apricot Cottage. The Fellowship itself began a year later.'

'Was Tathal one of the originals?' Edeard asked. The convoluted finances the nest had surrounded themselves with sounded like something Bise would concoct. And he was sure Ranalee made an excellent tutor.

'Yes, his name's on the residency application for the cottage.'

'All right, so what about Colfal?'

Jaralee smiled happily again. 'His herbalist shop is on the way down. It's getting so bad he hasn't even filed his tax statement this year, which is a big risk. The inspector is getting ready for compulsory submission proceedings. I checked round his usual suppliers. He's made some bad decisions lately. Income is drying up. The finance houses are asking for payment.'

'So Colfal is in desperate need of a new partner, especially one who has a lot of cash,' Edeard observed.

'True,' she agreed. 'But Colfal has been a herbalist for over seventy years. It's only this last year he's started to make bad decisions.'

'That's what seventy years of smoking kestric does to a brain,' Golbon remarked.

'These are really bad decisions,' Jaralee countered. 'He's been changing his normal stock for stuff that hardly anyone buys.'

'Who did he get the new herbs from?' Edeard asked sharply.

She nodded agreement. 'I'm looking into it. This can't be done quickly.'

Standing in the Apricot Cottage's lounge, facing the nest, Edeard finally knew that legal details like who bought what from whom were of no consequence whatsoever. The nest were very different to Buate; they weren't going to be blocked by any tax investigation.

'It's not a term we favour,' Tathal said in amusement. 'But it does seem to have caught hold.'

A multitude of fast thoughts flashed through the air around

Edeard. The nest were all communicating with each other, it was like the swift birdsong of a complex gifting. Except Edeard couldn't comprehend any of it. Real unease began to stir in his mind.

'I'm surprised,' he said, keeping the tone level, affable. 'Nobody wants to say much about any of you.'

'We discourage attention,' one of the women said. She was sitting to Tathal's left, covered in a deep purple shawl of thick wool. It didn't disguise her pregnancy.

The constant flow of mental twittering shifted for a moment, purifying. 'Samilee,' Edeard said abruptly, as if he'd know her for years, even thought she was only twenty-three, and her current favourite food was scrambled Qotox eggs with béarnaise sauce and a toasted muffin. The cravings were quite pronounced with only five weeks to go until her due date. Her son's father was either Uphal or Johans.

Edeard shivered in reaction to the knowledge.

'Welcome Waterwalker,' she replied formally.

Thoughts swirled again, as if the lacework shadows were in motion around the lounge.

'Can you blame us?' That was Halan. Twenty-eight years old, and so delighted to have found a home in the city after a decade and a half of unbearable loneliness in Hapturn province. His exemplary financial aptitude placed him in charge of the nest's principal businesses.

'Look what the establishment tried to do to you when you showed them your ability,' Johans said. Twenty-nine, and a very conscientious follower of city fashion, he designed many of his own clothes, and those of the nest's male members. Three of the most renowned outfitters in Lillylight district belonged to him. Their original families had been eased out in that way the nest specialized in.

'A whole regiment deployed with the sole intent of killing you in cold blood,' Uphal remarked. Their chief persuader, the one who whispered strongly to the weak, the inferior who swarmed the city like vermin.

'History,' Edeard told them. 'A history I evolved so that we could all live together no matter what our talents and abilities.'

'That *they* can live together,' Kiary and Manel sneered in unison. The young lovers, who had such a fun, wild time in the tunnels and elsewhere in the city: the Mayor's oval sanctum, the altar of the Lady's church, Edeard and Kristabel's big bed on the tenth floor of . . .

Tathal snapped his fingers in irritation as Edeard turned to glower at them.

'Enough,' Tathal chided. Tathal, the first to realize his dawning power, the gatherer of lost frightened kindred, the nurturer, the teacher, the nest father. Father to seventeen of their impressive second generation.

'Oh Ladycrapit,' Edeard muttered under his breath. He hadn't been this scared for a long long time. Decades. And even then he'd had youthful certainty on his side.

'So you see, Waterwalker,' Tathal said. 'Like you, we are Querencia's future.'

'I don't see that at all.'

'You said that you thought stronger psychics were emerging as a sign of human maturity in the Void,' Halan said.

'What?'

'I talked to Kanseen once,' Hala said with a dreamy smile. 'She has such fond thoughts of you, a little thread of longing never extinguished. I believe that's why she recalls your time in the Jeavons squad together so clearly even after all this time. Back then, after your triumphant day of banishment you told her that was your reason to enlist Marcol as a constable, to tame him, to bind him to your vision. You saw the strong emerging from the masses, that's very prophetic. We respect that.'

'And you've been keeping an eye out for others of strength ever since,' Uphal said. 'Bringing them into the establishment. The establishment whose throne you've claimed. Indoctrinating them with your ideals.'

'But that was then,' Tathal said. 'When the strong were few, and afraid. Now our numbers are growing. Soon there will be enough of us that we can emerge from the shadows without fear. One day, all humans will be as us. As you.'

'Really?'

'You doubt your own beliefs? Or do you dare not put a voice to them? You know we are right. For we are here, are we not?'

'What exactly do you see yourselves becoming?' Edeard asked.

The nest's thoughts swirled round him again, faster than ever. This time he knew their amusement, tinged with derision, perhaps even a scent of disappointment. The great Waterwalker: not so impressive after all.

'We are the children of today's people,' Tathal said. 'And as with all children, one day we will inherit the world from our parents.'

'Okay,' Edeard cleared his throat. 'But I don't think you're the type to wait patiently.'

'We are simply readying ourselves for every eventuality,' Tathal said. 'I do not delude myself that the transition will be smooth and peaceful, for it is never a pleasant realization that your evolution has ended and a new order is replacing you.'

'Unbelievable,' Edeard shook his head wearily. 'A revolution. You're going to replace the Grand Council with your own followers. Is that the best you can do?'

'We have no intention of replacing the Grand Council. Can you not understand what we are? We don't need to make the kind of empty political promises which Rah made to the masses, his ludicrous democracy. He knew the right of it when he established the families of the District Masters. That was where he expected our true strength to emerge. The Grand Families tried: for centuries they have chosen their bloodstock on the basis of psychic strength. But we have supplanted them as the true heirs of Rah. Evolution is inevitable, yet it is also random. Isn't that utterly wonderful?'

'So the weak don't get a say in the world you control.'

'They can join with us,' Uphal said. 'If their thoughts are bright enough, they will belong. That's what we are, a union of pure thought, faster and more resolute than any debating chamber full of the greedy and corrupt that rules every town and city. It is democracy on a level beyond the reach of the weak. Your children will be a part of it, especially the twins. Marilee and Analee are already open and honest with each other, that is a big part of what we are, what we offer. It's a wondrous life; nobody alone, nobody frightened. And there are more of us out there, more than you know, Waterwalker.'

Edeard gave him a thin smile. 'I suggest you don't threaten my family. I suggest that quite strongly.'

'I'm not threatening anyone.'

'Really? I've seen how you use dominance to bind people, to deny them free will. That's how you've come this far. Control seems to be what you're actually about.'

Tathal grinned. 'How is your campaign for Mayor coming along? Dinlay is putting an election team together for you, isn't he? Always the loyal one, Dinlay. His admiration for you verges on worship. Do you discourage that?'

'If I become Mayor it will be because the people who live in this city say I can. And when that mandate is over, I will step down.'

'Your nobility is part of your appeal. To their kind.'

'You talk as if you're different. You're not.'

'But we are, and you know it. And to make your guilt burn even brighter, you belong with us.'

'Dominance is psychic assault. It is illegal as well as immoral. I want you to stop using it against other people. You can start with Colfal.'

Kiary and Manel laughed derisively. '*This* is why we're cautious? Come on, he's an old man we can squash like ge-chimp crap.'

Tathal waved them into silence. 'Don't do that,' he said to Edeard. 'Don't fall back on righteous indignation, it does not become you. You were the first. You have a duty to your own kind. You are the bridge between us and the others. If you want to retain your self-respect, your grandeur, you will work with us. Continue as that bridge. People trust you, they will need your reassurance that what is happening here is inevitable. You are essential for the transition, Waterwalker. You cannot stop us, we are nature. Destiny. Help us. Or do you consider yourself above that?'

Edeard held up a warning finger, grimly aware of how pathetic that must appear to the nest. 'Stop interfering with other people's lives; leave their minds alone. You are not their superiors. We are all . . .'

'One nation?' Tathal enquired; the mockery was palpable.

Edeard turned and left the room. He was somewhat surprised he was still alive and allowed to do so.

*

Mirnatha was in the ziggurat when a shaken Edeard arrived home. He'd completely forgotten she was visiting. She was up on the tenth floor, along with Olbal, her husband, and their children. Kristabel was on the floor in the private lounge entertaining the two toddlers while the older ones were playing with Marakas and Rolar's children in the big playroom on the other side of the ziggurat. The children's excited laughter and squealing echoed down the vast stairwell, causing him to smile regretfully as he climbed the last few stairs. He passed the short corridor leading to his bedroom, and gave the closed door a pensive look. Kiary and Manel creeping in unseen to have their dirty little thrill was far too much like the time Mirnatha had been kidnapped. *Too many memories*, he told himself.

By the time he reached the main lounge he'd managed to compose himself and strengthen his mental shield. He smiled widely as Mirnatha rushed across to kiss him effusively, then he shook hands warmly with Olbal. Everyone had been surprised when Mirnatha had married him. She'd spent her teens and twenties enjoying every delight and excitement the city could offer a supremely eligible Grand Family daughter. Then suddenly Olbal had come to town and the next thing Julan, Kristabel and Edeard knew was her engagement being announced, and a wedding six weeks later in Caldratown, the capital of Joxla province. Kristabel had worried it would never last. Edeard had a little more confidence. He rather liked his brother-in-law, who owned a huge farming and woodland estate in Joxla province, to the north of the Donsori mountains. Olbal didn't care much for the city and its politics and its society events, he was a practical man, whose brain was occupied with agricultural management and food market prices. Such a man offered the kind of stability Mirnatha needed. And here they were, still together thirty years down the line with nine children.

'So what's new?' Mirnatha asked as she settled back into a sofa and reclaimed her tea-cup from a ge-chimp.

Edeard hesitated. *You really don't want to know that.* 'Not much. Still being bullied.'

Mirnatha clapped her hands delightedly. 'Excellent. Well done, sis. Keep them on a short leash, I say.'

Edeard and Olbal exchanged a martyred look.

'We've said nothing, but he's finally going to run for Mayor,' Kristabel said.

'Really?' Olbal asked, intrigued.

'It's all down to timing,' Edeard explained.

'Will you change anything?'

Not me. But my word doesn't count for much now. He looked at Alfal and Fanlol, the two toddlers, and smiled grimly. 'I think things are pretty good as they are now. I'll try and keep them that way.' His third hand poked playfully at Alfal as the boy banged an old wooden cart against a chair leg. Alfal turned around, a mischievous smile on his sweet little face, and pushed back with his third hand. The force was surprisingly strong: in fact, very strong indeed for a three-year-old.

'He's a tough one, my little man,' Mirnatha said adoringly. 'But then they all are. That's what growing up in the fresh air does to you. You two should spend more time outside the city.'

'I'd love to,' Edeard said. 'I always wanted to take a long voyage across the sea to find some new continents.'

'Like Captain Allard, hey?' Olbal asked. 'Now that would be quite something. I might even join you.'

'Over my dead body,' Mirnatha said.

'Families would be voyaging with us,' Edeard told her reasonably. 'After all, it would take years.'

'What? Including the children?'

He shrugged. 'Why not?'

'There aren't any ships that big,' Kristabel said.

'So we build them.'

'A fleet,' Olbal said. 'I like that idea.'

Kristabel and Mirnatha looked at each other. 'Man dreams,' Mirnatha exclaimed. 'It'll never happen.'

After dinner Olbal asked Edeard for a moment together, and they went out on to the hortus. Ku and Honious were both bright in the night sky, Honious in particular, with its bulbous ruby clouds braided by sulphurous wisps surrounding a dark centre where lost souls were said to fall. People were taking it as a bad omen that it was sharing the night with the Skylords. They were just visible above the horizon, five scintillations, growing steadily larger each night.

Edeard eyed them carefully. Normally he'd be excited and content at their impending arrival, but now he knew the true nature of the nest he couldn't help but feel the doomsayers might be right.

'Are you all right?' Olbal asked.

'Yeah, sorry. Just distracted by this whole Mayor thing.'

'That I can understand. Rather you than me.'

Edeard gave him a false grin. 'What was it you wanted to ask?'

'Ah.' Olbal leant on the thick rail, and looked out across the Grand Central canal. 'I know this sounds stupid, that I'm probably making a big fuss of nothing.'

'But?'

'My nephew, Constatin, he arrived in Makkathran three weeks ago. He was here to negotiate with merchants directly this year, agreeing a price for this season's apples and pears. We normally deal with Garroy, of the Linsell family; and I wanted to keep that arrangement going.'

'I know the Linsell family, they bring a lot of fruit to Makkathran's markets.'

'Yes, well . . . the thing is, Constatin has disappeared.'

'Are you sure you didn't just miss him on the road?'

'He was with Torran. It was Torran who told me he didn't come back one day.'

'Okay. What happened?'

'It was a Tuesday. Constatin had arranged to meet Garroy for lunch at the Blue Fox off Golden Park to thrash out the new deal.'

'I know it,' Edeard said stiffly.

'He never got there. Garroy called at Torran's inn that evening wanting to know what happened. He wasn't there. Torran searched for a day and a half before going to the Ysidro Constable Station. There wasn't much they could do, but the desk sergeant promised he'd keep his farsight stretched. Since then, we've heard nothing.'

'I see.'

'I didn't think there were any gangs in Makkathran these days.'

'There aren't,' Edeard said flatly. It *was* strange. But then several station captains had mentioned the number of missing people reported over the last couple of years had risen slightly. It was to be expected given how many visitors Makkathran was receiving, and how unfamiliar they were with the city streets.

'It was morning, Edeard, broad daylight. What could have befallen him? Torran checked the hospitals, and even the cemetery.'

Edeard put his hand on Olbal's shoulder, trying to push through a sensation of reassurance. 'I'll speak with the station captain. I doubt it was a priority for them, at the least I can rectify that.'

'Thank you, Edeard, I hate to use family like this, but my sister is badly worried. He is an only son.'

'That's okay.' Edeard frowned, thinking about what else he should be asking. Mysteries like this were rarities in Makkathran.

There was only one person he knew who solved such strange puzzles, but that was ridiculous, she was nothing but a figment of his bizarre dreams. However, she used a method of elimination to determine suspects, and gathering all possible information was essential to that method. 'You said you wanted to deal with the merchants directly this year. Is that unusual?'

'Not really. I normally use their agents, they have them in every province. And Garroy visits us every few years to keep up a personal contact; I have dinner with him whenever I'm in town. You need that level of trust if you are in business.'

'So what's different, why send Constatin here this time?'

'I was contacted by some new merchants seeking to buy our produce. They were offering a good price, a very good price.'

'Is that bad?'

'No. And I fully expect to sell them a substantial percentage of our crop. However, I want to maintain our trade with the Linsell family; they are a reliable buyer, and the future is what I must look to, especially with so many children.' He smiled fondly. 'New merchants come and new merchants go. Constatin was sent partly as reassurance that although we obviously wanted to squeeze the price up we would not abandon the Linsell family.'

'Who are the new merchants?' Edeard asked. He was getting a bad feeling about this.

'They worked for a supplier here in the city called Uphal.'

'What's the matter?' Kristabel asked. She was sitting up in bed, watching Edeard pull his silk pyjamas on. 'And don't say: nothing. You've been quiet since you got back this afternoon.'

'Yeah,' he said, and rolled on to the bed. The walls remembered nothing, Kiary and Manel had taken away the memory usually contained within the city's substance. He was going to have to find out how to do that for himself. 'Sorry, but it's not good news.'

'I'm a big girl.'

He smirked. For once she was wearing a sheer black negligee with a plunging neck. Even after seven children she was still slim, and with her hair worn loose, very alluring. And she knew it. There was a calculating smile playing across her lips.

'I'll bear that in mind,' he said, giving her figure an openly admiring look.

'Did somebody die?'

'No. There are some psychics in Makkathran who are at least as strong as I am. And there's a lot of them.'

'Oh. But you've found plenty of powerful psychics over the years; there's Marcol, and Jenovan, and what's that new girl who came to you last year?'

'Vikye. No, darling. What they're doing is a lot bigger than anything we can handle.'

'Why, what are they doing?'

'Same thing Ranalee and One Nation were trying. Except this isn't about establishing good snobbish blood as overlords, this is about strength pure and simple. If you're a strong psychic that means you have the right to rule everyone else.'

'There's a lot of us to try and quash.'

'I know, and that's what frightens me the most. Owain had guns and fear to keep people in line, the nest have dominance, which they haven't been afraid to use. They also have the same skill I have with the city.'

Kristabel gave him a sober look. 'Oh. If their strength comes from numbers, then you pick them off one at a time.'

'Won't work,' he said apologetically. 'They call themselves a nest for a reason. They're like a family of the mind. It's quite weird to see them together. Back when old Chae was training us he made sure our farsight was always aware of where the others of the squad were. The nest have a more sophisticated version of that technique. I'd never be able to isolate one of them.'

'Ladycrapit, what are you going to do?'

'I don't know. But they're young and they want to forge ahead in their own fashion. They've never learned how to accommodate other people because they've never had to; if they're allowed to carry on the way they are they never will. That means I might have a small opening.'

'To do what?'

'They asked me to be a bridge, between them and the "weaker" people.'

'Weaker?' she snapped indignantly.

'Yes. That's their way of thinking. That's what has to be broken.'

'Do you really think you can do that? Edeard, I know we never talk about Owain and Buate and all the others that vanished, and I never asked, but ... You couldn't make them change their minds, could you?'

'No,' he sighed. 'But this time I really have to try.' *Lady, but I don't want to have to do that kind of thing again.*

'So they share their thoughts all the time?'

'Sort of. They claim it's a development of democracy. They're still all individuals, but for decision-making they communicate on a very deep level, they have their own mental language. I suspect that's how they overcome anyone else with strength. They can gang up in perfect union. And the more they embrace, the stronger they become.' He'd been intrigued by that union they had ever since the encounter. To share thoughts so easily must be a wonderful thing, except they'd perverted it, using dominance to rid the concept of all equality. He suspected Tathal to be the cause of that. If the nest could have started without that malign influence it might have had a chance to develop in a positive, beneficial manner. After all, he'd concluded years ago that psychic abilities in the newer generations were significantly higher than among his own age. People were changing, adapting to their easier life.

Kristabel gave him a worried look. 'Embrace or get subsumed?'

'Good question. Dominance isn't my specialty, and the Lady knows I never found out how to reverse it.'

'No,' she growled.

'The one good thing is the way they've covered their tracks and set about amassing wealth.'

'How can that be good?'

'It shows they aren't that different to the rest of us after all. They chase after wealth and power just like everyone.'

'Taralee doesn't,' Kristabel said immediately. 'And you're the ultimate champion of democracy. After all, you could have been emperor.'

'Yes, but . . . Once you become part of the nest you become part of what they are, what they aim for.'

Kristabel wrinkled her nose up. 'A blatant psychic aristocracy.'

'Yes. And then what happens to those who won't or can't become a part of it? They lack any signs of compassion.'

She stroked a hand across his cheek. 'Poor Edeard. You have to find a way.'

'Easily said.'

'If you can't, who will?'

'I know. At least they've offered to listen to me.' *Which wasn't quite what Tathal had said.*

'Are they really stronger than you?'

'Who knows? Individually, I expect we're about the same. Though Marcol certainly panicked when he was trying to contain Tathal. It's this union of theirs that has me worried.'

Kristabel was frowning as she considered what he was telling her. 'It sounds like Tathal is the leader.'

'He is.'

'But if they have this mental democracy, surely they wouldn't need a leader. If he's as strong as you think, especially when it comes to dominance, isn't this nest just another gang with him as the boss? The rest of them won't even know, they just think they have free will. That's always the worst aspect of dominance, how the victim just embraces it.'

'They did seem to be contributing to the union. But to be honest, I couldn't interpret any of their combined thoughts.'

'He's the key, isn't he, this Tathal?'

'I think so. But the chances of me ever getting him by himself are slim.'

'He was on his own when Marcol confronted him.'

'Yeah. You're right.'

She grinned. 'Of course I am.'

'So, perhaps you wouldn't mind telling me how I watch someone who knows I'm going to be looking for an opportunity, and is in control of the city the same way I am.'

'You're the Waterwalker.' She pulled him closer, arms twining round his neck. 'You tell me.'

*

'You did it,' Salrana said. 'I didn't believe you could, or you would. I suppose . . . Thank you, Edeard. I mean that.'

'Timath has withdrawn his objection?' a surprised Edeard asked. He'd completely forgotten, hadn't even talked to the Grand Master of the Lawyers Guild.

'Yes. It's all over. Once Garnfal accepts the Skylord's guidance, his estate passes to me.'

'I see. That's wonderful news. Er, did Timath say why he wasn't going to challenge the will?'

'Not really. Just that he'd changed his mind.'

'Okay. I'm glad for you, really I am.'

Changed his mind, my arse, Edeard thought. *The nest couldn't have been more blatant if they'd bludgeoned Timath with a wooden club. They want me to know. They want to see what I'll do.*

*

It was surprisingly easy to work out some of Tathal's possible weaknesses. Edeard put Argain on tracking down Constatin's final movements. The constables at Ysidro Station might not have made much of an effort (and why should they?) but if he'd left any trace, any impression with people along his route to the Blue Fox, then Argain would find it. Edeard at least expected

Argain to find out roughly at which point he'd vanished, the street at least. That would mean he could check the memory within the city structure. Any gaps would be as incriminating as seeing Constatin being abducted by members of the nest.

His second possibility was the other missing people. Golbon and Jaralee had been bemused at first. It was an odd request, seeing if they could tie in anyone who had gone missing during the last few years to the nest's business deals, but they soon set to cross-referencing files. It was what they excelled at, and they had begun to enjoy the scent of the chase again. They even talked about bringing back other members of the old committee.

That just left the last two leads. They were the ones he needed to follow personally. And without a great deal of surprise, his first one only took three hours to confirm. After all, a station captain led a busy life. Especially Dinlay, who structured his days with meetings and inspections and appointments with civic notorieties and even made sure he went out on patrol with his officers three times a week. That left his wife with a lot of time to fill during the day.

Edeard floated in the middle of a transport tube, eyes closed, drifting along slowly as he kept pace with Gealee. She moved through Lillylight's central streets, wandering in and out of shops. Midmorning was taken up with meeting her girlfriends in a coffee house, for gossip and admiring each other's morning purchases. Edeard didn't use farsight, rather he pulled the images directly from the city's substance, feeling the weight of her high heels walk along, receiving the splash of colour her bright orange and black coat made amid the throng, hearing her voice growing sharp with shopgirls, the scent of her perfume wafting through the air. Then just before midday she walked over Steen Canal into Abad, where she went into one of the little cylindrical cottages behind the Jarcon family's mansion. It was the home of the family's second farrier, a hulking twenty-three-year-old with thick ebony hair that tumbled down over his shoulders. Gealee particularly liked twining her fingers through that hair while her lusty beau pounded away on top of her on the bed, on the lounge floor, on the awkward stairs . . .

'Missing your honeymoon already?' Edeard asked.

Gealee didn't start or feign surprise when he emerged from the shadows of a deep alcove on Spinwell Lane, a dark narrow passage barely a couple of yards wide in some places. She was using it as a quiet shortcut back to Steen Canal.

Instead she took the moment to adjust her wide-brimmed hat. 'Did you enjoy watching?' she retorted.

'Not really. Dinlay is one of my oldest friends.'

'And I'm his wife. I am quite devoted in that respect. He wants for nothing, I assure you.'

'Did Tathal tell you to make sure of that? Did you even have a choice?'

Her lips pushed together into a pout as she gave him a shrewd glance. 'Clever,' she said with a reluctant sigh. 'But then I never did think you got to be Waterwalker by brute strength alone. How did you know?'

'Tathal knew I was going to put myself forward for Mayor. I trust the people Dinlay has spoken to about making up my team, just as I trust Dinlay and the Master and Mistress of Sampalok. That leaves you.'

'Well done. But it doesn't really help you, does it?'

'I'm not sure. How do you think Dinlay will react when I tell him you used domination on him?'

Gealee laughed. 'Oh but we didn't, that's the beauty of it. I'm his type. You know that well enough, you've seen all his wives and the girlfriends between. All we needed to do was put me in the same room as him, and wait. It was inevitable. Actually, he's quite endearing – for someone his age. So dedicated, to the rule of law, to you.'

'You leave Dinlay alone. Do you understand?'

'You want me to leave him? To break his heart? Once more?'

'I want you to wait a decent interval until he realizes he's made another mistake.'

'Why don't you just tell him? A true friend would.' She tilted her head to one side, regarding him thoughtfully. 'You don't know what to do about us, do you? Which means you know you can't defeat us.'

'You're the ones who think in those terms.'

'We're the same as you. The only difference is that we're family, not loners. Why don't you join us? You know we're the future. Why else are so many of us appearing? It is our time. You can't argue against that. But you can play such a large part in birthing a new world, a new way of life. That's what you were sent here to do, that's why you're the first: to lead the way.'

'We cannot split society between those who have and those who don't. People the Lady has blessed with an exceptional talent have a duty to use it for the greater benefit. I've seen what happens when the ruling group begins to think only of itself. You weren't even born, but that's what Makkathran was like when I arrived. Your way of thinking isn't the future, it's the dead past. You have despoiled your gift; that is what I will end.'

Her smile became cold. '*Join us.*'

The command was so strong Edeard's eyes actually watered. It was like having a needle of ice penetrate his brain. 'Ladyfuck.' He staggered backwards, struggling to shield his mind.

Gealee made no move, no attempt to follow up her demand. 'You see, Waterwalker? That was just me, and I'm not even the strongest of us. Do you really think *anyone* can resist the entire nest?'

He shook the stupor from his head, staring at her with a mixture of anger and fright.

'Now you've found out what I am, I can hardly spy on you any more,' she said in a chillingly level tone. 'I'm going to return to the nest now. You're Dinlay's friend, you tell him why he doesn't have a wife any more.' She adjusted her orange and black coat, and walked off down the alley, her heels making loud *clicks* on the pavement.

Edeard watched her go, still shaken. His trembling palm wiped cold sweat from his brow. *So much for using her to expose a weakness.* But it did illustrate the kind of lengths the nest would go to in order to find out what he was doing, what he was capable of. And he had one ability left, of which they had no clue. The ultimate sanction. *If I have to use it, I won't be so brutal as before. I'll go back and try to reason with Tathal, to persuade him to share his talent before he becomes a selfish power-seeker.* Somehow the notion didn't leave him feeling as confident as it should have. Mainly because there was only one person left to ask about the origin of the nest's leader. He really didn't want to do that. But there weren't a whole lot of choices left.

*

With three days left until the Skylords arrived, the throng around the towers of Eyrie was so tightly packed that any movement within the district was becoming difficult. Some families resolutely refused to move on, setting up camp with enough food to see themselves through the duration. Constables struggled to keep pathways open. Mothers and their Novices suffered abuse for not allowing the eager aspirants up into the towers. The Mayor's appeals for calm and tolerance went completely unheeded. After all, none of the visitors had voted for him, or even against him. He wasn't their authority figure.

Edeard sat under a canvas awning and wove a seclusion haze around himself as his gondolier sailed past the edge of the district. It was early evening, and the smell of food cooking on open fires trickled across the canal. Open fires were of course banned in Makkathran. He gritted his teeth and ignored the violations. *Something* was going to have to be done about the stopover visitors before the next Skylords arrived. But right now he had something a lot more important, not to mention personal.

The gondola travelled the length of Great Major Canal to Forest Pool. Edeard alighted at a mooring platform. He could just see the ships berthed at the docks, their sails furled amid a forest of rigging. Natran had confided to him that the number of passengers his ships were bringing in for guidance had risen sevenfold over the last eighteen months. Some fleet captains were talking about commissioning a whole new class of ship, one without any cargo holds, just to bring people in from the furthest coastal cities.

There were times when Edeard believed half of Querencia's population was on the move to Makkathran so they might ascend from the towers. He watched the ships for a while before admitting to himself he was just finding excuses. So he turned his back on the docks and walked into Myco.

The House of Blue Petals was open, but this early in the evening there were hardly any customers. As always, there were two burly men on the big front door. They gave him a very surprised look when he walked past them, but said nothing. He sensed their urgent direct longtalk up to the office above.

His third hand pushed the door open. He wondered just how many times he'd come to this place over the years. How many confrontations had there been now? Weariness and malice mingled to produce a rogue thought: *I should just demolish this place, get the city to make a park.* But the nest would likely reverse the action.

Ranalee was waiting. Hair perfectly styled in narrow curves; wearing a long pale-grey dress of fine-knit wool. The soft fabric clung to her, revealing a belly heavy from the fifth month of pregnancy.

It was a sight which brought Edeard up short. All the words he'd rehearsed, ready to snap at her, withered away.

She caught his surprise and smiled complacently. 'Dear Edeard, is something the matter?'

'I ... didn't know.' He waved a hand towards her, embarrassed, mainly at himself.

'And why should you? You have a city to run.' She poured some wine and held the glass out to him. 'It's a lovely Sousax, try it; I can't have any myself, not in this delicate condition.'

'No thank you.'

'Afraid I'm trying to poison you?'

He sighed. 'No.'

Her smile turned mocking and she let out a theatrical moan

as she sank down into a long settee. 'Then why are you here? Kristabel not interested in you any more? I have several truly lovely girls at the moment, they're all very discreet.'

'Don't push me, Ranalee.'

'I'm trying to be helpful.'

'Then tell me about Tathal.'

Her glance slipped down to her full belly. 'What about him?'

'Did you ever . . .' Then he realized why she was looking at her unborn, and groaned. 'Oh Lady, it's not?'

'Of course it's his.' Her hand touched the bulge fondly. 'He is stronger than you in so many ways. My own deceits were nothing before him; he saw through me so easily, swifter than you ever did. But he forgave me, he allowed me to join the nest, and in return I taught him my art.'

Edeard examined what he could of her thoughts shimmering beneath a thick shield. The gaps were the tops of chasms opening into darkness. It was as if her head was filled with ebony shadow. That wasn't Ranalee. 'He used domination on you.'

Her smile was one of sensual recollection. The shadows began to take shape, revealing themselves as the nest members. They engulfed her, obliterating sight, sound. She couldn't move, couldn't cry out. Then she was suddenly no longer alone in the darkness, *he* was there with her, fear was surpassed by consummate pleasure. She welcomed it, turning to the source, weeping her gratitude. 'It was so exciting, to see all I'd hoped for finally come to pass. His strength is intoxicating, Edeard. He is raw, like you used to be; but not the shackled fool that you were. He is free and unafraid. My child will be as glorious as his father.'

'That's not you talking.'

'Wrong as always, Edeard. I didn't need the encouragement the others of the nest received. My thoughts already ran along these paths. He held my hand and took me *exactly* where I wanted to go. That was a kindness you never showed.'

'So you taught him domination.'

'He already knew. I simply showed him subtlety where all he had before was crude strength.'

'Lady! Do you have any idea what you've helped create? What you've let loose on the rest of us?'

Her hands tightened on the bulge. 'Yes,' she hissed. 'I'm not blinded by him Edeard, I'm not like the rest of the nest. I admire him. I belong with him, he knows that, why else would he take me as consort? My child will be a part of Querencia's future, a big part.' She laughed. 'Perhaps he will even be stronger than his father.'

'Your dream,' he said brokenly. 'But he's taken it for his own.'

'Join us, Edeard,' she said, leaning forward eagerly. 'This could be your moment, your real triumph.'

He turned and walked for the door. 'You know the answer to that.'

'Yes.' She paused. 'Thankfully, not all of your family is as stupid and reactionary as you.'

He stopped, knowing he was doing exactly as she wanted. A puppet to her manipulations again. 'What do you mean?'

Her answer was a triumphant smile. 'I told you once, we would have your blood.'

'What have you done?'

'I have done nothing. But all children leave their parents behind eventually. You know this in your heart.'

People turned round to look in astonishment as the Waterwalker slid up through the solid pavement of Boldar Avenue. None of them said anything, none of them moved. They simply watched as he strode purposefully to the door of Apricot Cottage, his black cloak flapping as if a hurricane was blowing. Only then did he notice their placid interest, the identical calmness. The residents of Boldar Avenue belonged to the nest.

Edeard sensed them inside, upstairs in the big lounge. Marilee and Analee were with them, their thoughts content, fluttering with excitement. Not quite their thoughts as they used to be.

Enraged, Edeard's third hand smashed down the front door. He marched up the stairs.

Tathal had a knowing smile on his lips as Edeard burst into

the lounge. It was echoed by the faces of the nest. Marilee and Analee wore it, too. They were standing on either side of Tathal; Marilee with her head resting on his shoulder, Analee with her arm around his waist.

'Undo it,' Edeard demanded.

Tathal gave Analee an indolent look, then glanced round at Marilee. 'No,' he said. Marilee smiled adoringly up at him.

'I will destroy you.'

'If you could, you would have done so by now. This was all the proof I needed. Besides, your daughters were almost a part of us already. They had learned to share.'

'Don't be cross, Daddy,' Marilee urged.

'Be happy for us.'

'This is so wonderful.'

'Belonging like this.'

'Now everyone can share and grow like we always did.'

'Everyone will be happy together.'

Tears threatened to clog Edeard's eyes. 'You did this to them.'

'We are together,' Tathal said. 'We are happy.'

'Because you tell everyone to be.' Edeard was certain he wouldn't stand a chance against them if he went on the offensive. That didn't leave him much choice.

'Please Waterwalker, join us, join me, you and I are equals. As Mayor, you can make the transition so smooth, so painless.'

'Not a chance, as the Lady is my witness.'

Tathal took a slow step forwards. 'You've already done it once.'

'What?'

'I've been so curious. Exactly what is your power? Is it more than communing with the city? We all have that now.'

'Give this up,' Edeard said. 'Now. I will not ask again.'

'So curious.' He took another step forwards. 'You know you cannot defeat us, yet you make threats. I see through you. You believe, you truly believe you have the upper hand.' He cocked his head to one side, regarding Edeard in fascination. 'What is it? What have I not got?'

'My daughters first.'

'I saw something when I studied you at Colfal's shop. There was a certainty about you, a confidence that I've never seen in anyone before. You think yourself unassailable. Why?'

It was all Edeard could do not to shrink away as Tathal moved closer still; it was like a kitten being stalked by a fil-rat. 'Let. Them. Go. Free.'

'I've already seen what happens if you win,' Tathal murmured.

'What?'

'Your words. Spoken in the seconds before you slaughtered Owain and his conspirators. I have watched the memory of the chamber below the Spiral Tower many times. You were impressively brutal, Waterwalker. Even Mistress Florrel was ripped apart by that frightening gun. An old woman; though not a harmless one, I imagine. But what did you mean by that? I have been sorely puzzled. You spoke as if you'd seen the future.'

Edeard said nothing, he was too shocked by the revelation of his dreadful act being uncovered.

'Is that it?' Tathal asked. 'Is that your secret? Your timesense?' A frown creased his handsome young face. 'But no. If you could see the future, you would know what I am, what I am to become.'

'You are to become nothing.'

'What are you?'

Edeard screamed as the question seared its way into his brain, falling like acid on every nerve fibre. He *had* to confess. Every one of the nest had joined their minds to Tathal's, offering their strength to the compulsion. Third hands closed around him, crushing his body, suffocating him. Their thoughts began to seep into his mind, corroding his free will.

He didn't have time to be neat and clever, nor did he have the time to summon up the focus to go far. He thought of when he was free, they allowed him that, the moments before he broke down the door to the Apricot Cottage. And reached for that—

*

Edeard gasped for breath as he slid up through the pavement of Boldar Avenue. Everyone was turning to stare at him, their heads filled with identical placid thoughts. Above him, the nest awaited.

He didn't even wait to sense if there was a glimmer of suspicion rising amid their unified mind. His memory conjured up that evening ... no just before then, a few hours earlier, the astronomer's parlour—

Edeard stood outside the House of Blue Petals, waiting patiently. It was late afternoon, and away at the other end of the city, the Grand Council was called to session. While over in the Tosella district, Finitan railed against his infirmity and pain.

Eventually, a young Tathal walked confidently across the street to the House of Blue Petals. He stopped abruptly, and turned to stare at Edeard.

'You've been watching me,' Edeard said.

Tathal's adolescent face screwed up into a suspicious grimace. 'So?'

'You're afraid I can stop you.'

'Ladyfuckit,' Tathal spat. His third hand began to extend as his mind was veiled behind an inordinately powerful shield.

'You have an extraordinary talent,' Edeard said calmly. 'Why don't you join me? The people of this world need help. There's so much good you can do.'

'Join you? Not even you can dominate me, Waterwalker. I'm nobody's genistar.'

'I have no intention of attempting that trick.' His gaze flicked to the House of Blue Petals. 'She tried it on me once, you know.'

'Yeah? Must be pretty stupid not to learn from that mistake. But I made her teach me a lot.' He sneered. 'I like that. She still thinks she's in control, but she bends over when I tell her to.'

'Honious! You've already started to bind the nest to you, haven't you?'

Tathal narrowed his eyes. Misgivings leaked out from his shield. 'What do you want?'

'Not you. You're too late.' Edeard remembered a day from a couple of years previously. Reached for it—

Edeard tried. He even impressed himself with his tenacity, seeking that one moment when Tathal had an ounce of humanity in his soul. If it existed, he never found it. In the end he doubted its existence.

But he tried. Waiting outside the city gates when a fifteen-year-old Tathal arrived with a caravan. That too was long after his personality had established itself. He'd already dominated the entire caravan, lording it over them in the master's wagon. It wasn't as subtle as the nest; men and women served him while their daughters became his stable of whores. The old and the recalcitrant had been discarded along the route.

Before that ... Edeard found Tathal came from Ustaven province. He missed Taralee's seventeenth birthday to travel to the capital, Growan, nine months before the caravan arrived and Tathal left with them. Just in time to sense the fourteen-year-old finally kill Matrar, his abusive father, with a display of telekinesis that was shocking to witness. Minutes later he threw his broken alcoholic mother out of their house.

Further back ... Five years previously, Edeard spent a month in Growan, drinking in Matrar's tavern, trying to reason with the miserable man, to steer him away from using violence against his family. To no avail.

Two years beforehand, and Edeard bribed the owner of the carpentry lodge where Matrar worked, promoting him so his life might be a little easier. There would be more money, and Matrar might see a brighter future opening up if he strove to better himself. But the new money was spent on longer binges, and his obvious failings bred resentment among the men he was supposed to supervise.

Eventually Edeard found himself outside the tavern Matrar favoured for the last time. It had taken some admirable detective work among the badly maintained civic records of Growan's Guild of Clerks, but eventually he'd tracked down Tathal's birth certificate. Not that he entirely trusted it. Which was why he was outside the tavern ten days before the probable night. He was dressed in simple fieldworker clothes and a heavy coat; with his face disguised by a shallow concealment mirage. Not even Kristabel would recognize him.

As a waitress squirmed between battered old wooden tables he surreptitiously tipped a phial of vinac juice into Matrar's ale. It was an act he performed every night for a fortnight.

Tathal was never conceived. Never existed, so could never be remembered, nor even mourned.

Edeard arrived back in Makkathran in time for Taralee's second birthday. Just as he recalled, she developed chicken pox two days later. Then in autumn that year a ridiculously happy Mirnatha announced her surprise engagement. Finitan was at the height of his powers, and supporting the special Grand Council committee on organized crime, which was producing good results.

He recalled it all. The events. The conversations. Even the weather. There was little he wanted to change. At first. Then he grew weary of the sameness. Knowing became a burden as he became exasperated with people repeating the same mistakes once more.

The only thing which differed now were his dreams; still bizarre, impossible, but fresh, new.

5

Cheriton McOnna was tired, irritable, and unwashed to the extent that his clothes were starting to smell; what he needed was coffee, proper sunlight and a decent blast of fresh air. The conditioning unit in the confluence nest supervisor's office was struggling under constant use by too many people. But Dream Master Yenrol was insistent that they kept a full watch for any sign of the Second Dreamer. That meant a special module grafted on to the nest itself, one with a direct connection to the team. It boosted perception and sensitivity to an exceptionally high level. Cheriton didn't like that at all; opening his mind to the gaiafield at such an intensity was equivalent to staring into the sun. Fortunately he had some filter routines which he quietly slipped in to protect himself. The other members of Yenrol's team weren't so well off. Slavishly obedient and devout, they scoured the emotional resonance routines for the slightest hint of their absconded messiah.

Around him, he could see their faces grimace from the strength of impressions pulsing down that singular linkage, yet still they loyally persevered. If they weren't careful they were going to suffer some pretty severe brainburns. Yenrol was adamant, though, convinced that whatever had happened over in Francola Wood was caused by the Second Dreamer. It was Phelim's strong belief, complacently accepted by the Dream Masters, that she was trying to return from Chobamba.

The brief ultrasecure message Cheriton had received from Oscar was clear that she hadn't emerged from the Silfen path. Not that anyone had the remotest idea of what had actually set off all the agents into yet another deranged fracas. The path had registered somehow within the gaiafield as it changed, but no one had walked out. Now it had inevitably shrunk away again in that way Silfen paths always did when scrutinized by curious humans. Cheriton knew that meant the Second Dreamer wouldn't be using it now, she was still out there walking between worlds – but try telling Yenrol that. The Dream Master was obsessed to the point of recklessness. He truly believed he was *this close*.

Cheriton snatched another quick look round the small stuffy office where his co-workers were crammed. Two flinched from some emotion twanging away on their raw neurones, shuddering from a near-physical pain. Yenrol himself was twitching constantly.

This is ridiculous, Cheriton thought. *She's not an idiot. The whole invasion force has one goal: to find her. She's not going to walk right back into the middle of them.*

Most of the ordinary Living Dream followers shared his logic. He could sense their despondency dripping into the gaiafield as they made their way reluctantly to the wormhole at Colwyn City's dock. Those of them that could. Surges of anger were also erupting into the gaiafield wherever Viotia's citizens physically encountered any of their erstwhile oppressors. If he chose to examine those particular stormwells of emotion closely, there was also fear to be found, and pain. After the first instances, Cheriton kept his mind well clear of them. More and more were occurring, especially in Colwyn City.

Some were close by. Despite his reluctance, he felt a mind he knew flaring out of the norm, boosted by terror: Mareble, with whom he'd grown familiar for all the wrong reasons. Against his better judgement he allowed the sensations to bubble in through his gaiamotes, seeing as she did the slope of a broad street falling away ahead of her. A street now cut off by the tumultuous mob.

'Oh crap,' he murmured under his breath. *Nothing I can do.*

Even as he observed the scene through a myriad emotional outpourings everything changed. A mind rose into the gaiafield, so close to Mareble and her prat of a husband; a mind of incredible strength, its presence flaring bright and loud. Cheriton's filter routines were just enough to shield him from its astonishing magnitude. Yenrol and the others screamed with one voice, their cry of anguish deafening in the confined office.

Mareble wanted nothing else but to be off this dreadful world. She and Danal had come here with such soaring spirits, believing they would be close to the Second Dreamer. But instead, their lives had degenerated with increasing speed, culminating in Danal's arrest by Living Dream. Those who had taken him away were not a part of the movement as she understood it. The Welcome Team moved with Cleric Phelim's authority, but they certainly lacked any of the gentle humility of the most devout. Men of violence and hauteur. What they'd done to poor Danal was an atrocity. Not that they cared.

Her husband had been released into her arms, a frightened trembling wreck, unrecognizable as the kind-hearted man she'd married. They couldn't even return to the pleasant apartment they'd bought. That was the reason Danal had been arrested in the first place. It was ridiculous, but the Ellezelin forces suspected them of colluding with the Second Dreamer herself. And Araminta being the Second Dreamer was the one thing Mareble could never quite bring herself to understand. Araminta, that pretty young woman, slightly nervous and on edge, eager to sell the apartment she'd been labouring over to renovate. Somehow, that just didn't connect. Mareble was expecting something quite different, but there had been no hint, no inkling when they'd talked and haggled over the price. She'd shared a cup of tea with the Second Dreamer and never known. Such a thing was simply wrong.

Danal didn't care about any of that when she tried to explain. When they were free of the Welcome Team he sank into a bitter depression, jumping at shadows and shouting at her. The things he shouted she tried to ignore; it wasn't him saying such hurtful things, it was the confusion and hurt left behind by his interrogators.

They spent days in a hotel together, living off room service, with her offering what comfort she could. Cheriton had recommended some drugs that ought to help, which she'd tried to get Danal to take. Sometimes he did, more often he'd fling the infuser away. So she waited patiently for her husband to recover while the insanity of the invasion raged on the streets outside. That was when the unreal news broke, that the Second Dreamer was Araminta; and worse, she'd escaped to some planet Mareble had never heard of on the other side of the Commonwealth. Bizarrely, the knowledge seemed to ease Danal's state of mind, at least he started taking the anti-psychosis drugs.

The calming effect was slow but constant; she began to see signs of the man she'd lost re-emerging. Which was when they realized they had to get away. It was a decision that seemed to be shared by most of the Living Dream supporters on Viotia. The hostility and violence directed at them from the rest of the population was never going to abate.

They decided to wait until midmorning before leaving the hotel. That way they figured there would be more people about, more Living Dream followers doing the same thing, more paramilitaries patrolling. It would be safest.

The hotel was only a couple of miles from Colwyn City's docks, where the wormhole opened to the safety of Ellezelin. When they made their way cautiously down to the lobby it was deserted. Mareble had tried to order some modern clothes from a local cyberstore and have them delivered by bot, but they'd never arrived. The store's management system insisted they'd been dispatched. She wanted the clothes in an attempt to blend in with everyone else on the street. Instead they made do with what they had. Danal wasn't too bad, his sweater was a neutral grey, which he wore above brown denim trousers. From a distance it would escape attention. Except for his shoes, which were lace-ups. Nobody else in the Commonwealth used lace-ups any more. Mareble was more worried by her own green and white dress; a dress was less suspicious, but the style was recognizable as belonging to Makkathran. In fact it was a copy of a dress Kanseen had worn one night in the Olivan's Eagle.

Standing in front of the door, she called a cab. There was a metro rail running along the street right outside the hotel. Her u-shadow reported that the cab companies weren't responding to requests, their amalgamated management cores apologized and said that normal service would resume as soon as possible.

'It's not far,' she said, more for her own benefit than his. 'Come on, we can get there. We'll be back on Ellezelin in an hour.'

Danal nodded, his lips drawn together in a thin bloodless line. 'Okay.'

The hotel entrance was sited on Porral Street, which was almost deserted when they walked out into the warm midmorning sunlight. They could hear distant airborne sirens as well as a suppressed buzzing like some angry insect, which Mareble just knew was a crowd on the hunt. Porral Street opened out on to Daryad Avenue, which was the main thoroughfare in this part of town, sweeping down the hill to the River Cairns. And just off to one side at the end of that slope were the docks. Simply looking down the broad avenue with its tall buildings and silent traffic solidos changing colour and shape for non-existent ground vehicles produced a surge of hope. Along its whole length she could see barely a hundred people in total.

An equally optimistic Danal linked his arm through hers, and they set off at a fast pace. A lot of the stores on either side had suffered damage. Windows were broken and covered up with big sheets of black carbon. Most of the adverts were cold and dark. Three smashed cab pods blocked the metro rails running down the middle of the road. The people they passed never met their gaze. Nobody was sharing anything in the gaiafield. Nobody wanted to be noticed. Mareble was acutely aware of other people heading down the slope – couples, groups. All of them were moving with that same urgent intent as her, yet trying to appear casual.

They were halfway down towards the smooth fast-flowing water of the river and starting to relax, when they crossed a side road. The shouts of the mob reached them at the same time. Mareble saw a man running frantically towards them. He was being chased by about fifty people.

'Run!' he screamed as he charged past. He was wearing a leather jerkin and blue cotton trousers, looking just like Arcton on the day of banishment. His black felt hat tumbled off as he turned down the slope. The mob was thundering up fast behind him, faces contorted with bloodlust and hatred. Mareble and Danal took off after him: it was pure instinct.

'Help,' Mareble yelled. Her u-shadow was sending an alert to the Ellezelin forces, which wasn't even being acknowledged. She cried into the gaiafield, only to receive the slightest ripple of sympathies from Living Dream followers. 'Somebody help!'

Danal was holding her hand, tugging her along. The dress was hindering her legs. Her ankle boots weren't designed to run in. It was at least a mile and a half to the docks. Fear began to burn along her nerves as the adrenalin kicked in. She thought of the Waterwalker on the mountain after Salrana's betrayal, with Arminel and his thugs closing in on the pavilion. Even then he had maintained his dignity. *I must be like him.*

Her foot hit something, and she went flying, landing painfully on the stone-block pavement, grazing her knees, tearing the skin on her wrists. The jolt thumped along her arms, and she wailed in dread knowing it was all over. 'Lady, please,' she whimpered as Danal hauled her to her feet.

The mob came up around them incredibly fast, surrounding them with a fence of savagely hostile faces. They carried lengths of wood and metal bars, a couple gripped small laser welders.

'No,' Mareble whimpered. Tears were already smearing her vision. She hated how weak she was, but they were going to hurt her. Then she would die before ever knowing the true wonder of the Void.

'I've called the paramilitaries,' Danal said defiantly.

A pole caught him on the side of his head, making a nasty *crack*. His mouth had barely opened to cry out in pain when another smacked across his shins. Danal dropped fast, his limp hand slipping from Mareble's arm.

'No!' she yelled. Her wild face looked directly at the man in front of her, pleading. He seemed ordinary enough, middle aged, dressed in a smart jacket. *He won't hit a woman*, she thought. 'We just want to go. Let us go.'

'Bitch.' His fist slammed into her nose. She heard the bone crunch. For the first second it didn't hurt, she was numb with shock and terror. Then the frightening pulse of hot pain pierced her brain. Mareble screamed, crumpling to her knees. To one side she saw a boot kick Danal's ribs. Blood was pouring down her mouth and chin.

'That's enough,' a woman's voice said calmly. A dark figure stepped into the middle of the mob.

Then *finally* the gaiafield was awash with sympathy and kindness. The amazing sensation grew and grew like nothing Mareble had ever known before. She gasped in astonishment, blinking up at the woman who was now opening her coat as if emerging from a cocoon. Underneath she wore a long cream robe, resembling those of the Clerics. It seemed to glow of its own accord. A pendant on a slim gold chain around her neck shone an intense blue light across Mareble's face and that, somehow, siphoned out so much of her fear. For a moment she transcended her own body to look out across the stars from a viewpoint outside the galaxy. The sight was extraordinarily warming. Then she was back on Viotia, and looking up in silent awe at the figure grinning down at her.

The front rank of the mob was hesitating, their first angry glances at the intruder fading to bewilderment. Even their hatred and rage couldn't stand against the blaze of serenity and comfort she poured into the gaiafield.

Danal raised his head, a look of incredulity rising over his pain. 'Dreamer!' he gasped in wonder.

'Hello, Danal,' Araminta smiled. She pushed some of the Skylord's contentment into the greeting, feeling it wash over the poor abused man, feeling his relief. Mareble was watching her worshipfully as she tried to staunch the flow of blood from her broken nose. While right across the Commonwealth Living Dream followers sent their welcome and thanks that she had finally come out of hiding to take up her destiny. The wave of goodwill was awesome in its extent, combining the emotion of billions, sending it sweeping across hundreds of worlds.

Then one of the mob finally managed to shake off the daze of sensation Araminta and the Skylord were radiating out into the gaiafield. It was the one who'd punched Mareble. 'You!' he spat. 'This is all your fault.' A metal bar was raised. Araminta stared at him, feeling *something* flow from the Skylord into her mind, elevating her thoughts still higher. And she recalled Ranalee's iniquitous ability. 'No,' she told him quietly, and changed his mind for him, draining away the fear and hatred.

His mouth parted in a silent gasp, and the metal bar clattered to the ground just as a squadron of capsules roared in overhead. Araminta grinned up at them as they descended, sharing the sight with everyone everywhere. She held a hand out, and helped Mareble to her feet as armour-clad figures shoved their way through the sullen silent mob.

'Thank you, gentlemen,' she said mildly as they came up right up to her, guns drawn to cover the throng. 'Please assist Danal.'

The officer in front hesitated. She could sense the uncertainty in his mind, the desperate wish to be anywhere else. 'You're to come with me,' he announced.

I AM THE DREAMER, Araminta proclaimed into the gaia-field, using the Skylord's strength to bolster the claim. The officer swayed back from the force of the thought, almost falling as his knees weakened. Behind him, people were flinching, cowering at the power of her thoughts. 'Did the Waterwalker travel by capsule?' she continued mildly. 'I think not. I will walk to the wormhole. Those of you who wish to follow the Dream may accompany me.' She gave the mob a calculated look. No one would meet her gaze now. 'Those who would hurt my followers will be dealt with.' She glanced at the officer again. 'Your name?'

'Darraklan. Captain Darraklan.'

'Very well, Captain Darraklan, your men will perform escort duty. There will be peace in this city. That is my wish.'

'Yes, ma'am,' Darraklan stammered.

Araminta raised an eyebrow. The hint of censure peeked out from her mind.

Darraklan bowed. 'Yes, Dreamer,' he corrected himself.

Araminta gave Mareble a gracious smile. 'Come.' The crowd parted, and she started walking down the slope towards the river and the docks. Bewildered Ellezelin troopers quickly helped Danal to his feet.

By the time she reached the bottom of Daryad Avenue she'd picked up quite a retinue. Happy Living Dream followers had rushed out of every intersection to greet her, disbelief and joy surging out of their minds. Captain Darraklan's troopers maintained a careful escort, not pressing in, yet forming a secure perimeter. Capsules drifted high overhead, keeping pace. Araminta ignored them.

There had been many protests outside the docks themselves. Several hundred hardy city residents had set up camp in front of the main entrance, only to be largely ignored by the capsules that flitted in and out over their heads. Now they formed a curious crowd, watching as Araminta led her procession towards them. Anxiety and uncertainty began to rattle along the front rank. It was one thing to taunt the unassailable, indifferent paramilitaries on the other side of the fence for the injustice they'd brought to Viotia, and quite another to face down a living messiah with mysterious telepathic powers. Araminta was still a hundred metres short of them when they began to part, leaving a clear passage to the dock entrance. Tall gates were hurriedly peeled open to reveal another batch of paramilitaries. These were headed by Cleric Phelim himself, who didn't offer anything by way of complicity or acceptance.

Araminta knew this was the first real test of her claim to be the Dreamer. Phelim wouldn't crumple like Darraklan. Though she was certain that ultimately he wouldn't be able to withstand Ranalee's dominance technique. She sincerely hoped the Skylord would lend its assistance again if she asked, if she showed an obstacle to bringing the faithful to the Void as she promised she would. In fact, it really shouldn't need the intervention of a Skylord. To the whole of Living Dream she had assumed her rightful position as their leader, their saviour. Clerics had become nothing more than administrators and bureaucrats, simple functionaries to facilitate her wishes. Judging from the expression on Phelim's face, and the few tightly controlled thoughts he did permit to be shared through the gaiafield, he was beginning to realize that too.

I just have to keep going, she told herself in that little core of identity she didn't share across the gaiafield, *be an unstoppable force just like I promised Bradley. The true followers won't stand for anyone interfering with me, not now I can deliver the Pilgrimage. That's what Living Dream stands for, it is everything to them.*

A phony respectful smile spread across Cleric Phelim's face. 'Second Dreamer,' he said, with a slight emphasis on 'second'. 'We are so glad you have chosen to come forth at last. Welcome.'

Araminta didn't even stop walking. She headed straight at the troopers lined up behind Phelim. They quickly shuffled aside. 'Part of the reason I remained concealed was the suffering you unleashed on this world,' she said as she led her supporters through the troopers. Mareble, who had stayed close by the whole way down Daryad Avenue, glared at Phelim. It was a common sensation directed at the man. Up ahead was the wormhole. Araminta could see the violet-blue Cherenkov radiation leaking out from the edge. A different sunlight shone through the centre.

Phelim's expression hardened as he struggled to restrain himself. 'I assure you, we did everything that we could to . . .'

He was moving with her now, ambling in an awkward sideways gait. She'd won. 'When I sit in the Orchard Palace

I will order a full and open enquiry into your part in this aggression,' she said dismissively.

'Wha—' Phelim managed to blurt.

'Violence was something the Waterwalker strove to eradicate: he devoted his lives to it. The cause almost broke him, but he succeeded. That is his true inspiration to us. And this monstrous invasion is the antithesis of everything Living Dream stands for. To believe you will go unpunished for such an atrocity is arrogant beyond belief.'

Cheering broke out all across the docks as Phelim abruptly stood still, watching with an open jaw as Araminta carried on to the wormhole. A lot of the enthusiastic jeering voices were rising from the protesters just outside the entrance.

Araminta smiled proudly, savouring the victory. The wormhole was directly ahead of her now, guarded by tall metal pillars studded with weapons and sensors. The Ellezelin forces parted before her. Helmets were discarded, showing grinning faces. The true believers were delighted she was here, was going to lead them onwards just as the movement had always promised. She was cheered and applauded.

'Thank you,' she told them. 'Thank you so much.' It was hard not to laugh outright. She'd accessed politicians working the crowds enough times, always hating the smug cynical bastards putting on a human persona whenever elections were due. Now she understood how they did it. Puppeting the crowds was apparently an inbuilt ability.

Just as she reached the wormhole she slowed and gripped Mareble's hands. The woman looked at her with an alarming degree of adoration, eyes bright above the dried blood staining her face and dress. 'You can go home now,' Araminta told the overwhelmed woman. 'I will lead us on Pilgrimage shortly, once the ships are ready.'

Mareble's lower lip trembled as she began to cry.

'It's all right,' Araminta assured her. 'Everything is all right now.' Which was a lie on the grandest scale possible. She was rather pleased with herself for carrying it off with such panache.

Araminta raised a hand to her newfound friends, and walked into the mouth of the wormhole where she was engulfed by Ellezelin's warmer, yellower sunlight.

*

'Holy crap!' Oscar muttered.

'That's not her,' Tomansio said.

'She's fucked us,' Beckia grunted. 'Totally fucked us. She's killed the whole galaxy.'

On the other side of the starship's cabin, Liatris shook his head, his mouth raised in a lopsided smile of admiration. 'Smart lady. They kept pushing her and pushing her, backing her into an impossible corner. There were only ever two options. Cave in, or come out fighting. They never expected her to do that.'

'Because that's not her,' Tomansio said confidently.

'Looked like her,' Oscar said. His u-shadow was still accessing the unisphere news feeds, showing the mouth of the wormhole, not half a kilometre from the Bootle and Leicester warehouse where the *Elvin's Payback* was secreted. It had taken a great deal of willpower not to run out of the starship and take a look at events for himself. The unisphere feed showed him hundreds of joyous people following their newfound messiah through the wormhole to Ellezelin. Unisphere coverage ended there. The other end of the wormhole was in a security zone.

The gaiafield, however, was still gifting Araminta's sight and emotions as she walked across the nearly empty staging field. Capsules rushed through the air towards her. People were breaking off from their tasks on the acres of machinery scattered about to cheer her arrival in Greater Makkathran. *And how is dear old Cleric Conservator Ethan going to react to this?* he wondered.

'So that's it,' Beckia said. She was still cranky at having to wear the medical sleeve on her arm, which was busy knitting the deep tissue repairs she'd undergone after the fight in Francola Wood. Three other enriched agents had swarmed her, and her integral force field had temporarily overloaded down her left side. Oscar had pulled her out of the fray just before the capsules landed. He considered her lucky Tomansio had managed to extract them; and the medical capsule repairing her had frankly performed a minor miracle.

'Maybe,' Oscar said. 'She must have a plan.'

'That's a dangerous assumption,' Tomansio said. 'Liatris got it right, she's been forced into this act simply to survive.'

'I thought you said it wasn't her,' Oscar countered.

Tomansio's handsome face shone with a bright smile. 'Touché.'

'It's her,' Oscar said.

'Still not convinced,' Tomansio said. 'This ... *empress* isn't the same girl we've been chasing after. Facing down Living Dream simply isn't in her psychology.'

'What then?' Beckia demanded.

'Double bluff,' Tomansio said. 'They got to her, they broke into her mind and installed their own operating routines. This is a puppet of Living Dream, one that's been pushed out centre stage to focus everyone's attention. Big bonus that she'll do what every follower wants, and lead them to Pilgrimage. It makes perfect sense for Ethan to do this, he gets everything he ever wanted.'

'Except lead Living Dream,' Oscar said. 'That's her next step, it has to be, she can't do anything else but claim the throne now.'

'It doesn't matter,' Tomansio said. 'He still gets what he wants, which is a ticket into the Void, and at the same time he doesn't get any of the blame if it all goes arse over tit.'

'Which it will,' Beckia said.

'I still don't buy it,' Oscar said. He remembered the expression of fear and determination he'd seen on Araminta's face when they met oh so briefly in Bodant Park; her magnificent run eluding not just his team, but the entire complement of agents from every power player in the Commonwealth. Besides, she was descended from Mellanie, and that meant *trouble* on a level these modern Greater Commonwealth citizens couldn't comprehend.

His lips registered a slight smile. *Something* about the whole situation wasn't quite right, Tomansio had the truth of that; but he had absolutely no idea what.

'Then what is she doing?' Beckia asked. 'She might have come out fighting from the corner they'd backed her into, but she's burned any options. She has to take Living Dream on Pilgrimage now. That's what her whole tenuous authority is based on.'

'Suicide?' Liatris suggested. 'She leads them into the Gulf, and the Pilgrimage ships get blasted apart by the warrior Raiel.'

'That'd work for me,' Beckia grunted.

Oscar grinned from the strength of his own conviction. 'Have a little faith,' he told the Knights Guardians. 'After all, she is a messiah now.'

Tomansio groaned. 'You mean you want us to stay on?'

'You've seen what's going on in the docks right now; every Living Dream follower on the planet is going to come running to the wormhole, and Phelim will have to shut off the weather dome to let them in. If we left now we'd definitely be seen, we'd blow our cover.'

'We don't need cover if the operation is over.'

'Give her a few days. She is rather busy right now, after all. And she has my number.'

'Don't we all,' Beckia muttered.

*

Araminta stood at the front of the big passenger capsule, looking through the transparent fuselage wrapped around her. Five hundred metres below, Greater Makkathran was laid out across the ground, a phenomenal urban sprawl which stretched to the horizon in every direction. Sunlight glinted and flashed off the crystal towers rising from lush parks; lower buildings shone with implausible colours. It was, she acknowledged, a beautiful city. However, her vision of the capital was slightly obscured by the sheer number of capsules rising up out of the designated traffic streams to wait for her to pass. Then they curved round to join the festive armada already flying along behind her. There were so many packed together, like a smoke cloud, she could actually see the hazy shadow they splashed over the ground.

Up ahead, the ocean appeared on the horizon where the city dipped down to a broad swathe of green park. And there, gleaming in the late afternoon sunlight, Makkathran2 was perched on the shoreline.

'Do you want to go straight to the Orchard Palace, Dreamer?' Captain Darraklan asked. He'd stayed with her after they walked through the wormhole, seemingly appointing himself as her personal guard. She wasn't about to argue. With his helmet off, he was actually quite handsome in a classic square-jawed way, his floppy chestnut hair reminding her of one of Mr Bovey's younger selves.

'No,' she said, without taking her gaze from the hauntingly strange reproduction city. 'Edeard first entered through the North Gate. Take me there. That will be fitting. I will walk to the Orchard Palace.' *Which will give Ethan plenty of time to throw up the barricades, if he dares.* She felt a grim amusement coming from Darraklan's mind as the capsule began to lose altitude. He must have been thinking the same thing.

They touched down on the vast circle of parkland surrounding the crystal wall. As she alighted on to the grass, she glanced back at the vast armada that was now tussling for groundspace. It really had turned the sky dark. She was sure none of them were obeying local traffic control orders any more. *That's good. A little knot of anarchy which I influence. They don't all obey Ethan's laws unquestioningly.*

So far everyone was waiting to see what would happen next. Pushing her along with their enthusiasm and her apparent newfound relish for the role of Dreamer. All she had to do was supplant Ethan, and the only way to do that was to show her ability and determination was greater than his. *Just like Bradley said.*

Araminta walked through the great arch in the crystal wall, with people pouring out of their badly parked capsules to form a carnival procession behind her. She didn't really get much of a look at Makkathran2 from ground level. High Moat, which the gate opened on to, was jammed with people; surely everyone who lived in their shrine city had turned out to welcome her. The cheer which arose at her arrival was deafening. A row of men in Makkathran constable uniforms (exactly like the Waterwalker's squad) saluted. Darraklan and their sergeant shouted back and forth while Araminta waved at the crowd – all the while moving forward. *Never hesitate, never slow.*

After a moment the constables fell in around her, easing her passage towards the bridge over North Curve Canal and into Ysidro.

She was wrong about the whole population being on High Moat. Ysidro's narrow twisting streets were packed solid with supporters, some crying openly. The eerily familiar Blue Fox tavern was there beside the ginger sandstone bridge, which took her into Golden Park where the sunlight was shimmering off the white pillars. Another sea of bodies thronged the vast open space, while the high domes of the Orchard Palace dominated the far skyline.

While she was walking along one of the park's elegant paths Darraklan leaned over to murmur in her ear, 'The Cleric Council has convened at the entrance to the palace.'

'Wonderful,' she replied. There were a lot of children lining the path, all of them with shining adulation in their eyes. It was hard to keep pushing on knowing she would ultimately betray that trust and reverence. *It is their parents who have misled them, not me. I will be the truth for them.*

By the time she reached the wire and wood bridge that crossed Outer Circle Canal her resolution had returned. The thousands of smiling faces that urged her on no longer even registered as she crossed the canal. Darraklan accompanied her, while the constables tried to stop the crowd pressing forward into the canal itself. They were all so desperate to see what happened next, their combined thoughts urging the Clerics to acknowledge their new Dreamer.

As Darraklan said, the Cleric Council was waiting for her just inside the Malfit Hall, resplendent in their scarlet and black robes. Ethan stood in front of them, his white robes shining far brighter than Araminta's own. Reasonable enough, she admitted, after all she'd sewn hers together from the lining of Mr Bovey's semiorganic curtains.

The Cleric Conservator bowed deeply. 'Dreamer,' he said, 'welcome. We have waited so long for this moment.'

Araminta gave him a sly smile; for someone who'd just been politically outmanoeuvred he was in surprisingly good humour. 'Be careful what you wish for.'

'Indeed. May I ask why you have finally come forward?'

'It was time,' she replied. 'And I wished to end Viotia's suffering.'

'That was most regrettable.'

'It is past,' she said lightly, knowing how angry her home-world would be at that. 'I am here to lead those who want a better life for themselves, those who choose to live as the Waterwalker did.' Again she appealed to the Skylord, who said: 'We await you. We will guide you.'

The gasp of joy from the crowd outside was audible through the hall's thick walls. She smiled significantly at Ethan: your call.

'We are honoured,' he said effusively.

'Thank you. Shall we move to the Upper Council chamber, now? We have much to settle.'

Ethan glanced along the line of Cleric Councillors, their uncertain hopeful faces. One of them smiled slickly. 'Of course, Dreamer,' he said.

'Rincenso, isn't it?' Araminta said.

'Yes, Dreamer.'

'I'm grateful for your support.'

'My pleasure.'

I'll bet it is, you unctuous little tit. 'Which way?'

Rincenso's bow was so deep it verged on parody. He gestured. 'This way, please, Dreamer.'

She watched the eternal storm playing across the ceiling, oddly saddened by the fact it was only a replica of the real Malfit

Hall, the vivid images above her nothing but a copy of Querencia's planetary system. Now she'd begun this course of action she was actually keen to see it resolved, to walk through the real Makkathran and see for herself the streets and buildings where Edeard's dramas had played out.

They walked silently through the smaller Toral Hall and into the Upper Council chamber. Araminta grinned at the solar vortex playing on its cross-vault ceiling; here the copper sun's accretion disc was still in its glory days, not as Justine had just seen it, with the brash comets dwindling and a new planet orbiting where it should never have been.

'You haven't updated it, then?' she enquired lightly as she walked straight to the gold-embossed throne at the head of the long table.

'This is the Makkathran of the Waterwalker, Dreamer,' Ethan said.

'Of course; not that it matters. We will soon be leaving here for good. Be seated,' she said graciously.

Ethan claimed the seat on her left-hand side, while Rincenso sat opposite him. There were just enough seats for everyone. *No Phelim*, she thought sagely. *Let's keep it like that.* The thin Cleric unnerved her somewhat.

'May I ask if you intend to keep sharing so widely with the gaiafield?' Ethan said.

'Until we pass into the Void,' she confirmed. 'The followers of Living Dream have had too much doubt and trouble intrude into their lives of late, in no small part due to you, Cleric. I feel they need the reassurance of seeing for themselves that I am honestly doing everything I can to lead the Pilgrimage. That is my only concern now. In that respect I will require this council to continue its running of the day-to-day aspects of Living Dream.'

She studied Ethan, curious how he'd react to the deal. It was so painfully obvious he didn't understand nor believe in her apparent conversion to the cause. He suspected something, but couldn't see what could possibly be askew.

'I will be delighted to help in any way I can,' Ethan said.

'We all will be,' Rincenso added quickly.

Araminta had to be stern with herself not to leak any disgust out into the gaiafield at the cleric's sycophancy. 'Excellent. So my first question is on the progress of the Pilgrimage fleet.'

'The hulls are all complete,' Cleric DeLouis said. 'Fitting out is going to take a while, but hopefully no more than a month.'

'And the drives?' Araminta asked.

It probably helped that Ethan was less than a metre away from her, but there was no way he could hide the little burst of dismay from her. She turned to fix him with a level stare. 'By my estimation, it will take nearly half a year to reach the Void using a standard hyperdrive.'

'Yes, Dreamer.'

'There is also the problem of the warrior Raiel. Justine barely made it through.'

'We are making arrangements,' Ethan said grudgingly.

'Which are?'

He made a small gesture with his hand. 'They are confidential.'

'No more. This unhealthy obsession with secrecy and violence ends now. It has done untold damage to Living Dream. Inigo and Edeard would not have tolerated such vice. Besides, we are no longer members of the Greater Commonwealth, and you are under my protection. Now what arrangements have been made?'

'Are you sure you—'

'Yes!'

'Very well. I organized delivery of ultradrives for each Pilgrimage ship. The journey time should be less than a month.'

'Good work. And the Raiel warships? How do we get past them?'

Ethan was completely impassive. 'The same manufacturing facility will also provide force fields capable of withstanding an attack by the warrior Raiel.'

'I see. And the cost?'

'It's budgeted for. We do have the wealth of the entire Free Market Zone at our disposal, after all.'

Araminta's voice hardened. 'The cost, please, Cleric, specifically the political cost for this technology?'

Everyone at the table turned to look at Ethan. The pressure of curiosity from the gaiafield was extraordinary. Even the Skylord was displaying a minor interest, engaged by the volume of emotion.

'Our supplier is to be taken into the Void with us.'

'Logical,' Araminta said. She smiled graciously. 'Thank you one and all for attending me. We'll convene formally tomorrow when I've had a chance to settle in. Ethan, I will be using the Mayor's staterooms here in the Orchard Palace as my residence until we depart.'

'Yes, Dreamer.' He seemed surprised there had been no censure concerning his Faustian deal.

Darraklan peered in through the door as the subdued yet relieved Cleric Council filed out. Araminta held up a finger to him. 'A moment more, please.'

'Yes, Dreamer.' He bowed and shut the doors after the last Cleric had left. Araminta allowed herself a slow look round the Council chamber, her gaze falling once again on the radiant image spinning endlessly on the ceiling. She wondered how Justine was getting on inside the Void, if she had reached the real Makkathran yet. But no, that would take days – weeks – even with the Void's accelerated time. Although the *Silverbird* should arrive before the Pilgrimage ships reached the boundary. *Ozzie! I hope she and Gore can do something to salvage this crock of shit before then, or I'm well and truly screwed. It sounded like Gore had a plan, or at least an idea. He owes me, too. Maybe he'll get in touch.* Somehow, she suspected she was going to have to do most of the work. But for now, there was the real threat to face. She took a breath, feeling the billions of Living Dream followers share her mind with a sense of trepidation as her own unease leaked out.

'Aren't you going to talk to me?' she asked the chamber. Her own voice reverberated off the hard walls. 'I know you're sharing me.' Again, the chamber was silent. Empty. Araminta let out a mildly exasperated sigh and allowed her ire to show. 'I am talking to *you*; that which emerged from Earth's prison. You have to speak with me at some time, for I am the only way to reach the Void. Let us begin now. Don't be afraid. You've seen I am both reasonable and practical.'

The curiosity within the gaiafield grew more intense as everyone strained to perceive what she was talking to. Her u-shadow reported the Upper Council chamber's secure communication net was activating. A solido projection appeared at the other end of the table. Not a person, but a simple dark sphere scintillating with grim purple light. Araminta faced it impassively.

'Congratulations on your ascension, Dreamer.' Its voice was female, melodically sinister.

'And you are?'

'Ilanthe.'

'You must be the one supplying the ultradrives and the force fields.'

'My agents arranged that with Ethan, yes.'

'Will the force fields be strong enough to protect us from the warrior Raiel?'

'I believe so. They are the same type currently protecting Earth.'

'Ah. And for this bounty you expect to be taken into the Void?'

'Without my assistance you cannot reach the boundary.'

'And without me you cannot get inside.'

'It would seem we need each other.'

'Then we have reached a concord.'

'You will take me?' Ilanthe's voice carried a note of surprise.

'The Void welcomes all who seek fulfilment. Whatever you are, you obviously believe you need what the Void can offer. Therefore I will be happy to bring you to it. It is, after all, my destiny as Dreamer to help those who yearn to reach the Heart.'

'That's very noble of you. And completely unbelievable.'

'You are evil.'

'No, I am driven. It is not just Inigo and Edeard who had a vision of a beautiful future.'

'Nonetheless, you are inimical to the Commonwealth and its citizens.'

'Again you are misjudging me. I simply wish to achieve a different goal to the mundane aspirations which have so far existed among our species. A wonderful uplifting goal that everyone can share. I require the Void's assistance to do that.'

'Then I wish you well on your voyage.'

'Why?'

'Because the Void will obliterate you. The Heart will not tolerate malevolence no matter the intent behind it, deluded or deliberate. You cannot avoid it, you cannot elude it. Despite my many misgivings I do genuinely believe in the goodness of the Heart, for I am twinned with the Skylords who truly know its munificence. If necessary I will travel there myself to expose you and your machinations.'

'Good luck with that.'

'Knowing this, knowing I will oppose you; do you still wish to come with us?'

'Yes. Do you still wish to take me?'

'Yes.'

'So be it. Our fate will be decided within the Void.'

'That it will.'

The sphere faded out and the solido projector switched off. A long breath escaped through Araminta's pursed lips. She grinned nervously for the benefit of her billions-strong spellbound audience. 'Lady! I wonder what day two is going to be like?'

Paula was curious about that herself.

'She's up to something,' Oscar insisted over the ultrasecure link. 'This self-coronation is only the start.'

'I don't see what else there can be for her,' Paula said.

'Well yeah ... If it was obvious, everyone would suss it out and it'd be pointless.'

'I do love your optimism. It was always your most endearing quality. You probably believe Ilanthe will see the error of her ways before long.'

'You sound bitter.'

Paula rubbed a hand over her brow, surprised to find it was trembling. But then she hadn't slept for days, even biononics could only keep her fatigue at bay for so long. 'I probably am. We're the good guys, Oscar, we're not supposed to lose.'

'We haven't lost; we're nowhere near losing. The Pilgrimage ships haven't even been finished, let alone launched. So tell me how many ways covert operations can sabotage them?'

'Hundreds, but that's only a delay. It's not a solution.'

'I want to keep going. I want to see if Araminta contacts me.'

'She won't. Everyone in the galaxy can observe every second of her existence. It's actually quite clever. Sharing like that puts her beyond mere Dreamer status, she's almost achieved the same level Edeard had. Every moment of her life is available for her followers to idolize, just like his was. But they'll only keep supporting her if she does what they want, and takes them into the Void. There's no escape.'

'Humour me. I have faith in her too. Different to everyone else, but faith nonetheless. She's not stupid, and she's descended from Mellanie.'

'If that's what your faith is based on we're in serious deep shit.'

'Yeah, I noticed that, too.'

Paula smiled wearily. 'All right, Oscar, I certainly haven't got anything else for you to do. Stick with the original mission, see if you can make contact with the Second Dreamer.'

'Thank you.'

'What do your colleagues think about the notion?'

'They're still on the payroll.'

'Are they all okay? Francola Wood seemed unnecessarily violent.'

'Wasn't me, honest.'

'You were there.'

'We were. And I still don't understand what happened. The

path became active somehow. We all knew that. Hell, we *felt* it. But she never came through.'

'And yet she turned up in Colwyn City right after.'

'Exactly. See, there's more to her than we understand. I trust you noticed what she's wearing round her neck?'

'Yes.'

'And she knew about Ilanthe. I didn't.'

'It was classified. The Navy knew she'd escaped.'

'So she's getting her information from somewhere. She understands what's going on. Which means she knows what she's got to do.'

'I hope you're right, Oscar.'

'Me too. So what are you going to do now?'

'Follow up leads, act on information. The usual.'

'Good luck.'

The link ended. Paula lay back in the couch, closing her eyes for a moment to summon up the willpower to place her next call. It was all very well being tired, but the situation was moving on with or without her.

Symbols appeared in her exovision and her secondary routines pulled out the technical results. *Alexis Denken* was currently in full stealth mode fifty thousand kilometres above Viotia's equator. The smartcore had been running a painstaking search across local space for signs of anyone else lurking above the planet. The first eight starships were easy enough for its sensors to detect; she suspected they were back-up vessels for various agent teams on the planet. Now it had found another, the faintest hyperspatial anomaly a quarter of a million kilometres out from the planet. The stealth effect was first-rate: anything less than *Alexis Denken*'s ANA-fabricated sensors wouldn't have been able to find it. That just left her with the question of who it was. And even if it mattered.

Her u-shadow opened a secure link to Admiral Juliaca. 'I wasn't expecting this,' she said.

'Neither were we,' the admiral confirmed. 'The President is not happy with today's events.'

'You mean the President is frightened.'

'Yeah. Our best guess is that someone captured her and broke into her mind. They're just remote-controlling her now. It's probably Ethan himself if it isn't Ilanthe.'

'That doesn't quite fit. I don't believe Ethan and Ilanthe would want their shabby little arrangement to be public knowledge. And how did Araminta know about Ilanthe?'

'Exactly, she has to have been taken over.'

'Or she communed with the Silfen Motherholm while she was on the paths. After all, we still haven't got a clue how she returned to Viotia, and it would appear she's been named a Friend.'

'Okay,' the admiral said. 'So why would the Silfen want Living Dream to go on Pilgrimage?'

Paula pressed her fingertips into her temple again, massaging firmly. 'I haven't got a clue. I'm just saying it's possible Araminta has decided to step up her game.' She could barely believe she was repeating Oscar's hopes, but what else was there to explain such extraordinary behaviour?

'Then her new game is going to kill us all.'

'Will the Navy destroy the Pilgrimage fleet?'

'President Alcamo is still trying to decide what to do. We're as compromised now as we were before, if not worse. If Ilanthe does make good her promise and supply Sol-barrier force fields to the ships, then they'll be invulnerable to anything we can hit them with. That just leaves us a small window while they're on the ground under construction.'

Paula immediately saw the problem with that. 'They're being built next to Greater Makkathran.'

'Actually, they're inside the urban boundary; which means they're under the city's civil defence force fields. If we take them out, we'll destroy half the city at least, probably more. Paula, even if I gave the order I'm not sure the Navy ships would carry it out. I wouldn't even blame them. Sixteen million people live there.'

'Billions of people live throughout the Greater Commonwealth. Trillions of entities live in the galaxy.'

'I know.'

'Covert sabotage will be easy enough. It doesn't have to be a frontal assault.'

'Believe me, we're drawing up those plans right now.'

'But that's only going to delay things.'

'If we have long enough, ANA might break out.'

'If we delay the Pilgrimage too much Ilanthe might offer Araminta a ride on her ship. Then we'd really be in trouble.'

'We're more concerned by what the Void would do,' the Admiral said. 'It already began an expansion the first time Araminta tried denying it. If we block her, there's no telling how it'll react to that. To put it bluntly: it knows where we live now.'

'So we still need an alternative.'

'We do. Paula . . . Do you have any idea what Gore is up to?'

'No, I'm afraid not.'

'Damn. Well that leaves us with just about nothing.'

'I thought the Raiel answered our request to attempt to break through the Sol barrier.'

'Yes, Qatux has agreed to help. We're expecting the *High Angel* will depart for Earth within the hour. The Navy is evacuating its core staff down to Kerensk, including me – after all we don't know if it'll come back.'

'I regard their involvement as promising. Nothing much stirs the Raiel these days.'

'I think Ilanthe and Araminta have managed to focus their attention.'

'Quite.'

'Have you got anything else for me?'

'I'm sorry, Admiral, but the only other possibility left is if Inigo is alive and on the *Lindau*.'

'How does that help us? He started this Ozziedamned non-sense in the first place.'

'Exactly. He may be able to stop it. He certainly had a large enough change of heart to dump Living Dream. Several powerful people believed that warranted expending considerable effort and energy on finding him.'

'What do you suggest? Intercepting the *Lindau*?'

'Not a good option. Not yet. This Aaron character is single-minded in his mission, and has already killed countless in his pursuit. If he is threatened he may well have instructions to eliminate Inigo.'

'Or he may not.'

'Granted. But if Inigo is our last remaining chance and he's on board that scout ship, we can't risk it. That's a small ship. Aaron has no fallback, nowhere to run. Prudence would suggest waiting until it reaches the Spike. That opens up our options from a tactical point of view.'

'All right Paula, but it's a loose end I don't want to ignore. We need every glimmer of hope we can muster.'

'I won't let it slip I assure you. I have a ship which can reach the Spike quickly when the need arises.'

*

Once again he ran across the vast hall with its crystalline arches high above. People scattered before him, frightened people. Children. Children with tears streaming down their sweet little faces.

Of all his uncertainty and confusion he knew that should not be so. A thought he held steadfast. A lone conviction in a world gone terribly wrong. Human society existed to protect its children. That was a bedrock he could rest easy upon. Not that such assurance meant anything to the physical reality he was surrounded by.

Weapons fire burst all around him, elegant coloured lines of energy forming complex criss-cross patterns in the air. Force fields added a mauve haze to the image. Then came the cacophony of screaming.

He ran, flinging himself across a cluster of wailing children. It was no good: the darkness followed him, flowing across the huge room like an incoming tide. It curled around him. And he felt her hand on his shoulder amid a clash of sparkling colours. The pain began, searing in through his flesh, seeking out his heart.

'You don't leave me,' she whispered silkily into his ear.

He struggled, writhing frantically against her grip as the pain was slowly replaced by an even more frightening cold. 'Nobody leaves me,' she said.

'I do!' he yelled with a raw throat. 'I don't want this.' Away along the fringe of darkness, more garish coloured lights exploded. He heaved against her iron grip—

—and fell out of the cot, to land painfully on the cabin floor. A weird ebony fog occluded his vision as he tried to focus on the *Lindau*'s bulkhead. It pulsed in a heartbeat rhythm with strange distensions bulging out, as if something was attempting to break out of his nightmare. He groaned as he squeezed his eyes shut, attempting to banish the creepy intrusion. The pain was real still, throbbing behind his temple like the devil's own migraine. Then he remembered a crown of slim silver needles contracting round his head, puncturing the skin, slipping effortlessly through the bone to penetrate his brain, and terrible red light shone into his thoughts, exposing every miserable segment of himself. 'Do it,' he yelled into the nothingness. 'Just do it now.' Sharp merciless claws reached in and started to rip out the most vital segments. And now his screams were silent, going on and on and on as his mind was shredded until finally, thankfully, there was nothing left. No thought remained so he ceased to think—

Aaron woke up with his cheek squashed uncomfortably on the deck, his neck at a bad angle. It was as if he was regaining consciousness from a knock-out blow. His skin was cold. He shivered as much from shock as anything. 'Oh crap, this has just got to stop,' he moaned as he slowly pushed himself up into a sitting position.

The captain's cabin was still a mess. He hadn't bothered to organize a servicebot to clean up yet. Personal environment wasn't a priority for him, unlike the other two, who seemed quite fastidious about their small, shared cabin. He ordered a fast biononic field scan to check on his captives. And relaxed fractionally when exovision displays showed them in the main cabin. Now their status was confirmed he followed it up by a review of the *Lindau*'s systems. Plenty of components were operating on the edge of their safety margins thanks to the damage they'd received back on Hanko. But they were still functioning, still in hyperspace and on course for the Spike.

Aaron took a moment to wipe himself down with a towel soaked in travel-clean before pulling on some clothes he'd found in the cabin's locker. The *Lindau*'s captain had been almost the same size as him, so the bots only needed to make a few adjustments before he could wear the conservatively styled shirts and trousers. So, dressed in fawn-coloured two-third-length shorts and a mauve sleeveless sweatshirt, he joined the other two for breakfast.

Corrie-Lyn gave him a sullen glance as he entered the main cabin, then returned to her bowl of yogurt and cereal. Aaron didn't need to run any kind of scan to know she was hungover. He'd given up trying to stop the one remaining culinary unit producing alcohol for her; its electronics were in a bad way, the last thing it needed was a software war raging inside its circuitry.

'Good morning,' he said politely to Inigo. At least the ex-Dreamer gave him a brief acknowledgement, glancing up from his plate of toast and marmalade. Aaron ordered up a toasted bagel with poached egg on smoked salmon, orange juice and a pot of tea.

'Why do you smell of bleach?' Corrie-Lyn asked.

'Do I?'

'You've used travel-fresh,' she accused. 'There is a working shower, you know.'

The culinary unit pinged, and Aaron opened its stainless steel door. His breakfast was inside. He hesitated at the slightly odd smell before transferring it all to a tray. The remaining chair at the table had broken as it was trying to retract, leaving a grey lump protruding from the floor, with an upper hollow that wasn't quite wide enough or deep enough for sitting in. Aaron squirmed his way down into it. 'The shower is in your room,' he pointed out.

'And you rate our privacy above your hygiene? Since when?'

Inigo stopped chewing and glanced silently up at the ceiling.

'Corrie-Lyn, we're going to be on board together for a while,' Aaron said. 'As you may have noticed this ship is on the wrong side of tiny, and there ain't a whole lot of it working too good. Now I don't expect you to be gushing with mighty gratitude, but it's my belief that basic civility will get us all through this without me ripping too many of your fucking limbs off. You clear on this?'

'Fascist bastard.'

'Is it true Ethan kept you on the Cleric Council because you were his private whore?'

'Fuck you!' Corrie-Lyn stood up fast, glaring at Aaron.

'See?' Aaron said mildly. 'It's a two-way street. And you can't rip my limbs off.'

She stomped out of the main cabin. Inigo watched her go, then carried on eating his toast. Aaron took a drink of his orange juice, then cut into the egg. It tasted like rotten fish. 'What the hell . . .'

'My toast tastes like cold lamb,' Inigo admitted. 'The fatty bits. I used biononics to change my taste receptor impulses. It helps a bit.'

'Good idea.' Aaron's u-shadow was interrogating the culinary unit to try and identify the problem. The result wasn't promising. 'The texture memory files are corrupted, and it doesn't look like there are any back-ups left on board, a whole batch of kubes got physically smashed up. It'll be producing this kind of crud all the way to the Spike.'

'Corrie-Lyn doesn't have biononics. She can't make it taste better.'

'That'll make her a bucketful of fun for sure. We'll have to inventory the prepacked supplies, see if there's enough to last her.'

'Or you could simply connect to the unisphere with a TD channel and download some new files.'

Aaron looked at him over the rim of the glass of orange juice – which tasted okay. 'Not going to happen. I can't risk an

326

infiltration. The smartcore's in the same condition as the rest of the ship.'

'That was a bad dream you had last night,' Inigo said quietly. 'You need to watch out for aspects leaking into your genuine personality.'

Aaron raised an eyebrow. 'My *genuine* personality?'

'All right then, the one that keeps you up and functional. I'm getting concerned about the Mr Paranoia who won't risk down-loading a food synthesis file.'

'Okay, for future reference, this very same personality has kept me alive through all my missions, and helped me snatch you. And that barely took a couple of weeks after I'd been assigned to you, whereas everyone else in the Commonwealth had spent seventy years on the hunt for you. So you might want to rethink your poor estimation of my operational capabilities.'

Inigo's hands fluttered in a modest gesture of acquiescence. 'As you wish. But you have to understand I am curious about your composition. I've never encountered a mind quite like yours before. You have absences, and I don't just mean memory. Whole emotional fibres seem to have been suppressed. That's not good for you; the emotions you have permitted yourself are abnormally large, you're out of balance as a result.'

'So Corrie-Lyn keeps telling me.' He tasted his egg again. His biononics had changed his taste receptors. This time the yolk had a mushroom flavour. It was weird, but he could live with it, he decided.

'You've been unkind to her,' Inigo said accusingly. 'Small wonder she hates you.'

'I found you for her. She's just ungrateful, that's all. That or she doesn't want to admit to herself how willing she was to pay the price.'

'What price is that?'

'Betrayal. That's what it took to trace you.'

'Hmm. Interesting analysis. All of which brings us back to our current situation. So you're taking me to the Spike to see Ozzie. What then?'

'Don't know.'

'Your unknown employer must have given you some hint, some rough outline. To be an effective field agent you have to constantly re-evaluate your alternatives. What if the *Lindau* was knocked out by the opposition – whoever they are. What if I'm taken away?'

Aaron smiled. 'Then I kill you.'

The cabin Corrie-Lyn and Inigo were sharing was small. It was meant for five crew, but in theory the Navy duty rota they followed should mean that only two would ever be using it at the same time, with changeovers every few hours. Inigo reckoned they'd all have to be very intimate with each other. The bunks were both fully extended, and locked at a ten-degree angle with the edges curling up as if they were heat-damaged. All of which left little space to edge along between them. And they were useless for sleeping in. Instead, Inigo had just piled all the quilts onto the floor to make a cosy nest.

When he came back in after breakfast, Corrie-Lyn was sitting cross-legged in the middle of the crumpled fabric, drinking a mug of black coffee. An empty ready-pak was on the floor beside her.

'Taste good?' he asked.

She held the foil ready-pak up. 'The deSavoel estate's finest mountain bean. It doesn't come much better.'

'That should help the hangover.' He perched awkwardly on the edge of a bunk, feeling it give slightly beneath him. It shouldn't do that.

'It does,' she grunted.

'I wonder if we can find a bean to help with the attitude.'

'Don't start.'

'What in Honious happened to you?'

Corrie-Lyn's dainty freckled face abruptly turned livid. 'Somebody left. Not just me, they left the whole fucking movement. They got up and walked out without a word, a hint of why they were going. Everything I loved, everything I believed in was gone, ripped away from me. I'd given decades of my life to you and the dream you promised us. And as if that wasn't enough, *I didn't know*! I didn't know why you'd left. Ladyfuckit, I didn't even know if you were alive. I didn't know if you'd given up on us, if it was all wrong, if you'd lost hope. I. Didn't. Know! Nothing, that's what you left me with. From everything – a fabulous life with hope and happiness and love, to nothing in a single second. Do you have any idea what that's like? You don't, clearly you don't, because you wouldn't be sitting there asking the stupidest question in the universe if you did. What happened? Bastard. You can go straight to Honious for all I care.'

'I'm sorry,' he said, crestfallen. 'It's . . . that final dream I had. It was too much. We weren't leading anyone to salvation. Makkathran, Edeard, that whole civilization was a fluke, a glorious one-off that I caught at just the right time. It can never be repeated, not now, not now we know the Void's ability. The Raiel were right, the Void is a monster. It should be destroyed.'

'Why?' she implored. 'What is that Last Dream?'

'Nothing,' he whispered. 'It showed that even dreams all turn to dust in the end.'

'Then why didn't—'

'I tell you?'

'Yes!'

'Because something as big, as powerful, as Living Dream can't be finished overnight. There were over ten billion followers when I left. Ten Billion! I can't just turn round to them and say: Ooops, sorry, I was wrong. Go home and get on with your lives, forget all about the Waterwalker and Querencia.'

'The Inigo I knew would have done that,' she said through gritted teeth. 'The Inigo I knew had courage and integrity.'

'I let it die, or so I thought. It was the kindest thing. Ethan was the finest example of that, a politician not a follower. After him would have come dozens of similar leaders, all of them concerned with position and maintaining the ancient blind dogma. Living Dream would have turned into an old-style religion, always preaching the promise of salvation, never producing the realization. Not without me. I was the one who might have been able to pass through the barrier. You know I was going to try, really I was. Go out there in a fast starship and see if I could make it, just like the original old ship did. That's before we knew about the warrior Raiel, of course. But once I had that dream I knew the ideal was over. Ethan and all the others who should have come after him would have killed off Living Dream in a couple of centuries.'

'Then along came the Second Dreamer,' she said.

'Yeah. I guess I should have realized the Void would never let us alone. It feeds off minds like ours. Once it had that first taste, it was bound to find another way of pulling us in.'

'You mean it's evil?' she asked in surprise.

'No. That kind of term doesn't apply. It has purpose, that's all. Unfortunately, that purpose will bring untold damage to the galaxy.'

'Then,' she glanced at the closed door, 'what are we going to do about it?'

'We?'

She nodded modestly. 'I believe in you, I always have. If you say we have to stop the Void then I'll follow you into Honious itself to bring that off.'

Inigo smiled as he looked down at her. She was wearing a crewman's shirt that was several sizes too large, which made it kind of sexy as it shifted around, tracing the shape of her body. He'd watched her yesterday with considerable physical interest, the simple sight of her teasing out a great many pleasurable memories of the time they had spent as lovers. But she'd been drunk and spitting venom about Aaron and their situation and who was to blame for the state of the universe. Now though, as he slipped off the bunk to kneel beside her, there was a look of hope kindled in her eyes. 'Really?' he asked uncertainly. 'After all I've put you through?'

'It would be a start to your penance,' she replied.

'True.'

'But . . .' She waved a hand at the door. 'What about him? We don't know if his masters want you to help the Pilgrimage or ruin it.'

'First off, he's undoubtedly listening to every word we're saying.'

'Oh.'

'Secondly, the clue is in who we're going to see.'

'Ozzie?'

'Yes, which is why I haven't tried anything like the glacier again.' Inigo grinned up at the ceiling. 'Yet.'

'I thought you didn't like Ozzie?'

'No. Ozzie doesn't like me. He was completely opposed to Living Dream, so I can only conclude that Aaron's masters are also among those who don't want the Pilgrimage to go ahead.'

Corrie-Lyn shrugged, and pushed some of her thick red hair away from her eyes. Intent and interested now, she fixed him with a curious look. 'Why didn't Ozzie like you?'

'He gave humanity the gaiafield so that we could share our emotions, which he felt was a way of letting everyone communicate on a much higher level. If we could look into the hearts of people we feared or disliked we should be able to see that deep down they were human too – according to his theory. Such knowledge would bring us closer together as a species. Damn, it was almost worth building a Faction round the notion, but the idea was too subtle for that. Ozzie wanted us to become accustomed to it, to use it openly and honestly. Only when we'd incorporated it into our lives would we realize the effect it'd had on our society.'

'We have.'

'Not really. You see, I perverted the whole gaiafield to build a religion on. That wasn't supposed to happen. As he told me, and I quote: The gaiafield was to help people to understand and appreciate life, the universe and everything, so they don't get fooled by idiot messiahs and corrupt politicians. So I'd gone and wrecked his dream by spreading Edeard's dreams. Quite ironic really, from my point of view. Ozzie didn't see that. Turns out he doesn't have half the sense of humour everyone says he has.

He went off to the Spike in a huge sulk to build a "galactic dream", as a counter to my disgraceful subversion.'

'So he hasn't succeeded, then?'

'Not that we know of.'

'Then how can he help?'

'I haven't got a clue. But don't forget, he is an absolute genius, which is a term applied far too liberally in history. In his case it's real. I suspect that whatever plan is loaded into Aaron's subconscious expects Ozzie and me to team up to defeat the Void.'

'That's a huge gamble.'

'We're long past the time for careful certainty.'

'Do you have any idea how to stop the Void?'

'No. Not a single glimmer of a notion, even.'

'But you were an astrophysicist to begin with.'

'Yes, but my knowledge base is centuries out of date.'

'Oh.' She pushed the empty coffee mug to one side with a glum expression.

'Hey,' his hand stroked the side of her face. 'I'm sure Ozzie and I will give it our best shot.'

She nodded, closing her eyes as she leant into his touch. 'Don't leave me again.'

'We'll see this through together. I promise.'

'The Waterwalker never quit.'

Inigo kissed her. It was just the same as it had been all those decades ago, which was a treacherous memory. A lot of very strong emotions were bundled up with the time he and Corrie-Lyn had been together. Most of them good. 'I'm not as strong as the Waterwalker.'

'You are,' she breathed. 'That's why you found each other. That's why you connected.'

'I'll do my best,' he promised, nuzzling her chin. His hands went down to the hem of the big loose shirt. 'But he never faced a situation like this.'

'The voyage of the *Lady's Light*.' She began to tug at the seam on his one-piece.

'Hardly the same.'

'He didn't know what he was coming home to.'

'Okay.' He pulled back and stared at her wide eyes. 'Let's just find our own way here, shall we?'

'What about . . . ?'

'Screw him.'

Corrie-Lyn's tongue licked playfully round her lips. 'Me first. I've been waiting a *very* long time.'

Inigo's Twenty-Ninth Dream

'Land ahoy,' came the cry from the lookout.

Edeard craned his neck back to see the crewman perched atop the main mast of *Lady's Light*. It was Manel, grinning wildly as he waved down at everyone on the deck. The young man's mind was unshielded as he gifted everyone his sight. Which right now was looking down on their upturned faces.

'Manel!' came a collective sigh.

His amusement poured across the ship, and he shifted his balance on the precarious platform to hold the telescope up again. Despite regular cleaning, the lenses in the brass tube were scuffed and grubby after four years of daily use at sea, but the image was clear enough. A dark speck spiked up out of the blue on blue horizon.

Edeard started clapping at the sight of it, his good cheer swelling out to join the collective thoughts of those on the other four ships which made up the explorer flotilla. Everyone was delighted. The distant pinnacle of land could only be one of the eastern isles, which meant Makkathran was no more than a month's sailing away.

'How about that,' Jiska exclaimed. 'He did get it right.'

'Yeah yeah,' Edeard agreed, too happy to care about the needling. Natran, who captained the *Lady's Light*, had been promising sight of the eastern isles for five weeks now. People were getting anxious about his navigational skills, though the captains of the other ships concurred with him. Jiska had spent that time supporting her husband's ability. After a four-year voyage, people were starting to get understandably fretful.

Kristabel came up beside Edeard, her contentment merging with his. He smiled back at her as they linked arms, and together they made their way up to the prow. It was getting quite cluttered on the middeck now, which Natran was generally unhappy over. As well as the coils of rope and ship's lockers, a number of wicker cages were lashed to the decking, each containing some new animal they'd discovered on their various landings. Not all had survived the long voyage home. Taralee's cabin was full of large glass jars where their bodies were preserved in foul-smelling fluid. She and the other doctors and botanists had probably gained the most from their expedition, cataloguing hundreds of new species and plants.

But no new people, Edeard thought.

'What's the matter?' Kristabel asked.

A few of the crew glanced over in his direction, catching his sadness. He gave them all an apologetic shrug.

'We really are alone on this world,' he explained to Kristabel. 'Now we're coming home we know that for certain.'

'Never certainty,' she said, smiling as she pushed some of her thick hair from her eyes. It was getting long again. They'd been eight days out from Makkathran when Kristabel simply sat down in the main cabin and got one of the other women to cut her already short (by Makkathran standards) hair right back, leaving just a few curly inches.

'It's practical,' she'd explained calmly to an aghast Edeard. 'You can't seriously expect me to fight off my hair on top of everything else storms will throw at us, now can you? It's been bad enough for a week in this mild weather.'

But you managed with a plait, he managed to avoid saying out loud. Kristabel without her long hair was ... just plain wrong somehow.

Edeard could laugh at that now. Besides, she was still rather cute with short hair, and elegant with it. It was the least of the changes and accommodations that they'd collectively made. He couldn't even remember the last time he'd seen a woman in a skirt aside from the formal dinner parties held every month without fail. They just wore trousers – and shorts in summer – with the exception of the flotilla's Mother, who'd maintained her traditional decorum at all times. The small revolution meant they were able to help with the rigging and a dozen other shipboard tasks that were usually the exclusive province of sailors. Indeed there had been a lot of grumbling from the Mariners Guild at the very thought of women going on such a voyage; while the general Makkathran population had been mildly incredulous – the male population in any case. Edeard had received a huge amount of support from the city's women-folk.

Scepticism about taking women, shaken heads over the prospect of repeating Captain Allard's grand failure, more con-sternation from Kristabel's endless flock of relatives concerning the cost of five such vast vessels. At times it had seemed like the only ones in favour were the Guild of Shipwrights and a horde of merchants eager to supply the flotilla. Such a dour atmosphere had lurked across Makkathran's streets and canals from the time he announced his intention until that day three years later when the ships had been completed. Then, with the five vessels anchored outside the city, attitudes finally began to mellow into admiration and excitement. There wasn't a quay large enough or a port district channel deep enough to handle the *Lady's Light* and her sister ships, adding to their allure. Trips around the anchored flotilla in small sailing boats were a huge and profit-able venture for the city's mariners. To lay down the keels, Edeard had even gone to the same narrow cove half a mile south of the city that Allard had used a thousand years ago to build the *Majestic Marie*. It all fostered a great deal of interest and civic pride. This time the circumnavigation will be a success, people believed. This is our time, our ships, our talent, and we have the Waterwalker. It probably helped that Edeard announced his intention the week after the first Skylord arrived to guide Finitan's soul to the Heart.

Edeard prided himself he'd held out that long. He never wanted to go back so far into his own past again. Querencia might have been saved from the nest, but the personal consequences were too high. It was a terrible burden to live through every day again, watching the same mistakes and failings and wasteful accidents and petty arguments and wretched politics play out once more when he already knew the solution to everything from his previous trip through the same years. Time and again he was tempted to intervene, to make things easier for everyone. But if he began he knew there was no limit to what he could and should do once that moral constraint was broken; there would be no end to intervention, constant assistance would become meddling in the eyes of those he sought to help.

Besides, those repeated events he endured weren't so bad for everyone else – especially now the nest hadn't arisen this time around. People had to learn things for themselves to give them the confidence to live a better life in their own fashion. And ultimately ... where would he draw the line? Stopping a child falling over and breaking an arm wouldn't teach the child to be more careful next time, and that was a lesson that needed to be learned. Without caution, what stupidity would they do the next day?

So with the exception of preventing several murders he recalled, he restrained himself admirably. Which was why he was so desperate to build the ships and sail away on a voyage that would last for years. As well as satisfying his curiosity about the unknown continents and islands of Querencia, he would be doing something different, something new and fresh.

And it had worked; the last four years had been the happiest time he'd known since he'd come back to eliminate Tathal. Kristabel had gladly responded to that, even relishing being free of the Upper Council and its endless bickering politics. They were as close now as they had been on their wedding day.

Back on the middeck Natran was the centre of an excited crowd, receiving their congratulations and thanks with good-humoured restraint. His little son, Kiranan, was sitting happily on his shoulders. Born on board three years ago, the lad was naturally curious about living in the big city the way Edeard and Kristabel described it to him. In total, twelve children had been born on the *Lady's Light* during the epic voyage, with another thirty on the other four ships. Which is where things had, finally, wonderfully, begun to change. Rolar and Wenalee had stayed behind to manage the Culverit estate and take Kristabel's seat on the Upper Council; Marakas and Dylorn had also chosen to remain in Makkathran. His other children had all joined the flotilla. Jiska and Natran were married, which they hadn't been in this year before. Taralee had formed a close attachment to Colyn, a journeyman from the horticultural association (which might well qualify for guild status after this voyage). But it was Marilee and Analee who had surprised and delighted him the most. He'd simply assumed the twins would stay behind and carry on partying. Instead they'd insisted on coming. Of course, they just carried on in their own way through shipboard life, almost oblivious to the routines and conventions around them. Not long out of port, they'd claimed Marvane as their lover, a delighted, infatuated, dazed, junior lieutenant, and enticed him down to their cabin each night. (Not that they needed to try very hard; his envious friends amid the flotilla swiftly named him Luckiest Man On Querencia.) It was a relationship which lasted a lot longer than their usual, for he was actually a decent worthy man.

Little Kiranan stretched his arms out towards his grandma, and squealed delightedly as Edeard's third hand plucked him from his father's shoulders and delivered him to Kristabel's embrace.

'I wonder if it's changed?' Kristabel murmured as she made a fuss of the boy.

Kiranan pointed at the horizon. 'Island,' he announced. 'Big home.' His mind shone with wonder and expectation.

'It's close, poppet,' Kristabel promised.

'It won't change,' Edeard declared solemnly. 'That's the thing with Makkathran, it's timeless.'

Kristabel flashed him a knowing smile. 'It's changed since you arrived,' she said smartly. 'Ladies in shorts, indeed.'

He smiled, glancing down. She was wearing a white cotton shirt with blue canvas shorts, her legs lean and tanned from years of exposure to the sun. 'There are worse revolutions.'

'Daddy,' Marilee called as she made her way along the deck.

'We'll be back in time,' Analee said, accompanying her sister, the two of them linking arms instinctively against the swell. *Lady's Light* was making a fair speed in the warm south-westerly wind.

'Not that we don't trust Taralee.'

'Or the ship's surgery.'

'But it will be a comfort to be back in the mansion with all of the Doctors' Guild on call.'

'Just in case.'

They grinned at him. Both of them were six months pregnant, and gloriously happy despite the constant morning sickness they both suffered from. And on board that was a very public morning sickness; nobody was completely shielded from the twins' nausea, which had brought about a lot of sympathetic barfing among the exposed crew.

'That'll be a close call,' he said, trying to be realistic. Not that the twins had ever paid much attention to that. 'Even with good winds it'll take a month from here.'

'Oh Daddy.'

'That's so mean.'

'We want to have landborn children.'

'Really?' he asked. 'What does Marvane want? He's a sailor, after all.'

Marilee and Analee pulled a face at each other.

'He's a father now.'

'And our husband.'

'Yeees,' Edeard said. Natran had married the three of them a year and a half ago. A beautiful tropical beach setting, everyone barefoot while the bright sun shone down and wavelets lapped on the white sands, the twins ecstatic as they were betrothed to their handsome fiancé. Querencia had no actual law against marrying more than one person at a time, though it certainly wasn't endorsed in any of the Lady's scriptures, so it had to be the senior captain rather than the flotilla's Mother who conducted the ceremony. With Marvane's title now irrefutable, the elated trio spent their honeymoon in a small shack the carpenters had built for them above the shore, while the expedition took an uncommonly long time to catalogue the flora and fauna of the island.

'So he's going to settle with us,' Marilee announced as if it should have been obvious.

'In some little part of the Culverit estate on the Iguru.'

'Where we can raise babies and crops together.'

'Because this voyage is a lifetime's worth of sailing.'

'For anyone.'

'And Taralee has found us some fabulous new plants to cultivate.'

'Which people are going to love.'

'And make us a fortune.'

Edeard couldn't bring himself to say anything, though he could sense Kristabel becoming tense with all the twins' daydream talk. *But then why shouldn't it come true? Stranger things have happened, and as daydreams go it's sweet. Besides, that's what we're all ultimately aiming for, isn't it? An easier, gentler life.* He was saved from any comment when he sensed Natran's longtalk to the helmsman, ordering a small change of course. 'Why?' he enquired idly.

'We need to identify the island,' Natran replied. 'There are eight on the edge of the eastern archipelago. Once I've got an accurate fix, navigating home will be easy.'

'Of course.'

'Are you ready for home?' Kristabel asked quietly.

'I think so,' he said, though he knew it to be true. *It's all new from now on.* Living in Makkathran again would be easy. Anticipation stirred a joy in him which had been missing for so long. He guessed she knew that, judging by the contentment glowing within her own thoughts.

'We could always go the other way round the world,' she teased. 'There're both poles to explore.'

Edeard laughed. 'Let's leave that to the grandchildren, shall we? You and I have enough to do taking up our roles again. And I think I might just consider running for Mayor at the next elections.'

The look she gave him was as if she'd never seen him before. 'You never stop, do you?'

'Wonder who I learned that from, Mistress?'

She grinned and cuddled Kiranan tight as the boy strained to see the city he knew was out there somewhere. 'And you,' she told the boy, 'you're going to meet all your cousins.'

'Yay-oh,' Kiranan cooed.

'Who probably make up half the city's population by now,' Edeard muttered. The rate Rolar and Wenalee produced offspring was prodigious, and he knew from last time round that Marakas and Heliana were keen to get started.

'Daddy!' the twins chorused disapproval.

'I wonder if Dylorn will be wed,' Kristabel said softly; there was a brief pang of regret at being parted from her children for so long.

'Without us there?' Analee sounded shocked.

'He wouldn't dare.'

'You two did,' Edeard pointed out.

'That's different.'

'We had you there.'

'Which makes it proper.'

Edeard sighed, and grinned at the horizon. 'Not long now. And Lady, we're going to have the reunion party of all time.'

*

Makkathran appeared over the horizon just before noon on the thirty-eighth day after Manel had sighted the first eastern isle. The crew of the *Lady's Light* knew it was near. Cargo ships had been a regular sighting for days, and early that morning they'd passed the outbound fishing fleet from Portheves, a village not ten miles from the city itself. Once they'd recovered from their shock, the fishermen had stood and cheered as the giant boats of the flotilla slid past.

By midmorning, they had a loose escort of a dozen traders heading towards the coastline. Good-hearted, curious longshouts from their new companions were thrown their way as they ploughed through the crisp blue water. Then Makkathran emerged, its sturdy towers the first aspect to rise up over the horizon, their sharp pinnacles piercing the cloudless azure sky. A fervent rush of farsight swept out from the city to wash across the flotilla, accompanied by astonishment and a burst of exultant welcomes. Everyone was up on deck to see the city they'd left behind just over four years ago. Edeard thought the ships would just fly onwards through the water even without any wind, so strong was the compulsion to make it home now. They must have been quite a sight to those in the city. Each magnificent ship had set out with three full sets of snow-white sails; now the *Lady's Light* was rigged with a grubby patchwork of canvas stitched together from whatever sails remained after years of sun-bleaching, storms, and frozen winters where ice crystals hung heavy from every seam and rope. Both the *Lady's Star* and the *Lady's Guidance* had broad repairs of a softer tropical wood on their waterline where the coral of the Auguste Sea had breached them despite the crew's best telekinetic efforts to snap the vicious submerged spines. Several ships had new masts to replace those that were snapped off in various gales.

But we made it, despite everything this world threw at us. Edeard grinned at Makkathran as the wondrously familiar out-line of his home grew clearer. *You can see that, you can see our triumph in the patches and the damage and the cargo of knowledge we've returned with. We've opened up the whole world for everyone.*

Slowly, though, his grin began to fade as he took notice of the thoughts swirling among the vast districts. The city's mental timbre had changed. For a while he was puzzled by the flashes of anger shivering beneath the surface clamour of excitement at the flotilla's return. Then he gradually became aware of the minds grouped together outside the north gate, thousands of them. Among those bright knots of rage and resentment he could find no hint of excitement or jubilation at the flotilla's arrival. They were completely at odds with the rest of the city.

'Uh oh,' he mumbled under his breath. His farsight reached out to see what in Honious was going on. The first thing he sensed was the militia, deployed around the gate and in long dug-out formations along the road through the greensward into the encircling forest. By tradition, that area outside the city was always kept empty and uninhabited. Not any more. Dozens of huge camps had sprung up on the meadowland, and from what he could determine, a lot of the ancient trees had been felled – presumably as fuel for the campfires.

'What is it?' Kristabel asked as he struggled to shield the dismay growing in his own mind.

'Some kind of siege, but that's not quite it.' He grudgingly gifted her his farsight.

'Oh Lady,' she grumbled. 'Where did they come from?'

He shrugged, trying to find some kind of clue. But such a feat was beyond farsight, especially at such a distance. 'We'll find out soon enough. And then everyone will expect the Waterwalker to put it right.' He just couldn't help how martyred he sounded, not to mention self-pitying.

'Edeard,' she gently rubbed the top of his back between his shoulder blades, 'why do you always punish yourself like this?'

'Because I'm the one who always has to sort everything out. Oh Ladycrapit, it just never stops. Every time I think I've got it right someone comes along with a fresh way to foul things up.'

'Darling Edeard, you're really far too hard on yourself.'

'No I'm not,' he said bitterly. 'It's my responsibility. I'm responsible for this whole world. Me. No one else.'

'Don't be silly, Edeard.' Kristabel's voice and mind hardened. 'Now please don't do this whole intolerable burden thing again, I had enough of it before. What's important now is to get the twins ashore; they need to get to the mansion to give birth, poor things. Concentrate on that if you have to have something to moan about.'

'Intolerable burden thing?' he asked quietly; he could barely believe what she'd just said.

'Yes,' Kristabel said firmly, giving him an uncompromising look. 'The Lady knows how impossible you'd become before we built the flotilla. That's the main reason I agreed the estate would pay for it all. And this voyage worked, Edeard. For the Lady's sake, you were back to normal. You were you again. Now this. We haven't even got ashore yet and already you're moaning that everything's going against you.'

Lady damn it, you have no fucking idea! He glared at her furiously and stomped off down the deck.

'Daddy?' Jiska asked with a worried frown.

But he was in no mood to talk, not even for her.

Thousands were lining the quays and wharfs of the port district as the flotilla's longboats made it through the great waterside opening in the city walls into the port district. There were fifteen boats in the first batch, all of them rowed by a regulation team of ge-chimps sculpted with broad shoulders and muscular arms so the oars fairly whizzed through the water. Edeard was on the second boat; Kristabel and Taralee had taken the twins and Marvane ahead on the first. Edeard had a fast directed longtalk to an elated Rolar, making sure a couple of family gondolas were waiting in the port to take them straight back to the ziggurat. The twins were in a great deal of discomfort; in Edeard's belief a condition partly owing to their fixation of giving birth on land. Taralee had privately confirmed they weren't due for another couple of days yet, though they were complaining as if their labour had already begun.

So he kept company with Jiska and Natran and Manel and a half-dozen officers and their wives and children; a merry group, all of whom were waving frantically at the cheering crowds. Except him. He simply couldn't summon the enthusiasm and sat at the back of the longboat in a private sulk.

'By the Lady, we'd given up on you at least a couple of years back,' Macsen's directed longtalk declared. 'Did you walk round the world instead? It's taken you forever.'

Finally, Edeard consented to a grin. There was his friend standing at the head of the very hastily assembled official welcome committee of grand councillors, district representatives, officials and family. A huge group of them squashed on to Wharf One, anxious that no one should move about too much, else those on the front rank would topple into the sea. They'd dressed in their most colourful and expensive robes, whilst the strong sea breeze blew their hair and hems about in an undignified manner. Macsen and Dinlay were at the forefront, of course, waving wildly. Dinlay had one arm round a tall, powerfully built girl. Edeard didn't care that he didn't know her. It wasn't Gealee, which was all that truly mattered. His gaze switched to Macsen, who was by himself. The Master of Sampalok had put on a disturbing amount of weight over the intervening years.

However, standing beside Macsen was Doblek, Master of Drupe. It was he who wore the Mayor's robes.

That's different, Edeard mused. Before, it was Trahaval who was Mayor at this time. He tried to convince himself that was a good thing, even though he remembered Doblek as a mildly inadequate District Master who admired the old traditions. *Not a reformer, by any means.*

The longboat reached Wharf One. Once the dock handlers had secured them, Edeard made his way up the wooden steps to mounting roars of approval from the waiting crowds. It was an invigorating sound, sending the timid seabirds wheeling still higher above the port district. *Just like the Banishment, but without the violence and turmoil.*

Not too grudgingly, Edeard raised an appreciative hand and grinned back at everyone on the docks who was producing such an effusive greeting.

'Waterwalker!' Mayor Doblek opened both arms wide and stepped forward to embrace Edeard. 'This is a joyful day. Welcome, yes, welcome back. Did you really voyage around the whole world?'

The city quietened slightly, hanging on to the Mayor's gifting, awaiting the answer.

'We did,' Edeard announced solemnly, but he couldn't help the smile widening his lips.

The cheering began again.

Edeard disengaged himself from the Mayor's clutches, turning slightly. 'Mayor, I think you know my senior captain: Natran. And my daughter Jiska.'

'Of course,' the Mayor moved along the line of arrivals, delighted with more official duty, keeping himself firmly at the forefront of public attention.

'It's crazy good, Grandpa,' little Kiranan said, clinging to Edeard's leg while his parents were swamped by the Mayor.

'What is?' Edeard asked.

'The city. Is this everyone in the whole world?'

Edeard hadn't thought of that. Kiranan had never known anyone other than the crews in the flotilla, now he was confronted by the city's jubilant population. Small wonder he was more subdued than usual. 'Not even close,' Edeard assured the boy. He pushed his farsight out to the smaller wharf on the other side of the port entrance where Kristabel and the twins were transferring to the family gondolas. Rolar was embracing his mother; and a host of grandchildren were jumping about excitedly, threatening to capsize the glossy black boat. Burlal wasn't among them. Edeard was nonplussed by that. Instead of his young grandson, a little girl was cavorting around Rolar and Wenalee, maybe five months younger than the boy he was expecting to see. It wasn't something he'd considered, that with this world diverging from what had gone before his own grand-children would be different. He knew now he should've been prepared for it. For a start, he'd been blessed with Kiranan, as well as the twins' pregnancy – neither of which events had gone before. But he'd really loved little Burlal, the boy was such a gem. He gave the girl a sharp scrutiny, which she responded to with a start; then looked back at him across the water before burying herself in Wenalee's skirts.

'So who's this, then?' Dinlay asked.

Edeard's smile returned in a weaker form. *No Burlal?* Edeard was still thinking. *Lady, but he didn't deserve oblivion like Tathal. That's not right, not right at all.* 'This is my new grandson, Kiranan,' he managed to say levelly as he ruffled the lad's hair.

'Grandpa!' the boy twisted away. 'You're Dinlay. You were shot, once. Grandpa has told me all about you.'

'Has he now? Well, you come and see me one day, and I'll tell you about him. Everything he thinks you shouldn't know.'

'Really? Promise?' The boy looked up admiringly at his new friend.

'Promise on the Lady.'

'Welcome home, Edeard,' Macsen said, and took Edeard's hand warmly.

'So where's Kanseen?' Edeard asked.

Macsen's wide smile froze. 'We called it a day,' he said with what was an attempt to maintain a jovial attitude. 'Best for both of us.'

'No! I'm . . . sorry to hear that.' *Lady, you can't do this me. They were still together before.*

'She said she'll see you later.'

'Okay then.'

'And this is Hilitte,' Dinlay said proudly, ushering the tall girl forwards. 'We've been wed these last seven months.'

This bit was easy. Edeard had done this many many times in every time he had begun again. So yet again and as always he kept a composed face and smiled politely as he held out his hand to the robust girl. 'Congratulations.' No disapproval shown, no surprise at her youth (younger than Jiska, easily), no confusion at the somehow familiar features smiling coquettishly back at him.

Macsen moved behind him, his mouth brushing past Edeard's ear as if by chance. 'Nanitte's daughter,' he whispered.

Edeard coughed, hoping to Honious he was covering his shock.

'Thank you, Waterwalker,' she said in a husky voice – yes, definitely similar to her mother. And that coquettish smile deepened, becoming coy, appraising.

Edeard quickly turned back to Macsen. 'Lady, it's good to be back.'

'So you really went the whole way round the world?' Dinlay asked.

'We certainly did. Ah, the stories I have to tell you.'

'And?'

Edeard knew exactly what the question was. 'There's only us. No one else.'

Dinlay's disappointment was all the more pronounced amid the rejoicing inflaming the city. 'Ah well,' he sighed.

'What's going on outside the North Gate?' Edeard asked.

'Those bastards!' Macsen began.

'Macsen,' Dinlay said awkwardly. 'The Waterwalker hasn't even seen his family yet – after four years. We've held the peace for this long, we can wait a day more. Edeard, it's nothing to worry about, we have the situation under control.'

Macsen gave a reluctant nod. 'Of course, I'm sorry old friend. This is wrong of me. There's so much I want to hear about.'

'And by the Lady, you shall,' Edeard promised.

*

It was several days before Edeard found the time to meet privately with his old friends. The first two days were spent happily enough greeting his family and getting to know the latest additions; then for one day he was banished to a lounge on the ninth floor of the ziggurat with the other senior males of the family, to feel worthless and faintly guilty while Taralee, two midwifes, several Novices and Kristabel and even Marvane helped the twins give birth. For once they didn't synchronize perfectly; Marilee gave birth to her two daughters a good five hours before Analee produced a son and daughter. After that, of course, was the formal Culverit tradition of the Arrival Breakfast where an overwhelmed Marvane sat in a daze receiving congratulations from his new family.

So lunchtime on the fourth day after the flotilla arrived back saw Edeard take a gondola down to Sampalok. He walked along Mislore Avenue to the square at the centre of the district. Every building he passed was occupied. No matter how small or awkward, every cluster of rooms had someone living there; bachelor, bachelorette, couples, small young families, stubborn old widower or widow. There was nothing left for any newcomer.

At the end of the avenue the six-sided mansion was a welcome sight. He always felt a mild satisfaction every time he saw it, something he'd created, something oddly reassuring.

This time, the square around it had none of the makeshift camps of stopover visitors awaiting guidance. It was back to a pre-Skylord normality, with Sampalok residents strolling around the fountains while kids played football and hoop-chase in the sunshine. Stalls on either side of Burfol Street were doing a good trade in sugared fruits and cool drinks.

People smiled graciously at the Waterwalker in his customary black cloak. Once, there was a time when he would have welcomed such a greeting from the citizens of Sampalok. Now he found it hard to return that smile. *But I'm being unfair, it's not just this district that's to blame.*

He went into the mansion via the archway on the lavender-shaded wall and hurried up the stairs to the fifth floor where Macsen had his private study. It was a simple room opening on to a balcony. Today the tall windows were shut. The desk was covered in leather folders, often with the ribbons untied to let the papers spill out; the tables were also piled high, as were various shelves and cabinets. Some of the chairs were also pedestals for the chaotic paperwork. It used to be an immaculately tidy room, Edeard reflected. As if reading his thoughts directly, Macsen gave a conciliatory grin as he got to his feet. 'Before you ask: yes, it has only got like this since she left.'

Edeard eyed the food (or wine) stains down Macsen's shirt; but said nothing. Some of the chairs already filled with paperwork had cloaks and robes draped over them. 'Something that big will take a while to adjust to,' he said diplomatically.

'Have you seen her?'

'No. Not yet. Kristabel visited her last night.'

Macsen shook his head and sank back into the chair behind the desk. 'She doesn't even live in Sampalok any more.'

'Do you want to tell me what happened?'

'Oh Lady, no. She said I was losing my focus or drive or something; the usual rubbish women spout. You know what they're like. Nothing I did was ever right.'

'Yeah, I know what they're like.'

'What? Even Kristabel?' Macsen seemed pathetically eager for confirmation, to know he wasn't alone in his suffering.

'Especially Kristabel,' Edeard assured him, wishing he was being completely dishonest. *But . . . Lady, she's changed since we got back. And it's all supposedly my fault.*

Macsen picked up a crystal decanter and poured out some double-blended spirits which the Rassien estate was famous for. He squinted at the golden brown liquid as it swirled round the tumbler, then swallowed it down in one go. The decanter was held out to Edeard.

'No thanks.'

'You pity me, don't you?' Macsen burped loudly.

Oh Great Lady, I don't need this. Not on top of everything else. 'I don't pity you. I'd like the old you back, but I'm prepared to wait.'

'Oh Edeard, how I wish we'd gone with you. None of this would've happened. No Our City movement, no Doblek winning the election, none of the squalid blockade camps.'

'I heard they called themselves Our City, Rolar told me. Of course, I sensed the camps and the militia as soon as we reached port.'

'The militia has to be there to keep the peace. I even voted in favour of Doblek's proposal to deploy them, may the Lady forgive me. There was no choice, Edeard. We were facing citywide riots, possibly a massacre worse than anything Buate ever planned. Ilongo had endured two days of anarchy after Our City prevented the stopovers from using any of the free housing. What else could we do?'

'You did the right thing,' Edeard assured him. 'You acted to save lives. That's what we always did, that's what we'll always do.'

'What's happening to the world, Edeard? Didn't we do enough saving it from Bise and Owain and the bandits? I tell you, in the Lady's name the Skylords will stop coming if we don't mend our ways, Edeard. They will, I know it.' He reached for the decanter again, only to find Edeard's third hand clamped firmly round it.

'Dinlay will be here soon,' Edeard said. 'We'll talk about the blockade and Our City then.' His farsight had already identified Dinlay walking across the square outside the mansion. 'So tell me, do you both still attend the Upper Council?'

Macsen shook his head, on the verge of tears. 'Jamico has been going on my behalf this past half-year. I couldn't face it any more after the vote for the regiment. He's a good man, I'm proud to be his father. He'll do better than I ever did.' His hand swept round in an expansive gesture. 'I try and keep up with the petitions, Edeard, really I do, but people expect so much. I am not Rah, but they don't understand that. They whisper I'm turning my back on them as Bise did. Can you imagine that? To be accused in such a fashion? There's nothing I can do to stop the insidious, malicious, *vicious*, whispers. It's Bise's old people behind it, you know, I'm sure of it.'

Edeard wanted to use his third hand and haul Dinlay through the air to the study's balcony. Anything to break up this bitter tirade of self-loathing. 'Dinlay's almost here. Speaking of whom . . .'

'Ha!' Macsen managed half a smile as he shook his head. 'You saw her. Exactly the same as all the others. Edeard, I swear on the Lady that somewhere out in the provinces there's a secret guild that just keeps using the same mould to produce them. How else does he find so many of them?'

Edeard smiled. 'A Dinlay-wife-sculpting Guild. I like it. But Nanitte's daughter . . . ?'

'Aye! Ladydamn. I knew it the minute I saw her; she didn't even have to tell me who she was. It triggered all those memories, the ones I'd tried so hard to forget. Then she claimed she and her mother quarrelled incessantly and she couldn't stand living at home any more, so she's spent the last four years on the road before she came here. Viewing the world, she claims. You know, I was one of the first people she came to. She said her mother had given her the names of people in the city who would help her if she ever got here. Not much of a quarrel then, eh? I bet the bitch sent her here to ruin us all.'

'Knowing Nanitte, more than likely.' Edeard checked again. Dinlay was through the archway in the dapple-grey wall, and asking a servant where the Master of Sampalok was. 'Where did Nanitte make her home eventually?'

'She worked her witch-magic on some poor rich bastard in Obershire, apparently. He married her a month after she arrived, and they live in a fine house on a big farming estate.'

'Good for her,' Edeard muttered.

Macsen snorted in contempt.

'But don't you see?' Edeard responded. 'She's changed. She's become a part of our society. It's an acknowledgement we are the right way forward for us all. A timely reminder we mustn't falter, if you ask me.'

'Whatever,' Macsen said wearily. 'Anyway, it took Dinlay all of half a minute to fall head over heels for the daughter. As usual.'

'Well maybe this time he'll get it right. He's certainly had enough practice.'

'Not a Ladydamned chance.'

Edeard remembered that flirtatious smile Hilitte had bestowed him as they met. *Macsen's right, the omens aren't good.*

Dinlay opened the door, giving Macsen a cautious look.

'Good to see you,' Edeard said and gave his friend a warm hug.

Dinlay returned the embrace, contentment and relief apparent in his mind. 'We really were starting to get worried, you know.'

'I know, and I thank you for that concern. But it's a big world out there, and we know so little of it. Honestly, the sights I have seen . . .'

'Really? Tell us!'

'There were huge rock-creatures in the southern seas like coral islands that float. I even stood on one. And trees! Lady, the trees on Parath – a whole continent on the other side of Querencia – I swear they were the same height as the tallest tower in Eyrie. And the animals we found, have you seen the ones we brought back? They were just the small ones. There was something on Maraca, the continent beyond Parath, that was the size of a house, it had blue skin and skulked about in swamps. The jungles, too! Around the equator on Maraca they make Charyau's temperature look like a mild winter; they're like steam baths.'

'You've never been to Charyau,' Macsen accused.

'But Natran has,' Edeard countered. 'And he gifted me the memories.'

'Lady, I wish I'd come with you,' a wistful Dinlay declared.

'I've already said that,' Macsen grumbled. 'See what happens when you leave us in charge.'

'We're hardly to blame,' Dinlay said hotly.

Edeard and Dinlay exchanged a private look. 'All right,' Edeard sighed. 'Tell me what's been happening in my city.'

The Our City movement began soon after the flotilla departed, Dinlay explained. Some argument in Tosella sparked it off, apparently. A newlywed couple who had found themselves a cluster of empty rooms in a big mansion between the Blue Tower and Hidden Canal. The rooms were up in the eaves, and had odd split-level floors with a rolling step, which was why they'd never been claimed. However, there was a good-sized room at one end where the man could set up his jewellery workshop. But they didn't register their residency until after the wedding, as is tradition in Makkathran. That's when the trouble started. They came back from their honeymoon and found a stopover family had moved in.

'Temporary,' Macsen grunted. 'That's all. Two brothers had brought their mother from Fandine province to Makkathran for a Skylord's guidance. She was arthritic and was succumbing to the onset of dementia. They just missed one Skylord by a week, and there were no approaching Skylords sighted by the Astronomy Guild, so it was probably going to be several months until the next one arrived. In the meantime the brothers couldn't afford to rent a tavern room for that long, or take one of the new inns out in the villages. The empty rooms were a logical solution.'

'The newlyweds told them to get out,' Dinlay said. 'At which point one of the sons went and registered their residency claim with the Board of Occupancy at the Courts of Justice. As they'd lived in the rooms for the required two days and two nights they were entitled.'

'Oh Lady,' Edeard moaned. He knew how this tale was going to unfold. There had always been resentment at the number of stopover visitors. He and Mayor Trahaval had talked about the problem before he'd confronted the nest. There hadn't been an immediate solution, though the inns being built in the coastal towns and out on the Iguru had seemed like a scheme that would ultimately solve everything. It was only by the grace of the Lady that there hadn't been an 'incident' like this one back then.

The jeweller and his new bride both had large families, and they were well connected, Dinlay continued. Worse, no other empty cluster of rooms would do – for the newlyweds or the stopover brothers. It had to be this one. So the couple made their stand: Makkathran buildings for Makkathran citizens. It was a popular cause. The stopover brothers and their mother were forcefully evicted. By the time the constables arrived they were already out on the street and in need of hospital treatment from a beating. The newlyweds were installed along with their furniture; and a huge crowd of their relatives blocked the entrance to the mansion. Not that they really needed to – the constables who arrived on the scene weren't entirely unsympathetic. All they did was cart off the brothers and their mother.

That might have been the end of it. But legally the rooms were registered to the brothers. So the newlyweds brought in legal help to revoke the residency and make it their own.

Edeard closed his eyes in anguish. 'Please! Lady no, not him.'

'Oh yes,' Macsen said with vicious delight. 'Master Cherix took the case.'

Because the couple were legally unequivocally in the wrong, and everyone knew it, all Cherix could do in court was fight a holding action. A registration of occupancy could only be overturned by an order of the Grand Council. In order to get that, the legal case had to become a political campaign. The Our City movement was born four weeks before the elections. Mayor Trahaval was strictly in favour of existing law and order – as espoused by the Waterwalker, as he was fond of repeating at every speech. Doblek, up until then a simple formality opposition candidate, chose to support Our City. He won a landslide majority, as did a host of Our City representatives.

The Our City movement was something its members took very seriously. By the end of the first week every single vacant space in every building in Makkathran was occupied and registered by one of their own. And the visitors arriving with their dying relatives had nowhere to stay; like the brothers before them, most couldn't afford the inns for what might be months. It all came to a head in Ilongo a week after Doblek was sworn in at the Orchard Palace. Some newly arrived visitors, outraged at being told they couldn't stay in the city that their dearly beloved were due to be guided from, tried to squat in some of Ilongo's central mansions. There were riots which the constables alone couldn't quell (not that they tried particularly hard). That was when Doblek acted with impressive resolution, and ordered the militia in to stamp down hard on the disturbance.

From that day on anyone who came to Makkathran to be guided by a Skylord (and couldn't afford a tavern room) was prevented from passing through the city gates until a day before the great event, when the Lady's Mothers organized their passage up the towers. Even then, relatives who'd been camping outside were discouraged from accompanying them to Eyrie.

'Doblek really thought he was emulating you on the day of banishment,' Macsen said. 'Throwing them all out and forbidding them to come back was what you did to Bise and the rest. And enough stupid people think the same, they applaud how tough he was.'

'I'm surprised he had the courage to suggest such a thing,' Edeard said. 'That's not the Doblek I remember.'

'Power changes people,' Dinlay said simply, giving Macsen a sharp look. 'And necessity. What else could he do?'

Edeard realized this was an old argument between his friends.

'I could accept that if he'd made any attempt to alter things since then,' Macsen said. 'But he hasn't. He doesn't know what to do; and more people are arriving each day. Did you know we've only just started getting our first visitors from the most distant provinces? And I include Rulan in that.'

'Cheap,' Dinlay muttered.

'Not really. The volume of people coming here is still rising. Doblek has done nothing to address that. Nothing! He had to deploy another militia troop to safeguard the route into Makkathran. The people he'd forced outside were starting to waylay merchant carts and caravans. So now we have a permanent presence of militia extending well out into the Iguru, and the stopover camps are hacking down the forests outside for fuel. You know those trees were planted by Rah and the Lady themselves.'

'The area circling Makkathran was designated a forest zone by Rah,' Dinlay said wearily. 'He didn't go around planting seeds himself, that's One City propaganda.'

'Whatever,' Macsen said. 'The problem is Doblek's actions, or rather lack of them. What does he think is going to happen? That it'll all sort itself out? And, Edeard, we've heard rumour that the Fandine militia is on the march through Plax.'

Edeard gave Macsen a puzzled look. 'Why?'

'Because we've used our militia against their citizens. They're claiming the right of protection.'

'Oh Great Lady!'

'It's the distance,' Dinlay said. 'That's our trouble. Rumour grows with each mile. A report of what was a grazed arm and a bloody nose in Makkathran has become some kind of mass murder of innocents by the time it reaches Fandine.'

'So is it true about the Fandine militia then?'

'General Larose sent fast scouts out last week. We'll know soon enough.'

'Militias fighting on the Iguru,' Edeard muttered in disbelief. The loss of life during the last campaign against the bandits had appalled him. He thought such horror had ended then. It certainly couldn't be allowed to happen again. He had never forgotten the carnage Owain had unleashed. 'I must speak with Doblek.'

'To what end?' Macsen asked. 'You think he'll back down and order the militia back inside the gate?'

'He was elected courtesy of Our City,' Dinlay said. 'He'll never go against the cause that put him in the Orchard Palace.'

Edeard briefly thought about using domination. He'd learned enough of that technique from Tathal and the nest in those last few seconds to change anyone's mind for them. But the Mayor was only one man. It would solve the immediate problem – that's if there even was a Fandine militia marching on the city with revenge in mind. It was the whole situation which had to be calmed. A situation which the Skylords had created. *And how's that for irony?*

He recalled that meeting he'd had with Macsen and Kanseen just after Dinlay had returned from his honeymoon with Gealee. *The time when dear Burlal existed.* Then, Mayor Trahaval had come nowhere close to finding a solution to the massive influx of people awaiting guidance. Edeard had told the others he'd try to find out why the Skylords would only accept people from Eyrie's towers. But there'd never been time to ask them before his final confrontation with the nest; and this time around he'd never bothered. Such things had been abandoned in favour of the voyage.

If I can get the Skylords to visit other towns on Querencia then this will all just go away. In the meantime he had to do something about the stopover refugees outside North Gate. *All that animosity on both sides is going to corrode the fulfilment which the Skylords judge us by.*

'All right,' Edeard said. 'Just how intractable is Our City?'

'It's a one-cause movement, which means they simply can't be moderate,' Dinlay said. 'There will never be any kind of compromise with them, so if you're going to take them on it will have to be a direct election and you change the law after you're Mayor.'

'Sounds drastic.' Edeard sucked in his cheeks. 'I'd better go take a look for myself, then.'

Our City had appropriately enough set up their headquarters in Ilongo. Dinlay had told Edeard with grudging admiration how their political ability had grown since their hurried formation. Eight of the current district Representatives had stood on the Our City ticket, forming a powerful bloc in Council. But their greatest influence over the lives of citizens came directly from the residency issue. Today if you were a Makkathran native searching for somewhere new to live, you had to ask Our City for their cooperation. Now their members had legal occupancy of every previously-vacant room and dwelling they were the ones who had to relinquish their claim before someone else could move in. So only when they'd confirmed you were a genuine born-in-the-city applicant would one of their members vacate the place you wanted. In effect, Our City now controlled who lived where. Another reason for ordinary people not to antagonize them. And as with all political parties, they traded advantage and made deals with rivals and other groups in Council and down on the streets and canals, insinuating themselves deeper and deeper into the city's political structure.

Edeard walked into the Ilongo district from a gondola platform on North Curve Canal. The narrow streets in the centre were a notorious maze. Most of the district was comprised of boxy buildings with walls at quite sharp angles, creating alleys of narrow tunnels with only a slim line of sky visible along the apex. Slim streets opened into unexpected squares which were like wells of light amid the overhanging walls; fountains bubbled away cheerfully as if to celebrate the sudden glare of the sun.

It was the first Makkathran district he'd ever walked through, he remembered, he and Salrana gazing in delight at the weird buildings and more than a little nervous at the sheer number of people walking through the narrow streets and passageways. They'd pressed together for comfort and maybe just enjoying each other, believing hard in the future they would share.

He jammed his teeth together, hating the memory, hating that, despite everything he could do, so much had gone wrong. That young happy Salrana was lost now, gone beyond his ability to recover. As was dear little Burlal. *Unless of course I go back far enough, and repeat the atrocity deep below Spiral Tower of the Weapons Guild.* Even then, it would only save Salrana. Burlal would never be born into the world which would emerge from that.

It's no good, I can only ever save one even if I could bring myself to confront a living Owain again. I can only ever go forwards.

Unless, he acknowledged darkly, he lived both lives. Went back and saved Salrana from Ranalee and herself, and lived that life until it was time for Salrana to be guided to Odin's Sea. Then at the very last moment, instead of accepting guidance for himself, dive back to the time when Burlal was alive and somehow defeat Tathal another way.

Useless, he acknowledged in anguish. *There is no way to defeat Tathal other than the way it's already been done – I spent years trying. Burlal is truly beyond my reach now. My poor gorgeous grandchild.* And worse, attempting such a rescue would banish Kiranan into nothingness along with the twins' new babes. *Unless I live this life first, then . . . Oh sweet Lady, why did you ever curse me with this gift!*

He came out into Rainbow Square, named after the seven walls each with its fur-like growth of moss. The actual surface was porous, weeping a steady trickle of moisture, like a sponge being squeezed. Vivid emerald moss thrived in such an ambience, its perpetually damp fronds tipped by tiny droplets which glistened brightly under the sunlight boring down the centre of the square, creating a prismatic haze.

Unlike the rest of Ilongo's crowded streets, this one was empty. The Waterwalker's black cloak stirred in agitation as he waited in front of the tallest building whose wall leaned back away from him. In the middle was an arching double door of some ancient black wood. A smaller inset door opened.

The leadership of Our City emerged slowly. Nervous of the Waterwalker, some of them old enough to remember the city's power he wielded on the great day of Banishment. One of them no doubt full of poison about the Waterwalker's malice and iniquity.

'Oh Ladycrapit,' Edeard groaned softly at the sight of the man who was first out of the door. Dinlay had never warned him.

Vintico gave the Waterwalker a defiant stare; a lanky man with his mother's eyes and his father's pettiness and greed. Edeard might have guessed that Salrana would somehow get herself ensnared in this debacle.

There were about twenty people crowding into Rainbow Square behind Vintico, all of them staring directly at him, curious and nervous, but determined, too; resolute that their advantage and position would not be taken from them by the Waterwalker, the epitome of 'old' Makkathran.

Edeard addressed them all, remaining calm and quiet, demonstrating how reasonable he was. 'This has to stop,' he said. 'People are suffering outside the city wall. That cannot be right.'

'No indeed, it isn't right,' Vintico said to the murmurs of approval goading him on. 'Why should good Makkathran families who followed Rah himself here out of the chaos be denied a place to live? We have rights too. When do we ever hear of those spoken by you and your cronies on the Council, hey?'

'The Lady herself has brought us to this time when the citizens of this world are fulfilled. They must be guided to the Heart by the Skylords. This is not in dispute.'

'We don't dispute it,' Vintico said. 'We simply ask to be allowed to reach our fulfilment. How can that happen when our families are wandering the cold streets without a roof over their heads. Do you think that enriches them, eh Waterwalker? Does that make them fulfilled?'

Edeard nodded in understanding even as he was reminded of something Finitan had said to him once in an unguarded moment: 'Most people who have failed miserably in life itself have one last resort left available to them, they become a politician.' Now Edeard began to appreciate what he'd meant. 'I understand your frustration,' he said. 'But resolving such a massive problem to everyone's satisfaction will take time. Something like communal waystations have to be built.'

'Then build them,' Vintico said. 'Leave us to get on with our lives.'

'It would all go a lot easier if you could help overcome the short-term problems. Come, we know this is going to be a difficult time. I will speak with the next Skylord who comes to Querencia and ask if they can guide souls from other places, not just the towers of Eyrie. I will also lobby the Mayor for a large building enterprise outside the city. Together we can overcome this.'

'Then join us,' Vintico said. 'We would be happy to accept you. And you would be showing your approval of us.'

'You're too insular,' Edeard told him. 'I can see that. Everything Our City embraces is a rejection of others. You must look outward, be welcoming. Closing yourself off like this, pushing the problem on to others, achieves nothing but antagonism and conflict. What kind of world will that build?'

Vintico grinned maliciously, a bad humour which rippled through the clique in the square. 'You mean, we must become like you? Join you? Acknowledge your way as the right way?'

'It's not like that, not about "ways". True life is the understanding and support of other people, of selflessness, of charity, of kindness.'

'Of being abused and exploited, you mean,' Vintico replied. 'That's what's happened to Makkathran. We were being overrun by these parasites. They threw our hospitality and welcome back in our faces. Well no more! We will not give up our claim on our city, our birthright is absolute. And soon everyone will join us in our goal.' His voice and longtalk rose, summoning up support from his audience, who shouted agreement.

Edeard stared into the man's stubborn expression, examining the minds glimmering angrily across the square around him; discovering the strength of resolution behind the words. Vintico meant everything he said. There would be no persuading them, no deal to broker, no halfway accommodation. Which even for a novice politician was odd. He gave Vintico a shrewd examination, wondering just how he'd come by so much confidence. 'Why would everyone join Our City?'

There was the smallest flash of triumphalism shimmering through Vintico's mental shield. 'You'll see. Even you will have to help defend our rights.'

'Oh Lady,' Edeard murmured barely audibly as he realized what Vintico had to mean. 'The Fandine militia is coming, isn't it?'

Vintico sneered. 'Not just them. The Colshire regiment is marching against us, as is the Bural. Three provinces seek to attack Makkathran. You will have to decide which side you're on Waterwalker. Ours or theirs, which is it to be?'

A grimace of pain crossed Edeard's face. Those closest to him took a nervous half-step backwards as a terrible anger rose through his mind, spitting out flares of misery and depression that made flesh judder and tenacity waver amid even the most stalwart in the square.

'In the Lady's name, what do you want from me?' Edeard yelled furiously. They were backing off fast now. 'Every time, every Honious-fucking time I do whatever I can to make things right, and this is what happens. Every time, something or someone comes out of the darkness to screw things up.'

Vintico's mouth twitched uncertainly. 'Waterwalker, we simply wish that our own children have the chance to—'

'Shut! UP!' Edeard bellowed. 'I have lost my grandchild to bring you this world today. My beautiful lovely little boy who brought no misery and suffering. Unlike you and your wretched kind who generate nothing else. I unmade him to give you a chance. And now I must do it again, because clearly I'm not allowed to go off voyaging around the world. Because when I do, you appear and ruin what peace and hope there is. The militias can't be stopped now they are on the march just as you oh so cleverly intended. They have to be stopped before they leave, they have to be stopped from leaving. In fact they must never have a reason for leaving. And the only way to do that is prevent your Lady-damned Our City from being formed. Do you understand what that means, you piece of shit? They have been born but two days! Why should I unmake them for you? Eh? Answer me that? Why should I not just exterminate every one of you here and now? That would have the same result. They'll never be born again, for sure as a genistar shits in the forest that voyage won't happen next time around because I can't leave Makkathran before the stopover problem is solved; so they'll never meet Marvane, and he'll never be crowned Luckiest Man. Will he?'

Vintico took a defiant step forward, even though he didn't understand what was being said to him. 'You can never exterminate all of us. Together we are strong.' To prove it, the minds of those in the square began to combine their telekinesis, strengthening a broad shield to ward off whatever terror the Waterwalker would unleash.

'Yeah,' Edeard barked. 'Don't I fucking know it.' With a final snarl of anguish he reached back for a memory—

—to land on the ground at the foot of the Eyrie tower. The crowd exclaimed in admiration, several people applauded. More cheered at the resurgence of the Waterwalker.

He started round in a daze. It was as if the sights and sensations of the city were muted somehow, as if this time lacked the solidity of true life. *I don't take part in life any more, I just respond to the old events as I believe I ought. What kind of existence is this?*

Kristabel scowled at the flamboyant display of his ability.

'Daddy,' Marilee scolded.

'That was so bad.'

'Teach us how to do that.'

He gave the twins a weary look. They had never looked happier than holding their babes barely a day ago in his own personal time. *Now that is never to happen, not even if I engineer a meeting with Marvane for them.* 'The Skylord comes,' he told them dully, hoping that would be enough to silence them for a while. It always had before.

Out across the Lyot Sea the massive shimmering bulk of the Skylord had risen above the horizon. Far above, on the tower platform, Finitan's astonishment at the arrival was echoed by the whole city. Awe turned to trepidation as the size of the Skylord became apparent to everyone.

So no voyage, he mused as the great creature flew effortlessly above the choppy sea. *And Kristabel said I had become almost intolerable at this point. So now instead of alleviating that with the voyage I must do something about the mass of stopover visitors. Lady, please understand, I cannot take much more sacrifice in my life. Truly, I cannot.*

6

The Delivery Man spent the flight accessing what information the smartcore had on the Anomine. There wasn't much. They were an advanced race who had travelled along the standard evolutionary development route for biological species, zipping from agricultural age to industrial age right up to a benign civilization with ftl starflight and a kind of cellular-based replicator technology that meshed with their own forms. That development had allowed for a lot of diversification before their various blocs and genealogies eventually reunited and elevated themselves to post-physical status. From the small snippets of true history which Navy expeditions had uncovered it seemed like the trigger factor for reunification was the threat posed by the Prime.

Sitting in the antique styling of the *Last Throw*'s cabin with an uncommunicative Gore, the Delivery Man couldn't help but wonder if the Anomine had found the Prime a little too much like looking into a mirror for comfort. Bodies which had merged into machinery? Albeit the Prime capability was set at a more primitive level. There but for the grace of God go I. Grace in this case being the Prime's biogenetically embedded xenophobia. The Anomine were only too well aware of what would happen if the paranoid, aggressive, and heavily armed Prime ever escaped their home star system, as they were already attempting in slower-than-light starships. Concerns vindicated by their observation of the first Prime ships to reach the closest star system, Dyson Beta, with its existing civilization. The peaceful aliens of that world never stood a chance.

Within ten years of the genocidal invasion, the Anomine had thrown up force-field barriers around the stars which humans came to know as the Dyson Pair. Where the Dark Fortress generators had come from, indigenous construction or borrowed from the Raiel, was still a point much argued over by a small specialist section of human academia. But it was that effort which had brought the diverse Anomine back together; barely a hundred and fifty years after the barriers went up, the majority of the Anomine went post-physical.

'There's nothing about the elevation mechanism,' the Delivery Man said as the *Last Throw* streaked towards the Anomine star at fifty-five lightyears an hour. They were fifteen minutes out, and the starship's sensors were starting to obtain high-resolution scans of the system with all its planets.

'Classified,' Gore replied smartly. 'Some aspects of government never change no matter how benevolent and transparent they strive to be. Secrecy is like oxygen to politicians and defence forces, there's always got to be some of it to keep them going.'

'But you've got the files, right?'

'I've accessed the summaries.'

The Delivery Man gave Gore a suspicious look. 'I thought you had this all planned out?'

'I do, sonny, so stop with the panicking.'

'Have you got those summaries?'

'Not actually with us here today, no; but I remember most of the critical stuff.'

'But . . . You do know how to get it working again, don't you? You said that.'

'I said that we think it's intact.'

'No!' The Delivery Man sat forward abruptly, almost ready to fly out of the chair and go nose to nose with Gore. 'No no, you said, and I quote: they went post-physical and left their elevation mechanism behind.'

'Well obviously they didn't take the fucker with them.' Gore gave a chirpy grin. 'If you're post-physical you can't, because the mechanism is physical. We saw that with the Skoloskie; their mechanism was still there, rusting away on their abandoned homeworld. Same goes for the Fallror. It's what happens. Jeezus, relax will you, you're acting like a prom virgin who's made it to the motel room.'

'But. You. The. Oh shit! Tell me the Navy has seen the Anomine mechanism, tell me you know it's on their homeworld.'

'The Navy exploration parties that did manage to get through communicated with the old-style Anomine left on the planet. They had legends of their ancestral cousins leaving. The legends are quite specific about that, they departed the homeworld itself. QED: that's where the mechanism must be.'

'You don't *know*! I trusted you! Ozziedamnit, I could be making progress, I could have opened the Sol barrier by now.'

'Son, Marius would have shredded you like a puppy stuffed into a food blender if I'd let you go off after him. You're good at what you do, delivering stuff to my agents and the odd bit of observation work. That's why I recruited you, because everyone knows you're basically harmless, which puts you above suspicion. Face it, you've just not got the killer instinct.'

'My family is trapped back there. I would do anything—'

'Which has made you angry, yes, which is driving you on. But that's bad for you. It would mean there comes a point where you hesitate or get a nasty dose of doubt and remorse and decency when you were sawing off Marius's fingers and making him eat them.'

The Delivery Man wrinkled his nose up in revulsion. 'I wasn't going to—'

'Son, you just said you'd do anything. And that would be the least of it. These people don't roll over because you ask them nice. You'd have to strap Marius down on the dungeon table and *make* him tell you how to take down the barrier. And I'll lay you good odds the only person who can actually deactivate the barrier is Ilanthe, and she's not available. No. The only way for you to achieve anything right now is by helping me. So will you please stop the fuck whingeing, and let me work out how to find the mechanism.'

'Crap!' The Delivery Man slumped back down again, furious at being taken in again, and even more furious that Gore was right. Because somewhere in his mind was an image of himself threatening Marius, maybe firing a jelly gun close to his head, which would make anyone capitulate. Right? He shook his head, feeling foolish. Then he gave Gore a sharp look. 'Wait a minute, you said the ones that got through.'

'What?' Gore paid him little attention. His eyes were closed as he lounged back in his orange shell chair, analysing the smart-core's data.

'The Navy exploration ships that came here. You said *some* got through?' There was no reply. The Delivery Man requested the raw sensor data, building up a coherent image of what they were approaching. The star's cometary halo seemed to have some kind of active stations drifting through it. Large stations, with force fields protecting them from any detailed scan.

'Oh yeah, them,' Gore said eventually. 'The borderguards are a good security team. They're left over from the last of the high-technology-era Anomine, and they don't like anyone contaminating the old homeworld.'

'The whats?' It didn't sound good, not at all. But Gore never had time to answer him. That was when the *Last Throw* dropped out of ultradrive, and the smartcore was showing him an image of the borderguard not a kilometre away. It measured over five kilometres across, though most of it was empty space. The primary structure was of curving strands arranged in a broad ellipsoid, but they bent around sharply in the thick central section, forming three twisting cavities which intersected in the middle. Each strand appeared to be transparent, filled with a thick gas which hosted a multitude of dazzling green sparks. They swarmed along the strands as if there were a gale blowing inside. Floating in the heart of the cavities was an identical shape to the one formed by the green strands; this one was barely a tenth of the size, and filled with a sapphire gas complete with swift sparks. At its centre was a crimson shape, while inside that was a yellow version, and that had a lavender speck nestled within it. Passive sensors couldn't make out if there was another miniature version contained by its haze, and a strong force field prevented any active examination.

'Now what?' the Delivery Man whispered.

'We talk very fucking quietly in case they're listening in,' Gore snapped back.

The Delivery Man actually cringed from the look of contempt Gore gave him. He cleared his voice. 'All right. Is it going to shoot at us?'

'I hope not.'

'So what do we do?'

'We ask permission to go through.'

'And if it says no?'

'Pray it doesn't. We'll have to kill all seventeen thousand of them.'

'Can this ship actually . . . ?' He broke off and kept silent. The smartcore shot a simple communication pulse at the border-guard. Sensors showed another five of the gigantic stations appearing out of odd spatial distortions a few thousand kilo-metres away.

'Why are you here?' the borderguard asked.

'We are representatives from the human race, two of us are on board.'

'What type?'

'Higher. You have dealt with us before and were favourable. I ask for that consideration to be shown again.'

'Your species has withdrawn all information valid to you from those who stayed behind.'

'I understand. We seek data on those who left. We are a subsect of our species which believes we should try to evolve as the final Anomine did. We seek information on their society.'

'You carry weapons; they are of a sophisticated nature. Those of your species who came before did not carry weapons.'

'There is an active conflict among our species and the Ocisen

Empire. Other species are emerging who are hostile. Interstellar travel is a dangerous endeavour right now. We reserve the right to protect ourselves.'

'We have detected no conflict.'

'It is coming. The Void underwent a small expansion recently. Species across the galaxy are becoming alarmed by its behaviour.'

'We detected the Void expansion.'

'In which case we would ask that you grant us permission to try and emulate the ultimate success of your species.'

'You may have access to those items left behind by the final Anomine. You may examine them with any means except physical alteration or destruction. You may not remove any item from our ancestral world. All items must be left in place when you leave.'

'We thank you for the generosity you show us.'

The *Last Throw* fell back into hyperspace, and raced in for the Anomine homeworld. The Delivery Man observed its course display with some curiosity as they performed a wide arc around the G3 star. The starship started to drop the confluence nest satellites one at a time. They finished up spaced equidistantly in an orbit two hundred million kilometres out from the primary. *Last Throw* headed in for the Anomine homeworld.

There was a lot of junk in high orbit, out beyond the geosynchronous halo. All of it was ancient, inactive. Vast spaceship docks and habitation stations that had slowly been battered by micrometeorites and larger particles, subjected to solar radiation for millennia coincident with thermal extremes. Consequently they were no more than brittle tissue-thin hulls now, drifting into highly elliptical orbits as their atmosphere leaked out and tanks ruptured. Chunks had broken off, tumbling away into their own orbit, bashing into each other, fracturing again and again. Now millions of them formed a thick gritty grey toroid around the old world.

The *Last Throw* darted gracefully through the astronautical graveyard and flew down to a standard thousand-kilometre parking orbit above the equator. From there, the starship's optical sensors showed a planet similar to any H-congruous world, with deep blue oceans and continents graded with green and brown land dependent on climate. Huge white cloud formations drifted through the clear air, their fat twisted peaks greater than any of the mountain ranges they blanketed.

'So now what?' the Delivery Man asked.

'Find a haystack then start searching for its needle.'

The Delivery Man deliberately didn't glare at the gold-faced man sitting in the shell chair opposite. No point. 'This planet is bigger than Earth,' he read from his exovision displays. 'Surface area nearly eighty million square miles. That's a lot of land to search with any degree of thoroughness.'

'What makes you think it's on land?'

'Okay, what makes you think it's even here? Was that in the summary? The Anomine had settled in eight other starsystems that we know of.'

'And they're all deserted. That's a goddamn fact. They came back here, every type of them. Another dumbass pilgrimage. This is where they elevated from.'

'Oh Great Ozzie,' the Delivery Man moaned. 'You don't know, do you? You've no bloody idea. You're hoping. That's all. Hoping there's an answer here.'

'I'm applying logic.'

The Delivery Man wanted to beat his fists on the chair. But it wouldn't be any use, not even as emotional therapy. He'd been committed from the moment he left Gore's asteroid. 'All right. But you must have some idea how to find the damn thing, right?'

'Again, we're going to apply logic. First we perform a complete low orbit mapping flight and scan every centimetre of the place for exotic activity, or gravity fluctuations, power generation, quantum anomalies – anything out of the ordinary.'

'But that'll take . . .'

'Several days, yes.'

'And if we don't find anything?'

'Go down and talk to the natives, see what they can tell us.'

'But they're an agrarian civilization, human equivalent to

mid-nineteenth-century. They're not going to know about machines that can turn you into an angel.'

'They have legends, we know that, they're proud of their history. The Navy cultural anthropology team did some good work. We can even talk to them direct. And they're more advanced than our nineteenth century – that I do remember from the files. Not that the comparison is entirely valid.'

'Okay. Whatever.'

Gore gave the briefest of nods, and issued orders to the smartcore.

'Why did you bring me?' the Delivery Man asked. 'You and the ship can handle this.'

'Back-up,' Gore said flatly. 'I might need some help at some point. Who knows?'

'Great.'

'Get yourself some rest, son. You've been wired tight for days now.'

The Delivery Man admitted he was too tired and edgy to argue. He went over to his private cubicle, and rolled on to the small but luxurious cot which expanded out of the bulkhead. He didn't expect to sleep. He was still too wound up about Lizzie and the children. The ship's TD link to the unisphere remained connected, so he could access all the news from back home.

High Angel had arrived at the Sol system. After six hours Qatux had diplomatically announced to the President there was nothing the huge arkship could do. The force field that the Accelerators' Swarm had deployed was too strong to break with any weapon they had.

After switching through several ill-informed news shows, the Delivery Man fell into a troubled sleep.

*

Corrie-Lyn woke up with a start, disorientated and unsure what had hauled her up out of such a deep sleep. She glanced round the small, darkened cabin, listening intently. But there was nothing. Sometimes the *Lindau*'s poor battered systems would produce odd sounds, pipes gurgled and bubbled, and the service-bots hammered away as they worked through their repair schedule, then there was that one time when she swore she'd heard the hull itself creak. But tonight it was silent aside from the constant hum of power – which was vaguely reassuring even though it shouldn't be that loud. At least they still had power.

Inigo stirred briefly beside her, and she smiled down gently at him. It was so *good* to have him back, physically as well as emotionally. Even though he wasn't quite the messiah of yore, he was still her Inigo. Concerned about different things now, but still as determined and focused as before. She felt so much happier now he was here to help, despite still being unable to escape Aaron.

The name acted like some kind of recognition key. *He* was why she'd woken. Her mind was abruptly aware of the turmoil bubbling out from the agent's gaiamotes. There were images her own brain instinctively tried to shut out, repulsive sensations of pain – not direct impulses but memories of the suffering which verged on nauseous, but worst of all were the emotions of guilt and fear which bridged the gap between them, plunging her into his nightmare of darkness and torment. She was suffocating in some giant cathedral where men and women were being sacrificed on a crude pagan altar. She was standing behind the high priest as the curved dagger was raised again. Screams blasted out from those awaiting an identical fate as the blade flashed down then rose again, dripping with blood. The figure in the white robe turned, and it wasn't a male priest. *She* smiled gleefully, the front of her robe soaked in scarlet blood, making the fabric cling obscenely to her body, emphasising breasts and hips.

'You don't leave me,' she explained as the smile widened. Lips parted to reveal fangs which grew and grew as the cathedral faded away. There was only darkness and her, the robe was gone now, blood glistened across her skin. The mouth opened wider, then wider still. There was no face any more, only teeth and blood. 'Come back where you belong.'

He wanted to scream, joining the clamour kicked up by the

others lost somewhere out there in the impenetrable blackness. But when he opened his mouth blood poured in, filling his lungs, drowning him. Every muscle shook in the terrible struggle to be free, to be free of her, of what she'd made him do.

'It's all right, son,' a new, soothing voice chimed in. 'Let me help you.'

A soft irresistible force closed around his body, solidifying, immobilizing him. He stopped gagging for breath as bright red laser fans swept across the darkness, quickly arranging themselves into a spiral web with his head in the centre. They contracted sharply, sending light pouring into his brain. Pain soared to unbelievable heights.

'Yetch!' Corrie-Lyn shook her head violently, closing off her gaiamotes. The sickening sensations vanished. Now she heard a sound, a muffled yell from the captain's cabin on the opposite side of the narrow companionway. 'Sweet Lady,' she grunted. No mind could survive that kind of psychological torment for long, not and remain sane and functional. She stared at the cabin door, fearful he would come bursting through, his weapon enrichments activated. But he didn't. There were another couple of defiant cries, then some whimpering like an animal being soothed before silence claimed the starship again.

Corrie-Lyn let out a long breath, seriously alarmed by just how great the threat of him going completely insane had become. Her skin was coated in cold sweat. She pulled the tangle of quilts off herself and wriggled over to the ablution alcove. Taking care to be quiet so she didn't wake Inigo, she slowly sponged herself down with a mild-scented soap. It cooled her skin, leaving her feeling a little better. Nothing she could do about the sensations crawling along the inside of her skin – the residual shock of the dream.

If that's what it is.

It was all a little too coherent for comfort. Not a brain naturally discharging its accumulated experiences orchestrated by the peaks of lingering emotion, the way humans were designed to cope with everyday experiences. These were like broken memories pushing up from whatever dark zone of the psyche they'd been imprisoned in. 'What in Honious did they do to you?' she murmured into the gloomy cabin.

The next morning the servicebots had finished tailoring down some of the fresh clothes as she'd instructed. 'Not bad,' Inigo said admiringly as she pulled on the Navy tunic with shortened sleeves. She grinned as she wiggled into a pair of tunic trousers. They were tight around her hips. 'Not bad at all.'

'I need some breakfast first,' she told him with a grin. The one – and only – advantage of their weird imprisonment was the amount of time alone they could spend catching up.

They held hands as they went into the lounge. Inigo of course used the culinary unit to prepare some scrambled eggs and smoked haddock. She delved into the pile of luxury supplies the crew had stored on board. The only thing the unit made which she could force down were the drinks, and that was pretty much limited to tea and tomato juice – neither of which was a firm favourite. So she tucked into a mix of toffee banana cake and dried mortaberries, gulping the tea down quickly so she could convince herself the taste was Earl Grey, albeit with milk and strawberry jam.

Aaron came in and helped himself to his usual poached egg and smoked salmon. Without a word, he shuffled himself into his broken chair almost at the other end of the lounge.

'Who is she?' Corrie-Lyn asked.

'Excuse me?'

'The high priestess or whatever she was. The one with all the blood. The one that scares you utterly shitless.'

Aaron stared at her for a long time. Just for once, Corrie-Lyn wasn't intimidated. 'Well?' she asked. 'You shared last night.'

It wasn't embarrassment, she suspected he was incapable of that, but he did lower his gaze. 'I don't know,' Aaron said eventually.

'Well you must—' She stopped and took a breath. 'Look, I'm actually not trying to needle you. If you must know, I'm worried.'

'About me? Don't be.'

'Nobody can take that kind of punishment night after night and not have it affect them. I don't care what you've got enriched and improved and sequenced into every cell. That kind of crap is toxic.'

'And yet here I am each morning, functioning perfectly.'

'Seventeen hours ago,' Inigo said.

'What?'

'You were supposed to be on the bridge monitoring the ship. You actually slipped into the reverie. I felt it.'

'My operational ability is unimpaired.'

'It's being undermined,' Corrie-Lyn said. 'Can't you see that? Or is it that you just can't admit it?'

'I can help,' Inigo said.

'No.'

'You have instructions for just about every eventuality,' Inigo said. 'Is there one for your own breakdown?'

'There is nothing wrong with me a bit of hush in the morning won't fix. A man likes to break his fast in godly contemplative silence.'

'Contemplate this: if you go gaga, how are we going to reach Ozzie?'

Aaron grinned contentedly. 'You want to?'

'Yes,' Inigo said with great seriousness. 'I don't know who programmed you, but I think they might be right about getting the two of us together.'

'Now ain't that something, progress at last.'

'The only thing that can stop us reaching the Spike now is you,' Corrie-Lyn said.

'I imagine that if bits of me start to fall off I will...' He stopped, the humour fading from his face.

'Suicide?' Inigo supplied.

Aaron was staring at a point on the bulkhead, his coffee cup halfway to his mouth. 'No,' he said. 'I'd never do such an unrighteous thing. I'm not that weak.' Then he frowned, and glanced over at Corrie-Lyn. 'What?'

'Oh Lady,' Inigo grunted.

Corrie-Lyn was fascinated, suspecting that the real Aaron had surfaced if only for a moment. 'You're not going to make it,' she said flatly.

'We've got barely two days to go until we reach the Spike,' Aaron said. 'I can hold myself together for that kind of timescale. Trust and believe me on that.'

'Nonetheless, it would be prudent for you to load some kind of emergency routine into the smartcore,' Inigo suggested.

'I can match that, in fact I can top it in a big way on the survival stakes. I would strongly suggest, now you've figured out that I'm not on the side of harming you, and that you and the great Ozzie are going to be best buddies standing before the tsunami of evil, that you think about how to stop the Void.'

'It can't be stopped,' Inigo said. 'It simply *is*. This I know. I have observed it from Centurion Station, and I have personally felt the thoughts emanating within. Out of all of humanity, I know this. So believe me when I tell you that if you want to exist in the same universe you have to find a way around it. Our best bet would be to turn round and ask the *High Angel* to take us to another galaxy.'

Aaron drank some of his coffee. 'Someone thinks differently,' he said unperturbed. 'Someone still believes in you, Dreamer, someone believes you can truly lead us to salvation. How about that? Your real following is down to one: me. And for now I'm the only one that counts.'

They began to feel the Spike's weird mental interference while they were still a day and a half out. At first it was nothing but a mild sensation of euphoria, which is why they didn't notice at first. Corrie-Lyn had cut down on her drinking, but there were still some seriously good bottles cluttering up the crew's personal stores. Be a shame to waste them. A couple, the Bodlian white and the Guxley Mountain green, were reputed to have aphrodisiac properties. Definitely a shame. Especially as there was nothing else to do on board ship.

So in the afternoon she'd got a bot to make up, or rather unmake, a semiorganic shirt so that just a couple of buttons held the front together. Satisfied the end product was suitably naughty, she stripped off and stepped into the ablution alcove. While she was in the shower the bot also remade a thick wool sweater into a long robe – which was scratchy on her arms, but what the Honious.

She'd left Inigo in the lounge reviewing astronomical data on the Void. Now he hurried to their cabin when she called him, saying something important had happened.

'What is it?' he asked as the door parted. Then he stopped, surprised then intrigued by the low lighting and three candles flickering on nearly horizontal surfaces. The culinary unit might be rubbish at food, but it could still manage wax easily enough.

Corrie-Lyn gave him a sultry look, and ordered the door to close behind him. He saw the bottle of Bodlian and two long-stem glasses she was holding in one hand.

'Ah.' His gaiamotes emitted a simultaneous burst of nerves and interest.

'I found this,' she told him in the huskiest voice she could manage without giggling. 'Shame to waste it.'

'Classic,' he said, and took the proffered bottle. She kissed him before he'd even got the cap off, then began to nuzzle his face. He smiled and pressed himself up against her while she toned up the mood her gaiamotes were leaking out. Together they undid the belt of the crude robe. 'Oh dear Lady yes,' he rumbled as the wool was slipped off to reveal what remained of the shirt.

Corrie-Lyn kissed him again, the tip of her tongue licking playfully. 'Remember Franlee?' she asked. 'Those long winter nights they spent together in Plax.'

'I always preferred Jessile.'

'Oh yes.' She sipped some of the wine. 'She was a bad girl.'

'So are you.' He poured his own glass, and ran one hand down her throat, stroking her skin softly until he came to the top button. His finger hooked round it, pulling lightly to measure the strain.

'I can be if you ask properly,' she promised.

Two hours later Aaron fired a disruptor pulse into their locked cabin door. The malmetal shattered instantly, flinging a cloud of glittering dust into the confined space. Corrie-Lyn and Inigo were having a respite, sprawled over the quilts on the floor. Inigo held a glass of the Bodlian in one hand, carefully dripping the wine across Corrie-Lyn's breasts. Secondary routines in his macrocellular clusters activated his integral force field instantly. Corrie-Lyn screamed, crabbing her way back along the floor until she backed into a bulkhead.

'Turn it off!' Aaron bellowed. His cheeks were flushed as he sucked down air, jaw muscles worked hard, clamping his teeth together.

Inigo rose to his feet, standing in front of Corrie-Lyn. He expanded the force field to protect her from direct energy shots, knowing it would ultimately be futile against Aaron. 'The force field stays on. Now in the Lady's name what's happened?'

'Not the fucking force field!' Aaron juddered, taking a step back. Weird unpleasant sensations surged out of his gaiamotes, making Inigo flinch. It was a torrent of recall from the strange cathedral with the crystal arches, terrified faces flashing past, weapons fire impossibly loud. Each memory burst triggered a devastating bout of emotion. Even Inigo felt tears trickling down his cheeks as he swung between fright and revulsion and defiance and guilt.

'The mindfuck,' Aaron yelled. 'Turn it off or I swear I'll kill her in front of you.'

'I'm not doing anything,' Inigo yelled back. 'What's happening? What is this?'

Aaron sagged against the side of the ruined door. 'Get them out of my head!'

'Deactivate your gaiamotes, that'll kill the attack.'

'They are off!'

Inigo's skin turned numb with shock – his own emotion rather than the chaotic barrage coming from Aaron. 'They can't be. I can feel your mind.'

Aaron's hand punched out, knuckles finishing centimetres from Inigo's face. Enhancements rippled below his skin, squat black nozzles slid out of the flesh. 'Turn it off.'

'I'm not doing anything!' Inigo yelled back. Ridiculously he felt exhilarated, this was *living*, the antithesis of the last few decades. He cursed himself for hiding away rather than facing up to everything the universe could throw at him. Which was stupid . . .

Four ruby-red laser targeting beams fanned out of Aaron's enrichments, playing across Inigo's face. 'Switch. It. *Off*,' the crazed agent growled. Somewhere close by dark wings flapped in pursuit. The edge of the cabin began to shimmer away as if the darkness was claiming it molecule by molecule. Her presence was chilling, seeping through Inigo's force field to frost his skin.

Aaron flung his head back. 'Get away from me, you monster.'

'It's not me,' Inigo whispered, fearful of whatever stalked them through the gloom which was now busily eating away at the edge of his own vision. He could see her smile now, predatory teeth bared. If she did break through to whatever Aaron believed to be reality there was no telling what would happen.

The laser beams started to curve through the air, sliding smoothly round Inigo to cage him in red threads. Their tips studded Corrie-Lyn's naked body.

'I can be as bad as her,' Aaron purred with smooth menace. 'After all, she taught me. I can make this last for hours. You will hear Corrie-Lyn plead with you to switch it off, she will beg you to kill her as the only way to stop the pain.'

'Please,' Inigo said. 'Listen to me, I'm not doing this to you.'

The arching lasers grew brighter. Corrie-Lyn's skin sizzled and blackened where the tiny points touched her. She gritted her teeth against the pricks of pain. 'Wait,' she gasped. 'Where are we?'

Aaron was shuddering as if someone were shoving an electric current through his body. 'Location?'

The darkness surrounding the cabin pulsed with a heart's rhythm, stirring up a gust of air that pushed against them.

'Yes!' Corrie-Lyn demanded. 'Our location. Are we near the Spike?'

'It's two hundred and seventy lightyears away.'

'Is that close enough for the dream? Is that what we're feeling?'

Aaron cocked his head to one side, though his hand remained steady just centimetres in front of Inigo's face. A drop of saliva dribbled out of his mouth. 'Dream? You think this to be a dream? She's here. She's walking through the ship. She's here for me. She never forgets. Never forgives. For that is weakness and we are strength.'

'Not your dream, you fucking moron,' Corrie-Lyn said. 'Ozzie's dream. The galactic dream he left the Commonwealth to build.'

'Ozzie's dream?' The curving lasers dimmed slightly. Corrie-Lyn wriggled away from their enclosure.

'That's right,' Inigo cried. 'This effect is like an emotion amplifier. I knew the sex was good, but . . .'

Corrie-Lyn stopped rubbing her burns. 'Hey!'

'Don't you see?' Inigo urged. 'He's heightened our emotional responses through the gaiafield. But with your screwed-up psyche that's simply helped with the destabilization. Whatever controls your masters installed are starting to crack under the pressure.'

The blackness pulsed again. Inigo swore he could feel the pressure increase on his inner ears.

'My gaiamotes are closed,' Inigo hissed.

'They can't be! I'm witnessing your dreams.'

'He's right,' Corrie-Lyn said. 'My gaiamotes are shut, too, but this fucking nightmare is terrorizing us all. It's not the gaiamotes.'

Aaron's targeting beams snapped off. 'What then?' he demanded. His knees nearly buckled. 'I cannot risk my mission failing in this fashion. It will leave you open to capture ... We will have to die.' His hand moved to clamp his fingers over Inigo's face. Inigo's exovision was suddenly swamped by warning symbols as his force field began to glow a weak violet. 'Your memorycell, too,' Aaron said. 'Nothing of you must survive to fall into the hands of the enemy, especially her.'

'He's circumvented it,' Inigo said, trying to keep calm. Violence wasn't the solution to this, he had to break through Aaron's neuroses. 'This is Ozzie's dream, it doesn't need the gaiafield any more. He's propagated the feelings through space-time itself.'

'This is an attack,' Aaron vowed.

'It's not. I promise. He's a genius, an authentic off-the-scale live genius. The gaiafield was just a warm-up for him. Don't you see, he's created real telepathy. Ozzie has made something that can make mind speak directly to mind just like he always wanted. It's internal, do you understand, your instability is coming from within.'

'No.' Aaron fell to his knees gasping for breath, pulling Inigo down with him.

'You are the cause of the mission failure. The damage is coming from your own subconscious.'

'No.'

'It is.'

'Make it stop. She can't get me. I can't allow that. Not again.'

'There is nobody there. She is just a memory, a screwed-up memory you don't know how to contain, there's so much fear embedded with the experience.'

Aaron suddenly let go of Inigo, stumbling round to face the broken door in a martial art pose. 'She's here.'

'Aaron, listen to me. Ozzie's dream is corroding your rationality because it was never designed to deal with circumstances like these. You have to let them go, you have to let the real you out of those constraints your boss imposed. You must come forward. This artificial personality can't cope.'

'Not good enough?'

'The real you is more than adequate. Come out. Come on, it's the only way you can beat this.'

'Damage control . . .' Aaron slowly sank to his knees, then his back curled as he dropped his head between his legs. His breathing started to calm. The eerie semi-hallucinations around the periphery of the cabin began to melt away.

Inigo and Corrie-Lyn gave each other an anxious look. 'Do you think . . . ?' she asked.

'The Lady alone knows,' he murmured back.

They stood up. Corrie-Lyn hurriedly pulled her woollen robe back on, then they both approached the crouched figure cautiously. Inigo reached out tentatively, but didn't quite have the courage to touch Aaron. He wondered if that was the dream field – or whatever – amplifying the worry. But it seemed sensible enough. Surely an emotional enhancer would boost his sympathy correspondingly. Maybe that was the way it worked, everything raised equally, so everything stayed in the same balance as before – no alteration to personality, just a greater perception or empathy.

Aaron's head came up and his biononics performed a thorough field scan of the starship. He stood up and looked at Inigo and Corrie-Lyn. His weapon enrichments sank back down into his hand; ripples of skin closed over them.

'Hello?' Corrie-Lyn said hopefully. 'Aaron, is that really you now?'

Inigo wasn't so sure. There wasn't a trace of emotion coming from the man. In fact . . .

'I am Aaron,' he said.

'That's good,' Corrie-Lyn said hesitantly. 'Have the disturbances gone?'

'There are no disturbances in my head. My thought routines have been reduced to minimum functionality requirement. This mission will be completed now. Arrival at the Spike is in eighteen hours. Inigo will accompany me to Oswald Fernandez Isaacs. You will then both be given further instructions.' He turned and walked out of the door.

'What in Honious was that?' a startled Corrie-Lyn asked.

'The last fallback mode by the sound of it: probably installed in case his brain got damaged in a firefight. He's running on minimum neural activity. Whoever rebuilt him must have had a real fetish about redundancy.'

She shivered, clutching at the robe. 'He's even less human than before, isn't he? And he was never much to begin with.'

'Yeah. Ladydamnit, I thought this was our chance to break his conditioning.'

'Crap.'

'But at least we know I don't get shot before we meet Ozzie.'

'Oswald? I never knew that was his name.'

'No, me neither.'

She let out a long breath, then narrowed her eyes to stare at him. 'The sex wasn't that good naturally?'

'Ah. I had to say something that would shock him.'

'Really?' She glanced round the cabin. Tiny shards of sharp metal debris glinted on every surface. 'Honious, this is a mess.'

'Hey, don't worry, we'll get through this.'

'I'm not worried.'

'Yes you are, I can sense it.'

'What? Oh!' Her eyes widened as she realized she could sense his mind as clearly as if they were fully sharing within the gaiafield.

He smiled weakly. 'That Ozzie, he's really something. Over two hundred and fifty lightyears away, and it already affects us. Whatever *it* really is.'

'Do you think it can be used to connect everyone with the Void?'

'I have no idea. But I suspect we're going to find out. Maybe that's why Aaron's controllers want me there; I have a proven access to thoughts from the Void, maybe they want to see if I can connect directly to the Heart.'

'So what can this effect do?' she mused.

They spent the next few hours experimenting. The effect was remarkably like the longtalk they knew so well from the Void. When one of them carefully formed words or phrases the other could perceive it, though they never worked out anything like the directed longtalk available to the residents of Querencia. But it was the constant awareness of emotion that was the most disquieting. If they hadn't already been so intimate, and adept at using the gaiamotes to connect emotionally, Corrie-Lyn thought they would have had real trouble with guilt and resentment at such openness. As it was, the effect took a long time to accept at an intellectual level. Being so exposed, and having no choice in the matter, made her apprehensive. She was all right with Inigo, but knowing the machine-like Aaron could perceive her every sentiment was unpleasant at the very least; and as for the prospect of every alien on the Spike being able to see into her mind . . . She wasn't sure she could cope with that.

The one time she gave a bottle of Rindhas a longing look she immediately knew of Inigo's disapproval, which triggered her own shame to new heights. No wonder the cranky old Aaron had broken down under the mental stress. It was a weird kind of human who could cope with having their heart on their sleeve the entire time.

And yet, she told herself, *that's what we were all wishing to undergo in the Void. Especially the all-inclusive telepathy as it was in the Thirty-seventh dream. Perhaps it's just people who are at fault. If I didn't have so much to hide I wouldn't fear this as much. My fault I'm like this.*

They went to sleep a few hours later, with Inigo using a low-level field scan to monitor Aaron – just in case. They woke in time for a quick breakfast before they reached the Spike.

The *Lindau* dropped out of hyperspace fifty AUs above the

blue-white A-class star's south pole. The emergence location allowed it an unparalleled view of the star's extensive ring system. Visual sensors swiftly picked out the Hot Ring, with its innermost edge two AUs out from the star and a diameter of half an AU. A hoop of heavy metallic rocks glittering brightly in the harsh light as they tumbled round their timeless orbit. Three AUs further out, the Dark Ring was a stark contrast, a slender band of carbonaceous particles inclined five degrees out of the ecliptic, so dark it seemed to suck light out of space. The angle allowed it to produce a faint umbra on the so-called Smog, the third ring, composed of pale silicate dust and light particles, combined with a few larger asteroids which created oddly elegant curls and whorls within the bland ochre-tinted haze. Beyond that, at seventeen AUs, was the Band Ring, a thin very dense loop fixed in place by over a hundred shepherd moonlets. After that there was only the Ice Bracelet, which began at twenty-five AUs and blended into the Oort cloud at the system's edge.

There were no planets, which was an idiosyncrasy that sorely puzzled the Commonwealth astronomers. The star was too old for the rings to be categorized as any kind of accretion disc. Most wrote it off as a quirk caused by the Spike, but that had only been in place for at the most fifty thousand years; in astrological time that was nothing. Unless of course it had obliterated the planets when it arrived, which would make it a weapon of extraordinary stature. Again highly unlikely.

From their position poised above the system, Aaron asked for approach and docking permission. It was granted by the Spike's AI, and they slipped back into hyperspace for the short flight in.

The Spike was in the middle of the Hot Ring; an alien artefact whose main structure was a slim triangle that curved gently around its long axis, which measured eleven thousand kilometres from the top to an indeterminate base. There was no way to determine the exact position of the base because that part of the Spike was still buried within some dimensional twist. To the Navy exploration vessel which had found it in 3072 it was as if a planet-sized starship had tried to erupt out of hyperspace with only partial success, with the nose slicing out clean into space-time while the tail section was still lost amid the intricate folds of the universe's underlying quantum fields. The only thing that ruined that big-aerodynamic-starship image was the sheer size of the brute. On top of the triangle was a five-kilometre-diameter spire that was a further two thousand kilometres in length – function unknown.

Contrary to all natural orbital mechanics, the Spike remained orientated in one direction, with the tip pointing straight out of the Hot Ring ecliptic. Its concave curve also tracked the star as it travelled along its perfectly circular orbit, like some heliotropic sail-shaped flower always following the light. So the anchoring twist which held its base amid the whirling rocky particles was obviously active, although its mechanism was somewhere within the unreachable base. Few people still believed it was a ship, though the notion remained among the romantically inclined elements of the Commonwealth's scientific community and more excitable Raiel/Void conspiracy theorists.

Contact with the fourteen known alien species living inside, which was remarkably easy, didn't advance the exploration starship's understanding of the Spike's origin or purpose one byte. All the species who'd found a home among the myriad habitation chambers had arrived there relatively recently – with the Chikoya the longest-established, having been there four and a half thousand years. They, and all those who had found a home in the Spike over the millennia, had made their adaptations and alterations to the basic structure to a point where it was difficult to know what was original any more.

When the *Lindau* emerged from hyperspace again they were eight hundred kilometres sunward and level with the top of the Spike, so the massive spire stabbed up into the southern star-field above them. The smartcore accelerated them in, matching the massive structure's errant velocity vector. Ahead of them the curved inner surface was segmented by crystalline chambers like a skin of bubbles, with the smallest extending over a hundred kilometres wide, while the largest, an Ilodi settlement, stretched out to a full three hundred kilometres in diameter. Eight tubes wove around and through the chambers, each of them a convoluted loop with a diameter of thirty kilometres, acting as the Spike's internal transport routes. Seven of them had an H-congruous oxygen/nitrogen atmosphere; the eighth supported a high-temperature methane/nitrogen environment.

Aaron directed them in to a metal mushroom sprouting from one of the H-congruous tubes. There were hundreds of similar landing pads scattered randomly along all the tubes. They didn't look original at all: some of them were crude, little more than slabs of metal with a basic airlock tunnel fused on to the tube. When the *Landau* settled on it, a localized artificial gravity field took over, holding the starship down at about a tenth of a gee.

Inigo and Corrie-Lyn were standing behind Aaron in the starship's small bridge compartment, with images of the Spike projected out of a half-dozen portals all around them. They could see a lot of movement on the surface. A huge variety of drones were crawling, rolling, sliding, skating and hopping along the tubes and chambers, performing various repair and maintenance functions. All of them were operated by the controlling AI, itself a patchwork of processor cores that had been grafted on to the original management network by the residents who had come and gone over the millennia.

'The effect's no stronger here than when it first hit us, it must be uniform,' Corrie-Lyn said wonderingly as she tried to sort through the multitude of foreign sensations which Ozzie's telepathy effect were allowing to impact on her mind. She could feel Inigo's mind as before, and the odd unemotional threads buzzing through Aaron's brain, but beyond them was a sensory aurora not too dissimilar to the gaiafield. Human minds were present, though she wasn't sure how many, probably no more than a few thousand. Alien minds were also intruding, which were intriguingly weird, possessing a different intensity and emotions that were subtly different.

'What I'm feeling can't represent everyone on the Spike,' Inigo said, perceiving her interest. 'For a start, there's over a million of the Ba'rine sect Chikoya who settled here after they got kicked off their homeworld. They're aggressive in their beliefs, and not afraid to show it. That level of animosity is absent. Then there's the Flam-gi and their whole nasty little species-ism superiority – they're definitely not sharing. And Honious alone knows who or what's in some of the sealed chambers.'

'So they're not all part of Ozzie's dream, then?'

'It would seem not.'

'Why?' Even as she asked it, she could sense his dismissal.

'I don't know. We'll just have to ask him. Aaron, do you know where he is?'

'No.' The agent's head didn't move. He was studying a projection of the Spike's entire inner surface. Some kind of mapping program was active, sending flashes of colour across sections and down tubes. 'The controlling AI has no information on him. U-shadow-based data retrieval routines do not function effectively in the network, and some compartment sections are blocked; I cannot check the data with any accuracy.'

'Reasonable enough,' Inigo said. 'There's no overall government as such. From what I remember you just turn up and find somewhere that supports your biochemistry and move in.'

'So what now?' Corrie-Lyn asked.

'We will visit the largest human settlement and ask them for Isaacs's location.'

'And if they don't know?' Inigo asked.

'He is renowned. Someone will know.'

'But he already knows we're here,' Inigo said.

Aaron turned to stare at him. 'Have you signalled him?'

'No. But this telepathy effect exposes everything to everybody. That's what he came here to do. Therefore he is aware of our arrival.'

'Can you determine the source of the effect?'

'No.'

'Very well. Come with me now.' Aaron walked out into the companionway.

Inigo gave Corrie-Lyn a bemused shrug, and the two of them followed meekly behind Aaron as he went into the scoutship's main airlock.

The landing pad had extruded a malmetal cylinder that was compatible to the starship's seal. The outer door expanded, showing the cylinder curving down. Aaron stepped through and glided forward in the low gravity. The cylinder bent in a sharp double curve to take them through the tube wall. They passed through a translucent pressure curtain that shivered around them, and they were inside a small blue-metal building with open archways. The temperature and humidity rose sharply to subtropical levels. They walked through the arches onto a broad paved area. The tube's inner surface was covered in lush pink-tinged grasses and long meandering grey-blue forests. Fifteen kilometres above their heads, a sliver of dazzling white light ran along the axis of the tube, shining through the thick smears of helectical cloud that drifted along the interior. As soon as they'd stepped through the pressure curtain Corrie-Lyn had felt the gravity rise to about two-thirds Earth standard, which gave her the visual impression of standing at the bottom of a cylinder where anything moving on the solid roof above her should fall straight down, while intellectually she knew damn well that every point of the landscape arching above her had the same gravity.

She puffed her cheeks out, partly from the heat, partly from the improbability of the vista. 'And this is just the transport route?'

'One of them,' Aaron replied. 'There are short-length worm-holes and some T-spheres operational within the structure. However they are under the control of the species which installed them. The tubes provide a general connection between chambers.'

'We walk?' she asked incredulously.

'No.' Aaron looked up.

Corrie-Lyn followed his gaze, seeing a dark triangle descending out of the glaring light straight towards them. As it grew closer she could see it was some kind of aircraft, maybe twenty metres long and quite fat given its otherwise streamlined appearance. Human lettering was stencilled on the narrow-swept tailfin, registration codes which made no sense. Landing legs unfolded neatly fore and aft, and it settled on the tough wiry grass. A door swung open halfway along its bulging belly. *No malmetal, then*, she mused. She couldn't see any jet intakes either. Whatever propelled it must be similar to ingrav.

The cabin interior was basic, and somehow primitive to anyone accustomed to the Commonwealth's ubiquitous capsules. She sank into a chair that could only have been designed for a human body. The hull wasn't transparent either, which disappointed her. A feeling Inigo picked up on. 'There's a sensor feed,' he told her, and gave her u-shadow a little access routine which wasn't like any program she was familiar with.

'How do you know that?' she asked as the aircraft's camera views unfolded in her exovision. They were already lifting fast, not that the acceleration was apparent.

'I'm monitoring Aaron's datatraffic,' he replied levelly.

After it rose above the thick winding clouds the aircraft shot forward. The speed made Corrie-Lyn blink. 'Wow,' she murmured.

'As best I can make out we're doing about mach twenty,' Inigo said. 'Even with the way this tube bends about you can probably get from one end of the Spike to the other in a couple of hours.'

'So what's the place we're going to?'

'The chamber has been named Octoron,' Aaron said curtly.

'How far?'

'Flight duration approximately three minutes.'

She rolled her eyes, hoping her mind wasn't showing just how unnerving she found this machine-like version of Aaron. Though presumably he no longer had the thought routines that bothered about such emotional trivia. When she concentrated on the few thought impulses inside his head they were all calm and cool, so much so it was hard to sense them at all.

Their little plane looped casually halfway around the axial

light, and then slowed quickly to begin its vertical decent. They landed close to a broad low dome of some silver-grey fabric that had wide arches around the base. It was obviously a transport hub, as several other planes were landing and taking off. People came and went from the cathedral-sized dome, dressed like any citizens of the Outer Commonwealth Worlds in a mix of styles from ultramodern toga suits down to the whimsy of centuries past.

Sitting right at the centre of the airy dome was a gold-mirrored sphere whose lower quarter was hidden below ground. People were walking in and out of it, pushing through the surface as if it was less substantial than mist. As she walked towards it, Corrie-Lyn was conscious of the suspicion and curiosity starting to emanate from the minds around her. Her consternation that Inigo at least would be recognized was acting as positive feedback. Several people stopped to stare. She felt their astonishment as recognition dawned. It was swiftly tinged by anger and resentment.

Just before they reached the gold surface Aaron took Inigo's hand. 'Do not attempt to evade me,' he warned.

'I have no intention to,' Inigo told him.

Aaron was still holding him as they all went through the sphere wall. Corrie-Lyn felt the surface flow around her like a pressure curtain. Then she was falling slowly as gravity shrank away again. It was gloomy inside. Her macrocellular clusters ran vision-amplifying routines, enabling her to see the wide shaft she was dropping down. It was a variant on a nul-grav chute, about three hundred metres long. Aaron and Inigo were a couple of metres ahead of her.

The descent took barely a minute. Whatever gravity distortion gripped her, it began to flip her round so she wound up rising to the far end of the chute. It was covered by a murky barrier identical to the one at the other end of the chute. Her skin tingled as she passed through.

*

Emergence location: plaza.

Active> grade-three integral force field

Active> Level-two biononic field scan. Scan summation: plaza one hundred seventy-eight point three metres major diameter. Three main access roads, five secondary streets. Immediate population eighty-seven adult humans, subdivision fifty-three Higher; nineteen children under twelve. No alien lifeforms. Surrounding buildings average height twenty-five metres, facade composition high-purity iron. Domestic power supply one hundred twenty volts; high-rate communication net. Visible transport: bicycles. Gravatonic fluctuation indicates seven ingrav drive units operational within three kilometres.

Preliminary assessment: secure environment. No threat to subject alpha. Subject alpha restrained by physical grip; maintain restraint condition.

Primary mission commencement: Determine location of Oswald Fernandez Isaacs. Four options.

Initiate option one: ask.

'You.'

Octoron citizen one: male, height one point seven two centimetres; biononic functionality moderate: 'Yes?'

'Where is Oswald Fernandez Isaacs?'

Octoron citizen one: 'Who? Hey, aren't you Inigo?'

Subject alpha: 'Yeah, fraid so.'

Octoron citizen one: 'You bastard. You stupid selfish bastard. What are you doing here?'

Subject alpha: 'Look, I'm sorry. This is complicated. Please answer his question. We need to find Ozzie.'

Octoron citizen one: 'Hey, why can't I sense your thoughts?'

'Irrelevant. Do you know where Isaacs is?'

Octoron citizen one: 'You're with Inigo? Go screw yourself.'

Scan>Octoron citizen one altering biononic field functions. Skin temperature rising, heart rate increasing, muscle contraction, elevated adrenalin. Analysis: possible aggression.

Threat.

Response.

Activate> biononic weapons field.

Armed> disruptor pulse. Target: midsection Octoron citizen one.
Fire.

External sound level increasing. Human screaming.

Subject beta: 'Oh great Lady! You killed him.'

'I neutralized the threat.'

'Threat? What fucking threat, you monster.'

Primary mission: option one failure. Go to option two.

'You.'

Octoron citizen two: female, one point five eight centimetres, zero
biononics, full Advancer macrocellular sequence. Running.

Capture.

'You.'

Octoron citizen two: 'What? I haven't done anything. Let me go. Help!
Help!'

Subject beta: 'Put her down, you bastard.'

'Is Oswald Fernandez Isaacs resident in the Spike?'

Octoron citizen two, no response.

Option two, second level.

Octoron citizen two: incoherent scream.

'Is Oswald Fernandez Isaacs resident in the Spike?'

Octoron citizen two: 'Yes, yes he's here. Oh shit that hurts. Stop it,
please. Please.'

Subject beta: 'Let her go.'

Subject alpha: 'Stop this now.'

Scan summation: twenty-three Higher humans activating high-level
biononic fields. Approaching. Inter-person data exchanges
increasing.

Threat imminent.

Response grade one to hostile enclosure situation.

'Halt now, or I will kill her.'

Subject beta: 'Stay back. Back. The maniac means it. Please, stay
back.'

'Where is Oswald Fernandez Isaacs?'

Octoron citizen two: 'I don't know. Please.'

'Who knows where Isaacs is?'

Three Octoron citizens, simultaneously: 'Let her go.'

Scan reception> eight target sensors locking on.

'I will kill her unless he is brought to me.'

Subject alpha: 'Stop this. Let me talk to them.'

'No.'

Enclosure threat elevated to grade five.

Response. Random target selection twelve citizens, three buildings.

Armed> Disruptor pulse. Sequential firepattern.

Armed> Ion beam. Sequential firepattern.

Scan> Level five> Successful penetration of debris cloud and atmospheric ionization. Zero immediate threat.

Surrounding sound level high.

Humans in plaza retreating. Casualties fifteen. Fatalities five.

Octoron citizen two struggling. Uncooperative.

Primary mission: option two failure. Go to option three.

U-shadow download general broadcast into local communication net.

'This is an open message for Oswald Fernandez Isaacs. I mean you no harm. It is imperative that you contact me. I have Inigo with me. Together you can resolve the Void catastrophe.'

Subject beta: 'Oh that should do it, you moron dickhead. I'd be rushing to call you if it was me.' Voice level raised/condition hysterical.

'Be silent.'

Subject alpha: 'Aaron, this has to stop. Do you understand, you are wrecking your own mission.'

Analysis.

Claim refuted.

'I know what I have to do. Don't interfere.'

Subject alpha: 'You don't know. You're dealing with humans. You need an emotional component in your reasoning. And you don't have that any more.'

'This environment is hostile to my emotion-based routines, it corrodes my rationality. They cannot be permitted.'

Subject beta: 'Oh shit. Shit, what do we do?'

Subject alpha: 'I don't know.'

Alert> T-sphere establishing across Octoron. Emergence of eleven
   objects – distance fifty metres. Scan> Level eight> Intruders
   identified: adult tristage Chikoya encased in armour. Multiple-
   weapon hardware attached. Force fields active.

Surrounding sound level increasing – human screaming.

Subject beta: 'Great Lady, what are they?'

Chikoya one: 'You are the human messiah.'

Analyse: how did they know that and locate Subject alpha so quickly?
   Time elapsed since landing seventeen minutes.

Subject alpha: 'I am Inigo, yes.'

Situation analysis. Chikoya engaging deployment manoeuvre. High
   tactical advantage in successful encirclement.

Probability of protecting subjects alpha and beta from synchronized
   Chikoya weapons fire: minimal. Option one: discard subject beta.

Chikoya one: 'You have initiated a devourment phase in the Void.'

Subject alpha: 'I haven't been in contact with Edeard for over a century
   and a half.'

Chikoya one: 'You initiated contact. You are responsible. You must stop
   it.'

'All Void activity will be ended. We will see to it. Now leave
   Octoron.'

Chikoya one: 'Messiah, you will come with us. Your threat to the galaxy
   must be ended. Come now.'

'Not permissible. Remove yourself and your kind from this place.'

Chikoya one: 'Your messiah comes with us.'

'Inigo, raise your integral force field to its highest setting.'

Subject alpha: 'What about Corrie-Lyn? Damn you, she's naked out
   here.'

Subject beta: 'What's happening? Inigo, don't go with those things,
   please. Aaron you have to—'

Alert> Chikoya weapons activation.

Multiple target acquisition.

Armed> Disruptor pulse. Sequential fire.

Armed> Neutron lasers. Sequential fire.

Electronic countermeasures. Engaged. Full power.

Armed> Microkinetics. Smart acquisition. Free fire authority.
Ceasefire.

Scan> Active Chikoya immediate area withdrawal. Redeployment.
>Tracking.

Current tactical situation poor. Move. Subject alpha to accompany.

Subject alpha holding subject beta, force field extended to protect
her.

'Let go of her.'

Subject alpha: 'Fuck you.'

Scan.

Move into Building-A. Utilize the cover it provides.

'Come with me.'

Moving. Subject alpha, subject beta, accompanying.

Alert> Multiple target acquisition.

Greatest tactical location: stand in Building-A doorway.

Armed> Disruptor pulse. Sequential fire.

Armed> Neutron lasers. Sequential fire.

Armed> Ion beams. Sequential fire.

Armed> Microkinetics. Smart acquisition. Free fire authority.

Armed> Ariel smartseeker stealth mines. Chikoya profile loaded.
Dispense.

Alert> Teleport emergence, eighteen armoured Chikoya.

'We can't get away. They know you're here.'

Ceasefire.

Subject alpha (shouting): 'Tell me something I don't know.'

Exit doorway. Weapons fire impact weakening Building-A structure.

'This way.'

Enact exit strategy.

Scan> mapping Building-A layout. Exit route confirmed. U-shadow
established in local communications net, infiltrating adjacent
transport capsules.

Alert> Chikoya access of Building-A.

Targeting Building-B structural load points.

Armed> Disruptor pulse. Fire.

Integral force field strengthened to resist partial Building-A collapse.
Fire outbreak. Scan through smoke. Three Chikoya disabled.

Subject alpha: 'Where do we go?'

'We must leave the immediate area. Switch off your force field.'

Subject alpha: 'What? In the Lady's name you've got to be joking.'

'Negative. They are tracking your presence through the telepathy
   effect, it is completely pervasive and leaves you exposed wherever
   you are.'

Subject alpha: 'So?'

'Switch off your force field. I will render you unconscious. If you are not
   thinking, your thoughts cannot betray our location.'

Subject beta: 'Inigo! No! He'll kill us both. He will, it's what he
   does.'

'You are no use to me dead.'

Alert> Target acquisition: Building-C rooftop.

Armed> Microkinetics suppression barrage. Fire.

Target eliminated.

Subject alpha: 'But I can't stop the Void if I'm unconscious.'

'When I acquire Isaacs I will insist he switches off the telepathy effect.
   No one will be able to find you then.'

Subject alpha: 'Oh sweet Lady.'

Subject beta: 'No no no.'

Subject alpha: 'You look after Corrie-Lyn, too.'

'I will.'

Alert> Nine Chikoya deploying in acquisition formation.

Subject alpha: 'Aaron, whatever's left of the real you in there, I'm
   holding you to that.'

Exit capsule approaching. Landing zone designated to u-shadow. Three
   decoy capsules en route – safety limiters disabled.

'You can rely on me.'

Subject alpha: 'Very well.'

Subject beta: 'No! Inigo, no, please.'

Scan confirmation, subject alpha force field deactivated. Targeting.

Armed> Microkinetics, minimal tissue damage mode selected, neuro-
   sedative tip loaded. Fire.

Subject beta: 'No! Oh lady you've killed him. Get away from me. Get
   away, you monster.'

Subject beta attempting to run.

Targeting.

Armed> Microkinetic, minimal tissue damage mode selected, neuro-sedative tip loaded. Fire.

Alert> Five Chikoya approaching, open assault formation.

Multiple target acquisition.

Armed> Disruptor pulse. Maximum power rating. Sequential fire.

U-shadow update: landing exit capsule behind Building-D.

Armed> Neutron lasers. Maximum power rating. Sequential fire.

U-shadow update: decoy capsules on collision vector. Mach eight. Accelerating.

Armed> Microkinetics. Enhanced explosive warheads. Free fire authority.

Armed> Ariel smartseeker stealth mines. Chikoya profile loaded. Dispense.

Alert> New targets.

Fire.

Fire.

Fire.

*

The Delivery Man's biononics ran a last scan over the weird active-molecular vortex and the way it spun down through the quantum fields. It was an interesting chunk of superphysics technology, certainly, yet he had no idea what its function might actually be, though he suspected it was an elaborate experiment. Whatever it was, he was fairly sure it wasn't the elevation mechanism.

His u-shadow opened a link to Gore. 'Washout,' he reported.

'Yeah, me too.'

'I'm coming out.' There was little light in the vast cave, a few cold blue patches up amid the multitude of stalagmites eighty metres above his head. The bottom quarter of the cave had been cut smooth and flat, leaving the natural rock formations above. Even two and a half thousand years ago, when the advanced

Anomine had set it up, the cave couldn't have been a terribly practical place. That was the thing with the Anomine, everything had an aesthetic aspect.

Water dripped out of the deep fissures and off the end of the stalagmites, creating long pungent algal ribbons down the rough walls. Drainage channels had clogged, leaving dank puddles spreading across the floor. The vortex carried on regardless; moisture and murky air were never going to affect its composition or function.

As he retraced his steps along the winding passage back out to the surface, the Delivery Man was puzzled by the lack of any communication system connected to the vortex. If it was an experiment, surely they would need to monitor the results, same for a control system. *Or maybe I'm missing something,* he thought wearily. *Maybe there is an ultrasophisticated net covering the whole planet that biononic scans are simply too primitive to discover.* He was grasping at straws and knew it. The *Last Throw*'s sensors were good. They'd detected a hundred and twenty-four advanced devices still functional on the planet, of which the vortex was the eleventh they'd examined. If there was some kind of web linking them, *Last Throw*'s sensors would have revealed it.

A quarter of an hour later, the Delivery Man walked out into the evening sunlight. Tall cumulo-nimbus scurried through the darkening sky, splashed a pale rose-gold by the vanishing sun. From his position, high up a plateau wall, the countryside swept away to the south-east, its furthest fringes already turning to black. Several rivers traced bright silver threads across the mauve and jade vegetation. Then there was the city to the east, larger and more imposing than any of Earth's cities even at the height of the population boom. A forest of tall towers stretched over a mile into the air. Elaborate spiked spheres and curving pyramids filled the ground between the soaring spires like foothills. Lights were still shining through windows and open arches as the service machinery maintained the city in perfect readiness for occupation.

It was completely devoid of anyone, which he'd found

strangely sad, like a spurned lover. The remaining Anomine chose to live in their farm villages out in the open land. He could even see several of their little settlements amid the darkening land, flickering orange lights growing as the nightly fires were lit. He never did get that philosophy, living in the shadow of a past civilization, knowing that at any time they could simply move into the giant towers and live a life of unrivalled luxury, and challenge their minds once again. Yet instead, they rejected any form of technology beyond labour-animal carts and ploughs, and filled their days tilling the fields and building huts.

The *Last Throw* came streaking in over the mountains behind him, to finish up hovering a few centimetres above the succulent spiral grass-equivalent. He drifted up into the airlock.

'This is getting us nowhere fast,' Gore grumbled as the Delivery Man arrived in the main cabin.

'It's your procedure. What else have we got? There's not too many of these things to examine.'

'They're all small-scale. We have to look big.'

'We don't know that, remember,' the Delivery Man chided as he settled in a broad leather-cushioned scoop chair. 'We simply don't know what it is. That vortex I just examined. It had to be linked with the elevation mechanism.'

'How?' Gore snapped.

'I think it was some kind of experiment, probing the local quantum structure. That kind of knowledge could only help to contribute to going post-physical, surely?'

'Don't call me Shirley.'

'What?'

Gore ran a hand over his forehead. 'Yeah. Right. Whatever.'

The Delivery Man was mildly puzzled by Gore's lack of focus. It wasn't like him at all. 'All right. So what I was thinking is that there has to be some kind of web and database in the cities.'

'There is. You can't access it.'

'Why not?'

'The AIs are sentient. They won't allow any information retrieval.'

'That's stupid.'

'From our point of view, but they're the same as the border-guards, they maintain the homeworld's sanctity, the AIs keep the Anomine's information safe.'

'Why?'

'Because that's what the Anomine do, that's what they are. They're entitled to protect what they've built, same as anyone.'

'But we're not damag—'

'I know!' Gore snarled. 'I fucking know that, all right. We have to work round this. And listening to you sitting there, whingeing twenty-four-seven is no fucking help at all. Jezus, I should have lived a fucking normal twenty-first-century life and died properly. Why the hell do I fucking bother to help you moron supermen? Certainly not the gratitude.'

The Delivery Man only just stopped himself from opening his jaw to gawp at the gold-skinned man sitting in his antique orange shell chair. He was about to ask what the problem was, then realized. 'She'll be out of suspension soon,' he said sympathetically.

Gore grunted, shoving himself further back in his chair's cushioning. 'She should've been there by now.'

'We don't know. In the Void we just don't know. Timeflow there isn't uniform.'

'Maybe.'

'The confluence nests are functioning. She will dream Makkathran for you, she'll be there.'

'It'll mean crap if we don't find the mechanism.'

'I know. And we've still got Marius to deal with when we do.' The Delivery Man had been perturbed when the sensors showed them Marius had got past the borderguard stations. The Accelerator agent's ship had immediately dropped back into stealth mode once it was inside the cometary belt. Currently it was lurking amid the orbital debris cloud above the Anomine home-world, watching them zip over the planet. It wouldn't take much to work out what they were doing.

'Ha. That dick. We can take him whenever we want.'

'We don't know that.'

'It takes smarter and tougher than him to catch me with my ass hanging out.'

The Delivery Man shook his head. He couldn't decide if the machismo was worse than the insecurity. 'Well let's just hope it doesn't come to that.'

'Oh yeah. Wishful thinking, that's what keeps the universe ticking.'

The Delivery Man groaned and gave up.

Gore's golden lips parted in a small smile. 'The Navy teams didn't exactly push the AIs.'

'Uh huh,' the Delivery Man said warily.

'We've got another hundred or so of these tech highspots left to examine, right? So that's not going to take more than four or five days if we hustle.'

'That sounds about right.'

'Then we do it. If we draw a blank we go to plan B.'

'Which is?'

'Did you know I actually knew Ozzie?'

'I didn't, but it doesn't surprise me. You were contemporaries.'

'He pulled off two of the greatest thefts in human history.'

'Two? I knew there was some dispute with Nigel about taking the *Charybdis*.'

'Dispute? Jezus, do they even teach you people history these days? Nigel nearly killed him, and that's not a metaphor.'

The Delivery Man just ignored the 'you people' crack. After two weeks cooped up in the *Last Throw*'s cabin with Gore, it was almost a compliment. 'So what was the first crime?'

Gore grinned. 'The great wormhole heist. The smartass bastard cleaned out the Vegas casinos, and nobody ever knew it was him. Not until after the War, and Orion let it slip. Can you imagine that?'

'No, I truly cannot.'

'Well, sonny, you and I are going to steal the knowledge of an entire species. If that's what it takes to find this goddamn mechanism, then that's what we're going to do. Nobody will remember Ozzie's legend then, so screw him.'

I didn't know it anyway, the Delivery Man complained silently. He had no idea how Gore was planning to circumvent the Anomine AIs, but he suspected it wouldn't be a quiet method.

Inigo's Thirty-Third Dream

'We can visit any place on your world where we sense those who are fulfilled gathering in readiness for our guidance to the Heart,' the Skylord had said in answer to Edeard's question.

'So the towers of this city where you have come today play no part in guidance?'

'Those who inhabited this world before you built them to bid their kind farewell. They are where we came before, therefore they are where we come now. You use them as they did.'

'Then we can call you to gather us from anywhere?'

'Of course. My kindred welcome all those who have reached fulfilment. It is our purpose.'

Edeard kept dreaming that single crucial event over and over. It was one of the few natural dreams he ever had. Though even that faded after a few years – in his personal timescale.

*

The two Skylords had been visible on the horizon every morning for eight days, moving slowly across the pantheon of the Void's nebulae as they approached Querencia. Edeard stood on the highest balcony in the Orchard Palace, staring up into the pale sky as a cool breeze wafted in off the Lyot Sea. If he really stretched his farsight he could just sense the placid thoughts of the massive creatures.

Two, where every time before it has been four. Why? Why should that be? The whole city is a unified society. I have made sure we've achieved contentment within ourselves this time. That makes us better people. So why have only two come?

He didn't like how much that disturbed him. Even on the occasion two times past, when Oberford's Great Tower of Guidance was being built and the whole economy was falling apart as if Honious was establishing its very own kingdom of bedlam across Querencia, four Skylords had come. It was the start of autumn on the fifth year after Finitan's death. One of the few constants linking his attempts to change the world for the better.

Ladydamnit, four always come now!

The breeze played over his bare skin, and he rubbed his arms absently at the chill. Those two gauzy stars were still too far away for him to talk with them directly. But when they were within his range, he would be asking. Yes indeed.

High above the compact streets and blue pointy roofs of Jeavons, a couple of ge-eagles were floating lazily on the updrafts. They weren't any he was familiar with, and their long circling flight meant that one of them was always turned towards the palace. He scowled up at them, but resisted hauling them down out of the sky. Someone was interested in him. Hardly news. Though none of the independent provinces were a direct threat to Makkathran. *That I know of. Perhaps they're just running scared and want to spy on me to satisfy their paranoia.* Knowing the provinces and the trouble they'd caused this time around it wouldn't surprise him. But still, the brazenness; watching the Waterwalker, the absolute Mayor of Makkathran, in his own city. That took some gall. Which in itself narrowed it down to three provinces – or rather their governors. Mallux in Obershire, Kiborne in Plaxshire, or more likely Devroul in Licshills. Yes, any one of them would dare; they were all busy establishing their claims as unifiers to rival him. Each fierce in their independence. Greedy in their desire to absorb their neighbour. Exactly the opposite of what the world should be; what he was trying to make it.

He went back into the master bed chamber. Kanseen had always enjoyed the Orchard Palace's state rooms. It was what all the city buildings should be like, she'd claimed, a blend of old Makkathran architecture and more practical human adaptations. Theirs had been a pleasant two years together; though in truth after Kristabel's increasing sourness anyone else would have been a relief. But in parallel to the breakdown of his own marriage Macsen had become intolerable for Kanseen, so the two of them finally winding up with each other was almost inevitable.

Since he moved out of the Sampalok mansion, Macsen's downfall had continued at a rate that even upset Edeard. Not that there was anything he could do to help – not yet. Macsen cut himself off from everyone, his old friends, his children, political allies, anyone that might stand between him and his food and drink and miserable self-pity. He also completely rejected Edeard's unity. Not for him the growing solidarity of the city, an extended family whose open minds would sympathize and care for him and help him regain his dignity and purpose in life.

The last time Edeard had farsighted the former Master of Sampalok, three weeks ago, he had made a woeful figure. Living in some squalid room in a Cobara household by himself, spending his coinage in nearby taverns whose forte was cheap beer and cheaper food. His reaction to the intrusion had been a viciously personal diatribe that went on for almost an hour before it finally spluttered away when he succumbed to a drunken slumber.

Edeard had withdrawn then, guilty and angry in equal measure. Macsen was one of his oldest friends; he ought to have been able to do something. Yet he despised the way Macsen had just let go and given in to whatever Honious-born spirits now possessed him; he was stronger than that, Edeard knew. Yet Macsen in his alcohol-and-kestric-derived state blamed Edeard for the way his life had tumbled into the abyss, with his rejection of unification at the heart of it. Edeard knew the trust and understanding he'd brought to Makkathran was the true way forward. He couldn't stop now, not for one person, no matter how much his friendship used to mean.

Being with Kanseen hadn't helped Macsen's condition. That was just the most personal way to wound Macsen there could be. It insured there would be no reconciliation now, Edeard knew, no last-minute mellowing and putting aside of pride – not on either side. So his own triumph in establishing the unification in the city had come at the cost of his friend. And, if he wasn't careful, his friend's soul, for in the end what Skylord would ever guide Macsen's embittered, unfulfilled soul to the Heart? He had no choice, he knew. Each day now was simply spent putting off the inevitable. Soon a subtle domination would have to be applied, gently guiding Macsen back into the embrace of those who loved him.

Edeard padded over to the wide circular bed, and pushed aside the gauzy curtains that surrounded it. A hazy patch on the ceiling above the soft mattress radiated a warm copper light, its dusky illumination just enough to reveal the outlines of her body as she slept. The sheet had slipped down past her shoulders, exposing skin that still gleamed from the oils that the two younger girls had massaged in at the start of the evening. It was a pleasurable entertainment, variants of which he enjoyed most nights now. Proof, as if he needed it, that the city was now on the right course to provide fulfilment for everyone. Nobody censured any more, nobody criticized or fought or complained. They cooperated and helped each other succeed in their individual endeavours. He had brought them liberation of themselves, the sure route to the kind of fulfilment that the Skylords sought.

Edeard bent over and kissed her gently on the lips. Hilitte stirred, stretching herself with indolent grace; not fully awake, yet smiling when she saw him. 'What time is it?' she mumbled.

'Early.'

'Poor Edeard, couldn't you sleep?' Her gathering thoughts were tinged with genuine concern.

'There are things I worry about,' he admitted with voice and mind. *Honesty with each other, that is the key to true unity.*

'Even now? That's so wrong. So unfair.' Her arms rose up to twine round his neck. 'Let's think of something else for you to occupy yourself with.'

For a second he resisted, then allowed her to pull him down so he could lose himself in simple physical delights and forget all about the rebel provinces and Macsen and the others who struggled against the city's unity. For a while at least.

Not surprisingly, Edeard didn't wake again until the sun was well above the horizon. He and Hilitte bathed together in the oval pool in the bathroom where water gurgled in along a long raised chute which he'd crafted to resemble a small stream. It also showered down on them from a bulge in the curving ceiling when they asked; since he moved into the Palace state rooms after the election he'd been modifying things so he could have any kind of spray from a heavy jet to a light mist. He lounged in a sculpted seat at the side of the pool, watching Hilitte rinse herself off under the fast rain of droplets, deliberately stretching and twisting so he might appreciate her lithe figure. Which he did, but ... Kanseen had enjoyed the new improved shower, he recalled with a touch of melancholia. That wasn't the problem that ultimately came between them. They'd differed over Makkathran's unification. How he wanted to go about creating an atmosphere of trust, how to use family and political supporters and those who eagerly sought the Waterwalker's patronage; building so many allies, seeding the districts with unity groups, that the outcome would be inevitable. She never fully agreed with the concept, regarding it as a branch of domination.

What Kanseen did not understand, and he could never explain, was just how badly wrong the nice and open and honest approach had gone – twice in a row. How the time before, the one after the whole Oberford Tower disaster, the method of inclusion, which he'd so carefully crafted from his horrendous experience with the nest, and had given freely so Querencia might live as one, had been warped and subverted by the malcontents of the emerging generation of strong psychics (and

Ranalee, of course) to build new, small, versions of the nest centred around themselves in what was almost a reprise of Tathal's time. Bitter struggles ensued, tipping the world yet again into chaos and hurt, leaving him with no choice this time around but to launch the unification in a way that enabled his governance to be paramount. Restricting dissent was a small price to pay for such an achievement. Even now, strong psychics out in eight provinces had managed to subvert the gift, declaring independence from Makkathran's benign governorship – the Waterwalker's menacing empire, as they called it. Their own petty little fiefdoms were hardly beacons of enlightenment. He was still considering if and how he should move against them; as with the original nest, they wouldn't allow anyone to leave of their own free will.

'What's the matter, sweetie?' Hilitte asked, suffused with concern.

'I'm fine.'

She struck a sultry pose under the shower. 'You want me to bring the girls in to help me wash under here?'

'We did enough of that last night, and we will again tonight. I'm going to get breakfast now.' He stepped out of the bath and snagged a big towel with his third hand. Behind him Hilitte gave a small pout and ordered the shower off.

That was the one trouble with her, he realized, she really was too young to be anything else but a bedmate. He couldn't talk to her about anything, exchange ideas, argue problems through, reminisce about events. They never went to the Opera House together, and she swiftly grew bored at the more formal dinner parties he was constantly invited to – so much so she rarely went to any these days, which was just as well. But she did have a delectably dirty mind and a complete lack of inhibition. It all came as something of a revelation after being married for so long. However unfair that was on Kristabel, Hilitte's bedroom antics provided a grand way of getting his mind off the troubles of the day.

Which makes her more convenient than visiting the House of Blue Petals. Not necessarily cheaper, though.

Breakfast was taken in the huge state dining room with its long roof forever showing intense orange images of the sun's corona from the vantage point of some endless orbit a million miles above the seething surface. Underneath the fluctuating glare the long polished blackash table was capable of hosting city banquets for a hundred and fifty guests. This morning it had been set for the two of them. The kitchen staff had laid out big silver ice-bed platters on one of the dozen bolnut veneer sideboards, laden with an array of cold smoked meats cut as thin as parchment. Petal-pattern segments of fruit, cheeses and glass jugs of yogurt were laid out next to them like small works of art. Warm dishes contained scrambled eggs, poached eggs, fried eggs, tomatoes, mushrooms, bacon and sausages and crisp mashed potato. Five earthenware pots contained the mixes of cereal, while a small charcoal grill was ready to toast any of the five different types of bread or just warm his croissants for him.

Edeard sat down and stared over at the ridiculously extravagant spread of food without really registering any of it. He directed a ge-chimp to bring him a tall glass of apple juice and a bowl of cereal. Hilitte sat next to him dressed in a thick towelling robe with fluffy pink house-socks. She gave him a warm smile before issuing a whole batch of instructions to the ge-chimps.

They ate in silence for a few minutes as Edeard considered what he was going to ask the Skylords. He was sure they'd be in range by the following morning, or a day later at the least.

What could possibly have upset their appearance? Change originated from him. He'd travelled back to start again enough times to know that by now. Everyone else would just carry on as before unless he did something to alter their path through life. It was influence that mattered the most – he did something different, so the people interacting with him had their ordained life altered to varying degrees, and so the effect spread out like a sluggish ripple. The major difference he made each time since the epic voyage around the world was explaining how the Skylords didn't need the towers of Eyrie to accept people for guidance, which out in the provinces always led to a rush to build some kind of homage tower in every town and city – to the detriment of the economy. His repeated clarifications that it didn't need to be a tower, just a broad open space for people to gather, was always blithely ignored (witness the tax revolt following the Great Tower of Guidance fiasco).

For all the change he brought, it was only lives he affected. He couldn't change the weather or make the planets orbit any differently. *So why are there only two this time?*

The only possible answer was one he simply couldn't accept.

Dinlay arrived soon after Edeard started munching away on his second slice of toast. The Chief Constable's humour was as pleasant as always. Dinlay had joined the unification almost unknowingly and certainly very willingly; the acceptance of such a gentle universal communion was after all the thing his subconscious had yearned for all these years. Even then, some things about Dinlay had never altered.

Edeard watched closely for any sign of envy or jealousy from his old friend regarding Hilitte (he'd made very sure that this time he was the first to meet her as soon as she arrived in Makkathran armed with her mother's lists of contacts). *That old Ashwell optimism just never dies, does it?* But no, Dinlay was unconcerned by Edeard's latest girl; after all he'd just married Folopa, who was lofty even by his standards.

Dinlay sat next to Edeard and placed his smart uniform hat on the table, aligning it with the edge. His open mind revealed how satisfying that was, how it fitted in with the view that the world should be an ordered place.

'Help yourself,' Edeard said, gesturing to the sideboard. He couldn't help the wistful memories of when he and Dinlay had moved into the Constable Tenement after they'd finished their probation. Nearly every morning until he'd married they'd had breakfast together. *The best days. No! The easiest.*

A ge-chimp brought Dinlay a cup of coffee and a croissant. 'You need to watch what you eat,' Dinlay said, eyeing the huge spread of food. 'You'll wind up Macsen's size if you're not careful.'

'No, I won't,' Edeard assured him softly. Dinlay and Macsen hadn't spoken for over a year now, which pained him. *Maybe I should go right back to the beginning?* Except he knew that was the most pitiful of wishful thinking. This was the time when he'd got everything so close to being right. All that was left for him now was to bring those remaining provinces into the unification, along with a few recalcitrants left over in the city. When that was done he could truly, finally, relax.

'Some news came in last night that you're going to enjoy,' Dinlay said. 'It would seem the Fandine militia is on the march.'

Edeard endured a nasty chill of déjà vu at the claim. The Fandine militia had last marched when he was voyaging on the *Lady's Light*, but that was for another reason altogether. 'Against Makkathran?' he asked sharply.

Dinlay's thoughts were happy at providing his friend with a surprise, and being able to reassure him. 'Against Licshills. It would seem Devroul's expansionist ambitions were too great for Manel.'

'I see.' Edeard didn't allow anyone to know his own dismay that this time around Manel had fallen to the bad again, and had set himself up as the Lord President of Licshills. 'When did this happen?'

'Five days ago. Larose's fast scouts brought the news as quickly as they could.' Dinlay sipped at his coffee, waiting for Edeard's response.

'Five days. Which means they'll be a fifth of the way there by now.'

'Are you going to try and stop them?'

'Oh Edeard,' Hilitte exclaimed. 'You have to stop them. There would be so many people killed if you don't. The Skylords would never come again.'

Edeard gave Dinlay a shrug. 'She has a point.'

'Yes, but ... Who would the city's militia regiments side with?'

'Neither. We oppose both, of course.' Edeard was trying to work out what course of events they could play out. Clearly, the city forces would have to stall the provincial regiments while domination was used against the individual militiamen, pulling them in to Makkathran's unification. But ultimately there would be a showdown with the strong psychics at the core of each independent province. It was a situation he'd been avoiding for two years, hating the idea of yet more confrontation. But the only alternative was travelling back for yet another restart, making good the mistakes and problems before they emerged; and that was something he could simply not contemplate. *Not again. I can't do it. Living those same years yet again would be a death for me.*

Dinlay nodded sagely. 'Shall I tell Larose to prepare?'

People were going to die; Edeard knew that. The number would depend on him. Riding the city militia into the conflict was the only way to keep the number of deaths to a minimum. 'Yes. I'll ride with them myself.'

'Edeard—'

He held a hand up. 'I have to. You know this.'

'Then I will come with you.'

'The Chief Constable has no business riding with the militia.'

'Nor does the Mayor.'

'I know. Nonetheless, it is my responsibility, so I will be there to do what I can. But someone with authority must remain in the city.'

'The Grand Council ...'

'You know what I mean.'

'Yes,' Dinlay admitted. 'I do.'

'Besides, we don't want to make Gealee a widow now, do we?'

Dinlay glanced up from his croissant. 'Gealee? Who's Gealee?'

Edeard grimaced as he silently cursed his stupidity. 'Sorry.

My mind wanders these days. I mean Folopa. You can't take the risk. You're barely back off honeymoon.'

'There's an equal risk.'

'No, Dinlay, there isn't. We both know that.' He pushed. Ever so slightly, sending his longtalk whisper slithering into Dinlay's thoughts to soothe the agitated peaks of thought. Dinlay's reluctance faded away.

'Aye, I suppose so.'

'Thank you,' Edeard said, hoping his guilt wasn't showing. 'I know this isn't easy for you.'

'You normally know what you're doing.'

It was all he could do not to bark a bitter laugh. 'One day I will. Now come on.' He rose and gave Hilitte a quick kiss. 'We have to get to the sanctum. Argian and Marcol are the first meeting. They seem pleased with themselves.'

'It's nothing,' Dinlay said, finishing his coffee before getting to his feet. 'Information on the criminals resisting our city's embrace. They have some new names for you.'

'They're not criminals.' *Not yet*, he added silently, wondering where all his guilt was coming from this morning. *As if I don't know, those Ladydamned Skylords.*

'They should be,' Dinlay muttered darkly.

It was the way of his days now. Meeting with people who were at odds with the city's unity. Acting as moderator, smoothing the way for understanding between everyone. A version of being Mayor he'd never quite envisioned during the caravan trip to Makkathran too many decades ago. He'd always thought he'd be elected in a free vote, arguing with his opponents and winning people over. Instead, he'd been the only candidate in a city where everyone's mind was attuned to his. *Well, not everyone*, he admitted, *and that's a big part of the problem*. Some people knew how to resist or deflect dominance. But they still gave the appearance of sharing, of unity with everybody else. Everything would be running along smoothly for weeks, then one morning the constables would be called to premises which had been smashed up, or a gondolier yard where boats had been broken. More worrying were the warehouses where fruit and meat had been ruined, chopped open or doused in cartloads of genistar excrement. That was happing too often for his liking, and it was always performed by genistars, leaving no trace of the perpetrator, even in the city's memory.

So Argain and Marcol and Felax tracked down those resisting the unification one by one, but their true numbers were unknown. Rumour had it in the thousands. Edeard suspected a few hundred. Which left him content that his dedicated team would gradually wear down the resistance. It was almost like the good old days of the Grand Council committee on organized crime. Except even that was an illusion, a memory which when examined properly wasn't so joyful. It was just another achingly long time spent shuffling reports and dossiers.

If anything was becoming a true constant in his life, it was the mountains of paperwork and those endless boring meetings. *Can that really lead to my fulfilment? And if not, what?*

The evening didn't start well. One of the girls Hilitte brought to the bed chamber wasn't used to so much food being available and ate too much during the meal beforehand, which led to her feeling sick when they all retired to the master bed chamber. With unity came minds wide open to each other. That meant the sensations of her nausea spread like a contagion.

After she'd hurried out, leaving those left behind to take deep breaths and calm their queasy stomachs, Edeard decided a quiet night spent by himself might be preferable to the usual frenetic physical performance. Sure enough, his day had been long, uneventful and ultimately thankless. His one attempt to longtalk Jiska had resulted in the usual quick rebuff. His children had all taken their mother's side. It was probably the main reason he'd turned to Hilitte and the others. Their cheap adoration was an easy way of easing the pain of loss, no matter how shallow and flimsy the act. His one genuine thread of comfort amid the estrangement came from knowing that a unified world would provide them with fulfilment, and that he hadn't failed them, even though they would never acknowledge it.

He asked Hilitte and the remaining girl to leave him. Hilitte stomped out in a wake of hurt feelings and sourness with just an undercurrent of worry that her time as favourite was drawing to a close. Such was his languor he couldn't be bothered to reassure her. He wove a thick shield around his feelings, cutting himself off from the mellow reassuring contentment of the unified minds glowing around him, and fell asleep.

He was woken out of his outlandish dream by the strength of worry from the approaching mind. For a second he was back in the forest with the other Ashwell apprentices on their galby hunt, beset with fear without knowing why. But it was only Argain, breezing his way past staff with cool purpose, ignoring any requests to wait for the sleeping Waterwalker to be formally woken and informed of his presence.

'It's all right,' Edeard longtalked through the bed chamber's closed door. 'Come in.' His third hand hauled a robe over as Argain strode in. Now Edeard was shaking off the sleep he became aware of just how deep the currents of anxiety were running in the man's mind. Bitter regret was like the burn of bile. 'What is it?' Edeard asked in trepidation.

'We caught them,' Argain said, but there wasn't a trace of elation in the tone. That morning he and Marcol had been excited at the new leads they'd gathered, the information that there would be a raid on a shipyard in the port district that night, where two half-built trading schooners would be burnt.

'And?' Edeard asked.

'They fought back.' There were tears glinting in Argain's eyes now. 'I'm so sorry, Edeard. Her concealment was good, we didn't even know she was there.'

Edeard became still, the hot blood pounding round his body suddenly turning to ice as he perceived the picture forming amid Argain's thoughts. 'No,' he moaned.

'We didn't know, I swear on the Lady. Marcol hauled her out of the flames as soon as we farsighted her.'

'Where is she?'

'The hospital on Half Bracelet Lane in Neph, it was the closest.'

Edeard flung his farsight into the district, pushing through the thick walls of the hospital. As always, the sense revealed only gauzy radiant shadows, but he could perceive the body that lay on a cot in the ground-floor ward, he knew the signature anywhere. It was ablaze with pain. 'Oh great Lady,' he groaned in horror.

The travel tunnels took him down to Neph in minutes. As he passed under Abad, he sensed someone else flying along ahead of him. Two girls, holding hands as they hurtled headfirst, radiating fear and concern as their long dark skirts flapped wildly in the slipstream.

'Marilee? Analee?' he called. He had no idea they knew of the travel tunnels. Their thoughts vanished behind an astonishingly strong shield. The rejection was as shocking as it was absolute.

He rose up through the floor of the hospital a few seconds behind the twins. They were already hurrying towards the ward, glimpsed as shadows in the dark corridors, their heels clattering on the floor. He followed, every step slower than the last. The farsight of his whole family was converging on the hospital, their presence like malign souls.

Jiska was lying on a cot, a terrible reedy wail bubbling out of her throat. The level of pain filling the long room was enough to make Edeard's legs falter. He was crying as he approached. Three doctors were bent over his daughter, trying to remove the burnt cloth from her ruined skin. Potions and ointments were poured over the blackened, crisping flesh, doing little to alleviate the awful thudding pain.

He took another step forward. Marilee and Analee moved quickly to form a barrier between him and the bed, minds fiercely steadfast. They were clad in robes similar to his own signature black cloak, hoods thrown over their heads leaving their faces in shadow. Steely guardians of their mortally injured sister, determined to prevent any last violation of her sanctity.

'She has suffered enough, Father.'

'She doesn't need you here to make it worse.'

'Jiska,' he pleaded. 'Why?'

'Don't do that.'

'Not here.'

'Not now.'

'Don't pretend your ignorance is some kind of innocence.'

'You're not ignorant. Nor innocent.'

'You are evil.'

'A monster.'

'We will do whatever we can to ruin your empire.'

'And destroy you.'

The two black-clad figures wavered in his vision, and he saw them on the tropical beach as it had never happened so many years ago, both in long cotton rainbow skirts, bare feet on the hot sand, both clinging adoringly to Marvane, rapturously happy as Natran performed the marriage ceremony.

'I do this for all of you,' Edeard wept. 'I am bringing you fulfilment. The Lady knows I try to bring fulfilment to the whole world. Why do you reject me?'

'Your evil would enslave everyone on Querencia, and you ask us why.'

'Evil. Evil. Evil man. Honious will take you.'

Jiska convulsed. Edeard groaned through clenched teeth as he forced himself to share every aspect of her agony. He deserved nothing less. His legs gave way.

'We will bring you down.'

'We are still free.'

'We have taught others how to liberate themselves.'

'Your slaves will rise up against you.'

'Domination does not deliver eternal loyalty.'

'Already your hold on the provinces crumbles away.'

'You?' he asked through the sickening pain. 'You are the resistance?'

Then the longtalk he dreaded most spoke. 'Who else was left?' Kristabel asked. 'Whose mind has your megalomania left unbroken?'

Jiska's head turned slightly.

'Don't move, don't move,' the doctors chorused in concern.

Red scabbed eyelids fluttered, sending a yellow fluid seeping out of freshly opened cracks. The remaining good eye stared right at him. 'We will beat you,' Jiska's weak longtalk told him determinedly. 'My soul will wonder the Void, but I will die knowing this. I am fulfilled, Father, but not how you desired me to be, thank the Lady.'

Edeard fell to his knees. 'You're not to be lost. I can stop this,' he told her with a whisper. 'I can.' *Two hours, that's all. Just go back two hours and stop the fire from ever happening. I'll talk reason to them. We will find common ground.*

'If you try—'

'—you will have to kill us first.'

'All of us,' Kristabel longtalked.

Edeard raised his head to the shadowed ceiling. 'You do not die. Not again. Not ever while I live. I have suffered too much for that to be allowed.'

In the streets outside the hospital, minds were emerging from their concealment. Their presence shocked him. Rolar, Dylorn, Marakas, even Taralee. The oldest five grandchildren, all emboldened and resolute. *But not Burlal – he at least is spared this.* And they weren't alone. Macsen and Kanseen emerged with them, as did their children. Then at the last Kristabel came forth.

'You can rule this world,' they told him with a loving unity whose nobility was infinitely more beautiful than any he had ever imposed. 'But we will not be a part of it. One way or another.'

'But we must be one,' he shouted back frantically. 'One—' *Nation.* With that he crumpled to the ground and cried out in anguish as the shock of what he now believed in hit him with a physical impact. *Oh my great Lady, I have become my enemies: Bise, Owain, Buate, the Gilmorn, Tahal, all the others I struggled to overcome. How was I so weak to let them win, to adopt their methods? This cannot stand. This is why fewer Skylords have come. Fulfilment is slipping away from me, from all of us. I knew that. Lady, I always knew that.*

He had sworn not to go back again, but that was an irrelevance now – he *was* going back to save Jiska. Not two hours. That would not be salvation. There was only one option left.

'You are right,' he told them, and opened his mind so they could see whatever love and humility he had left. 'I have fallen to arrogance and sin, but I swear to the Lady I will show no more weakness.' And reached for that wretched moment—

—to land on the ground at the foot of the Eyrie tower. His ankles gave way and he stumbled, falling forwards. Strong third hands reached out to steady him. A blaze of concern and adoration bathed his bruised thoughts.

The crowd drew its collective breath in a loud: 'Ohoooo,' at his dangerous landing. Then as he straightened up they began to applaud the ostentatious resurgence of their old Waterwalker.

For a moment he feared his jumbled recollections and shaky emotions meant he'd completely misjudged the twisting passage through the Void's memory. But there was no powerful farsight following him, no Tathal, no nest. This was the time immediately after he had vanquished that foe, when events were so close to what they had been the first time, the genuine life he'd forgone so long ago.

Macsen gave him a derisory sneer, while Dinlay's hardened thoughts registered his disapproval at the madcap jump from the tower. *As they always do, thank you Lady.*

Kristabel's expression was one of unwavering anger. He looked at her, and smiled weakly. 'I'm sorry' he whispered inaudibly. 'I'm so sorry.'

Her fury subsided as she measured the confusion and sadness filling his mind. He held his arms out to her. After the briefest hesitations she walked over.

'Daddy,' Marilee scolded.

'That was so bad.'

'Teach us how to do that.'

Edeard nodded slowly. 'One day I might just do that. But for now there's a young man I want you to meet, a sailor.'

'Which one of us?' Analee asked, playfully mistrustful.

'Both of you. Both of you should meet him. I think you all might be very happy together.'

The twins turned to give each other a look of complete astonishment.

Kristabel moved into his arms. 'What's wrong?'

Edeard took a long time to answer. 'I'm sorry for the way I've been lately. I'm going to stop that now.'

She shrugged awkwardly inside his embrace. 'I can't be the easiest person to live with.'

He pointed out across the city to the Lyot Sea. 'The Skylord comes.'

'Really?' Like everyone in Makkathran, she extended her farsight to the horizon as the astounded residents of Myco and Neph gifted their sight of the giant creature.

'It will bring such change to our lives,' Edeard said quietly. 'I think I know how to moderate any difficulties. But I don't know everything, I truly don't. I will need help. It will not be easy.'

'I'm here,' she said with a soft reassuring hug. 'As are all your friends; and together we will live through this. So just banish that horrible old Ashwell optimism, Edeard Waterwalker. This is the life you were made for.'

'Yes.' *And this is the last one, whatever happens, this is what I will live with. Sweet Lady, please, in your infinite wisdom, give me the strength to get it right.*

7

The capsule came down close to the centre of Octoron's little township. Acrid smoke layered the air. Several of the buildings surrounding Entranceway Plaza were damaged. Energy weapons had briefly turned the iron structures molten, causing them to sag and twist as they started to lean over. The wreckage of crashed capsules was sticking out of the ruins. Heat from the impact in combination with all the munitions had ignited a great many fires, which the chamber's drones were only just extinguishing. They'd used a lot of crystalfoam, covering vast swathes of the plaza in blue-green mush that was still emitting sulphurous belches.

Human paramedics were scuttling round, performing triage. Serious cases were carried to waiting capsules to be ferried off to the hospital on the edge of town. Fifteen heavily armoured and badly pissed Chikoya were strutting round, getting in the way of the human emergency teams. Resentment was starting to rise on both sides. There'd be another clash if tempers didn't start cooling quickly.

The capsule's door dilated, and he stepped out. It wasn't a bad entrance, he felt; he was wearing some really quite stylish mauve shorts and a loose-fitting shirt of semiorganic white silk open down the front, like the top half of a robe. Top-grade Advancer-heritage genetic sequences and a decent diet had toned him up, and his slightly elevated position gave him that commanding full-of-confidence appearance, as if he'd arrived ready to take charge and everyone else could now relax. The frayed leather flip-flops admittedly detracted from the image, but he'd been in a hurry so nothing he could do about that now. In any case, no one was looking at his feet. They were all looking up at him. Except the fifteen armoured Chikoya, who had swung their weapons round to splash their targeting lasers across his pristine shirt.

'Well this sucks,' Ozzie said.

He trotted down the capsule's three stairs to the ground and gave the big aliens his best untroubled grin. The Chikoya resembled medium-sized dinosaurs with vestigial dragon wings. Beefed up with armour that resembled black-metallic crocodile skin, they were imposing demonic creatures. And really very pissed, Ozzie decided, as their minds radiated the paranoia and aggression which only their species could produce in such quantities.

'So what's up?' he asked.

'You are Ozzie?' the lead one asked. Its thick neck curved down, putting its helmet tip inches from Ozzie's nose.

'Sure thing, dude.'

Three mirrored lenses in the helmet's centre swivelled slightly to focus on Ozzie's head. 'Where is the human messiah?'

'I don't know. I like just got here. Right?'

'You are the one who broke through into the realm of the all-perception. You can use it at the highest level. You must know where he is.'

Ozzie took a sad moment to reflect how semantics always betrayed the universe-view of each sentient species. 'I don't know,' he said patiently, pushing an intense feeling of benevolence out into mindspace. 'The messiah is powerful. He has mysterious ways of camouflaging himself from the rest of us.' Which was a slight exaggeration. Ozzie was sorely puzzled how Inigo had actually managed to conceal himself. One moment he'd been there, his raging thoughts glaring out into mindspace, the next he'd gone, vanished, the mind extinguished. It was as if he'd died. Which judging by the amount of carnage let loose in the plaza, was a high probability. Except there had been others with him, a woman and some kind of psychotic special forces bodyguard – who also oddly didn't register in mindspace. For all three to vanish without leaving a visible corpse between them just wasn't going to wash. Either they'd teleported out somehow, which he didn't believe because the AI was showing the damaged Navy scout ship still sitting on the pad. Or they knew a way of circumventing mindspace. Which he wouldn't put past that slippery, gloating, little shit Inigo.

'Why is he here?' the Chikoya demanded. Oval vents at the front of its helmet clunked open, allowing a misty stream of phlegm to come spitting out.

Ozzie dodged gracefully, managing to clamp down on his feelings about that particular Chikoya body function. 'As I haven't met him, I don't know.'

'He is a danger to all living things on the Spike. The Void may know of his presence here. It will seek us out, we will be the first to be devoured.'

'I know. Real crock of shit, huh. When I find him I'm going to kick his ass right off the Spike. I'm going to be hunting hard.'

'We will locate the messiah. We will make him stop the Void.'

'That's wonderful. We both want the same thing. But, dude, you just gotta make sure to let me know when you find him, please. I got me special super-secret weapons that will cut the bastard to shreds no matter what kind of force fields and military protection he's brought with him.'

'You have weapons?' Sensor clumps mounted on the Chikoya's armour rose up like time-lapse mushrooms to scan over Ozzie as another jet of phlegm spat out.

'Hey-ho, I used to be one of the Commonwealth's rulers, you know. Check your database to confirm. That means I had full access to its pre-post-physical technology. *Of course* I have superweapons with me, dude.' He pushed a starburst of sincerity and determination into his mind, and held it there. 'I don't want any more of your herd to be hurt or killed by his soldiers, so please, if you find him, please call me. I can squash him like a Kantr under a Folippian.' *Whatever they are.*

'We will inform you if he is troublesome.'

'Thank you. That's very kind.' Ozzie smiled again at the monster's helmet and walked round it into the plaza. The other Chikoya let him pass. His macrocellular clusters reported a quick surge in encrypted data between the big aliens. They began to holster their weapons.

Oh yeah. Still the Man.

Which was exactly what he'd come to the Spike to get away from. He went over to one of the triage teams. 'Hi Max.'

'Uh? Oh, hi Ozzie,' the medic replied. He was kneeling beside an unconscious woman who'd suffered a lot of burns.

'So what happened?'

'The guy was a fucking lunatic. He took on a whole army of Chikoya by himself.'

'Did you see it?' Ozzie asked.

'Just the end.' Max applied some pale-green derm3 to the woman's black and red legs. The jelly spread out evenly over the terrible damage and began to bubble like sluggish champagne. 'And I had to wait until that was over before I landed. Anything moving down here got trashed. I guess weapon enrichments have come on some since I left the Commonwealth.'

'Yeah, looks like it.' Ozzie's field scan told him the Chikoya were starting to teleport out.

Coleen, the medic working with Max, broke off from implementing the stem support module she'd applied to the woman's throat. 'What the hell is Inigo doing coming here?'

'Sounds like he wants to talk to me,' Ozzie admitted.

'Why?'

'Don't know for sure, but just a wild guess here: the Void.'

Max had cut away the smouldering fabric of the woman's dress, and started applying the derm3 to the side of her abdomen. 'Can you stop it?'

Ozzie gave him a bitter laugh. 'No. I wouldn't know where to begin.'

'Then why—'

'Dunno, man.' Ozzie spread his arms wide in surrender. 'She going to be all right?'

'She's not Higher,' Coleen said. 'But she should be able to avoid re-life. I think she's stable enough to make the trip to hospital now.'

'I'll take her,' Max said.

'How many hurt?' Ozzie asked. He didn't want to know, but his conscience was prodding him. That was something that hadn't happened in a long time. *And it shouldn't be happening now, damnit.*

'Eleven got bodylossed,' Coleen said. 'We've shipped eight live criticals back to the hospital, and there's another five bad ones waiting. Maybe two dozen more with minor injuries.'

Ozzie gave a tight nod. 'Could have been worse.'

'The Chikoya aren't going to get over this in a hurry,' she said.

'I know.'

'They think the Spike belongs to them.'

'It doesn't.'

'But this . . .'

'They'll get over it. We've all got to get along.'

'So you keep saying,' she said.

Ozzie was disappointed by the amount of bitterness and resentment in her mind, and Coleen was good at toning down her feelings.

'I'll sort this out,' he assured her.

'Good.' She hurried off to another victim, her boots squelching through the whiffy crystalfoam.

Max gave Ozzie a sympathetic look. 'I don't blame you.'

'Very big.'

'But it's *Inigo*, Ozzie! The Dreamer himself. Things have to be bad if he's come to you.'

'I know.'

'And that bodyguard—'

Ozzie held his hand up, palms outward. 'I'm on it, man.' He

turned and walked slowly back to the capsule, stopping briefly to study the broken buildings. No doubt about it, they were going to have to rebuild the whole centre of town. 'Connect me to him,' he told his u-shadow.

The code embedded in the general message made a connection instantly. 'This is Ozzie.'

'You are the eighth person to claim this.'

'That's gotta be a bummer for you. And what if I've cloned myself? Would any of us brothers do, or did you want the original?' He waited for a reply, slightly mystified by the delay.

'I need the original.'

'Then this is your lucky day, pal.' Ozzie's u-shadow informed him that a very sophisticated infiltrator was trying to take over the capsule's smartnet. 'Let it in,' he told the u-shadow. 'But if we land in deep shit, I want to be able to wipe it.'

'Confirmed,' his u-shadow reported. An exovision display showed him the infiltrator's progress.

'I will require DNA verification that you are Oswald Fernandez Isaacs.'

'Nobody calls me that.'

'That is your name.'

'It was my name.' Even after all the re-life procedures and biononic regenerations he'd undergone in the last fifteen hundred years, with all their associated memory edits he'd never quite let go of the childhood persecution that name had brought down upon him. 'Now I'm just Ozzie; always have been, always will be.'

'Very well, Ozzie, I am loading a coordinate into your capsule. Please do not attempt to deviate from the route.'

'Dude, wouldn't dream of it.'

A map of Octoron compartment flipped up, with his u-shadow showing him the route that the infiltrator was preparing to fly. Ozzie studied it, but the destination was a nowhere, a remote stretch of land past one of the water columns, about thirty kilometres away. Just the kind of nowhere outlaws would choose to lie low in a decent Western.

The capsule lifted silently and curved round over the town. Ozzie watched the buildings shrink away while the resentment built in his mind. The Spike was his escape from the shitty vibes of life in the Greater Commonwealth, and the one man who'd subverted and ruined his hopes for the gaiafield: Inigo.

Nigel Sheldon had offered him another way out, a berth on the Sheldon family armada of colony starships. They weren't just going to the other side of the galaxy to set up a new society, oh no, not Nigel, he was off to a whole new galaxy to begin again. A noble quest, restarting human civilization in a fresh part of the universe. Then in another thousand years a new generation of colony ships might spread to further galaxies. After all, as he'd pointed out, this one is ultimately doomed with the Void at the centre, so we need somewhere that's got a long-term future. Ozzie grabbed the logic, even as he'd argued back that humans would have gone post-physical long before the Void would ever present a real tangible threat.

Ha! Yeah right. Goddamn Nigel, always gets the last laugh.

The Spike had been a kind of compromise for Ozzie. A withdrawal from Commonwealth life for sure, but not a complete retreat the way Nigel had chosen – not that he saw it as a retreat. He did it because there was a slight chance he could still turn it around, and reclaim the dream that he'd lost to Inigo, Edeard, and the insidious Void.

He had intended the gaiafield to allow humans and aliens to understand each other better, eliminating conflict and confusion across the galaxy. The oldest liberal dream of all, *if we just keep talking* ... And now the gaiafield could back the talk up with sincerity and understanding. Except as always the human race had found a way to fuck it up, and turn it into the carrier wave of the latest and stupidest of all religions. So he came to the Spike with an idea of how to make something bigger than the gaiafield and communing with the Silfen Motherholm, a wonderful union of the mind which couldn't be subverted by selective, edited, thoughts like Inigo's seditious dreams with their sole purpose to entrap people.

Mindspace was a good start, except it worked better with human thoughts than anyone else's, especially the ratty little Ilodi. But the Chikoya were coming round to accepting the state, even though the stupid monsters were hanging a whole load of their own religious connotations on the 'all-perception realm' which had sparked some old dumbass racial lore.

A little bit of fine-tuning was all it would take. Something he'd been analysing and rationalizing – well sort of – for the last forty years. Then every sentient species in the galaxy would be aware of every other species. Which would be truly wonderful. Unless there was something else like the Prime out there. And pre-science/rationality species would probably think their Gods were calling. Oh, and greedy little psychopaths like the Ocisen Empire would use it to provide a map of worlds to conquer.

Yeah, fine tuning. That's all.

Which he would have got round to. Eventually. Except now the Commonwealth and its incredible idiocies and Factions and violence had followed him to the Spike. His basic instinct was to just cut and run again. But Inigo's boneheaded stupidity was finally paying off, with the Void going apeshit and everyone desperate for a solution. To what, Ozzie wasn't sure. But sure as bears shit in the woods, they came searching him out for it, treating him like the ultimate guru.

So once again, here he was doing the *right thing*, which would have appalled the him of centuries past. Today, he just figured that this was the quickest way to get them the fuck off the Spike.

The capsule approached the water column, one of twelve massive support structures that stretched from the chamber's landscape right up to the opaque roof forty kilometres above. They always reminded Ozzie of giant cocktail swizzle sticks, huge narrow cylinders with ridges that spiralled the entire length. It was part of the chamber's irrigation system; water flowed constantly down them, racing round and round in a white-foam cascade. Every couple of kilometres along the top third the twists had sharp angled kinks that sent thundering bursts of spume swirling off in long clouds that traced huge arcs as they fell downwards and outwards until they'd evolved into ordinary stratus scudding through the air before eventually drizzling on the ground far below.

He flew directly underneath one of the churning ribbons of thick white mist and began a steep descent. It was a broad expanse of Octoron's purple and green grass below, with a herd of sprightly tranalin racing away from the lake at the base of the water column. Ozzie expanded his biononic field scan function, and probed the ground directly below. Three human figures were waiting for him, which was odd because he couldn't perceive any incursion of thoughts within mindspace. He frowned and refined the scan. One was standing waiting, integral force field active; the other two were lying on the grass, unconscious.

'Ah,' he grunted as realization dawned. 'Clever.'

The capsule touched down and he emerged to face the standing man. No doubt that he was the bodyguard-type who'd unleashed hell back in the town. The man's biological appearance was mid-thirties, which was slightly older than Highers usually maintained their physical looks. He had short black hair, but Ozzie was drawn to his eyes, which were grey with weird flecks of purple. His Commonwealth Navy tunic was simple grey-blue semiorganic, with several burn scars where energy weapons had fired out from subdermal enrichments. But it was the expression, or rather lack of it, which was most intriguing. He didn't express a single flicker of emotion. Whatever thoughts were animating the body were extraordinarily simple, like those of a small animal. Ozzie had to get within ten metres before he could even sense them.

'Yo dude, you hurt a lot of people back there. Some are going to have to be re-lifed, and that hospital doesn't have a whole lot of medical capsules.' He had to raise his voice above the crashing white-water waves of the column as they poured into the lake behind him. Very humid air was surging out. His semiorganic shirt hardened slightly to become water resilient; but he could feel it starting to saturate his Afro hairstyle.

The man put his hand out. Ozzie raised an eyebrow.

'I need to confirm your DNA,' the man said.

'Ho brother,' Ozzie touched his palm to the one offered, allowing the biononic filaments to sample his dermal layer cells.

'You are Ozzie,' the man declared.

'Really? I thought I was just fooling myself.' In itself the confirmation was interesting: that particular data was extremely hard to get hold of in the Commonwealth. Ozzie had made sure of that before he left, and ANA enforced the proscription on access. You'd need to be quite the player to get hold of it.

'No, you are not. Please turn off the telepathy effect.'

'*Say what?*'

'Turn off the telepathy effect. It allows the Chikoya to track Inigo.'

'Ah, I get it. Smart. No.'

'I have brought Inigo to you. You cannot function effectively together if we are constantly interrupted by hostile elements.'

'Man, I don't want to function effectively or any other way with that little turd.'

'You have to.'

'No, dude, I don't.'

'I will exterminate the woman if you do not switch it off.'

'Jezus fuck! Why? Who is she?'

'Corrie-Lyn. A past member of the Living Dream Cleric Council, and Inigo's lover.'

'So why kill her?' Ozzie was getting a bad feeling about the way the man's thoughts functioned. In fact he was beginning to wonder just what kind of biology was nestling inside the human skull. And who it belonged to.

'She is my leverage. If you do not comply I will find others to kill until you do.'

'Okay. I'll accept that threat is real for the moment. What does Inigo want with me?'

'He doesn't know yet. I am following orders from another source to bring you both together.'

'Shit. Who wants that to happen?'

'I don't know.'

'Come on! Seriously, dude?'

'Yes.'

'Wow. So what do you expect us to do when we're up and talking?'

'I do not know. Those operational instructions will not activate until that stage of the mission has reached active status.'

'You're not human.'

'I was.'

Yep, *very* bad feeling. 'I know of this kind of conditioning. The last time it was used on humans was by the Starflyer. And I'm pretty sure we got rid of that bastard.' Ozzie grinned evilly. 'But you never know, do you?'

'I do not know who I work for.'

'So I have to take a chance, huh?'

'Yes. And spare Corrie-Lyn's life.'

'Hum. I guess the only reason your boss would get me and the dickhead messiah here together is if he or she or it thinks we can do something about the Void. And for that reason, and that alone, I'll switch it off. I'm curious to see what you think I can do.' He directed his u-shadow to deactivate the device. 'This will take a while.'

'How long?'

'I have no idea. Maybe half an hour. It's never been switched off before.'

'I will wait.'

Ozzie watched him. The man wasn't kidding. What followed was no vaguely awkward interval where they occasionally made eye contact and hurriedly looked away, nor was there any attempt to talk. He just stood there, his field scan sweeping round; otherwise he had no interest in anything. That wasn't human. His thought routines such as they were resembled machine code in their simplicity. In one respect that was a relief, Starflyer conditioning was different.

After a while Ozzie felt mindspace withdrawing, collapsing in on itself. It was akin to closing down his gaiamotes. The minds glimmering all around him faded away, most of them expressing sorrow and alarm as they felt mindspace fading. The loss was more profound than he was expecting, even though he knew it was temporary. But he'd lived with and embraced mindspace for so long now it was a part of his existence.

'It's done,' he said grimly, and pushed his hair back off his forehead. It had absorbed so much of the vapour thrown out by the water column it had begun to sag and tangle in unpleasant rat-tails.

A tic started on the man's left cheek. Expression slowly emerged on his face, like colour filling a pencilled-in outline. He let out a long sigh, the kind a witness to something awful would make. 'Okay then, that's good.'

A thoroughly fascinated Ozzie gave him a very curious look. 'What's happening?' He had a strong urge to switch mindspace back on and feel the man's thoughts again. But it would take days for the device to re-establish the state.

'My normal thought routines are back.' The man gave Corrie-Lyn's unconscious form a quizzical glance. 'That ought to go down well in some parts.'

'So what was firing away in your brain before?'

'It's a kind of minimal function mode, in case of neural injury.'

'Uh huh.'

'In my profession there's a big chance my neural structure will suffer physical damage during a mission. This allows me to remain functional in adverse circumstances.'

'Cool reboot. Uh, what adverse circumstances hit you here?'

'The telepathy effect was affecting me in an unfortunate way.'

'Right,' Ozzie drawled. 'So who the hell are you, dude?'

'Aaron.'

'Okay. Top of the list, huh.'

Aaron grinned. 'Yes. And thank you for agreeing to meet with me. My minimal version doesn't have a lot of tact.'

'Man, that's the biggest understatement I've heard in a century. But you said you've no idea why you're here.'

'Partially true. When Inigo wakes up I'll know what I have to ask the pair of you to do. I'm expecting it'll be to stop the Void devourment phase.'

'Oh sure. I've got time before lunch. Shall I tell my super-warship crew to get ready to fly? Or are we going to sneak in through the back gate and steal the bad guy's unguarded power supply?'

Aaron smiled like a particularly tolerant parent. 'Is that the back gate on the Dark Fortress?'

'Man, I don't like you.'

'I appreciate this isn't easy.'

'You have no idea.'

*

Some mornings after she'd woken, Araminta would walk out onto the balcony overlooking the vast expanse of Golden Park to enjoy the sunrise, watching the first rays touch the tips of the white pillars along Upper Grove Canal. Over a thousand people were usually there to greet her with waves and cheers and thoughts of thanks directed through the gaiafield. They camped there overnight, much to the annoyance of the city authorities. But Araminta had told the Clerics to grant them permission to stay, knowing that the more people were watching her, the less anyone could do anything about her. She still gifted everything she saw and heard and felt to the gaiafield, which had led to a storm of embarrassment for the first few days as she used the toilet – she soon learned to stop gifting anything but sight at those times, and was careful where she looked. And she really didn't want to think about what it was going to be like when it was her time of the month. Mercifully, it was a kind of mutual embarrassment, and no one who came into contact with her was crass enough to mention it.

She was thankful for the control she could exert upon her own mind (sometimes resorting to the melange program for support). Without that discipline she would have been completely exposed to the impact of thoughts within the gaiafield. Those of her devout followers she held back from, content to simply know their existence through the outpouring of gratitude. From everyone else – the deluge of emotion from the billions upon billions of humans who didn't admire her – she kept herself as remote as possible. Even with that detachment it was impossible not to be aware of their hatred and vilification. Hour after unceasing hour, she was subject to the superlative abuse and loathing from the majority of her entire species. The intensity was awesome in its extreme. They despised her as pure evil that had taken on human form. Which was justified, she acknowledged weakly. After all, she was going to trigger the event which was most likely going to kill every single one of them.

She gave the Golden Park crowd a swift wave of appreciation and went back inside. The pool in the bathroom was almost big enough to swim in; and of course no one from the Dreamer down to the Cleric Conservator had ever entertained the notion of installing a decent modern spore shower in an unobtrusive corner. If the residents of the state rooms wanted to get clean they jolly well had to do it the old-fashioned way. Araminta walked down into the body-temperature water and started slathering on the liquid soap. All that ever did was make her think of Edeard and the string of floozies he'd enjoyed during the dark time that'd befallen him in dreams Thirty to Thirty-three. She ordered the shower on and sluiced the bubbles off, mildly worried about how similar the whole episode was to starring in a porn show.

Sure enough, and despite her resolve, she could just feel the physical admiration of male Living Dream members seeping into the gaiafield as the water ran across her skin. And no little amount of appreciation from females, either. Worse still, a lot of her foes were registering their enjoyment of her flesh.

When this is over I'm going to have to walk down the Silfen paths to the other side of the galaxy and live like a hermit for evermore. Her gaze was drawn down to the pendant as it dangled between her glistening breasts – *oh Ozziecrapit, look away!* It wasn't warm, and the light inside was dim, as if a wisp of phosphorescence had been caged within the crystal, but it still made its presence known. On the other side of it was the infinite comfort and wisdom of the Silfen Motherholm. That at least gave her some reassurance. She wasn't entirely alone.

Three Mr Boveys smiled in gentle sympathy as they sat down to a late dinner at home.

She ordered the shower off and stepped out of the pool. Then all she had to do was rub herself down with a towel, which she did while looking at the ceiling. A small growl came out of her throat as she grew cross with herself. She hurriedly struggled into her vest top and briefs, then slithered her long white robe on top. The belt was one modified by the Palace security detail, and contained a force-field generator. They'd insisted and she wasn't going to argue. So dressed and chaste at last, she made her way through the long ornate halls to the state dining room.

Underneath the glaring ceiling, the huge polished wooden table built for a hundred and fifty guests was set for one. *At least Edeard had Hilitte for company*, she thought. *And how would he have coped with body functions and sex and life in general if he'd ever known of his audience?* She wasn't sure if a table this size set for two was more or less ridiculous than it was with just her lonely cutlery. But then Edeard was often joined by Dinlay for breakfast. All she had were five super-efficient staff to serve her anything she wanted from the bolnut veneer sideboard that was loaded up with an authentic Edeard-style breakfast from the Thirty-third dream. She remembered the later dreams when he'd been properly elected as Mayor. He and Kristabel had never had breakfasts like that; but then he'd never taken up residence in the state rooms then either. Perhaps the Palace staff were being ironic. If so, the subtlety was lost on her.

Just to be difficult she ordered a hot chocolate to have with her croissant. One of the girls in a maid's uniform scurried off to the kitchens. As she tore the pastry open, Araminta reflected on how it would be nice to have someone here for company. She was a little sad that Cressida hadn't been in touch, but she could certainly sympathize with her cousin wanting nothing to do with her.

Her chocolate arrived in a huge cup, the top covered in whipped cream dotted with strawberry marshmallows. Darraklan walked in with the maid. He'd taken to wearing the long burgundy waistcoat, white shirt and yellow drosilk cravat of the senior Orchard Palace personnel. He'd slipped very easily into the job of chief of staff, helping her to settle in. 'Good morning, Dreamer; Cleric Rincenso requests a moment of your time.'

Araminta noticed Darraklan didn't have any gaiafield emission relating to the Cleric whatsoever. But then in his own repellent arse-kissing way Rincenso was also striving hard for favoured status. She could use that. He'd want to score points by exposing any of his colleagues who doubted or schemed against her.

'Show him in,' she said.

The Cleric came into the dining room as the corona of Querencia's sun erupted with flares all across the ceiling. The bright rippling light shining off his robes and highlighting his eager smile had an almost aquatic property. He bowed politely. 'Dreamer.'

Araminta gazed at him as she sipped her chocolate. It was delicious. *Thank Ozzie, being a Galaxy-killer should have some perks, surely.* 'Did you find them for me?'

'Yes, Dreamer. The women were at the mansion on Viotia. He was actually already here, our security services have been holding him.'

'Why?'

Rincenso's smile became stretched. 'It was thought he might be shielding you from our Welcome Team.'

'Ah. He wasn't. I eluded them by myself.' A pause for emphasis. 'It wasn't that difficult.'

'Not for you, Dreamer.'

He was so smooth he almost spoilt the taste of the chocolate for her. 'Is he here now?'

'Yes.'

'Bring him in.'

Rincenso hesitated. 'Dreamer, he was *interrogated* very thoroughly.'

'Thoroughly? You mean . . .' She didn't like to dwell on that too much. *I make a truly rotten despot.*

'He was given a memory read, yes.'

'Honious! Bring him in.'

The man led through the dining-room doors needed the support of a burly security guard in a constable's uniform. The man had the body of Liken, but the spirit was definitely withered. Any lingering anger she felt towards him was immediately banished. She got up and pulled out the chair next to her. The security guard helped him into it. There was no evidence of any physical damage, but his limbs were shaking badly, and he hunched up as if he was cowering from some omnipresent tormentor.

'I'm sorry,' Araminta said. 'I didn't know.'

'You,' he said with a bitter snarl. 'There was always something about you.'

'You were quite the personality yourself.'

'That's not what you told me when we parted.' He glared round the big room. 'That's on record now. You know I'm telling the truth.'

'They will give all the copies back to you. I wish it to be so,' she said with simple authority. Rincenso nodded discreetly. 'You can destroy them if you'd like.'

'Ha. And what use will that be when the boundary comes reaching out of the stars to obliterate all of us?'

'A question I'm sure you asked yourself when you facilitated Viotia's compliance with Conservator Ethan's scheme. That whole monstrous invasion was dedicated to one purpose, to find me. What did you think the Second Dreamer was going to do once I ascended to the Orchard Palace?'

He forced his head to shake despite the jerkiness of his muscles.

'Like all non-believers you considered us to be foolish and deluded,' she continued. 'You put your own greed before anything.'

'I do not let greed drive me. I have strategy, I have logic and planning.'

'Likan . . . I'm not interested. Whatever there was between us is long gone. You're here today to correct an injustice.'

'I fuck your apology all the way to hell. I hope the warrior Raiel blow your Pilgrimage fleet to shit. The rest of us will have the greatest party history has ever known to celebrate your death.'

'I'm not apologizing for your interrogation, you brought that upon yourself.'

'Yeah? Well I'm going to plead with the Raiel to turn you over to the Prime. And we all know what they do to humans, don't we?'

She could feel billions urging him on, hoping his desire succeeded. 'I'm prepared to let you go free,' she said.

'What?'

'Free to go back to Viotia, perhaps? Our wormhole will be closing today or tomorrow now all my followers have returned home. Free for the Viotia authorities to question you about your part in the government's corrupt submission to Cleric Phelim and the invasion – oh, Phelim's coming back to Ellezelin and joining the Pilgrimage fleet. Who will that leave to face trial do you think? And I will look favourably on any request to turn over your read memories to them for examination. What evidence of treason will that turn up?'

His whole body juddered. 'You said . . .'

'I said I'd like to release you. But there is an injustice to right first, one that only you can do.'

'Bitch!'

'Phelim took your harem into custody. They're already here. I've got the best genetic team on Ellezelin ready to treat them. The problem is, we didn't read your memories from that long ago.'

Likan glared at her fearfully.

'Which three, Likan? Once I know, you'll be released, you have my word as the Dreamer on that. A starship will take you wherever you wish to go. We can even reprofile you first if you'd like.'

'What's the point?' he wailed, close to tears.

'The point is success. Do you think that ultimately I will succeed? Or will you and your way of life? I know which choice Nigel Sheldon would make. Do you?'

His head dropped. When he brought it up again the shakes and tics were overridden by a ferocious snarl. The old Likan was glowering out at her. 'Oh yes, madam Dreamer. I'll take your deal. I will comply. But remember, it will leave me free to hunt you down when you fail, because a miserable fuck-up like you couldn't pull off something this grand in a million years, not a chance.'

'We'll see,' she growled back.

'Marakata, Krisana, and Tammary,' Likan said.

'Thank you.'

'They'll kill you, your new friends, even if I don't get there first. Once you've given them what they want, they'll kill you. This is too big for you. You were small-time when I picked you up and screwed you, and you're still small-time now.'

'Win-win for you, then,' she said coolly. At the back of her mind the Skylord was showing an interest in why she was becoming so agitated. 'Get rid of him,' she told the security guard.

Likan was hauled roughly to his feet. There was a starship waiting for him at Greater Makkathran's spaceport. She'd organized it all last night, using her u-shadow to send messages to Phelim and Rincenso and Ethan in private, editing it all out of what she released into the gaiafield. Phelim had few troops left on Viotia, but he was desperate to redeem himself so he expended every effort. She knew poor little Clemance and the others would have been terrified as the remnants of the Welcome Team snatched them. Bundled into a capsule when the rest of the planet was rejoicing the lifting of tyranny, not knowing where they were being taken, nor why. Then being forced through the wormhole to Ellezelin itself. If the Dreamer Araminta was now regarded as the devil, then this planet was surely her realm.

But in a couple of hours they'd be reunited with Likan – those who wanted to be. The starship would fly them to an Inner World of his choice. She'd supplied untraceable funds, she'd supplied new identities. There was nothing more she could do.

The three he'd violated would spend a couple of months in a womb-tank here in Greater Makkathran having their psychoneural profiling reversed. When they came out they could make their own choices again. *That's if there's a galaxy left to come back out into.* It didn't matter, she'd done the right thing.

She looked over at Darraklan. 'Is Ethan ready?'

'Yes, Dreamer.'

'Right then.' She got to her feet, starting to resent Inigo's stupid proscription that no capsules should be allowed to fly above Makkathran2. It meant such long walks or gondola rides (which she actually quite liked) or riding on horseback – and no way was she going to do that; her one time on a pony when she was seven hadn't ended well.

A squad of bodyguards in constable uniforms fell in around her as she left the back of the Orchard Palace. They went down the sweeping perron and into Rah's garden with its sweet roses and immaculately shaped flameyews. Clerks peered out of their offices as she carried on through Parliament Building on the other side. Then she was out in the open and walking over the Brotherhood Canal bridge into Ogden. That at least was a short straight path to City Gate. People were running frantically across the meadowland to greet her. She didn't even need Likan's old melange program to help her slip into her mildly aloof public persona. Greeting a privileged few overawed followers with a handshake, a murmured word of thanks for their support. Smiling graciously at the rest while allowing her squad to keep her moving past them.

The crowd at City Gate was a lot larger. But more guards were there, in ordinary clothes. She suspected the shimmering semi-organic fabric covered up some muscle enrichments; they certainly seemed extraordinarily strong as they pushed people aside. Three capsules were parked just outside the Crystal wall, waiting for her; with another five defence force capsules drifting overhead. Ethan stood beside the door of the largest capsule. He bowed graciously as Araminta approached.

'Your morning has gone well, then?'

'It certainly did, thank you,' Araminta said. 'I appreciate your help in preparing the medical treatments.'

'My pleasure, Dreamer.'

They stepped up into the capsule and sat at the front while the bodyguards took the rear seats. It flew swiftly along the coastline, keeping Greater Makkathran on one side, heading for the broad estuary to the north of the city. With the security forces flying escort, no civilian capsules tried to approach. It left Araminta with a clear view of the landscape through the transparent fuselage. Once again she marvelled at the vast metropolis sprawling across the land beyond Makkathran2.

Living Dream built all of this out of nothing, she thought. *If they can do that, if they are so creative, why do they want to go to the Void? The reset ability isn't that different from our own regeneration. Humans have been able to start again from scratch for over a thousand years.*

It had to involve not a small amount of avarice lurking in everyone's heart, she realized sadly. Effectively it was a universe where only you could regenerate, giving you a vast advantage in terms of knowledge and experience over everyone else. That and the whole telepathy and telekinesis thing, that was raw power.

'Oh Lady,' she muttered as the starship manufacturing field came into view. She recalled the last time she'd seen it was on a unisphere news report a while back, when the ground was being prepared by big civil construction machinery. Regrav units had propelled streams of raw earth and crushed rock through the air as massive bots crawled across the bare soil driving in thick support stanchions and spraying down acres of enzyme-bonded concrete.

She'd expected to see huge hangars spring up where thousands of bots would crawl along scaffolding gantries, bringing together a million components that formed the starships. Instead, the starships were assembled out in the open, floating in the middle of regrav fields. The bots were there, though. Tens of thousands of busy little black modules buzzing about like wasps around their hive entrance.

'That is something else,' she admitted. For once she didn't bother restraining the emotion that swarmed out of her into the gaiafield. 'Did you organize all this?' she asked Ethan.

'I wish I could take credit,' he said ruefully. 'But the plans for the Pilgrimage were begun back in Dreamer Inigo's time. Indeed, the main driving factor behind Ellezelin's economic dynamism was to provide us with the resources to build the fleet when the time was right. These ships have been in the design stage for over fifty years, constantly being improved as new techniques were developed. The National Industrial Ministry also had to match production systems to the requirements, making sure we had sufficient capacity. Nearby Commonwealth planets complained that we were unfairly subsidising our manufacturing corporations, while in actuality we were preparing for this moment. Every section and component can be fabricated either locally or on a Free Market Zone World.'

'Incredible,' was all she could say.

The entire fifteen square miles of the construction yard was cloaked by five layers of force fields, capable of protecting it from just about every known weapon system. Unlike the weather dome that Colwyn City could throw up, this one went right down to the ground, then carried on binding soil and rock molecules together to guard against any possible subterranean threat.

Twelve of the mile-long cylinders hung gracefully above the vast expanse of concrete, each one the centre of its own airborne cybernetic swarm. The hulls were all complete, leaving the thick streams of regrav-propelled machines to wind in and out of huge ports and access hatches. Thousands of tonnes of equipment was being delivered to each ship every hour. The majority of it now was made up of the identical dark sarcophagi of suspension chambers: twenty-four million of them. They were being produced all over Ellezelin and the Free Market Worlds, Ethan said, churned out by replicator systems that were close to level-three Neumann cybernetics. 'All we have to do is provide the chambers with power and basic nutrient fluid. Essentially, that's all the ships are, warehouses full of suspension chambers with an engine room at the back.'

The capsule slipped down towards one of the five matériel egress facilities spaced equidistantly round the rim of the force field. Their capsule with its escort flew through a series of sophisticated scans before landing outside the entrance of a thirty-storey office tower; one of fifty ringing the yard. They were greeted by quite a crowd of senior project personnel headed by Cleric Taranse, the overall director. For once the gaiafield wasn't just filled with excitement and admiration for her. Everyone working in the construction yard was devoted to the project, delivering a strong and very pleasing sense of achievement. That didn't stop thousands of them from taking a break and pressing up against the windows to watch her. Araminta slipped back into full politician mode, thanking the group with the director for their extraordinary effort.

As they walked alongside the first massive cylinder she was struck by how arid the air was inside, almost as bad as the desert around Miledeep Water. An errant thought made her wonder how Ranto was doing right now. Searching the desert in vain for his beloved bike, or had he bought a flashy new one that would boost his status among his peers by an order of magnitude?

The dryness was nothing compared to the noise. With so many machines operating inside the dome, the humming and buzzing was constant, all-pervasive and loud. Araminta heard the ponderous motions of larger systems through her rib cage. And the sheer quantity of metal flying around on regrav units stirred up small fast gusts that whirled along each avenue between hulls like microclimate winds in perpetual conflict. Her hair and robe fluttered about with every step. And the giant regrav fields supporting the ships induced disconcerting effects on her inner ears as she moved. Walking in the yard was akin to keeping balance in an earthquake zone, a mere couple of paces through the invisible conflicting fields could bring on unexpected queasiness which secondary routines in her macrocellular clusters had difficulty suppressing.

To counter the nausea she tried picking a point in the distance and focusing on it; which led her to look up. The metallic-grey fuselage curved away above her, presenting an impression of size and weight almost as great as the one given by the length of the damn thing stretching on ahead. Holes the size of skyscrapers were open all the way along the side, with fleets of bots and freight sleds zipping in and out. Now she could see them up close, she noticed that most of the sleds were carrying identical consignments. *Twenty-four million medical suspension chambers*; she couldn't quite get her head around that number. It was more than the population of Greater Makkathran. But not of Ellezelin; and as for the billions of followers across the Greater Commonwealth . . .

'I've heard this referred to as the first wave,' she said.

'Yes, Dreamer,' Cleric Taranse said cheerfully. He had the appearance of a man in his biological fifties, even down to thinning hair and wrinkled skin; the deliberate *elder* image, she suspected, was an attempt to give him an aura of experience and confidence. But then a lot of Living Dream followers allowed themselves to appear to age – because in the real Makkathran, everyone grew old. 'Now the production systems have been established they can continue at remarkably little cost. Ellezelin can certainly afford to keep on producing them.'

'But won't Ellezelin's population be the first to leave? When they've travelled into the Void, who will keep the economy going?'

'We are ultimately hoping that some kind of bridge can be

established between Void and Commonwealth,' Ethan said smoothly. 'Such a thing can hardly be beyond the ability of the Heart.'

Araminta remembered the way the boundary had distended out to swallow Justine's little ship. 'Most likely.' She glanced up again as she moved through another clash of regrav waves. The sight of the starship was drawing the Skylord's attention, building anticipation. One question she was never going to ask it was: *Can you reach us here?*

'I will need to be awake during the voyage,' she said.

Both Ethan and Taranse smiled an indulgent smile, not quite belittling her, but close.

'The life-support section is in the centre of the ship, Dreamer,' Taranse said. 'Each will have a crew complement of three thousand. There are a lot of systems to maintain even with smartcore and bot support.'

'Of course. That's very reassuring.'

'The cabins will be fully equipped with every luxury. Your voyage will be spent in complete comfort and security. You have nothing to worry about.'

He wasn't joking, she realized. 'How do we stay in contact with Ellezelin during the flight?'

'The ships will be dropping relay stations at frequent intervals, just like the Navy link with Centurion Station. As well as TD channels ours will also have confluence nests.'

Araminta felt very reassured by that; she'd been worried about what might happen if she passed out of range from the bulk of her followers. The ships would no doubt be crewed by Ethan's loyalists. 'So now we just need the ultradrives and force fields,' she said as she checked the timer in her exovision. There were only a couple of minutes left.

'I have every confidence,' Ethan said easily.

'Oh I'm sure it wants us to get there all right,' Araminta said.

He stopped and gave her a look of reluctant admiration. 'You were correct in what you said to Ilanthe. The Void will always triumph. I was . . . gladdened by your faith in it.'

'Do you have any idea what that thing wants to achieve inside?'

'No. But it will be some soulless technocrat scheme to "improve" life for everyone else. It is the sort of delusion of which her kind dream constantly. That is why I never really concerned myself about it.'

'Yes, I thought as much.' For several nights after her arrival in the Orchard Palace, Araminta had tried to feel for Ilanthe's thoughts, to try and gain a sense of what her intentions were. Bradley and Clouddancer had said the Silfen Motherholm had sensed whatever it was emerging from the Sol system, but either Ilanthe had somehow slipped from the Motherholm's perception, or the Silfen in their wisdom weren't sharing. She thought the latter unlikely.

'They're here,' Cleric Taranse announced happily.

Icons from Ellezelin's civil spaceflight directorate were popping up in Araminta's exovision. She'd never realized just how much information even a nominal head of state such as herself was supposed to absorb on a daily basis. How actual heads of state coped she had no idea; expanded and augmented mentalities, presumably.

Thirty-seven large commercial freighters had just dropped out of hyperspace two thousand kilometres above the planet. A secure link to the Ellezelin defence force fleet headquarters informed her that five squadrons of Ellezelin warships were emerging around the freighters in a protective formation. This was the critical stage, the one window of vulnerability left to those who opposed the Pilgrimage. Until the freighters got under the construction yard's force fields they were dangerously exposed.

The freighters were given clearance to descend. Sure enough, eight craft lurking in orbit dropped their stealth effect and opened fire. Weird mauve and green light flooded across the ground at Araminta's feet at the same instant the exovision displays reported what was happening. She tipped her head back in reflex to see what was going on, but the dome had opaqued above her. All she saw was rapidly expanding coloured blotches in the greyed sky, like borealis storms as bright as sunlight.

More icons appeared, assuring her that the Greater Makkathran force fields were also up, and protecting citizens from the terrible torrent of hard radiation slicing through the atmosphere. She even felt a start of anxiety leaking out of Ethan's gaiamotes, and smiled in sympathy. The Pilgrimage fleet could probably make it with standard hyperdrives, but without the force fields the Raiel would reduce the ships to radioactive fog.

Though the Void might just be able to stop them, she thought. *The Raiel could never beat it.*

Her u-shadow told her the head of planetary defence, Admiral Colris, was opening a secure channel. 'Dreamer, we've eliminated the enemy ships.'

'Are our ships all right?'

'Three badly damaged, eight took temporary overload hits but they're still flightworthy.'

'How badly damaged?'

'We'll recover the crews, don't worry, it's what we train for, Dreamer.'

'Thank you. Was there any damage to the freighters?'

'No. Lady be praised. It looks like those new force fields are as tough as advertised.'

The whole Greater Commonwealth that was gaiafield-attuned blinked at the burst of Araminta's surprise. 'The freighters are protected by Sol-barrier force fields?'

'Yes, Dreamer.'

'I see. Please pass my thanks to your crews.'

'Of course, they'll appreciate your concern, Dreamer.'

Ethan and Darraklan were both watching the force field overhead gradually clear. The sky beyond was reverting to its usual pristine blue. A few violet scintillations burned through the ionosphere as disintegrating wreckage hurtled downwards. Ethan's delight and relief were open. 'Those would be the best ships our opponents could deploy,' the Cleric said.

449

'Yes,' Araminta replied, not quite knowing if she should be celebrating or not.

'We can begin installation at once,' Taranse said.

'How long until we're ready?' she asked.

'If the systems function in accordance with the details they supplied, we'll be looking at a week.'

'Excellent,' she said. *Then I can finally try and stop this madness. I just hope there's enough time left.*

They waited in the construction yard as the freighters dropped down through the atmosphere. Taranse left them to organize the unloading. Araminta and Ethan watched the operation begin from the front of the big office tower where their capsule was parked. She was a little disappointed at how dull it all was. The units were all encased in smooth metal shells, providing no hint as to their function. For all she knew they were just water tanks.

'Your moment draws near, Dreamer,' Ethan said.

She wasn't surprised by the way he was studying her so intently. She'd felt his curious thoughts wiggling through the gaiafield, trying to gain a hint of her true feelings. She suspected that when they arrived in the Void he would prove a formidable telepath.

'It does indeed,' she said levelly. 'Where do you suppose all this came from?'

'It is irrelevant now. That it is here is what matters.'

'And because of that we can reach the Void. Yes. That just leaves me and the Skylord now.'

'I will be honoured to fly with you in the flagship to offer what support I can.'

'Which one . . .' Her hand waved idly at the row of ships.

'That one. The *Lady's Light.*'

Araminta had to smile at that. 'Of course. But shouldn't that be *Lady's Light Two*?'

'If you wish it to be so, Dreamer.'

'No. The original has been unmade, and it was a redoubtable ship. Let us hope our own voyage is as successful.'

Ethan's smile was tight. He clearly still couldn't work out

what Araminta's game was. Which was exactly how she wanted it.

The capsule lifted through a thick sea mist that was rolling in fast from the shore. As soon as they were above it Araminta saw the change that had spread across the fields and forests that stretched away from the city's perimeter. The lush green squares of grassland and crop fields had become a sickly yellow. Long lines of wildfire burned furiously through the forests.

'What happened?' she asked in confusion.

'Radiation downspill,' Ethan explained. 'The orbital fight was directly above us. Those who understand such things explained to me last time that starship weapons today are extraordinarily powerful.'

'Last time?'

'Two ships fought above Ellezelin shortly before you came forward. We never did find out why.'

'Great,' she so nearly said Ozzie, 'Lady. What about people caught outside the city force field?' The mist as well, she realized, was a part of it. Surface water flash-boiled by the energy deluge.

'Not good. A majority of Living Dream followers don't have biononics or memorycell inserts.'

'Because the Waterwalker didn't.' It almost came out with contempt.

'Quite. But the clinics will be able to re-life those who did.'

'May the Lady watch over the souls of those who didn't,' she said, appalled by how pious she sounded.

'We're a long way from the Lady,' Ethan said.

'Not for much longer.'

*

'Araminta is disgusted with them,' Neskia declared as the gifted vision swirled around her, partially blocking her view of *the ship*'s cabin. 'It didn't leak into the gaiafield, but I could tell how horrified she was when Ethan told her the moronic faithful didn't even have memorycells because of their belief.'

'That's reasonable enough,' Ilanthe said. 'I'm equally disgusted.

451

They chose to remain animal when they could elevate themselves. They certainly don't deserve pity.'

Neskia's head swept from side to side as her long neck undulated sinuously. 'If she's truly taken up the cause of Living Dream and become their Dreamer as she claims, then she would exhibit sympathy. This is simply evidence she is attempting some kind of subterfuge.'

'I fail to see what she can do. She is committed now, as few have ever been. She has claimed her position as the head of Living Dream on the promise of delivering Pilgrimage. To go back on her word now would bring dire personal consequences. At the least, Ethan would break into her mind and compel her to communicate with the Skylord. In that he would have the tacit support of most followers. Either way I gain entry to the Void.'

Exovision images showed Neskia the inversion core resting cleanly in *the ship*'s one and only cargo hold. There was no gaiafield connection so she couldn't determine the timbre of Ilanthe's thoughts – if that's what they could still be called. 'Her conversion was too swift, too complete. I do not believe in her.'

'Nor do I,' Ilanthe agreed. 'But in gaining political power, choice has been taken from her. You heard her, she trusts the Void will defeat me.'

'And how did she find out about you? She was all alone and running from everyone.'

'I suspect the Silfen.'

'Or she has allies among the remnants of the Factions. Gore is still at large; the Third Dreamer. That could indicate a connection.'

'Gore told Justine to travel to Makkathran. Whatever he's planning it involves a connection between him and his daughter, not Araminta. None of us knew her identity until a few days ago; she was never part of any of Gore's schemes.'

'He's going to go post-physical, isn't he? That's what he's doing on the Anomine homeworld. It has to be; the Anomine elevation mechanism must still be there. Such an advance will grant him the power to ruin everything.'

452

'If that is his goal, he will fail.'

'How do you know?'

'I researched the Anomine elevation mechanism a century ago. It won't elevate Gore.'

'Why not?' Neskia asked.

'He is not an Anomine.'

Neskia's long throat trilled with delight. 'I had no idea.'

'The process I am committing to is not one I undertook lightly. Every option was reviewed.'

'Of course. My apologies. But you really should get Marius to eliminate him.'

'Marius may or may not succeed in such an endeavour. Gore's ship is undoubtedly the equal to the one Marius is flying, and the borderguards will intervene.'

'You can't risk him interfering with Fusion,' Neskia insisted.

'You say that because you do not understand what I will initiate when we enter the Void. Gore and all the others are a complete irrelevance. Araminta is all that matters now.'

'We will initiate Fusion. I understand and approve.'

'No. Fusion was a misdirection. The inversion core is destined to seed a far greater revolution.'

Neskia became still, perturbed by this change of direction. Everything she had become was dedicated to the Accelerator goal of Fusion. 'What?' she asked, mildly surprised she was questioning Ilanthe's purpose. But still . . .

'The Void is rightly feared because it requires energy from an external source in order to function. It is the epitome of entropy, the final enemy of all things. But the Void is a beautiful concept – mind over matter is the ultimate evolutionary trait. I propose to achieve the full function of the Void without the failing of its energy demands. That will be the Accelerator gift to existence itself.'

'In what way?'

'I was inspired by Ozzie. His mindspace works by altering the fundamental nature of spacetime to accommodate the telepathic function. I don't know how he worked out the specific alteration to make such a thing viable, but its implementation was a phenomenal achievement, sadly underappreciated thanks to his sulky withdrawal from the Commonwealth. But to change the very nature of spacetime across hundreds of lightyears is remarkable. It opened vistas of possibilities I had never conceived of before. I realized I should be aiming so much higher than simply wedding the Accelerator Faction to the Void. The potential of the Void is far greater. That it is locked away behind the boundary, dependent on a dwindling source of power, is a disaster for the evolution of sentience everywhere. It needs to be liberated, for the boundary to be thrown down.'

'You mean you want to bring all sentient species into the Void?'

'Quite the opposite. As Ozzie's mindspace is only a localized alteration, powered, presumably, by the Spike's anchor mechanism; so the Void can only function as long as it has mass to feed on, and that is finite. What the inversion core will do is instigate a permanent change. It will grasp the fundamental nature of the Void and impress spacetime to that pattern, forcing reality itself to transform. The Void's final magnificent reset of everything will begin. Change will shine out from the centre of this galaxy – in time, a very short time, illuminating the entire universe. Entropy will no longer exist because its principles will simply not be a part of the new cosmos. With the laws of spacetime itself rewritten, the true controller of reality will become the sentient mind, allowing evolution to reach a height impossible even for the post-physicals which this limited, flawed universe can gestate.'

'You're going to change the fundamental laws of the universe?' a shocked Neskia murmured.

'Such a goal is the pinnacle of evolution, elevating an entire universe. We will be the instigators of a genesis from which our mythical gods would cower in awe. Now do you see why I don't concern myself with the antics of Gore and his kind? I will simply wish them out of existence. And it shall be so.'

Inigo's Forty-Seventh Dream:

The Waterwalker's Triumph

It was Mattuel who had the privilege of helping Edeard up the long winding steps to the top of the tower. Edeard wouldn't put up with it from any of his other children, nor grandchildren, nor great-grandchildren, or even the great-great-grandchildren and certainly not the great-great-great-grandchildren, most of whom were just children. And Grolral, the first of his fifth-generation offspring and whom he adored, was only seven weeks old and really not interested in much apart from feeding and sleeping. But Mattuel was the favoured son, mainly because he'd been born so much later than the others, four and a half years after Finitan's guidance. Which shouldn't have made him any more special – and by that time none of the first seven cared about such things – but Edeard always regarded him as proof of success in living this life as he'd sworn to do. By the time the four Skylords appeared in Querencia's skies, events across the planet weren't going too badly this time around. Each town and most larger villages had a big park designated for the gathering of those who sought guidance. The open areas were based on the Waterwalker's solemn advice that the Skylords didn't really like the towers of Eyrie, and only used them out of respect for the bygone race that had sculpted them in the first place. Simple and cheap, the parks avoided any economic problems and petty rivalries. It also meant nobody trekked across half the continent to the towers of Eyrie, and all the problems that entailed.

Except that today Makkathran was once again host to crowds not seen in a hundred years. The last time so many thronged its streets was when the eight huge galleons of the flotilla had returned from their exploratory voyage circumnavigating the world. Edeard had sailed with them, enjoying the occasional bout of nostalgic sadness as they discovered the coastlines and seas he recalled from over a century before on his own private timeline. This time he'd made sure the problems afflicting Querencia in the wake of the Skylords were well and truly eliminated before setting out. There were no more attempts to dominate and bind people to a cause or family or individual. The newer generations of stronger psychics of were welcomed and integrated into a society whose prosperity was on a steady climb thanks to the expansion of the Eggshaper Guild and an abundance of genistars. New lands were being opened in what had once been the western wilds. Even the youngsters of Makkathran's Grand Families were encouraged to seek their fortune amid the fresh opportunities to extend the old estates and businesses – though that process was clearly going to outlast him by some considerable period.

This day was the day when Querencia paid tribute to the Waterwalker for transforming their world to one of enlightenment and potential. Already his era was being proclaimed as the planet's golden age.

'I hope to the Lady they're right,' he'd muttered to Kristabel as they woke together that last morning.

She'd given him a warning stare as one of their great-great-granddaughters helped comb her thin strands of white hair. 'Don't give me the Ashwell optimism now. Not today.'

Amusement and appreciation made him smile, which triggered a nasty bout of coughing deep in his chest. Two of the Novices attending him eased him forward on the bed. One proffered a steaming potion for him to inhale. He almost refused out of pure age-driven obstinacy, but relented when he recalled

Finitan's last days. The sweet girls were only trying to help. So he breathed the vapour down, and was relieved to find the muscle quakes subsiding. 'Yes dear.'

'Ha!'

He smiled again. One of the Novices started unbuttoning his bedshirt. 'I can still manage that, thank you,' he told her smartly. Of course he couldn't, not with his hands, horrible, swollen, gnarled things that they were now. The potions the doctors made him drink did nothing for his terribly arthritic joints any more. But thankfully his third hand remained more than capable. Finitan had remarked on something similar, he recalled.

When he blinked and looked round, everyone in the big room was staring anxiously at him. 'What?' he asked.

'You drifted off there, again,' Kristabel said.

'Honious! Let's hope I last till they arrive.'

That earned him another disapproving stare from Kristabel, while the Novices drew sharp nervous breaths and assured him he would. 'Actually, I was thinking of Finitan, if you must know,' he told the bedroom full of too many people.

'Goodness, I can't even remember what he looks like any more,' Kristabel said regretfully.

'It was nearly two hundred years ago,' Edeard reminded her. 'But we'll be seeing him again soon enough.'

'Aye, that we will.'

Edeard smiled at her again, blocking out the awful indignity of their well-meaning attendants bustling round. His farsight found the rest of his family assembling in the lounges on the upper floors of the ziggurat, all of them abuzz with conflicting emotion. Contrary to expectation their presence actually comforted him. There were so many, and all had done well – or at least hadn't turned to the bad. That was his true measure.

Eventually, he and Kristabel were dressed in their finest robes without too much assistance. He'd decided against the Water-walker's black cloak. At his age it would have made him look ridiculous. Besides, after eleven tenures as Mayor, he felt the robes of office were more appropriate.

Edeard managed to walk out of the bedroom to the first big lounge, but that was about as far as his muscles could manage without a decent rest. Mattuel's third hand steadied him as he sank down into a tall straight-backed chair. He was about to throw the youngster an angry look, but relented. In truth, he'd needed the support. Landing on his arse at the start of this ceremony was hardly dignified.

'Thank you,' he said quietly. Not that Mattuel could ever be considered a youngster any more – his own two hundredth birthday had been celebrated a few years back. Edeard couldn't quite remember when.

One by one, the family came up to him and Kristabel for one last embrace and a few words of comfort. The tradition had grown up in the last century and a half. It was a good one, he decided. *Clears the air, allows reconciliation for any too hasty words and stupid feuds. Not that I have any.* That particular harsh lesson had been learned two hundred years ago, and learned well.

So now he could greet them all gladly, and receive their wishes for a safe journey without any regrets. If there was sorrow it was from seeing how his children had aged. Rolar and Wenalee, who would surely be seeking guidance themselves the next time a Skylord visited. Jiska and Natran, and their huge brood of eleven children, fifty-seven grandchildren, and he didn't know how many after that except this morning they had to be accommodated on the eighth floor and longtalk their farewells – there was simply no room on the tenth. Marilee, Analee and Marvane, still together, and with eighteen children between them. Edeard clutched the merchant captain warmly when it was his turn. 'You can still come with us if you like,' he offered with a chuckle. 'I expect you could do with the respite.'

'Daddy, that's horrible.'

'He doesn't want a respite.'

'We treat him nicely.'

'When he's good.'

'And better when he's bad.'

Marvane spread his hands wide. 'You see?'

'I've always seen,' Edeard told him fondly.

Marakas and Jalwina were next. Happily married these last forty years. But then Marakas had plenty of practice, she was his seventh wife after all. Even then he was still way behind Dinlay's count.

Taralee in her own Grand Mistress robes, even though she had resigned the Doctors Guild Council thirty years before. 'Are you all right?' she asked in concern. 'I have some sedatives, ones from the folox leaf.'

'No,' he said firmly.

'You'll do all right,' she said with a grin. 'Goodbye, Daddy.'

'See you soon.'

See you soon, it was a murmur that swept round the lounge, then a chorus of well-wishing that was taken up by those on the ninth floor, and further, all the way to the third. And nowhere in the ziggurat was Burlal. He at least was spared the indignity of age, his brief years were always those of happiness.

Edeard was doing his best not to cry as his dynasty said its final formal farewell. He and Kristabel were lifted gently by third hands and carried down the central stairs with hundreds of their family leaning over the railings and now cheering them raucously.

'You know, we really did bump your dear old Uncle Lorin out of here in the end, didn't we?' he said as he waved at the blur of faces.

'Thank the Lady for that,' she said.

The largest family gondola was waiting for them at the ziggurat's mooring platform on Great Major Canal. They sat on the centre bench and looked round. The entire canal was lined with people come to wish the Waterwalker well on his way. They waved and clapped and cheered as he and Kristabel set off on the very short journey down to Eyrie's central mooring platform. All were dressed in their best clothes, transforming the route to a splendid colour-washed avenue.

'Remember the flowerboats from the Festival of Guidance?'

he asked his wife. 'They were as colourful as this. That used to be such a lovely day. It's a pity they had to end it.'

'Not a lot of point to it after the Skylords started arriving,' Kristabel said. 'And I'm hardly likely to forget. That's the day we met. Remember?'

'Mirnatha's kidnapping,' he said, remembering a few details of the day. He hadn't thought of it in decades – probably longer. 'Bise was holding her in the House of Blue Petals.'

'We never found out exactly who took her, and they held her in Fiacre.'

Owain, he knew. *Owain and his clique ordered her kidnapping; but I could never tell Kristabel that. I would have needed to explain what had ultimately become of Owain, and Bise, and – Lady forgive me – Mistress Florrel. And why it was essential they were eliminated. What would she say if she knew the secret of this universe? What would she do? What would any of them do?*

'Wake up,' Kristabel chided. 'We're here.'

'I wasn't asleep,' he complained as the gondola was being tied to the mooring. Up above the canal, the crooked towers of Eyrie were jabbing up into a cloudless summer sky. Those who sought guidance were already being aided to their places on the upper platforms. Mattuel and a few of the third-generation relatives were already on the street above, looking down, readying their third hands to lift Edeard and Kristabel. They'd all hurried over behind the gondola, walking across the surface of the canal – they were all strong enough to do that.

The streets between the towers were packed solid with representatives from across the world who had come to honour the Waterwalker and bid him farewell. They cheered and waved. On the steps of the Lady's church, the Makkathran Novice choir began to sing. The verse and chorus was taken up by the entire city.

Edeard asked Mattuel to pause a moment as the tune rang across Makkathran, allowing him to savour the music one last time. It was Dybal's *Bittersweet Flight*, the old musician's last and finest composition. Both simple and haunting, it had become quite the anthem since he was guided by a Skylord some eighty years before.

'Respectable at last,' he murmured as the song ended. All around him, people were bowing their heads. Standing still for the customary minute's silence.

'How poor Dybal would hate that,' an amused Kristabel replied.

'Yes. I must tell him when we get there.'

Friends were well placed amid those circling the tower itself. Edeard managed a weak wave at several familiar faces. There was no Salrana, for which he still felt remorse, though it was dulled now by the centuries; she'd taken guidance over ten years ago. Edeard had observed from the hortus as the Skylord swooped across the city, anxious that her soul would be accepted. He was sure it had been. For which he was glad. Even though they had never been reconciled, she had found her own fulfilment in the end.

Ranalee, too, had gone, contemptuous and antagonistic to the very end. In her own way she had accomplished much, with a host of descendants whose successful avaricious enterprises extended their influence far and wide.

Edeard closed his eyes as he was gently elevated upwards. *This is when I must make my choice. It has been a good life, today is proof of that. Not perfect, but it never could be. Do I go back and live it again? And what would be the point of that? I know I can only live those centuries again if I do it differently. Perhaps now would be the time to go back beyond Owain's death? I could go right back to Ashwell and stop my parents being killed. Salrana would never be corrupted . . .* He shook his head with only the mildest regret. That was not the life for him. Too many bad events would have to be played out again in one form or another so that the final two centuries could be lived in the peace and hope he'd enjoyed this time around. He would have to make things different to make them remotely bearable. The risk was immense.

I will take guidance.

The central stairway winding up the tower was too cramped for an entourage, so it was Mattuel who performed the honour of carrying his father to the top, accompanied by the Pythia herself. Honalee carried her grandmother, while the rest of the family surrounded the base of the tower.

'Dear Lady, I haven't been up here since the day Finitan was guided,' Edeard said as they neared the top.

'Yes, Father.'

'You know, this is the same tower which Owain's thugs pushed me off.'

'I know, Father.'

Edeard smiled softly to himself as they rounded the last curve and went out into the bright sunshine. Eight tall spires guarded the edges, their tips bent inwards slightly. As always, the wind was a lot stronger on the open platform than it was down on the ground. It whistled faintly as it blew around the spires.

A gaggle of Novices and Mothers were clustered round the entrance to the stairs, each of them openly anxious to see the Waterwalker as he was settled on to a pile of comfortable cushions. They had escorted the others who sought guidance, of which there were fifty on the platform. Most of them resting on similar cushions, though a few were stubbornly insisting on standing to face the Skylord's arrival.

'About time you turned up,' Macsen said.

Edeard tipped two fingers to his old friend. Even as he did he wondered how on Querencia the Mothers and Novices had ever got the enormous Master of Sampalok up the tight stairwell. Macsen seemed be almost globular these days. He hadn't managed to get out of bed unaided for over four years.

Edeard looked round at his friends, humbled and delighted that they would all be travelling together. Kanseen on a bed of cushions next to Macsen, her terribly frail frame struggling to breathe. Dinlay, standing of course, gaunt yet with a straight back, his Chief Constable's uniform immaculate, dignified at the last. He was by himself; to everyone's amazement his final marriage had lasted thirty-two years (a record) and remained current, but his wife was eighty-seven years younger.

'Everyone together,' Edeard said.

'No matter what,' they all chorused.

The Pythia bowed to Edeard. 'Waterwalker, may the Lady Herself bless your journey. She will greet you soon I'm sure. What you have done for this world is beyond praise. The Heart awaits you with eagerness, as do your friends who dwell there now. You go there with the undying thanks of all of us who live on Querencia, whose fulfilment you have worked so hard towards.'

Edeard looked up into her face, kind and stern as all the Pythias seemed to be, but radiant with concern. A concern that extended a great deal further than the tower. *Should I tell her?* Somehow, he couldn't risk the woman's disapproval, so all he said was: 'Thank you.'

The Novices and Mothers began their walk back down the tower's spiral stair.

Macsen let out a comfortable groan as he slumped back onto the cushions. 'Right then, we've got a minute, anyone bring some booze?'

'I think you've had enough now, dear,' Kanseen longtalked quietly. Watching her juddering breaths, Edeard knew it was willpower alone which kept her body alive. Dinlay came over and perched beside Edeard. The lenses in his glasses were like balls of glass they were so thick. Edeard knew very well he was virtually blind. It was only his farsight which allowed him to move around these days.

'Do you think Boyd got there?' Dinlay asked.

Edeard smiled wistfully. 'If he didn't, we'll have to organize a search of the Void for him.'

'I'm sure a Skylord would help,' Kanseen longtalked. 'He deserves his place in the Heart.'

'Wouldn't that be something?' Kristabel said. 'A voyage across the universe; a bigger version of our trip around the world.'

'Yes, my love, it would be quite something.'

He saw her head turn to stare at him, eyes narrowing in that oh so beautifully familiar expression. 'Is there something wrong?'

'Not wrong, no. But tell me this, all of you: if there was something you knew, an ability you had which could change everything, the way you lived, your beliefs, the way you thought, even, would you keep it to yourself?'

'What ability?' Macsen asked keenly. 'The way you talk to the city?'

'No, something much greater than that.'

'Would it change things for the better?' Kristabel asked.

'It just brings change. How it is applied, for better or worse, depends on the user.'

'You cannot judge people,' Dinlay said. 'Not even you, Water-walker, have that right. We have our courts of law to maintain order, but to decide the nature of a person's soul is not something we are worthy of. The Heart alone decides.'

'If the ability exists, it exists for a reason,' Kanseen longtalked.

'I thought so,' Edeard said.

Down below, the city gasped then cheered as the Skylord rose above the horizon. The tremendous flood of rapturous blessings directed from Makkathran's crowds rose to a crescendo. It was enough to bestow Edeard's body with a final surge of strength. He reached out with his third hand, and drew his friends to him. They held hands as the Skylord swept in across the Lyot Sea. Wind rushed on in front of it, causing their robes to flap about. All around them, the spires of the tower began to glow, a vivid corona of light that spilled out across the platform, filling the air with sparks, as if the stars themselves were raining down.

'Will you accept us?' Edeard asked of the Skylord. 'Will you guide us to the Heart?'

'Yes,' the giant creature replied benevolently.

Tears of gratitude seeped down Edeard's cheeks as the light grew stronger and the shadow of the Skylord slid across Eyrie. This was his last chance.

The light flared, overwhelming his eyes. He sensed his body

starting to dissolve into whatever force the towers unleashed. Yet his mind remained intact, if anything it grew stronger, his thoughts clearer than they had been in decades. His perception expanded, taking in the whole of the city.

'I have one last gift for you,' he spoke to the glittering enraptured minds below. 'Use it well.' And he showed them how to travel back through their own life to begin again where they chose.

'That's how we always won?' a laughing Macsen asked.

Edeard's soul shone with happiness. Rising beside him into the giant fluctuations of light that ran through the Skylord's body, Macsen's spectral form had returned to his handsome adolescent self.

'Not always,' he promised his friends. 'And not for two hundred years. I swear upon the Lady that your achievements here are your own.'

'Whatever will they do with it?' Dinlay asked, looking down at the world shrinking away below the glare of their disintegrating bodies.

'The best they can, of course,' Kanseen said.

'You did the right thing,' Kristabel told him.

Edeard cast his perception up, growing aware of the songs calling down from the nebulas. They seemed to speak directly to him, a promise of such glory he was filled with wonder and anticipation. 'They're so beautiful,' he exclaimed. 'And we'll soon be there.'

8

Oscar munched away absent-mindedly on his chocolate twister as he reviewed the astrogation charts his u-shadow was extracting from various files. On the other side of the exovision displays Liatris McPeierl was running through an energetic exercise routine, stripped to the waist to show off perfectly proportioned chest muscles which were gleaming rather nicely with sweat. A sight that was not a little distracting; Oscar found it hard to concentrate on trans-galactic navigation with all that joyous hunk-flesh flexing lithely just a couple of metres away.

Liatris finished his routine and reached languidly for a towel. 'I'm for a shower,' he announced, and twitched his bum in Oscar's direction as teasingly bogus thoughts of lust burst out into the gaiafield.

Oscar bit firmly down into a big chunk of his pastry, inhaling a lot of the dusty icing sugar it was coated with, which made him cough, and that made him look really stupid. He took a drink of tea to clear his throat. When he'd finished, Liatris was gone and Beckia was giving him a piteous smile from the other side of the starship's main cabin.

'What?' he grumbled.

'Liatris is spoken for back home,' she said.

'Back home is a long way away.'

'You're a wicked old Punk Skunk.'

'And proud of it. Wanna take a look at my scorecard?'

'You just have no dignity at all, do you?'

He flashed her a lecherous grin, and ordered his u-shadow to pull files from the unisphere on all previous known and rumoured trans-galactic flights. 'Part of what makes me lovable.'

'Part of you is lovable?'

Tomansio and Cheriton rose up through the airlock chamber into the centre of the cabin, both of them wearing toga suits with quite flamboyant iridescent surface shimmers, and gaiamotes emissions toned down to zero. Letting everyone know they were staunch Viotia citizens and nothing to do with Living Dream in any respect.

'It's not getting any better out there,' Cheriton complained.

For a couple of weeks now the team had been accessing and experiencing the attempts of Viotia's government as it tried to re-establish normal services and deal with the damage caused by the invasion. An operation not helped by the lynching of their Prime Minister two days after the Ellezelin troops had withdrawn from the capital, Ludor. It had been a messy affair with a mob storming into the National Parliament building while the guards had been content to stand back and let natural justice take its course. The rest of the cabinet, fearful for their own bodyloss, had been reluctant to stand up and issue instructions. Relief was mainly being coordinated by local authorities while tempers were given time to cool.

Given that Colwyn City had sustained by far the worst damage, its infrastructure was still limping along as repairs and replacement operations were implemented. Bots and civil engineering crews were hard at work, aided by equipment delivered by starships flying in from across the Commonwealth. But commerce was sluggish, and a surprising number of businesses still hadn't reopened despite the urging of the city council.

'I think they've done well, considering the general apathy,' Tomansio said. 'It's going to take a couple of years before everything gets back to pre-invasion levels. It doesn't help that Likan's company is currently shut down. It was a huge part of the planetary economy. The treasury will have to step in and refloat its finances. And the cabinet isn't strong enough to orchestrate that right now. There'll have to be an election to restore public confidence in government.'

'Which is the main problem,' Oscar said. 'What's the point? Our gloriously idiotic Dreamer is going to launch the Pilgrimage fleet in seven hours. You're not going to get an election if there's nothing left of the galaxy to hold an election in.'

'So remind me while we're still here?' Tomansio said.

Oscar was going to launch into his usual impassioned plea for hope and faith based on that five seconds of raw face-to-face impression he'd gained of Araminta back in Bodant Park. He had been so utterly certain that she was playing Living Dream somehow. But the team had heard it all so many times from him, and now here he was examining ways to flee from the galaxy in one of the finest starships ANA had ever constructed. 'I don't know,' he said, surprised by how hard the admission was. It meant the mission was over, that they could do nothing, that there was no future.

He wondered what Dushiku and Anja and dear mercurial Jesaral would say when he landed outside their house in a stealthed ultradrive starship and told them they'd have to flee the galaxy. It had been so long since he'd spoken to them they were actually starting to drift away from his consideration. Which wasn't good. He really could survive without them. *Especially now I'm living life properly again.*

A dismayed groan escaped his lips. *Oh, you treacherous, treacherous man. Beckia is right, I have no dignity.*

Cheriton, Tomansio and Beckia exchanged mildly confused glances as the rush of conflicting emotion spilled out of Oscar's gaiamotes.

'What will you do when the expansion starts?' he asked them.

'The Knights Guardians will survive,' Tomansio said. 'I expect we will relocate to a new world in a fresh galaxy.'

'You'd need to find such a world,' Oscar said cautiously. 'For that you'll need a good scoutship. An ultradrive would be perfect.'

'It would. And we would be honoured for you to join us.'

'This is difficult,' Oscar said miserably. 'To acknowledge we have failed so completely, not just the five of us but our entire species.'

'Justine is still inside the Void,' Beckia said. 'Gore may yet triumph. He clearly intends something.'

'Clutching at straws,' Oscar told her. 'That's not strong.'

'No, but part of what I believe in is having the strength to admit when you've been defeated. We didn't secure Araminta, and she's made her own choice – despicable bitch that she is. Our part in this is over.'

'Yeah,' he acknowledged. He still wasn't sure how his life partners would react to all this. Not that he was so shallow he'd fly off without making the offer to take them. But they all had family, which made an exodus complicated. Whereas he was truly alone. Probably the closest connection he had to anyone alive today was Paula Myo. A notion which made him smile.

Every one of Oscar's exovision displays was abruptly blanked out by a priority protocol as his u-shadow reported someone was activating a link from an ultrasecure onetime contact code.

'Bloody hell!' he blurted.

'Hello, Oscar,' Araminta said. 'I believe you told me to call.'

*

Even with a combination of smartcores and modern cybernetics and replicator factories and a legion of bots and effectively bottomless government resources, not to mention the loving devotion of every single project worker, building the twelve giant Pilgrimage ships was a phenomenal achievement by any standards. But for all that, the prodigious amount of processing power and human thought which had been utilized to manage the project was primarily focused on planning and facilitating the fabrication itself. It was unfortunate, therefore, that a proportional amount of consideration hadn't been given over to working out the embarkation procedure for the lucky twenty-four million.

Mareble had been reduced to tears when she and Danal had received confirmation that they'd been allocated a place on board the *Macsen's Dream*. She actually sank to her knees in the hotel room and sent the strongest prayer of thanks into the gaiafield, wishing it towards Dreamer Araminta for the kindness she'd shown towards them yet again. For days afterwards she'd gone through life in a daze of happiness. Her brain was stuck in such amazing fantasies of what she would do when she walked the streets of Makkathran itself that it was a miracle she even remembered to eat. Then her wonder and excitement was channelled into preparation; she was one of the chosen ones, an opportunity she must never waste. So she and Danal spent hours reviewing the kind of supplies they wanted to take. Allocation was strictly limited to one cubic metre per person, with the strong advice not to bring any advanced technology item.

It was her deepest wish that she could somehow become an Eggshaper, like the Waterwalker himself. For years she'd studied the techniques he'd employed in those first dreams; she was sure that she could emulate the ability if she could just get into proximity with a pregnant default genistar. So once the basic clothes and utensils and tools were packed, she set about filling the precious remaining space with the kind of tough coats and jeans and boots that were essential to any branch of animal husbandry, with practical veterinary instruments occupying the last remaining cubic centimetres. Danal filled his container with some luxury food packets and a range of seeds; but mostly his allowance was taken up by old-fashioned books printed on superstrong paper by a small specialist replicator unit he had bought for the occasion. He wanted to be a teacher, he told her, which was why he also took pencils and pens and all the paraphernalia necessary to make ink.

Embarkation began three days after the drives and force fields arrived. Before she'd met Dreamer Araminta, the unsavoury origin of the technology would have troubled Mareble. But now she'd witnessed Dreamer Araminta confront the disquieting Ilanthe-thing, she had confidence that their Pilgrimage wasn't being perverted for a Faction's sinister agenda. Araminta was quite right: the Void would prevail over any wickedness. So when their capsule arrived at the construction yard she was carefree and dizzy with the prospect of the flight itself. Everything her life had been devoted to was about to be consummated.

The capsule had to wait outside the yard's force-field dome for seven hours, stacked three hundred metres above the ground in a matrix resembling a metallic locust swarm, all of them awaiting landing clearance. When they finally did get down outside one of the matériel egress facilities, bots loaded their containers on a trolley, which quickly slipped away through the air. Mareble and Danal had to walk through the facility past an array of scanners and sensor fields before they were finally out under the domes which cloaked the evening sky in a pale purple nimbus. Long braids of trolleys buzzed high through the air, forking and flowing like a dark river tributary network as they glided to their designated ship to offload. Staring up at the appallingly complex, fast-moving streams, Mareble glumly resigned herself to never seeing her personal container again.

Below the trolleys, a strata of solido signs hovered above the wide avenues between the starships, carrying directions and stabbing out flashing arrows. To complement that, her u-shadow received a series of guidance instructions that would take her to entrance ramp 13 of the *Macsen's Dream*. Her and two million others. What those instructions amounted to was: join the three-hundred-metre-wide queue filling the avenue and shuffle along for five hours.

With darkness falling, the hulls of the giant ships curving away above her created an unavoidable impression of being trapped in a metallic canyon with no end. The regrav fields supporting the ships pulsed oddly, creating unpleasant effects in her stomach. There were no toilets. Nothing to eat or drink. Nowhere to rest. The noise of everyone talking and complaining together, along with crying distressed children, was unnerving and depressing. Only the gaiafield with its shared sensation of anticipation kept her spirits up.

Five hours pressed up next to a band of boisterous women who boasted about their genetic reprofiling to Amazonian twenty-year-olds. They wore T-shirts with embroidered slogans: Dinlay's Lurve Squad. Badder Than Hilitte. I'm Gonna Get DinLAYd.

Mareble and Danal exchanged a sardonic look, and closed their ears to the bawdy talk and dirty laughter. It was amazing how some people interpreted the fulfilment the Pilgrimage was bringing them to.

Eventually, after far too long in a Honious-like limbo they arrived at the base of ramp 13. After the chaos she'd endured, she let out a quiet sob of relief.

'It's real,' she whispered to Danal as they began the slow walk up the slope. The Dinlay girls followed them up, but the crowd here wasn't so bad. Thousands more were still trudging slowly along the avenue behind and below her. She was rising above them now in every sense.

He gripped her hand and squeezed tight as his mind let out a surge of gratitude. 'Thank you,' he told her. 'I would never have made it without you.'

For one brief instant she thought of Cheriton, and the short hot comforting time she'd spent with him after Danal's arrest – how in turn he'd given her the fortitude to get through that period of misery and disorientation. Somehow she didn't let the pang of guilt out. After all, even the Waterwalker had lapsed when he tried to bind the world to his faulty notion of unity. From that he had emerged triumphant.

'We made it though,' she said. 'I love you. And we're going to wake up in Makkathran itself.'

'Och, that's very sweet,' a loud amused voice said.

Mareble fixed on a blank smile and turned round. The man behind her on the ramp wasn't quite what she was expecting – not that she had any preconceptions, but . . .

He was taller than Danal, dressed in a kilt and very bright scarlet waistcoat with gold buttons. Not something she ever remembered anyone on Querencia wearing. She was about to say something when a flicker of silver and gold light shone through his thick flop of brown hair, distracting her.

'They call me the Lionwalker,' he said. 'But I got that label a long time before our very own Waterwalker came along, so that's okay, then. Pleased to meet you.'

'Likewise,' Danal said stiffly as he introduced himself.

'So are you two lovebirds going to get hitched in the Lady's church?' Lionwalker asked.

'Mareble is my wife,' Danal said with such pride that she ignored how rude the stranger was being and smiled up adoringly at her husband as his arm tightened around her.

'Aye, well yes, but a marriage blessed in that church would be a blessing indeed, now wouldn't it? And take it from a man who's seen more than his fair share of every kind of bride and groom there is, a marriage needs every bit of help it can get.' Lionwalker pushed his hand up in salute, showing off an antique silver hip flask. 'Cheers and bon voyage to the pair of you.' And he took a long nip. 'Ahaa, that'll keep the cold off my toes on the voyage.'

'We don't need extra help,' Mareble spluttered.

'If you say so. Mind, it's a particular person who needs no advice in life.'

'I'll thank you to keep your homilies to yourself,' Danal told him. 'Our guidance comes from the Waterwalker himself.'

They'd reached the top of the ramp, which frankly Mareble had wanted to achieve under slightly more dignified circumstances. The Lionwalker took another nip, winked lecherously at her, and sauntered off inside the *Macsen's Dream* as if he owned the starship.

'Well!' Danal grunted indignantly. 'Some of us clearly have a lot longer to go before reaching fulfilment than others.'

The chamber behind the airlock was a junction of seven corridors. Small, neat solidos flowed smoothly along the walls, indicating the zone where their assigned medical capsules were located.

'Come on,' Danal said, gripping her hand.

Mareble narrowed her eyes, staring along the corridor down which the Lionwalker had vanished. 'I know him,' she said uncertainly. The memory was elusive. But then the squad of Dinlay Girls were shrieking wildly and running down their corridor like a football team going onto the pitch, which made her chuckle. She let Danal lead her into the labyrinthine interior of the starship. Instinctively, she reached for Dreamer Araminta's gift, finding her standing on the observation deck of the *Lady's Light*. Alone and resolute, staring out through a huge curving transparent section of the forward fuselage.

Reassured her idol was watching out for all of Living Dream, Mareble strode on with renewed confidence.

*

The SI's icon appeared in Troblum's exovision, requesting a connection. At least it was asking, he thought, rather than intruding.

Mellanie's Redemption was still secreted away in transdimensional suspension above Viotia. Troblum couldn't quite help that. He had been completely taken by surprise at Araminta's defection to Living Dream. Given how long she had spent trying to elude them, suddenly turning up and claiming their leadership lacked any kind of logic, at least the kind he understood. He did assume it was some kind of ruse, again not one he could fathom.

So he waited for her endgame to become clear. After all, if he took flight to another galaxy and, however unlikely it was, she resolved the whole Pilgrimage problem, he'd never know.

'Even if they don't Pilgrimage, there's still the Accelerators and Ilanthe and the Cat,' Catriona had pointed out.

'A solution to the Pilgrimage will by definition have to include and neutralize them,' he explained patiently.

'I thought you were keen to find out what happened to the trans-galactic expeditions?'

'I am. But the timescale is so short now before we know if Araminta succeeds in getting the Pilgrimage fleet through the barrier I can afford to wait and see if the expansion begins as predicted. If it does, we can outrun it now we have ultradrive.'

'What about Oscar? The SI said it knows where his ship is.'

'Irrelevant now. All that's left are Gore and Ilanthe, the two real players. This is their war.'

'Are you scared to meet Oscar?'

'No. There's simply no point.'

'You might be able to open the Sol barrier.'

'No!' Which was the truth. He'd spent day after day analysing the files in his storage lacuna, working through the theories and equipment they'd developed during his time on the Accelerator station building the Swarm. There was no way round it that he could see, no way to overwhelm the barrier. And he didn't have enough data on the individual components of the Swarm to see if there was a backdoor. In any case, most of it had been constructed after he left; all he'd done was help set up the manufacturing systems. They would have made a lot of changes and improvements over the decades. He wasn't current.

So the *Mellanie's Redemption* stayed above Viotia, because it was as good a place as any to wait. After his futile attempt to analyse the Sol barrier he even managed to catch up on some sleep. Time was spent on reviewing the starship's basic systems, getting up to date on maintenance procedures, fabricating some replacement components in the small high-level on-board replicator. There were also a great many files his u-shadow acquired for him from the unisphere; information and entertainment which would make a life of exile in another galaxy more bearable.

When the SI's icon appeared Troblum didn't authorize the link at once. First of all, he was busy. And then ... The last couple of weeks had eased him into a state of acceptance. He knew he was leaving. It was simply a question of timing now. And he didn't really even have to make that decision. The Void's final expansion phase would begin and he would leave. It was that simple.

The SI, though, that would bring complications back into his life.

'I know you,' Catriona Saleeb said. 'Not knowing what it wanted to tell you will eat you up. And it's being polite. It could have forced its way into the ship's link with the unisphere.'

'Yes,' Troblum sighed. He cancelled the blueprints in his exovision display and looked down at the micromanipulator he was using. Underneath its transparent dome, the clean-environment unit contained a scattering of newly replicated components which he was slowly assembling into a solido projector. He'd obtained enough base programs to construct a reasonable I-sentient personality. It would be himself, he'd decided, a younger, physically fitter version, which would be able to share Catriona's bed. He'd redesigned the sensory correlations with his own biononics so they were a lot higher than a standard version, allowing him to enjoy the experience to the full. Incorporating those customizations took time. By itself, it was an intriguing problem to solve, one which had absorbed his intellect for several days. It was almost like becoming multiple. Catriona had said she was looking forward to it as well.

His u-shadow opened the link.

'I have an interesting development to report,' the SI said.

'What?'

'Oscar Monroe has just received a secure call from someone at Bovey's Bathing and Culinaryware. That's a macrostore in the Groby touchdown mall in Colwyn City.'

'So?'

'The originator claims to be Araminta. The link was established through a onetime code which Oscar issued. Nobody else knew about it except him and the person it was given to.'

'And you. So any decent e-head could find it.'

'I only know about it because I'm monitoring all the links going in and out of Oscar's hidden starship. Once I'd intercepted it, cracking the code was tough even for me. It would be beyond most e-heads in the Commonwealth.'

Troblum frowned at the tiny electronic components inside the micromanipulator case glittering like so many diamonds. 'But it can't be from Araminta.' His u-shadow had put the

Pilgrimage departure into a peripheral exovision image, he could see the Pilgrimage fleet on Ellezelin. They had finally finished their chaotic embarkation. Several live feeds were showing Araminta standing in the observation deck of the *Lady's Light*. 'She's in the flagship. They're about to launch.'

'Exactly. So why is a onetime code given to her personally by Oscar being activated from Colwyn City?'

'I don't understand.' Though it did make the puzzle of why she'd defected to Living Dream more absorbing. Troblum liked puzzles. Not that it changed anything. 'What did they say?'

'Nothing much. She asked Oscar to meet her in a restaurant on Dryad Avenue in fifteen minutes.'

'But . . .' Troblum pulled the news feeds to centre. The protective force fields over the construction yard were powering down, leaving the skies wide open for the colossal ships to launch. 'She's on board the *Lady's Light*. I'm accessing the feed right now.'

'Yes. So either she's bringing the entire Pilgrimage fleet to Viotia for a quick visit, or there's something else going on.'

'What?'

'Are you taking an interest, Troblum? Are you considering contacting Oscar now?'

'I'm not talking to him. For all I know this is some trick of yours.'

'If it is, it's a little late in the day.'

'What do you want from me?'

'I'm infiltrating nodes inside the restaurant. Oscar's team is running checks to provide cover for their man. They're good but I can elude them. Would you like to observe the meeting?'

Troblum closed his eyes. Images from the starship's sensors showed him Viotia as a vast intrusion within spacetime's gravity field. The planet was only a hundred thousand kilometres away, although the SI didn't know that. *Or perhaps it does.*

The fear and worry which had slowly ebbed away over the last week suddenly resurged, elevating his heart rate. Tiny beads of sweat oozed up out of his pores, chilling his skin. Biononics smoothly countered the physiological aspects, but they couldn't quell his anxious thoughts. He couldn't begin to guess what was going on. *I don't understand people, fuck it. Why is Araminta doing this? Why is she trying to kill the galaxy? Why is she calling Oscar? And he must know she won't be meeting him.*

'You said Oscar's people are checking out the restaurant?'

'Yes. Two of them are physically deploying to cover the building. He's already on his way.'

'But he knows where Araminta is; he knows she won't be there. It must be a trap, yet he's going into it.'

'A trap set by whom? And why? And why now? No weapon in the galaxy can stop the Pilgrimage ships, we know that. Your Commonwealth Navy can't break through the force fields Ilanthe has provided, nor can the warrior Raiel.'

'Are you saying it isn't a trap?'

'I'm telling you what's happening, and offering to share.'

'Why? Why do you want to involve me?'

'To finally achieve what I've so often wrongly been accused of doing: influencing the outcome of human affairs. We must have more options ranged against Living Dream and Ilanthe. And the Cat, of course. You may yet be able to play a true part, Troblum. Do you want that?'

He looked across the cabin at Catriona, who was bestowing on him that worshipful look again. He put his head in his hands. *She's not real. Nothing I have is real.* With biononics amplifying his strength he suddenly thumped his fist down on top of the micromanipulator unit. It made a dull thudding sound, and some of the tiny components jittered around inside. His fist rose again. This time his biononics added a weapons pattern to the impact. The dome shattered, and the delicate little mechanisms inside were crushed beyond salvation. Electronic components scattered across the decking, ruined by both the violence and the air that contaminated their flimsy molecular structure.

'Show me,' he told the SI. 'And who is Mr Bovey?'

*

'Come alone.' Araminta had been insistent about that.

Oscar appreciated the sentiment, but ... Some things were just too big to leave to goodwill and pleasantries. He took a table in the middle of Andrew Rice's restaurant at the bottom of Daryad Avenue, an ancient (by Viotia standards) wood and carbon-panel building barely a mile from the docks where *Elvin's Payback* still sat in the warehouse, overlooked and unnoticed by the managers trying to restore order to the docks. There weren't many people in; the windows had just been replaced after being smashed. Oscar was sure it should have had more tables, too; the remaining ones were certainly spaced unusually far apart. Perhaps some had been looted. *Who loots a table?*

A human waiter came over to take his order, and he asked for a salad. He rather liked the look of the enormous steak and kidney pies a couple of blokes were eating at a corner table, but he'd only just finished his tea and twister. It had taken less than ten minutes to walk to Rice's from the *Elvin's Payback*, which was cause for mild suspicion. Did Araminta know their location? It was hard to see how.

Beckia was out in Daryad Avenue, keeping watch as she browsed through a recently reopened store opposite the restaurant. Cheriton had taken up position in a lane at the back, also scanning round for any sign of other agents or some kind of trap, or just something out of the ordinary. Oscar still couldn't figure out what was going on. The gaiafield quite clearly revealed Araminta standing in the observation deck of the *Lady's Light*, where she had remained for the last couple of days. Ethan and Taranse walked across the empty chamber to her, and bowed in unison.

'Embarkation is complete, Dreamer,' Taranse said. He looked exhausted but supremely content, a man who'd achieved his goal in life.

'Thank you,' she said. 'You have done a remarkable job.' She turned to Ethan. 'Are we ready to launch?'

'Yes,' he said with open delight. 'The ultradrives appear to be functional.'

'Very well. Please ask the captains to lift and set a course for the Void.'

'It will be done.'

'Is there any sign of Ilanthe?'

'No, Dreamer.'

'No matter. I'm sure she will make herself known before we reach the boundary.' She turned back to the tall strip of transparent fuselage in time to see the construction yard's last layer of force fields deactivate. It was dawn outside, a bright yellow-gold radiance illuminated the colossal Pilgrimage ships, and she smiled at the sight. Then the decking trembled and the *Lady's Light* slowly lifted out of its regrav suspension, rising into Ellezelin's clear sky.

'Holy crap,' Oscar grunted. He truly had no idea what he was doing here now. In fact he started to worry that Tomansio was right and Living Dream had broken into her mind so they could clear up any possible remaining problems. Which was bollocks, he knew. *Why wait until now?*

His salad arrived. He gave it a dispirited look.

'Ah, life just got interesting again,' Beckia said. 'Here we go.' Her link showed him a Mr Bovey climbing out of a cab on Daryad Avenue just outside the restaurant. It was the middle-aged black-skinned one Oscar had talked to before.

'Yes! Your money is mine,' Cheriton declared. 'Pay up.'

The team had been running a pool on who would actually show up at the restaurant. Oscar had put his money on the elusive cousin Cressida.

'Anything suspicious?' Oscar asked the rest of the team. Liatris, who was flying coverage over Colwyn City in a modified capsule, said no, the area was clear of any covert activity. Back in *Elvin's Payback*, Tomansio also reported a clean sweep.

The Mr Bovey walked straight into the restaurant and sat down next to Oscar. He was wearing a conservative grey toga suit that barely shimmered, which made him look quite dignified.

Oscar's biononics threw a small privacy cloak around the table. 'Mr Bovey,' he began in censure, which he was about to follow up with something along the lines of *what's she up to?* when the man simply grinned and shook his head. 'No,' he said emphatically. 'That's Mr Bovey over there keeping an eye on you.'

Oscar twisted round. The two men eating steak and kidney pies waved solemnly. 'I don't get . . .'

'I'm Araminta. Araminta-two, I suppose. I borrowed one of my fiancé's bodies. This one to be precise. I always liked this one.'

'Ungh?' Oscar grunted.

'I'm starting to go multiple. It's an interesting lifestyle, don't you think?' And he gave Oscar a lopsided smile.

'Fuck me.'

'Quite. You said you could help?'

'Oh shit yes!' Oscar's skin was actually tingling from astonishment. He couldn't help it: he started laughing in delight. *Maybe there is hope.* 'If you'd like to come with me . . .' Biononics and secondary thought routines had to regulate his neural responses, filtering down his adrenalin rush so he could concentrate properly on the mission. He had to stay focused.

Araminta-two gave him a modest shrug and stood up.

'Cover us,' Oscar told Beckia and Cheriton. 'Liatris, get us out of here.'

'Way ahead of you,' Liatris said.

Oscar couldn't remember being both elated and terrified to such an extent. If they were going to be intercepted, it would be now after this version of Araminta was identified for what s/he was. As they walked to the door he wanted to shove his integral force field up to full strength, activate all weapons enrichments. *Keep cool. Keep calm. It's a brilliant manoeuvre. No one could anticipate she'd do this.*

Liatris brought the ingrav capsule flashing down directly on to the pavement outside the restaurant, earning several angry glances from pedestrians who had to dodge out of the way. The door opened and Oscar virtually shoved Araminta-two inside. Then they were rising fast, already curving towards the docks.

Araminta-two nodded cheerfully at a thunderstruck Liatris, then looked round briefly. 'You know, some people think ingrav shouldn't be allowed in this city.'

'Right,' Oscar said.

'There's a chance it screws up the deep geology. There could be earthquakes.'

'Uh-huh.' This was so the opposite of anything Oscar was prepared for it had shifted over to vaguely surreal.

Their capsule dipped down to hover in front of the Bootle and Leicester warehouse. The doors curtained apart and they nudged forwards. Oscar just knew that was going to draw attention from the dock staff. It didn't matter any more. They had Araminta, so nothing else mattered. *Actually, one Araminta, not the whole person. Maybe that's why she – he – whatever – is a bit . . . flaky.*

Tomansio was in the middle of the starship's cabin as the three of them rose up through the airlock. The floor solidified underneath them. Oscar couldn't help the vast grin on his face. He jabbed a finger at Tomansio. 'I told you so!'

'Yes,' Tomansio said softly.

That was when Oscar's biononics told him Tomansio was executing an extremely thorough field scan of Araminta-two. He almost protested, then realized he should have done it back in the restaurant.

'Clear,' Tomansio declared. 'In fact, very clear. You don't have biononics, even your macrocellular clusters are basic.'

'Mr Bovey is multiple,' Araminta-two said. 'He doesn't depend upon the technocentric systems other Commonwealth cultures revolve around.'

Tomansio dipped his head. 'Of course. But you do understand what you're saying is difficult to accept without proof.'

'I know. Watch through me.'

The Dreamer's gifting to the gaiafield revealed her view through the front of the *Lady's Light*. From her position she could see the curvature of the planet starting to fall away below as the starship rose ponderously out of the atmosphere. The dawn terminator line was etched by a gold corona which skittered off ocean and clouds alike. The Dreamer's mouth opened. 'Trust me, Tomansio, I am very real,' she said.

Across the gaiafield, those billions of Living Dream members watching in envy as the Pilgrimage began reaffirmed their devotion to her. Tens of millions wondered who Tomansio was.

Araminta-two lifted an eyebrow at Tomansio. 'So?'

'Okay, that was pretty convincing. A multiple of two. Who'd have guessed?'

'Not you,' Araminta-two said.

'Let's hope I'm not alone.'

Oscar grinned again. 'I was right. She didn't betray us.'

'Oscar, I love you dearly,' Tomansio said. 'But if you don't shut up about that, I will shove you headfirst into—'

Oscar chuckled. 'Yeah yeah.' The smartcore showed him two capsules arriving in the warehouse. Beckia and Cheriton came sprinting out. It took the edge off his humour, slightly. He ordered the smartcore to launch as soon as the other two were in the airlock.

Tomansio gave him a startled look as the *Elvin's Payback* punched clean through the warehouse roof and accelerated vertically at twenty gees. The internal gravity countered some of the force, but they all had to sit down quickly in the couches extruded by the cabin floor.

'A little drastic?' Tomansio mused.

'Tactically smart. Up here we can run if we have to.'

'You're the boss.'

Beckia and Cheriton emerged from the airlock, and gave Araminta-two incredulous looks as they lumbered over to their acceleration couches.

Oscar's initial jubilation was draining away. Viotia spaceflight control was directing a lot of queries and warnings at them, but nothing appeared to be in pursuit. Space above the planet was relatively clear; none of the starships the sensors could detect were threatening. 'All right,' he said to Araminta-two. 'What the fuck is going on?'

'I was running out of options,' Araminta-two replied. 'Becoming the Dreamer is a diversion.' His confidence faltered for a moment. 'I hope. That's where you come in.'

'I wasn't lying,' Oscar said. 'We're here to help in any way we can.'

'Why? I know who you are, I checked. But I'd like to know who's backing you.'

'Fair enough; it was ANA, but now we're just hanging on by ourselves. Hoping for something to turn up. And . . . you did.'

'What do you need?' Tomansio asked. 'Are you going to crash the Pilgrimage fleet into the boundary or something?'

Araminta-two's dignified face produced a sad smile, making him look even older. 'There are twenty-four million people on those starships. Idiots, yes, but still people. There is no way I will slaughter them as an example to the rest of the galaxy not to go in. No, if they arrive at the Void boundary before we can stop them, then I'll have get the Skylord to open the way for them. So you see, I really need help.'

'Name it,' Oscar said.

'Bradley suggested I find Ozzie. He said Ozzie is a real genius, and if anyone can come up with a solution it will be us in combination.'

Oscar's skin chilled right down. 'Bradley?' he asked lightly. The others gave him a curious look. It must have been because of what his emotions revealed.

'Bradley Johansson,' Araminta-two said. 'I met him on the Silfen paths.'

'Bradley Johansson is alive?'

'Bradley is a Silfen now.'

'Holy crap.'

'Do you speak the truth of this?' Tomansio demanded almost in anger.

Araminta-two faced him down. 'I speak the truth.' He turned back to Oscar. 'Bradley told me you and he fought together in the Starflyer War, he said I could trust you, Oscar. And you did help me back at Bodant Park.'

'Bradley a Silfen,' Oscar said in wonder. 'How about that? We both survived the Planet's Revenge in our own ways.'

'He lives,' an incredulous Beckia murmured. 'The greatest of us all, our founder, humanity's liberator. He lives! Do you realize what . . .' She broke off, too overwhelmed to speak.

'I don't wish to disappoint,' Araminta-two said. 'But he's not coming to help. I'm afraid the best he could do was send me.'

'And he wanted you and Ozzie to team up?' Oscar queried.

'Yes. Um, he was also worried about the Ilanthe-thing and what it is now. Even the Silfen are concerned about that, as much as they are about anything.'

'Nobody knows much about Ilanthe,' Oscar said. 'So let's concentrate on what we can achieve.' He opened a secure link to Paula.

'Take her to Ozzie,' Paula said as soon as he'd finished explaining.

'Really?'

'Bradley is right. The Dreamer and Ozzie together would make a formidable combination.'

'All right then.'

'And . . . Araminta really met Bradley?'

'Yeah, so she says. Something, huh?'

'Indeed.'

'So where's Ozzie these days?'

'The Spike.'

'No shit, Paula, that's seven thousand lightyears away.'

'I know. But face it, what else have we got? We're that desperate now.'

'Okay.' The *Elvin's Payback* had finished its initial acceleration. It was curving into a wide elliptical orbit above Viotia. Oscar grinned at Araminta-two. 'Ozzie's in the Spike. It'll take five days to get there.'

'Then let's go.'

'Great.' He gave a relieved smile.

'A word of caution,' Paula said, which brought Oscar down fast.

'Yeah?'

'I believe someone called Aaron has possibly taken Inigo to the Spike for exactly the same reason you're going, to link up with Ozzie.'

'Oh crap.' He glanced round to see the team all giving him a vaguely accusatory stare. 'Inigo? They found Inigo?'

'Yes. Which I'm hoping is good. If you can bring together the First and Second Dreamers along with Ozzie, that may really give us the kind of edge we're going to need to—'

'Take out the Void? Blow up the Pilgrimage fleet? Eliminate Ilanthe?'

'I'd settle for any one of those right now.'

'So who is this Aaron character and who is he working for?'

'I'm sorry, I don't know. But logically he belongs to a Faction inimical to Pilgrimage. And be careful, he can be very trigger-happy, and he's known to be somewhat aggressive with it. Your team should be able to protect Araminta from him if he turns hostile.'

'Okay. What about you, Paula, what are you doing?'

'Working on a couple of leads, as always.'

Feeling slightly let down by her reply, Oscar ordered the smartcore to go ftl and take them to the Spike. Then he and the others started questioning Araminta-two in earnest.

'What will you do now?' the SI asked Troblum as the *Mellanie's Redemption* tracked Oscar's starship going ftl. It suddenly vanished from his exovision. None of the sensors could track it when it was stealthed.

'I don't know,' he said unsteadily. The conversation between Oscar and Paula, which the SI had intercepted, had left him badly shaken. Both Dreamers and Ozzie coming together to solve the problem was cause for some tentative hope. 'I can't make a difference.'

'You know more about the Sol barrier than any other individual. They might need that.'

'I don't know.' It was too big, too much, and getting horribly personal again. But it was a huge unexpected relief to solve the Araminta puzzle. She hadn't betrayed anyone, she was doing what she could. *And . . . Araminta, Inigo, Oscar and Ozzie together. That's going to be history.*

Catriona came over and sat on his lap. She was wearing a thin lacy top and tight jeans. The feel of her resting there, human scent and musky perfume, her perfect form centimetres from his eyes. It was comforting somehow.

'We should go,' she told him softly.

'Yes.' Even that made him feel good.

Sensors showed Paula the *Elvin's Payback* flash into hyperspace and activate its stealth. She could track it of course, though few other ships in the galaxy could.

After a minute, the ship hanging in suspension a hundred thousand kilometres above Viotia also pushed back fully into hyperspace, and followed Oscar at ultradrive speed. Its stealth wasn't as good as the ANA ship, but its drive seemed more than capable; and the real giveaway was the mass. It was identical to the *Mellanie's Redemption*, which Paula had last seen departing Sholapur at mere hyperdrive speeds.

'And then there was one,' Paula muttered.

The remaining stealthed ship started to move. Its drive signature was one the *Alexis Denken* was also familiar with from Sholapur, as was the much superior stealth effect. Paula ordered the smartcore to follow the other three starships to the Spike, then opened a secure link to the *High Angel*.

'Hello, Paula,' Qatux said.

'So you can't break through the Sol barrier?'

'No. Our trip here was largely symbolic, a statement of Raiel support for the rest of the Commonwealth.'

'I don't expect empty political gestures from you.'

'If there is any way we can influence the Living Dream from their Pilgrimage we are obliged to enact it.'

'They've just launched.'

'I know. Paula, if you would like to come with us when this galaxy falls, I will be happy to take you.'

'I know the purpose of the *High Angel* is supposed to be to save life from this galaxy, but something is happening, Qatux, something my instinct tells me is crucial. So I'm going to need a favour. A very big favour.'

*

The lake measured over ten kilometres across, its shoreline made up of attractive sweeping coves. Two thirds of the surrounding land was smothered by a thick wild forest, with vegetation scrambling down over the stones which lined the rippling water. The remaining third was an alien city whose globes and spikes dominated the skyline. Deserted for millennia, its iron structures were a similar construction to those of Octoron's little human township. But this metropolis was put together on a much grander scale. Perhaps a little too imposing: humans living in the chamber had never attempted to settle there.

Ozzie's old capsule skimmed above the thin towers and dropped down towards the huge semicircular harbour bay on the other side. There were several small islands dotted across the water. They were heading for the largest, which had a wide sandy beach guarded by rocky prominences on either side. Behind the beach itself the land was a cluster of long dunes before the ground started to slope up into the island's central mountain. A simple whitewashed stone house stood alone, poised between dunes and the forested slope. It was surrounded on three sides by a veranda that had a leafy canopy of thick vines draped over an ancient, sagging wooden frame. Tall sash windows had wooden shutters on the outside, giving the place the appearance of a farmhouse from rural Provence.

The capsule touched down in front of the solitary building. Aaron scanned it briefly. Another human was lurking behind the wide slatted doors that opened from the lounge to the veranda decking. She had biononics, but they weren't weapons-configured.

There were some additional enrichments that he didn't recognize, but their low power usage argued against them posing any kind of threat. The house itself had a few technological items, a culinary unit, medical capsule, two very sophisticated replicators, a fleet of old-fashioned maidbots, and five smartcores larger than he'd encountered before. In short, the perfect retreat for someone like Ozzie.

'Okay, we can go out,' Aaron said.

Ozzie gave him a long look. 'You sure?'

'Yes.'

'Well okay, but be careful of the mutant squids in the lake.'

'I appreciate this intrusion is unwelcome, we'll be gone as soon as we can.' Though Aaron couldn't be sure of that. Ideas were starting to form in the back of his mind in anticipation of Inigo regaining consciousness. He gave the sleeping messiah a quick look. It wouldn't be long before he was awake.

'And remember never to leave the house at night,' Ozzie said with an innocent tone which nonetheless mocked.

'Why?'

'Vampires.'

Aaron bit back on his response. He wasn't quite sure how much of Ozzie's attitude was driven by irritation at having his hermit life violated. If it was genuine, things might get unpleasant. Aaron hoped not.

Ozzie walked out of the capsule, leaving Aaron to deal with the two unconscious people sprawled on the curving leather couch at the back of the passenger section. 'Greatly done,' he muttered and picked Inigo up, fumbling him into a traditional fireman's lift. For a long moment he was tempted to shoot another sedative (or ten) into Corrie-Lyn, but Inigo wouldn't be happy about that. And having two bolshie living legends with overblown egos pissed off with him would be a definite disadvantage.

Aaron carried Inigo over the dunes, and up the grey wooden steps to the veranda. He dumped the inert body onto a sunlounger and went back for Corrie-Lyn.

Ozzie was nowhere to be seen by the time he got back to the veranda. A quick low-level field scan showed him upstairs in the house's biggest bedroom with the woman. Aaron abruptly cancelled the scan, trying to quash his feeling of dismay at Ozzie's attitude and behaviour. He hadn't expected quite this much irrational stubbornness.

Inigo groaned and stirred. His biononics assisted a quick rise to full awareness. He sat up and looked round the shaded veranda, then took a moment to stare at the vista of the ancient alien city facing him across the bay.

'We made it then?'

'We made it.'

Inigo gazed over at Corrie-Lyn on the next sunlounger. 'How is she?'

'Stable. She should wake up in half an hour or so. Your biononics give you an advantage.'

Inigo nodded slowly. 'You kept your word. Thank you.'

'I know she hates me, but truly I'm not one of the bad guys. I just have a job to do.'

'Indeed.' Inigo started flexing his limbs, grimacing at the chemical-induced stiffness. 'What do you do for fun?'

'I don't.'

Inigo gave the city another look. 'That looks deserted.'

'It is. Ozzie has fully embraced his whole living recluse legend.'

'Great Lady, you actually found him?'

'Yes.'

Inigo peered round, unable to contain his excitement. 'So where is he?'

Aaron held up a finger for silence. On cue a woman's rhythmic groans could be heard from the open bedroom window.

'Ah,' Inigo muttered. 'What's he like?'

'Not pleased to see me, and especially not you.'

'Yeah. We never did hit it off.' He stood up cautiously and

went over to Corrie-Lyn. His field scan ran a fast check. 'So what's the plan?'

'I'll tell you when Ozzie comes down.'

'Whatever.' Inigo wandered into the house and found the kitchen. After a burst of enthusiastic compliments at discovering the culinary unit sitting amid all the historic cooking appliances he started issuing it with a complicated list. Several maidbots followed him back out to the veranda carrying contemporary dishes. A meal for two.

Corrie-Lyn finally shook off the sedative amid a flurry of cursing and groans. After a moment hugging a relieved Inigo she shot Aaron a vicious glare. 'Bastard.'

'We're alive. The Chikoya can't locate us. And I've found Ozzie.'

'So where is he?'

'I'm sure he'll join us soon.'

'He's not happy about this,' Inigo explained.

'Tell him to get in line.' But she relented when Inigo led her over to the table where the maidbots had laid out the meal. 'Oh wow, real food.' She hesitated.

'It's genuine,' Inigo reassured her.

She grinned her gratitude and started wolfing down the keanfish starter, dipping the tassels into a plum and rador sauce. Aaron went into the kitchen and ordered up his own meal from the culinary unit, eating it alone on the scrubbed pine table.

An hour later Ozzie still hadn't come down. It was pushing the screw-you point a little far, Aaron decided. Inigo and Corrie-Lyn were chatting happily on the veranda, holding hands at the table like a couple on a first date as they finished their second bottle of wine. All the scene lacked was candles and twilight. The chamber's light hadn't varied since they'd arrived.

Aaron went upstairs and knocked politely on the bedroom door. There was no answer. Ozzie was being deliberately difficult, which was understandable but unacceptable. He went into the room. It was dark inside, with the big wooden shutters closed and the slats down. Ozzie and the woman were cuddled up on the bed. The woman was sleeping. Colourful patterns on her space-black body glowed in phosphorescent hues, shifting slowly in time with her breathing. Aaron hesitated at that. They reminded him of OCtattoos – a technology from so long ago he didn't even understand where the memory had come from. Ozzie raised his head and peered at Aaron. 'What, dude?'

'Quicker we start, the quicker it's over.'

'This is the middle of the night, you moron.'

Aaron gestured at the light spilling in through the open door.

'Yeah? So? The light never goes out in Octoron. You make your own days here, man. And this is my night. Now take a hike.'

'No. You come downstairs now and greet Inigo.'

'Or what?'

'I start getting unpleasant.'

'Fucking fascist.' Ozzie slithered off the bed muttering. 'Drown in your own shit,' He found a silk robe and tugged the belt tight emphatically. 'Used to some goddamn respect in my own home.' He combed his fingers through his mass of wavering wayward hair.

'I know. Turn your back for a moment and the whole Ozziedamned universe falls to barbarism.'

Ozzie glared at him for a long moment. It actually made Aaron nervous. Secondary routines poised to activate his bion-onic defences.

'Don't push it, creepy-boy,' Ozzie growled out.

'Sorry, but you're not making my life easy.'

Ozzie stomped past him out onto the first-floor landing. 'That's not what I was born to do.'

'So what with all this daylight I guess I don't have to worry myself too much over those vampires?' Aaron said to the legend's back.

Inigo and Corrie-Lyn glanced round as Ozzie walked out onto the veranda, looking for all the world like guilty school kids. Inigo started to get up. 'This wasn't my idea, but I'm genuinely pleased we can finally—' he began.

'No shit, asshole.' Ozzie dropped down hard in one of the chairs round the table. He gave the remains of the meal a suspicious look, and picked up a tantrene sausage. 'Get on with it.'

'Okay then. So what's the plan?' Inigo asked Aaron.

Aaron sat at the table, trying to project the impression of reasonable moderator. 'My original goal was to take you into the Void,' he told Inigo. 'The intention was to establish a link with the Heart or nucleus, or whatever it is that has sentient control of high-level functions in there. With that communication channel open it was hoped to initiate negotiations.'

Ozzie shrugged. 'Makes sense in a lame-ass sort of way. We know we can't shoot the thing down or blow it up. Who would negotiate?'

'I'm not aware what form the negotiations were to take. My job was to secure the link. After that . . . I'd know.'

'How in the Lady's name was I supposed to start talking to the Heart?' Inigo asked incredulously. 'Haven't you people shared any of my dreams? You only reach the Heart after you have achieved fulfilment.'

'There is a methodology, I know,' Aaron said. 'That is, I'm certain I have procedures to follow once we get inside.'

Inigo threw up his hands and slumped back in his chair for a sulk.

'Told you so,' Corrie-Lyn said smugly. 'This whole mission is a complete waste of time. You murdered hundreds of people for *nothing*.'

'So why come here, man?' Ozzie asked. 'Why me? Everyone who knows me in the Commonwealth knows I don't do this kind of shit any more. And your boss knows me, too much.'

'There are several ways I would expect you to help. One would be an ultradrive ship we can use to fly to the Void.'

'Dude, you need to stay current. Okay, first off I don't have an ultradrive. If I need that kind of shit ... well let's just say I've got an arrangement with ANA. It'll send me one if I ask. But we can't ask any more, can we? Second, your replacement,' he stabbed a forefinger at Inigo, 'has just launched.'

'The Pilgrimage?' Corrie-Lyn asked. There was awe in her voice.

'Oh yeah, babe. They're truly that dumb.'

'How do you know?' Aaron asked.

'Myraian grooves all that cruddy gossip from the Commonwealth.'

'Myraian? The lady upstairs?'

'Yeah. The lady upstairs. Who, I'll tell you for free, is mighty peed off with all of you right now, not least over mindspace crashing; so watch your mouth. I got a private TD link from the Spike to the Commonwealth. So even if you're out of *my* gaiafield's range you can still get to dig what Araminta's been doing.'

Inigo ignored the jibe about the gaiafield. 'It will take them months to reach the Void, so—'

Ozzie's harsh laughter cut him off. 'Seriously, man, you need to get current. I'm going to open my house net for you to access. Catch up, and we'll talk again in the morning. You know, before you leave in a cloud of gloom and defeat.'

He left them on the veranda and went back upstairs. At the last he opened his gaiamotes a fraction.

Inigo didn't like the arrogance he exuded one little bit. It verged on smugness. Standard communication icons were slipping up into his exovision as the house's nodes acknowledged his u-shadow. 'We'd better see what's been going on,' he said.

'Yeah,' Aaron agreed. His gaiamotes gave nothing away, but he sounded troubled.

Ozzie's temper had improved mildly when he came down for breakfast the next morning. That was deliberately quite a while after he'd woken the first time. He and Myraian had gone at it like they had the night before, and after that he'd dozed contentedly for an hour. Then there was a shower, none of that modern itchy spore crap that clogged up his hair, a proper hot water and scented gel affair. Myraian hadn't joined him, which was a shame but you couldn't have everything in life – well actually you could if you'd lived as long as him, but then you learned not to be too demanding of people. They were transient enough without the stresses and strains everyone unwittingly put on a relationship. It had taken a long time for him to learn why it was women never stayed with him beyond a couple of decades, so now he knew how to treat them right. Or at least fake treating them right.

Myraian was dressed and ready when he finally came out of the bathroom in his shorts and T-shirt. She'd resequenced herself back to her mid-twenties then tweaked various chromosomes to produce a great figure; which in combination with a mind that was away mushrooming with fairies most of the time made her utterly irresistible to him. *No accounting for some things, but she's perfect for me at this time of life.* He took an enjoyable look at the thin ankle-length skirt of sky-blue cotton and black mesh shirt that, with her skin colour, made it look like she was wearing nothing at all. Her skinlight patterns shone through the thin weave, creating weird diffusion ripples. 'Cool combo,' he told her. 'Kinda earth-mother meets dominatrix.'

'Thank you.' She shook her hair, allowing the long blond, auburn and pink tresses to sway round her head in an underwater slow motion as the fluff-fronds elevated it.

And no way was he ever putting them in no matter how much she nagged. 'Let's go catch them crying into their tea cups.'

She pouted. 'You should stay up here. I'll teach them not to bully my baby Ozzie.'

'They're not nice people,' he told her again, hoping it registered this time. 'Don't let them bug you. And really, man, don't get cross with them. I don't want any of that.'

'I'll eat them up, scrummy yummy,' she promised.

'Yeah.' *Okay, maybe it's not so much the mind that's the attraction.*

He found Aaron, Inigo and Corrie-Lyn in the lounge,

slouched across the couches and looking slightly dazed, like a bunch of students from his time at Caltech pulling an all-nighter. The only thing missing was the pizza boxes. They did stare a little at Myraian but didn't say anything. Ozzie wasn't really surprised when it was Corrie-Lyn who rounded on him first. She reminded him of not a few ex-wives.

'You knew! You knew you're going to die in the expansion and you won't do *anything* to help us?' she barked.

'I normally have orange juice, coffee and toast for breakfast. Man, the old habits are the hardest to break, don't you find?' His u-shadow gave the culinary unit its instructions.

She just growled at him.

'You don't get it,' Ozzie told her. 'You don't get *me*. Dude, I'm over one and a half thousand years old. I've seen it all, and I do mean all! I can live with dying.'

'But what about the rest of the galaxy? All the people who don't get a chance to live as you have? The children?'

'Wow! Dude, *big* shift there from one of the most truly devout Living Dream disciples *ever*.'

'Cleric Councillor,' Myraian said distantly as her hair fronds swam about lazily. 'The Dreamer's lover. Chief prosecutor in the Edgemon heresy tribunal.'

'That was not . . .' Corrie-Lyn ground to a halt, furious.

'If you're so worried about what you've unleashed on the rest of us, why don't you rush into your precious Void and be safe?' Ozzie challenged.

'Enjoy your victory,' Inigo said softly. 'The Void is not our salvation. I was wrong to hold it out as a symbol of attainable nirvana, of a life that can be perfect. It is none of those things. I. Was. Wrong.'

'Crap,' Ozzie muttered. It wasn't often he was rendered speechless, but a messiah renouncing his life's work could certainly do it every time. 'I'll make that a big pot of coffee. You'd better all join me for breakfast.'

'We all understand the Void threat well enough,' Aaron said as the maidbots slid around the table in the kitchen, delivering plates and cups. 'I'm interested in your take on whatever Ilanthe has become. That could be a big factor in the expansion.'

'She was the leader of the Accelerator Faction,' Ozzie said as he accepted his glass of chilled orange juice from the maidbot. 'The original idea was that they elevate themselves up to post-physical status courtesy of the Void. Thing is,' he scratched at his hair, 'the Accelerator Faction is trapped behind the Sol barrier along with the rest of ANA, so they can't pull off their whole Fusion concept. And the Silfen Motherholm is worried about her, which is new to me. Nothing gets that placid goddess riled. Nothing. Till now. Draw yourself a map.'

'The Silfen Motherholm?' Corrie-Lyn asked cautiously.

'Sure, babe, I'm a Silfen Friend.' He tried not to sound too smug, settling for merely superior. 'I know what's going down across the galaxy.'

'Ozzie is the father of our species' mind,' Myraian announced; her skinlight glowed a proud mauve.

There was a polite silence for a moment.

'Of everything that's happened I find her involvement the most disturbing,' Inigo said. 'It was inevitable Living Dream would be corrupted and manipulated after I turned it over to the Cleric Council – that was the point of me abandoning it as I did. But I never envisaged anything like this. Ultradrives, unbreakable force fields . . . this was not meant to be.'

Aaron turned to Ozzie. 'Do you know anything about these technologies?'

'Not really my field,' Ozzie said quietly. He waited.

'It used to be,' an omnidirectional voice spoke up. Ozzie let out an exasperated breath. It was his own voice. 'Just shut the fuck up,' he told it.

'You'd like that, wouldn't you? Nobody can run from their past. Not forever, *dooode*.'

'What is this?' Aaron asked.

'I told you, dude,' Ozzie said with an edge. 'I'm ancient. Human bodies aren't designed with this kind of lifespan in mind. Grab the "in mind" bit there? Back in the first-era

Commonwealth when all we had was rejuve we used to edit memories and store the ones that *weren't important*. Then there were memorycells, and neural augmentation chips. Biononics added a whole load of new memory capacity. And there's always an expanded mentality network.' He raised his head and glared at a random point on the ceiling. 'That's if you want to carry all that junk round contaminating your body. I didn't. Not any more.'

'So he dumped me,' the voice said. 'Literally. I'm Ozzie. The real Ozzie.'

'You're a goddamn me-brain-in-a-jar and don't you forget it,' Ozzie told it crossly.

'Seriously,' the voice said. 'I'm one and a half thousand years of memories, while you're what? Twenty years' worth? Who's the most real of them all?'

'Only one of us got to keep the personality, man,' Ozzie shouted back. 'I'm the biochemical, hormonal, awkward, sonofa-bitch soul of a human. You're the hardwired Xerox that's frozen in the past.'

'You can mouth off all you like, but I'm the one with the knowledge and talent that these fine and sincerely desperate people need. You got rid of all the serious physics and math and shit clogging up your little meat brain. Admit it, tell them. Be a man. As much as you can be with so much missing.'

'Ozzie lacks nothing,' Myraian said calmly. 'He has purged himself at a spiritual level to make himself complete again. You are the contamination that was holding him back, preventing the angel within from spreading his wings. He's been clean for decades now, and grown because of it.' She smiled wide.

Ozzie caught the narrowing of Aaron's eyes as he noticed the tiny fangs which that otherwise blissful smile revealed.

Aaron blinked and put his hands down on the table. 'Okay. Please tell me you can access and assimilate whatever knowledge you need from . . . you?'

'From the me-brain-in-a-jar? Sure. I retained autonomous integration for the smartcores I stuffed it into – me into.'

Inigo gave Ozzie a bemused grin; there was respect in there, too. 'I'm sure you can. But let's face it: there's you, me, and him.' He jabbed a thumb at Aaron. 'A smartass smartcore and a reasonably good replicator. Doesn't matter how good we all are in combination, we're not going to bootstrap ourselves a superweapon to smash open the Sol barrier, or an even faster ultradrive that'll get us to the Void before Araminta charges in. And that's not even talking about the Ilanthe-thing.'

'Yeah,' Ozzie admitted. 'But, man, on the plus side I can get us out of here safely. Qatux owes me. The *High Angel* will stop by and collect us on its way to Andromeda or wherever the hell it's going.'

'No,' Aaron said. 'You're not abandoning hope after half an hour. And I don't believe I even have to threaten anyone or anything to make that come about, now do I?'

'No,' Inigo sighed.

'Our goal is to connect you somehow to the Void Heart,' Aaron said. 'Now I'm not the greatest self-thinker any more but you're the smartest guys I know with the weirdest of blessings. You'll come up with something.'

'Fair enough,' Inigo said. 'What about your telepathy effect, Ozzie? Can we talk to the Void that way?'

Ozzie shoved the empty glass away and reached for the plate of toast. 'Okay, this is how it works. The gaiafield is a broadcast medium: you transmit your thoughts out through the motes and they zip across space to connect with everyone else's motes. Confluence nests are just powerful amplifiers and relay stations, they're what turn it into a "field". Admittedly it's a big field, but step outside the Commonwealth and you're on your own. Now there are other, similar, fields out there, with the Silfen commun-ion the biggest of them all. It's truly galaxy-spanning, dude. I know. I'm tuned in. But it's not so dense as the gaiafield, that's down to species psychology. The superelves don't have the same urge to carry every boring stream-of-consciousness drivel as humans crave.'

'So?' Aaron asked.

'We can't use the gaiafield, it can't extend to the centre of the galaxy.'

'Not quite right,' Corrie-Lyn said. 'The Pilgrimage fleet will be dropping a series of confluence nests en route. That was always the plan, and Ethan won't change that aspect. They'll do for the gaiafield the same as the Navy TD relays did for Centurion Station. The idea is to open a permanent dream channel to the Void so the faithful who weren't in the fleet can witness everyone reaching fulfilment, and rush to follow them.'

'And the instant we try using that, Ethan will shut it down,' Inigo said.

'Last resort,' Corrie-Lyn said. 'The hack might last long enough, especially as it's you, the true original Dreamer. You still have more clout than anyone else in the movement.'

'I doubt that now Araminta has appeared,' Inigo said.

'Yeah, useful to know,' Ozzie agreed. 'Okay, mindspace. Now that's something different. I rearranged spacetime's quantum structure so that it becomes a conductor for thought, same as air conducts sound. Admittedly it works best for human thoughts, that's what I worked with to synchronize it with at the beginning. Aliens are aware of it, but for them it's like the Silfen communion is for humans: vague. Unless you're the goddamned Chikoya, then you think it's a doorway into the thoughts of your ancestors. What is it about avian culture that makes them worship their ancestors like that? It's got to be a hundred thousand years since their wings were big enough to actually carry them, yet every space habitat they ever built is zero gee so they can flap about with all the grace of a chicken falling off a wall. Even here they're in a lograv compartment.'

'They will find enlightenment in the end,' Myraian said. 'You are worthy of that. Your galactic dream will lead all of us out of the darkness.'

'Thanks babe,' he said. 'The point of it was to have something which allows people to share their thoughts in a more open way. Confluence nests contaminate the purity of thoughts, they allow distortions, partial thoughts with the emphasis where the origi-nator desires, perverting the whole truth.'

'Do we have to do this now?' Corrie-Lyn asked with deceptive lightness.

'Just telling you the why of it so you'll understand. That's the reason I set up mindspace. But both notions have the same problem: reach. Bluntly, they need power to stretch that far.'

'What powers the mindspace?' Inigo asked.

Ozzie winced. 'Ah, well, see, I kinda *adjusted* the Spike's anchor mechanism to propagate the change to spacetime which makes mindspace work. There's a device, sort of a parasite, really. But its emissions aren't directional. You can't squirt it round like a laser. The whole concept of mindspace was to embrace all sentient entities in the galaxy.'

'But it doesn't,' Aaron said curtly. 'Aliens have trouble utiliz-ing it.'

'Yeah, well, this is the marque one, dude. I just need to do some fine-tuning is all. The theory works.'

'He's had decades,' the voice from the house's smartcores said. 'All he's done around here since we built the anchor modifier is bum around finding his inner geek. Progress zero.'

'Hey, screw you,' Ozzie snarled. 'Experimenting on alien brains might be your bang but it ain't mine, not any more.'

'You don't have to experiment on anything. You were just frightened, that's all. Frightened different minds and exotic thoughts would find a way of corrupting mindspace the way the gaiafield went.'

'I'm observing the psychosocial implications of mindspace's impact on alien cultures, and you goddamn well know that. A genuine galactic dream isn't something you rush into. I made that mistake before.'

'And the kind of freaks who come to the Spike for refuge are such good representatives of their societies.'

'Damn, I used to be a bigot.'

'You used to be honest with yourself. You know goddamn

well you're struggling with the right of imposing it on species who have no understanding of what they are relative to the universe. It is cultural imperialism in its worst possible form. Our way of thinking is better than yours, so come join us.'

'Universal understanding might have prevented the Pilgrimage.'

'Is there any way you can increase the power from the anchor?' Inigo asked. 'Maybe just on a temporary basis?'

'No way, man. And I don't need my brain-in-a-jar thoughts to confirm that. We're at the limit of the anchor's capacity now. Hell, mindspace reached over two hundred and fifty lightyears, that's pretty goddamn phenomenal. In any case, there's no knowing if the Heart would mesh with mindspace.' He took a drink of the coffee before it cooled down any further. 'So that leaves us with you.'

'Me?' Inigo queried.

'You dreamed the Void from thirty thousand lightyears away. No booster circuitry involved. You have an inbuilt connection. How did you do that?'

'I don't know, I never did understand. The best anyone came up with was that Edeard and I were related somehow. Could be, but we'll never know. I connected to a human. There aren't any left in the Void now. The Skylord was quite clear about that when Justine asked.'

'You mean a Skylord like the one Araminta is talking to? She can do it. Have you even tried?'

'Whatever curse she has it's different to mine.'

'Have you tried?' Ozzie asked more forcefully.

'No.'

'No, of course not.' He turned to Aaron. 'And you, you're desperate for this link. Did you ever consider hunting Gore down? The Third Dreamer, Lord help us. He's got a working connection to Justine who is right where you need her.'

'That's outside ... I don't have, that is I'm not aware of contingencies to contact Gore.'

'Because it's a new development,' Corrie-Lyn said scathingly.

'You can't think for yourself. And the Lady knows nobody else is allowed a say in your universe.'

'So, big thanks there for all the drama yesterday,' Ozzie said. 'But actually you already have two proven methods of getting your voice heard inside the Void.'

'Can you reach a Skylord?' Aaron asked Inigo.

'Dreaming is not a function I can simply activate by touching its "go" icon. I have to admit, Araminta seems to have a lot more control over the ability than I ever had.'

'A Skylord would never go to the Heart, not even for the Dreamer,' Corrie-Lyn said. 'This we know above all else. They only take those who are fulfilled.'

'I doubt it would even understand the concept of talking to the Heart for us,' Inigo said.

'So your safest bet is to scram back to the Commonwealth and ask Gore to help,' Ozzie observed. 'He was acting like he knew what he was doing.'

'This mission is based on getting Inigo physically into the Void,' Aaron said. 'In a last-ditch emergency mental contact is permissible providing it allows the next stage to progress. I will not deviate from that.'

'What next stage?' Ozzie asked in fascination.

Aaron thought for a moment, his face drawn up to reflect inner discomfort of some nature. 'When we make contact I will know what to do.'

'Dude, if I'm going to help I need to know more. Look, I've got a really advanced medical module down in the basement. What say we drop you in and allow some neural unblocking?'

'No.'

Ozzie grunted disapproval. He wasn't surprised, but Aaron's crazy mental programming was starting to bug him.

'What part of the Void are you supposed to take me to?' Inigo asked.

'Makkathran,' Aaron replied without hesitation.

'Interesting. Not a Starflyer. Does that destination still apply now we know Querencia is no longer inhabited by humans?'

'I think so, yes.'

'I never bothered with your dreams,' Ozzie said. 'What's in Makkathran that can put us in touch with the Heart?'

'Nothing,' a puzzled Inigo admitted.

'If we don't have an ultradrive ship available, and mindspace cannot reach the Void from here, is it possible to move the Spike until we're within range?' Aaron asked.

Myraian let out a wild giggling laugh.

'You've got to be fucking kidding me,' Ozzie barked.

'So the anchor mechanism isn't an ftl drive?'

'No.'

'It is unlikely, but we don't know for sure,' the house's smart-cores said.

Aaron gave Ozzie a quizzical glance.

'Oh yeah,' Ozzie snapped. 'We can examine its unmapped functions, work them out and get it to fly across the galaxy all in a week. Dude you've got to break through that brainlock and start thinking for yourself. The Spike's anchor mechanism is bigger than this whole chamber, and that's just the chunk that's in spacetime.'

'I need to be sure you are considering all options,' Aaron said.

'Grab this straight. I am not going to start messing with the anchor mechanism. No way, no how.'

'If that is the method by which we can connect with the Heart then that is what will have to be done.'

'There's a universe of choice out there, dude. Go exploring one day.'

'So will you help us find a way of connecting to the Heart?' Inigo asked.

Ozzie studied the ex-messiah for a long moment, trying to work him out and failing miserably. Eventually he gave up. 'Okay, I just don't get it. I've had my share of doubts, and I've screwed up plenty of times in my life so I can be big enough to admit them from time to time. But this? What the fuck happened, man? You had a gospel powerful enough to attract billions to your cause. What could there possibly be to make you turn your back on them? Edeard was a bit of a dick, for sure, but he came good in the end. That's the moral message all religions pump out, it's a standard hook. Humans triumph over adversity. Throw in a bit of suffering along the way and people dig that bigtime. And your guy won.'

'No he didn't,' Inigo said sadly.

'All right, I lied before. I took the occasional peek at your dreams. That last one: man, he went to the Heart knowing the world he left behind was the best it was possible to build. Then on top of that he gave everyone the chance to perfect their individual lives like he'd done. How's that for total selflessness? If he'd been around out here three thousand years ago he'd be a genuine saint, or worse.'

'Perfection,' Inigo said, 'is what we strive for, it is never what we should achieve. There is no such thing as utopia. Life by its nature is a struggle. Take that away and you take away any reason to exist.'

'What happened?' Corrie-Lyn entreated. 'Please Inigo, what did you dream after Edeard accepted guidance to the Heart? Just tell us. Tell me. I trust you with this. I always will. But I think I deserve to know.'

'I dreamed of perfection.'

Inigo's Last Dream

I wish to fly.

My mind elevates my body. Thus do I fly with arms out-stretched to feel the wind upon my face. It is pleasurable. I open my eyes. A hundred feet below me is Great Major Canal. Dark water cool and calming fills its long channel. Sunlight ripples across its surface. Traditional gondolas are slivers of blackness amid its elegance, manifested for this hour alone. A harmonious song rises through the air from the gondoliers themselves, a sweet melody evoking an older, poignant time.

Honour.

We do honour the great ancestor, our Waterwalker. This day a thousand years ago he ascended to the Heart which calls us all. So do all of us who remain upon this blessed world gather in this ancient place to pay tribute.

Pride.

I have pride to be the Waterwalker's bloodline descendant. Through his twins I was birthed into existence no less. Joy I feel at their fullness of life. Their grandson's granddaughter is my mother. From that I reach for his nobility, his strength.

My family.

My family flies with me. Full seven of us soaring above the

ancient buildings of this revered city. Laughing, delighting in the sight of such wonder. Deep deep below us the citymind slumbers onwards towards the end of time. It is sorrow that radiates outward from its slow dreams. Sorrow we also feel at its submission to misplaced destiny. Respect we show for its right to be. Though today all have the strength, none will wake it.

Our life.

Our life is lived in a home on the slopes above the sea in far Tolonan. An island discovered by the Waterwalker's flotilla so long ago. A lush place of warmth and beauty, its trees bloom with flower the full year around, their scent enriching the air. Vineyards and orchards still thrive on the old terraced slopes, producing abundance. Such traditions we still follow, commemorating our ancestors and the life they struggled through to bring us to the light of our day. The fruit is succulent and flavoursome, the wine sweet. Our bellies fill each day. We lack for nothing. We experience everything. For this we give thanks.

The towers.

How beautiful the pinnacles of Eyrie are, tall yet curving with exotic grace and style. We fly around them like spirited birds, twisting through the platform spires as we laugh exuberantly, then suddenly veering upwards to soar vertically like an essence ascending to those who guide. What exhilaration, what elation.

My choices.

To kindle the gift of thought, and ponder the rich occasions and chances sentience brings. So much I have considered throughout my existence. So many sights I have seen on this world. I have lived on every continent. I have tasted every plant that is eatable, raced with fastfoxes, flown with eagles, dived with whalfish. Each season has been lived through and admired for the change it brings. I have learned to appreciate nature, and through that life in every form.

*

My world.

I have known it all. I have exchanged thought with all ten thousand of us remaining. We have admired and discussed that which we know, that which we aspire to. I have dwelled within the flights of fancy those more imaginative than I have conjured. I have manifested places that do not exist in reality, calling them out of the folds of darkness which lurk beneath our universe, and embellished them with my whimsy. I have heard dark echoes from the past which filled me with dread. I have bathed in the tears of triumph and delight that rose from adversity. I have filled my head with the merry songs of success.

They come.

Those who guide fall from the sky in a tide of sparkling light that shines through my very skull. My family and I streak downwards to hurtle along the narrow jagged streets of Makkathran. Fast, so fast, that the walls and windows and roofs merge into a single blur of colour. I manifest wings, flowing out of my arms to turn and twist against the heady rush of air. My body spins and gyrates with the elegance of those born to the air. Our shouts of admiration are the only sounds to fill the alleys and squares for over a century.

Our welcome.

We fly across the sea outside the city's port. Dipping and weaving around the armada of elegant yachts which delivered us all to this place and time from across our world. Grand white sails curve against the gentle sea breeze just as they did in days of yore. For art's sake, for completion of form. Such ocean-ranging beauties deserve to be more than functional, and so it is. Our family yacht needs only my will to propel it across the water, yet the sails billowing out bring comfort and rightness to the mind, as easing as a child's night-toy.

The gathering.

A wind blows strong ahead of those who guide as they sweep

along the air road they have returned to time and time again. Bringing rippling half-shadows and vivacious starlit twinkles to dazzle and deceive the eye, they blow the yachts playfully across the skittish water beneath them. Tumbling mischievously in their wake, our wings flapping with slow grace, we crowd together and cheer with minds and voice alike. Both cries lost amid their ethereal glamour. The accord cannot last, and soon we separate. I bid farewell to those four of my family who have fulfilled their lives here on this planet of bounty and promise. I bid my farewell to the splendid thousand who are to pay the ultimate tribute this day, this moment.

Departure.

Cold sparkling light streaks from the towers of Eyrie, great flames of opalescence that reach out with such yearning to stroke the ever-shifting crystal bodies of those who guide. Into the flares flies the essence of those who would ascend to the Heart of the Void. Now as always the power of the towers thrusts them on their way as their bodies bloom to dust. Then they are gone, flashing upwards to dwell as colourful shadows amid the fantastical geometry of crystal. Gone to destiny's reward.

I descend.

Gently gently, dissolving my wings back into nothingness. Growing clothes about my form. I land upon Golden Park to observe with mind and sight as those who guide launch themselves back into the empty chasm of space which lies between us and the nebulas of this universe. I am content that yet more of us have gone to join our ancestors and all those who used to live within this eternal Void that is gracious enough to provide us a warm comforting home amid the raw chaos burning outside its boundary. I am sad that so many have left. I am sad that so few of us now remain. But not disheartened.

That which remains.

Is small. I will not bear any more children. Nor will my

two remaining children. That time is over now for us. Any new mind born into this world would only learn what we have already experienced. We are history now. We are the pinnacle of life.

Identity.

The cells of which I am composed yearn to continue. Such desires are inbuilt. They are me, entwined with my essence. I recognize that is right, for to deny it is to renounce myself. Purpose grows from many sources. None should be ignored. I will live for a while more. But not forever.

My journey.

I have only one voyage left now. I walk across Golden Park admiring and acknowledging the times and events that have played out here. The rich past is become a ghost memory. So much suffering, so much endeavour has gone to bringing me to this place and time. This is my milieu and I am grateful to those who came before. I wish them to know nothing was in vain, no word they spoke, no deed they performed, all of it went into my making. I am the nexus of their existence, and I am content to be such.

A tribute.

My acknowledgement is simple. My mind elevates the fabric of this universe as I manifest my will. Suddenly Golden Park is filled with people one last time as past intersects present, the air thickens with sound and smell. I am jostled good-naturedly by those who never envisioned me as they go about their business. Over there are Rah and the Lady alighting from their small boat to stare in wonder at the domes of the Orchard Palace for the first time. There goes the exquisitely pretty young maiden Florrel to entrap her first lover. Here I see a dejected Akeem trudge back to his guild, the first steps along his path to self-imposed exile. A furtive Salrana hurries by on her way to that fateful meeting in the Blue Fox tavern. And there he is, the Waterwalker in all his glory, following his never-to-be love, knowing in his heart that he is about to witness a haunting grief.

Love.

I love them all, worshipping them from afar. And so my manifestation ends, and the city is empty again save for me and my kind walking along empty streets, making our way back to our yachts, and from there to our homes. We will not return.

Life.

I have succeeded in living. Soon now, when my home is in order, I will rise up to those who guide, knowing all that can be done has been done. We have achieved so much. There is nothing left here now. Nothing.

The future.

What is to come? I cannot know the most beautiful mystery of all. Not yet. It awaits us within the Heart of the Void. A song which grows stronger with each passing day.

9

Dawn arrived as the *Last Throw* lifted silently back into the chill air above the Delivery Man. Ahead of him the sun was rising, a sliver of rose-gold incandescence emerging above the mountains on the horizon. He could feel the weak heat on his face as he started to walk down the slope. Thin strands of mist were stirring above the tiny coils of grass-equivalent, filling the folds in the land to form wraithlike streams. Local birds were already calling out in their guttural warbles, taking flight from the black trees as the light grew stronger.

The Delivery Man watched them lumber upwards, amused by the sight. It looked like evolution hadn't got it quite right on this world; what they lacked in grace they made up for in bulk.

A sleeping herd of quadruped beasts grunted and shook themselves, greeting the new day in their own laborious way. Ponderous creatures the size of a terrestrial rhino, and imbued with almost the same temper. Their heavily creased hide was a dapple of rust-brown and grey, while legs as thick as the Delivery Man's torso could plod onward all day with prodigious stamina. These were the animals which the Anomine kept to pull their ploughs and wagons.

The Delivery Man skirted the herd before they noticed something strange walked among them. It would hardly do to stampede the animals before he'd had a chance to greet the natives.

He could smell smoke upon the breeze as he neared the

village. Fires that had blazed throughout the night were finally dying down to embers now they had performed their task and warned off the wilder animals during the long hours of darkness.

The *Last Throw*'s sensors had run a passive scan across the village as they came down to land, revealing a broad semicircular sprawl of buildings along the banks of a small river. There was little evidence of stonework aside from a few low circular walls that appeared to be grain silos. The buildings all employed a wooden construction. Retinal enrichments gave him a good look at them as he covered the last half-mile to the village. Their houses stood on thick legs a couple of metres above the dusty ground. Roofs were tightly packed dried reeds overhanging bowed walls made up from curving ovals of polished wooden frames that held some kind of hardened translucent membrane. He could just make out shadows moving within the houses he was approaching.

A couple of Anomine tending one of the village's five fire pits stopped moving, and twitched their antennae. They were elderly. He could tell that from the dark lavender colour of their limbs and the way their lower legs curved back, reducing their height. Youngsters were a near-uniform copper colour, while adults in their prime had a jade hue. These ones were also larger around the trunk section. Weight-gain clearly didn't just affect humans as they got older.

He walked into the village as his u-shadow ran one last check through the translator unit hanging round his neck on a gold chain. It was a palm-sized rectangle, capable of producing the higher-frequency sounds employed by the Anomine language. Navy cultural anthropologists had resequenced their vocal chords so they could speak with the Anomine directly, but it hadn't been an unqualified success. The effort had been appreciated, though; the Anomine really didn't like machines more advanced than a wheel.

The Delivery Man studied the etiquette profile file displayed by his exovision. 'I greet you this fine morning,' he said, which immediately came out as a series of squeaks and whistles similar to dolphin chatter. 'I have travelled from another world to visit you. I would ask you to share stories of your ancestors.' He bowed slightly, which was probably a gesture wasted on the aliens.

They were taller than him by nearly a metre, especially when they stood up straight, which they did to walk. Their tapering midsection was nearly always bent forward, and the upper knee-joints of the triple-segment legs folded the limbs back to balance.

The one whose limbs were shading from purple towards black replied. 'I greet you this morning, star-traveller. I am Tyzak. I am an old-father to the village. I can spare some time to exchange stories with you.'

'I thank you for showing me such a kindness,' the Delivery Man said. If there was excitement or curiosity in Tyzak's posture he couldn't gauge it. Unlike the weight issue there was no human-parallel body language, no jittering about, or understandable agitation. It would have been hard, he admitted to himself. Their skin was almost like scales, making subtle muscle motion imposs-ible. And as for the classic darting eyes, their twin antenna were a uniform slime-grey of photosensitive receptor cells waving up from the small knobbly head that was mostly mouth, giving them a wholly different visual interpretation of their world to that of a human. The brain was a third of the way down inside the torso, between the small mid-arms and larger main upper arms.

'Your true voice is silent,' Tyzak said.

'Yes. I cannot make the correct sounds to speak to you directly. I apologize for the machine which translates.'

'No apology is required.'

'I was told you do not approve of machines.'

The two Anomine touched the small claws of their mid-arms. 'Someone has been less than truthful with you,' Tyzak said. 'I am grateful you have come to our village that we might speak the truth with you.'

'It was my own kind who informed me of your aversion to machinery. We visited a long time ago.'

'Then your kind's memory has faded over time. We do not dislike machines, we simply choose not to use them.'

'May I ask why?'

Tyzak's middle and upper knees bent, lowering him into a squatting position. The other Anomine walked away.

'We have a lifepath laid out by this world which formed us,' Tyzak said. 'We know what happens to us when we choose a lifepath centred around machines and technology. Our ancestors achieved greatness, as great as you, even.'

'Your ancestors reached further than we have done, in so many ways,' the Delivery Man said. 'Our debt to them is enormous. They safeguarded so many stars from an aggressive race, for which we are forever grateful.'

'You speak of the oneness which lives around two stars. It sought to devour all other life.'

'You know of them?'

'Our lifepath is separate from our great ancestors, for which we feel sorrow, but we rejoice in their achievements. They went on to become something other, something magnificent.'

'Yet you didn't follow them. Why was that?'

'This planet created us. It should choose the nature of our final days.'

'Sounds like another goddamn religion to me,' Gore said over the secure link.

'More like our Factions,' the Delivery Man countered. 'Their version of the Accelerators went off and elevated, while the Natural Darwinists wanted to see what nature intended for them.'

More Anomine were coming down from their houses, jumping easily on to the ground from narrow doorways several metres above the ground. Once they were on the ground, they moved surprisingly swiftly. Long legs carried them forward in a fast loping gait, with each stride almost a bounce. As they moved they bobbed forward at a precarious angle.

Their balance was much better than a human's, the Delivery

Man decided, even though the motion sparked an inappropriate comparison to a pigeon walk.

A group of younger ones bounded over. He was soon surrounded by Anomine children who simply couldn't keep still. They bopped up and down as they chattered loudly among themselves, discussing him, the strange creature with its odd body and clothes and weak-looking pincers and fur on top. The noise level was almost painful to his ears.

He heard Tyzak explaining what he was.

'Where do you come from?' one of the children asked. It was taller than its fellows, getting on for the Delivery Man's height, and its apricot skin was darkening to a light shade of green.

'A planet called Earth, which is lightyears from here.'

'Why are you here?'

'I search out wisdom. Your ancestors knew so much.'

The children's high-pitched calls increased. The translator caught it as a round of self-reinforcing: 'Yes. Yes they did.'

'I eat now,' Tyzak said. 'Will you join me?'

'That would please me,' the Delivery Man assured him.

Tyzak stood swiftly, scattering several of the children who bounded about in circles. He started walking towards one of the nearby houses, moving fast. His lower curving legs seemed to almost roll off the ground. The Delivery Man jogged alongside, keeping pace. 'I should tell you, I may not be physically able to eat most of your food.'

'I understand. It is unlikely your biochemistry is compatible with our plants.'

'You understand the concept of biochemistry?'

'We are not ignorant, star-traveller. We simply do not apply our knowledge as you do.'

'I understand.'

Tyzak reached his house and jumped up to a small platform outside the door. The Delivery Man took a fast look at the thick posts the house stood on, and swarmed up the one below the platform.

'You are different,' Tyzak announced, and went inside.

The membrane windows allowed a lot of light to filter through. Now he was inside, the Delivery Man could see oil-rainbow patterns on the taut surface, which he thought must be some kind of skin or bark that had been cured. Inside, Tyzak's house was divided into three rooms. There wasn't much furniture in the largest one where they entered. Some plain chests lined up along an inner wall. Three curious cradle contraptions which the Delivery Man guessed were chairs. And five benches arranged in a central pentagon, all of which were covered by fat earthenware pots.

First impression was that half of them were boiling their contents. Bubbles fizzed away in their open tops. And the air was so pungent it made his eyes water. He recognized the scent of rotting or fermenting fruit, but so much stronger than he'd ever smelt before.

After a moment he realized there was no heater or fire in the room even though the air was a lot warmer than outside. The pots really were fermenting – vigorously. When he took a peek in one, the sticky mass it held reminded him of jam, but before the fruit was properly pulped.

Tyzak pulled one of the pots towards him and bent over it, opening his clam-mouth wide enough to cover the top. The Delivery Man had a brief glimpse of hundreds of little tooth mandibles wiggling before the Anomine closed his mouth and sucked the contents down in a few quick gulps.

'Would you like to sample some of my >no direct translation: cold-cook conserve/soup<?' Tyzak asked. 'I know the sharing of food ritual has significance to your kind. There must be one here harmless enough for you to ingest.'

'No thank you. So you do remember members of my species visiting this world before?'

'We hold the stories dear.' Tyzak picked up another pot and closed his mouth around it.

'No one else seems interested in me, except for the younger villagers.'

'I will tell the story of you at our gathering. The story will spread from village to village as we co-gather. Within twenty years the world will know your story. From that moment on you will be told and retold to the new generations. You will never be lost to us, star-traveller.'

'That is gratifying to know. You must know a lot of stories, Tyzak.'

'I do. I am old enough to have heard many. So many that they now begin to fade from me. This is why I tell them again and again so they are not lost.'

'Stupid,' Gore observed. 'They're going to lose a lot of information like that. We know they used to have a culture of writing, you can't develop technology without basic symbology, especially math. Why dump that? Their history is going to get badly distorted this way; that's before it dies out altogether.'

'Don't worry,' the Delivery Man told him. 'What we need is too big to be lost forever; they've certainly still got that.'

'Yeah, sure, the suspense is killing me.'

'I would hear stories of your ancestors,' the Delivery Man said to Tyzak. 'I would like to know how it was that they left this world, this universe.'

'All who visit us upon this world wish this story above everything else. I have many other stories to tell. There is one of Gazuk whose bravery saved five youngsters from drowning when a bridge fell. I listened to Razul tell her own story of holding a flock of >no direct translation: wolf-equivalent< at bay while her sisters birthed. Razul was old when I attended that co-gathering, but his words remain true. There are stories of when Fozif flew from this world atop a machine of flame to walk upon Ithal, our neighbouring planet, the first of our kind ever to do such a thing. That is our oldest story, from that grow all stories of our kind thereafter.'

'Which do you want to tell me?'

'Every story of our beautiful world. That is what we live for. So that everything may be known to all of us.'

'But isn't that contrary to what you are? Knowledge lies in the other direction, the technology and science you have turned from.'

'That is the story of machines. That story has been told. It is finished. We tell the stories of ourselves now.'

'I think I understand. It is not what was achieved by your ancestors, but the individuals who achieved it.'

'You grow close to our story, to living with us. To hear the story of what we are today you must hear all our stories.'

'I regret that my time on your world is short. I would be grateful for any story you can tell me about your ancestors and the way they left this universe behind. Do you know where this great event took place?'

Tyzak gulped down another pot. He went over to the chests and opened the hinged lids. Small, bulging cloth sacks were taken out and carried over to the benches. 'There is a story that tells of the great parting which will never fade from me. It is most important to us, for that is how our kind was split. Those who left, and those who proclaimed their allegiance to our planet and the destiny it had birthed us for. To this time we regret the separation, for we will never now be rejoined.'

'My people are also divided into many types,' the Delivery Man said as he watched Tyzak open the sacks. Various fruits and roots were taken out and dropped into pots. Water from a large urn at the centre of the benches was added. Finally, the alien sprinkled in some blue-white powder from a small sachet. The contents of the pots began to bubble.

'I will listen to your stories of division,' Tyzak said. 'They connect to me.'

'Thank you. And the story of the place where your ancestors left? I would very much like to know it, to visit the site itself.'

'We will go there.'

Which wasn't quite the reply the Delivery Man was expecting. 'That is good news. Shall I call for my ship? It can take us anywhere on this world.'

'I understand your offer is intended to be kindness, however

I do not wish to travel on your ship. I will walk to the place of separation.'

'Oh crap,' Gore said. 'This could take months, years. Just try and get the damn monster to tell you where it is. Tell him you'll meet him there if necessary.'

'I regret I am not able to walk very far on your world,' the Delivery Man said. 'I need my own kind of food. Perhaps we could meet at the place?'

'It is barely two days away,' Tyzak said. 'Can you not travel that far?'

'Yes, I can travel that far.'

'Hot damn,' Gore was saying. 'Your new friend must mean the city at the far end of the valley. There's nowhere else it can be.'

The Delivery Man's secondary routines were pulling files out of his lacuna and splashing them across his exovision. 'We checked a building there four days ago, right next to a big plaza on the west side. You went in. There was an exotic matter formation, some kind of small wormhole stabilizer. Non-operational. We assumed it was connected to an orbital station, or something that doesn't exist any more.'

'That just shows you how stupid it is to assume anything about aliens,' Gore said. 'We've found fifty-three exactly like it, and dismissed them all.'

'They were all in different cities,' the Delivery Man said, reviewing a planetary map in his exovision. 'Well distributed, geographically. I suppose they could be an abandoned transport network, like the old Trans-Earth-Loop.'

'Yeah, that was before your time, but I used it often enough. Whatever, I'm on my way to the city now. I'm going to scan and analyse that mother down to its last negative atom. I'll find out what the hell it does before you've had lunch.'

Tyzak walked through into one of the back rooms. The Delivery Man considered it a minor miracle the old alien didn't bash its antenna on the ceiling. But each movement was deft, it ducked under the doorway without pausing.

'Lucky we picked a village close to the actual elevation mechanism,' the Delivery Man responded. He couldn't believe it himself. Probability was staked way too high against such a thing.

'About time we got a break,' Gore replied.

The Delivery Man knew damn well he didn't believe it either. *Perhaps Tyzak is just going to use the wormhole to take us to the elevation mechanism? Maybe that's what the transport mechanism is for. No, that's stupid. If he won't use a starship to fly to the city he's not going to use a wormhole. Damn!*

The Anomine came back into the main room dressed in what resembled loops of thick cloth, dyed in bright colours and embellished with stone beads. It was actually an elaborate garment, the Delivery Man acknowledged, covering the long tapering abdomen while allowing the legs and arms complete freedom of movement.

They set off straight away, walking down the slope through the village, then crossing the river on an arched stone bridge that was old enough for the outer stone to be flaking away.

'How long has your village been here?' the Delivery Man asked.

'Seven hundred years.'

The fields and orchards on the other side of the water were neatly tended. Anomine adults moved along the rows of trees, reaching up to snip the fruit stems with their strong upper arm pincer claws. They were mostly the mothers, the Delivery Man guessed from their coloration. Anomine lifecycle followed a simple progression from neutral youngsters to adult female to elder male. With each stage lasting about twenty-five years. It was very unusual for an adult to live past eighty.

That he simply could not get his head around. He knew they'd had complete mastery of genetic manipulation in the past, giving them the ability to extend their lives. So that too had been rejected and neutralized so they could follow their original evolutionary path. There was no human Faction that would ever follow such a tenet; even the Naturals went in for good old-fashioned rejuvenation every thirty years. The desire to cling to life was screwed into the human psyche deep beyond any psychoneural profiling to remove.

Like hope, he thought. *I'm carrying on this ridiculous charade of Gore's because it gives me hope. It's the only way I know that might possibly deliver me back to Lizzie and the kids. Ozzie alone knows what madness Ilanthe has planned when she reaches the Void, but no one else has any idea how to stop her. If only this wasn't so . . . frail. If only I could bring myself to believe in what I'm doing.*

The Delivery Man raised his head. High above, the ancient orbital debris band shimmered faintly through breaks in the cloud, like a motionless strand of silver cirrus. He sighed at the sight. *Signs and portents in the sky, that's what I'm searching for now. How pathetic is that? And I think the Anomine are weak and strange because they re-embrace their primitive life. A life that doesn't threaten the galaxy. A life which doesn't tear fathers from their families.*

He opened the link to Gore. 'What are you going to do after? If we win?'

'Get back out of this goddamn meat animal for a start, back into ANA where I can think properly again.'

'But isn't that the problem? Look what our evolutionary drive has pushed us to.'

'You think we're suffering overreach, sonny? You think arrogance is the root of all this?'

'In a way, yes.'

'Ha, in a way: for fucking certain. That's why we need to keep going, keep pushing the human development boundary. All of us need to boost our responsibility and rationality genes to the maximum. It's the only way to survive peacefully in a galaxy as dangerous as this one.'

'That's an old argument.'

'And completely valid. Maybe the one argument that has remained relevant for our entire history. Without education and understanding the barbarians would have outnumbered us and swarmed the city gates a long time ago.'

'She's making a pretty good go of it right now, isn't she?'

'Ilanthe? Typical case, educated way, way beyond her IQ, with ambition stronger than ability. She's just another cause fascist, son; and that's the worst kind, they always know they're right. Anyone who dissents for whatever reason is evil and an enemy, existing only to be crushed.'

He wouldn't have believed it could happen, but the Delivery Man actually felt himself smile as he walked on through the alien groves and meadows. 'So very different from your liberalism, huh?'

'You got it, sonny.'

Before long the cultivated fields gave way to the valley's tangled grassland. Tyzak chose a small path that curved round to run parallel with the major river several miles away. That put the Delivery Man facing the giant empty city that straddled the mouth of the valley; its grandiose towers and arresting domes barely visible through the late morning haze.

That vision. The clean air. The bright sunlight. Walking to a definite goal. Whatever the reason, he actually began to feel a sense of purpose again. Not confidence exactly, but it would do for a start.

'I can go faster,' he told Tyzak.

The big alien started to lengthen its stride, bouncing along in an effortless rhythm. The Delivery Man matched it, relishing the urgency which their speed brought. *I'm doing it*, he told Lizzie and the kids silently. *I'm coming for you, I promise.*

*

Ozzie didn't let anything slip about his opinion. Myraian smiled in that dreamy way of hers and said: 'Sweet.' Then she relived Inigo's Last Dream again.

Corrie-Lyn was the most affected. She knelt in front of Inigo and looked up, as if pleading for it not to be true. 'They had it all,' she entreated. 'They succeeded. Their minds were beautiful.'

'And it is worthless,' he told her in turn. 'They are no longer human. They have anything they want, which takes away any dignity and purpose they might have had. Their lives are day after day of ennui. All that concerns them is the past. Visiting places because they have already been discovered, that's not gaining experience, that's a dismal nostalgia trip. They no longer contribute because there's nothing to contribute to.'

'They reached fulfilment,' she said. 'Their minds were so strong. Inigo, they flew!'

'But where did they fly to? What did they use such a gift for? To please themselves. Querencia became a playground for characterless godlings.'

'They succeeded in throwing off the kind of mundane physical shackles that grind our lives down. This is what the Waterwalker gave them. They lived in splendour without having to exploit anyone, without damaging anything. They understood and loved each other.'

'Because they were all the same. It was self-love.'

'No.' Corrie-Lyn shook her head and walked out onto the veranda. A few moments later Ozzie heard the sound of her shoes on the creaky old wooden steps down to the garden.

A dismayed Inigo rose to follow her.

'Don't do it, dude,' Ozzie said. 'Let her work it out for herself, it's the only true route to understanding.'

For a long moment Inigo hesitated, then slowly sank back into the tall-backed chair at the kitchen table. 'Damnit,' he grunted.

'So that was it, huh?' Ozzie said. 'Bummer.'

Inigo shot him a thoroughly disgusted look.

'I don't get it,' Aaron said. 'They achieved something approaching the classical heaven on Earth.'

'Fatal, man,' Ozzie said. 'I've been there myself. Trust me: plutocrat with a decent brain and the finest rep available during the first-era Commonwealth. Wine, women and song all the way; I had it so totally better than those guys. Well . . . except for the flying bit. I gotta admit that was way cool. I always wondered why Edeard couldn't do that. Man, if I ever got into the Void

I'd be trying from dusk till dawn. Oldest human wish fulfilment there is.'

'I don't understand,' Aaron said. 'They had reached fulfilment. All of them. That is admirable. It was the final validation of the entire whole Living Dream movement.'

'A dung beetle that gets its turd home is fulfilled. We're talking levels, here, dude. Am I right, Inigo?'

'You're right.'

'See, be careful what you wish for. Utopia at our biological level just doesn't work out. Once you've achieved everything, there is nothing left, you take out the core of being human: the striving. Edeard's descendants had reached a state where fulfilment was inevitable. You didn't have to work for it. That's less than human, they were starting to un-evolve. And in their own way they knew it. Their population was way down on Edeard's time, and still shrinking. There was no point in having children, because there was nothing new for them. They wouldn't be able to contribute anything relevant let alone profound to the Heart.'

'In which case this Last Dream doesn't help our situation in any way I can fathom,' Aaron said.

'Not your mission, no,' Ozzie told him, curious how that would affect the man's strange mentality. 'But I guess if we release the Last Dream it might cause the rise of a few doubters in Living Dream. Mind, they'd be the smart ones, and, face it, they're in a minority in that religion.'

'Too late,' Inigo said. 'Even if the majority acknowledged the result of a Pilgrimage into the Void is ultimately a lost, sterile generation, it won't affect the Pilgrimage itself. And you saw Corrie-Lyn's reaction. She doesn't believe the Last Dream is an indication of failure. If I can't convince her . . .'

'Throwing away your belief is always hard, man, look at you.'

Inigo rubbed his hands wearily across his face as he slumped down in the chair. 'Yeah, look at me.'

'I'm sorry about that, man. No, really I am. That was one tough mother of a fall. How long have you bottled that Last Dream up?'

'About seventy years.'

'No shit. That's gotta be good to let it out finally. Tell you what, tonight you and me are going to get major-league hammered together. It's the only way to put shit like that behind you. And if anyone's going to understand a colossus of a disaster, it's yours truly.'

'That's almost tempting,' Inigo admitted.

'You can do that afterwards,' Aaron announced. 'Now we've determined the Last Dream is not relevant to us, I need you both to focus on what is achievable.'

'Man, you never give up, do you?'

'Did you give up when the Dreamer emerged and subverted your gaiafield?'

'Please, don't try that motivational psychology bullshit on me. Whatever you are, you're not up to that. Trust me, stick with the psycho threats.'

'As you wish. Stick your pleasantries, and stay with me now. Our task is to get the Dreamer into the Void.'

'It may not be,' Inigo said. 'I actually think Araminta's faith in the Void isn't entirely misplaced. The Heart will be able to defeat Ilanthe.'

'You're right about that,' Ozzie said. 'The Silfen believe in Araminta, I can feel it, man. It's their strongest hope right now.'

'Again, irrelevant,' Aaron said.

'No it's not,' Inigo said stubbornly. 'The Ilanthe side of the problem didn't emerge until well after your mission was started. Given how big a factor she is, we have to start taking her into consideration. It would be irrational to do anything else.'

'Our mission is to get you, Dreamer, into the Void.'

'No. Kills me to say it,' Ozzie admitted, 'but Inigo is right. Ilanthe is clearly part of the original problem, even though your boss didn't take that into account when he preloaded all that mission crap in your brain. You've got to start thinking about her, man. Come on, there must be some room to manoeuvre in that metal skull of yours.'

'Fair enough, I can see she is a factor in the ultimate outcome.

But if we're not in the Void we can't confront her, now can we? So will you two please start putting your genius brains together and solve this problem of how to get Inigo inside.'

'Can't be done,' Inigo said. 'Even if you still had that ultra-drive ship you lost on Hanko, it couldn't get us to the Void boundary before the Pilgrimage. Basically, whoever gets inside first wins.'

'Don't big it up like that, dude,' Ozzie said. 'If you'd gotten there first you might have stood a chance of a win. But nothing is certain, especially not in there. Now you can't get in, we all need to start thinking about a dignified yet fast exit.'

'That is not permissible thinking, and I'm getting mighty tired of telling you,' Aaron said. 'Don't make me ram the point home, because I'm through talking metaphors. Now how do we get the Dreamer into the Void?'

Ozzie hunched his shoulders up. The agent was starting to annoy him, which wasn't good. He knew he wouldn't be able to resist pushing Aaron to the limit, just to find out what the limit was. *Just like the Chikoya at Octoron.* 'So can we still plan for that emergency telepathic link up if everything else fails?' he asked innocently.

Aaron's arm came off the table. Weapon enrichments bulged up out of the wrist skin. 'Don't.'

Myraian's eyes fluttered open. She smiled up from the depths of some narcotic state. 'Bad boys. You won't get any supper.'

'I want my supper,' Ozzie said.

Aaron gave him a long warning glance, then the enrichments sank back down. 'Okay then, let's examine this in a sweet progressive fashion. We're now a little more than eight thousand lightyears behind the Pilgrimage ships, the *Lindau* is terminally screwed. So we need something faster than the Commonwealth's ever produced. What's available on the Spike?'

Ozzie let out a sigh. 'Hey, you heard the man, me-brain-in-a-jar, what have we got out there?'

'The Spike's AI is currently registering three hundred and eighty-two alien starships docked,' the smartcores replied. 'None are known to be faster than a Commonwealth hyperdrive. The fastest local sensors have observed is the Ilodi ships, which can reach twenty-two lightyears per hour.'

'No use to us,' Inigo said.

'You two could steal one and get back to the Commonwealth,' Ozzie suggested. 'If Inigo publicly reappeared maybe your boss would get in touch and tell you what the hell to do next.'

'That would be a last resort if even a telepathic link to the Heart failed,' Aaron said. 'You said that the *High Angel* would pick you up if the expansion phase begins.'

Ozzie suddenly wished he hadn't shot his mouth off earlier. This line of thought could only go one way. And Aaron wasn't about to drop it, not him, not ever. 'It might. Depends on how busy it is.'

'Your precise words were: "Qatux owes me. The *High Angel* will stop by and collect us on its way to Andromeda or wherever the hell its going." That means you can call the *High Angel* here.'

'Dude, I could ask. There's no guarantee . . .'

'Ask.'

'What's the point? You want to get inside the Void. Qatux is heading in the opposite direction. A long long way in the opposite direction.'

'The Raiel are the only known species able to break through the Void boundary. They can get us inside.'

'Can but won't. Don't even have to ask.'

'Humour me.'

Ozzie gave Inigo a frozen help-me-out smile. The ex-messiah just shrugged his shoulders and said: 'Welcome to my world.'

'It's not easy to make contact,' Ozzie said. It was lame. This was a losing battle and he knew it.

'For someone with his own private TD channel to the Commonwealth?' Aaron queried lightly.

'Ain't going to work,' Ozzie said.

'I'm almighty pleased for you about that. You deserve a moral victory over me around about now. Maybe I'll shut up and leave you alone afterwards.'

Ozzie gave him an evil stare, and told his u-shadow to open a link to the *High Angel*.

'Expand this end of the link to include us, please,' Aaron told him.

Ozzie couldn't remember being quite this pissed off for some centuries. It wasn't that he didn't want to help get Inigo inside the Void. But that he might have to actually accompany him was deeply worrying, and Qatux might not agree to loan them the *High Angel* unless he came along. Ozzie did not want to go into the Void for the simple reason that no one had ever been known to get out.

The link was accepted by *High Angel*. 'Ozzie,' Qatux said. 'It has been many years.'

'Yeah. Listen, we'll do the old buddy-buddy catch-up crap later; I've got a couple of people here on my end of the link who need to get into the Void before the Pilgrimage. Any chance you or your species can make that happen?'

'Ozzie, as always you are never what I expect. This is why I always delight in knowing you. Is Aaron with you?'

'I am here,' Aaron said. 'How did you know that?'

'This link stretches over seven thousand lightyears, it also passes through many nodes within the unisphere. I do not believe it to be totally secure. Please remember that. However, I am glad you have survived. Our mutual friend Paula Myo has been keeping me informed of your travels.'

'Ah. Right.'

'And the other person with you, this is the man you were searching for when we met?'

'Yes.'

'That is excellent news.'

'I'm glad you think so. I hope you understand that this third person may be able to neutralize this whole situation if you can get them into the Void ahead of the Pilgrimage. Can you or the warrior Raiel do that?'

'No.'

'I am making a sincere offer. What harm will it do getting us through the boundary? Two people, when there are now twenty-four million en route.'

'I regret we are not able to help. It is a physical impossibility. Even our ships do not have the speed to perform such a task. However, I do have an alternative for you to consider.'

'Yes?'

'Someone else is on their way to meet Ozzie. Someone who is possibly more important than the person already with you. They will be with you in three days. I urge you to wait for them.'

'I'm not sure I can do that. I have a mission.'

'That is a great shame.'

'I'll wait for them,' Ozzie said.

'Thank you, Ozzie. They are accompanied by an old friend of mine, Oscar Monroe. He will act as guarantor for what you will hear.'

'Holy shit. Oscar? Really? Is he out of the slammer already? Damn, I so lose track of time.'

'He is very much out. I hope that together you will be able to find a solution to this terrible situation. Please convince Aaron's companion to wait.'

'Do my best, dude.'

The link closed. Ozzie gave Inigo a pensive grin. 'Someone more important than you, huh? Now who could that be?' He couldn't figure it out for himself, which was hugely annoying. Qatux wouldn't lie, so ... someone more important than the Dreamer with regard to the Void. There wasn't even a list.

'We have been compromised,' Aaron said. He stood up, and activated a low-level integral force field, creating a tiny purple nimbus around his stolen Navy tunic.

Ozzie chuckled. 'Something you need to know about Paula Myo. Apart from being able to freeze your balls off at ten paces with a single look, that chick seriously rocks. Wouldn't be surprised if she's your secretive boss. She's done groovier things in her time.'

'I cannot allow my mission to be terminated.'

'Relax, if Paula wanted you stopped, you wouldn't be here.

Qatux was telling me to chill. The old big-Q, he's not stupid. We need to wait for Oscar. Man, fancy him still kicking around. Tell you, my confidence just went up like ten notches.'

'Who in Honious is Oscar Monroe?' Inigo asked.

'Oscar the Martyr,' Aaron said quietly. 'He sacrificed himself so Wilson Kime could steer the Planet's Revenge and save the human race from corruption and extinction. If it truly is Oscar coming here . . .' He hesitated, which was something Ozzie hadn't seen him do before.

'So I guess we wait, then?' Ozzie said, curious to see what reaction that would trigger. For someone who didn't have many memories, it was strange in the extreme that Aaron (or his boss) had room to include a fact that obscure. Yet knowing Oscar was on his way actually seemed able to divert his otherwise rigid fixation on the mission.

There was a noticeable pause before Aaron said: 'We must continue to consider methods of getting Inigo into the Void. That cannot stop.'

'But we can do that sitting here, right?' Ozzie insisted.

Again, Aaron hesitated. 'That is permissible.'

'Cool. But you can forget getting inside the Void. If the Raiel can't get here, pick you up, then overtake the Pilgrimage fleet, no one can.'

'Qatux said the link was suspect.'

'Dude! There's caution and there's paranoia. I think we all know which road you walk down.'

'All right,' Aaron turned to Inigo. 'Ethan told Araminta that Living Dream hoped the Void would open a gateway within the Commonwealth for the rest of the followers.'

'It was an idea we were kicking round before I left, certainly,' Inigo replied. 'I never gave it a lot of credit.'

'If you can contact a Skylord, you must ask it to reach for you.'

'Oh, Lady, come on . . .'

'Every option must be examined. If physical flight to the boundary is now denied us, then we must try this method or at the very least see if it is possible. You have to Dream the Void again. How could it possibly make the situation worse?'

Corrie-Lyn appeared in the kitchen doorway. Ozzie was fairly sure she'd been hovering outside for some time.

'I will be with you if you try that,' she said to Inigo, and walked over to embrace him. 'For now and evermore.'

He rested his head on her shoulder. 'Thank you. For everything. For understanding.'

'You were right. Their lives were futile, worthless. They were blessed beyond our wildest aspirations, yet they never thought to look outward. Their bodies flew but their souls were moribund. That's so sad. We can't let such a fate befall our followers. They will be lost and the galaxy will fall.' She took his hands in her own. 'Lead us away from that, Dreamer, don't allow the Void to destroy our spirit.'

'My love.' Inigo gave her a tender kiss.

It was so intimate Ozzie was almost embarrassed to be a witness. Almost. The two lovers were staring longingly at each other, smiling with happiness and relief. No one else existed.

'Dude?'

Inigo's smile widened. Corrie-Lyn laughed.

'Yes, Ozzie?'

'Just a suggestion: Give your followers the Last Dream.'

'What?'

'Corrie-Lyn's right, you've got to start fighting back. So do it, show them how their dream of the Void is going to go horribly wrong, that they're going to condemn their children to emptiness and extinction. What is it your guy was always saying? *Sometimes you have to do the wrong thing to do the right*? It'll devastate all your loyal followers; they may understand, they may not. Who gives a shit, man? You were never going to get them all back on side anyway. At the very least you'll give Ethan and Ilanthe a seriously bad day. And if you're lucky you might even spark a mutiny amid the fleet.'

'Yes,' Corrie-Lyn said, suddenly animated. 'They deserve to

know. They have waited so long to know you again. Give them their true hope back. It is what Edeard would have wanted.'

'Yes,' Inigo rose to his feet. His gaiamotes opened, and the Dreamer gifted his thoughts once more. All of them.

*

If Tyzak had been human, then he and the Delivery Man would have been best friends by the time they reached the abandoned city at the end of the valley. Two days hiking together through the countryside was a superb bonding opportunity. The well-tended fields and pastures clustered around the village had given way to wild meadowland after the first three hours. With few animals grazing, the coiling grass-equivalent grew thick and tall, curling blades tangling to produce a difficult carpet to traverse. Tough plants as tall as a human knee were common, their spiky leaves containing a mild toxin that made Tyzak steer well clear. That made their path less straight than the Delivery Man wanted. He stuck with it, telling Tyzak about his life, his family.

'It sounds as if your kind are diverging as our ancestors once did,' the old Anomine said.

'Our story has similarities with yours, certainly. From what we know of your story, you were a lot less antagonistic. That is admirable. I wish we would strive for that.'

'There are stories that tell of conflict among our ancestors. Some believe they have lost their power as they are told with grudging voice. It would be strange indeed if our past was completely without strife.'

'That may also be common ground. So many of us like to talk about the good old days from a thousand years ago. Those I've met who actually lived through such times say the years between always distort reality.'

'Who would wish disdain upon their ancestors? They did deliver us to the present day.'

As well as the stinging plants the streams also caused an irritating degree of diversion. Tyzak weighed a great deal more than a human. He had to be careful of the mud; many an incautious traveller had been trapped in some treacherous patch of marshland he explained as they tramped along a gurgling rivulet searching for a stony stretch to cross.

In return for his selectively edited life story the Delivery Man was finally told the tale of Gazuk on the collapsing bridge, and Razul, and Dozul and Fazku, and a dozen other terrifically boring incidents all too characteristic of a pastoral society. Finally the story of Fozif was forthcoming, which was a great deal more lyrical than the others. The Delivery Man was amused that the first rocket flight to another world remained so revered while all the Anomine had accomplished afterwards as a starfaring race was delivered in a few short sentences. But it did allow him to respond appropriately with the story of the Cold War space programme and Neil Armstrong, which kept Tyzak quiet for a good forty minutes.

That first night they made camp on the edge of a small forest of tall trees with broad weeping branches. The Delivery Man took a hand-sized cylindrical condenser unit from his belt, which whirred quietly as it propelled air along its short length. Its water sac slowly expanded out from one end like a sallow tumour as it extracted moisture from the air. When it was full, he pumped the clean water into flat packets of food concentrate. It didn't taste too bad, though he would have preferred something hot. Tyzak just gulped down a couple more potfuls of his cold gloop, which he'd carried in a backpack.

As the dark fell, so night animals began their calls. The Delivery Man expanded his tent up and out from a square of plastic. Tyzak thanked him for the offer of sharing the tough little shelter, but refused, saying he preferred to rest outdoors. The Anomine didn't sleep as deeply as humans, instead they spent the night in a mild doze. They certainly didn't dream.

Secondary routines woke the Delivery Man a little after midnight local time. His biononic field scan had detected three largish animals approaching. Outside, the city at the end of the valley glimmered with a vivid iridescence, as if the buildings were now made from stained glass wrapped around a fissure of daylight. It was a stark contrast to the black cliff of the forest beside him, animated with wind-rustling and sharp warbles. He faced the trees and reconfigured his biononics to produce a complex low-level energy pulse. The approaching animals chittered frantically when he fired it at them; thrashing about in the darkness before rushing off, snapping low branches and tearing up the grass in their hurry to flee. He had no idea what Tyzak felt about killing local creatures, so the shot would have been the equivalent of giving them a damn good smack on the nose, with a modest electric shock thrown in to emphasize the point.

'I thank you,' Tyzak said, rising from the grass where he'd lain. 'Three >no direct translation: night beasts< would have presented even me with a problem defending us.'

'You see, machines can be useful occasionally.'

'I have my >no direct translation: cudgel axe< to aid me,' the Anomine said, holding up length of wood with a couple of spiral carvings along its length and a wicked curved spike on the top. 'It has never failed me yet.'

The Delivery Man turned back to the radiant city and opened a link to Gore. 'Have you figured it out yet?'

'Partly, the damn thing is stabilizing a zero-width wormhole, but it's currently not extended. The *Last Throw* sensors are starting to examine its quantum composition, but that's not easy in a collapsed state. I should have an idea where the wormhole used to lead in a few hours or so.'

'So it's not the elevation mechanism, then?'

'Not unless it leads directly to Anomine heaven, no.'

'If it is zero-width then nothing physical travels along it.'

'I know. But it's early days. I'm probably overlooking something. How are you doing?'

'Oh great. I'm in the middle of a boy's own wilderness adventure. Should be with you in another day.' With that he bid Tyzak goodnight and went back to the wonderfully soft mattress in the tent.

*

They started off again soon after first light. Thin tendrils of mist slithered along the floor of the valley, mirroring the river course in the early light until the sun cleared the hills and burnt if off. A constant wind blew in over the city, which now gleamed in the morning light.

It was a long way, but the Delivery Man was confident they'd make it before nightfall.

'Do you have a story which tells where the planet will take your kind?' he asked the old Anomine.

'We still live within the story. From there the ending cannot be seen.'

'Surely you have some notion? It must be a powerful belief which caused you to stay behind when your ancestors left to become something else.'

'There were many stories of hope told at the parting that will endure forever. Some believe that we will eventually sink back to the more simple-minded creatures which we evolved out of and the planet will bring another mind forward.'

'Isn't that the opposite of evolution?'

'Only from a single-species perspective. A planet's life is paramount. It is such a fragile rare event it should be treasured and nurtured for the potential it brings forth. If that means abdicating our physical dominance for our successors then that is what we will accept. Such a time is a long way in our future. In terms of evolution we have only just begun such a journey.'

'How do you know if you've reached your pinnacle? That you should already be making way?'

'We don't. I live in the time of waiting. We expect it to last for several tens of thousands of years. It may be that we will finally understand ourselves through our stories. Many think that once such comprehension is reached we will simply cease to be. Then there are also those who expect us to carry on in harmony with the planet until the sun itself grows cold and all life is ended. Whatever our fate I will never know. I am a simple custodian of our life and essence for a short period. That is my purpose. I am content with that and the wondrous stories

I will hear in my short time. Can you say the same with your life?'

'How well you know me already, Tyzak. No, my life lacks the surety and tranquillity of yours. Perhaps if I am successful in knowing what I wish to know of your ancestors things will get better for me.'

'I have sorrow for you. I will do what I can to help your story finish well.'

'Thank you.'

'It's the local star,' Gore announced mid-afternoon.

The Delivery Man glanced up through the canopy of furry branches overhead. He and Tyzak were tramping through a forest where the hot air was still and humid, heavy with a pepper-spice pollen. He squinted against the sharp slivers of sunlight slicing down past the lacework of dangling blue and green leaves. 'What's wrong with it?'

'Nothing. The zero-width wormhole used to extend a hundred and eighty million clicks. That's how far we are from the primary. There's nothing else at that distance. The *Last Throw* ran a sweep.'

'That's a huge volume of space to cover with one sensor sweep. It could easily have missed something, especially if it was stealthed. Or maybe the station changed orbit.'

'You're thinking like a human. Stop it. The Anomine didn't have anything to hide.'

The Delivery Man gave a loud laugh, which startled several of the big clumsy birds from the tree-tops. 'They hid the elevation mechanism well enough, didn't they?'

'It's not hidden, we just don't know how to look for it through their perception.'

'That sounds like the argument of a desperate man.' *Or worse, a crazy obsessive.*

'Son, you're following a monster through a forest on an alien planet hoping it'll ultimately take you back to your family. Please don't talk to me about desperate, okay?'

'All right, but answer me this, why would you want to open a wormhole into the middle of a star? You'd kill the planet on the other end.'

'It's a zero-width wormhole, nothing physical passes down it.'

The Delivery Man could picture Gore's face perfectly, gold skin at the side of his eyes creased slightly as he frowned in annoyed perplexity. 'Okay, so what information can it gather from a star?'

'Not the star directly, there must be some kind of sensor bobbing about under the corona. Or maybe deeper. We know they love their research experiments.'

'We do, but we need the end result, remember?' He took a guess what Gore's next question was going to be, the impatience was obvious.

'How long until you get here?' Gore asked.

The Delivery Man smiled at the forest. 'Give us another five hours.'

'For Christ's sake!'

'We're making good time,' he objected. 'Tyzak isn't exactly the youngest Anomine in his village.'

'All right. I'll be waiting.'

The Delivery Man thought it best not to point out that five hours would only just bring them to the edge of the city.

Dusk had already drained the sky of vitality when they began traversing the flat grassland which skirted the Anomine city. It was a curiously unnerving walk. Unlike a human city, there was no gradual build-up of the urban zone. Here it was clearly defined. One minute the suspiciously level and uniform grass was underfoot, the next the Delivery Man was treading on a concrete-equivalent street with a bulbous skyscraper rising high into the ash-grey sky in front of him. Lights were starting to come on inside every building. There didn't seem to be windows in the human architecture mode; these massive structures had a skin which was partially translucent. Staring at it hard, the Delivery Man thought he saw some kind of movement in the faint moiré threads which suffused the substance, as if it was a very slow moving liquid. That was when he realized it was the high-technology version of the membranes in the village houses.

The deeper they walked into the city, the darker the sky above became. It was mere minutes before the Delivery Man was completely surrounded by the hulking buildings. He'd been in enough Anomine cities since they'd arrived in the system not to be perturbed by the layout and profiles; but something about being with Tyzak made this experience different. It seemed . . . not as deserted as it appeared. Warm soft light illuminated the streets, creating a blend of multicoloured shadows playing across each surface. More than once he thought he caught them fluttering from the corner of his eye. The sensation of being watched was so great that he finally gave in and ordered his biononics to run a fast field scan.

Obviously there was nothing. But that cold logic did nothing to dispel the haunting sensation.

'Do you have stories of ghosts?' he asked Tyzak.

'Your translation machine is struggling with the word. Do you mean an essence which lingers after the living body has died?'

'Yes.'

'There are stories of our ancestors who transferred their thoughts into machines so they might continue after their biological bodies failed.'

'Yes, humans do that, but that's not quite what I mean. It would be an existence without physical form?'

'That is where they went after the separation. This is the method which you seek.'

'No. Not quite. This is something from our legends, stories that may be fiction. It is a nonsense, but it persists.'

'We have no stories of such a thing.'

'I see. Thank you.'

Tyzak continued along the street in his long fast bobbing motion, not even turning to focus on the Delivery Man. 'But the city does speak to me with the smallest stories.'

'It does?'

'Not a sound. But a voice nonetheless.'

'That's interesting. What story is it telling you?'

'Where my ancestors left this place. This is how we will find it.'

The Delivery Man wanted to say: but you don't use machines. Because he knew that's what the communication must be, a download into the Anomine equivalent of human macrocellular clusters, a little genetic modification that the remaining Anomine hadn't purged from themselves after all.

'We made assumptions again,' Gore said. 'We thought Tyzak was familiar with the elevation mechanism. But he's got to ask the surviving AIs.'

'No,' the Delivery Man said. 'That's not what he'd do; I know him well enough by now. He'd rather risk getting torn apart by wild animals at night than use a decent weapon to defend himself with. This is something else . . .' He ran a more comprehensive field scan. 'Nothing is being transmitted, at least that I can detect. Yet I'm still getting the creeps about this place. You've been here two days, has it bothered you?'

'Ghosts and goblins? No.'

Typical, the Delivery Man thought. But he was still disquieted by the city, and Tyzak was receiving information of some kind, which was impacting in a fashion his biononics couldn't detect. He ran another scan. Sonic. Chemical. Electromagnetic. Visual/ subliminal. Microbial. Surface vibration. Anything known to discomfort a human body.

The city wasn't active in any way. Yet when he'd walked through previous Anomine cities without Tyzak, he'd felt none of this. *So if the effect isn't impacting from the outside . . .* The Delivery Man opened his gaiamotes fully, and searched amid his own thoughts.

It was there, hovering out of reach like a foreign dream on the fringes of the gaiafield generated by the nests they'd left orbiting above. A mind, but woven from notions very different to those human sentience was comprised of. Colours, smells, sounds, emotions were all amiss, out of phase with what he perceived as correct.

'Hello?' he spoke to it.

There was a reaction, he was sure of that. A tiny strata of the strange thoughts twisted and turned. There was even a weak sensation, not a thought or memory but an impression: an animal curled up sleeping, contracting further as something pokes its skin.

So we can understand each other. Except the city didn't want to, because he was not part of the city, not part of the world. He didn't belong, didn't connect. He was alien. There was no regret, nor even hostility within the somnolent mind. The city didn't hold opinions on him, it simply knew he wasn't a part of itself or its purpose.

'The AI is neural-based,' he told Gore. 'I can sense it within the gaiafield. It's semi-active but only responds to an Anomine's mind. We're never going to get any information out of it.'

'Shit.'

'How ironic is that: one wish, one thought from a native, and the whole city will revive itself to provide them a life they can't even imagine any more. Yet they're happy with the whole been-there-done-that philosophy.'

They were trotting down a long boulevard which led up a steepening slope. Slim arches linked the buildings on either side, each one glowing with a uniform colour, as if the bands of a rainbow had been split apart, then twisted round. His exovision was displaying a map. 'You know, we're heading your way.'

'Yeah, I see that.'

'Actually, we're heading directly for you. That can't be co-incidence.'

'Sonny, I've given up on being surprised by anything this planet pitches at us.'

It took them another hour to navigate through the city's broad streets. Tyzak walked on unhesitatingly. Though towards the end the big alien did seem to be labouring to bounce forwards with quite the vitality he'd possessed that morning. Even the Delivery Man's bionomic-aided muscles were starting to feel the strain. They'd been walking for fifteen hours with only a few short breaks.

But with the stars barely visible through the cloying light-haze cast by the buildings they finally came out into the open plaza. It was a broad empty circle seven hundred metres in diameter, with long garden segments of dense green-grey shrub trees ringing the outside. Towers and elongated globes over a kilometre high stood around the edge, something about their height and proximity giving the impression that they were leaning in protectively.

It was a slightly incongruous setting for the *Last Throw*, but Gore had brought the starship down on one side of the plaza, close to a swollen cylindrical tower with a blunt dark apex. The gold man was already striding over the plaza to greet them, casting a range of pale harlequin shadows in all directions that shifted like petals as he approached. He stopped in the middle of the plaza and bowed gracefully to the old Anomine.

'Tyzak, I am honoured that you should spend time telling us the story of your ancestors' departure.'

The Delivery Man raised his eyebrow as he realized the sharp chittering sounds of Anomine language were coming directly from Gore's throat.

'It is a joy to do so,' Tyzak replied. 'Your coloration is different. Are you more advanced than your species colleague?'

'In this form, I am not, no. My body is from a time long past. Circumstances required me to adopt it once more.'

'I am glad you have. You are interesting.'

'Thank you. Can you tell us where your most sophisticated ancestors departed this world from?'

The Delivery Man almost winced at the bluntness.

'Right here,' Tyzak said.

Gore pointed a golden forefinger at the matt-glass surface of the plaza. 'Here?'

'Yes.'

Gore turned full circle, almost glaring at the shiny surface of the broad plaza. 'So we're actually standing on the machine which changed them into their final form?'

'Yes.'

The Delivery Man's biononics performed a deep field-function scan on the substance below his feet. Gore was doing exactly the same. The plaza was actually a solid cylinder extending nearly five hundred metres down into the city's bedrock. Its nuclear structure was strange, with strands and sheets of enhanced long-chain molecules twisting and coiling around and through each other like smoke tormented by a hurricane. They were all cold and inert. But they did seem to be affecting the underlying quantum fields to a minute degree, an effect so small it barely registered.

He'd never seen anything like it before. The smartcore certainly couldn't identify it or any of the functions which the weird molecular arrangements would produce if they went active. When he opened his gaiamotes he could just sense the elevation mechanism's soft thoughts, even more abstract than those of the city's mind. With a despondent curse he knew there was never going to be any possible connection between it and a human. It would take Tyzak or his kind to coax it back to awareness and functionality.

'They really didn't want anyone to follow them, did they?' Gore said pensively.

'Looks that way.'

'Huh. Then along came me. Right then.' His hands went onto his hips as he looked up at Tyzak. 'Will you ask the machine to switch on for me, please?'

'The machine which separated our ancestors from us is not a part of my life. It has discharged its purpose. The planet has destined us for something different.'

'That's it? That's your last word on this?'

'How could it be other?'

'The galaxy may be destroyed if we don't establish how your ancestors left this universe.'

'That is a story which I would not repeat at any gathering. It lacks foundation in our world.'

'And if I could prove it was true?'

'If that is what awaits this planet, then it is what awaits us also. The planet carries us.'

'Goddamn fatalists,' Gore muttered.

'Now what?' the Delivery Man asked. It was hard to keep a tone of defeat from his voice.

'Stop whingeing, start thinking. We'll just have to hack into it, is all.'

'*Hack* into it?'

'The control net, not the actual machine. Once you've got control of the power switch you're in charge, period.'

'But we're hardly talking about a management processor. This thing is a cross between a confluence nest and meta-cube network. You can't subvert it, the bloody thing's sentient, half-alive.'

'Then we physically chop the connections and insert our own command circuitry into the mechanism itself. Now shut up. Have you run a comparison review of the other fifty-three zero-width wormholes we found?'

'What? I . . . No.'

'Stay current. Every one of them is right next to an open space like this plaza. In other words, there are at least fifty-four elevation mechanisms on the planet. Makes sense, really. There were too many high-level Anomine for a single gathering point, especially if they really did all come back from their colony worlds. The upgrade to post-physical must have gone on for a long time.'

'Yes, I'm sure it must.'

'Good. So how did they power it? If you're bootstrapping yourself up to archangel status, that's going to take a lot of energy, especially when you're using a machine that's nearly half a cubic kilometre of solid-state systems.' He turned to stare at the bulging tower that backdropped the *Last Throw* and wagged an accusatory gold finger at it. 'But if you've got a cable that plugs directly into the nearest star, power is the least of your worries.'

'Ah, the wormhole doesn't carry information . . .'

'No way. They've got some kind of energy siphon swimming about in the photosphere or maybe deeper, it sends all the power they need back along the zero-width wormhole. Okay, that works for me. We'd best go see if the siphon's still there.'

For a moment, words refused to come out of the Delivery Man's mouth. 'Why?'

'What part of I-don't-give-up-easy is hard for you?'

'The wormhole isn't extended. Everything is managed by machines that have their own *psychology*, and it's anti-us psychology.'

'One step at a time. First we check it all out. If everything is still there in standby mode just like they left it, then we start an infiltration strategy. Human-derived software is the most devious in the galaxy, our e-head nerds have had a thousand years to perfect their glorious trade, God-bless-em, and I'd stack them against *anyone*. Certainly a race as sweet and noble as this lot.'

'But we don't have any with—' The Delivery Man caught the expression on Gore's golden face and groaned as comprehension kicked in.

'And if I can't re-establish something as fucking simple as a de-energized wormhole then I'm already dead and this is hell taunting me. Now come on.' Gore started marching across the plaza to the *Last Throw*.

'Are you leaving?' Tyzak asked.

'For a short while only,' the Delivery Man assured the old Anomine. 'We have to fly to check on something. It should take less than a day. Will you stay here?'

'I wish to hear the end of your story. I will remain for a while.'

The Delivery Man resisted the urge to spill out an apology, and hurried after Gore.

*

In the time it took to dive into hyperspace and re-emerge three million kilometres out from the star's photosphere the culinary unit had produced a batch of lemon risotto with diced and fried vegetables. Lizzie used to make it, standing over a big pan on the cooker, sipping wine and stirring in stock for half an hour while the two of them chatted away at the end of the day. The Delivery Man instructed the unit to produce a side plate of garlic bread, and started grating extra Parmesan cheese over the steaming rice. Lizzie always objected to that, saying it dulled the flavour of the vegetables. Gore shook his head at the offer of a bowl.

'You're still worrying about Justine, aren't you?' the Delivery Man said.

'No I am not worried about Justine,' Gore growled out. 'We're still well inside the time-effect it should take her to reach Querencia.'

'Okay then.'

'Even if something has happened it's not as if we can launch a rescue mission.'

'Unless that witch Araminta persuades the Skylord to abandon the *Silverbird*, I don't see anything which could interrupt her flight.'

'That wouldn't stop my Justine. Maybe slow her down some, but nothing worse. You have no idea how stubborn she can be.'

'Where does she get that from, I wonder?'

Gore gave him a small grin. 'Her mother.'

'Really?'

'No idea. That is one memory I made sure I junked a thousand years ago.'

The Delivery Man put a slice of the garlic bread into his mouth, and ended up sucking down air to cool it. 'I don't believe that.'

'Son, I'm not a fucking soap opera. I can't afford to be. My emotional baggage level is zero. I haven't had anything to do with that woman since Nigel watched Dylan Lewis take his epic step.'

'What?'

'Kids today! The Mars landing.'

'Ah, right.'

Gore sighed in exasperation.

The Delivery Man wasn't sure just how much of that attitude was for his benefit. As he forked up some more risotto the *Last Throw* emerged back into spacetime. Warning icons immediately popped up in his exovision, along with a series of external sensor feeds. A quick status review showed the force fields could cope with the current exposure level of radiation and heat. Hysradar return of the corona and photosphere was fuzzy, distorted by the massive star's gravity. Even the quantum-field resonance was degraded.

'We need to get closer,' Gore announced.

The Delivery Man knew better than to argue as they began to accelerate in toward the star at ten gees. He just hoped that Gore wouldn't try to tough out the heat. The way the gold man was wired it was a distinct possibility.

There were no borderguards within ten million kilometres of the star. The few that did cover that section of the Anomine solar system showed no interest in their flight. Nor were there any other kind of stations, only a host of asteroidal junk and burnt out comet-heads. The closest large object was the innermost planet at seventeen million kilometres out, a baked rock with a day three and a half times the length of its year, allowing its surface to become semi-molten at high noon. It was only the starship that had followed them from the Leo Twins that showed any interest in their exploratory flight, remaining five million kilometres away, and still keeping itself stealthed.

The *Last Throw*'s safe deflection capacity limit was reached at approximately a million kilometres above the fluctuating plasma of the photosphere, leaving them swimming through the thin, ultra-volatile corona. Giant streamers of plasma arched up from the terrible nuclear maelstrom below, threatening to engulf the little ship as they expanded into frayed particle typhoons rushing along the flux lines.

Sensors probed down into the inferno, seeking out any anomaly amid the superheated hydrogen. The starship completed an equatorial orbit and shifted inclination slightly, scanning a new section of the star's surface. Eight orbits later they found it.

A lenticular force field two thousand kilometres below the surface of the convection zone. Hysradar revealed it to be fifty kilometres wide. Intense gravitonic manipulation was keeping it in place against the force of the hydrogen currents which would otherwise have expelled it up into the photosphere at a respectable percentage of lightspeed.

'That's definitely our power siphon,' Gore said. Hysradar showed them the flux lines swirling round the disc in odd patterns. The force field appeared to be slightly porous, allowing matter to leak inwards at the edge.

'Why not just use a mass-energy converter?' the Delivery Man mused.

'Check the neutrino emissions; only a mass-energy converter will give those kind of readings,' Gore said. 'And look at it. All it's doing now is holding position, and see how much mass it's converting just to do that, because sure as Commies whinge about fairness that intake ain't flowing out anywhere afterwards. This is the mother of all turbo-drive converters.'

'Okay, so we've proved it's there and still functioning. Now what?'

'Our force fields wouldn't get us halfway, but the only way we can access it and infiltrate is go down and rendezvous – possibly even dock, or at least cling on and start drilling into the thing's brain.'

The Delivery Man gave him a frankly scared look. 'You're shitting me?'

'Wish I were, son. Don't panic, the replicator we have on board is high-order. We'll have to churn out some advanced force-field generators to upgrade the *Last Throw's* defences. Once they're beefed up to Stardiver standard we'll drop into the convection zone and switch the power back on to the elevation mechanism. Well . . . When I say us, I mean you.'

*

'It looks impressive,' Catriona Saleeb said.

'Yes.' For once Troblum felt content. He looked at the feature-less suit of matt-grey armour standing in the middle of the cabin with its round helmet almost touching the ceiling. It was big, adding about twenty-five per cent to his existing bulk. That didn't matter. The electromuscle bands could move it around easily enough. Walking would be effortless. As would flying, thanks to the little regrav unit he'd incorporated. There were no weapons, of course. He couldn't even think along those lines. But the defences . . . He would be safe anywhere. In other words, he could even face the Cat and not piss himself like he had on Sholapur.

I should have built one of these a long time ago.

At his order the two small assemblybots crawled down the suit like oversize spiders and scuttled away. He reached out to the table where his snack rested, and picked up a wedge of the club sandwich.

His exovision display showed him the Spike, now a mere three lightyears away. Its anchor mechanism was creating a huge distortion that extended out from spacetime to warp the sur-rounding quantum fields. He found the effect fascinating. It was nothing like a human hyperdrive. Unfortunately, the *Mellanie's Redemption* lacked the kind of sensors which could run a truly comprehensive scan.

Troblum finished the snack, washed it down with some Dutch lager and started putting on the armour suit. By the time he was comfortably ensconced, the starship dropped out of hyper-space two thousand kilometres out from the Spike's sunward side. Visual sensors showed him the fantastic curving triangle of metallic chambers glistening in the bright sunlight like silver bubbles. Dark tubes wove between them in complex convolu-tions. He immediately understood why the crew of the Navy ship which had discovered it believed they'd found the galaxy's biggest starship: the shape was intrinsically aerodynamic. Space on either side of the giant alien habitat was filled with dull glimmer of the Hot Ring arching away to infinity; bolstering the notion that it was frozen in mid-emergence.

He flew the starship across the sunward surface, accelerating to match the structure's unnatural orbital vector. Bright flashes of blue-white sunlight burst from the mirror-facets of the sail-shape as *Mellanie's Redemption* moved above the uneven segments. Sensors scanned landing pads dotted all along the winding H-congruous transport tubes, searching out a specific profile. The *Mellanie's Redemption* certainly hadn't been able to track their target in stealth mode during the flight; he was just hoping they'd arrived in time.

'There they are,' he said finally.

'Oscar's ship?' Catriona asked.

'Yeah. They've landed close to Octoron. That figures. It's the largest human settlement.' He ordered the smartcore to put them down on an empty pad two kilometres from Oscar's ship. A weak localized gravity field came on as soon as they touched down, but Troblum kept the ultradrive powered up just in case. The smartcore aimed a communication laser at the starship he'd followed from the Greater Commonwealth. 'I'd like to speak to Oscar Monroe, please,' he asked when his u-shadow told him a connection had been accepted.

'And you must be Troblum,' Oscar said.

The burst of fright which came from hearing his name made him twitch. Electromuscle amplified the motion. His armour helmet hit the cabin ceiling. Secondary thought routines immediately brought up the command for *Mellanie's Redemption* to power straight into hyperspace and flee. A single thought was all it would take to trigger it. 'How did you know my name?'

'Paula Myo said you might make contact.'

'How did she know ...?' Even as he asked he knew the SI had told her, had betrayed him.

'Damned if I know,' Oscar said. 'She scares the shit out of

me, and we go way back. Then again, how did you know I was on board the *Elvin's Payback*?'

'Is that the name of your ship? What was he like?'

'Adam? Like me, misguided in that way only the truly young can be. Is that what you wanted to ask?'

'No. I may be able to help.'

'How's that?'

'I know about the Swarm, I helped build it. Ozzie, Araminta and Inigo might find that useful.'

There was a long pause. 'I'm sure they would. We've already made contact with Ozzie. There's a capsule coming to collect us from our airlock in ten minutes. Why don't we fly over to yours straight after?'

'Okay. I'll wait for you.'

*

Afterwards he stood on a vast snow-swept tundra, completely naked yet feeling no pain. Somewhere in the distance tall mountains with fearsome rocky pinnacles guarded the edge of the rough icy country, a geological wall between civilization and the wild where he had come from. He wasn't cold, despite the harsh wind and flurries of snow brushing against him. This was home, after all, his one refuge against the rest of his life and all the anguish it brought whenever he lived it.

It was daytime, yet the sun was invisible behind the low grey cloud which filled the sky. He walked across the frozen ground, his feet leaving crisp indentations in the firm-packed snow. From somewhere out amid the rolling folds of this austere landscape he could hear the snorting and stamping of horses. Then a wild herd of the giant animals charged over a distant crest, tossing their mighty heads, horns slashing at the frosty air. He smiled in delight, remembering times when he'd ridden the breed for no reason other than enjoyment, taking trips to other villages, meeting friends, practising his saddle skills, the formalized ancient fighting techniques which all the youngsters sought to master. Back before—

It wasn't snow brushing against his skin any more. He plucked one of the slow-drifting particles out of the air only for it to disintegrate between his fingers. Ash. Powder puffed up from beneath the soles of his feet as each footfall became soft. Ash covered the land, choking grass and tree alike. Ruining the rich living terrain. The blanket of ash blew away from a high mound ahead of him, revealing it to be the corpse of a huge winged creature. Feathers fell like autumn leaves to expose dry skin pulled tight over a sturdy skeleton.

'No,' he exclaimed. The king eagles were the most magnificent of Far Away's creatures. Countless times he had sat astride one and soared through the splendid sapphire sky.

Orange light shimmered across the desolate landscape. He spun round to see the mountains erupting, their sharp pinnacles disintegrating as lava gushed upwards. Massive explosion plumes clotted the sky, surging outward.

There were footfalls in the ash carpet behind him. The stench of burning flesh grew and grew until he thought he would choke on the cloying fumes.

'This is not your sanctuary,' she said. 'This is where I nurtured you. This is where your heart belongs. This is mine. You are mine.'

He couldn't turn round. Couldn't face her. To do so would be to lose, to be consumed by pain and diseased love.

Gold sunlight speared through the suffocating shroud of ash. A single incandescent ray falling across him. He shielded his eyes from it, cowering.

'Come on, son,' a kindly voice said. 'This is the way. This is your future. This is your redemption.'

Ash clouds boiled high and fast, towering above him, taking form. The beautiful golden light held. He stretched his arms out, reaching for—

'Wooah!' Aaron woke and sat up fast, arms windmilling against the thin sheet that was wrapped round him. 'Shitfuck!' His body was sweating profusely, making the silk sticky against him.

The room was on the first floor of Ozzie's house. With a

single bed in the middle, some crude wooden furniture, and a window with the big shutters firmly closed. Nonetheless, light was stealing round the edges. Allowing him to see—

'Shit!' he yelped.

Myraian was sitting on the end of the bed, her legs folded neatly as she regarded him thoughtfully. Today her hair was green and blue. Purple skinlight shone through a loose white lace top.

'You're losing,' she said with a sweet smile.

He gave those fangs of hers another mistrustful look. Even though he'd been sleeping there was no way she should have been able to creep up on him, biononics should have detected her approaching. Tactical secondary routines were supposed to inform him of any proximity violation, bestowing an instinctive knowledge when he awoke. Hell, even natural instincts should have kicked in. He hadn't been this surprised for a long time. *That's bad.* 'Losing what?' he asked sourly. Biononics scanned round, making sure there were no other surprises like a fully armoured Chikoya waiting for breakfast downstairs.

'Your mind.'

He grunted and rolled off the bed, finally freeing himself from the sheet. 'It'll be joining yours then.'

'You dreamed of home when she came for you. You can't retreat much further. Your childhood will be an even worse defence. No child could withstand her.'

Aaron paused as he was reaching for trousers which Ozzie's replicator had fashioned for him. 'Her who?'

She giggled shrilly. 'If you don't know, I can't.'

'Sure.' He was trying to ignore the dream. But it was more than a dream and they both knew it. Besides, it was worrying him at a fundamental level. Something deep in his mind was *wrong.* It wasn't a war he understood, and there was certainly no tactical withdrawal.

Unless I go basic again.

But today was going to require patience and diplomacy. Not his best features even with full faculties engaged.

Myraian skipped off the bed and stretched her arms behind her back, linking her fingers. Her head rocked from side to side in time with an unheard beat. Aaron was unimpressed by the whole fairy princess routine, suspecting she was covering something.

'So are you a physicist?' he asked.

'I'm just good for my Ozzie,' she said in her silly light voice.

'Okay.' He pulled on a black T-shirt.

'You should have someone for yourself. Everyone should. This is not a universe to be lonely in, Aaron. Besides, you need help to hold her back.'

'I'll think about that.' He put his feet into his boots, allowing the semi-organic uppers to flow over his ankles, then grip.

'They're here.'

'Huh?'

'The starship. Oscar called eleven minutes ago.'

A message his u-shadow should have monitored and told him about. He started to get concerned about the string of tactical failures. They couldn't all be coincidence. 'Great, did he say who he'd brought with him?'

'No, but I'm going to fetch them now. I'll be back soon.'

He wanted to go with her and greet the arriving starship himself, but he couldn't abandon Inigo. Taking him along would increase exposure risk. No choice, he had to wait and rely on Myraian. *Which is pretty much an oxymoron.*

Downstairs, Ozzie and Inigo were sitting at the big table in the kitchen. Dirty plates and cutlery had been pushed to one side. Ozzie was drinking coffee, Inigo had a pot of hot chocolate. Corrie-Lyn was slumped in the fat old sofa at the far end of the room, looking incredibly bored.

'A great-grandfather on my mother's side was allegedly a Brandt,' Inigo was saying. 'My mother was always telling me that her grandmother had some kind of trust fund when the family lived on Hanko. I don't know how much that was a fable about the old homeworld and how much better life had been back then. If the money ever existed then it got lost in the Starflyer

War and the move to Anagaska. All anyone brought through the temporal wormhole was what they could physically carry with them. We certainly didn't have much money when I was growing up. If we were Brandts the hard-core left us to sink or swim by ourselves.'

'Sounds like a dynasty, okay,' Ozzie said.

'But you covered up your family history,' Aaron said as he made his way over to the culinary unit. 'I was at the Inigo museum in Kuhmo, there's nothing about any connection to a dynasty.'

'You know why I did that,' Inigo said. 'I was born Higher. My mother was basically raped by one of the radical angels, my aunt, too. You think I want the Greater Commonwealth drooling over that piece of personal history? And they would, my opponents would have loved that.'

'Sure I dig that. But even if that Brandt lineage gives you a family connection to a colony ship that doesn't explain how the ship got inside the Void in the first place.'

'Same way as Justine, I suppose.'

'No. She was close to the boundary. This has to be something else, a long-distance teleport.'

'The dynasty colony ship could have got up close if they were trying a quick route to the other side of the galaxy.'

'Not a chance. The Raiel have been acting as traffic cops ever since their invasion failed. They turn everyone round before they reach the Gulf, starting with Wilson on the *Endeavour*.'

'I'm not disputing that,' Inigo said. 'But, equally indisputable, a human ship got inside. That was the foundation of our hope the Void would be able to open some kind of portal to the Commonwealth.'

'See, this is where theory just collapses with a big sigh of bad air. How did the Void know the colony ship was there? It seems to have a lot of trouble with the whole "outside" concept.'

'The Skylords do. You can't claim the same for the Heart. It has to be a lot smarter.'

'But that implies a perception that can reach just about

anywhere. If it wanted minds, why not just teleport each sentient species off its homeworld as soon as they developed a coherent thought?'

'It doesn't have to be perception. Araminta dreamed a Skylord. Other connections are available to it.'

'Not its own, they piggybacked the Silfen Motherholm presence to get Araminta's attention.'

'That doesn't disqualify.'

Aaron collected his bacon roll and a mug of tea from the culinary unit and went to sit next to Corrie-Lyn. 'Still at it, then?'

'Oh yeah,' she grunted.

Five days solid now. Inigo would try and dream a Skylord, an endeavour which had so far proved fruitless. Between his attempts, he and Ozzie would argue about the nature of the Void and try to conjure up possible methods of getting through the boundary. Which was exactly what Aaron wanted. He just wasn't quite prepared for how mindbreakingly dull their conversations would be. Every minute, an irrelevant concept was dragged out and discussed at extreme length. They didn't seem to develop ideas so much as entire wishful philosophies. In other words, after four days neither one of them had produced a single helpful notion.

'Have you talked to Myraian at all?' he asked.

Corrie-Lyn gave the briefest shrugs. 'She talks? Sense?'

'Yeah, got a point, there.'

'I have been watching the Greater Commonwealth through the unisphere.'

'And?'

'The Last Dream; it's not popular. Living Dream's new Cleric Council denounced it as a fake, but everyone knows Inigo's thoughts. There's some hefty infighting breaking out among the faithful. More than I expected have said they're worried by the outcome of travelling into the Void.'

'But everyone on the Pilgrimage fleet is in suspension.'

'Yes. So it was too little too late. It's confirmed what all the non-followers believed about us, but they're irrelevant as always.

None of the crews on the Pilgrimage ships are showing any sign of rebellion.'

'Ah well, at least we can all die with a clear conscience.' He bit into the bacon roll. There was far too much butter; it dribbled down his fingers.

Corrie-Lyn gave him a strange look, crinkling her cute nose up. 'That's a first.'

'What is?'

'You mentioning the possibility of defeat. Even if it was a joke. I didn't know you could think like that.'

'Just trying to appear human, put you at your ease. Standard tactics.'

'Your dreams are getting worse again, aren't they?'

'Sleep is not my highpoint right now, I'll admit. Or is that too much weakness as well?'

'Defensiveness now? Gosh, we'll break through that conditioning yet.'

Something will, he thought bleakly. It had taken several minutes for his fear to sink away after he'd woken. That was a first, having the dread follow him out of the nightmares into the waking world. Another aspect of *her* growing strength. 'Pray you don't,' he muttered and glanced back at the table.

'I could find out eventually, I suppose,' Ozzie said. 'I still have clout with what remains of the Brandt dynasty, but your heritage will only ever be a footnote. Even if you're a long-lost Brandt, that doesn't explain how the colony ship got inside in the first place. Besides, think how many other Brandts there are left in the Commonwealth. What makes you special?'

'Is there a list of how many Brandts had a tour of duty at Centurion Station?'

'Irrelevant. Your talent doesn't allow you to talk to a Skylord, which is what we need right now.'

'Knowledge is not irrelevant. Any theory has to be built on a foundation of fact.'

'Sure, man, but that's the wrong foundation.'

'All information about the Void is what we need to determine ...'

Aaron wolfed down the remnants of the roll. 'I'm going outside to wait for them.'

'Don't blame you,' Corrie-Lyn said.

He stood on the veranda, facing the daunting alien city across the still water of the bay. The dreams he was cursed with and whatever was struggling to rise from his subconscious was troubling him. He deflected the worry with a diagnostic review of his biononics and tactical routines, the ones which had so failed him this morning. There was no clear answer how Myraian had crept into his bedroom. The field scan had registered a movement, but it wasn't sufficient to trigger the beta-grade alert routines. And by sitting on the end of the bed she'd been ten centimetres from triggering an alpha-grade alert. Was that distance a coincidence? If so, they were mounting up.

But at least his u-shadow determined why it hadn't intercepted Oscar's call to Ozzie. The house's smartcores had shielded it with some very sophisticated software. *So Ozzie hasn't quite rolled over. Figures.*

The capsule appeared against the strong sheen of the Spike compartment's translucent crown. Biononics filtered his retinas so he could maintain visual acquisition. His field-function scan swept through it. There were seven people inside. Myraian, of course; three men and a woman with biononics configured to low-level defence, allowing him little acuity – however they weren't weapons-active; that left an ordinary human male with no biononics, and a very large human in an armour suit with a force field already powered up. That alone made Aaron bring several weapon enrichments to active status.

He sent an identity ping into the capsule, which was returned by everyone except the ordinary human. He took a guess that he was the important one Oscar was escorting to meet Ozzie.

The old capsule settled on the swathe of purple and green grass between the lake and the house. Its door opened and the passengers started to clamber out. Myraian was first, waving gaily; which Aaron ignored. Beckia and Tomansio ran a quick field scan across the area – but not Oscar, which was interesting. Only then was the natural human allowed out. He was slightly older than Commonwealth-standard, and quite dignified-looking. The armoured figure of Troblum was last, having to squirm about to get through the door.

Ozzie, Inigo and Corrie-Lyn came up behind Aaron to watch the visitors approach. Ozzie was grinning. 'Holy crap, it really is Oscar.' He raised his voice. 'Yo dude, been a while there.'

Oscar tipped his forefinger to Ozzie, smiling sheepishly.

But it was Tomansio's reaction which held Aaron. He was staring right at him, a look of incredulity on his handsome face. 'You!' Tomansio gasped. 'You're alive.'

'Never better, man,' Ozzie said cheerfully. He turned to Inigo. 'See, legendary genius trumps messiah every time.'

'Go fuck yourself,' Inigo told him.

'I don't think—' Corrie-Lyn began as she looked from Tomansio to Aaron.

'The Mutineer,' Tomansio whispered. He still hadn't taken his gaze from Aaron.

A brief memory flickered up into Aaron's mind as if tearing silently through some vital membrane. *Her* face smiling coyly at him as she lay on the bed beside him. The same woman he'd encountered back in Golden Park the day Ethan had been selected as Cleric Conservator. Different hair, but still her. *Bad News.* 'What?' he croaked. 'What did you call me?'

Ozzie and Inigo were both frowning now, glancing over at Aaron.

'The Mutineer. It is you. It is!'

'No,' Beckia exclaimed. 'It can't be.'

'Who?' a puzzled Oscar asked.

'Lennox. Lennox McFoster, how can this be?' Tomansio demanded angrily. 'How can you be here?'

'The Knights Guardians spent centuries searching for you,' Cheriton said. 'Where have you been?'

'Sorry,' Aaron said. 'But I really don't know what the hell you're talking about.'

Even after ten minutes, the natural man still hadn't been introduced, and Troblum had been completely silent. The Knights Guardians were astounded by Aaron's existence, and quite forcefully insisting he was who they believed him to be. The son of Bruce McFoster, another old legend who had been captured and subverted by the Starflyer, and subsequently killed by Gore Burnelli. Lennox had been an infant at the time, they said, brought up by his mother Samantha as a Guardian. He'd been one of the first converts to the Cat's vision, desperate to find a new role for the Guardians of Selfhood as they teetered on the verge of self-destruction.

Their talk made Aaron nervous. Names and events were certainly registering somewhere in his mind, just not in the conscious section. He didn't doubt that he could originally have been one of the Knights Guardians; theirs was the kind of ability he had in abundance. Which made the rest uncomfortably plausible . . .

'What kind of mutiny did I lead?' he asked curiously. It was a question he shouldn't have asked. It was irrelevant.

'Pantar Cathedral,' Troblum said in a strangely neutral tone. 'It's on Narrogin. The Knights Guardians were brought in to help one of the local political movements achieve dominance over their rivals. The Cat herself took command in the field. There was a hostage situation. Demands were made with a deadline. Then she started slaughtering them anyway. Including their children. You stopped her. You stood up to the Cat.'

'That's when our whole movement changed,' Beckia said. 'We finally acknowledged the Cat's flaws. After that, we rejected her leadership. But not yours.'

'The majority of us rejected her,' Cheriton said slightly awkwardly. 'There was something of a schism. After all, she was our founder, bringing us out of the wilderness following the Starflyer

War and uniting us with the Barsoomians. Though legend says that part was your idea.'

Aaron knew he had to get the mission back on track; he should find out who the natural human was, make everyone talk to Ozzie and Inigo. *Get Inigo into the Void.* That was the universe – all that mattered. But for once the compulsion was weak. Her smile lurked behind his thoughts now. Sometimes he could see it without having to close his eyes.

Bad News.

She hadn't been kidding, apparently.

'Did I save them?' he asked faintly.

'Who?'

'The children. You said she was killing children when I stopped her.'

Tomansio and Beckia shared an uncomfortable look, which was an eloquent enough answer.

'Do you remember anything since then?' Cheriton asked.

Aaron shrugged. 'I don't even remember that. There's ... nothing,' he lied as the vision of a vast crystalline ceiling shimmered like flame somewhere in his mind.

'You were never caught,' Tomansio said. 'Never stood trial. Nobody knew what happened to you.'

'Including me, it appears,' Aaron said. It actually appealed to his sense of irony.

'Somebody did this to you,' Beckia said tightly. A great deal of anger was leaking out of her gaiamotes. 'Somebody gave you the galaxy's biggest mindfuck.'

'Could it have been her?' Tomansio mused.

'No,' Aaron said, not knowing where certainty came from, but knowing it anyway. 'It is my choice to be as I am. And I will retain this personality despite what you believe me to be.'

'But you're not working too good, are you?' Corrie-Lyn said. 'Your conditioning is breaking down.'

'I'll survive,' he said grimly. 'I have a mission to complete.'

'Which is?' Oscar asked.

Aaron pointed at Inigo. 'The Dreamer must be taken to Makkathran inside the Void. Or at least establish contact with the Heart.'

As one, Oscar and the three Knights Guardians looked at the natural man. He stepped forwards and put his hand out to Inigo. 'Dreamer,' he said. 'I'm Araminta-two.' His gaiamotes released a flood of thoughts and emotions, including the gifting from the observation deck on the *Lady's Light*.

'Great Lady,' Inigo grunted.

'Oh yeah,' Ozzie grinned. 'That is so cool, man.'

'I'm here to help,' Araminta-two said. 'The Pilgrimage has to be stopped.'

'Now tell them who suggested you team up with Ozzie,' Oscar said smugly.

At least it got them all talking, Aaron admitted. Even though it was little more than 'Gosh,' and 'Wow,' as various stories unfolded. But they sat around Ozzie's kitchen table, testing snacks and drinks from the culinary unit. All except Troblum, who stood at the head of the table, refusing to come out of his armour suit.

'I met the Cat,' was all he'd say on the subject. Everyone accepted that was a pretty good excuse for extreme paranoia.

The only other thing Troblum said was: 'Ozzie, it's a great honour to meet you; I am a descendant of Mark Vernon.'

'Yeah? That's nice, dude,' Ozzie said, and turned back to Araminta-two. 'We've been trying to figure out if the Void can bring people inside like some kind of teleport effect,' he said. 'Can you ask the Skylord that?'

'I can ask,' Araminta-two said.

Aaron kept watching Troblum. The big man had rocked back a fraction as Ozzie dismissed him. There was no hint of a gaiafield emission. In fact, there was no way of telling exactly what was in that suit.

According to Oscar, Troblum had helped build the Swarm.

Again something both Ozzie and Inigo seemed completely uninterested in. Aaron was interested, but only in that such information might break Earth out of its prison. But right now that was a long way down any list of possible actions to take to get Inigo into the Void. Besides, given the Raiel couldn't break through the Sol barrier, he suspected that might take even longer than accomplishing his primary mission.

'Is there any way you or the Heart can reach out and bring me into your universe?' Araminta-two asked the Skylord.

Aaron glimpsed an amazing golden web of nebula dust, fluorescing from dozens of dim glimmer points within as stars contracted to their ignition points. Skylords shone against the drifting eddies, their vacuum wings fully extended.

'You approach,' the Skylord said. 'I feel you growing. Soon you will be here. Soon you will reach fulfilment.'

'I will be with you sooner if you could reach for me.'

'The Heart reaches for all. The Heart welcomes all.'

'I am still outside your universe. I fear I cannot reach you. Can you reach out for me as you once did for others of my race?'

'Those of your kind grew here upon the solid worlds. My kindred will take you there.'

'But first we have to get to you. Can you make that happen?'

'I feel you growing. It will not be long now.'

'How did the first of my kind arrive in your universe?'

'They emerged, as do all.'

'Did the Heart help them emerge?'

'The Heart welcomes all who emerge here.'

'I can no longer reach you. My voyage to your universe is over unless the Heart helps me. Ask it to reach for me, please. I wish to visit the world where my kind dwelled before.'

'You will come.'

Araminta-two's thoughts hardened. 'I will not.'

'You continue to grow closer. Your voyage is unbroken. We will welcome you. We will guide you.'

Araminta-two growled and shook his head as the Skylord's presence dwindled to a background murmur at the very brink of perception. 'Ozziedamnit.'

'I will if you want me too, man, but I doubt it'll do much good,' Ozzie said.

Araminta-two gave him an abashed look. 'Sorry. Force of habit.'

'It hardly matters,' said Inigo. 'Ever since you started talking to the Skylords it's been obvious they simply don't comprehend the concept of "outside". Their thoughts aren't configured for that.'

'But the Heart or nucleus or whatever's running the place does,' said Oscar. 'It listened to you when you asked it to take Justine inside. That was quite a night.'

'It was still relayed through the Skylord,' Ozzie said. 'And that request was a lot easier to comprehend.'

'So we have to work out how to make the message simpler,' Inigo said. 'All we have to do is establish some kind of conduit to the Heart. It will understand exactly what we want.'

'Dude, you can't get a message more simple,' Ozzie protested. 'It's convincing the Skylord to talk for us which is difficult.'

'Suspiciously so,' Inigo said. 'I find it hard to believe something that can manipulate the Void fabric as the Skylords can do are genuinely unable to grasp new concepts.'

'The control processes seem instinctive,' Ozzie countered. 'Direct willpower is the driving force for any modification within the Void itself.'

'Yes, but—'

Aaron felt a sigh building in his chest as they started to argue again. *Her* smile became mocking.

'I can get you there in time,' Troblum said.

Everyone turned to the giant dull grey figure looming over them. Myraian let out the faintest giggle.

Ozzie pushed a big frond of floppy hair back from his forehead. 'Dude, how are you going to do that?'

'I have the Anomine planetary ftl engine in my starship.'

Silence again.

'The what?' Oscar asked.

'The Anomine didn't build the Dyson Pair force-field generators, they acquired them from the Raiel. To get them into position they used an ftl system big enough to move a planet. I have it. Or a copy of it. Actually, it's a copy of what I believe they built.'

Aaron didn't care how uncertain the others were. 'Is it faster than an ultradrive?' he asked.

'Yes. It's effectively instantaneous. It's a wormhole.'

'A wormhole big enough to shove a planet through?' Ozzie's voice had risen a notch with incredulity.

'Yes.'

'Not possible.'

'Actually, it's perfectly possible,' the house smartcores announced.

Ozzie growled and shot the ceiling a furious look.

'Wormhole structure is dependent on the power source,' the smartcores said. 'The greater the available power, the bigger the size you can achieve – theoretically.'

'That's right,' Troblum said.

'Okay,' Ozzie said. 'So what do you use to power the mother of all wormholes?'

'A nova. Nothing else approaches the required output peak.'

'Well that's handy, dude. We'll just hang around and see if one happens.'

'You don't need to,' the smartcores said in the same voice, but with a gloating edge.

'Ah,' Aaron smiled. 'Nova bomb.'

'Yes,' Troblum said. 'With a diverted energy function.'

'Clever,' Inigo said.

'You've gotta be fucking kidding me,' Ozzie yelled.

'I think it will work,' Troblum said.

'You mean you haven't tried it?' Tomansio asked.

Myraian started giggling again, louder this time.

'No. Not yet.'

'And it can get us to the galactic core ahead of the Pilgrimage fleet?' Aaron persisted.

'It should. I envisaged transporting a Saturn-sized planet five hundred lightyears as a test. But there are variables. If we make the wormhole diameter smaller—'

'You can increase the reach,' Inigo finished. 'So for something the size of a starship . . .'

'I estimate we can extend the wormhole approximately twenty-five to thirty thousand lightyears. If we trigger it today, it will put us ahead of the Pilgrimage fleet.'

Ozzie stood up. 'Okay then. My work is done. Good luck to all of you.'

'You're not coming?' Inigo asked.

'Hey, dude, I'm an ageing irrelevancy with only half a brain, remember. And then there's—' He frowned expressively, clicking his fingers. 'What was it? Oh yeah: I want to stay alive!'

'Ozzie, you'd be a valuable member of any team working to prevent the expansion phase,' Corrie-Lyn said.

'No he wouldn't,' Myraian said. She smiled sweetly at Corrie-Lyn. 'Ozzie stays here, where I can cuddle him safe.'

'Can't argue with that,' Ozzie said triumphantly.

Aaron was beginning to question exactly what Myraian was. He'd assumed she was just some worshipful groupie, one with a dipsy habit. But now he'd been here a few days he was realizing she actually had quite a say in the relationship. No doubt it was a strange relationship, but then that was Ozzie for you. Even with his reduced memories Aaron knew Ozzie could be extremely quirky, and those memories were a couple of centuries out of date. 'All right then, Ozzie isn't essential. Inigo is, and Aramintatwo. I have to go. So how many more can your starship hold, Troblum?'

'Hey!' Corrie-Lyn snapped.

'I'm dealing in practicalities,' Aaron explained patiently. 'There are minimum requirements for mission success. The Dreamer and Second Dreamer are the absolute priority for this flight.'

'Who the fuck put you in charge?' Tomansio asked.

'Do you have a viable plan for shutting down the Void? I'm sure we'd all like to hear it if you do.'

'By all accounts, you haven't got much of one yourself. You know more about who you are than what you're doing.'

'But I do have a plan. And I'm the Mutineer, remember? The one Knight Guardian you can rely on above all the others. Even yourself.'

'You might have been the Mutineer, but I'm damned if I know what you are now. And you certainly don't.'

They all turned to look at Ozzie, who was laughing boisterously.

'What?' Tomansio asked.

'Seriously? Have you dudes even been listening to yourselves? The Dreamer. The Martyr. The Second Dreamer. The Mutineer. Jezus H, all you need is masks and some spandex capes and we'd have us a regular superhero convention going. At least Troblum's got himself a costume already. Good one, too, big man, by the way.'

'Are you saying we shouldn't go?' Tomansio asked.

'By all the rules of probability and statistics you shouldn't even have made it this far, not any of you, because you are seriously fucking clueless. But you have got here, and someone knows what they're doing loading whatever plan they have into the Mutineer's brain. So grab this, as far as I can make out you guys are the last chance we've got to stop Ilanthe and the Void itself. I don't know what Aaron's boss has got in mind for when you get to Makkathran, but ... Tomansio, he's right; unless you've got an idea, then this is the one you bust your balls to make sure works. Tell the kids how it is, Oscar. You and I have gone face to face against odds like this once before. You know when something is real.'

'Yeah,' Oscar said grudgingly. 'Ozzie's right. This is looking like our one shot. Both Dreamers together? If anyone can stop this it's going to be them. Somehow.'

Tomansio shrugged. 'Okay. I'm just saying, we don't know which side the Mutineer is on.'

'Logically it's a Faction opposing the Accelerators,' Inigo said. 'I've been through all this. I actually do trust him.'

'Ha!' Corrie-Lyn said.

'All right, so Troblum, how many of us can your starship hold?' Cheriton asked. 'And does it really have wings?'

'Life support will sustain fifteen people, but that's cramped. And they're thermal dissipator fins,' Troblum said.

'There's only ten of us,' Oscar said. 'We can all fit in easy, then.'

Ozzie cleared his throat. 'You're still not thinking. How long did it take Justine to reach the fake Far Away?'

'Oh crap,' Aaron said. 'Void time.'

'That's right, man. So your actual question is how many medical chambers has Troblum got on board? Because you're going to need suspension once you make it past the boundary.'

'One,' said Troblum.

'There are five in the *Elvin's Payback*,' Oscar said. 'They were installed in case we got simultaneous casualties.'

'You always did lack real faith in us,' Tomansio grinned. 'We need four more, then. Are any available in this compartment, Ozzie?'

'Not right now,' Ozzie said in a suspiciously neutral voice. 'They're all very busy for the first time in decades. Don't worry, my replicator can put some together for you.' He raised his voice. 'Is that right me-brain-in-a-jar?'

'Already started,' the house smartcores replied.

'I suppose our replicator can produce them as well,' Oscar said. 'That should shrink our departure time.'

Troblum still wouldn't take his armour suit off. Oscar didn't quite know what to make of that. Paula's u-shadow had sent him a largish file on the ex-Accelerator agent. But that just kicked up a whole load of additional questions.

Tomansio had been right to question Aaron; but Oscar was a lot more concerned about the strange big man with enough personality flaws to fill entire psychology texts. *And an ftl system big enough to shift entire planets? Gas-giant planets? Come on.*

Then again it was all past worrying about. They were committed now. If everything worked and Aaron's unknown boss got to talk with the Heart the entire Void/Pilgrimage nightmare could be over within a week.

Yeah, that's going to happen.

Ozzie was right, though. That was all they had left. So he sat at the kitchen table without complaining or analysing, eating some of the bagels and salmon which Ozzie's culinary unit had provided for their brunch. It would have been nice to chat to Ozzie, he reflected; not that they'd ever been close, but they certainly had a lot of shared history. It wasn't to be. Ozzie and Inigo seemed to spend the entire time arguing with each other. And in the short intervals when they had to take a breath Tomansio was busy interrogating Aaron.

The house smartcores (and that was pretty weird even by Ozzie standards) and Liatris said the new medical chambers would be fabricated within the hour. That just left installing them on the *Mellanie's Redemption*. Another blast-from-the-past name which Oscar could have done without. *But then when you're as old as me I guess everything is connected.*

'I hope you never restart mindspace,' Inigo said heatedly. The voice was getting loud, everyone had to drop their own conversations and listen in. 'It's the end of humanity, sending the mind down a rotten branch of evolution.'

'Psychology is an evolutionary trend?' Ozzie grunted back. 'Gimme a break.'

'You're imposing it on every sentient. At least the gaiafield had a provision for individuals to withdraw. This doesn't. It's mental fascism, and the worst of it is you think it's benevolent, for our own good. Blanket the galaxy with mindspace and you'll turn us into the kind of society I found in the Last Dream. Don't you get it: utopia is boring; ennui is our true enemy. You and the Void both have to be stopped. You were wrong about sharing thoughts just like Edeard in his dark phase. Both of you were seduced by the Heart's version of perfection, which is nothing more than taming and enslaving the human soul.'

Aaron sat down next to Oscar, holding a plate of waffles. Oscar leaned over and whispered. 'Liatris says the replicator will be finished in eighteen minutes.'

'Maybe there's something to be said for the Void's time acceleration after all,' Aaron muttered back.

'Have they been like this all the time?'

'Five days, nonstop. I encouraged them to explore options.'

'So what do you make of our big silent friend?' Oscar nodded gently at the hulking armour suit.

'Neutral for the moment. I can accept his concern about the Cat. If he keeps it on inside his own starship then I'll have to make some decisions.'

'Yeah. And you really don't know what's going to happen once we reach Makkathran?'

'No. But I like your optimism.'

Oscar gave him another look. He liked to think he could tell. But Aaron had this human shell wrapped over something very odd indeed – almost a void in itself. He mimicked personality rather than possessing one of his own. And Corrie-Lyn hadn't been subtle about the near-breakdowns.

'Individuality cannot stand as it has always done,' Ozzie protested. 'The human race has to become collective. For fuck's sake, we have nova bombs, M-sinks, quantumbusters, enough weapons to smash the galaxy to shit without the Void even having to wake up. That power has to be restrained. Ask the Mutineer over there. Don't you ever stop and think what'll happen if someone like the Cat gets hold of them and goes on a rampage. For fun! There has to be an inbuilt protection mechanism in a society as technologically sophisticated as ours. And that is *trust*, man. It's all it ever can be. Mindspace will make trust inevitable. You really will be able to love your neighbour.'

'Mindspace is exactly the same as giving a psychopath a

Commonwealth Navy warship. There are aliens out there who have thought processes so utterly different to ours they'll think you're trying to take them over or evangelize and alter their culture.'

'That is a serious bunch of crap, what do you know about—'

A red exovision tactical warning sprang up over Ozzie and Inigo, and secondary thought routines supplied Oscar's mind with a definition of the problem. A T-sphere was establishing all around Ozzie's house. 'Shit!'

His integral force field came on. As it did, he saw Troblum's suit blacken to deepest night. *Son of a Bitch, that's Sol-barrier technology.*

Full field-function scan showed seventeen Chikoya teleport onto the grassy slope just above the lake shore. A quick follow-up scan revealed they were heavily armoured, weapons active.

'Liatris, come get us. Now.'

'On my way,' Liatris replied.

Another twenty-three Chikoya teleported in, completing their encirclement of the house. A six-strong squad charged forward across the front lawn. Oscar was about to ask Tomansio what attack formation he wanted to use when his field scan reported something very odd happening to Ozzie's quantum structure. Accelerant-flooded nerves reacted fast, spinning him round, targeting graphics swept across the abnormality zone, focusing on Ozzie, who was already becoming transparent as his body's molecules *changed*, attenuating. There was just enough of him left to reveal an apologetic expression on his spectral face. He raised a hand in a half-hearted wave.

'Wait!' Oscar yelled. 'You're leaving?' it came out as sheer disbelief.

'This kinda thing really isn't me any more,' Ozzie replied faintly.

'Yes it is! You're Ozzie. Help us.'

'You dudes have it pretty much covered. But hey, one day I might join in again. Don't hold your breath.' And with that his outline vanished. Some kind of disturbance stirred the underlying quantum fields. Something way beyond Oscar's field-function scan to analyse.

'Fuck me!' Beckia gasped. 'Where's he gone?'

'Irrelevant,' Tomansio said. 'Mutineer, you safeguard the Dreamers. Everyone else, let's meet and greet. Compass-point deployment, beat them back from the house.'

Oscar crunched his way straight through the kitchen wall and leapt from the veranda, flying a good fifteen metres over the dark grass. He landed on the lawn that sloped down to the lake. Tomansio was on his right, heading for the spinney that bordered the garden. Beckia was on his left, where the land started to curve upwards before breaking into rough terrain. Oscar was gratified to see how well he fitted into the team, knowing at an automatic level how to position himself.

He'd never seen a Chikoya before, never mind six at once. It was a shock, but all he was concerned about was a tactical analysis of the armour, weapons and manoeuvrability. A small traitor section of his mind wondered what Dushiku or Jesaral would make of something that big in knobbly black armour rampaging towards them with husky weapons swinging round to shoot. All he saw was the exovision targeting structure, with secondary routines coordinating fire control for his enrichments. Electronic warfare emissions hammered the Chikoya suit circuits, hashing and confusing their sensors. Energy beams and distortion pulses blasted through the air. Two Chikoya went tumbling backwards, their armour smouldering, spraying jets of a dark purple blood from gaping wounds. The others went for cover, firing as they went.

Masers slashed across Oscar's integral force field, which deflected them easily. Then his macrocellular clusters warned him of a targeting scan, and he jumped again as an electron laser detonated the ground where he'd been standing half a second before. He somersaulted at the top of his jump trajectory, twisting left, landing at a crouch and sending a massive distortion pulse at the Chikoya who was hefting the enormous beam gun.

On either side of him the Knights Guardians were hopping between cover points, their speed amplified by accelerants and biononic muscle reinforcement. A range of suppression fire lashed out, forcing the Chikoya back from the house.

Oscar was sprinting along the scorched grass as one of the aliens followed his movement with some kind of neutron beam which was gouging through the soil and stone, creating a fantail of lava and flame in his wake. He dispensed a hail of micro-missiles at the origin. Something exploded. The shockwave buffeted him. There was no more neutron beam.

'Anyone know what they want?' Beckia asked as she rolled over a clump of boulders. A flight of smartmines arched out to bombard the Chikoya squad slithering through the boulders on the slope above her.

'The Dreamer,' Aaron told her.

'Why?' Oscar asked. Two Chikoya were charging right at him, masers and machine guns firing enhanced explosive grenades that pummelled the ground and air all around as he dodged along a narrow drainage gully that led down to the lake. He sprang up and got a clean electron laser shot at the magazine on an opponent's underbelly. The explosion shredded most of the alien. Steaming lumps of gore and fragments of armour rained down.

'Never quite got that far into the conversation,' Aaron said.

A tactical display showed Oscar how the Knights Guardians were successfully pressing the Chikoya away from the house in a rough expanding circle. However, some were still close to the other side of the house, creeping forwards. Cheriton was having a hard time of it prising them free from their cover on the steep forested slope. 'Liatris, where are you?'

'Two minutes,' Liatris promised.

The Chikoya were starting to regroup along the shoreline ahead of Oscar. Several of them splashed through the shallows.

Oscar began to designate targets for his smartseeker munitions. Then his field scan showed him Myraian dancing across the smoking remains of the lawn towards them. He risked sticking his head out from the gulley to watch her. She was skipping and twirling as if she was in some elaborate ballet performance. Her gauzy blouse with its wing sleeves spun around her as she waved her arms, creating serpentine loops in the air. Chikoya targeting lasers converged on her.

'What the fuck . . . ?' Oscar grunted. His field scan couldn't detect any kind of integral force field. 'Get down!' he screamed at her. The crazy woman must be doped up on something. She seemed totally unaware of what was going on.

Myraian sang as she danced, the kind of warbling verse Oscar would've expected to hear from a Silfen, not a human. The ground around her feet rippled as tatters of loam and gravel were churned up by the storm of kinetic projectiles missing her. And they kept on missing her. The Chikoya simply couldn't get anything to hit. The armoured aliens began to fall back as she approached. Their weapons fire stopped. Myraian finished her madcap dance directly in front of one of the massive aliens. She giggled and swept her arms out wide to bow gracefully, bodylight glowing an exotic orange through her flimsy clothes. The Chikoya didn't move, its extended suit sensors tracked her carefully. Then she raised herself on her tiptoes, looking pitifully small and weak compared to the armoured monster towering above her. She kissed the alien on the tip of its helmet.

The Chikoya collapsed on the ground. Dead.

Myraian pirouetted away as the rest of the Chikoya squad opened fire. Again they couldn't get a fix. She was almost invisible behind a blaze-cloud of grenade detonations and stark purple ionization contrails.

Oscar realized he needed to breathe again.

'Let's give her some support,' Tomansio ordered.

A cascade of smart weapons fell on the Chikoya squad. They broke and ran, leaving the shore strewn with fatalities. Myraian skipped gaily through the shallows, following them like some demented pixie storm trooper, kicking at the spume as she went. Her fluffy plimsolls were stained grey-blue with alien blood.

Oscar jumped up out of the long drainage gully and stared in disbelief. Two of the Chikoya being chased by Myraian teleported out. 'Holy crap,' he murmured. *What is she?* Although exact definitions didn't really concern him at this moment. He was just relieved she was on their side.

Five kilometres overhead, the *Elvin's Payback* arrived in a burst of sharp violet light as it decelerated hard. Above it, Oscar could just make out a ragged black hole punched through the compartment's dome; crumpled metallic shards tumbled silently through the tortured air on their long fall to the ground. Thin strands of mist grew in density around the rent, stretching and curving up to pour out into the vacuum beyond. The glowing cometary sphere suddenly flared, shoving out eight vivid pseudopods of dazzling flame. They separated from the starship, and accelerated downwards towards the beleaguered house. His biononics felt the combatbots' first sensor sweep.

The Chikoya must have known what was coming. Another three teleported out.

'Ozziedamned monsters,' Cheriton exclaimed. Seven of them on higher ground were targeting him with a barrage of energy beams and a ferocious kinetic broadside, pushing his integral force field dangerously close to its limit.

'Priority target,' Tomansio ordered Liatris. 'Take out the hostiles surrounding Cheriton.'

A massive spear of incandescence lanced down out of the turbulent sky to strike the incline behind the house. Parts of Chikoya spewed upwards. Aggressive flames swirled over trees and bushes populating the slope. Cheriton was still being targeted by four Chikoya.

Oscar's scan showed him a T-sphere locus establishing itself around his team mate. 'Counterprogram,' he yelled.

'Can't,' Cheriton replied.

Oscar, Tomansio, and Beckia immediately launched a volley of smartmissiles over the roof of the house. While he was fending off such an intense attack, Cheriton's bionomics wouldn't be able to counterprogram the T-sphere as well as maintain his integral force field. The combatbots fired again, eliminating more Chikoya. This time the energy impact kicked up a long wildfire line across the forest, the formidable heat igniting whole trees. Thick smoke billowed up, cutting off all visual observation. But Oscar's field-function scan could still slice clean through. He watched his exovision display showing Cheriton being teleported away.

'Fuck it! Liatris, where did they take him?' Oscar demanded. 'Where's the T-sphere centre?'

The combatbots were barely five hundred metres overhead. They fired down continuously, adding to the conflagration now burning around half the house. The surviving Chikoya were teleporting out as fast as they could.

'It's centred in the Farloy compartment, about twelve hundred kilometres along the Spike. That's one of the major Chikoya settlements.'

'Are you getting any kind of signal from him?' Tomansio asked.

'Negative. Shall I fly over there and run a detailed sensor sweep?'

'No,' Tomansio said.

Oscar eyed the wall of fire that was creeping down the slope to consume the trees closest to the house. Thermal imaging was showing him some alarming temperatures blossom across the walls. The T-sphere shrank to zero. He admitted Tomansio was right. Not that it was easy.

'Land by the house,' he told Liatris. 'I need the Dreamers safe on board before we get an entire Chikoya army teleporting in. Aaron, bring them out, please.'

'Confirm,' Aaron said.

Oscar turned round and ran a sweep along the shoreline. There were nine dead Chikoya scattered across the blackened lawn, two of them lying in the water. His bionomics couldn't find any trace of Myraian. He shook his head in bemusement at the fantastical woman. In a strange way he was rather glad she'd disappeared; it meant he didn't have to think about her.

Elvin's Payback thumped down out of the sky, sending out a shockwave that shattered the house's remaining windows and brought roof slates skittering down. It hovered five metres above the ruined garden. Oscar and the remaining Knights Guardians closed in, ready to provide cover as Aaron led the two Dreamers, Corrie-Lyn and Troblum out across the veranda and underneath the starship. Its airlock bulged upwards and Inigo rose into it. Corrie-Lyn was next.

A couple of large trolleybots floated out of the house, each one carrying a medical chamber. Flames were flickering along the roof, gaining hold on the rafters. Smoke curled out of the gaping first-floor windows.

'What do we do?' Oscar asked Tomansio as they backed towards the starship. 'Do we go after him?'

'No. He's true Knights Guardians, he's not expecting us to. That would jeopardize the mission.'

'Jesus? What will they do to him?'

'If I was a Chikoya I'd worry about what he'll do to them. Human biononics are a damn sight meaner than anything they've ever built.'

The medical chambers were lifted smoothly up into the starship. It was just Oscar, Tomansio and Beckia left. The starship's force fields came on around them.

'But they targeted him,' Oscar said; even inside the protective shields he couldn't relax. 'It was deliberate. They must have known he wasn't a Dreamer.'

'Maybe they thought he was me,' Aaron told them. 'I had quite a run-in with the Chikoya before you arrived.'

'Irrelevant,' Tomansio said. He gestured at Oscar to step under the open airlock. 'We have a job to do.'

'Not irrelevant,' Oscar insisted as he began to float up into the fuselage. He knew he was missing something, and it was making him very cross. 'Surely he can get some kind of signal out? Liatris, are you seeing any sign of a firefight in the Farloy compartment?'

'No. Nothing registering.'

Oscar slid up into the cabin to find the Dreamers and a miserable, shaking Corrie-Lyn giving him an anxious look. Troblum's helmet almost touched the ceiling. His armour had reverted to shabby grey again. He still hadn't opened it up.

Beckia arrived, swiftly followed by Tomansio. The cabin was feeling quite cramped even with the furniture withdrawn.

'Up and out,' Tomansio said. 'Come on Oscar, let's go.'

Oscar bit back any immediate comment and told the smartcore to take them back through the hole Finitan had created in the dome above. 'We could make one flyover,' he said.

'They could have teleported him to any compartment on the Spike by now,' Beckia said sadly. 'Or even into a starship. He could already be ftl.'

'No he's not,' Oscar said, reviewing the sensor records as they passed through the mini-hurricane surrounding the hole and emerged back into space. 'Nothing's gone ftl in the last ten minutes.'

'Oscar, drop it,' Tomansio said. 'He's gone, and hopefully he took a whole bunch of the Chikoya bastards with him. When we get back to Far Away you're welcome to attend the ceremony of renewal. We'll grow him a new body and download his secure memory store into it. He'll spend the whole evening teasing you about worrying.'

Oscar wanted to hit something. 'All right.' *But I know something is wrong.* He concentrated on the starship's sensors. The *Mellanie's Redemption* had left its landing pad at the same time as the *Elvin's Payback*. Now it was holding station five thousand kilometres on the Spike's darkside. He told the smartcore to rendezvous with it.

'Troblum, we're safe now.'

'Good,' the armoured figure said.

'You can take your helmet off.'

There was a long pause while the big figure did nothing. Then horizontal lines of malmetal on the helmet flowed apart, leaving three segments on each side. They swung open.

Oscar tried to be neutral. Troblum's face was fat and heavy, his skin an unhealthy pallor, and dribbling with sweat. Patchy stubble coated his cheeks and chins. 'Hello,' he said sheepishly to his audience. He couldn't meet anyone's gaze.

'Thank you for offering your help,' Inigo said. 'We appreciate it.'

Troblum gave a rough nod, but didn't say anything.

Oscar didn't like the idea of relying on him one bit, there didn't seem to be any empathy. Troblum was not a likeable person, and he'd decided that from just the half-dozen sentences the man had spoken. Not that there was anything they could do about it. *I'm committed. Again. Let's hope I don't have to die this time.*

'So how did the Chikoya find you?' Liatris asked Inigo.

'Plenty of people in Octoron would know where Ozzie lives,' Aaron said. 'I'm surprised it took them this long, actually.'

'I'm just glad you arrived before they did,' Corrie-Lyn said. She was still trembling, even though she'd got a chair to extend and was sitting all hunched up. 'We wouldn't have stood a chance otherwise.'

'Don't be so sure,' Beckia said. 'Whatever that Myraian had was more than they could deal with.'

'Is she a Silfen?' Tomansio asked.

'No,' Araminta-two said. 'I would have known that. She was human.'

'I think "was" is right,' Oscar said. 'She's not post-physical, but she's certainly more than Higher.'

'Speaking of not being physical,' Aaron said. 'Ozzie?'

'Lady alone knows,' Inigo said. 'My physics is centuries out of date, but whatever he did was seriously advanced.'

'He transmuted his quantum state,' Troblum said. 'Somehow he went outside spacetime.'

'Personal ftl?' Corrie-Lyn asked incredulously.

'Probably not. You have to time-phase to do that.'

'So is he post-physical?' Oscar asked.

'I'd say not in the classical sense, but I don't have any empirical evidence,' Inigo said. 'Normally, post-physicals don't hang around afterwards. And he was dedicated to helping the human race in many ways. I know, we discussed it at length.'

'Certainly did,' Aaron murmured.

The *Elvin's Payback* drew alongside *Mellanie's Redemption*. The two starships manoeuvred for a few seconds before their airlocks touched and sealed. Troblum was the first through, moving surprisingly quickly. The others let him go without comment, though Oscar knew they were all a little perplexed by the enigmatic Higher.

He followed Troblum through the airlocks, emerging into a cabin that was almost the same size as the one he'd just left. A very attractive girl was waiting there, dressed in old-fashioned clothes; her hands pressed anxiously against the chest of Troblum's armour as she asked if he was all right. Oscar frowned at the sight. There'd been no mention of a companion. And with the best will in the universe, he couldn't imagine a girl like that partnered with Troblum. Perhaps she was his daughter? But there'd been no reference to a family in his file.

The others were crowding into the cabin; they all shared an identical mildly surprised expression as they saw the girl. Gaiamote emissions were hurriedly reduced.

'This is Catriona,' Troblum mumbled.

'Hello,' she smiled shyly.

Oscar saw Tomansio staring at an electronic device on the cabin's lone extended table. It looked vaguely familiar. Secondary routines ran a comparison search through his storage lacunae. 'Oh,' he said softly. His retinas switched to infrared, which confirmed it. Catriona was a solido projection.

Then a trolleybot glided in carrying a medical chamber and everyone was suddenly busy making room. The next trolleybot appeared, and Oscar started to think some of them were going to have to go into suspension before they reached the Void. *And given I'm just about redundant now...*

Troblum opened a low hatch into a companionway. 'We can stack some of the medical chambers here.'

'Is this all the space there is?' Inigo asked dubiously.

'Once the planetary ftl has launched we can use the forward cargo hold. Until then, we'll just have to squeeze in.'

The medical chambers kept coming. Two fitted into the narrow companionway. Troblum got the cabin bulkhead to extrude thin shelves. There was just enough height for the big dark sarcophagi to be stacked three high. That left everyone else with standing room only, and pressed uncomfortably close.

'I'll join you later,' Catriona said, and faded away. Troblum pretended not to notice. His armour suit opened up and he stowed it in a broad luggage cylinder that telescoped up out of the decking. The toga suit he wore was about the shabbiest Oscar had ever seen.

'Are there any sleep cubicles?' Beckia asked.

'Three,' Troblum told her.

'One for me,' she said quickly. Corrie-Lyn claimed the second. Somehow no one asked to use Troblum's personal cubicle.

It was still cramped in the cabin as the last medical capsule was secured and the airlock flowed shut.

'So how does this work?' Tomansio asked.

'We need an uninhabited star system,' Troblum explained. 'Also, the radiation from a nova can sterilize neighbouring star systems. So we really need a star that's fifteen lightyears away from any H-congruous planet to be safe. There are three candidates within fifty lightyears, an hour's flight time.'

'Closest one then,' Inigo said.

'That's the one furthest from the Void.'

'Oh. Well, how far to—' He stopped in surprise.

Oscar was suddenly aware of a personal gaiafield emission. The emotional content alone was enough for him to identify Cheriton. A sensation of panicky urgency made his heart flutter in sympathy. The emission strengthened into a gifting. 'Hello,' Cheriton's thoughts said softly. The need for reassurance was overwhelming.

Inigo and Araminta-two exchanged a meaningful look. 'We're here,' their minds choroused.

'No!' Aaron yelled. He raised his fists in silent exasperation and glared at the two Dreamers.

The gifting had no sight or sound or scent, just Cheriton's small befuddled thoughts. He was alone, unable to sense anything from his body. Only training and excellent self-control were keeping the fear at bay.

'Ah.' Another mind spoke with unnerving serenity. 'I hadn't thought of a gaiafield connection. I see you have an unusual number of gaiamotes, with some interesting little tweaks to their structure.'

Oscar thought the newcomer might not even be human. There wasn't the slightest timbre of emotion to be found anywhere.

'Go ftl,' Tomansio told Troblum. The big man had a scared look on his face. He was trembling. Catriona rematerialized in the cabin, and hugged him tightly.

The gifting expanded as Cheriton's eyes opened. He was staring up at some dark-grey ceiling. A head appeared above him, badly blurred. Focus was gradual, as his sluggish eyes responded to the pale oval shape. It was a woman's face, framed by short dark hair, smiling benevolently.

'Oh bollocks,' Oscar groaned.

'Hello, boys and girls,' said the Cat. 'I can feel you out there. How lovely, you care so much about your friend.'

'I can't move,' Cheriton reported. His self-control was starting to crack. Little bursts of fear were interrupting the gift as if it was conveying electric shocks.

'Sorry about that,' the Cat said. One hand lifted up into view; it was drenched with blood. Drops splashed down off each fingertip. 'But I couldn't have you running away, now could I?'

'Cheriton,' Tomansio said very calmly. 'You have to trigger your biononic overload. I'm so sorry. We'll hold the ceremony of renewal when we return home. I swear it.'

'I can't,' Cheriton's wretched thought came back. 'I can't.'

'We have your secure store. You will lose nothing.'

'I can't.'

A sleep cubicle door expanded. Corrie-Lyn ran out and clung to Inigo. She was fighting back tears.

'Cheriton,' Tomansio continued, his thoughts becoming stern. 'You have to do this. She'll infiltrate. The mission will be compromised.'

'Help me.'

'Oh my dears.' The Cat's smile hung above them, exuding an icy presence into the cabin even though she was nowhere close. Her lips widened into a mournful smile. 'The poor boy is telling the truth. He can't suicide. That's a weakness, and we all know what I think about being strong, now don't we? So I'm helping him. I took a nice big pair of scissors to his biononic connections.' She looked at her glistening scarlet hand, as if puzzled by the colour. 'I seem to have accidentally cut through a few nerves, too. Well, when I say cut I mean hacked. But on the positive side, nothing will hurt now, so that was kind of me, wasn't it?'

'Devil whore,' Tomansio sent. 'When this is over, I will find you.'

The Cat laughed. 'Better than you have tried. But I'm curious, exactly what is "this"? It's all very exciting, this gathering of yours. I'd like to be a part of it.'

'Go ftl,' Aaron said sharply. 'We have to get a head start. She will find out.'

'Yes,' the Cat agreed. 'Leave him. Leave him with me. All alone. We'll have such a party together.'

'Go,' Cheriton said. 'Just go. It will be over quickly. I'll not survive what she's done to me.'

'Oh now, my dear, that's just a big bad lie. I have a medical capsule and I'm not afraid to use it. The two of us will spend what seems like an eternity together. I might even make you Aaron's replacement. How lucky can you get?'

'Never.'

'How lovely. You believe you are strong.'

The gifting was suddenly flooded by a sharply defined image

surging up out of Cheriton's memories. A startled Cheriton found himself seven years old and sitting at the table eating a meal with his parents and two sisters. It was a pleasant time, with his mother and father talking to their children, interested in their day, encouraging questions. A delightful period of his life, suffused by happiness.

Then his father stood up. 'Come here,' he beckoned to Cheriton. As the young boy got to his feet his father activated several weapons enrichments.

'No!' Cheriton's frantic thoughts pleaded. 'No, no, this is me, this is my life.'

'It was boring, my dear. It makes you weak, and that's no use to me. I'm going to make it so much more interesting, and a little bit dirtier.'

'Stop this,' Aaron said.

'Or what?' the Cat asked over the sound of young Cheriton's distraught sobbing. The sizzle of weapons fire was deafening, blotting out the screams of his sisters. The stench made Oscar want to throw up.

'Now they don't exist any more, so let's edit them out of the rest of your life shall we?' the Cat said. 'And while I'm doing that, I'll have a think about what I can replace them all with. Something yummy, I feel. Something that is going to make you love me.'

'They are real,' Tomansio sent with a surge of conviction. 'Believe it, Cheriton. Know the truth. They did not die like that.'

The gifting degenerated into a chaotic swirl of images and sounds and sensations. Flashes of Cheriton's family slipped past them, draining to grey nothingness.

'Bring them back!' Cheriton wailed.

'Troblum,' Tomansio said. 'Get us out of here.'

Troblum only tightened his hold around Catriona. 'It's me she wants. She'll never stop, not ever. She never does. I know her. I studied what she is. Ask him.' He pointed at Aaron.

'I don't know,' Aaron said. 'This is what was done to me.'

'Bring who back?' the Cat asked lightly, her mind radiating gentle concern. 'Who, my dear?'

'What?' Cheriton's thoughts were confused.

'If she does want you there's only one place you can go to be safe,' Oscar said urgently to Troblum, worried by how distraught the big man seemed to be. He clearly wasn't thinking logically. 'Take us there,' he urged.

'Oh look,' the Cat said enthusiastically.

Another memory was jerked out of Cheriton's brain. This time Oscar found himself on a picnic by some small stream. Now Cheriton was the father. His wife and small son were with him.

A deep disquiet bubbled up into Cheriton's thoughts. This was a lovely time, yet he instinctively knew something was wrong.

'Stop this,' Tomansio said. 'You can extract what you need easily enough.'

'But this way I get to play first,' the Cat said. 'If my Cheriton is to belong to me, he can't have affections for anyone else, now can he?'

'Don't!'

'Troblum,' Aaron said with a menacing insistence. 'Get us out of here.'

'Please,' Araminta-two whispered. Her emotional output was rising to a fearsome level as she responded to Cheriton's terrible degradation. Oscar found the tears welling up in his own eyes at her distress.

'Like father, like son,' the Cat said.

Cheriton looked down to find himself holding a pump-action shotgun. 'No!' he screamed. 'No no no no. Stop her, in Ozzie's name, don't let her do this.'

'We can't leave him,' Corrie-Lyn sobbed. 'Not with her. Nobody can face this alone, it's inhuman.'

A ruby targeting laser stabbed out of Aaron's fist. It splashed on the solido projector. 'Now!' he hissed.

'Troblum!' Catriona wailed.

Cheriton's finger pulled the shotgun's safety off. It produced a nasty *snick* that echoed round the starship's cabin.

'It's not real,' Inigo vowed. 'Know this, Cheriton, and remember.'

'Oh dear Jesus,' Oscar moaned.

'Do it, you motherfucker,' Aaron yelled.

The *Mellanie's Redemption* flashed into hyperspace.

Justine: Year Forty-Five

Justine eased herself up into a sitting position, for once feeling every year of her age. Suspension over such a long time was a killer. Every muscle ached. She swore she could hear her joints creak as she moved them. Hunger pangs battled against nausea.

Secondary routines told her it was fifteen years since she'd last been out of the medical capsule for a brief inspection of the *Silverbird*. Exovision displays and secondary routines gave her a fast review of the starship's current status. Most on-board systems were functioning within acceptable parameters, though the degradation over the last forty years was noticeable.

Her u-shadow ordered the culinary unit to produce a banana-based protein drink. She grabbed the plastic cup with her third hand and hauled it across the cabin. A couple of minutes after she finished the gooey stuff she actually began to feel a bit better. Her muscles still ached, but with biononic support it was relatively easy to clamber out of the chamber. She wobbled her way over to the bathroom cubical, and ordered the cabin to extrude a shower compartment. Not a spore shower, but a decent original deluge of hot water that she could stand under and feel pounding on her skin. The heat soaked into her flesh, defeating the toxic stiffness that had built up during suspension. Then she rubbed on the gel, relishing the cleansing sensation – as if she really was washing away lethargy. Her skin began to tingle pleasurably. It was only after a while she realized she was probably broadcasting the whole soaped-up-girl-in-a-shower scene to most of the human race. *Through Dad!*

'Aww crap!'

A quick sluice of cold water promptly blew away any possible sense of erotica. She stepped out and picked up a thick towel. This whole sharing the body thing was going to take some getting used to. Not that she was particularly prudish, but still, *every* sensation . . .

Dried and dressed in a decent semi-organic blouse and trouser set she settled back into her favourite chair and reviewed the external sensor images. They were still travelling at point nine lightspeed, streaking through a star system. Two lighthours ahead of them was the unnaturally vivid blue and white speck of an H-congruous world. She began to smile as the sensors found the desert planet Nikran, orbiting thirty million miles closer to the star, while Gicon's Bracelet was almost on the opposite side of the star, showing as a bright cluster of lightpoints. No doubt about it, the Skylord was taking her directly towards Querencia.

Across the surrounding starfield the nebulas familiar from so many of Inigo's dreams were visible. The spectacular blue and green smear of Odin's Sea, crowned by its scarlet reefs; Buluku, the twisting river of violet stardust beset with impossible lightning storms up to half a lightyear long; and of course the glowing entwined folds of topaz and crimson that was Honious in all its dire glory.

Now she was actually here, Justine experienced something weirdly close to déjà vu. It was as if she had suddenly found out that a childhood fable was true, and the colourful monsters she'd read about were finally emerging from the pages of the book. It wasn't scary, but profoundly exciting; this was true pioneering. *Or maybe archaeology is closer to it.*

Her longtalk reached out for the Skylord. 'I thank you for bringing me to this world. My ship can fly and land by itself now.'

'I can take you closer,' it replied magnanimously.

'I would feel happier if my ship landed by itself. I am here now. I am content, for which I thank you.'

'As you wish,' the Skylord said.

Justine braced herself. Not that it did any good. The *Silverbird* was once again gripped by strange acceleration forces as the Skylord exerted its temporal manipulation ability. The star ahead transformed back to a yellow radiance as they slowed drastically. Red-shifted stars behind grew in magnitude and intensity. Querencia's clouds and icecaps darkened as its oceans fell to a deep sapphire. Iridescent colours swirled around the *Silverbird*'s fuselage as the Skylord's vacuum wings swept past it. Then they were separating swiftly.

'Watch for my kind, they will be here soon,' Justine sent. Receiving a serene flicker of acknowledgement in return.

Justine concentrated on the planet ahead. The Skylord had left her a hundred and fifty thousand kilometres out, and approaching fast. She ordered the smartcore to produce a vector which would put her into a twenty-degree inclination orbit a thousand kilometres out. From memory, Makkathran had been on the edge of the temperate zone. That orbit should allow her to see it visually. Somehow she couldn't imagine it had gone. Makkathran was a constant, whatever it was. Acting as a refuge for whatever race had the misfortune to stumble into the Void. It had been there for a long time before humans arrived, she was sure it would remain even today.

As soon as the *Silverbird* began its fifteen-gee deceleration she switched the confluence nest back on. It wasn't a memory she loaded in, more a belief, hopefully verging on obsession – that everything on board the starship would work. *Even if it's no more than a pathetic wish, it might be enough to keep the systems functional long enough to give me a proper landing.*

With that in mind she started thinking about practical items she might need after she arrived. The replicator was soon humming away, producing a wide range of clothes for every season. Food followed; fruit preserves and dried or cured meats, half-baked bread in sealed sheaths, basic packaged microbe-free meals that would take a long time to go mouldy or putrefy; juices and the odd bottle of wine. To cook it all she had the replicator fabricate a small barbecue grill (with bags of charcoal). After that she dragged up truly ancient memories of camping back at high-school, when she'd been equipped with (relatively) simple tools like a compass, and firelighters, pots, plates, cups, cutlery. Washing-up liquid. Soap. Shampoo! Several decent pairs of boots. Knives of various sizes, including the fattest Swiss-Army type she could pull from the smartcore's memory, which would virtually build her another starship if she could just figure out how to work the gadgets it contained. Rope. An old-fashioned tent. It seemed an endless list, which kept her absorbed right up to the moment when the *Silverbird* curved round into its designated orbit. After that she sat in the chair watching high-resolution projections of the world as it rolled past below.

The smartcore had made a reasonable job of mapping the planet's basic geography during the approach phase, capturing about two thirds of the continental outlines. Despite that, she couldn't really correlate what she was seeing with any of Edeard's landscapes. The shorelines, which should have given her the greatest clues, were unfamiliar from an orbital vantage point. So it was five orbits before she started to fly over mountains that could well be the Ulfsen range, which Edeard had first traversed with the Barkus caravan on his journey to Makkathran. *With Salrana*, she thought sadly. Their tragic, doomed romance had never meant much to her before, but now she was here where it had played out she felt a surprising emotional resonance stirring her. *Stupid meat body*, she cursed, and concentrated on the projected image.

No doubt about it, the Donsori Mountains were next. The Iguru Plain swept into view, a vast lush green expanse with those strange little volcanic cones. Then there it was straddling the coastline: Makkathran.

She stared at the big urban circle, marvelling at the familiar shapes of its districts as delineated by the dark curving canals.

Sunlight glimmered off the crystal wall, revealing it as a thin line encircling the city; dipping down into the sparkling Lyot Sea at the port district with its distinctive fishtail profile.

Under her direction the smartcore ran a final check on all drive systems. With the exception of the ultradrive, they were all working at above eighty per cent efficiency. Glitches were minimal.

'Take us down,' Justine told the smartcore. The starship began its final deceleration phase. That just left her one thing to decide. A decision she'd admittedly been putting off since arriving in orbit. *Do I take a weapon?* She was reasonably confident she could ward off any animal with her third hand, but what if a whole pack of dogs or fastfoxes rushed at her? So much time had passed that the dogs would have lost any trace of domesticity. And it wasn't just animals. She had no idea who was going to arrive in Makkathran over the next few weeks, or years, or decades – or however long she was going to have to spend here before Gore's plan became apparent.

Files of schematics flowed across her exovision. She chose one, and shunted the blueprints into the replicator. Two minutes later out slid a semi-automatic pistol with guaranteed jam-free mechanism. Next came five replacement magazines and five boxes of bullets – which really should be enough.

Ingrav had killed the *Silverbird*'s orbital velocity, allowing it to drop vertically. The starship hit the upper atmosphere, whose thin molecules started a faint scream from the buffeting impact. A long wavering trail of lambent ions stretched out behind the craft as it fell deeper and deeper.

Amber exovision alerts began to appear, warning Justine the force fields were edging close to overload. She shared her desperate desire that their generators would hold with the confluence nest, willing them to succeed. The amber alerts blinked off.

Regrav took over at fifteen kilometres altitude, slowing the descent. She began to study the city as the visual images built up. Deeper sensor scans were hazed as they began to probe the surrounding rock, denying her a clear picture of whatever lay beneath Makkathran. Though she could just make out the faint threads of several travel tunnels radiating out through the ancient lava field which was the Iguru Plain.

So I still don't know what it is, she thought in mild annoyance. But anything which could manipulate gravity, as it used to do to propel Edeard along the tunnels, had to be a high-technology intruder into this universe. The city's thoughts had admitted as much to Edeard when it told him about the Void's reset ability. *The night Salrana betrayed him*, she remembered, wishing the thwarted lovers didn't bother her quite so much. *Come on, girl, it was thousands of years ago. Their bodies are dust and their souls are partying in the Heart.*

Again – not the most comforting of thoughts. *If I die here I'll either wither away wondering through space, or be absorbed by the Heart. Or Honious.*

Cross with herself for showing off such weaknesses, she concentrated on the city that was expanding across the projections. A landing site was her priority now. There were so many places she wanted to see. And she would, but they were all in built-up areas. She could make out the larger buildings now, the domes of the Orchard Palace in Anemone, the odd twisting towers of Eyrie standing guard around the Lady's church. Her eyes darted towards Sampalok, and sure enough there in the central square was the six-sided building that Edeard had created out of the ruins of Bise's mansion.

'Oh holy crap,' she muttered. 'It *is* real.'

Fright or determination, she didn't know which, made her concentrate properly now. The thick band of meadowland between the crystal wall and the outer ring of canals made up of the High Moat, Low Moat, Tycho and Andromeda was a likely candidate, though it was terribly overgrown. She could see clumps of trees down there, which certainly hadn't been growing in Edeard's time. According to the radar sweep and mass scans what looked like grass from altitude was mostly bushes and vines.

Golden Park, then. The old flat fields within the pristine white pillars were as shaggy as the meadows outside, and the original avenues of huge martoz trees had multiplied and grown wild, but radar showed there were plenty of relatively level patches.

Silverbird continued its descent, twisting slightly to align itself over the westernmost part of the park, between the curves of Upper Grove Canal and Champ Canal.

Two warning icons appeared, telling her the regrav units were having to draw extra power to maintain a steady rate of descent. It was as if gravity was increasing, pulling the starship down.

And how do you wish gravity was less?

More warnings began to appear, reporting glitches in secondary systems. She felt a faint vibration starting to build up, and ordered her chair to grip her tightly. It responded sluggishly.

'Oh crap, here we go,' she groaned.

The starship was only a kilometre above the city as it started to pick up speed. *Nothing fatal*, she told herself. *Not yet*. The landing legs bulged out of the fuselage. *So something wants me to land okay*. Velocity was increasing more than she was comfortable with. She sent a series of instructions into the smartcore, composing her own procedures for a Void-style landing.

Five hundred metres and the Silverbird was ass down as it should be, with the nose tracing a slight arc in the sky as it wobbled. The exact landing spot she'd picked received a final radar sweep, confirming it was solid and stable.

Her thoughts slammed into the confluence nest, *demanding* normality. Power from the reserve D-sinks was channelled into the regrav units, pushing them up to their safety margins. She saw the towers of Eyrie come level with the starship, and beyond them, over in Tosella, the tip of the Blue Tower was now higher than her.

Silverbird's last hundred metres were a perfect landing profile, slowing to relative zero velocity ten metres above the wild vegetation. Then a half-metre-a-second descent until the landing legs touched. Spongy layers of leaves and moss and grass compressed, and only then when the base of each leg registered and confirmed solid contact did the regrav units shut off.

As if in sympathy, power drop-outs bloomed all over the

starship. Justine really didn't care. This had been nothing like as traumatic or dramatic as her touchdown on the replica Mount Herculaneum.

'Houston,' she said solemnly to the silent cabin. 'This is Golden Park base. The *Silverbird* has landed.'

10

Araminta had remained on the observation deck of the *Lady's Light* right from the start of the Pilgrimage. The room was as big as the Malfit Hall back in the Orchard Palace, and twice as high. Its floor was empty apart from a chair and a bed which had been brought in at her request. Araminta used the chair as little as possible, preferring to stand and stare ahead through the vast transparent section of fuselage. There was nothing to see, there hadn't been since hyperspace enfolded the massive ship. It was blank outside, with the occasional cascade of blue sparks slipping across the surrounding pseudofrabric their ultradrive was creating. Imperfections within the quantum-field interstice, Taranse had explained when she'd asked what they were. What caused such imperfections he didn't say – probably didn't know. She rather liked them, they provided the illusion that some material substance was outside, and the twinkling flaws registered their progress through it.

For five days she watched the nothingness flow past, gifting it to the billions of her followers back in the Greater Commonwealth. On the sixth day Araminta began to cry. Tears rolled down her cheeks as her shoulders quaked. The sorrow she radiated out into the gaiafield was so profound that the majority of beholders began to weep in sympathy. They were aghast, flooding the gaiafield with concern. 'What's wrong?' they asked in their bewildered billions, for nothing and nobody was in the observation deck with her. 'We love you, Dreamer.' 'Can we help?' 'Let us help, please.'

Araminta gave them no response. She stood resolutely in front of the disintegrating flecks of light, mute and distraught. Her personal staff were dismissed with a curt gesture when they ventured out on to the sleek expanse of floor. Even the loyal Darraklan was sent away without a word.

Inevitably, as she knew he would, Ethan appeared, and began the lonely walk towards her. Those sharing her dismay felt the anguish recede as she straightened herself. She made no attempt to wipe the tears from her eyes. Then her followers were standing on soft grassy land which fell away to a shoreline encased by high dunes. Sunlight shimmered off the idle waves that spanned the ocean's clear waters. A Silfen stood before her, majestic and ominous with his dark leather wings extended, tail poised high. 'You can do this,' he assured her.

'I know.'

The pendant around her neck flared with the joyous azure light of affirmation. And there was Ethan standing in front of her on the observation deck, his eyes narrowed against the cold light radiating from the pendant on its slim chain which now rested outside her white robe.

'Second Dreamer,' he said formally.

'Cleric Ethan.'

The absolute hatred directed by the followers of Living Dream at their ex-Conservator was staggering in its passion. He hesitated, then recovered with a sure smile which simply confirmed his dishonour before his audience.

'Perhaps you would like to tell your people what dismays you so,' he suggested smoothly.

'Are you aware?' she asked.

'Yes, Dreamer.'

'There is only one person in the universe who could have told you.'

'Indeed. However the messenger is not important. What she told me is.'

'In this case the message and the messenger are one, nor is the method by which the message was procured insignificant. She is the cause.'

'Nonetheless she has named you false.'

'Ilanthe lies. That is what she is now. The serpent among us all.'

'Is it true? Are you many?'

'I am.'

'Then I must question your intent.'

'Of course you must. Yet I will keep my word. I will lead this Pilgrimage into the Void as I promised.'

'You seek to thwart us,' he spat.

'I seek our true destiny. I seek to avoid the folly and fate of the Last Dream for the devout. I seek the Void's own fulfilment.'

'By allowing those who would destroy it to enter. That cannot happen.'

'I tell you now what I told Ilanthe and what I have also told Inigo. Our fate will be decided within the Void. It will be decided by the Void. Not by you, nor by anyone else. I have been chosen as the instrument to open a path into the Void, that is all. I am not a gatekeeper. All those who seek their fulfilment, whatever its nature, are free to enter the Void. Simply because their vision is different from yours and that of Living Dream does not entitle me to deny them passage. I do not judge, Cleric. Unlike you, I do not consider myself infallible.'

Ethan's uncertainty couldn't be more apparent if he'd allowed it to shine out through his gaiamotes. 'You have spoken to Inigo?'

'We are both Dreamers. We are together even now. Didn't your dearest Ilanthe tell you that?'

'Ilanthe is no friend of mine.'

'And yet you defer to it, whatever it is, whatever it seeks. The Dreamer Inigo released the Last Dream as a warning. Do you really think that dreary destiny of bored supermen is one to which we should aspire for our children?'

'I believe we have the right to choose our future. I wish to live my life on Querencia and achieve fulfilment and be guided to the Heart. You and Oscar and Aaron are trying to prevent that.'

Araminta gave him an icy smile. 'Sometimes to do what's right you have to do what's wrong.'

Ethan glanced about the massive observation deck as if seeking allies. 'If you deny us the Void it will go badly for you. That I promise. My *life* has been given to serving Living Dream. All I have done, all I have sacrificed, has led to the launch of this Pilgrimage. I will not tolerate betrayal.'

'You will enter the Void, Cleric. You will yet walk upon Querencia. You have my word on it. Now why don't you go and ask Ilanthe what future she desires for all of us? Or perhaps she doesn't trust you enough to answer.'

He nodded impersonally. 'As you say, the Void will ultimately triumph. I don't worry about Ilanthe's intent. What any of us do, our petty schemes and conspiracies, are an irrelevance in the face of the Void's majesty.'

'I'm glad we are as one in that view. Now don't bother me again.' She turned away from him and waited. Finally, she heard him walk away.

The gaiafield was awash with confusion and dismay. Her followers needed her to explain what was happening, what the Dreamer Inigo was doing.

'You'll see,' she assured them. 'In the Void there will be truth.'

*

It was a yellow star whose meagre family of planets consisted of a couple of airless solid worlds and a single gas giant that boasted over twenty moons. None of them ever had a chance to evolve life; wrong orbits and lack of volatile organic chemicals had seen to that. Now they were just circling endlessly waiting for the star to run through its main sequence and inflate into a red giant, devouring them all.

Mellanie's Redemption emerged from hyperspace eighty million kilometres from the star, and immediately activated its stealth systems. Inside the overcrowded cabin the mood was bleak. Oscar wasn't sure he could take many more emotional swings on this kind of scale. Abandoning poor Cheriton to the Cat had been tough on them all, though strangely Araminta-two had been the most affected. Tears had streamed down his face as the starship fled from the Spike. No amount of comforting from Inigo and Corrie-Lyn helped.

Then both Dreamers had abruptly joined in surprise as Justine's dream of landing at Makkathran came rushing through whatever tenuous contact they had with the Void.

'She made it,' Beckia exclaimed in surprise as the *Silverbird* touched down gently in Golden Park and the dream faded.

'Never expected her to do anything less,' Oscar said. 'I remember her from my first life. The Burnellis were a formidable lot.'

'Is she part of your plan?' Tomansio asked Aaron.

'Not as far as I know. Her voyage certainly doesn't trigger any alternatives or imperatives. We proceed as agreed.'

'Okay. Troblum, how long does this thing take?'

Oscar was interested to see that Catriona had gone away during the short flight. Once he was on his own, Troblum hadn't said ten words to them, and there certainly hadn't been anything given away from his gaiamotes. In fact, Oscar wasn't certain Troblum had gaiamotes.

'I'll bring the device up to active status now,' Troblum said.

'Great. So how long?'

'The wormhole parameter will have to be reformatted. I was working on that during the flight. Loading it in shouldn't take more than quarter of an hour. After that, we simply have to launch it into the star.'

'How long, then?'

'That depends on the distance we launch from. The smart-core is reviewing the corona's radiant output for a definitive safe distance, but I'd say it'll be about a million kilometres. The device itself will activate when it reaches the upper corona. It only needs a reasonably dense plasma layer to initiate a chain-reaction propagation within the quantum instability. I based that part of it on our standard novabomb.'

'Troblum. How long until the wormhole forms? From right now?'

Oscar was seriously impressed by Tomansio's restraint.

'Oh. About twenty-five minutes.'

'Good work,' Aaron said, obviously amused by Tomansio's suppressed frustration. 'And how far will the new wormhole reach?'

'I think, now I've got the new profile, twenty-eight thousand lightyears.'

'That'll put us twelve to fifteen thousand lightyears ahead of the Pilgrimage fleet,' Araminta-two said. 'Will that give you enough time?' she asked Aaron.

'All I know is we have to get to Makkathran.'

Oscar gave him a considered look. 'Gore was adamant that Justine go to Makkathran.'

'It's the one place we know for sure is H-congruous inside the Void.'

'Gore told her that after she landed on the replica Far Away.'

'His actual words were "that's where humans are centred in the Void",' Beckia said. 'Which is logical. It is where everyone is going.'

'I bet Ilanthe isn't,' Corrie-Lyn grunted.

'We don't know if the replica Far Away is still there,' Tomansio said. 'Justine reset the Void to before she dreamed for it.'

'I think you're all overreacting,' Inigo said. 'Or at least reading too much into this. Makkathran as a destination isn't coincidence, exactly, but there wasn't a whole lot of choice involved in either case.'

'Do you ever remember meeting Gore?' Liatris asked Aaron.

'I don't remember anything.'

Liatris showed a modicum of unease. 'He did kill your father.'

'Irrelevant.'

'Bruce McFoster was a Starflyer agent when Gore eliminated

him,' Tomansio said. 'The actual Bruce was killed years before when he was taken captive by the Starflyer.'

'But you have to admit the coincidences are starting to—'

'Uh oh,' Araminta-two said.

Everyone was still as he gifted them the scene in the observation deck of the *Lady's Light*, where a determined Ethan was walking towards her. As the confrontation unfolded, Inigo put his arm round Araminta-two's shoulder. 'I am here,' he whispered, pushing his support through the gaiafield union. 'Show him no weakness. You are the Dreamer now. You are right in your belief. It is the Void which will decide this for all of us.'

Oscar drew a sharp breath as the winged Silfen shimmered within his thoughts. *Bradley*, he knew, and smiled. *Way to go, man. You look great.*

A thwarted Ethan walked away. Everyone in the *Mellanie's Redemption*'s cabin burst into spontaneous applause. After a moment, even Troblum joined in.

So he does have gaiamotes, Oscar thought.

Araminta-two smiled round sheepishly. 'Thank you,' he told Inigo. Corrie-Lyn gave him a swift kiss.

'Troblum,' Tomansio said, 'let's get going.'

'The device is almost at active status. Another five minutes.'

Aaron smiled encouragement.

Troblum's tentative humour faded away. His big round face paled. 'Oh no,' he gasped.

Oscar's u-shadow was pulling sensor imagery from the starship's smartcore. Troblum had permitted everyone a general-level access.

A sleek-looking ultradrive ship not too dissimilar to the *Elvin's Payback* had emerged ten kilometres away. It opened a communication link. Oscar's shoulders slumped. He *knew*.

'Hello, my dears,' said the Cat.

A pulse of pure misery swept through the cabin.

'What kind of defences have we got?' Aaron asked.

Troblum shook his head. He was close to tears.

'Weapons?'

Troblum started trembling. His legs gave way, and he sank to his knees. 'I can't let her capture me. I can't.'

'What do you want?' Oscar asked the Cat. If it was dead, they would've been that already.

'That's a whole load of talent you've got on board there with you, Oscar my dear. It's not often I'm impressed, but just this once I'm going to admit it. You did good.'

'What have you done to Cheriton?' Corrie-Lyn demanded.

'Don't interrupt the grownups,' the Cat said. 'You'll get a smack where it hurts most for that.'

Oscar made a frantic cutting hand signal at Corrie-Lyn. She gave him a disgusted glare.

'You told Ilanthe about us,' Oscar said.

'Oh I'm sorry. Did that spoil things? I thought you dealt with that little shit Ethan quite beautifully, Araminta.'

'What do you want?'

'You know that, Oscar. Same thing as I always do, some fun.'

'We'll invite you to the victory party.'

'Don't push your luck. The Void is where this is all going to finish. I need to be a part of that, and you're going to take me there.'

'What is Ilanthe doing?' Oscar asked.

'She's set her little metal heart on something called Fusion.'

'No,' Araminta-two said. 'It's not that. She has become something *other*.'

'Then you'll be able to ask her yourself soon enough, won't you?'

'Can the Cat affect us once we're inside the Void?' Aaron asked Inigo.

'You mean apart from blowing us all to shit?'

'Surely your mind is stronger?'

Inigo gave Araminta-two a worried look. He looked equally alarmed.

'I just don't know.'

'Oscar, my dear, it's rude to keep a lady waiting,'

Oscar didn't know what the hell to do, apart from use the

obvious smartarse answer – which in this case might just prove terminal. And nobody was offering any suggestions. Suddenly he was flinching, cowering halfway to the decking. Space outside was ablaze with hard radiation as a range of enormously powerful weapons were fired. His u-shadow reran events, analysing it in millisecond increments. He saw another ultradrive starship materialize directly between the Cat's ship and *Mellanie's Redemption*. It opened fire instantaneously, at the same time its force field expanded, deflecting the Cat's return salvo away from *Mellanie's Redemption*.

A communication channel opened.

'Oscar, get the hell out of there,' Paula said. 'Leave the Cat to me.'

'Go,' Oscar screamed at Troblum.

For the second time in an hour, the *Mellanie's Redemption* fled into hyperspace.

'You're going to deal with me?' the Cat asked. There was a mocking tone in the voice.

Paula was frantically reviewing the *Alexis Denken*'s defence status. The force fields were struggling under the energy impact of their first weapons exchange. Whatever the Cat's ship was equipped with, it was stronger than she had expected. The beam weapons were somehow transferring some of their energy through hyperspace, circumventing the force fields. Local gravity was doing strange things, its twists exerting unnatural stresses throughout the *Alexis Denken* which the on-board compensators weren't designed to cope with.

'Always do,' Paula sent back. On her instruction, the smartcore fired a couple of quantumbusters. They shot away, accelerating at two hundred gees. 'And this is the last time.' The quantumbusters went active. Eighty kilometres away, the small chunk of asteroidal rubble they targeted was less than thirty metres in diameter. The entire mass was converted directly into energy in the form of ultra-hard radiation. For a microsecond its output rivalled that of the nearby star.

Exovision warnings leapt up as the force fields strained to deflect the appalling radiation torrent. Paula sent the starship back into hyperspace and flashed towards the gas giant. The Cat came after her. Neither was making any attempt at stealth.

Fifty thousand kilometres above the seething pink and grey cloudscape, Paula stopped, and the *Alexis Denken* hung in transdimensional suspension while the force-field generators began to stabilize.

One of the gas giant's large outer moons exploded. A quantum-buster had converted a couple of its more substantial craters directly into energy, a detonation big enough to fracture the moon down to its core. The entire globe ruptured, with vast segments moving ponderously apart, while a billion rock fragments came tumbling out of the expanding fissures into the outburst of raw energy. The physical damage was an irrelevancy. The quantum-buster had a diverted energy function, shunting a high percentage of the explosion's power into hyperspace.

Paula went flying painfully across the cabin as the colossal exotic energy wave smashed into the starship. *Alexis Denken* fell back into spacetime as its overstressed ultradrive failed. Outside, the remnants of the moon were creating a giant translucent shocksphere twenty thousand kilometres across that glowed an ominous spectral blue as it inflated at half lightspeed. The Cat's ship came streaking out of the garish aurora, force fields glimmering a malevolent crimson as it headed straight for the *Alexis Denken*. Dark missiles punched forwards at a hundred gees.

The smartcore identified them as Hawking M-sinks. Force fields wouldn't protect Paula from those.

Another moon exploded. Sequential ripples of exotic energy swept outwards, blocking any return to hyperspace. Paula powered the *Alexis Denken* straight down towards the gas giant, accelerating at fifty gees. Internal gravity compensators could only shield her from about thirty of those. Biononics had to support her body physically as the punishing force tried to crush her into a puddle of flesh across the decking. Even with that enrichment it was tremendously difficult to breathe. She'd got her left leg at a slight angle; it made a bad sound as it flattened out.

One of the small inner moons was below her, a cratered rock two hundred kilometres in diameter, three thousand kilometres further along its orbital track from her vertical vector, and moving sedately away. She fired a quantumbuster at it, modifying the effect field format. When the weapon activated it converted a quarter cubic kilometre of rock right at the moon's core. The moon shattered instantly. Millions of rocky shrapnel fangs detonated outward from the micro-nova in a lethal super-velocity cloud. The particles vaporized as they went, blowing off expanding flares of indigo and topaz ions like primeval comets. Space was filled with a dense clutter of energized mass. The Hawking M-sinks flew into it and began to absorb the deluge of lively atoms. Vapour or rock shards, it made no difference; the event horizons sucked everything down. In doing so their courses wobbled slightly. As the drives attempted to compensate, their efficiency fell off due to the near-exponential increase in mass they were now propelling.

The *Alexis Denken* raced away from the underside of the hellish fireball, hurtling straight for the agitated stormscape below.

Mellanie's Redemption flicked back into space one and a quarter million kilometres above the yellow star. She hung there for a couple of seconds while the forward cargo bay opened and the fuselage force field started to fizz with violet stress patterns. The planetary ftl device shot out, and Troblum took the starship straight back into transdimensional suspension.

'How long?' Aaron demanded.

'Ten minutes to initiation,' Troblum said. Catriona was back at his side, her beautiful face tragic with concern. 'Establishment will take longer. And no, I don't have a fucking clue how long. Nothing more I can do, we just sit and wait now.'

Oscar was keeping track of the hysradar return. He winced when one of the gas giant moons broke apart within a bloom of exotic energy. That was one hell of a fight, as bad as Justine and the warrior Raiel. *Oh crap!* 'Hey!'

Everyone looked at him. In the packed cabin that was quite intimidating.

'You didn't think this ship could survive anything the Cat threw at it,' he said to Troblum. 'Why?'

'Because it couldn't,' Troblum replied. Catriona was directing an aggressive stare Oscar's way, which he ignored.

'But you have the Sol-barrier technology. That can withstand any Commonwealth weapon.'

'*Mellanie's Redemption* doesn't have that kind of protection,' Troblum said.

'But ... your armour does.' *So I assumed the ship would as well. Shit!*

'Yes. I just built my armour. But before now I couldn't ever use the design the Accelerators developed from the Dark Fortress. That would have revealed what we'd got.'

Oscar wanted to grab the front of Troblum's toga suit and give the huge man a shake. 'But if we haven't got that kind of force field, how the hell do you think we'll get past the warrior Raiel?'

'They'll let us past. Won't they?' Troblum said in a puzzled tone that verged on hurt. 'When we explain that we're on a mission to shut down the Void.'

'Shit,' Tomansio grunted.

For once even Aaron was startled.

'Troblum,' Oscar said very firmly. 'Give me full access to your TD linkage. Now.'

'What are you doing?' Inigo asked.

'Calling the one person who might be able to help.' He grimaced as another of the gas giant's moons was blasted into a tsunami of exotic energy. 'If she's still alive.'

The *Alexis Denken* hit the upper atmosphere at fifty kilometres a second. Paula ordered an immediate deceleration as they plunged towards the first truculent cloud layer. It didn't seem to make much difference. Disintegrating gases gouged a five-hundred-kilometre tail of incandescence in their wake, a giant pointer for the Cat's sensors. The juddering was phenomenal; as an indicator of how much punishment the starship was encountering it was badly worrying. Acceleration forces were still crushing her down on to the decking.

Far above, the first flaming debris from the small rock moon was following her down. Dazzling points of light churned through the atmosphere, jetting out vast plumes of black smoke. The terrible buffeting broke them apart into hundreds of smaller chunks, which then shattered again and again. A vast plane of electrical fire sank down towards the clouds. The basic energy which the impact was spinning off created enormous lightning discharges that flared for thousands of kilometres through the higher atmospheric bands.

It made sensor coverage difficult. But just before she sank into the second cloud layer, hysradar located the Cat's ship chasing her down.

Paula hurriedly changed her direction, angling the regrav units' propulsive effect sharply to try and flatten out her trajectory, but still heading down.

'I see you,' the Cat called through an interference-saturated link.

'If you stop now and rendezvous with your force fields down I will simply place you in suspension with your original self,' Paula replied. 'Any other course of action will result in your termination.'

'Darling Paula, this is what I love about you. That psycho-neural profiling is actually the installation of blind stupidity. Come to me, I can remove it for you.'

The *Alexis Denken*'s sensors detected another M-sink being fired. Now the entire gas giant was doomed – though its final destruction would be weeks away. Paula suspected the Cat had done that to make sure there would never be any hiding place beneath the gas giant's furious storms. Paula fired a quantum-buster, then she angled the *Alexis Denken* down through the fourth and final cloud layer. Below that was a zone of perfectly clear hydrogen extending for several hundred kilometres. Huge vertical pillars of lightning snapped on and off within the gap. At their base, a smog of hydrocarbons eddied uneasily atop the pressure boundary where the atmospheric compounds were finally compressed into a liquid. The sight vanished in a blaze of white light as the quantumbuster activated.

'Naughty, darling,' the Cat taunted. 'My turn.'

The hysradar showed Paula two missiles curving up from the Cat's ship, arching through the clouds where the density was reduced. And of course they could accelerate far faster than the poor *Alexis Denken*, which was tunnelling through the compacted hydrogen.

They started to plummet down again.

'Oh fuck,' Paula grunted, and dipped ever closer to the smog band.

Her smartcore surprised the hell out of her when it announced Oscar was calling through a TD link.

'Little busy,' she sent.

'Appreciate that. But we're in trouble.'

'Doesn't it work?'

'That almost doesn't matter. This ship has no protection from the warrior Raiel. Can you ask Qatux to have a word, please.'

The missiles were quantumbusters. They activated a hundred kilometres ahead. A solid wall of energy hurtled towards the *Alexis Denken*, only partially slowed and absorbed by the enormous density of the lower atmosphere. Paula dived into the hydrocarbon soup.

'Do what I can,' she promised. Some remote part of her brain was chuckling over the irony.

The jolt of impact was enough to cause a momentary blackout. Her tormented flesh was already at its limit. When she recovered she was still barrelling forward, but her speed was sluggish even with the ingrav and regrav units operating at their maximum. The force field was heading towards overload and she was only five kilometres deep. Blood was pouring out of her nose. A small medical icon in her exovision reported she was also bleeding from her ears; there were internal lacerations, too.

The Cat's ship sliced cleanly through the hydrogen zone until she was directly above the *Alexis Denken*. Eight missiles curved elegantly down towards the smog, spreading out in an exemplary spider-leg dispersal pattern. They'd act like old-fashioned depth charges, Paula realized. If they didn't force her up and out into the open, the pressure pulse would crush the fuselage. *Perfect!*

From somewhere deep inside the star, oblivion was surging up through the superdense matter. The planetary ftl device had triggered a terminal mass-energy explosion sequence far below the photosphere, whose gigantic shockpulse was now slowly flowing down towards the core, creating an unsustainable fusion surge as it went. Energy levels were building fast from the accelerated reactions. Not even the enormous gravity gradient and ultracompressed hydrogen of the star's interior could contain it.

But as the runaway energy thrust its languid way upwards, other, stranger forces came into play as the device's exotic matter functions began to blossom, fed by the star's own amplified output. Like a parasite growing larger as it consumed more of its host, the device exerted an intolerable stress on an infinitesimal point of spacetime, which promptly ruptured. The throat of the wormhole opened. Behind it, the corona began to darken as more and more power was drained away through hyperspace to sustain the new exotic energy manifestation. The wormhole's terminus began to strain for its designated emergence coordinate over twenty-eight thousand lightyears distant. Half of the rapidly expanding photosphere was now falling into darkness as the wormhole usurped more and more of its escalating output.

Troblum actually smiled at the sensor image as the *Mellanie's Redemption* emerged into spacetime. The starship's curving fins glowed a strong magenta as they threw off the heat that was still seeping through the force fields. Directly ahead, the surface of the violated star was being distorted by the imminent nova eruption. Yet the very pinnacle of the distortion was cascading into night as mass and energy vanished through a dimensional rift. In the middle of that emptiness a tiny indigo star was shining as Cherenkov radiation gleamed out from the exotic matter of the wormhole's pseudofabric.

'It's stabilizing,' he gasped.

'How long will that hold for?' Inigo asked gently.

Troblum shook himself. 'Not long,' he admitted. For a moment he regretted not using the original configuration, a wormhole wide enough to swallow a gas giant. This was only a kilometre across. But it did extend for twenty-eight thousand lightyears.

It works. I was right. I was right about everything. The Anomine, the Raiel. Everything.

'I win,' he said softly, then shouted it. 'I fucking win! And the universe knows it.'

'Take us through,' Aaron said.

Troblum wiped his sleeve across his eyes, getting rid of the moisture. 'Right,' he acknowledged. The *Mellanie's Redemption* slipped forward, accelerating hard as it passed into the wormhole's haze.

The Cat's exovision showed her the eight quantumbusters activate fifty kilometres below the surface of the compressed hydrocarbon ocean. Their titanic pressure waves inflated, merging.

Hysradar scanned incessantly, trying to discern the *Alexis Denken* amid the turmoil. But hydrocarbon fluid at that density was strange stuff, and the massive energy deformation didn't help. If Paula didn't make a dash for freedom up to the hydrogen layer, she'd be dead. No starship could withstand the kind of force currently cascading through the hydrocarbon.

Still nothing.

The smog rippled apart as the hydrocarbon eruption began. It was like seeing a perfectly rounded volcano erupt. The cone kept rising – five, ten, twenty kilometres high. As it lifted up into the hydrogen zone where the pressure was far less, it began to boil violently, spewing out great columns of spray like rocket exhausts that just kept thundering upwards. Within seconds the hydrogen zone for hundreds of kilometres was clotted by the weird chemical fug. Optical-band imagery was reduced to zero as the greasy vapour surged round her starship. Regrav units strained to hold position as the gales rushed past.

'So fuck you, then,' the Cat told Paula's cold, gigantic funeral pyre.

Sensors showed her the upsurge was still growing, which was surprising but hardly threatening. The crest reached a full hundred kilometres, drawing down a barrage of almighty lightning strikes from the belly of the cloud layer far above.

Mountainous waves began to gush ponderously down the eruption's flanks to the ocean below. The Cat still couldn't see anything, but the starship's sensors provided her an excellent graphics-profile image. The hydrocarbon was draining away from something solid. Something vast that was still impossibly rising upwards.

'What the—' she spluttered. Then the profile began to resolve. Fourteen mushroom-shapes were shrugging off their cloak of glutinous liquid and filthy gas to expose the crystalline domes which roofed them. They were attached to the main bulk of the thing, which measured just over sixty kilometres long.

High Angel cleared the unstable cleft in the hydrocarbon ocean, shedding a tempest of seething smog.

A communication channel opened – without any authorization from the Cat's u-shadow. 'Hello Catherine Stewart,' Qatux said.

'Fuck.' She sent her starship into a seventy-gee climb, not even able to scream against the abysmal force crushing her body. Bones snapped, flesh and membranes tore.

'You don't remember my wife, do you?' Qatux asked.

'Your *wife*? No!'

'Nor will you ever.'

Exovision showed the Cat an energy pulse blasting straight up from the *High Angel*. It struck her starship.

The shot was powerful enough to warp spacetime in a very specific fashion, so although the starship was blown apart in milliseconds, time within the explosion stretched on and on and on ... To the Cat the utterly excruciating instant of her death lasted for hour after long terrible hour. Though she never realized, it was exactly the same amount of time it had taken Tiger Pansy to die 1,199 years ago.

*

Nine thousand lightyears from the boundary of the Void, and five lightyears from the closest star, a wormhole terminus swirled open, spilling its gentle indigo light out into interstellar space. Thirty seconds later the streamlined shape of the *Mellanie's Redemption* flew out.

'FucktheLady,' Corrie-Lyn exclaimed. 'We made it.' She smiled incredulously and kissed Troblum before he could stop her.

Behind them, the weak light faded away as the wormhole closed, leaving them as isolated and alone as any humans had ever been. Comprehension of their status quickly spread through the cabin, amplified and reinforced by the tiny self-generated gaiafield. It drained away any sense of elation.

Inigo gave Corrie-Lyn a quick hug in the uncomfortable silence which followed.

'What do you think happened?' Araminta-two asked.

'The important thing is, that deranged bitch didn't follow us,' Oscar said.

'And Paula?'

Oscar had to grin at that. 'Trust me, if anyone in this universe can take care of herself, it's Paula Myo.'

'So what do we do now?' Inigo asked.

'There is no question,' Aaron said. 'We go into the Void.'

'I meant, what do we do about the warrior Raiel?'

'Two options,' Oscar said. 'If Paula survived, we might already have a clear passage confirmed. If not, we really do try what Troblum suggested, and ask nicely.'

'We got this far,' Corrie-Lyn said.

'That's the kind of mad optimism I like,' Oscar said. 'Troblum, let's go.'

'We need to start installing the medical chambers,' Tomansio said.

Oscar grinned. 'Another optimist.'

'Just being practical.' Tomansio patted one of the capsules stacked up against the bulkhead. He didn't have to move his arm far.

'So next question,' Liatris said. 'Who gets to sleep off the next part of the voyage?'

'Me, happily,' Oscar said. 'So long as you bring me out when we go through the boundary. That I have to see.'

'We're going ftl,' Troblum announced. 'I'll get the bots to prepare the forward hold.'

'How long to the Wall stars?' Aaron asked.

'A hundred and sixty hours.'

Paula teleported into Qatux's private chamber, for which she was grateful. She certainly couldn't have walked. There was a fat warming sheath around her left leg. Twelve semi-organic nodules were stuck over various parts of her torso, their slender filaments weaving through her skin to combine with biononic systems deeper inside her body, helping to repair the damaged cells. She wore a loose robe over all the systems, and limped along as if she was an old woman – which was appropriate enough, she acknowledged grimly.

A human-shaped chair rose silently out of the light-blue floor, and she eased herself into it. Directly ahead the silver-grey wall continued its gentle liquid rippling. Tiger Pansy's face smiled back gleefully at her through the odd twisting motions.

You can rest easy now, Paula thought. *Wherever you are.*

The wall parted and Qatux walked in. One of his medium-sized tentacles stretched out, and its paddle tip touched Paula on her cheek. There was a phantom sensation of warmth which lingered after the touch ended, perhaps a sensation of sympathy and concern, too.

'Are you badly damaged?' Qatux whispered.

'Only my pride.'

'Ahhh,' the Raiel sighed. 'The old ones are the best ones.'

'Thank you for your help.'

'And yet her real self lies dormant in Paris.'

'Where it should be. Not resurrected to act as some human political movement's agitator. Not that she ever did as she was told in whatever incarnation.'

A couple of tentacles waved about in what could have been agitation. 'As you said, the universe needs to be rid of her.'

'I was sure if anything could make her termination definite it would be *High Angel.* Navy ships have the firepower, but she'd detect them.'

'Not quite what my race intended this arkship should be used for, but we live in extraordinary times.'

'I hope I haven't got you into trouble, Qatux.'

'No. We Raiel do not lack for empathy. However, I believe some of the humans in residence are slightly shocked by events. Not to mention the Naozun.'

Paula couldn't remember any race called the Naozun. 'Good. It's about time we stirred things up.'

'We have grown, you and I, Paula.'

'I should certainly hope so, we've had long enough.'

Air whistled softly out of Qatux's mouth. 'Indeed.'

'Did the wormhole open as Troblum predicted?'

'Yes.'

'Finally! Something went right for us. Whatever the hell that something is. I just hope Aaron's controller knows what they're doing. On which note, I have yet another favour to ask.'

'Yes.'

'The *Mellanie's Redemption* needs to get into the Void. Can you get the warrior Raiel to let it through the Gulf unharmed? I genuinely believe it might be our only chance to prevent a catastrophic expansion phase.'

'I will explain why they should. I can do no more.'

'Thank you.' She rubbed at the sheath on her leg, knowing

that was never going to get rid of the itch. 'Where are we going now?'

'Back to the Commonwealth.'

'Not out of the galaxy, then?' Paula was faintly relieved. The Raiel obviously still had hope.

'No. That time is not yet here. As you said, there is little which prevents it.'

'What about the DF spheres? Are they capable of stopping the Void?'

'We don't know. But understand this, Paula, the warrior Raiel will attempt to stop the Pilgrimage fleet. They do not indulge in sentiment about that many lives when the very galaxy is threatened by their actions.'

'I understand, and I do not hold you to account. We have to be responsible for ourselves. If that many humans want to try to endanger all life in this galaxy, they must not be surprised if others attempt to prevent them.'

'Yet your own kind did not.'

Paula hung her head, mainly in shame, but there was frustration there, too. 'I know. Those of us who were free to do so did what we could. The level of the conspiracy took us by surprise. In that, we failed so many.'

The Raiel touched her cheek again. 'I do not hold you to account, Paula.'

'Thank you,' she managed to say.

'I do have some privilege as captain of an arkship. We are in communication with the warrior Raiel. Would you like to see the galactic core defences in action? I imagine the last stand of our species will make quite a spectacle.'

*

The Delivery Man waited patiently while the trolley glided across the plaza, and rose up to the *Last Throw*'s midsection hatchway. The chunk of equipment it was carrying only just fitted through the opening, but it managed to get inside. The assembly-bots, which the replicator had produced a couple of days earlier, started to ease the equipment off the trolley. Once they began the integration process he'd go up and inspect.

He was useful again, which had lifted his spirits considerably. His physics and engineering knowledge was hardly up there at Ozzie and Nigel levels, but his recent cover job analysing technology levels made him competent enough to oversee the integration. The systems the replicator was producing were all geared towards giving the *Last Throw* additional strength. *Strong enough to ward off a star's energy from zero-range.* It was a very special kind of crazy who contemplated such a procedure. The design in the smartcore memory had been developed by the Greater Commonwealth Astronomical Agency for its Stardiver programme. None of the probes they'd dispatched had ever carried human passengers.

The Delivery Man glanced across the plaza to where Gore was talking to Tyzak. It was like observing a devoted priest and a confirmed atheist locking horns. Their conversation, or argument, or discussion – whatever – had been going on for days now. There'd even been pictures for emphasis. Gore had brought a holographic portal down from the *Last Throw*, showing Tyzak various images of the Void, the Gulf, the Wall stars, DF spheres, even views of Makkathran, Skylords, and the Void nebulas taken from Inigo's dreams.

Not once in all that time had he let up in his efforts to convince the Anomine to talk to the elevation mechanism. Then they received Justine's dream of landing at Makkathran, and Gore's determination went off the chart. The Delivery Man found it hard to credit the Gore he knew had so much patience. But then even he'd punched the air when the *Silverbird* touched down in Golden Park. It was quite a moment.

Tyzak was interested, some parts of the story he found fascinating. But none of it inclined him to help ward off the end of everything. The old Anomine insisted that the future, specifically his race's future, could only be determined by the planet itself. That prohibited using relics from the past.

'But it's not your future that will be affected in any way,'

Gore was saying. 'All I need is a little help from a machine which you don't even use any more. Do your beliefs prohibit charity?'

'I understand your problem, but you are asking me to abandon my entire philosophy, my reason for existence, and delve back into the past we have completely rejected.'

'You would be knocking on the door. I would be the one passing through.'

'You are attempting to differentiate the entire act into degrees. That is not applicable. Any act of renunciation is ultimate.'

'How can helping others be renunciation of yourself?'

'It is the method, as you very well know, friend Gore.'

'How do you think your ancestors would respond to this request? Their generosity helped other species before, when you isolated the Prime aliens.'

'I cannot know, but I suspect they would reanimate the machine for you.'

'Exactly.'

'But they are gone. And they were an aberration in our true line of evolution.'

'Your inaction means you'd be killing trillions of living things. Doesn't that bother you in the slightest?'

'It is a cause for concern.'

The Delivery Man stiffened. That was the first time the slightest concession had been made to reasonableness on Tyzak's part. Reasonableness on human terms, anyway.

'The space fortresses that guard your solar system, the cities that never decay, this machine beneath our feet which slumbers, all these things were left behind by the ancestors you dismiss. They wanted you to have options. That is why they bequeathed them to you. So much of what they had is now dust.' Gore's hand waved loosely up at the lustrous band of debris orbiting the planet. 'But these specific artefacts remain because they knew that one day you might need them. Without the fortresses many species would be here plundering the riches your ancestors left behind. A large part of evolution is interaction. Isolation is not evolution, it is stagnation.'

'We are not isolated,' Tyzak answered. 'We live within the planet's will; our every second is determined by the planet. It will deliver us to our destiny.'

'But I've shown you what will happen to your planet if the Void's final expansion phase begins. It will be destroyed, and you with it. That is not natural, that is an external event of pure malice, the cessation of evolution not just here but on every star system in the galaxy. Such a thing cannot be factored into your belief of planetary-guided evolution, for it is not inborn. If you truly wish to continue your evolution on this world you have to protect it. Your ancestors left you the ability to do that, to ward off the unnatural. You don't have to do anything other than to ask the machine to awake. It and I will do everything else.'

The Delivery Man held his breath.

'Very well,' Tyzak said. 'I will ask.'

Gore tipped his head back to look the old Anomine directly in the eye, and sighed. 'I thank you from the bottom of my heart.'

The Delivery Man hurried over to the two of them. Dusk had fallen now, its fading light bathing the plaza in a cool grey illumination. All around them the imposing city buildings were responding to oncoming night with their own internal radiance. Pale colourful streaks shimmered over an igloo-style shelter they'd expanded close to the parked starship where the replicator had been set up. The second, smaller shelter housed the intrusion apparatus Gore had created in case the elevation mechanism should prove reluctant.

Last Throw's smartcore reported that it was initiating a deep field-function scan of the elevation mechanism, mapping out functions and control pathways. The Delivery Man couldn't help the ridiculous burst of optimism lightening his heart as he drew close to the two figures profiled by the harlequin glow of a deep city canyon on the other side of the plaza. It was almost symbolic of the moment, he thought, the two wildly different species finally coming together in the face of adversity. *If only I wasn't such a cynic.*

Just as he reached them he saw something move down the

glimmering canyon beyond. Retinal inserts provided a clearer resolution. 'No bloody way,' he grunted. It was a Silfen, riding some huge quadruped animal with thick scarlet fur. The Silfen himself was clad in a long, magnificently gaudy honey-coloured coat embedded with thousands of jewels that sparkled energetically in the city's luminosity.

'Gore!'

Gore turned round. 'What?'

But it was too late, the Silfen had ridden off down an intersection. 'Doesn't matter.'

Tyzak had become very still. When the Delivery Man concentrated on his own diminutive awareness of the city's thoughts he could just make out another stream of consciousness out there somewhere. Like the city's these were precise and cool. Not quite aloof, though, for there was definite interest in why they had been roused.

'I feel you,' the elevation mechanism said. 'You are Tyzak.'

'I am.'

'Do you wish to attain transcendence from your physical existence?'

'No.'

'I exist for that purpose.'

'I wish to transcend,' Gore told the mechanism.

'You are alien. I cannot help you.'

'Why not?'

'You are alien. I exist to lift Anomine to their next stage of life.'

'Our biochemistry is essentially the same. I am sentient. It would not be difficult for you.'

'No. Only Anomine may lift themselves through me.'

'Are you sentient?'

'I am aware.'

'There is a possibility that an event at the heart of the galaxy may destroy this planet and with it all the surviving Anomine. If I am elevated to the next stage of life I will be able to prevent this from happening.'

'Should such an event occur the remaining Anomine will be assisted to transcend, if that is what they wish.'

'Do you still have the power to do that?'

'Yes.'

'And the rest of us? You would abandon every sentient in the galaxy to death?'

'I lift Anomine. I cannot reach the rest of the galaxy.'

'You can reach me.'

'You are not Anomine.'

'Are you unable to rise above your original constraints?'

'I am what I am. I exist to lift Anomine to their next stage of life.'

'Yeah. Got that.'

The elevation mechanism's thoughts retreated, shrinking its consciousness back to the somnolence where it had spent the centuries that passed it by.

'You were not given the answers you were hoping for,' Tyzak said. 'I feel sorrow for you. But the machine's story is an ancient one, it will not change now.'

'Yeah, I know. See you in the morning.' Gore rose to his feet and headed back to the *Last Throw*.

It took the Delivery Man by surprise. He got up and hurried after Gore, wishing in vain he didn't feel like some pupil bobbing round his all-wise guru master. 'So now what?'

The city's shifting opalescence produced strange reflections across Gore's golden face. If his expression did possess any emotion it wasn't anything the Delivery Man could read. 'We got a pretty good functionality schema, which thankfully included a route into the wormhole when it checked its main power supply.'

'Ah. So you can hack it?'

'I don't know. It's extremely complex, which is what I expected from a machine that has its own psychology. But at least we know how to attempt it. There are physical junctions which are critical to its routines, they can be breached.'

'So are you going to start that now?'

'Certainly not. The other systems on this planet share an awareness of each other. I doubt I'd have more than a few minutes' primacy before they put a stop to my evil alien incursion.'

'Oh, right. So we do need to reactivate the siphon first?'

'Siphon and wormhole. How long until the modified force-field generators are finished?'

'A few days,' the Delivery Man said reluctantly.

'Good. We need to be ready to launch this part of the plan as soon as everyone in the Void is in place.'

'Everyone in the Void? You mean the Pilgrimage ships?'

'No. I'm expecting an associate to arrive.'

'An associate? In the Void?'

'Yes.'

'When?'

'Justine will let us know.'

*

The Raiel warship was *big*. Aaron studied the return which was coming from the hysradar. Most of the image was fuzzed, denying him any details. Some small part of his mind wasn't sure he wanted details. *Which is hardly strong of me*, he thought with a cool amusement. *That part of the Knights Guardians has obviously been lost*. Again, that wasn't something which disturbed him. Even the name Lennox meant nothing, which he knew on an instinctive level was a good thing, that he wanted to be free of what was. *She* dwelt there in the past, slithering though the banished memories, taunting, bleeding poison, leaving only shadow in her wake. It was the only place she could hurt him now.

He recalled Cheriton's last terrified thoughts. The pleading.

Not relevant. A definitive conclusion which gave him a great deal of confidence in himself. *I'm still here, still me.*

The warrior Raiel ship was matching course with *Mellanie's Redemption* now. Ten lightyears ahead was the fringe of the Wall stars, the close-packed multitude of globular clusters throwing out a screen of blazing light which blocked any glimpse of the Gulf beyond and the true dark core of the galaxy.

'What now?' Troblum asked.

His remaining passengers appeared uncertain. Oscar and his Knights Guardians team had gone into suspension, though Corrie-Lyn refused to leave Inigo, and as Aaron suspected the Raiel might need proof from the original Dreamer, that left five of them still awake and moving round. Which even with the medical capsules all installed in the forward cargo hold, still made for cramped conditions. It didn't bother Aaron, but he could see how the others were getting agitated. Troblum's non-existent personality didn't help. And as for the amount the big man ate at every meal . . .

'They haven't blown us to shit yet,' Aaron said. 'That's got to be good. So we ask them if they'll let us go through the Wall and into the Void.'

'What are you going to say to them?' Corrie-Lyn asked. The presence of the warrior Raiel was having quite an effect on her. The tentative relief she'd shown after they came through the wormhole had shrunk away as soon as the warship rendezvoused with them.

Aaron ignored her. 'Inigo, Araminta, I think this one's for you.'

The two Dreamers exchanged a what-the-hell look.

Araminta-two sighed. 'I'll do it.'

Aaron opened his gaiamotes to sense the Second Dreamer reaching for the giant warship. Riding passively in conjunction with Araminta's thoughts was making him aware of whole aspects of the gaiafield he'd never known before. There was certainly some kind of consciousness registering out there, and not a human one. It was too composed for that. He also felt the first direct touch with the Skylord, which sent a chill firing along his nerves. *So close now.*

'We are the human Dreamers,' Araminta-two told the Raiel.

'Yes. You are two Dreamers. The third of your kind is a long way from here. And part of you is elsewhere.'

'That's correct,' Araminta said, mildly surprised by the summary. 'We seek to travel into the Void. We believe we may be able to prevent the final devourment phase.'

'We know this. Qatux has spoken with us. You may pass through.'

'I thank you.'

'You understand that the ships which you also lead will be intercepted.'

'Yes. I understand this.'

'If we succeed, then millions of your kind will be destroyed. Why do you not cease to appease them?'

'It is not that simple. However I believe in what we are doing. I believe this will resolve the threat which the Void holds over this galaxy without any loss of life.'

'As you wish.'

'I would ask one other thing. There is an entity called Ilanthe travelling with the Pilgrimage fleet whose nature is uncertain. If there is any way it can be prevented from reaching the Void, I would urge you to implement it.'

'We are aware of Ilanthe. We remain vigilant for it.'

'Thank you.'

The warrior Raiel ship slid away.

'It's fast,' Troblum said admiringly. 'Faster than we are. I wonder what kind of drive theory they have.'

Inigo put his hand on the big man's shoulder. 'When this is over I'm sure they'll be delighted to give you a full tour.'

Troblum's face produced a grimaced smile. He clearly wanted to wrench himself away from the hand.

An awkward Inigo quickly snatched it back. His thoughts were apologetic even though he said nothing.

Corrie-Lyn gave Aaron a shrewd look. 'So now do you know what happens in the Void?'

He grinned back as annoyingly as he could. 'We're not there yet.'

'We will be soon,' Araminta-two said. 'And the Skylord knows that.'

*

Oscar and the Knights Guardians were brought out of suspension for the passage itself. The cabin was once again crammed up with too many people, but this time it wasn't so bad. This time everyone was jokey and excited, eager to see what lay outside the fuselage. Eager to be inside the obdurate, mysterious boundary.

The *Mellanie's Redemption* was slowing as it approached the black wall. It dropped out of hyperspace fifteen lightyears away – the same distance the *Silverbird* had been when the distended cone opened for it.

Radiation alerts sprang up in everyone's exovision. Far behind them the loop burned a dangerous burgundy as high-energy photons smashed relentlessly through the clouds of dark mass swirling through the plane of the Gulf. All around the starship streaks of irradiated matter swarmed in towards the boundary, like a particulate ocean with a solitary eternal tide.

Araminta-two actually looked nervous, even though he was in constant contact with the Skylord. Still entwined with the Second Dreamer's thoughts, Aaron could sense the great creature's interest and expectation growing.

'Remember to ask it to pull us through somewhere close to Querencia,' Tomansio said. 'We don't want a forty-year voyage like Justine.' He didn't actually give the cabin a pointed look, but everyone knew his opinion on the starship's reliability. Perhaps it was the proximity of the Void, but they were now sharing quite intimately.

Araminta-two gave him a tight nod, then spoke to the Skylord. 'We are here. Please call to the nucleus, please urge it to bring us into your universe so we may achieve fulfilment.'

'I have waited so long for this moment,' the Skylord said.

'When we come, we need to be near the solid world where humans lived.'

'There were several such worlds,' the Skylord replied.

Inigo gave Araminta-two a shocked look as her concentration faltered briefly.

'Shit,' Tomansio muttered.

'I thought there was only one,' Oscar said out loud.

'There's more than one?' an incredulous Corrie-Lyn said. 'How many were there?'

'It took Justine to Querencia,' Aaron said urgently. 'Go specific.'

'What did she ask...?' Araminta-two shook his head irritably, and concentrated again. 'The world we seek is the one where a member of our species is already waiting for us. She arrived recently. It has a city there, a city that did not arise within the Void.'

'I know the world you seek,' the Skylord replied.

'I hope it does,' Troblum said. 'Because it's starting.'

'Will you be there?' Araminta asked. 'I need you there to guide me. Without your help I will never reach fulfilment.'

'I come,' the Skylord promised.

Hysradar showed them the surface of the boundary expanding at hyperluminal speed, a great protrusion heading up directly for the starship. Just like the planetary ftl wormhole, but on an unimaginably vast scale. They watched in silence as the smooth crown opened. Once again the glorious undulating nebula-light shone out into the wretched desolation of the Gulf, casting a single beam of elegant luminosity across the *Mellanie's Redemption*.

The starship accelerated forward eagerly, passing through the small aperture. Behind it, the boundary closed again, shutting off the pale light. The pinnacle sank back down, merging back into the featureless surface of infinite darkness.

'So where are we?' Aaron demanded. The starship's visual sensors were working perfectly, showing stars and nebulas all around. There was no sign of the boundary.

'Working on that,' Troblum said. He was sweating profusely.

'Well whadda you know,' Tomansio said. A cup of tea was floating in mid-air, ten centimetres from his outstretched fingers. It lifted a little, then wiggled from side to side. He grinned wildly. And his mind was radiating smugness and satisfaction for all of them to perceive.

'Oh crap,' Corrie-Lyn exclaimed. Her mind shimmered rapidly in everyone's farsight, its surface lustre dimming as she ponderously fought down the exuberant emotions, shielding them from psychic perception like a mother folding her arms protectively round a crying babe. Images and memories persisted in flashing out: Edeard scrambling to shield his own thoughts, the techniques he employed. After a short while the surface of her mind hardened to an impermeable screen from which nothing leaked, not a single emotion or memory or sensation.

There was a long minute while everyone struggled with the same technique with varying degrees of success. No one was surprised when the two Dreamers shielded themselves perfectly. But no matter how hard he tried, Oscar simply couldn't contain his ebullient thoughts. The best he could achieve was to tone them down a bit. 'This group's Edeard,' he said ruefully. 'He could never protect himself fully. Personally I see it as a sign of superiority to the lot of you.'

Everyone allowed a glimmer of amusement to trickle out. Except Troblum. His shield was darker than most, and the thoughts below were convoluted. His emotions didn't match anything familiar.

Aaron was satisfied with his own protection, though the others were giving him curious looks. Their emotions were hurriedly wrapped away from perception. 'What?' he asked. His longtalk matched his voice in intensity.

'It's like you're at war,' Corrie-Lyn said. 'Your thoughts are shining out, yet they make no sense because they have so many contrary facets. You are anger and conflict.'

He gave her his old concessionary grin. 'But I still function.'

'So?' Tomansio asked, his inexorable curiosity infecting them all. 'We're in the Void. What next?'

'Makkathran,' Aaron said solemnly.

Tomansio let out a growl of frustration.

Araminta-two looked at something far beyond the cabin's bulkheads. 'It's here,' he said in wonder.

Aaron's farsight felt the Skylord approach. A benevolent

concentration of thoughts which intimidated through sheer size. Somehow it seemed to negate worry, sharing satisfaction on a level that was impossible to refute.

'You are here,' it told Araminta-two.

'Part of me. The rest will follow as I bring those who seek fulfilment.'

'My kindred welcome you. They welcome those who are to join us here in the Void.'

'Makkathran,' Aaron whispered.

'Will you guide us to the world we spoke of before?'

'Yes.'

Aaron instinctively reached out to grab hold of something and steady himself. *Mellanie's Redemption* was twisting round, gravity shifting in strange swelling motions. Exoimage relays from the fuselage cameras showed him the huge crystalline folds of the Skylord's body rotating spryly against the flexing ribbon of violet phosphorescence that was the Bulku nebula. Then the stars ahead were brightening as the Skylord executed its temporal acceleration function, and the starship was flashing towards the hot blue light points at close to lightspeed. Behind them, the Void shifted down to a dull carmine.

Araminta-two inhaled sharply, his hand pressing flat on his chest.

'What's wrong?' Oscar asked him.

'It's very weird, like I'm being torn in two. You seem fast, yet I'm not slow, or part of me is. The Pilgrimage fleet is hardly moving until I concentrate on it. Arrrgh. Ozziedamn, this is so strange.'

'Temporal rate difference,' Troblum said. 'You are conscious on both sides of the Void boundary, which means you're living at two different speeds. It will be hard to reconcile.'

'You'd better go into suspension,' Tomansio said.

'No!'

The spike of alarm from Araminta-two's mind was enough to still them all.

'Sorry, but no,' he said. 'I – this body – has to live through this. If this me goes into suspension, that means it'll be just her left, I'll be out there all alone. If they come for me with those brain infiltrator *things*, I won't have any refuge.'

Tomansio nodded in understanding. 'How far are we from Querencia?' he asked Troblum.

'We're heading for a star system about three lightmonths away,' Troblum said. 'I guess it's Querencia.'

'Three months. Well, I suppose it's better than three years.'

'Or thirty,' Oscar said. He was leaking sympathy and concern.

Araminta-two fumbled for his hand. 'Thank you, Oscar.'

Now embarrassment was added to the emotional blend he was betraying. 'I think I'd better head straight back into suspension,' Oscar said. 'Who else?'

'Us as well,' Tomansio said.

Inigo and Corrie-Lyn consulted on some unknown level. 'We'll sleep it out,' Inigo said. 'There's nothing for me to do until we reach Makkathran. Is there?'

'No,' Aaron confirmed. 'How about you?' he asked Troblum. 'Me what?'

'Okay then. That's myself, Araminta-two and Troblum staying up for the rest of the flight.'

'I'm sure you'll all be very happy together,' Corrie-Lyn said. Her mental shield allowed no feeling to show through.

It didn't matter. Aaron knew how much she was laughing inside.

*

Everyone in the Commonwealth was desperate to know what the hell that confrontation between Araminta and Ethan had been about. She was many? Like a multiple? But she wasn't. So was she referring to the other Dreamers? She claimed to be with Inigo. And why had he chosen now to release the Last Dream? Had Araminta asked him to?

Nobody knew. And for all her apparent devotion to Living Dream, Araminta resolutely refused to enlighten her desperate followers back in the Commonwealth, or her equally vociferous opponents. Strangely, Ethan gave nothing away either.

So the Pilgrimage fleet flew on at fifty-six lightyears an hour towards the Void for day after day with no change. It was apparent now that nothing could stop it apart from the warrior Raiel.

Or perhaps Justine and the Third Dreamer, some suggested. Gore certainly had some kind of idea. He, too, proved elusive.

They were odd days that marked the flight of the Pilgrimage fleet. The whole Commonwealth knew that if it was successful then that was the end of everything. That if they were lucky the Heart would become aware of them, and bring their stars and planets unharmed through the Void's boundary as it swept out to engulf the galaxy. Devoid of ANA's guidance, Higher worlds were turning their replicator systems to producing armadas of starships in preparation to flee the galaxy. On the Outer Worlds, anyone lucky enough to own a starship was busy modifying it to make an inter-galactic trip. While the Greater Commonwealth government contingency was to have everyone update their secure memory store, which would then be carried by Navy ships to whatever cluster of stars was selected to establish the New Commonwealth, a plan of action invoking the spirit of the New47 Worlds of a millennium ago. Knowing your new self would be resurrected in an alien galaxy at some unknown time in the future wasn't quite as reassuring as it should have been, not when that meant you'd have to watch your immediate doom smashing down out of the sky.

Odd days. And that was without the declaration of absolute war by the Ocisen Empire. Further threats of hostile action from eight of the sentient species the Commonwealth had contact with. Appeals for technological help and starships from another three races including the Hancher.

Odd days, confused even more when the *High Angel* reappeared back in Icalanise orbit, and its human inhabitants started broadcasting their sojourn in a gas giant's atmosphere, complete with the brief conflict they'd witnessed through the smog. A conflict *High Angel* refused to comment on.

Odd days, where those who instigated the crisis in the first place started to falter. The followers of Living Dream left behind began to question their commitment in the light of the Last Dream; to such an extent that the preparation for the second Pilgrimage fleet was openly challenged. A great many argued that the new ships would be better used fleeing the expanding boundary rather than seeking refuge within, where their ultimate future was now less than certain.

Days where even the sudden surge of fortitude and determination was still tempered by so many who insisted on immersing themselves in Araminta's gifting. Hour after hour the Pilgrimage fleet faithfully dropped relay stations as they went, providing a straight electronic channel back to Ellezelin and the unisphere as well as stretching the gaiafield contact across the galaxy.

Araminta saw only the scattering of turquoise glimmer-points flowing past on the other side of the observation deck. Hysradar revealed the crowded band of globular clusters which comprised the Wall growing closer and closer. Then came the definitive quantum signature of ftl ships approaching from the centre of the galaxy. Over fifty of them. Even that didn't stir the Dreamer's cool composure as she led her followers onward to their promised destiny.

Unisphere access to the sensor feeds rose sharply as the entire Greater Commonwealth sought to witness the outcome. Gaiamotes were opened wide to receive Araminta's gifting.

The imagery and sensations ended without warning. Two hundred lightyears behind the Pilgrimage fleet, eight relay stations failed simultaneously. Nobody knew what was happening.

Paula did. She was sitting in Qatux's private chamber, watching a display similar to a holographic portal projection. The warrior Raiel had taken out Living Dream's relays. Now the main attack force was converging on the twelve giant ships.

Over the next nine hours eighteen gas giants were obliterated, their dying mass converted to exotic energy. Some resulted in omnidirectional distortion waves slicing through hyperspace. Others were subject to incredibly complex formatting architecture, producing coherent beams targeting specific Pilgrimage ships.

The Sol-barrier force fields protecting the ships resisted every attack tactic, every weapon the warrior Raiel had. As well they might. They were the best it was possible to create. If anything, the Accelerators had improved the design they'd reverse-engineered from the Dyson Alpha generator.

When the Pilgrimage fleet was halfway across the Gulf, the warrior Raiel withdrew, allowing the fleet to continue unimpeded.

'I feel shame this day,' Qatux said.

'I feel anger,' Paula told him. She rubbed her hand across her face, unpleasantly weary from watching the aborted interception. 'Did they find any trace of Ilanthe?'

'Regrettably not. If it is there, it is exceptionally well stealthed.'

'Crap! We know the ship that picked it up was equipped with high-level stealth. But I never expected it to elude your warrior class.'

'Even if they had detected the ship, there would be nothing they could do about it. The force fields the Accelerators built were flawless.'

'There's nothing else left then?'

'Our warships are abandoning the Gulf where they have patrolled for these past million years. Now there is only one option remaining: the containment.'

'What's that?'

Qatux waved one of his two large tentacles at the glowing images which floated across the chamber. 'See. It begins.'

Ever since their invasion armada failed to defeat or even return from the Void, the Raiel had been preparing for what they regarded as the inevitable catastrophic expansion phase. The strategy was centred around the largest machines the Raiel ever constructed. Humans called them DF spheres, which they first encountered at Dyson Alpha generating the shield which imprisoned the entire Prime solar system. The second encounter was at Centurion Station, which indicated they had more than one function.

Once the Raiel had established their production facilities in a dozen star systems the gas-giant-sized spheres were distributed throughout the Wall. Over ten million of them had been made over the course of a hundred thousand years, of which only seven had ever been diverted to deal with other problems: two were loaned to the Anomine, three to species who faced similar difficulties, and two to imprison stars that were going nova in order to protect nearby pre-starflight civilizations that would have been eradicated by the radiation.

Now, courtesy of Qatux's status, Paula was observing the overview of their activation. During the Void's last brief expansion when Araminta had denied the Skylord, the DF spheres had all moved in to a close orbit around the stars they were orbiting in preparation for their final phase. Now they began to exert colossal gravity fields, increasing the gravity gradient within their host stars, accelerating the fusion rate.

Throughout the Wall, supergiant stars started to brighten, chasing up through the spectrum to attain the blue-white pinnacle.

'Their raised power levels will be consumed by our defence systems to produce bands of dark force much like the force fields your Accelerators learned how to create,' Qatux explained. 'They will link up into a bracelet, and ultimately expand into a sphere which englobes the entire Gulf.'

'The containment,' Paula murmured in amazement. The Raiel had conceived a true marvel, an endeavour that until today she'd have said could only possibly belong to a post-physical. It almost made her feel sorry for the Raiel: to have devoted their entire race to such a feat meant they had nothing else. Their commitment to overcome the Void had imprisoned them as surely as if they were inside it.

After a few hours the glittering band of stars circling the chamber was showing a filigree of black lines multiplying along its inner edge, slowly coalescing into a wide bracelet.

'Will it hold the Void?' she asked as she watched the slow progress of the lines.

'We don't know. We have never dared use it before. Our hope is that it can last long enough so the Void consumes all the mass left within the Gulf as it actualizes the reset dreams of everyone inside. Once its fuel is exhausted it will collapse. If the Void is able to break through, the resultant surge may well be so fast as to overwhelm any starships seeking to leave the galaxy.'

'So if it works, everyone inside the Void will die?'

'And the galaxy will live.'

Justine: Year Forty-Five

Day Thirty-One

Justine woke as dawn sent gold-tinged sunlight streaming in through the bedroom's big window. She groaned at the intrusion, and rolled over in her sleeping bag. Underneath her, the spongy mattress rippled gently with the motion. Edeard had got that particular piece of furniture absolutely perfect, she thought drowsily. The thick beam of sunlight slid slowly across the floor, advancing inexorably towards her. She watched its progress idly, knowing she ought to be getting up. But early rising had never been her strongest personality trait. Those first thirty years living the East Coast party scene had established a habit that nearly a thousand subsequent years spent living in a meat body had never quite managed to break.

Eventually she unzipped the sleeping bag and stretched, yawning widely, before finally rolling off the bed. It was a large bed, fusing seamlessly into the floor. But then it was a large bedroom, as was appropriate for the Master and Mistress of Sampalok.

Justine padded barefoot across the floor to the panoramic window, and looked down on the district's central square. The expanse was remarkably clean, something she'd noticed through-out her exploration of the city. Dirt and leaves certainly started to pile up along the edges of buildings and in various clefts and narrow gaps. But it never got to the stage where weeds would take root. She supposed the city absorbed any large accumulation of muck. Back in Edeard's time teams of genistar chimps had cleaned up the rubbish produced by the human inhabitants.

As she watched the small fountains playing, she could see several animals slinking about around the edges of the square as they began their day's foraging or hunting. She'd been right about the dogs: there were several nasty packs thriving in Makkathran. Native animals were also nesting in the empty buildings. The city seemed to tolerate them.

Justine slipped on her denim shorts and a clean tangerine T-shirt, then went into the lounge she was using as her base. Most of her equipment was set up, including a simple camp chair which the ship's replicator had managed to produce after the landing during one of its infrequent functional periods. The one remaining chair in Makkathran, she told herself in amusement. She picked a quarter-litre self-heating coffee canister from the food stack and settled into the simple canvas and aluminium frame. The coffee started steaming half a minute after she pulled the tab, and she sipped appreciatively while she peeled the foil off a buttered almond croissant. There was jam, but she couldn't be bothered to fetch that. The daily routine was a quick breakfast, a packed lunch, then in the evening she took the time to light the barbecue charcoal and cook herself something more elaborate – which helped pass the time. Despite the city's pervasive orange light, she didn't venture out at night.

After half an hour she began getting ready. A small backpack carried her food and waterproofs, along with some simple tools and a powerful torch. She hung a knife on her belt, along with the semi-automatic pistol and a spare magazine. Before she clipped the cattle-prod on she gave it a quick test, satisfied with the crackling spark that arced between the prongs. Along with the torch, it was one of the few electrical devices that worked reliably.

Ready to face the new day, Justine walked down the four flights of broad stairs to the entrance hall. The wooden doors of the arching doorway were long gone, rotted away centuries ago.

However, the decorative outside gates which closed across them remained. Their intricate gurkvine lattice must have been made from a very pure iron, Justine decided. Rust was minimal, and most of the ornamental leaves were intact. They were robust enough to stop any large animal getting in at night – one of the big contributing factors for choosing the Sampalok mansion.

She'd been curious why they were still in place. After all, every other human artefact attached to a wall was rejected and expelled after just a few years. But when she examined them in detail she found the city's substance had actually been fashioned into the thick hinge pins which the gates were hung on. It had taken all of her telekinetic strength and some liberal applications of oil, but eventually she'd managed to prise the gates open.

Now they swung aside easily as her third hand pushed them. She walked into the square. The hot humid air constricted around her, bringing perspiration to her brow. It was mid-summer, with a correspondingly intense sun sliding up over the city's minarets and towers and domes. Justine put her sunglasses on as she sent her farsight searching round. There was nothing threatening nearby. A couple of fil-rats and some terrestrial cats scurried away. Seabirds circled overhead, their high-pitched calls echoing through the empty squares and alleys. She carefully closed the gates behind her, and set off down one of the wide streets which led away from the square, heading for Mid Pool.

None of the signs were up on the walls any more, so it had taken her a while to place the original names to various streets and alleys. She soon realized she'd never be able to name more than a fraction – not even the dreams had fully portrayed the sheer complexity and numbers of the passages and lanes and streets that made up Makkathran's districts. The closest Inigo's dreams had ever come to conveying the bewilderment of the urban maze she'd felt for the first couple of weeks after her landing was the day Edeard and Salrana arrived and walked through Ilongo and Tosella.

Now she strode along the twisting length of Zulmal Street, which would take her to the concourse around Mid Pool. The width of the street varied almost with every step. For the most part it had been shops here, she recalled. Which fitted the wide bulging windows on the ground floor of most buildings. There were no doors any more. They had all vanished ages ago; as had all the interior fittings. At first she'd been curious about the general lack of debris until she realized the city absorbed fragments that threatened to clog its drains and produce soil mounds where grass and moss could flourish. But as she wandered in and out of buildings she found some remains. Metal items were the most prevalent: most homes had some cutlery and the odd piece of jewellery scattered across the floor, the sole testimony to the inhabitants who had left them behind so long ago. The items of precious metal held their shape best; the iron stoves which most households possessed were rusting and flaking down to unrecognizable sagging lumps. She'd also learned to be careful of the long, sharp fragments of crockery and glass that were lying about, making her glad her boots had thick soles. It was strange that these tarnished, almost unrecognizable trinkets were the only proof that an entire civilization of humans had once inhabited this world. If she wasn't careful, melancholia could shade over into loneliness and apprehension. From there it was only a short step to true dread, the kind that would send her hurrying back to the *Silverbird* and suspension – assuming the medical cabinet would function adequately. The Void's prohibition of technology seemed to be gaining ground against the little starship sitting in Golden Park. Even the confluence nest had erratic days. She was fairly certain the only way she'd ever get back into space now would be to once again reset the Void to a time before she landed.

Just before Zulmal Street opened out onto the concourse, she stopped and looked at a building. It was one she'd passed a dozen times before as she came and went on her daily mission of exploration, but the relevance had never registered before. This was the baker's where Boyd had been murdered by a deranged vengeful Mirayse. Justine's farsight expanded into the shop, finding nothing in the front rooms. But in the back she could just perceive a mound of decaying metal which must surely be the old baker's ovens.

Edeard, of course, had perceived Boyd's soul lingering after his death. She could sense nothing like that, although the whole memory now made her cold. It was so much easier to sneer and scorn the foolish simplicity of Living Dream's icons from the intellectual sanctuary of ANA rather than actually standing amid the movement's sacred heart experiencing its reality for herself. Just looking at the ancient shop's open doorway she finally understood why Inigo had decreed the construction of Makkathran2. It was the ultimate act of worship and devotion. This alien city was the embodiment of Edeard's triumph; a foreigner from some rural province had come here and given the citizens a hope they'd never known they'd lost and, from that, he inspired billions he never knew existed. All her lofty rationalized disdain could never weaken his phenomenal accomplishment. Here, tracing his footsteps in a very literal sense, she knew how small she was in comparison, on so many levels.

When she finally arrived on the concourse she'd recovered some self-esteem, but that moment of self-realization had left her more aware of her loneliness than she'd been since she arrived in the Void.

Come on, Dad, where are you? Whatever you're waiting for it must have happened by now, surely?

Up until the last few days she'd managed to keep herself busy enough. Setting up camp in the Sampalok mansion, exploring the rest of the city, testing out and developing her psychic abilities. All that had kept her occupied well enough, venturing into the truly significant places: the Culverit ziggurat, the Orchard Palace with its fabulous ceilings with their astronomical images, the Jeavons Constable Station, and of course the House of Blue Petals – weirdly, an anticlimax now it had cast off its signature bar and doors and thick drapes. Without such rigging it seemed to lack substance. Even the grand Lillylight Opera House had been a disappointment. With the private boxes of the Grand Families no longer cluttering the tiered ledges of the massive ampitheatre, it lacked the character she'd witnessed in the dreams, though she was impressed by the domed ceiling with its white and violet stalactites. Sadly she didn't quite possess enough courage to sing when she stood beneath them on the stage.

But now her interest in visiting the plethora of locations and buildings of significance to Living Dream was waning. All she seemed to be doing was reinforcing the core of Living Dream beliefs by her display of reverence and excitement.

I need to find something relevant to me.

The surface of the Great Major Canal was clotted with various green and purple puffweeds and fronds of the aquatic plants which flourished. They shivered occasionally as a fil-rat slithered through them, but other than that the whole length of the canal remained perfectly still. Only the centre of Mid Pool was clear, showing the dark water, which moved with a smooth slow flow as the Lyot Sea's modest breakers washed in and out of the port district.

Justine had often considered building some kind of boat or raft to sail along the canals. With her tools and third hand it wouldn't be that difficult, and it would at least keep her occupied.

She wondered if Rah and the Lady had felt this peculiar sense of expectancy when they first entered Makkathran. Something in human nature just called out to occupy and use the empty city.

The boat idea was a good one, she thought, both therapeutic and practical. It also overlooked the fact she'd never done any manual work in her life and didn't know the first thing about carpentry.

Maybe tomorrow.

She went over the flat pink bridge across Trade Route Canal and into the tip of Pholas Park. From there she had to walk along Lilac Canal for several minutes until she came to a blue humpback bridge into Fiacre. The human bridges of metal and wood must have been the first artefacts to disappear after their builders left. Now she had to use the city's own crossings. Her one attempt to do a Waterwalker and stabilize the surface of a canal with telekinesis hadn't been enormously successful. How they must have laughed at that dunking back in the Commonwealth. *Assuming Dad's still dreaming all of this for them.*

As she carried on parallel with Great Major Canal her farsight probed through the city substance below her feet, showing it as a thick shadow of brown grey, almost completely featureless. She didn't have anything like Edeard's perception range, but she had been able to glimpse the tunnels below the canals, which was a moment of extreme pride – even though they appeared like a particularly low-quality exovision display. Then when she added a biononic field function scan to the wavering spectre she was also aware of the faint fissures even further beneath her feet that represented the travel tunnels.

But that was definitely her limit. There was no way she could sense the city's slumbering mind so far underneath, let alone wake it. She wondered if the *Silverbird*'s neutron laser could cut down into a travel tunnel for her, and if it did what Makkathran's response would be. Field-function scans had confirmed that the city's orange lighting was all electrically powered. That evidence of a technological base convinced her that the travel tunnels could take her a great deal closer to the controlling core of the city – whatever the city actually was.

Again, that would be a project for another day. *If I just knew how long it's going to be before someone arrives. Surely the Pilgrimage fleet must be on its way by now? That must be what Dad was expecting when he told me to come here.*

Most of the buildings in Fiacre were covered in vines and creepers, growing out of the deep troughs that lined the streets. Without anyone tending them they now simply swamped the structures they were supposed to complement, sealing up the entranceways and cloaking the windows. Some of the narrower alleys were impassable tangles of dense vegetation. Even the wider streets were difficult to walk down. Fortunately the path along the side of the Great Major Canal was relatively clear.

The open bridge over Grove Canal was so smooth it verged

on slippery, and that was with the rugged soles of her boots. She vaguely recalled it had a rope rail and wooden slats pinned on back in Edeard's time. But she edged across it without falling into the water below. Then she was in Eyrie. The tall towers did have a distant kinship with human Gothic design, though no one on Earth had ever built anything quite so crooked as these. She walked though the broad thoroughfares between them, tipping her head back to try and glimpse the spires which formed a crown around each apex. The angle was all wrong, but she wasn't going to climb up one to gain a view from the platform at the top, not today.

It was late morning by the time she arrived at the Lady's church. *Cathedral would be more accurate,* she thought. The large central dome with its crystal summit radiated three long wings outward, each with five levels of balconies held apart by slim fluted pillars.

The doors had gone, as had all the pews. Justine walked in, feeling more nervous than she usually did when she scouted the notorious buildings. Sunlight shone down vertically through the huge transparent centre of the dome, creating a bright haze over the silver-white floor. Several default genistars gave her a curious look before shuffling away down one of the broad side cloisters where they were nesting. There were no sculpted genistars left, of course. Creating ge-chimps or maybe ge-hounds was another possible occupation for her, though the high probability that she'd mess up the sculpting made her squeamish. Even Master Akeem at the height of his ability had a regular quota of failures.

She thought she could see something moving on the other side of the bright shaft of light filling the centre of the church. Farsight and retinal zoom functions found nothing, but she was uncertain ... Something about the church was unnerving her, like a deep harmonic that she couldn't quite hear.

Stupid. Come on girl, pull yourself together.

She marched straight through the intense splash of light. The giant white-marble statue of the Lady had survived, standing alone where the altar had once rested. One of the cloisters opened up behind it, and again she thought there was some movement in the shadows. Goosebumps were rising along her arms. She moved forward, more cautiously this time. Her third hand pulled gingerly at the secure flap on top of her holster. Just in case . . .

She moved into the relative gloom of the cloister, allowing her retinas to adjust. Farsight showed her there was nothing but empty air. Then her father stepped out from behind a pillar twenty metres away.

Justine let out a small sob of relief and took one step forwards before freezing. A big alien had emerged beside him.

'Dad?'

'Hello, darling. Glad you made it here. Not that I was getting worried, but . . .'

He smiled his half-smile, the one that was so familiar and welcome she just wanted to rush over and hug him. However . . . 'Is that an Anomine?'

'Yep. Meet Tyzak, he's slowly showing an interest in our story.'

The Anomine twittered away in its high-pitched voice.

'He says he's pleased to see you,' Gore translated.

Justine sighed. 'And here I was just starting to think everything was making sense.'

'Trust me. You're doing fine. That was a good landing, by the way. Nicely judged.'

'What's happening, Dad? Why am I here?'

'You're my link into the Void. And that makes you critical. People are on their way.'

'The Pilgrimage fleet?'

'Yeah, they made it past the warrior Raiel. But there's someone else, too. That's important, Justine. They should arrive before the fleet. They may even be in the Void already.'

'Okay,' she said uncertainly. 'Who?'

'The other Dreamers.'

'You're kidding?' That made little sense. 'Really?'

'Yeah. An old contact told me they got ahead. Or at least,

they made it to the boundary. I don't know anything more. But if they made it through they'll head for Makkathran.'

'Why, though? Why them?'

'Because they're what I need in place along with you.'

'All right, Dad, I'll watch for them.'

'Thank you.'

'Have you got any idea of timescale?'

'Not really; I'm sorry, darling, you'll just have to sit it out.'

'Do I need to get anything ready?'

'No. Just survive, however long it takes.'

'I was thinking I might try and communicate with the city mind. Drill down into the deep tunnels or something,' she said with a hopeful tone.

'No point.'

'Can't you tell me anything?'

'I will, I promise. But I'm contending with small local problems that might become unpleasantly physical if I show my hand too soon. And I should warn you that Ilanthe is with the Pilgrimage fleet.'

'Ha! That bitch. I'll sort her out if she tries anything with me.'

Gore's golden features reflected anxiety. 'No you won't, darling. She's not what she used to be. She's taken on a different aspect which might be trouble, a lot of trouble. Even the Silfen are worried about her and what she's doing. '

'Oh. Okay.' Justine didn't like the sound of that at all; it took a great deal for Gore to show caution.

'I love you, darling.'

'Dad. Be careful, please.'

'My middle name.'

'I thought that was bulldozer.'

'I hyphenate a lot these days. Sign of the times.' He raised his arm, and gradually turned translucent. After a while he was gone altogether, and Tyzak with him.

Justine stared at the space where they'd been, then shook her head as if coming out of a trance. 'Oh crap.' She tried to press down on the sensation of anxiety, without any real success. But at least he'd given her a clear objective. *Stay alive.* 'Nice to know,' she muttered. Not understanding came hard to Justine: it showed an alarming lack of control. And that just didn't sit right at all.

Justine turned and walked back out into the cavernous central section of the church. If she was going to be staying in Makkathran for any serious length of time there were practical aspects she'd have to work out, not to mention contingencies should the *Silverbird*'s systems eventually fail. Food was the primary long-term requirement. She was sure there had been some sheep and goats roaming round on the Iguru; and seven days ago she'd actually glimpsed what looked like chickens on Low Moat. There must be seeds she could cultivate, too. The Grand Families all had kitchen gardens in their mansions, the plants must have survived in some form. And fishing ... She grinned. Fishing would be easy with a third hand.

It wouldn't be easy, but she could survive. After all, the city must have been in a similar unkempt state when Rah and the Lady arrived. Justine smiled up at the Lady's face high above her. 'And look what you did with the place,' she told the statue. The Lady gazed down with her unchanging sombre expression. Justine's smile began to fade. There was something about those features now she could study them closely – after all Edeard hadn't been a particularly regular visitor to the church. She had to dig deep amid memories she hadn't realized her body had retained, but there were connections sparking away in her subconscious. 'No,' she whispered in shock. This Lady as captured by the sculptor was a lot older than the time Justine had met her, and she had very different hair back then, not to mention figure. 'Oh no.' Justine's eyes began to water as the sheer emotional power of recognition engulfed her. 'It is, isn't it?' Her shoulders started to shake, and she giggled. 'It is you. Holy crap, it's really you!' Giggles gave way to hysterical laughter. She actually had to hug her belly it hurt so much. She couldn't stop. *This* was the Lady, venerated and worshipped by two separate civilizations. The epitome of dignity and grace. 'YES!' she yelled out, and punched the air. Then the joyful laughter made her double up again. She waved her hands helplessly, trying to wipe the tears away.

Well what do you know, the universe has a sense of irony after all.

11

The thin sleet of blue sparks cascading through hyperspace's pseudofabric faded away as power was withdrawn from the ultradrive engines of the *Lady's Light*, and the ship dropped back into spacetime. Blackness pressed in against the vast transparent wall at the front of the observation deck. Radiation from the glowing loop of interstellar detritus behind them struck the ordinary force field which was protecting them from the hostility of the Gulf, creating a disagreeable claret glow around the edges of the transparency. Araminta put on a pair of sunglasses, and stared through the polarized lenses at the greater darkness four lightyears ahead.

Ethan stood beside her, immaculate in his Cleric robes, leaking awe and expectation into the gaiafield. Taranse, Darraklan and Rincenso waited loyally behind their Dreamer, also subdued at the sight of the barrier which they had doubted they would ever witness for themselves.

'We're here,' Araminta told the Skylord. 'Ask the Heart to reach for us, please.'

It responded with a pulse of near-human happiness.

Exoimage displays showed her the starship's hysradar return. The Void boundary was rippling, distending upwards at hyperluminal speed. Reaching for the pilgrimage fleet. For her. Its summit opened.

A soft gale of nebula-light swept over the twelve pilgrimage ships.

Hysradar detected another ship emerging from stealth mode, tiny beside the waiting goliaths, but with an impenetrable force field.

'I wondered where you were,' Araminta said.

'You knew,' Ilanthe replied equitably.

Ethan's delight chilled rapidly at the reminder of the cost of his victory. 'What now?' he asked.

'We go in,' Araminta told him. 'Together. Correct?'

'Correct,' Ilanthe said.

'Taranse,' Araminta said. 'Take us through.'

He gave a dreamy nod. The *Lady's Light* accelerated forwards, with the other ships matching their course.

'My Lord,' Ethan's mind cried, his thoughts amplified by the three confluence nests on board, then reinforced by those on the remainder of the fleet. 'Please take us to the solid world which used to be inhabited by those of our species.'

Shit! Araminta shot him a furious glare. He returned a satisfied sneer. 'Did you overlook that part of the request, Dreamer?' he asked mockingly.

Araminta watched the tortured red glare fade from the edge of the transparency as the glow of the nebulas strengthened. Somewhere behind them, the boundary was closing again. For the first time in days the infestation of nausea and confusion from living at two speeds abated. Her thoughts cleared.

'And your uniqueness would appear to be at an end,' Ethan continued. Araminta's farsight showed her his thoughts, the malice which festered there, naked to taste as he slowly realized the abilities of the Void and recalled the techniques Edeard had applied. Farsight also showed her what he was hiding within the copious folds of his robe.

'True,' she said. 'But that leaves us leading the real life of the Void.'

Ethan reached for the old-fashioned pistol he'd concealed. Araminta's third hand picked him up and threw him across the

647

observation chamber. He screamed as much from shock as fright as he flew through the air, a cry that was cut off as he thudded face-first into the bulkhead. He crashed awkwardly to the floor, whimpering in pain from the broken bones. Blood was dripping from his mouth and nose.

'When Rah and the Lady came to Makkathran they had only politics and brute force to enforce their rule,' Araminta said lightly as she walked towards Ethan, who was trying to scramble away. 'How fitting that such gifts are also what we will be starting out with.'

Ethan went for a heartsqueeze. Araminta warded it off easily. She held out a hand, palm upwards, raising it. Ethan was abruptly tugged off the floor. A finger beckoned. He was drawn towards her.

'You were right,' she said to Aaron. 'I did need to practise. He's a sneaky little shit.'

Taranse, Darraklan and Rincenso were very still, all of them hurrying to establish their own mental shields lest the Dreamer should read their thoughts.

'You don't believe,' Ethan hissed through bloody lips. 'You never did.'

'But you believe in me, don't you?' she urged huskily, recalling Tathal's dreadful compulsive domination during the Twenty-Sixth dream – applying the ability against the squirming mind before her. 'It was me who brought you to the barrier. Me who called to the Skylord. Me who is bringing you to Querencia. Isn't that so?'

'Yes,' Ethan gurgled.

'And you are grateful for such an act of selfless generosity, are you not?'

'Yes.'

'How could you do anything but love the person who made it possible to finally live the dream?'

'I couldn't.'

'Do you love me, Ethan? Do you trust me?'

'Yes. Oh yes.'

'Thank you, Ethan, from the bottom of my heart.' She lowered him carefully to the decking, and smiled gently at her aghast audience. 'The ex-Conservator seems to have tripped in all the excitement. Please take him to the sick bay.'

Taranse nodded nervously, and knelt down to help Ethan. With Darraklan's help, they managed to pull him up between them.

Because she could show no weakness Araminta watched them with a passive smile, while over in the *Mellanie's Redemption* Araminta-two was puking his guts up at the atrocity he'd just committed.

'Dreamer, look,' Rincenso said in wonder. He was pointing at the front of the observation deck. On the other side of the transparent bulkhead, a flock of Skylords was approaching the pilgrimage fleet. For all she feared and resented the creatures, they looked glorious as they swam out of the sparse starscape.

As soon as the boundary closed behind them, Ilanthe ordered *the ship* to open its cargo bay doors. She could sense the abilities intrinsic to the Void's fabric pervade the inversion core. What the animal humans of Querencia crudely described as farsight allowed her mind to examine the fabric directly, plotting the effect her own thoughts had on it, the alterations and reaction they propagated. The symbiosis was fascinating. Already she'd learned more than a century of remote analysis of Inigo's stupid dreams. The Void's quantum architecture was completely different to the universe outside. But it was tragically flawed, requiring extrinsic energy to sustain itself even in its base state. When the functions enfolded within its extraordinarily intricate quantum fields were activated the power levels they consumed were far greater than she'd expected.

'The doomsayers were right,' she told Neskia. 'The pilgrimage animals would have wiped out the galaxy with their reset demands.'

'Will you prevent that?' Neskia asked.

Ilanthe regarded the concern swirling within her otherwise

faithful operative's mind with a detached interest. Even a Higher as progressive and complex as Neskia was betrayed by residual animal emotion. 'My success will render the question irrelevant.'

Ilanthe observed the flock of Skylords closing in. With their opalescent vacuum wings extended wide, the mountain-sized creatures were expanding quickly across the thin scattering of stars as they accelerated towards the fleet. The lambent twisted strands of the nebulas were distorted through the weird lensing effect of the wings, causing them to flicker and shift like celestial flames. Ilanthe examined the true functionality of the wings, how they rooted down into the Void fabric, manipulating localized gravity and temporal flow. A process of propulsion so much more sophisticated than the crude 'telekinetic' ability of manipulating mass location. Less energy-demanding, too, she noted approvingly.

When her thoughts tried to replicate the same interaction with the Void fabric there was some aspect missing. Instead she simply wished herself elevating out into space, employing some of the technique Edeard's descendant had employed in the Last Dream. The inversion core immediately flew clear of *the ship*. The method worked, which was gratifying, but lacked the elegance and capability of the Skylords.

Ilanthe felt the perception of the Skylords concentrate on the inversion core, seeking understanding of what she was. Her thoughts established a perfect shield around the shell of the inversion core, blocking their probes.

'Greetings,' she told the closest Skylord neutrally, and began to accelerate towards it. Her own perception ability listened to Araminta and several others from the pilgrimage fleet frantically warning the Skylords to be careful, claiming she was dangerous. Their responses were interesting, revealing their complete lack of rational intellect. They almost evaded the topic. Certainly they didn't seem to comprehend the meaning behind the concepts. It wasn't part of their world, therefore their mental vocabulary didn't accommodate it. Either they were artificial constructs designated by the nucleus with the specific task of gathering up mature minds, or they had once been fully sentient spaceborne entities who had de-evolved throughout the countless millennia since their imprisonment. With nothing new to experience inside the Void, no challenges to struggle with, their minds had atrophied down to instinct-based responses.

'I am fulfilled,' Ilanthe told the Skylord as she approached it. 'Please take me to the Heart.'

'I do not know if you are fulfilled,' the Skylord responded. 'You are closed to me. Open yourself.'

The tentative wisps of the colourful vacuum wings flowed around the inversion core as it glided in towards the Skylord's glimmering crystalline body. Ilanthe could perceive the texture of its oddly distorted geometry, a kind of honeycomb of ordinary matter and something similar to an exotic force; the two were in constant flux, which bestowed that distinctive surface instability. The composition was intriguing. But despite its subtle complexity, the thoughts which animated it lacked potency. Her own determination, amplified by the neural pathways available within the inversion core, was a lot stronger. 'I would be grateful if you would open yourself to me,' she told it.

'I withhold nothing.'

'Oh but you do.' And she reached for the Skylord, inserting her hardened, purposeful thoughts amid its own clean and simple routines. Lovingly entwining them. Taking hold.

'What are you doing?' the Skylord asked.

She suppressed the rising incomprehension, stilling its deep instincts to facilitate applications which would take it far from this place.

'Your intrusion is preventing me from functioning. Parts of me are failing. Withdraw yourself.'

'I am helping you to become so much more. Together we are synergistic,' she promised. 'I will guide you to the pinnacle of fulfilment.' Then the feast began.

'I am ending,' the Skylord declared.

'Stop!' Araminta cried. 'You're killing it.'

'Have you learned nothing about the Void?' Ilanthe retorted.

Dark spectres began to slither through the cheerful sparkles of the Skylord's vacuum wings, proliferating and expanding. The tenuous cloud of molecules which formed the physical aspect of the wings burst apart, dark frosty motes dissipating through space like a black snowstorm. Now the dark flames were shivering across the intricate optical quivering of the Skylord's surface, biting inwards.

Everything it was poured across the gap to the inversion core, an extirpation that allowed the abilities and knowledge of its kind to flow into Ilanthe.

At that point she almost regretted no longer having a human face. How she would be smiling now. Engorged and enriched by the Skylord's essence, her mastery of this strange continuum was rising towards absolute. Function manipulation began to integrate with her personality at an instinctive level. She heard the call of the nebulas, the trans-dimensional sink points of rationality twisting out through the Void's quantum fields, keening for intelligence with the promise of escalation to something greater, as yet unglimpsed. They must lead to the paramount consciousness, she knew. The Heart itself. From that nucleus everything could be controlled.

Local space was awash with despair and revulsion at the Skylord's demise. 'You will thank me soon enough,' she informed the insignificant human minds. One was different to the rest. A small part of her acknowledged the Dreamer Araminta, whose thoughts stretched away somehow, a method that didn't utilize the Void fabric. It wasn't relevant.

Once more Ilanthe's thoughts flowed into the pattern to manipulate the Void's temporal and gravitonic functions, this time correctly. A wide area around the inversion core began to sparkle as the surrounding dust was caught up in the effect, drifting into chiaroscuro spirals. Ilanthe accelerated hard, simultaneously negating the temporal flow around the inversion core's shell. The Pilgrimage fleet dwindled away to nothing in seconds as it achieved point nine lightspeed. Far ahead, the siren melody from the nebula which Querencia humans had named Odin's Sea grew perceptibly stronger.

Araminta hadn't moved throughout the whole atrocity. It had happened not ten kilometres directly ahead of the *Lady's Light* and there was absolutely nothing she could do about it. She'd seen the Skylord's vacuum wings dim to a frail grey travesty of their former grandeur, then even that feeble light was smothered. All the while her mind echoed with the Skylord's pitiable incomprehension.

It was too much. Tears leaked out from behind her sunglasses. 'I did this, I'm responsible, I brought that monster here.'

'No,' Aaron assured her. 'You were manipulated by Ilanthe, as were all of us. You have no guilt.'

'But I do,' Araminta whispered.

'Dreamer,' Darraklan said earnestly. 'This is not your fault. Ethan was the one who fell to that thing's sweet promises. It subverted him. You are blameless. You simply fulfilled your destiny.'

Out beyond the observation deck, the remaining Skylords were slowly circling round the cold husk of their dead kindred. She could feel their mournful thoughts as they scoured space for its soul. But of course Ilanthe had absorbed every aspect, leaving nothing.

'I'm so sorry,' she told the distraught Skylords.

'It is gone,' came the chorus of grief. 'Our kindred is gone. It did not go to the Heart. The *other* ended it. Why?'

'The other is unfulfilled and evil,' Araminta told them. 'This is what we bring wherever we go.'

The Skylords recoiled.

'We need them,' Rincenso said in alarm. 'Dreamer, please. The fleet needs guidance, more than ever now.'

'It's over,' she said brokenly. 'Ethan was right, I don't believe. Besides, it doesn't matter any more. Inigo will end this as he began it. At least I think that's right.'

When Araminta-two looked at Aaron for confirmation he shook his head angrily.

'What?' Araminta-two protested. 'That's the great and wonderful plan, isn't it?'

'The fleet is not part of the plan,' Aaron said.

'I got it safely through the barrier. That's it. That's all I ever said I'd do.'

'Get the Skylords to help,' Aaron ordered. 'Come on, don't wilt on us now.'

'Help do what?' Araminta-two asked. 'We're almost at Querencia. Nothing else matters. You don't need me now, and I never needed the fleet.'

'You talked about responsibility,' Aaron said. 'Those millions of dumb Living Dream followers placed their lives in your hands.'

'Waiting in space isn't going to hurt them. It won't be long. After all, this is about to end.'

'And if it doesn't end in our favour?'

From the other side of the cramped cabin of the *Mellanie's Redemption*, Araminta-two gave him a curious glance. 'You? You have doubts?'

'I've always known what I have to do even though I don't know why. It's comfortable that way.' His face twisted up in anguish. 'I've remembered too much of *her* now, and it's eating me alive. Memories of night and desolation are breaking loose. She thrives on them. I have to unknow again. I have to be free, I have to be clean. That or death. I would welcome death at this point. You, Corrie-Lyn, Inigo, the others, you all claimed that I needed to find myself, to be true to me. I don't. I cannot be. I need to be what I was granted in return for my new life. That is me. And none of you accept that.'

'But—'

'Things go wrong!' Aaron almost shouted.

It was the thing Araminta had feared ever since Corrie-Lyn told her about Aaron's near-total collapse in mindspace. He was the one who'd brought them all together, who'd relentlessly pushed them into the Void because of some plan his masters had conceived. He knew what to do. Even though his faith in that task was totally artificial, it had swept them all along. And now here they were, almost within reach of whatever goal they had to attain, and he was falling apart because of his past and the doubts it was inflicting.

'I'll talk to the Skylords,' Araminta-two said earnestly. 'I'll fix this. The pilgrimage fleet will land on Querencia. They'll be safe.'

He nodded, grimacing. 'Thank you.'

Darraklan was giving Araminta a curious look as agitation built amid his thoughts. She realized that some suggestion of Aaron might have escaped from her shield.

'Dreamer?' It was almost a plea. Like all of them, he'd invested everything he had in her.

'It's all right,' Araminta said, and held out her hand for him to touch. 'I will talk to the Skylords. I *will* get us to Makkathran.' She faced the front of the observation deck again, focusing on the bereaved Skylords. 'We seek fulfilment,' she told them calmly. 'We seek guidance.'

*

Everything was calm. That wasn't good.

The Delivery Man wanted some kind of evidence of the unimaginable nuclear hell that raged barely twenty metres from where he was sitting in the *Last Throw*'s cabin.

'This is really disturbing you, isn't it?' Gore said over the TD channel. 'Your emotions are hyping up the gaiafield. Why don't you play some soothing music?'

'FUCK OFF.'

And still the *Last Throw* remained perfectly still. The Delivery Man desperately needed proof that he was actually descending through the photosphere of a mid-range star – not that size truly mattered given the circumstances. Some shaking would be nice. Maybe the odd creak of the stress structure. And heat. There really, really ought to be an unpleasant amount of heat in the cabin.

There wasn't a chance of that. The super-reinforced force fields cocooning the starship would either work or they wouldn't. There was no little margin of error that he could get through by gritting his teeth and heroically enduring some hardship. For all the difference it would make he could quite easily be taking a comforting spore shower, or maybe a little snooze in his sleep compartment. *Oh yes, that's really going to happen.*

The *Last Throw* was navigating by hysradar alone. None of its other sensors would be of the slightest use. They couldn't even protrude through the ultra-silver one-hundred-per-cent-reflective surface of the outermost force field. Nothing material could survive the photosphere plasma.

So ... hysradar it was. The exovision display showed the macro-hurricanes of the photosphere rampaging around him. Particle gales so large and fearsome their size actually made their surges and twists predictable. The smartcore could track and predict the impact vectors of the magnetosphere squalls and granulation eruptions braking around them, allowing the ingrav and regrav units to compensate, keeping them on course.

They were driving down vertically, forcing through the barrage of escaping plasma towards the siphon – now three thousand kilometres below *Last Throw*, submerged within the convection zone where the temperature spiked up past two million degrees centigrade, with a density just over ten per cent that of water. And life was going to get extremely dangerous, because, as Gore had gleefully remarked, the photosphere was just the warm-up. The Delivery Man still didn't know what to make of that sense of humour.

His one talisman was the Stardiver programme, which had notched up some success over the centuries. Not that Stardiver probes were the most regular missions launched by the Greater Commonwealth Astronomical Agency. The hyperspace-spliced shielding perfected for them over eight hundred years hardly guaranteed success once the convection zone was entered.

The Delivery Man would have liked a few test flights first, each one dipping a little deeper, scientifically analysing the results, seeing how the modified and expanded force-field generators performed. Power consumption. Energy tolerance. Pressure resistance. Hyperspace shunts. But no . . .

'It either works or it doesn't,' Gore had said. 'There's no halfway here.'

That didn't mean you couldn't be prudent. It wasn't an argument the Delivery Man even bothered with. Besides, even he acknowledged it wouldn't do to pique the curiosity of the ship that had followed them. No Accelerator agent would ever permit any endeavour which might halt Ilanthe's attempt to Fuse with the Void.

Two and a half thousand kilometres.

The Delivery Man had launched five hours after Justine's last dream. And he hadn't worked out what was so incredibly funny about the Lady's statue. Gore – naturally! – had smirked, and gone: 'Well who'd have guessed?' So they both knew who she was, some figure from ancient history no doubt.

'How's your infiltration going?' the Delivery Man asked.

'Everything's in position,' Gore replied. 'I won't be starting the actual physical process until you've established command over the siphon.'

'What does Tyzak make of it all?'

'It's just another sensor system to him.'

'We could maybe tell him the truth.'

'Sonny, we're doing what we have to so we can protect our species – and his. He does what he has to do to guarantee his way of life. This is not a diplomatic negotiation so that we can find common ground. Both of us are genetically wired to be what we are. And right now there is no common purpose. That's a fucking great shame, but it's the way it is.'

'I know. I suppose I was hoping that meeting Justine might make him change his mind. If he could just understand what it is we're all facing.'

'That's the thing: he does understand. But that doesn't mean he can change, not to the degree we need, and certainly not in the timeframe we have.'

'I know. Are you really not going to tell me who the Lady is?'

'It's a complete irrelevance to this situation, besides it keeps you distracted.'

'Yeah, right.' The *Last Throw* was now three hundred kilometres above the surface of the convection zone. Energy usage was growing as the drives fought to keep the ship stable against the monstrous tides of plasma streaking along the quivering flux lines. There was also the problem of the star's own gravity. Five additional ingrav units had been included in the modification, whose sole purpose was to negate that awesome crushing force. They were operating right at their maximum loading. If one of them glitched for even a second he'd be squashed into a molecule-thick puddle of blood and flesh across the decking.

'Here it comes.' The Delivery Man braced himself as *Last Throw* approached the convection zone. There was no clean defining edge between the two. The photosphere simply grew hotter, with a corresponding shift in density.

The *Last Throw*'s ultradrive came on as the temperature rose from the relative cool of the photosphere, shunting excess energy from the force fields away into hyperspace. A flow rate which was increasing at a near-exponential rate. The Stardiver project engineers had soon learned that combining the force-field energy-dissipation function with an exotic component was the only way to deal with such extraordinary temperature loading.

'It's holding,' the Delivery Man said in surprise as the starship began to descend through the convection zone. Now the biggest danger lay with the bubble-like granulations that bloomed thousands of kilometres across almost without warning and raced for the photosphere. One of the primary mission objectives for Stardiver probes was to study the factors which contributed to their gestation. Even now, with centuries of research and observation, that prediction was a very inexact science.

'Good man,' Gore replied levelly. 'Keep it coming.'

'Right.' The Delivery Man was shaking now. He wiped a hand across his forehead, dismayed to find out how much sweat was forming there; then ordered his biononics to initiate an adrenalin suppressor. He had to keep a clear head, and fear was degrading his ability to think straight. *Yeah, as if staying sober and alert is going to help.* One flaw in a system, one dodgy component, a single poorly written line of code, and it would be over in microseconds. *At least I'll never know. Until I get re-lifed. Except I won't get re-lifed because according to Gore this is the galaxy's last chance. Oh shit, I miss the kids.*

This time the moisture staining his cheeks wasn't coming from his brow.

'So when do you think Inigo is going to get to Makkathran?' he asked to distract himself from death – which was surely going to hit any moment. He was still amazed at Paula Myo calling to tell Gore that Inigo, a weird duo-multiple Araminta and a team of her agents had somehow raced Troblum's starship ahead of the Pilgrimage Fleet.

'It really shouldn't be long, son. You'll be out of there and back with your girls before you know it.'

'Yeah, sure.' His one remaining satisfaction was knowing that he was doing something to help Lizzie and the girls. By contrast it would have been awful to be stuck inside the Sol barrier with them, not knowing what was happening outside, if there was any hope. *Not much, but enough,* he promised his family. Given the not-so-small miracle Gore had worked getting Inigo to help, he'd convinced himself there was a chance. A very small one, but it was real. All he had to do now was rendezvous with the siphon.

It took another fifty minutes to manoeuvre through the macrosurges of the convection zone's deathly environment before the fifty-kilometre circle of the siphon force field was directly underneath *Last Throw*. Hysradar showed the torrent of two-million-degree hydrogen streaming in through the rim. The Delivery Man guided the starship across the curving upper surface of the giant lens-shape then slowly down until it was nose-on to the edge.

'That's the weak part,' Gore said. 'Show me what you can do.'

The *Last Throw* eased forward until its force field actually touched the protective shield around the siphon. That was when the Delivery Man finally got to feel some physical aspect of the flight. A low thrumming reverberated through the cabin as the starship was caught between the force field and the plasma hurtling past. He could feel the decking vibrate, and grinned weakly. Maybe tranquillity was preferable after all.

Sensors could just manage to scan through the semi-permeable segment of the force field which it was pressed against. The smart-core began to probe what it could of the siphon's quantum signature, tracing ghostly outlines of the gigantic generator sheltered inside the force field. The map of its structure built slowly. Eventually there was enough for the Delivery Man to begin the second stage.

The *Last Throw* activated several TD channels, directed with impressive accuracy at the siphon's control network. Low-level connections were created, and a software analysis initiated.

'It's not the same kind of semi-sentient that controls the elevation mechanism,' the Delivery Man reported. 'More like a distributed AI routine; although the parallels with Commonwealth genetic software are minimal.'

'Can it be hacked?'

'There are a lot of safeguards including an external override which will have to be neutralized; but the smartcore says we have several infiltrator packages which should work.'

'Launch them.'

*

It's Gore. That was the thought which Oscar awoke to. The medical capsule's cover withdrew, showing a blurred figure peering down at him in the cargo hold's dim green-tinged light. *Gore is expecting someone to join Justine, and that's what Aaron was committed to. Gore is Aaron's controller.*

The face above him resolved into that of Araminta-two, whose mind was badly agitated.

'It's Gore,' Oscar croaked. Suspension had left him with stiff muscles everywhere and an embarrassingly full bladder.

'What is?' Araminta-two asked.

'The person behind Aaron, or at least one of them.'

'Oh. You mean because he's directing everyone to Makkathran? Yeah, I figured that one out a few months back. Even Aaron agreed.'

'Ah. Right. Need to pee.' Oscar levered himself upright on his elbows, and nearly banged his head on the ceiling of the forward cargo hold. There wasn't much room between the bulky medical cabinets. He saw three of them were already empty.

I thought I was supposed to be first out. 'Everything okay?'

'Just about,' Araminta-two answered with a whole load of glumness. Oscar gave him a good look; the Dreamer was wearing a baggy blue T-shirt and grey-green trousers that had a lot of spare fabric. For a moment Oscar thought he was dressing in Troblum's old clothes before acknowledging the style was deliberately feminine. 'What's up? Have we arrived?'

'Our Skylord is decelerating us into Querencia orbit. Troblum has already detected the *Silverbird*'s beacon, so we know where Makkathran is. No need for observational orbits.'

'That's good.' He *really* needed to pee.

'It's been touch and go with Aaron,' Araminta-two blurted.

'Why?'

'His memories of the Cat are breaking through. He spends longer and longer asleep wrestling with his nightmares. Yesterday he was only awake for five hours. And his body's having some kind of psychosomatic reaction; I think enhanced by his psychic ability.'

'Oh crap.' Oscar hunched down and made his way along the companionway to the main cabin. His u-shadow connected him to the smartcore, and an exoimage display showed him the planet ahead, expanding quite rapidly as they decelerated into orbit. 'Seventy-three minutes out? And we spent three and a half months travelling. Not bad.' He made it into the cabin to find Inigo, Corrie-Lyn and Tomansio waiting for him. 'Gotta go . . .' He pointed urgently at the washroom cubicle. They all waved him on, offering sympathetic thoughts.

He was just sealing his fly when the deluge of senses hit him hard, foreign thoughts slicing clean through his basic mental shield, bringing vertiginous light, sensation, sound, taste, along with a primeval fear that numbed his hands as he tumbled down into someone else's life.

It had been a fabulous holiday. When evening came they'd taken one of the hundreds of tourist boats that nosed around the piers of Tridelta City and headed up the Dongara River for a night of partying and native spectacle. The planet's native bioluminescent vegetation didn't disappoint, glowing vividly against the dark skies. And the lounges on the boat provided a lot of wild fun, impressing even the most jaded passenger.

They disembarked at dawn, and went back to their hotel on the top of the old Kinoki Tower three kilometres above the muddy waters of the rivers that shimmied round the city groynes. Daytime was spent eating, sleeping, and having furious sex. The Cat had no inhibitions, which was yet another reason he loved her so. Provocative and daring, she exhausted him and still wanted more, telling him what she expected his poor old flesh to perform.

'Let me have just one break,' he laughed, reaching for some of the chilled wine. But the bottle was lying on its side where it'd been kicked. He gave it a depressed stare, and told his u-shadow to connect to—

The Cat rolled him on to his back, and straddled him. A delightful victorious smile lit up her cute face. 'Wrong answer,' she said, grinning. Her hand closed round his wrist, and the skin burned beneath her fingers. He screamed as the charred flesh welded itself on to the mattress. She gripped the other hand, and seared that down too. 'Nobody denies me,' she told him.

He screamed again as she began on his ankles, spreadeagling him so he was held immobile by the stringy remains of his own smouldering flesh. Then her hands stroked nimbly along his chest. She stiffened her fingers, and powered them down like a knife. Bones cracked, blood welled up in deep punctures. 'With your body gone, I will take your mind and finally your soul,' she promised. He screamed and screamed, and twisted with all his strength to escape, prising himself free—

'Shit!' Oscar juddered back, cracking the side of his head on the bulkhead of the tiny compartment. 'Ow!' He pressed his hand to the rising bruise as biononics hurried to ease the damaged flesh. That was when he saw the red markings round his wrist. He stared at them in shock. They were an identical shape to the injury Cat had inflicted on Aaron – in the dream. 'Bloody hell.' He stumbled out into the main cabin, holding up both arms incredulously to show his colleagues the sores.

'Yeah!' Tomansio said heartlessly. 'You have to guard yourself against that. He got me half an hour ago. I just hope to Ozzie they're not genuine memories.'

A muffled scream sounded across the cabin. Everyone looked at the sealed door of the sleeping cubicle where Aaron was brawling with his own mind. 'Can't we wake him up?' Oscar's shield was as strong as he could make it, and he could still sense the nightmare flooding out of the sleeping man's mind.

'Troblum and I tried that once,' Araminta-two said. 'Won't be doing that again. Thankfully my third hand is stronger than his.' He gave a nervous smile. 'Actually, Aaron was the one who's been making me practise and develop my abilities.'

'We're losing him,' Inigo said. 'And if we lose him . . .'

'No,' Corrie-Lyn said. 'We won't lose him, not to her. Not before we reach Makkathran. He's stronger than that. I know.'

'Yeah but this?' Tomansio gestured at the sleeping cubicle.

'Less than two hours,' Corrie-Lyn said. 'And we'll be walking though Makkathran's streets. His subconscious knows that.'

'His subconscious is the problem,' Oscar muttered dourly. 'Where's Troblum?'

'Where he's been for most of the flight,' Araminta-two said archly. 'In his sleeping cubicle.'

'Has he got problems, too?' It came out before Oscar really thought about what he was asking.

A mildly guilty flash of amusement shimmered across the cabin, a brief intimate connection shared by everyone equally.

'Okay,' Oscar said, desperate not to let any thoughts wander in the direction of the big man's cubicle. 'Why?'

'Wouldn't like to guess, but his solido projector is in there with him.'

'Wow, this must have been a great trip for you.'

'Wonderful,' Araminta-two admitted. 'Being on the *Lady's Light* was just about preferable.'

'Did the Pilgrimage fleet make it through?'

'Yes. About a week ago. I had a spot of trouble with Ethan afterwards, but that's settled now.'

Oscar was curious, but instinct made him hold back asking for details. 'And Ilanthe?'

'Oh yes, it's here. It killed a Skylord, and consumed its abilities.'

'Christ. So where is it now?'

'The other Skylords say it's on its way to the Heart.'

Oscar almost wished they'd left him in suspension. 'Let's wake up the others,' he said.

Aaron emerged from his sleep cubicle just as Beckia was taken out of her medical cabinet. Oscar took one look at him, and drew in a sharp breath. Aaron was in a bad way. His face looked as if he'd had some kind of capsule smash, with scars and bruising contaminating his skin. Eyes bloodshot.

'Good to see you,' Oscar lied.

Aaron gave him a sour glance. 'Where's Troblum?' Without waiting for an answer he thumped his fist on Troblum's door. Oscar saw each fingernail was black and bleeding.

Troblum emerged, his mind spilling resentment into the cabin. He gave everyone a sullen glance, and dropped his gaze to the decking like a censured teenager.

'Land us,' Aaron said. 'Come on, we don't have time for your personal crap. You need to focus on this. Justine encountered some difficulties on the way down.'

'I'm ready,' Troblum replied sullenly.

Acceleration couches rose up out of the floor.

'Talking of personal crap,' Tomansio said levelly. 'Have you considered what you've been spilling into the Void?'

'What?' Aaron snapped.

'Well let's just hope your ex-girlfriend hasn't been replicated like Kazimir was. I'd hate to bump into her down there.'

Oscar gripped the sides of his couch. The first amber warnings flickered into his exovision. Several systems were glitching. He wished they'd left him in suspension until they were down and this particular hell was over.

*

It was late afternoon in the Anomine city, and the air was already starting to cool. Gore pulled on a black cashmere sweater as he moved along the intrusion systems lying like a giant spider web across the plaza. The strands were sticky, glistening black in the rose-gold sun. His field-function analysis of the individual strands was showing up few imperfections amid the long-chain molecules that were twined together round their active penetration filaments. Production quality had been high, which was impressive given the replicator had never been designed with anything quite like this in mind.

He gave Tyzak an unobtrusive look. The big old Anomine was squatting on his hind legs on the other side of the plaza, close to Gore's little camp. It still had no true idea of the web's actual purpose.

I guess mistrust and suspicion are greater in humans than Anomine. Shame, but there you go, it gives us an edge. And yet . . . they went post-physical. Though not this variety. It's almost as if they bred two strains of themselves, the go-getters and the naive.

A theory as good as any. Somehow he couldn't imagine Tyzak and his kind achieving post-physical status.

Maybe that's true biological evolution. Achieve the pinnacle and decline back into peaceful extinction, irrelevant once your true achievement has elevated itself out of this universe. Perhaps space-time has no other purpose than to be an embryo for sentience.

He tried to recall how many species the Navy Exploration

ships had found who had backed away from the apex of science and intellect without achieving the leap to post-physical. The statistics eluded him, but he didn't think there were many.

Something ripped noisily through the clean air above the city, bringing a wave of joy and relief. Tyzak hadn't heard it, therefore . . .

Gore smiled contentedly to himself. He felt surprising calm for a mere meat body as his u-shadow opened a link to the Delivery Man. 'How's it going?'

'Well, amazingly, I'm still alive. No change up here. The incursion package is loaded, I'm just waiting for you to say go to activate it.'

'Go.'

'What?'

'Initiate the wormhole, and start the siphon power-up sequence. We're going to need that energy soon.'

'Oh crap. Okay, I'll try.'

'Thanks. For everything.' Gore closed his eyes, opened his mind, and watched the sky.

*

The sonic boom crashed across Makkathran without warning, sending the local birds wheeling through the sky, their wings pumping in alarm. Panicked animals across the city started an ugly bawling. Justine looked up and smiled wide in utter relief. She *wanted* Dad to know this, a wish that surged out of her as strong as any Void-derived psychic ability. It took a moment, then she found the pure white contrail sketching a beautifully straight line high across the turquoise sky. The dark tip was already out across the Lyot Sea. It started to curve back round again.

'Finally!'

The starship vanished from sight behind the high wall surrounding the little courtyard garden at the back of the Sampalok mansion. Justine told the two ge-chimps to carry on raking the new section of the vegetable patch she was preparing. The funny little creatures swished the crude tools back and forth across the soil as she directed. Sculpting them had been one of the most satisfying moments she'd had in ages; even though the first had one arm longer than the other, and the second seemed to have a hearing difficulty.

Justine hurried out into the central square, and stood on the specific spot she'd been using for the last seven weeks. 'Take me down,' she asked the city. The ground beneath her feet *changed*, and she fell through the city substance to the travel tunnel underneath. And that was *the* single most satisfying achievement just about ever. She still hadn't talked to or even sensed the city's primary mind, buried heaven only knew how many kilometres below the buildings and canals. But she had finally managed to impress her thoughts on the more simple routines that regulated the fundamental aspects of the city structure. Whatever Makka-thran actually was, its management network was a homogenized one. Farsight had showed her that electricity powered the lights and some of the pump systems. Gravity was manipulated to make the travel tunnels work. All of which confirmed everyone's original belief that the city had come from outside the Void. But it still didn't tell her anything she wanted to know.

She descended into the dazzling illumination of the travel tunnel and pushed her sunglasses firmly back on her nose before asking the city to take her to Golden Park. Gravity began to shift, and she made sure she was leaning forwards as it altered. She'd made the mistake of falling feet first once, and didn't want to repeat that. Flying head first, now that was another matter. It was more exhilarating than Inigo's dreams had ever conveyed. She punched her fists out in front and whooped joyously as she performed her first corkscrew roll.

Justine rose up into Golden Park beside one of the white pillars along the Outer Circle Canal. The melded domes of the Orchard Palace gleamed with a burnished sheen behind her as she waited. After all the weeks of anticipation, half-convincing herself that she might have decades to wait, she was finally giving in to her body's hormonal rush of anxiety as she watched the starship appear above the port district. It was flying a lot slower now, though its wingtips were still trailing faint vapour trails across Makkathran's cloudless sky. *Wait ... Wings?*

The starship circled round over Ysidro district and began a steep descent. It was suffering the same way *Silverbird* had, Justine decided. The flight wasn't as stable or as slow as it ought to be, the Void was glitching its drive units. Once or twice she sucked down a sharp breath as it wobbled in the air. Then long landing struts popped out, and it dropped the last ten metres out of the sky to skid a way along the thick tangle of grass before coming to a halt not a hundred metres from the *Silverbird*.

A circular airlock opened in the starship's midsection, and some old-fashioned aluminium stairs slid out. People trotted down, radiating a mixture of joy and disbelief that Justine's farsight recognized easily. It was identical to her own.

There were nine of them standing together on the grass as she approached, a surprising number for a ship that size, even if they'd used suspension. Then their farsights perceived her and they turned to greet her as she jogged over.

Shouts of welcome reached her when she was still twenty metres away. Several were waving jubilantly. A couple of them even started to run towards her. They all seemed to be smiling wildly.

Not true, she corrected herself, and pushed her sunglasses up.

The big man standing at the back with a formidable shield around his thoughts, he wasn't smiling. Nor was the one who looked as if he'd been in a bad streetfight and lost. But the others were all genuinely happy to see her, which was good enough.

The one who was in the lead flung his arms wide and gave her an effusive hug. Something oddly familiar about his face ...

'Justine Burnelli,' he exclaimed. 'It's been a while.'

And that smile was so sinfully teasing she couldn't help but grin back. 'Sorry. Who ... ?'

'We met at the *Second Chance* departure party,' he said wickedly. 'Oscar Monroe, remember.'

'Oh. My. *God*. Oscar? Is that you? I thought you were still . . . I mean,' she shrugged awkwardly.

'Yeah, they let me out eighty years back. I didn't make a fuss about it.'

'Good to see you, Oscar,' she said sincerely. 'Gotta admit, I wasn't expecting you.'

'Nobody does. I think that's the point of being me these days.'

She laughed then glanced over his shoulder at the others. 'Inigo, isn't it?'

'Yeah.' Inigo didn't go for the whole hugging scene. He stuck his hand out formally. That was when Justine realized she might be slightly overdoing the whole Queen of the Wild City act. All she wore was boots, a small black bikini top, some denim shorts with the cattle prod, pistol and a machete hanging off her belt. The sun had tanned her skin a deep honey brown at the same time it'd bleached her hair almost white – and that hadn't been styled since she arrived; these days she just tied it back with some straps in a loose tail. Quite a change for someone who back at the start of the twenty-first century used to spend over a hundred thousand dollars a year on personal grooming – and that was before her clothes bill. All in all she must've been quite a fright-sight.

Slightly more self-consciously now, she allowed Oscar to introduce everyone else. Araminta-two – *two!* – was interesting, the Knights Guardians were about what she expected, Troblum she didn't know what to make of, Corrie-Lyn she took an instant mild dislike to, while Aaron just plain scared her. She wasn't alone in that, judging by the way everyone else reacted to him.

'All right,' Corrie-Lyn said to Aaron. 'We made it. We're here. Now for the love of the Lady will you tell us why we're here?'

Justine was expecting Aaron to smile wisely at least, as any normal human would. Instead he turned his bruised eyes to Inigo. 'We're here so that you can bring *him* forth,' he said hoarsely.

'What?' a startled Inigo asked. 'Oh sweet Lady! You are joking.'

'No. He's the only one who can help us now. And you're the one who has his true memory. You are connected with him. Especially here. You can reach into the Void's memory layer where he was. You don't even have to reset the Void any more, which was the original intention, we know that now; Justine showed us this with Kazimir.'

Corrie-Lyn went to Inigo and took both his hands in hers. 'Do it,' she whispered fiercely.

'The Waterwalker is gone,' Inigo said with infinite sorrow. 'He is a dream now. Nothing more.'

'You can bring him back,' Aaron said. 'You have to.'

*

—to land on the ground at the foot of the Eyrie tower. His ankles gave way and he stumbled, falling forwards. Strong third hands reached out to steady him. But there was no crowd as there always was, as there should have been. No family. No Kristabel.

'Honious! I am wrong,' Edeard stammered miserably. In his haste to escape the horror of the hospital in Half Bracelet Lane he had somehow misjudged the twisting passage through the Void's memory and finished up . . . He looked at the small group of people staring at him; they were dressed so strangely – yet not. His farsight swept out. Finitan was not atop the tower. He scoured the buildings in Haxpen and Fiacre to find them empty. The city was silent, devoid of its eternal telepathic chatter. He couldn't sense a single mind anywhere save the nine directly in front of him. 'No!' he spun round to face the ziggurat, farsight frantically probing every room on the tenth floor. They were empty of people, furniture . . .

'Where are they?' he bellowed. 'Where are my family? Kristabel!' His third hand drew back, ready to strike instantly.

One of the peculiar group walked forward, his thoughts calm, welcoming, reassuring. A tall man with a handsome face – a known face, though it was darker than it had been before, and the hair was brown instead of light ginger as it ought to be. Such trivia was irrelevant, for this was a face that could not possibly be here, not in the real world.

Edeard's third hand withered away. 'No,' he whispered. 'This cannot be. You are a dream.'

The man smiled. There were tears in his eyes. 'As are you.'

'Inigo?'

'Edeard!'

'My brother.' They embraced, Edeard hugging the man as if his life depended on it. Inigo was the only thing that made sense in the world right now; he was the anchor. 'Hold me,' Edeard begged. 'Do not let me go, the world is falling apart.'

'It's not, I promise. I am here to get you through this.'

Edeard's thoughts were awhirl, panicked, dazed. 'The life you lived,' he choked out.

'Nothing compared to yours,' Inigo assured him.

'But . . . those worlds you showed me, the wonders that dwell there. It's all real?'

'Yes. It's all real. That is the universe outside the Void. The place where the ships that brought Rah and the Lady came from.'

'Oh dear Lady.'

'I know this is a shock. I'm sorry for that. There is no way I could have warned you.'

Edeard nodded slowly and moved back to gaze incredulously at the one person he'd believed was forever beyond reach. 'I thought you were someone the Lady had sent to comfort me as I slept. You showed me what kind of life could be built if only we tried. And I have tried so *hard* . . .' His voice broke. He was close to weeping.

'You did more than that, Waterwalker, so much more,' a young woman said. She had dark red hair and a pretty freckled face, and she looked at him so worshipfully he was astounded. 'You succeeded.'

Edeard glanced shamefully at Inigo. 'You know what I have done, what I am fleeing from.'

'We all know your life. That is why we are here.'

'You can help me? Is that why you have come?'

'You don't need our help,' Inigo said. 'Your triumph was magnificent. Whole planets marvel at your achievements here in Makkathran.'

'I don't understand. I've screwed this up just as Owain and Buate and their ilk always claimed I would. I became what they were, Honious take me.'

'No you didn't,' the woman said earnestly. 'Edeard, listen to me. After the unity attempt failed your next effort to bring peace and fulfilment to Querencia worked. You never reset the Void again, you never needed to. You, and Kristabel, and your friends all accepted guidance to the Heart in old age. It was beautiful to behold.'

'You speak as if this has already happened.' Edeard gave the woman a curious look as some very uncomfortable thoughts began to gather in his mind.

'Edeard.' Inigo put a steadying hand on his shoulder. 'We've only just arrived in the Void. In here time flows much quicker than it does outside. Which is why only a few hundred years have gone by out there compared to the millennia here. You are our past. I brought you out of the Void's memory.'

'Are you saying I have already lived my life? All of my life?'

'Yes.'

'But . . .' His farsight swept out again, desperate to find anyone else. 'Where is everybody? If I succeeded the way you claim, what happened to the people I tried to help? Their grandchildren should still be here. Did they desert the city?'

Inigo appeared embarrassed. 'You created a society where it was possible for everyone to achieve fulfilment. Eventually, all the humans here accepted guidance. The last one left for the Heart several thousand years ago.'

'Gone?' he couldn't believe it. 'All of them gone? There were *millions* of us living on Querencia.'

'I know.'

'Why did you bring me back?' Edeard asked bitterly.

'We need your help.'

'Ha! Then Honious knows you picked the wrong man; Finitan is more worthy than me, or even Dinlay. And even if you had no choice, you should have brought back this future Edeard you spoke of, the one who is triumphant.'

'I chose you very carefully. You are exactly the Edeard I need.'

'Why?'

'Determination,' Inigo said simply. 'This is the you who resolved never to let anything beat him no matter what. You, the you of this day, are the best Waterwalker there ever was. This is the moment your triumph was built upon.'

'I find that hard to believe,' Edeard said weakly.

'I'm truly sorry this was how we had to meet. But we really do need your help.'

'How? How in the Lady's name can I possibly help people who have the power to travel between universes?' He was watching Inigo gathering himself to reply, when the really strange one with the battered face and tormented thoughts stepped forward.

'I am Aaron, and I have come here to ask you to take us to the Heart.'

Edeard almost laughed at him; but the man was in so much suffering, and so fired up with desperation he was clearly speaking the truth. 'Why?'

'Because that has to be what controls the Void. I must speak with it, or Inigo must, or even you. Whichever of us it will listen to.'

'What would you say to it?'

'You're killing us. Switch off.'

Inigo's arm went round Edeard's shoulder again. 'This is going to take a while to explain,' he said gently.

The bright sun was well on its way to the western horizon, coating the edges of Eyrie's towers in a familiar cerise haze. *And yet not familiar*, Edeard thought sadly. This Makkathran he found himself in was a sorrowful one indeed. The buildings were exactly as they should be – oh but the rest of the districts and canals. It didn't suffer decay, the fabulous city would never fall to that, but it had become *shabby*. Without its citizens it was a poor spectre of itself in its glory days. And there was so little left of the people who lived here, nothing more than blemished trinkets and stubborn dust. That they should have vanished with so little to show for their achievements was infinitely depressing. As was knowing he was forever separate from them all now. Though he supposed he could reset the Void once more, somehow he didn't have the appetite to plunge back in to what had been. Besides, according to Corrie-Lyn, he had already won his life's battle. And if he understood what his mind-brother Inigo was saying, he was responsible for unleashing devastation upon the true universe outside.

'More ships are coming?' he asked.

'Yes,' Inigo admitted. 'My fault. I was besotted with your life.'

They were sitting on the steps outside the Lady's central church, each of the visitors doing what they could to help him comprehend Inigo's story of what was happening in the galaxy outside, and what the Void actually was. It had taken hours.

'You showed people my life,' Edeard said, not quite accusing, but . . .

'I did. You never told anyone of mine.'

'They would have thought me mad, even Kristabel. Flying carriages. People who live forever. Hundreds of inhabited worlds. Machine servants instead of genistars. Cities where Makkathran would be naught but a small district. A civilization where justice was available to all. Aliens. More stars in the sky than it is possible to count. No, such marvels of my fevered imagination were best kept inside my skull. Except it wasn't my imagination, it was all you.'

'I hope I was of some help, some comfort.'

'You were.' Edeard finally gathered the courage he'd so far lacked, and asked the question: 'This future I lived, the one where I finally achieved guidance to the Heart . . . was Burlal part of it?'

'No. I'm sorry, Edeard. He was only ever here that one time.'

'I see. Thank you for your honesty.'

'Waterwalker,' Aaron said. 'Can you take us to the Heart, please?'

The edge in his voice, the way his raging thoughts threatened to burst out of his head, it made Edeard nervous. 'I understand the need for the Void to be contained. If I could do so, I would.'

'There is a way to speak with it,' Aaron said through clenched teeth. 'Once we get there, I know there is.'

'How?'

Aaron slammed his hands on to his face. Once, twice, three times. Blood trickled out of his nose where he'd hit it. 'She won't tell me!' he yelled furiously. 'I can't find it any more.'

Edeard's third hand gripped Aaron's arms, forcing them down.

'This is my mission! I am the mission. I have an objective. I must be strong. She likes that. She loves me.'

Tomansio stood next to the stricken agent. 'Hey, it's okay.' He reached out. 'We have two starships and the Waterwalker. We can take—'

Aaron's muscles went slack, and Tomansio caught him as he pitched forwards, unconscious.

'How did you do that?' Edeard asked.

'Very basic tranquillizer. Lucky our biononics are degraded here. Would have been quite a scrap otherwise.'

'I see.' Which he didn't quite. But these warriors from the outside universe were formidable. And they had honour. Somehow he was reminded of Colonel Larose from the Makkathran militia.

'Now what?' Corrie-Lyn asked with a sigh. 'Our pet psycho is going to go quantumbusting when he wakes up.'

'I'd hate to try a neural infiltration in this environment,' Tomansio said. 'The first glitch and we'd probably rip his brain apart. Besides, I think the way his mind was reconfigured implies it was resistant to that kind of inquisition. The information is hidden in the subconscious.'

'We do have the two ships,' Oscar said. 'And we know we have to fly to the Heart. Our problem is always going to be guidance.' He grinned at Edeard. 'I guess that's where you come in.'

'It's down to fulfilment,' Inigo said. 'If the Skylord believes Edeard to be fulfilled, it will guide him.'

'His soul,' Corrie-Lyn said sharply.

'We don't know that,' Inigo said. 'Humans have never been able to fly around inside the Void before. Maybe it'll show a living body the way.'

'I'll ask,' Araminta-two said.

His thoughts were gifted in a fashion Edeard was unaccustomed to; the clarity he was given exceeded any he'd known before. It was hard to throw off the sensation that he was actually in Araminta-two's body, breathing together, feeling together. And there was the shadow perception distracting him, standing in a giant room of metal and glass, watching the nebulas outside. A flock of Skylords guiding the incredible starships. That mind's perception shimmered underneath the connection Araminta had with the Skylord leading the fleet, and its awareness of the Void.

'Do I have to abandon my body to be guided to the Heart?' he asked.

'You have to be fulfilled,' the Skylord replied lovingly. 'Then I will guide you. Soon, I feel. Your mind is strong, you believe, know your way. You understand yourself. You lack only surety.'

'If I have that, if I gain what I need for fulfilment, would you take me, the living me, in this ship?'

'I would do that.'

Edeard shivered as the outlandish gifting ended. It was as if a gust of winter air had squalled around the church. He gave Araminta-two a curious look. 'You can longtalk across the Void?' Such strength of mind was incredible.

'Not really. That was my other body. And as for the Skylord, we are joined as you and Inigo once were.'

'I see,' he lied. *My other body!* He'd said it so casually. How he wished for Macsen at this time; Macsen who would make light of such confusion with a quip and a laugh, and the world would be right again.

'So now we find out if this Edeard is fulfilled,' Oscar said. 'And if he is, you fly him to the Heart.'

'It would seem that way,' Inigo agreed.

'Not yet,' Justine said. She stood up. 'This is too important for maybes. We need a very clear understanding of what we're supposed to achieve here. Follow me.' And she walked up the steps towards the church's open entrance.

Edeard observed everyone produce puzzled looks behind the blonde girl. A few shrugs were exchanged, but they all trooped dutifully after her. Justine's tone had been commanding.

When they'd been introduced Edeard had been dismissive of the sultry girl. Wary even – because of her crude clothing and wild hair she reminded him of the real bandits who lived in the wilds beyond Rulan province. But as the afternoon wore on he'd revised his opinion. For a start, she was one of the Commonwealth eternals. She might look as if she was barely out of her teens, but he knew she was older than anyone who'd ever lived in Makkathran. And despite her lack of clothing, she had a dignity and poise that would've intimidated Mistress Florrel. He also strongly suspected she was tough enough to rip Ranalee to shreds in any kind of fight, fair or otherwise.

The air inside of the church was cooler than outside. Seeing the interior bare apart from the big statue of the Lady was odd, emphasizing how cut off and alone he was now. A mere day ago in his own time he'd been Mayor, and the city bent to his will. These people meant well, he knew, but he couldn't help the resentment at the way they'd summoned him out of his true life. If it had been anyone but Inigo – but then only Inigo could do such a thing.

Stranger than the naked church was the golden man standing in the middle, waiting for them. Visible only because of some strangely pervasive gifting from Justine which he couldn't quite shield himself from; yet his farsight found nothing where the man stood, not at first. 'A soul,' Edeard exclaimed when he intensified his perception.

'A dream, actually. I'm Gore, pleased to finally meet you, Waterwalker. You're a very impressive man.'

'Gore is the one who guided us all here,' Inigo explained lightly. 'By various methods. Not all of them pleasant.'

'Just making sure you don't run out on your responsibilities, sonny.'

'My father,' Justine said proudly.

'You need to keep Aaron under,' Gore told Tomansio. 'His neural reconditioning was never going to be strong enough to withstand an encounter with the Cat. I wasn't expecting that. Goddamn Ilanthe.'

'Lennox,' Tomansio said coldly. 'His name is Lennox. One of our founders. As such, very important to all Knights Guardians. What have you done to him?'

'Exactly what he asked,' Gore said. 'Christ knows what kind of number the Cat worked on him, but he was a near-total basket case when my people recovered him. We erased what we could of that old personality, but the damage had seeped down into his subconscious. Now that can normally be suppressed providing it doesn't receive too many associative triggers. But as for an out-and-out cure, forget it. I did what I could. I patched him back up, and sent him out doing what he loved, what he was born to do. He runs every dirty covert mission the Conservative Faction needs to keep the good old Greater Commonwealth on the straight and narrow. I'm not his boss, I'm his partner for Christ's sake.'

'Dad, the Heart?'

'Yeah right,' Gore glanced round at all of them. 'It's a simple enough plan. Like Aaron said, you go in and engage the damn thing, reason with it. It has to be made to understand it's committing galactic genocide.'

'That's it?' Oscar asked.

'You got anything better?'

'Well . . . no.'

'Then that's it. One minor upgrade, I'm coming with you. I might have found something to persuade it.'

'What?'

'A new beginning. But we're going to have to be quick. Fuck knows what Ilanthe's up to in there.'

'All right, Dad. The Skylord will guide Edeard's body, assuming he's fulfilled.'

'That was the original idea.' Gore shot a meaningful glance at Inigo. 'We do need someone we know is fulfilled.'

'I understand.'

'I'll take the Waterwalker and Inigo in the *Silverbird*,' Justine said. 'It's in better shape than the *Mellanie's Redemption*. I think it will launch again. If not, we can reset to a few days before I land here.'

'No,' Gore said. 'Take this ship. Its fully acclimatized to the Void now, so functionality shouldn't be a problem any more. And we're probably going to need some serious badass firepower if we run into Ilanthe.'

'This ship?'

Gore gave her a pitying look. 'What do you think you're standing on?'

Standing atop the sweeping steps of the Lady's church with the others gathering round him, Edeard finally felt as if he was coming alive again. This whole time had seemed bizarre, like some kestric-fuelled dream. There was nothing for him to grasp, nothing to assure him he was living. Even encountering Inigo was something he imagined might eventually befall him in the Heart, which contributed to the sense of unreality.

But now . . .

Raw excitement accelerated his heart, sending hot blood pounding through his body. He was smiling as he sent his farsight racing down below the streets, past the travel tunnels, winding through the strange conduits and glowing lines of energy that pervaded the structure all the way down, and down.

Makkathran's mind slumbered on still, as unchanged as the buildings and canals, those giant thoughts pulsing in their slow sombre beat.

The Waterwalker's thoughts lifted rapturously as he gifted his perception to his new friends, welcoming the sheer flamboyance, the audacity of the moment. How Kristabel and Macsen would have loved this, and as for the twins ... 'I know what you are now,' he told the great sleeper, pouring sincerity, sheer *belief* into what he was saying. Sharing himself utterly. 'I know why you came to this universe. And you should know, others have followed you in. We think we can end this now. You can finish what you started.'

The vast thoughts began to quicken, their wide strands of gentle musings coming together into a cohesive whole. Makkathran's consciousness arose. 'You? I remember you. I thought you had gone, along with the rest of your kind.'

'I was brought back. I believe I am your way into the Heart.'

'You have forgotten much. I am content to end here.'

Edeard felt his soul brother grip his hand. Inigo's confidence, his surety, was astounding.

'We do not go there to submit to absorption,' Inigo told Makkathran unwaveringly. 'We are here to finish this. The time you feared has arrived. Millions of my species are on their way to this world, they know its secret. All of them are intent on resetting the Void to their own whim. The ensuing devourment phase will consume the galaxy.'

'It cannot be stopped,' Makkathran said. 'The Void is what it is.'

'There is a chance. I believe we can still reason with it.'

'The Void does not listen. We tried. I watched my kind die in their tens of thousands as they attempted to pass through the final barrier. It was all for nothing. The flames of their death outshone the nebulas that day.'

'An entity has arrived in the Void who may make things worse. The devourment phase is beginning. And finally we have the smallest, most fragile opportunity to speak with the nucleus, the primary sentience. It will accept one of us if a Skylord guides them to the Heart. Help us. Please. Your species is still out there on the other side of the barrier, doing what they can. In all the aeons since you came, they have never faltered. We owe them so much, we owe them this last attempt.'

'My kind still live?'

'Yes.'

'I thought so. I thought I heard one, once, not so long ago. I called out, but it was your race who came instead.'

'Please,' Edeard said. 'I was guided to the Heart once before. Whatever sacrifice I have to make to be guided again, I will do so, I swear upon the Lady.'

Makkathran's thoughts fluctuated, dousing them all in a wave of ancient sorrow. Edeard was humbled by everything the city had endured, its terrible loss.

'I did not expect change to befall me ever again,' it told them. 'I did not expect to be shown hope, however small. I did not expect to do what I was born to do; to fly against the greatest enemy once more. You have brought this to me. For that I should show thanks. If the galaxy is to fall, then it is fitting that I should fall with it. I will take you.'

'Thank you,' Edeard said.

'Thank you,' the others chorused.

They waited bunched together on the broad expanse outside the Lady's church, farsight probing round, alert for the first change to manifest. They waited with the irrepressible excitement of schoolchildren knowing they were to witness something wholly spectacular.

Justine caught it first. 'There,' she cried, her mind urging the others. 'There, look, the crystal wall.'

All around the city, the high translucent gold wall which defined the edge was growing upwards. It raced into the sky with astounding speed as the city put forth its will. Then they were tilting their heads back to gape in admiration as it curved overhead. Half an hour after the growth began the last shrinking circle of clear sky vanished as the crystal melded together. The city was encased in a perfect dome.

Makkathran exerted its wishes. A mind larger than mountains engaged the Void's elementary mass-location ability, demanding matter move in the manner it wanted.

Out beyond the sealed-off port district, the Lyot Sea parted. Two vast tsunamis of water rushed apart, surging away from the shore, exposing the seabed for tens of miles. Water was the easy part. Makkathran continued its manipulation. The naked seabed cracked open with a howl of destruction which shredded any organic matter within fifty miles. Fissures deepened, slicing down through the ancient lava as they raced inland to splinter the Iguru Plain.

Oscar was laughing helplessly as the ground shook furiously, triggering massive landslides over in the distant Donsori Mountains. It was the kind of semi-hysteria that was contagious. Edeard found himself grinning wildly in sympathy as he was toppled to his knees. Waves chased along the canals, sloshing over the edges as the earthquake's power built. He could see the tips of the Eyrie towers rocking from side to side. Agitated air was slapping clouds against the outside of the dome.

'Glad we brought you back now?' Oscar called tauntingly above the roar.

The Iguru Plain and the uncovered seabed had shattered down to a single level zone of undulating rubble. All the odd little volcanoes juddered about like disintegrating icebergs as their mass dissolved down into the churning debris. The city gave a sudden lurch, thrusting a hundred metres straight up as the land's grip was finally broken. Edeard yelled in delirious shock along with everyone else as the impetus knocked him flat. He gave Oscar a crazy thumbs up. 'Oh Lady am I ever,' he longspoke above the tremendous din that was penetrating the protective crystal. What the devastation must be like outside was something he couldn't conceive.

Frenzied clouds slid down the sides of the curving crystal as the domed city began to rise further. That was just the apex of the immense warship.

Makkathran, last survivor of the Raiel armada, soared back up into the sky it had fallen from a million years ago, and headed for the clean emptiness of space.

*

Gore Burnelli didn't often admit admiration for other people, least of all meat humans. But he had to acknowledge Araminta had done a fine job living in two different time-flows. Even though he'd been one of the pioneers of enhanced mentality, he was finding the going a little tough.

The segment of his mind designated to maintain the connection to Justine was racing on ahead, looking back at the ponderous events on the Anomine homeworld with something approaching contempt. It would be very easy to divest himself of his sluggish flesh and live fast and free in the Void. He had to focus hard on the other aspects of his mind and the requirements they served to dismiss the notion. The temptation was pulling with unrelenting tidal force.

For a heartbeat he watched from the entranceway of the Lady's church as Makkathran flew clear of Querencia's atmosphere then accelerated after the Skylord which had brought the *Mellanie's Redemption* just a few hours earlier.

Exoimage displays surrounded him, tracing the progress of the infiltrator filaments as they slithered through the molecular structure of the elevation mechanism, chasing down the network pathways and penetrating delicate junctions. Primary attention switch: to the massed ranks of code awaiting initialization so the packages could slide into alien software, mimicking the routines in order to subvert them. His accelerated mind watched the symbology flip round at a speed he could actually follow as they analysed the first impulses flashing through the junctions.

Incoming call: which he answered with another segment operating within his meat skull.

'We're in,' the Delivery Man said. 'I'm establishing control over all major siphon systems. The override is disengaged. Full wormhole initialization sequence is running. Power generation is increasing. I need to take that slow, there's nowhere to send it yet.'

'Well done.'

'I never knew Makkathran was a Raiel ship.'

'What else could it be? Haven't you ever visited *High Angel*?'

'No, actually.'

'Oh. Well, those domes are the real giveaway. They're identical.'

'Obviously.'

'Any sign of Marius?'

'I haven't got a decent sensor that can function down here in the innermost circle. Hysradar works but it's useless. He must be in stealth mode, still.'

'Keep watching. When he finally figures out we can stop his precious Ilanthe he won't take it well.'

'Oh crap. All right.'

*

Makkathran caught up with the Skylord just before it crossed Nikran's orbit, barely two million miles from the desert planet. Edeard stood in the square at the centre of Sampalok, staring at the small brown orb which appeared to be hanging just above the mansion. It was kindling a surprising amount of nostalgia. He could just make out some of the surface features as he'd done that other day, now lost in the broken past, when he'd sat in the Malfit Hall waiting to be called before the Mayor and handed his bronze epaulettes. His squadmates had teased him for his questions about other people living on Nikran. They never knew, as he did, that humans lived on hundreds of worlds. And now they never would.

Or maybe they do. Who knows what they see from the Heart?

Of all the revelations Inigo had brought, knowing that the Void was a danger to life everywhere was the hardest to accept.

'I always hated that Ladydamned thing,' Inigo said, glaring at the six-sided mansion.

'The mansion?' Corrie-Lyn asked in surprise.

'No, the arcology in Kuhmo. It dominated every day of my life while I was growing up. That's one of the reasons I offered the town council all that money to demolish the monstrosity, so kids wouldn't be so blighted in future.'

'It did fill your mind,' Edeard confirmed. 'I wasn't really sure what genuine human architecture looked like, and I was in a hurry that day. It was the obvious choice.'

'Thank the Lady you didn't build it full size.'

'I saw the fane you replaced it with,' Corrie-Lyn said dryly. 'It wasn't a whole lot better.'

Inigo grinned back at her. 'There's gratitude.'

Edeard sensed concern growing in Justine's mind. He glanced over to see her standing close to Gore, whose golden face had hardened with worry.

'What?'

'Some events are outside our control,' Justine said. 'I think you need to ask the Skylord now.'

The creature they were pursuing was still half a million kilometres away, a shimmering patch to one side of Nikran. Edeard eyed it reluctantly. If it declared he wasn't fulfilled then Inigo would have to delve down into the memory layer and bring out a version of himself who was. There were few enough certainties for him right now, but encountering his future self was something he knew he didn't want to endure. 'I'll try.' He felt for the Skylord, finding it on the edge of perception. Usually their thoughts were composed and content. He'd never known one to host such confusion before. It was grieving for its kindred which had succumbed to Ilanthe; and the colossal warship racing after it was also unsettling – there were ancient ancestral memories about such things: the time of chaos.

'You have nothing to fear from those I travel with, including the city,' Edeard assured it. 'They are my companions as I seek fulfilment.'

'I know this city now,' the Skylord replied. 'Its kind brought ruin to this universe. We have found no minds since they threw the planets of life down into the stars they orbited. None have emerged here other than your own species.'

'That time is over now. You know more of my species are already here. Minds are emerging again.'

'As is the *other* who kills.'

'That is why I wish to reach the Heart. I will carry the warning to it. I believe I am fulfilled, I believe the Heart will accept me. Is this right?'

The Skylord took a long time to answer. 'You are fulfilled,' it acknowledged. 'I will guide your essence to the Heart.'

'Guide me to the Heart as I am. This ship will take me. We will follow you.'

'It is the essence of every mind my kindred guide.'

'Guide me to the Heart. It will decide if it accepts me as I am or if I abandon my body and become pure mind.'

'I will guide you.'

'Thank you.'

Beyond the crystal dome, the stars began to chase short arcs across space as Makkathran turned to follow the Skylord. Then they started to accelerate again. Edeard experienced a long moment of dizziness. When he looked straight up again, he could see a small clump of stars directly above the apex of the dome. They'd all become bright blue-white. The rest of the universe around them was black.

'That's not fast enough,' Gore said. 'Ilanthe has a week of Void-time on you. Christ knows how close she is now.'

'We know this is as fast as the Skylords can travel,' Justine said.

'Yeah, but they're not exactly swinging from the top of the IQ tree, now are they? Ask Makkathran, it's had millions of years to figure out what passes for spacetime in the Void.'

Justine gave Edeard a questioning look.

'I'll ask,' he said.

'Faster?' Makkathran queried; its thoughts intimated curiosity.

'We were designed for every conceivable quantum state except of course this one. Here the mind is paramount, helping to seduce so many inferior mentalities. Long ago, I observed the fundamental connections between rationality and the multidimensional lattice which incorporates this universe's functionality. Speed is an aspect of temporal flow, which in turn is determined by thought. It is the application pattern which is the key, and those are actually quite simple to determine.'

Outside the dome, light exploded out of the emptiness. Stars began to streak past like rigid lightning bolts. Glaring nebula clouds formed hurricane curlicues, spiralling round and round as they streamed away in a resplendent blaze of colour.

'I think that was a yes,' an awestruck Oscar mumbled as multicoloured ripples of light flowed across his upturned face.

'So are we going fast, or is the Void slowing down?' Corrie-Lyn asked tentatively.

'That's not strictly relevant in here,' Inigo said. 'All that matters is the end result.'

*

In parallel to his conversation with the Delivery Man, Gore was monitoring the data that the infiltration software was surreptitiously accumulating. The elevation mechanism had started running internal scans as the filaments continued their invasion into its structure. He released the first batch of packages, a low-level torrent that swiftly insinuated themselves into the scan interpretation routines, falsifying the results so the elevation mechanism would find nothing wrong with itself at a molecular level.

Dream: Makkathran went ftl amid a spectacular lightstorm.

Visual observation: Tyzak was bouncing its way over the plaza, taking care not to step on the glistening black webbing that was humming gently.

That's all I need, a higher-secondary segment of Gore's mind thought. The Anomine translation routine in a storage lacuna went active.

'Others have come,' Tyzak said.

'From your village?' Gore warbled and whistled back.

'No. Others. Star-travellers who are similar to you, but very different. I do not know of their story.'

'Show me, please.'

Tyzak traced his way back across the plaza. One of his limbs extended, pointing down a broad street.

There were eight of them standing across the road a hundred metres short of the plaza. Pastel light from the buildings on either side glittered across their extravagant jewelled longcoats. One of them raised a long white spear, and bowed slightly.

'Silfen,' Gore sighed, resisting the urge to give them the finger in return. Instead he inclined his head. 'Just ignore them. They're the galaxy's greatest voyeurs.'

'Why should they come here?'

'To observe me.'

The infiltration packages flashed up a problem with the analysis routines they were trying to modify. There must have been hidden sentinels, because the analysis routines were resisting any attempt to subvert them. They had begun reformatting themselves with alarming frequency. It meant the packages couldn't establish themselves: there was no stable configuration to match. And the sentinels were routing more advanced routines to the scans, examining why the resistance algorithms were being triggered. That might well alert the elevation mechanism's principal consciousness.

Gore pressed his golden lips together. 'Oh shit; here we go.'

*

Hanging in transdimensional suspension two million kilometres above the Anomine star, Marius had directed his starship's sensor readings to a constellation of semi-autonomous secondary routines. Although the Delivery Man's ship had performed a truly astounding feat flying into the star's convection layer, it wasn't his main concern. He simply didn't understand Justine's dream.

That Gore had somehow manoeuvred Inigo and Araminta-two into the Void was seriously impressive. But then the notion faltered. To rationalize with the Heart as Gore claimed was their ultimate purpose must be a misdirection. He was sure of it.

Then the Waterwalker was resurrected. 'Remarkable,' Marius admitted. Which was as nothing compared to Makkathran awaking and lifting itself out of the gargantuan lava-filled impact crater it'd created when it crashed there in the aftermath of the armada's invasion.

And Gore announced they had to beat Ilanthe to the Heart. Makkathran performed the impossible, and went ftl inside the Void.

'No,' Marius said in alarm. Whatever scheme Gore had for when they were inside the Heart, he could not permit it. The risk was infinitesimal, but nonetheless it existed.

His mind moved the dream to secondary routines for monitoring, and brought the sensor readings back to his full attention. The Delivery Man's starship hadn't moved. It was still attached to the shielded circular object inside the convection zone. Whatever connection Gore envisaged between that and Makkathran was beyond understanding, but there was purpose to it. No one expended this much effort without a reason.

His quandary was that he didn't know if Gore was on board the starship, or back on the planet. Therefore the process of elimination would have to be both literal and simple. Ship first. If the dream continued, then Gore was on the Anomine homeworld.

Marius ordered the smartcore to drop them out of stealth. Active sensors came on line and performed a more detailed scan of the ship inside the convection zone. For all it incorporated Stardiver shielding to deal with the heat, its layered force fields had only received about twenty per cent strengthening. They remained vulnerable to combat strikes. The only real problem Marius had was choosing a weapon which would be able to reach it within such a radical environment. He started to activate the possibles.

*

They waited for the moment on the Sampalok square, just outside the mansion's entrance. Inigo and Corrie-Lyn holding hands, and sharing thoughts privately. Araminta-two never far from Oscar, the two of them providing each other with a strange variety of support and comfort. The three Knights Guardians in a tight group, keen and nervy. Justine and Gore side by side, proud and defiant, their determination shining as bright as any of the weird stars flashing past outside. That, oddly enough, left Edeard gravitating towards Troblum, who was waiting with a sulky, near-childlike pout.

The cascade of opalescent light drained away as quickly as it had arrived. Edeard gazed up at the dome, thunderstruck by the sight beyond the crystal. Makkathran was gliding through space above the centre of Odin's Sea. Directly above the apex of the dome a ruffled lake of aquamarine dust glimmered with a steady lambency, alive with deep currents and the flaring nimbi of protostars. Around its shores the scarlet reefs extended out for lightyears, slender twined braids of fluorescence that swelled at their tips to form silken veils around the stars they incarcerated.

'Sweet Lady I never thought to see such a sight,' Edeard moaned incredulously. And finally his mind heard the siren call; it wasn't a song but the sense of uncountable minds blending in peace and friendship, secure in their totality. Together they were whole, and combined with the Void's fabric at some ultimate level of existence. The promise of belonging to such an affiliation filled him with joy; the weariness and strife of a physical life would end, and he would be a part of the greater existence that reached for perfection. The urge to join them, to contribute his nature, was so strong that if his third hand could have elevated him up from the square and through the crystal he would have flown into the Heart there and then for the final consummation. It was nothing like the foolishly imagined near-physical heaven he had expected, where souls clung to their old form and lived in splendour among a city of golden towers. That kind of life was actually achievable back on Querencia if you tried hard enough and often enough, revisiting your own past until you finally eliminated all your failures and disappointments. No, the Heart looked to the future and a fate that was fresh and different to anything that had gone before. He would be a part of creating that.

'This hippy dippy shit is what everyone praises?' Gore snapped. 'Jeezus wept.'

Edeard struggled to keep his temper in check in the face of such blasphemous provocation. 'It is a glorious reward for a life lived true to oneself.'

'Uh huh, well let's not forget why we're here. We need to get inside.'

'There is no physical location,' Makkathran told them when Edeard asked to move closer. 'At least, not in relation to the Void fabric at this level. The Heart lies beyond rather than behind. That is the final barrier, the one which defeated us before.'

'Ask it to admit us,' Oscar said.

Edeard nodded slowly, reluctant at the last to begin the event that could lead to the demise of the entire Void. *What if they have lied?* Which he knew to be a foolish insecurity. *Good old Ashwell optimism, even here. Inigo does not lie, not to me.* 'How can something this splendid be so flawed as to threaten life everywhere?'

'Because it doesn't know it's a danger,' Gore said.

'How can that be?' he cried. 'It is awesome; it is the accumulation of billions upon billions of minds. How can you possibly be so arrogant to try and change its path?'

'Those lives it has consumed are doing nothing but dreaming their existence away. The souls who were guided here have been betrayed, the wisdom they brought, the continued life they were promised, it's all being wasted.'

'All right.' Edeard reached out for the Heart. *I am here,* he told it. *I am ready. I am fulfilled. Bring me to you.* He held his breath. Nothing happened. *I am here,* he repeated.

'Now what?' Tomansio asked.

'Stop trying,' Oscar said. 'Just let the urge take you. Chill down, and surrender to it.'

'You're already in there,' Corrie-Lyn said. 'Listen for yourself.'

'Very well,' Edeard said. It sounded stupid, but he closed his eyes, then withdrew his farsight, allowing the presence of the Heart to seep into him. He listened for himself. In truth there were others he wanted to hear, to join. Kristabel. Macsen. Dinlay. Kanseen. Akeem! Was he waiting? Had he found his way? Finitan surely would be there. And Rolar, and Jiska, and the twins, and Dylorn, and Marakas, and sweet Taralee. Perhaps even Salrana, who might have finally made her peace with him. He could never forget that night he discovered the true nature of the Void; in the pavilion, after her death, her soul had panicked, realizing she had strayed. Perhaps . . .

'The barrier falls,' Makkathran said.

Edeard opened his eyes in time to see Odin's Sea fading away. The light simply vanished, and they were surrounded by nothing. A perfect uniform blackness.

The Heart's thoughts grew more powerful. Edeard found himself strengthening his shield. His mind seemed to be expanding, moving to embrace the Heart, flowing out to join it.

'Edeard!' Inigo shouted.

His brother's fright was strong. He hesitated.

'Edeard, come back.' Inigo was compelling him, infusing their bond with love.

He opened his eyes again. This time the sturdy Sampalok mansion seemed faint. When he lifted up his hand it was growing translucent.

'It's absorbing him,' Gore said. Worry was flooding from the golden man's mind. 'Edeard you've got to hold on.'

'Without you we will be rejected,' Makkathran warned.

'Edeard, is there anything you can sense in there that'll talk to us?' Gore asked. 'A single coherent mind?'

Edeard had to laugh. 'The Heart is bigger than worlds. It is universal, it lies behind everywhere in the Void. And still it grows.'

'Fuck it,' Gore snarled. 'It's grown so big it's lost cohesion. All right, Edeard, it wasn't always like this. I need you to go back to when it was smaller.'

'What?'

'Get into the memory layer, trace it down to the origin. Come on son, you can do it.'

'Lean on me,' Inigo said. He gripped Edeard's hand, suffusing him with strength and love. 'I will help you.'

'And me, Waterwalker,' Corrie-Lyn said. Her firmness and fortitude made Edeard smile in gratitude.

Oscar came over, as did the Knights Guardians. 'Whatever you need,' Tomansio promised sincerely, which made Edeard regret he hadn't known the warrior for longer. Justine, smiling and determined, added her essence, buoying him along. Even Troblum was there, dependable and resolute.

There was a memory layer in this place, wherever they were, which surprised Edeard more than anything. Strangely uncluttered, it was easy to perceive, to follow back. He plunged into the past, saddened by how little changed. Then abruptly the Heart wasn't quite so large. This was the time before humans. He carried on back through it, pushing harder and harder.

There were many changes, coming eons apart, then further. Each alien species that'd come to the Void had contributed to the expansion in its own fashion. None had brought true cohesion. He found that wrong somehow, that the amalgamation always acted in the contrary direction to the Heart's purpose.

At the end he could think only of flying through the travel tunnels, soaring on into the unknown, content simply in the act of voyaging. He was quite surprised when it did finish. The memory layer grew thinner somehow, less cluttered. And there, right at the beginning of the Void, when the Heart was forming, were millions of connections to individual minds. They could communicate with the Heart. They were the link, the way in. He chased after one and embraced it, offering it up to the creation layer. Perceiving the entity take form again.

Edeard drew a startled breath, shaking himself free of the memory layer and the intimacy of his new friends. Right in front of him, standing in the entrance to Zulmal Street, an alien twenty feet tall was unfolding its disturbingly sinuous limbs as its thoughts churned with surprise and suspicion.

'Oh wow,' Oscar groaned, and took a step back. Even so, he was grinning effusively.

'A Firstlife,' Edeard announced simply. And he had to own up to being intimidated by so many curving, pointed teeth at the top of its fat central trunk as it opened the glistening mouth membranes to whistle at a painful volume.

Then something moved in the nothingness outside the dome. A dark sphere beset with deep purple scintillations slipped smoothly overhead.

'What are you doing?' Ilanthe asked.

*

Marius had been fascinated by the Heart and the notions it sang of. There really was no other way to describe it. In a way he was relieved that it was so vast, so aloof. Gore's stupid plan to talk to it, to make it see what he considered to be reason, would never transpire in such a milieu. The golden man was pissing in the wind.

Then he stood in Sampalok's central square, observing through Justine as Gore told the Waterwalker to search back through the memory layer for a younger, more accessible Heart.

'No no no,' he chanted in dismay. His exovision brought up the starship's weapons. He selected a couple of diverted energy function quantumbusters. They would activate in the photosphere, sending a huge exotic energy distortion wave smashing against the Delivery Man's ship. Its Stardiver shielding would never survive such an impact. Whatever part of Gore's scheme was being enacted down there in the convection zone would be obliterated. That would give Ilanthe the window of opportunity to enact Fusion.

The two missiles shot away, accelerating at a hundred and fifty gees. His exovision display threw up a sensor image, showing a hyperspace anomaly erupting fifty thousand kilometres away from his own location. One of the huge borderguards materialized out of the spacial deformation. Its concentric shells of elliptical strands were ablaze with aggravated neon light. The outermost strands darkened from a lurid jade down to an irradiated carmine. Marius's sensors showed the energy spectrum raging inside the borderguard leaping almost off the scale. It fired on the quantumbuster missiles, which burst into a dynamic vapour plume.

'Shit!' Marius discarded the dream altogether, and sent his starship hurtling towards the borderguard at thirty-seven gees. Weapons locked on to the garish nimbus. He opened fire.

*

No matter how hard he cursed, how fast his expanded mind activated infiltration packages, Gore knew it was coming. There was nothing he could do about it. His wild boast about Commonwealth webheads had proved vain and hollow. And everything in the galaxy was going to die because of it.

Unless . . .

'Shit. Go for it,' he ordered the Delivery Man. 'Initialize the wormhole. Shove some fucking power my way. Do it. Do it now.'

He ordered the packages to activate, to grab control.

Too late. Out of the city's subdued background murmurings Gore perceived that cool consciousness rising once again. It observed its environment with a host of strange senses.

'This is an act of hostility,' the elevation mechanism said. 'You are trying to steal my fundamental nature. It is not for you and your kind, and with good reason.'

'Yeah. So you said. And as I told you, the Void is about to

expand and wipe this star system from existence.' The dream showed him the big Firstlife in Sampalok, shaking its thick beefy body furiously as it tried to orientate itself. Then Ilanthe appeared overhead. 'Oh Godfuck, no!' Gore entreated. 'No, not her, not now.' The defeat was as strong as any physical blow, striking him to his knees in the middle of the plaza. All around him the glistening black strands of the infiltration web began to smoulder, filling the air with a thin acrid smoke. 'You're killing us,' he screamed into the night. 'All I needed to do was show the Heart, that's all, just show the fucker there's an alternative, prove it can evolve.'

Tyzak was approaching him cautiously, stepping gingerly over the spluttering web.

'Got it,' the Delivery Man called. 'Siphon's activated. Wormhole established. We did it!'

'Leave,' Gore told him flatly. 'Fly to a fresh galaxy, one that isn't cursed like this one. Don't let the universe forget us.'

*

The third borderguard imploded amid a searing flare of violet Cherenkov radiation. Broken strands from the concentric shells twirled away, venting thick sparkling gases at high velocity. Marius detected another five materializing out of their distinctive hyperspatial rents. He brought the ship about in a fast curve, chasing the debris that was expanding out of the last implosion. The trouble with combat this close to the star was the lack of mass for quantumbusters to work with.

Sensors tracked the three largest chunks of the shells, and he launched missiles at each of them. Diverted energy function quantumbusters activated, converting the tumbling mass to energy. Exotic distortions slammed into two of the borderguards as they were still exiting hyperspace, wrenching at the exotic pseudofabric. Unbearable contortions crushed the borderguards down to neutronium density. The wreckage immediately detonated out of its impossible compression state, saturating local spacetime with an inordinately hard neutron storm.

Seven energy beams burned across the force fields protecting Marius's starship. His exovision brought up severe overload warnings. He fired another nine Hawking M-sinks, which the surviving bodyguards had no defence against. *So far.* He watched in fury as the attackers opened up small wormholes, which swallowed five of the M-sinks. Another barrage of energy beams found his starship. Missiles were heading in towards him at ninety gees. And he still hadn't managed to knock out the Delivery Man's ship.

Sensors reported a zero-width wormhole establishing itself between the star and the Anomine homeworld. The smartcore dismissed it as a weapon. Marius ordered an urgent review. The wormhole was originating from the mysterious object which the Delivery Man's ship had rendezvoused with.

It had to be some kind of power system. But what needed that level of power? *The elevation mechanism!* Marius knew it with absolute certainty. Gore had found some way to switch it on. He was going post-physical. It was the only thing left which could threaten Fusion.

Marius activated the ship's ultradrive and flashed in towards the star. He emerged just above the swirling streamers of the photosphere where energized atoms from a multitude of spots and flares simmered away into solar wind. Every force-field warning turned critical as the starship received the full blast of the star's radiation and heat. Marius fired two novabombs straight down, then jumped back into hyperspace.

Behind him the borderguards were massing above the photo-sphere. Eighteen of the giant machines had rushed out of hyperspace, firing enough weapons down after the novabombs to break open a moon. None of it was any use. The nova-bombs were designed to function amid the outer fringes of a star, whereas the borderguards' weapons were just uselessly pumping more energy into the rampant solar furnace.

Thirty seconds before they detonated, Marius was already outside the Anomine system. The nova would eliminate the power station, then go on to wipe out the Anomine homeworld minutes later. Gore would never reach post-physical status now. The Accelerator objective was safe.

*

Edeard didn't know who to give his attention to, nor even that it would do any good if he could decide. The astounding Firstlife was straightening itself, turning several small black membranes at the top of its trunk towards the humans as well as directing a formidable farsight at them.

Above the dome the Ilanthe thing was also observing them. It scared him how non-human it was. His farsight couldn't begin to uncover its secrets, but the power it contained was evident. Whatever the Heart was, it seemed to be bending around Ilanthe's glossy surface.

But it was Gore who now concerned him the most. The golden man was stumbling, dropping to his knees. The anguished keening his mind emitted was dreadful, as if his soul itself was being violated.

'Dad,' Justine was yelling frantically. 'Dad, what is it? What's happening?'

'It caught me,' Gore told her weakly. 'The motherfucker found the infiltrator packages.'

'I could have told you the Anomine mechanism was obdurate,' Ilanthe said complacently.

The Firstlife took a step towards the humans, three of its feet slamming down on the surface of the square with a slap that Edeard could feel in his leg bones. 'What is this place?' the Firstlife's longtalk demanded. 'What are you? You are not us.'

Inigo squared up to the imposing creature. 'This is your future. You were recreated from the Void's memory.'

The Firstlife's farsight probed round again, its extraordinary reach allowing it to scan the city, and delve down into a fair percentage of the warship's main body. It also attempted to examine Ilanthe, who deflected it effortlessly.

'You are the omega?' it asked in surprise.

'No,' Inigo said. 'We originated outside the Void.'

698

'How can that be? There is nothing outside, only dead matter.'

'Are you the creators? Did your species build this?'

'Yes.'

'We and many others have been pulled inside so you could exploit our rationality.'

'That is not so. You cannot exist unless the omega formed you.'

'We do exist, and the Void did not make us. The Void is killing us.'

'You do not understand your purpose. This is why I was brought back.' The Firstlife was uncertain.

'No. You can communicate with the Heart, the mind that envelops us. This is why—'

'Wait,' Troblum said. He ignored the looks everyone gave him. 'In your time, were there any other sentient species in the galaxy?'

'There is only us. We are first and when we achieve omega we will be last.'

'First life,' Oscar said in wonder. 'The first race to evolve in the galaxy. How old is this thing?'

'Ancient,' Justine muttered. 'More ancient than we ever thought possible.'

'Since your time, countless species have evolved right across the galaxy,' Inigo said. 'You were first, but you are no longer alone.'

The Firstlife's thoughts reeled in astonishment. 'You are not us? You are original?'

'We are.'

The black membranes flapped about in agitation. Glistening honey-like droplets appeared on their tips. 'Why are you here?'

'This thing you built, this Void, now threatens the entire galaxy,' Gore said, climbing to his feet again. 'I understand why you built it, to evolve into something new, something exquisite. You haven't. Instead it has absorbed thousands of other types of minds which have pulled it in every direction. It cannot evolve, not in this state.'

'Exactly,' Ilanthe said. 'Ask these creatures what they would have you do. They want you to stop, they want all you have achieved on the way to your omega to wither away and die. They have nothing else to offer you. I do.'

'Is this why you brought me back?' the Firstlife asked. 'To end our evolution?'

'It cannot continue in its current form,' Inigo said. 'It is consuming the mass of the galaxy in order to power its existence. Every star will ultimately be devoured, and the species they have birthed will die with them.'

'Unless you act now,' Ilanthe said. 'Communicate with the amalgamated mind, tell it to adopt my inversion.'

'What is your inversion?'

'I will take the composition of the Void and implant it within the quantum fields which structure the universe outside. This core will ignite the chain reaction which will disseminate change across the entirety of spacetime. Entropy will be eliminated. Mind will become paramount. Every sentient entity will be given the opportunity to reach its own omega as you anticipated for yourselves. Your legacy will be the birth of a new reality.'

'You have got to be fucking joking,' Gore gasped. 'Any quantum-field transform wave will simply reverse once it expands past its initial energy input zone. All you'll be left with is a collapsing microverse that seals itself off from reality as soon as the implosion is complete.'

'Not if entropy is eliminated.'

'You can't eliminate entropy across infinity. That's the fucking point of infinity. It's forever and always.'

'Ask the amalgamated mind to give me the Void's governing parameters,' Ilanthe said to the Firstlife.

'Do not!' Gore shouted, thrusting his arm out at the Firstlife. 'Do not even think it. You will destroy this entire supercluster with her insanity.'

'And what do you offer?' Ilanthe mocked. 'The end of their journey to omega?'

'Since you built the Void, hundreds of species have evolved

to post-physical status, what you call omega,' Gore said. 'It can be done, but not like this. I'm sorry. You have made a mistake by building the Void. You have to get the Heart to stop the boundary's mass devourment, suspend the Void's functions, become stable. We'll show you how to achieve true evolution in a different way.'

'You can't,' Ilanthe said. 'Every species has to find its own way.'

The Firstlife didn't reply. A whistling sound was coming from the thin fronds around its mouth as air gusted in and out past the teeth. Edeard was aware of its thoughts pulsing out to be absorbed by the Heart. It wasn't anything he could copy, he knew he could never communicate with the Heart directly.

'Darkness eclipses us,' it said eventually. 'Something is growing outside our frontier, a shroud which would deny us the universe.'

'The warrior Raiel,' Ilanthe said. 'Sworn to destroy you. Ask this wretched remnant of their invasion if you require confirmation. They seek to cut you off from your source of energy, to starve you to death. They will be rendered irrelevant by the change I can instigate. In time, in the new universe, they will learn to celebrate your liberation.'

'Do you seek to destroy us?' the Firstlife asked.

'We require you to end your absorption of this galaxy, and the threat of extinction it brings to all life,' Makkathran said. 'If you will not undertake this freely, we have the right to stop you.'

'You don't have to stop,' Ilanthe said. 'Inversion circumvents everything. All of us will achieve the promise of our evolution. Give me your governing parameters.'

'Wait!' Gore demanded. 'I think my alternative just became available.' He lifted his golden head and gave Ilanthe a sweetly evil grin. 'And guess who made that happen.' And he dreamed of his life back outside the Void.

*

The Delivery Man watched in horror as the twin quantum signatures expanded at hyperluminal velocity. Marius had fired novabombs into the star. He couldn't believe it. This was genocide.

Diverted energy functions absorbed the energy liberated from the first activation pulse, modifying it to expand the annihilation effect. A volume of the star's interior the size of a superJovian gas giant converted directly into energy. The convection zone bulged around the periphery, the first act in a sequence that would see the star's core squeezed beyond stability.

Monstrous shockwaves raced towards the *Last Throw* at close to lightspeed. 'Ozziefuckit!'

By the time he'd said it, his accelerated thoughts had already ordered the smartcore to trigger the ultradrive. It was never designed to operate within a stellar gravity field, but he was dead anyway.

The universe clearly hated such an aberration, sending a vengeful force to tear savagely at the perpetrator. And finally the cabin was alive with noise and shaking and alarms just like he'd thought he wanted. Bulkheads split, hundreds of tiny cracks ripping open. Sparks and sprays of gooey fluid shot through the air, churned by a cyclone of gravity waves that pulled the Delivery Man violently in every direction. He screamed in terror.

Two seconds. The time it took the ultradrive to claw the *Last Throw* out of the star's stupendous gravity gradient. The time that an astonishing amount of pain went surging along the Delivery Man's nervous system. The time the ship's overstressed components had to hold together. Most of them did.

The Delivery Man's world steadied. Gravity stopped its wild fluctuations. The vibrations beating the starship's fuselage faded away. His screaming dribbled off to a whimper.

And far away in a dream Ilanthe was entreating the Firstlife to give her the key to the Void's nature.

'Gore!' he called.

'What's happening?' the golden man asked. 'There's a power surge from the siphon.'

'Hell, you mean it's survived that?'

'Survived what?'

'Marius! Sweet Ozzie, he used novabombs. Gore, the star is going nova. It's already begun. That fucking deranged maniac has killed everything in the system. Tyzak! Warn Tyzak. I'm coming to get you.' Already the *Last Throw* was approaching the Anomine homeworld. The Delivery Man was designating a vector to take him round to the city where he'd left Gore.

'They know,' Gore said.

The Third Dreamer had abandoned Makkathran to dream of the Anomine city. The fantastical lights within the empty buildings were blazing with solar glory now. In its last minutes the city was waking defiantly to face its doom. Gore turned to Tyzak, who was staring straight up at the few quiet stars still visible directly above the plaza. The small remaining patch of dark sky was fading away as the light of the buildings grew ever stronger. Finally the old alien's thoughts were slipping through whatever variant of the gaiafield was establishing itself around the planet. Every system and device the ancient Anomine had left behind was coming alive. Thousands of borderguards were materializing into orbit.

The Delivery Man knew it was all useless. Nothing could save the planet now.

'It was us,' Gore told Tyzak. 'Humans. We did this. I'm so sorry.'

'You did not,' Tyzak replied. 'Your song remains pure.'

'I have failed so many times today.'

'I believe you are to have your greatest success. They seem to think so.'

Gore saw the plaza was now lined with hundreds of Silfen, all of them keeping back from the rim of the elevation mechanism.

'This is the fate our planet has brought us to,' Tyzak said. 'I did not expect this, but what is, is. And perhaps the planet knew all along what it would be called upon to do. I will depart believing this one thing.'

Anomine began teleporting in, appearing all across the plaza. Hundreds, then thousands. Youngsters were agitated, squeaking loudly. It was happening in every city on the planet.

'Gore?' the Delivery Man asked. 'What's happening?'

Gore smiled at Tyzak even as he was being jostled by Anomine who were crowding in. 'Go home,' he told the Delivery Man. 'You deserve it.'

'Gore?'

Gore shut down the TD link. He folded all his secondary routines back into his mind. There was only one consciousness now, making him as close to human as he'd been for many a century. His dream showed him Justine with an expression of alarm spreading over her beautiful face. She knew.

Tyzak called for the elevation mechanism.

'I feel you,' the elevation mechanism said. 'You are Tyzak.'

'I am.'

'Do you wish to attain transcendence from your physical existence?'

'Yes.'

*

'Dad?' Justine asked.

Gore's thoughts had calmed. He brought his arms out, and glided gently across the square to the waiting Firstlife. 'This is evolution,' he told the giant alien. 'The omega you have sought for so long.'

'No, Dad, you can't, you're not Anomine.' Justine started to run. Edeard's third hand caught her.

'Today I am,' Gore said benignly.

'No!' she sobbed. 'Dad, please.'

Far outside the Void's boundary the elevation mechanisms on the Anomine homeworld absorbed the power thundering out of the escalating nova. They adapted it, and offered it up to the remainder of their species, and one other who waited with them.

Gore felt his mind began to change, to rise. His perspective of the universe grew elegant.

'This is how it is done,' he told the Firstlife as they grew apart, gathering up everything the elevation mechanism was performing, the method and the outcome he now rushed towards. The union was so tenuous now, infused with the poignancy of Justine's grief as she stretched herself between the two. 'This is what you can become. This is destiny. Leave your past behind and reclaim the dream you started with. Like so . . .' He gifted the whole experience of his elevation to the Firstlife, who in turn shared it with the Heart. And after a while he was gone.

Edeard stood at the head of the group, facing up to the Firstlife. 'You must choose,' he said to the daunting alien, aware of the Heart focusing on him. And Ilanthe.

'We do,' the Firstlife replied. 'We choose evolution. It is why we created this place, it is what we aspired to so long ago. Anything else would betray all we were, all we aspired to. It could never be any other way.'

'Thank you.'

'It is the wrong choice,' Ilanthe declared.

'You should go with the Heart,' Inigo told her in disgust. 'There is no place for you in this universe. You wanted to be a God and this is your chance. If it will take you.'

'You may come with us,' the Firstlife told the inversion core. 'We offer to take all of you.'

'Naaah,' Oscar told it. 'Not me. I'm not quite ready for that yet.'

Inigo gave the Firstlife a thoughtful look.

'No,' Corrie-Lyn entreated. She took his hands and pressed herself against him. 'Don't. I can't become that, nor can I lose you again.'

'There's going to be Honious to pay when we get home.'

'I'll face it with you.'

'All right.' He reached out a hand to Edeard. 'And you?'

'I have to see the worlds you gave me a glimpse of. And . . .' Edeard grinned sheepishly. 'And there are many things I would like to do.'

'Anyone else?' Inigo enquired.

'Justine?' Corrie-Lyn said uncertainly.

Justine rubbed the moisture from her eyes. 'No. It's over. Let's go home.'

The Wall stars now shone with a brilliance equal to the rest of the galaxy, a blue-white collar shackling the Gulf. Inside, the containment shell was almost complete. The bands of dark force produced by the Raiel defences had merged together. Only a few gaps remained, and they were reducing fast.

Within the dark shell, automated Raiel monitors continued their observation of the Void boundary as they had done for the last million years. It had remained quiescent since the pilgrimage fleet passed through.

'It begins,' Qatux whispered.

Paula tried to get a grip on her dazed thoughts. Gore's dream had left her reeling, delighted and awestruck. For an instant she wanted to be there, standing in Sampalok with the Firstlife, telling the Heart she would join it. *Thank you*, she told the aching absence in the gaiafield where the Third Dreamer had once been. *Despite everything, you deserve to be the first of our species to achieve transcendence. I just hope it's not too lonely out there.*

She drew a deep breath, and focused on the display that dominated Qatux's private chamber. The surface of the Void boundary was changing. A thin ridge rose out of the equator, extending all the way out to the glowing loop. As before, the dying mass of broken stars fell into the event horizon.

'This time it will be different,' Paula promised. 'This time it will absorb the energy to power evolution.'

'I feel you are right,' Qatux said.

The entirety of the loop was taken, absorbed below the boundary. The ridge began to retreat. Then the Void itself was shrinking. Gravity, the boundary's primary enforcer, lessened. The impenetrable cloak that had defeated nature for so long fell away, and the Void lay naked at the core of the galaxy.

'Oh my,' Paula said in wonder.

The Void reached transcendence.

After it was gone, after normal spacetime reclaimed all it had lost, the vast warships of the warrior Raiel flew in to examine the darkness their great enemy had left behind. Virtually no matter existed in the Gulf now, no radiation, no light. No nebulas.

Right at the centre they found a single star shining bright, with a lone H-congruous planet in orbit. And one of their own.

12

The Raiel warship slipped out into spacetime above Icalanise, dwarfing the *High Angel* five hundred kilometres away. Qatux and Paula teleported over, materializing in a circular compartment over a hundred metres wide. Like the Raiel quarters on the *High Angel*, the ceiling was hidden from sight, giving the impression the compartment extended upwards forever.

Paula regarded the waiting warrior Raiel with interest. She'd assumed they'd be bigger than Qatux. Instead they were only two thirds his size, but where his hide was leathery theirs was made up from hard neutral blue-grey segments. Small lights twinkled under the surface, making her think it was an artificial armour. Or perhaps by now it was sequenced in like macrocellular clusters in humans.

Neskia stood between them. Her neck waved fractionally from side to side like a snake rising vertically, its casing of gold rings sliding over each other without revealing any human flesh. The metallic-grey surface shimmer of her skin was subdued. Big round eyes blinked once as Paula appeared. That might have reflected puzzlement, Paula wasn't sure. She had certainly been startled by the news that the Accelerator agent had surrendered herself to the warrior Raiel without any fuss.

'You were complicit in the establishment of the Sol barrier,' Paula said.

Neskia said nothing.

'I would like the deactivation code, now, please.'

'And then what?'

'You will face an enquiry into your actions.'

'By ANA itself. So there's really not much of an incentive to hand over the code, is there.'

'A memory read is never pleasant.'

'A mild discomfort. But you would never be able to extract the code. I have several self-destruct routines embedded in my biononics.'

'So you are in an invincible position. Congratulations. Curious then that you allowed yourself to be intercepted. Your ship has a superb stealth capability, yet you chose not to use it. Why?'

Neskia's neck became rigidly straight. 'I have nowhere to go.'

'She didn't take you with her.'

'Obviously.'

'But then ascension to post-physical status through Fusion was never her aim.'

'I am aware of that now.'

'What deal are you looking for?'

'Total immunity. The right to settle on whatever world I select. And I retain ownership of *the ship*.'

'No to *the ship*. You are forbidden from taking part in any subversive activity ever again. You will permit removal of all combat-enabled biononics. You will not reinstate them or any further weapons enrichments. You will report any contact by criminal or proscribed organizations to my office immediately.'

'Free political association is the fundamental right of the Greater Commonwealth.'

'Without ANA the Commonwealth as we know it cannot exist. I fully intend to protect it from extreme ideologues.'

'Will it ban the Accelerators?'

'I suspect those members involved with illegal activities will be suspended. The rest will be free to pursue and continue lobbying for what they believe in. As is their right.'

'Very well, I agree.' Neskia's u-shadow sent the code to Paula, along with instructions how to apply it to a specific coordinate outside the Sol system.

'Thank you,' Paula said. 'So you're pissed at her then?'

'To put it mildly. I risked everything, devoted my life to the cause, and now I find it never actually existed.'

'What will you do?'

'I will found the real Accelerator Faction. I still believe in human evolutionary destiny.'

'Of course you do.'

*

The *Elvin's Payback* sank down out of the low grey clouds that were drizzling steadily across the rumpled verdant countryside. Oscar directed it to land on the grass next to the spinney of gangling rancata trees. He floated down out of the airlock and looked round contentedly. Seeing the raised circular house just as it always was kindled an unexpected bout of homesickness. While he'd been away he'd thought of it and Jesaral and Dushiku and Anja less and less, so much so he'd started to believe he didn't care about any of them any more. Now he was here and he didn't want to leave again.

Wild emotions of surprise and trepidation burst into the gaiafield. Oscar grinned wryly as Jesaral charged down the spiral stairs in the house's central pillar, and ran across the lawn.

'You're back,' Jesaral yelled. He flung his arms round Oscar and began kissing him with youthful eagerness. Rampantly erotic thoughts came percolating out through his gaiamotes. 'Oh Ozzie, I missed you.'

'Good to be home,' Oscar admitted.

Dushiku and Anja hurried up.

'I couldn't believe it when you showed up in Gore's dream,' Dushiku murmured as he hugged Oscar tight. 'You were in the Void! That was you in Makkathran right at the end.'

'Yeah that was me,' he admitted. It actually felt good to boast about it for once.

Anja finally got her moment with him. 'So this is what you are?'

'Some of the time,' he admitted.

The other starship dropped through the clouds and came in to land next to the *Elvin's Payback*.

'Who's this?' Dushiku asked in a resigned tone.

'And why does a starship need wings?' Jesaral asked.

'They're not wings, they're heat dissipators; and this is my new partner.'

Anja recoiled slightly. Dushiku merely gave a disapproving glance, while Jesaral was already powering up his outrage.

'Business partner,' Oscar assured them hurriedly.

The *Mellanie's Redemption* landed smoothly. The airlock opened and a set of aluminium stairs slid out.

Jesaral gave Dushiku a meaningful glance that ended up as a pout. Oscar put his arms round both of them, enjoying the flashes of jealousy.

The aluminium steps bowed as Troblum came down, raindrops trickling quickly down the worn fabric of his old toga suit. He gave Oscar's startled life-partners a brisk nod, and quickly looked away.

'What sort of business?' Anja asked curiously.

'Exploration,' Oscar said contentedly. 'The Commonwealth has sent out a lot of colony ships over the centuries. We thought it was about time we found out what happened to some of them. And who knows what else is on the other side of the galaxy? Wilson never did have a proper look.'

Anja raised her eyes skywards, and produced a sigh of disapproval in that way only she could. However, she stepped forward and held her hand out to Troblum. 'Good to meet you.'

'Uh, thank you.' He gave her hand a frightened look. By then it didn't matter, Anja was looking up at the second figure to appear at the top of the stairs. She was so surprised she forgot to prevent the emotion from revealing itself through her gaiamotes.

'This is my fiancée,' Troblum announced.

'Pleased to meet you,' Catriona Saleeb said. She smiled nervously as she came down the stairs, and fumbled for Troblum's hand.

Oscar knew he was leaking out all the wrong thoughts, but he just couldn't help it. He'd been the first to support Troblum when Catriona was made real. Troblum had seen that one last slender chance in the time after the Heart had decided to follow Gore and the moment it elevated itself. He hadn't analysed it, or paused for doubt, he'd simply gone for it; using the Void's creation layer to turn his solido into flesh and blood. An act which was perhaps the most human thing Troblum had done in his life.

Oscar was also pretty sure it wouldn't last, that Catriona would soon outgrow her initial thoughts, but then ephemerality was the summation of most human activities. The trick was to enjoy the time things were going right.

*

The *Silverbird* alighted gently outside the Tulip Mansion, its landing legs barely making dints in the gravel drive in front of the grand entrance portico. Justine floated down out of the airlock, taking a wonderfully reassuring breath of Earth's old air once again. There had been moments when she thought that might not happen ever again. Kazimir whooped joyfully as he followed her down to the ground. Manipulated gravity was just one of the delights he'd discovered in the short time since she'd summoned him out of the Void's creation layer.

He stood perfectly still, allowing his mouth to open wide as he stared up at the preposterously extravagant building. 'This is your *home*?'

'Yes, this is where I was born, and lived ever since.' Which was almost the truth. She didn't want to spoil things. It was going to take this naive Kazimir a while to adjust to everything the Greater Commonwealth offered. *And who better to act as his guide and tutor?*

'Would you like to look round?'

'Oh yes!' His arms flapped round for emphasis. 'Who else lives here?'

'Ah, no one at the moment. It's become a bit of a museum, I'm afraid. We'll find you a bedroom, a suite actually. There are some excellent ones in the west wing.'

He caught hold of her hand, and gave her *that* beseeching look with his lovely big adoring eyes. 'Will you be nearby, Justine?'

'Um,' she was blushing again. *Come on, girl, get a grip.* 'I will stay for a while to make sure you're all right. I'm going to be quite busy. There's a lot to sort out right now.'

He grinned. 'You have saved the galaxy. People will allow you time for yourself now, I am sure of it.'

'Probably.' The entrance doors were huge jet-black slabs of glossy stonewood, inlaid with a gold-leaf vine pattern. She paused as they swung open. *I never noticed before, that's so similar to the gates of the Sampalok mansion.* Oscar had sworn his first voyage of exploration would attempt to find the previous occupiers of Makkathran. She still couldn't quite get her head around that partnership. *But then in the Void anything is possible.* Kazimir was witness to that. And Catriona.

Kazimir peered in curiously as the lights came on along the length of the cavernous hall. 'How old is this place?'

'Over a thousand years,' she said with pride.

'Dreaming heavens,' he murmured as they walked inside.

'I used to rollerblade in here,' she said fondly. 'That's when I was your age, or maybe a little younger. Dad would scream at me and—' She stopped dead. A shiver ran up her body, strong enough to cause her to clutch at the doorframe for support. Shock that only a genuine flesh-and-blood body could know was threatening to reduce her to tears.

Gore was standing in the doorway to the White Room. As always his solido was the twenty-fourth-century version of himself, gold-skin body wearing a black shirt and trousers.

'Dad?' she gasped. In her nice rational tidy mind she'd known all along that he would be waiting here for her, that ANA would have reanimated his personality as soon as it confirmed his bodyloss on the Anomine homeworld. But back in Makkathran his transcendence had been so real, so vivid. Her meat body and brain knew her father's mind and body had gone on to something better. That Daddy had died. That everything afterwards was just the result of clever technology.

Sometimes basic human flesh and blood was far too painful.

'You did a great job out there,' he said. 'Not everyone operating in a meat body would hold it together under that kind of emotional stress. Thanks.'

'My pleasure,' she said weakly.

'So how about that? My original body finally gets fried up in a nova. Goddamn Marius, he's actually worse than Ilanthe in his own pathetically petty way. Funny thing, I didn't imagine I'd get nostalgic, but I think I'm going to miss it. The damn thing was like a psychological final safety net. I suppose I ought to clone another. Not that I'll ever use one again.'

'Good idea.'

'And I'm going to have to have a long talk to the Delivery Man; he can fill in the missing details. I accessed the kubes in Ozzie's asteroid as soon as ANA brought me out of suspension storage. They updated me back to the point I left on the *Last Throw*. But there's no accurate record of what happened on the Anomine homeworld between then and when that old Tyzak guy switched on the elevation mechanism. The way it played out I'm guessing there had to be some serious problems back there.'

'Yeah, that's how I read it, too.'

'Right. Well you wouldn't believe the fuss the radical Darwinist faction is kicking up in here. Conniving little shits. I could do with some help slapping them down. Are you coming back home now?'

Justine draped an arm round a very silent Kazimir's shoulders and gave the golden man a defiant look. 'Not just yet, Dad.

There's a few things I have to finish off out here. They might take a while.'

*

The ultradrive starship hung in transdimensional suspension five million kilometres out from the Leo Twins. Marius wasn't quite sure why he'd chosen this as his destination. Presumably his subconscious had identified it as the last place anyone would suspect him of fleeing to.

As to what he should do now, he had no idea. The onetime scrutineers he'd inserted into the unisphere were supplying a comprehensive picture of the political fallout from the Void's elevation and the fall of the Sol barrier.

ANA had carried out its threat and suspended the Accelerator Faction. Instructions were being issued to ANA representatives to locate and arrest the remaining Accelerator agents. The list was very comprehensive. He was at the top, charged with genocide. That wasn't something the authorities would quietly downgrade and forget after a couple of decades, or even centuries; certainly not if Paula Myo was involved. That meant he would have to leave the Commonwealth entirely.

His options weren't good. He didn't know where any of the colonies were, nor what kind of societies they'd developed. Conceivably he could start rescuing the other Accelerators on the list, form some kind of resistance. It would be dangerous, but he was more than capable of working in such an environment.

Alarms flared.

His ship was wrenched back into spacetime before even his accelerated thought routines had truly grasped what was happening. Sensors revealed nothing except a minuscule spatial anomaly directly in front of the fuselage. Then they failed, along with the drive. The starship's network crashed. Gravity cut out, leaving him in freefall. Cabin lights died. He couldn't access his u-shadow. A biononic field scan revealed the life-support system was off line.

715

A link opened to his macrocellular clusters. 'You're under arrest,' Admiral Kazimir informed him.

'For now,' Marius retorted. 'She'll be back.'

'She won't. None of them come back.'

*

As Araminta landed the big passenger capsule outside the sprawling white house her confidence suddenly deserted her. Even the little surprise she'd prepared for him seemed feeble. There was absolutely no way of knowing how he'd react. Sure, he'd helped her before, but that was when the Living Dream maniacs threatened his homeworld and his lives.

They were gone now, thanks to her and the deception he'd helped her with. Now Ellezelin would be paying compensation for all the physical damage its troops had caused during the invasion. Inigo had promised that as he went back there to assume the presidency she'd abdicated. It was going to take a long while to dismantle the Living Dream movement, but he was the best – the only – candidate for the job. After the Void's elevation, he was the person everybody trusted to do it right.

Two of hers stepped out onto the grass, her original body and Araminta-two. She looked round with all four eyes, relishing the familiarity.

Mr Bovey had been busy since she left. The house had been repaired and painted. But then if anybody could do a fast, quality refurbishment it was going to be him with all his contacts in the business.

Several of hims were coming out of the house, running towards her. And they were all smiling, which brought a lump to her throats. *He does care still!* Now she thought everything might be all right after all, she believed she might cry – that would be a lot of tears. The gaiafield was abruptly full of the relief hes were broadcasting loud and clear.

Eight of hims surrounded the two of hers. The young blond one gave her a tentative look. 'You came back.'

His uncertainty was too much. She just flung her arms round him. Then they were kissing.

'What you did was unbelievable,' the Asian him was saying to Araminta-two. 'You never backed down, not for a second. Ellezelin, the *Lady's Light*, you kept on and on. It was awesome.'

'They made me do it,' she told him. 'It was the only way I could survive.'

'I was frantic when the Raiel blew up the link. Then Gore started dreaming and you were on Makkathran. It was . . .' All of hims on the lawn started laughing in amazement. 'Ozzie, you were unbelievable. For a while there you were in charge of the whole universe.'

Araminta gave him a demure smirk. 'Did you think that was hot?'

The blond youngster cleared his throat. 'Could have done.'

'Let me give you back. Hang on.' She closed her eyes, concentrating on the way her thoughts were spread out through the gaiafield. Slowly and carefully she withdrew herself from the body she'd borrowed. When she opened her eyes he was right in front of her, that oh so familiar smile on his face. Then he looked down at himself. 'Thank you, you took good care of him.'

'Certainly did.' Araminta let go of the blond youngster one and went over to the original – she could never stop thinking of him in those terms. It was only slightly weird kissing the body she'd been a few seconds earlier. 'It was interesting being a man for a while,' she said in a teasingly husky voice.

'Really? Why?'

'I learned about . . . reflexes.' She was still pressed up against him. 'Specifically, the involuntary ones.'

'Uh huh.' His voice had become hoarse.

'And I was bad, too, while I was away.'

'That's always been one of your best qualities.'

'You don't understand. Once you learned how to use it, the Void could make all your wishes come true. It really could. *Anything*. And I wasn't strong enough to resist temptation. Mind you, I wasn't alone. Most of us were at it at the end, there. It was quite the little fantasyfest we had going on in the Sampalok mansion.'

'Oh.' He sounded disappointed. 'Well, you had just saved us all. I suppose that entitled you.'

'My thoughts exactly.' Araminta had forgotten how much fun it was to tease Mr Bovey. But the poor man was suffering, which he didn't really deserve, he was far too noble for that. 'I watched Justine and Edeard and Troblum all pulling lost loves out of the creation layer like rabbits from a hat.'

Mr Bovey frowned. 'Er . . .'

'So I thought: I haven't lost anyone I love, but someone I love might appreciate a lot more of me.' She gave him a wicked smirk and glanced over at the capsule. The rest of hers were emerging.

Mr Bovey watched with incredulous delight as fifteen identical Aramintas walked across the garden to hims.

'That conversation we had about what types of mes I'd have when I was multiple?' she said. 'I decided there's not much wrong with this one.'

'This one is absolutely perfect.'

'Good. So now all of yous can take all of mes to bed.'

'Oh yes!'

'Now, please.'

*

Last Throw fell smoothly through the miserable winter weather to land at the house in Holland Park. The Delivery Man didn't even waste time walking, he teleported straight into the lounge.

'Dadeeeeie!' The girls flew at him. Small arms clung with surprising strength. Wet sticky kisses smudged his face. Little Rosa was bouncing around, yelling for attention as her elder sisters wouldn't get out of the way. He scooped her up for big cuddles.

Lizzie was standing in the door, her eyes damp as she smiled at him.

'I'm back,' he told her.

'Yes,' she said. 'And Boy have you got some explaining to do. Don't you ever, *ever*—'

The Delivery Man kissed his wife.

*

Inevitably, the world was a pleasant one. The temperate zones where Araminta walked had vast rolling grasslands, tall snow-cloaked mountains, and extensive forests.

The three of them had been there for a couple of days, making leisurely progress along the narrow path, before she heard the singing. 'They're here,' Araminta told Aaron. He didn't react. Tomansio gently urged him forward toward the haunting non-human melodies. Aaron didn't protest, just went with his guides as he'd done ever since they'd left Makkathran. Saying nothing. He didn't have nightmares any more. He didn't have anything; his mind had shut down of its own accord.

The Knights Guardians had wanted to take him back to Far Away where there would be the best clinics and doctors and medical modules and memory edits. Lennox the Mutineer would be reassembled, they said. Araminta had said no, Aaron had suffered enough technology, he needed real healing. And she would take him to the one person who would grant that. Tomansio had been startled by the suggestion, and very quick to agree.

Several dozen Silfen were camping in the broad glade. A semicircle of wide marquees had been set up, with long heraldic flags fluttering from the tips of tall poles. A huge fire was blazing in the middle of the semicircle. Some Silfen sat around it, playing flute-like instruments. More were dancing.

Araminta wasn't entirely surprised to see a human woman among them. She was dressed in Silfen clothes, a simple white shirt with intricate dragons embroidered in gold and turquoise thread; a loose petal-layered cotton skirt that swirled and flared out as she danced. Her face was rapt, lost in the enjoyment of the music. Wavy golden hair swished around her head. Araminta could just glimpse a long chin and well defined cheekbones – similar to her own.

'Ozziebedamned,' Tomansio muttered. He was staring round at the scene as if the elves had enchanted him.

Then Clouddancer and Bradley were walking towards them. Araminta hurried over. The dancers encircled her, warbling approval and greetings.

'You did well,' Bradley said.

'Thank you,' she said. 'Thank you for believing in me.'

'In your case it came easy,' Clouddancer said, his circular mouth fluting out to laugh.

'I've brought somebody,' she said.

'We know.'

'Please help him. He suffers from terrible demons in his head like you once did,' she told Bradley.

Bradley's wings spread wide. 'And if the Silfen can cure me . . .'

'That's what I hoped.'

'He can walk with us,' Clouddancer said. 'Where he will go can never be foretold.'

'He's surefooted,' Araminta promised. 'Look what he did for everyone.'

'Oh how you have grown. You are a wonder, Araminta. Mr Bovey is a lucky man.'

She grinned back, slightly abashed.

'I think I'd better go and speak to your other friend before he explodes,' Bradley said.

Araminta laughed at how scared Tomansio looked as Bradley went over to him. The toughest superwarrior humbled by his idol. Speaking of which . . . She slithered through the dancers, finding herself swaying in time to the harmony. Somewhere by the end of the marquees two of the biggest Silfen she'd ever seen started drumming, pounding a compulsive beat.

The woman beckoned her over with both hands. 'I'm Mellanie,' she called above the music.

'Yeah, I know.'

'Of course you do. I'm proud of you, Araminta.'

'Thanks. That really means a lot.'

'It's all over now, so let's dance.'

*

They came from across the galaxy, the Raiel arkships and warships, congregating in orbit around the star where Centurion Station was based. From there the starscape was unchanged, the Wall stars still shone with their normal intensity, giving no hint of the endeavour they had just driven. It would be centuries before their leap in luminosity would be visible to any observer standing beside the ruins of the observation outpost.

Paula accompanied Qatux as they teleported into Makkathran. They arrived in Golden Park, where Querencia's seabirds were still flapping above them, calling out in confusion as they hunted their missing sea. Paula turned a full circle, as admiring as any tourist as she took in the tall white pillars and the sweeping domes of the Orchard Palace.

'I never expected to stand here,' she admitted.

Qatux was staring out over Padua to the towers of Eyrie beyond. 'Nor I,' he said. They made their way together through the overgrown park, following the curve of Champ Canal until it took them to Birmingham Pool. Paula was only too well aware of all Edeard's gallant events that had played out around the pool and down the canal; yet she kept her silence, knowing Qatux was here for only one thing.

As they started along the side of Great Major Canal to High Pool, Paula looked over the weed-saturated water to the unmistakable Culverit ziggurat. That was when she finally appreciated Justine's melancholia at how empty the city was. She was thrilled at just making this visit, but to have seen it during the Waterwalker's heyday, watching the intrigues unfold and meeting people she knew only from dreams – that would have been *glorious*.

There was a bridge she didn't remember across Market Canal,

taking them into Eyrie itself. When she glanced up at the crooked towers she could see past the crystal dome to the vast constellation of Raiel ships gathered protectively around their ancient comrade.

'What's going to happen next?' she asked.

'We will decide together,' Qatux told her. 'The change will come hard for us, I expect. The Void gave us purpose for so long it is a part of what we became.'

'You know you will always be welcome in the Commonwealth.'

'Your kindness does you credit. However we do have a responsibility to the other species living in the *High Angel* and all our other arkships.'

'Will you take them home?'

'Possibly. Some no longer have homeworlds they can return to. It has already been suggested we accept our original undertaking, and spread out to new galaxies to begin again.'

'And you, Qatux, what about you? Do the Raiel still have a homeworld?'

'Yes. But it is not one any of us recognize. Two other species have come to sentience there in the time since we declared war on the Void. There will be no going back for us.'

'Perhaps that is for the best. I tried going home once. I had grown too much while I was away. We all do.'

Finally they stood in front of the Lady's church. Qatux hesitated on the steps leading up to the entrance.

'You don't have to,' Paula said compassionately.

'I do.'

The church was silent inside. Light shone through its transparent central roof to illuminate the centre, leaving the vestibules in shadow. Right on the edge of the silver-hazed light, the Lady's white-marble statue stood resolute. Paula gazed up at the solemn well-crafted face, and the corner of her mouth lifted in an appreciative smile. 'She looks so different here,' she said. 'But then I only ever met her once. We parted as soon as we got to Far Away.'

'I remember,' Qatux said. 'It was the day I first met her.'

'I disapproved.'

'I loved her even then. She was so colourful, so flawed, so imbued with life. She taught me to feel again. I owe her everything.'

'How did she wind up here?'

'She was re-lifed, of course, after the Cat had finished with her. I supplied the memories for her new body, for I shared everything she felt right up until the last. That was why we parted. There was nothing left for us to know.'

'So she boarded a Brandt colony ship to start a new life. So many Brandts were disillusioned with the Commonwealth after the Starflyer War, they say almost a fifth of the senior dynasty members left. They would have welcomed her on board. She must have been quite solitary, poor thing.'

'It was for the best. Then Makkathran must have heard her as they flew around the Wall – somehow. It mistook her for a Raiel, for our minds had shared so much, and it called out.'

'And the Void did the rest. As it always does.'

'Yes.' Qatux extended a tentacle, and stroked the statue's cheek. 'Goodbye my beloved.' He turned and left the church.

Paula couldn't resist one final over-the-shoulder check, just to make sure she wasn't mistaken. For an instant she could've sworn the statue was grinning in that ridiculous carefree way Tiger Pansy always had when she was happy. But it was only a trick of the light.

*

From the switchback road high in the foothills, Salrana looked out across the Iguru Plain, not understanding what she was seeing. But then many things were puzzling her this day.

Someone coughed behind her. She turned nervously. 'Edeard!' she cried, for it was him ... but different, older. There was no mistaking that shy hopeful smile however. Try as she might she couldn't sense him with farsight and he wasn't five yards away. Nor did she have a third hand any more. 'What's happened?' she implored.

Edeard glanced down at the small boy whose hand he was holding. The boy looked back up adoringly. There were several shared features on their faces.

'Edeard!' she implored. She thought she might cry.

'This is so hard,' he said. 'I know. I have undergone this myself, but if you ever trusted me then please believe you are all right. Nothing is going to harm you.'

She took a tentative step towards him. 'Where are we? Where's Makkathran? Was there an earthquake?' She turned back to stare at the terrible devastation that had befallen the Iguru Plain. The farms and orchards and vineyards had vanished, wiped out by a smouldering desert of grey rock that extended out to the shoreline. But stranger than that were the ships. At least that's what she thought they were, for what else could they be? Twelve metal monsters lying around the edge of the destruction. Though to imagine anything of such a size flying was impossible.

'We are home,' Edeard said. 'Though it is not home, not truly, not any more. Makkathran is gone. But nobody died. They all lived, Salrana, they lived such amazing lives. And now we have a chance to live our life. Together.'

'Us?' she asked, still hopelessly confused.

'Well actually, the three of us.' He ruffled the boy's head. 'This is Burlal, my grandson.'

'Grandson? Edeard, please, I don't understand.'

'I know. Perhaps I was wrong to do this, for the Lady knows it is a very selfish act. But sometimes to do what's right—'

'—you have to do what's wrong.'

'Yes. You have just finished your training in Ufford Hospital haven't you?'

'I was due to leave tomorrow, but I woke up here.' She frowned. 'No, I arrived here somehow. Edeard, do I dream this?'

He took her hand, which made her ridiculously grateful. But then the touch of him had always done that, and she'd missed him terribly these long months away from Makkathran.

'We are no longer dreams, my love. We are as genuine as can

724

be. And out here, in this time, I chose you over everyone. I chose the you from now because you are still the real you. My brother taught me that trick.'

'What brother?'

He laughed. 'There is so much to explain, and I'm not sure how to begin. I never told you, did I, that I had dreams? Every night of my life I dreamed of life outside the Void. Well that's where those ships have come from. Outside, where the universe goes on forever.'

'Like Rah and the Lady?'

'Yes. Just like them. And the three of us are going on one of those ships. It's going to fly away, fly out of here. We're going to live out there, Salrana, out among the stars.'

She grinned, for he was being so foolish. But she could see how happy he was. Which she liked.

Edeard's arm went round her shoulder, which felt fantastic. For so many years now she had waited for such a sincere open gesture. Then she saw a tall, strangely dressed man coming down the road. He was wearing some kind of skirt with a colourful square pattern on it, and a bright scarlet waistcoat. Slim, curving lines of silver and gold light shone through his thick brown hair.

He stopped in front of them; looked them up and down, and promptly grinned broadly.

'I know you,' Edeard said in amusement. 'You're the Lion-walker, you were in charge of my brother's science station when first we dreamed of each other.'

'Aye, that I was. Good morning to you, Waterwalker. And young Salrana, of course. And I think you must be Burlal. Am I right?'

The boy gave a cautious nod, clinging tighter to Edeard's leg.

'Well congratulations and then some, Waterwalker, that was quite a sight. I've just spent the night up on top of the mountain where the air's clearest. Didn't want to miss anything. After all, it's not every day you get to see an entire universe evolve, is it?'

'My first time, as well,' Edeard told him.

'Aye well, it's over now.' Lionwalker Eyre gave Salrana a

roguish smile. 'It's nice for an old romantic like me to see you two back together.' A finger wagged at Edeard. 'Don't you go messing it up again, lad.'

'I won't,' Edeard said quietly.

'Well, I'd best be off. I expect you two have a lot to talk about.' He started walking briskly down the road.

'Wait,' Edeard called after him. 'Where are you going?'

'Onwards,' the Lionwalker replied with a wave. 'Always onwards.'

If you enjoyed *The Evolutionary Void*,
turn the page to read the prologue of *Pandora's Star*,
part one of the Commonwealth saga . . .

Prologue

Mars completely dominated space outside the *Ulysses,* the bloated dirty-ginger crescent of a planet that never quite made it as a world. Small, frigid, barren, airless, it was simply the solar system's colder version of hell. Yet its glowing presence in the sky had dominated most of human history; first as a god to inspire generations of warriors, then a goal to countless dreamers.

Now, for NASA Captain-Pilot Wilson Kime, it had become solid land. Two hundred kilometres beyond the landing craft's narrow, curving windshield he could pick out the dark gash that was the Valles Marineris. As a boy he'd accessed the technofantasies of the Aries Underground group, entranced by how one day in an unspecified future, foaming water would once again race down that vast gully as raw human ingenuity unlocked the frozen ice trapped beneath the rusting landscape. Today, he would actually get to walk through those dusty craters he'd studied in a thousand satellite photos, hold the legendary thin red sand in his gloved hands to watch little trickles slip slowly through his fingers in the low gravity. Today was the most glorious history in the making.

Wilson automatically started a deep feedback breathing exercise, calming his heart before the reality of what was about to happen affected his metabolism. No way was he giving those goddamned desk medics back in Houston a chance to question *his* fitness to pilot the landing craft. Eight years he'd spent in the USAF, including two combat duties based in Japan for Operation Deliver Peace, followed by another nine years with NASA. All that build-up and anticipation; the sacrifices, his first wife and totally alienated kid; the eternal VR training at Houston, the press conferences, the mind-rotting PR tours of factories; he'd endured it all because it led to this one moment in this most sacred place.

Mars. At last!

'Initiating VKT ranging, cross-match RL acquisition data,' he told the landing craft's autopilot. The coloured strands of light captured inside the windshield began to change their geometrical patterns. He kept one eye on the timer: eight minutes. 'Purging BGA system and vehicle interlink tunnel.' His left hand flicked the switches on the console. Watching the tiny LEDs come on to confirm the switch cycle. Some actions NASA would never entrust to voice-activation software. 'Commencing BGA non-propulsive vent. Awaiting prime ship sep sequence confirmation.'

'Roger that, *Eagle II*,' Nancy Kressmire's voice said in his headset. 'Telemetry analysis has you as fully functional. Prime ship power systems ready for disengagement.'

'Acknowledged,' he told the *Ulysses* captain. Turquoise and emerald spider webs within the windshield fluttered elegantly, reporting the lander's internal power status. Their sharp primary colours appeared somehow alien across the dull pallor of the wintry Martian landscape outside. 'Switching to full internal power cells. I have seven greens for umbilical sep. Retracting inter-vehicle access tunnel.'

Alarmingly loud metallic clunks rang through the little cabin as the spaceplane's airlock tunnel sank back into the fuselage. Even Wilson flinched at the intrusive sounds, and he knew the spaceplane's mechanical layout better than its designers.

'Sir?' he asked. According to the NASA manual, once the lander's airlock had retracted from the prime ship they were technically a fully independent vehicle, and Wilson wasn't the ranking officer.

'The *Eagle II* is yours, Captain,' Commander Dylan Lewis said. 'Take us down when you're ready.'

Very conscious of the camera at the back of the cabin, Wilson said: 'Thank you, sir. We are on line for completed undocking in seven minutes.' He could sense the buzz in the five passengers riding behind him. All of them were the straightest of straight arrows; they had so much right stuff between them it could be bottled. Yet now the actual moment was here they were no more controlled than a bunch of schoolkids heading for their first beach party.

The autopilot ran through the remaining pre-flight prep sequence, with Wilson ordering and controlling the list; adhering faithfully to the man-in-the-loop tradition that dated all the way back to the Mercury Seven and their epic struggle for astronauts to be more than just spam in a can. Right on the seven-minute mark, the locking pins withdrew. He fired the RCS thrusters, pushing *Eagle II* gently away from the *Ulysses*. This time there was nothing he could do to stop his heart racing.

As they drew away, *Ulysses* became fully visible through the windshield. Wilson grinned happily at the sight of it. The interplanetary craft was the first of its kind; actually quite an ungainly collection of cylindrical modules, tanks, and girders arranged in a circular grid shape two hundred metres across. Its perimeter sprouted long jet-black solar power panels like plastic petals, all of them tracking the sun. Several of the crew habitation sections were covered in big Stars and Stripes flags, implausibly gaudy against the plain silver-white thermal foam that coated every centimetre of the superstructure. Right in the centre of the vehicle, surrounded by a wide corrugated fan of silver thermal radiator panels, was the hexagonal chamber which housed the fusion generator that had made the ten-week flight time possible, constantly supplying power to the plasma rockets. It was the smallest fusion system ever built: a genuine made-in-America, cutting-edge chunk of technology. Europe was still building its first pair of commercial fusion reactors on the ground, while the USA had already commissioned five such units, with another fifteen being built. And the Europeans certainly hadn't got anything equivalent to the sophisticated *Ulysses* generator.

Damn it, we can still get some things right, Wilson thought proudly as the shining conglomeration of space hardware retreated away into the eternal night. It would be another decade until the FESA could mount a Mars mission, by which time NASA planned on having a self-sustaining base on the icy sands of Arabia Terra. Hopefully, by then, the agency would also be flying asteroid-capture missions and even a Jovian expedition as well. *I'm not too old to be a part of those, they'll need experienced commanders.*

His mind underwent just the tiniest tweak of envy at the prospect of what would come in the mid-term future, events and miracles whose timetable and budget allocations meant they might just elude him. *The Europeans can afford to wait, though.* While thanks to the dominant influence of the Religious Right over the last few administrations, the US had halted all genetic work centred around stem cells, the Federal government in Brussels had poured money into biogenic research, with spectacular results. Now that the early bugs had been ironed out of the hugely expensive procedure, they'd begun to rejuvenate people. The first man to receive the treatment, Jeff Baker, had died in a climax of global publicity; but in the following seven years there had been eighteen successes.

Space and Life. Those separate interests spoke volumes about the way the cultures of Earth's two major Western power groups had diverged over the past three decades.

Now Wilson's fellow Americans were beginning to re-evaluate their attitude to genetic engineering. Already there were urban myths of Caribbean and Asian clinics offering the rejuvenation service to multi-billionaires. While Federal Europe was once again attempting to narrow the American lead in space, desperate to prove to the world that it excelled in every field. Given the fractious political state currently afflicting the planet, Wilson rather welcomed the idea of the two blocs drawing closer together once more – that was, after Americans had landed on Mars.

'First de-orbit burn in three minutes,' the *Eagle II* autopilot said.

'Standing by,' Wilson told it. He automatically checked the fuel tank pressures, and followed that up with main engine ignition procedures.

Three hypergolic fuel rockets at the back of the little spaceplane fired for a hundred seconds, pushing their orbit into an atmosphere-intercept trajectory. The subsequent aerobrake manoeuvre lasted for over ninety minutes, with the scant Martian atmosphere pushing against the craft's swept delta wings, killing its velocity. For the final fifteen minutes, Wilson could see the faintest of pink glows coming from the *Eagle II*'s blunt nose. It was the only evidence of the violence being done to the fuselage by high-velocity gas molecule impacts. The ride was incredibly smooth, with gravity slowly building as they sank towards the crater-rumpled landscape of Arabia Terra.

At six kilometres altitude, Wilson activated their profile dynamic wings. They began to expand, spreading out wide to generate as much lift as possible from the thin, frigid air. At full stretch they measured a hundred metres from tip to tip, enough to allow *Eagle II* to glide if necessary. Then their turbine fired up, gently thrusting them forward, keeping speed constant at two hundred and fifty kilometres an hour. The westernmost edge of the massive Schiaparelli crater slid into sight away in the distance, rolling walls rising up out of the rumpled ground like a weatherworn mountain range.

'Visual acquisition of landing site,' Wilson reported. His systems schematics were tracing green and blue sine waves across the view. Ground radar began to overlay a three-dimensional grid of spikes and gullies which almost matched what he could see.

'*Eagle II*, mid-point systems review confirms you are go for landing,' said Mission Control. 'Good luck, guys. You've got quite an audience back here.'

'Thank you, Mission Control,' Commander Lewis said formally. 'We are eager for the touchdown. Hoping Wilson can give us a smooth one.' It would be another four minutes before anyone back on Earth heard his words. By then they should be down.

'Contact with cargo landers beacon,' Wilson reported. 'Range thirty-eight kilometres.' He squinted through the windshield as the autopilot printed up a red line-of-sight bracket within the glass. The crater rim grew steadily larger. 'Ah, I've got them.' Two dusty grey specks sitting on a broad patch of flat landscape.

For the last stage, *Eagle II* flew a slow circle round the pair of robot cargo landers. They were simple squat cones which the *Ulysses* had sent down two days earlier, loaded with tonnes of equipment, including a small prefab ground base. Getting them unloaded and the projected exploration campus up and running was the principal task awaiting the crew of the *Eagle II*.

'Groundscan confirms area one viability,' Wilson said. He was almost disappointed at the radar picture. When Neil Armstrong and Buzz Aldrin were landing on the Moon, they had to hurriedly take manual control of their Lunar Module and fly it to safety when the designated landing site turned out to be strewn with boulders. This time, eighty-one years later, satellite imagery and orbital radar mapping had eliminated such uncertainty from the flight profile.

He brought the *Eagle II* round on its pre-plotted approach path, engaging the autopilot. 'Landing gear extended and locked. VM engines pressurized and ready. Profile dynamic wings in reshape mode. Ground speed approaching one hundred kilometres per hour. Descent rate nominal. We're on the wire, people.'

'Good work, Wilson,' Commander Lewis said. 'Let's bump struts, here, huh?'

'You got it, sir.'

The landing rockets fired, and *Eagle II* began to sink smoothly out of the light pink sky. A hundred metres up, and Wilson couldn't stand it. His fingers flicked four switches, taking the autopilot off line. Red LEDs glared accusingly at him from the console. He ignored them, bringing the little spaceplane down manually. Easier than any simulation. Dust swirled outside the windshield, thick and cloying as the rocket jets scoured the surface of Mars. Radar gave him the final approach vectors, there was nothing to see visually. They settled without a wobble. The sound of the rockets died away. External light began to brighten as the agitated dust flurries dissipated.

'Houston, the *Eagle II* has landed,' Wilson said. The words had to be forced out, his throat was so tensed up with pride and exhilaration. He could hear that beautiful phrase echo along history, past and future. *And I made it happen, not some goddamn machine.*

A wave of jubilant shouts and cheering broke out in the cabin behind him. He wiped an errant drop of moisture from his eye with the back of one hand. Then he was suddenly involved with systems supervision, re-engaging the autopilot. External instrumentation confirmed they were down and stable. The spaceplane had to be put into surface standby mode, supplying power and environmental services to the cabin, keeping the rocket engines warm so that take-off wouldn't be a problem, monitoring the fuel tank status. A long, boring list of procedures that he worked through with flawless diligence.

Only then did the six of them begin to suit up. Given the cabin's chronic lack of space, it was a cramped, difficult process, with everyone jostling each other. When Wilson was almost ready, Dylan Lewis handed him his helmet.

'Thanks.'

The commander didn't say anything, just gave Wilson a look. As reprimands went, it didn't get much worse than that.

To hell with you, Wilson retorted silently. *We're the important thing, people coming to Mars is what matters, not the machines we come in. I couldn't allow a software program to land us.*

Wilson stood in line as the commander went into the small airlock at the back of the cabin. *Third, I get to be third.* Back on Earth they'd only ever remember that Dylan Lewis was first. Wilson didn't care. *Third.*

The tiny display grid inside Wilson's helmet relayed an image from the external camera set just above the airlock door. It showed a slim aluminium ladder stretching down to the Martian sand. Commander Lewis backed out of the open airlock, his foot moving slowly and carefully onto the top rung. Wilson wanted to shout, *For God's sake get a move on.* The suit's medical telemetry told him his skin was flushed and perspiring. He tried to do his deep feedback breathing exercise thing; but it didn't seem to work.

Commander Lewis was taking the ladder rungs one at a time, pausing on each one, then he finally reached the last one. Wilson and the others in the cabin held their breaths; he could feel a couple of billion people doing the same thing back on the old home planet.

'I take this step for all of humanity, so that we may walk together as one people along the road to the stars.'

Wilson winced at the words. Lewis sounded incredibly sincere. Then someone sniggered, actually sniggered out loud; he could hear it quite plainly over the general communication band. Mission Control would go ballistic over that.

Then he forgot it all as Lewis took his step onto the surface, his foot sinking slightly into the red sand of Mars to make a firm imprint.

'We did it,' Wilson whispered to himself. 'We did it, we're here.' Another outbreak of cheering went round the cabin. Congratulatory calls flooded down from *Ulysses*. Jane Orchiston was already clambering into the airlock. Wilson didn't even begrudge her that; political correctness wouldn't allow it any other way. And NASA was ever mindful of pleasing as many people as possible.

Commander Lewis was busy taking a high-resolution photo of his historic footprint. A requirement that had been in the NASA manual for the last eighty-one years, ever since Apollo 11 got back home to find that embarrassing omission.

Lieutenant Commander Orchiston was going down the ladder – a lot faster than Commander Lewis. Wilson stepped into the airlock. He couldn't even remember the time the little chamber took to cycle, it never existed in his personal awareness. Then it was him backing out onto the ladder. Him checking his feet were secure on the rungs before placing all his – reduced – weight on them. Him hanging poised on the bottom rung. 'I wish you could see this, Dad.' He put his foot down, and he was standing on Mars.

Wilson moved away from the ladder, cautious in the low gravity. Heart pounding away in his ears. Breathing loud in the helmet. Hiss of helmet air fans ever-present. Ghostly suit graphic symbols flickered annoyingly across his full field of vision. Other people talked directly into his ears. He stopped and turned full circle. Mars! Dirty rocks littering the ground. Sharp horizon. Small glaring sun. He searched round until he found the star that was Earth. Brought up a hand and waved solemnly at it.

'Want to give me a hand with this?' Commander Lewis asked. He was holding the flagpole, Stars and Stripes still furled tightly around the top.

'Yes, sir.'

Jeff Silverman, the geophysicist, was already on the ladder. Wilson walked over to help the commander with the flagpole. He gave the *Eagle II* a critical assessment glance on his way. There were some scorch marks along the fuselage, trailing away from the wing roots, very faint, though. Other than that: nothing. It was in good shape.

The commander was attempting to open out the little tripod on the base of the flagpole. His heavy gloved hands making the operation difficult. Wilson put out his own hand to steady the pole.

'Yo, dudes, how's it hanging? You need any help there?'
The question was followed by a snigger.

Wilson knew the voice of everybody on the mission. Spend that long together with thirty-eight people in such a confined space as the *Ulysses* and vocal recognition became perfect. Whoever spoke wasn't on the crew. Yet somehow he knew it was real-time, not some pirate hack from Earth.

Commander Lewis had frozen, the flagpole tripod still not fully deployed. 'Who said that?'

'That'd be me, my man. Nigel Sheldon, at your service. Specially if you need to get home in like a hurry.' That snigger again. Then someone else saying, 'Oh man, don't do that, you're going to so piss them off.'

'Who is this?' Lewis demanded.

Wilson was already moving, glide-walking as fast as was safe in the low gravity, making for the rear of the *Eagle II*. He knew they were close, and he could see everything on this side of the spaceplane. As soon as he was past the bell-shaped rocket nozzles he forced himself to a halt. Someone else was standing there, arm held high in an almost apologetic wave. Someone in what looked like a home-made space suit. Which was an insane interpretation, but it was definitely a pressure garment of some type, possibly modified from deep-sea gear. The outer fabric was made up from flat ridges of dull brown rubber, in pronounced contrast to Wilson's snow-white ten-million dollar Martian Environment Excursion suit. The helmet was the nineteen fifties classic goldfish bowl, a clear glass bubble showing the head of a young man with a scraggly beard and long oily blond hair tied back into a pigtail. *No radiation protection*, Wilson thought inanely. There was no backpack either, no portable life support module. Instead, a bundle of pressure hoses snaked away from the youth's waist to a . . .

'Son of a bitch,' Wilson grunted.

Behind the interloper was a two-metre circle of another place. It hung above the Martian soil like some bizarre superimposed TV image, with a weird rim made up from seething diffraction patterns of light from a grey universe. An opening through space, a gateway into what looked like a rundown physics lab. The other side had been sealed off with thick glass. A college geek-type with a wild afro hairstyle was pressed against it, looking out at Mars, laughing and pointing at Wilson. Above him, bright Californian sunlight shone in through the physics lab's open windows.

extracts reading groups
competitions books new
discounts extracts
competitions
books
new
events books
new extracts
new titles reading groups
interviews
reading groups
events extracts
discounts events
new books events
events new
discounts extracts discounts
www.panmacmillan.com
extracts events reading groups
competitions books extracts new